ROBERT LOUIS
STEVENSON

GREAT CLASSIC LIBRARY

ROBERT LOUIS
STEVENSON

KIDNAPPED

THE MASTER OF BALLANTRAE

THE STRANGE CASE OF
DR JEKYLL AND MR HYDE

CHANCELLOR
PRESS

Kidnapped was first published in 1886
The Master of Ballantrae was first published in 1889
The Strange Case of Dr Jekyll and Mr Hyde was first published in 1886

This collected volume first published in Great Britain in 1994 by
Chancellor Press an imprint of
Reed Consumer Books Ltd
Michelin House
81 Fulham Road
London SW3 6RB
and Auckland, Melbourne, Singapore and Toronto

Design and arrangement © 1994 Reed International Books Ltd

ISBN 1 85152 499 1
A CIP catalogue record for this title is available at the British Library

Printed and bound in Great Britain by Cox and Wyman

Contents

KIDNAPPED

1

THE MASTER OF BALLANTRAE

171

**THE STRANGE CASE OF
DR JEKYLL AND MR HYDE**

351

KIDNAPPED

⁜ Dedication ⁜

My dear Charles Baxter,

If you ever read this tale, you will likely ask yourself more questions than I should care to answer: as for instance how the Appin murder has come to fall in the year 1751, how the Torran rocks have crept so near to Earraid, or why the printed trial is silent as to all that touches David Balfour. These are nuts beyond my ability to crack. But if you tried me on the point of Alan's guilt or innocence, I think I could defend the reading of the text. To this day you will find the tradition of Appin clear in Alan's favour. If you inquire, you may even hear the descendants of 'the other man' who fired the shot are in the country to this day. But that other man's name, inquire as you please, you shall not hear; for the Highlander values a secret for itself and for the congenial exercise of keeping it. I might go on for long to justify one point and own another indefensible; it is more honest to confess at once how little I am touched by the desire of accuracy. This is no furniture for the scholar's library, but a book for the winter evening schoolroom when the tasks are over and the hour for bed draws near; and honest Alan, who was a grim old fire-eater in his day, has in this new avatar no more desperate purpose than to steal some young gentleman's attention from his Ovid, carry him awhile into the Highlands and the last century, and pack him to bed with some engaging images to mingle with his dreams.

As for you, my dear Charles, I do not even ask you to like the tale. But perhaps when he is older, your son will; he may then be pleased to find his father's name on the fly-leaf; and in the meanwhile it pleases me to set it there in memory of many days that were happy and some (now perhaps as pleasant to remember) that were sad. If it is strange for me to look back from a distance both in time and space on these bygone adventures of our youth, it must be stranger for you who tread the same streets – who may tomorrow open the door of the old Speculative, where we begin to rank with Scott and Robert Emmet and the beloved and inglorious Macbean – or may pass the corner of the close where that great society, the L.J.R., held its meetings and drank its beer, sitting in the seats of Burns and his companions. I think I see you, moving there

3

by plain daylight, beholding with your natural eyes those places that have now become for your companion a part of the scenery of dreams. How, in the intervals of present business, the past must echo in your memory! Let it not echo often without some kind thoughts of your friend.

R.L.S.

SKERRYVORE, BOURNEMOUTH

I Set Off Upon My Journey to the House of Shaws

I WILL BEGIN THE STORY OF MY adventures with a certain morning early in the month of June, the year of grace 1751, when I took the key for the last time out of the door of my father's house. The sun began to shine upon the summit of the hills as I went down the road; and by the time I had come as far as the manse, the blackbirds were whistling in the garden lilacs, and the mist that hung around the valley in the time of the dawn was beginning to arise and die away.

Mr Campbell, the minister of Essendean, was waiting for me by the garden gate, good man! He asked me if I had breakfasted; and hearing that I lacked for nothing, he took my hand in both of his and clapped it kindly under his arm.

'Well, Davie, lad,' said he, 'I will go with you as far as the ford, to set you on the way.'

And we began to walk forward in silence.

'Are ye sorry to leave Essendean?' said he, after a while.

'Why, sir,' said I, 'If I knew where I was going, or what was likely to become of me, I would tell you candidly. Essendean is a good place indeed, and I have been very happy there; but then I have never been anywhere else. My father and mother, since they are both dead, I shall be no nearer to in Essendean than in the Kingdom of Hungary; and, to speak truth, if I thought I had a chance to better myself where I was going, I would go with a good will.'

'Ay?' said Mr Campbell. 'Very well, Davie. Then it behoves me to tell your fortune; or so far as I may. When your mother was gone, and your father (the worthy, Christian man) began to sicken for his end, he gave me in charge a certain letter, which he said was your inheritance. "So soon," says he, "as I am gone, and the house is redd up and the gear disposed of" (all which, Davie, hath been done) "give my boy this letter into his hand, and start him off to the house of Shaws, not far from Cramond. That is the place I came from," he said, "and it's where it befits that my boy should return. He is a steady lad," your father said, "and a canny goer; and I doubt not he will come safe, and be well liked where he goes." '

'The house of Shaws!' I cried. 'What had my poor father to do with the house of Shaws?'

'Nay,' said Mr Campbell, 'who can tell that for a surety? But the name of that family, Davie boy, is the name you bear – Balfours of Shaws: an ancient, honest, reputable house, peradventure in these latter days decayed. Your father, too, was a man of learning as befitted his position; no man more plausibly conducted school; nor had he the manner or the speech of a common dominie; but (as ye will yourself remember) I took aye a pleasure to have him to the manse to meet the gentry; and those of my own house, Campbell of Kilrennet, Campbell of Dunswire, Campbell of Minch, and others, all well-kenned gentlemen, had pleasure in his society. Lastly, to put all the elements of this affair before you, here is the testamentary letter itself, superscribed by the own hand of our departed brother.'

He gave me the letter, which was addressed in these words: 'To the hands of Ebenezer Balfour, Esquire, of Shaws, in his house of Shaws, these will be delivered by my son, David Balfour.' My heart was beating hard at this great prospect now suddenly opening before a lad of sixteen years of age, the son of a poor country dominie in the Forest of Ettrick.

'Mr Campbell,' I stammered, 'and if you were in my shoes, would you go?'

'Of a surety,' said the minister, 'that would I, and without pause. A pretty lad like you should get to Cramond (which is near in by Edinburgh) in two days of walk. If the worst came to the worst, and your high relations (as I cannot but suppose them to be somewhat of your blood) should put you to the door, ye can but walk the two days back again and risp at the manse door. But I would rather hope that ye shall be well received, as your poor father forecast for you, and for anything that I ken, come to be a great man in time. And here, Davie, laddie,' he resumed, 'it lies near upon my conscience to improve this parting, and set you on the right guard against the dangers of the world.'

Here he cast about for a comfortable seat, lighted on a big boulder under a birch by the trackside, sate down upon it with a very long, serious upper lip, and, the sun now shining in upon us between two peaks, put his pocket-handkerchief over his cocked hat to shelter him. There, then, with uplifted forefinger, he first put me on my guard against a considerable number of heresies, to which I had no temptation, and urged upon me to be instant in my prayers and reading of the Bible. That done, he drew a picture of the great house that I was bound to, and how I should conduct myself with its inhabitants.

'Be soople, Davie, in things immaterial,' said he. 'Bear ye this in mind, that, though gentle born, ye have had a country rearing. Dinnae shame us, Davie, dinnae shame us! In yon great, muckle house, with all these domestics, upper and under, show youself as nice, as circumspect, as quick at the conception, and as slow of speech as any. As for the laird – remember he's the laird; I say no more: honour to whom honour. It's pleasure to obey a laird; or should be, to the young.'

'Well, sir,' said I, 'it may be; and I'll promise you I'll try to make it so.'

'Why, very well said,' replied Mr Campbell, heartily. 'And now to come to the material, or (to make a quibble) to the immaterial. I have here a little packet which contains four things.' He tugged it, as he spoke, and with some difficulty, from the skirt pocket of his coat. 'Of these four things, the first is your legal due: the little pickle money for your father's books and plenishing, which I have bought (as I have explained from the first) in the design of re-selling at a profit to the incoming dominie. The other three are gifties that Mrs Campbell and myself would be blithe of your acceptance. The first, which is round, will likely please ye best at the first off-go; but, O Davie, laddie, it's but a drop of water in the sea; it'll help you but a step, and vanish like the morning. The second, which is flat and square and written upon, will stand by you through life, like a good staff for the road, and a good pillow to your head in sickness. And as for the last, which is cubical, that'll see you, it's my prayerful wish, into a better land.'

With that he got upon his feet, took off his hat, and prayed a little while aloud, and in affecting terms, for a young man setting out into the world; then suddenly took me in his arms and embraced me very hard; then held me at arm's length, looking at me with his face all working with sorrow; and then whipped about, and crying goodbye to me, set off backward by the way that we had come at a sort of jogging run. It might have been laughable to another; but I was in no mind to laugh. I watched him as long as he was in sight; and he never stopped hurrying, nor once looked back. Then it came in upon my mind that this was all his sorrow at my departure; and my conscience smote me hard and fast, because I, for my part, was overjoyed to get away out of that quiet countryside, and go to a great, busy house, among rich and respected gentlefolk of my own name and blood.

'Davie, Davie,' I thought, 'was ever seen such black ingratitude? Can you forget old favours and old friends at the mere whistle of a name? Fie, fie; think shame!'

And I sat down on the boulder the good man had just left, and opened the parcel to see the nature of my gifts. That which he had called cubical, I had never had much doubt of; sure enough it was a little Bible, to carry in a plaidneuk. That which he had called round, I found to be a shilling piece; and the third, which was to help me so wonderfully both in health and sickness all the days of my life, was a little piece of coarse yellow paper, written upon thus in red ink:

TO MAKE LILLY OF THE VALLEY WATER – Take the flowers of lilly of the valley and distil them in sack, and drink a spooneful or two as there is occasion. It restores speech to those that have the dumb palsey. It is good against the Gout; it comforts the heart and strengthens the memory; and the flowers, put into a Glasse, close stopt, and set into ane hill of ants for a month, then take it out, and you will find a liquor which comes from the flowers, which keep in a vial; it is good, ill or well, and whether man or woman.

And then, in the minister's own hand, was added:

Likewise for sprains, rub it in; and for the cholic, a great spooneful in the hour.

To be sure, I laughed over this; but it was rather tremulous laughter; and I was glad to get my bundle on my staff's end and set out over the ford and up the hill upon the farther side; till, just as I came on the green drove-road running wide through the heather, I took my last look of Kirk Essendean, the trees about the manse, and the big rowans in the kirkyard where my father and my mother lay.

TWO

✤ I Come to My Journey's End ✤

ON THE FORENOON OF THE second day, coming to the top of a hill, I saw the country fall away before me down to the sea; and in the midst of this descent, on a long ridge, the city of Edinburgh smoking like a kiln. There was a flag upon the castle, and ships moving or lying anchored in the firth; both of which, for as far away as they were, I could distinguish clearly; and both brought my country heart into my mouth.

Presently after, I came by a house where a shepherd lived, and got a rough direction for the neighbourhood of Cramond; and so, from one to another, worked my way to the westward of the capital by Colinton, till

I came out upon the Glasgow road. And there, to my great pleasure and wonder, I beheld a regiment marching to the fifes, every foot in time; an old red-faced general on a grey horse at the one end, and at the other the company of Grenadiers, with their Pope's-hats. The pride of life seemed to mount into my brain at the sight of the red-coats and the hearing of that merry music.

A little farther on, and I was told I was in Cramond parish, and began to substitute in my inquiries the name of the house of Shaws. It was a word that seemed to surprise those of whom I sought my way. At first I thought the plainness of my appearance, in my country habit, and that all dusty from the road, consorted ill with the greatness of the place to which I was bound. But after two, or maybe three, had given me the same look and the same answer, I began to take it in my head there was something strange about the Shaws itself.

The better to set this fear at rest, I changed the form of my inquiries; and spying an honest fellow coming along a lane on the shaft of his cart, I asked him if he had ever heard tell of a house they called the house of Shaws.

He stopped his cart and looked at me, like the others.

'Ay,' said he. 'What for?'

'It's a great house?' I asked.

'Doubtless,' says he. 'The house is a big, muckle house.'

'Ay,' said I, 'but the folk that are in it?'

'Folk?' cried he. 'Are ye daft? There's nae folk there – to call folk.'

'What?' says I; 'not Mr Ebenezer?'

'Oh, ay,' says the man, 'there's the laird, to be sure, if it's him you're wanting. What'll like be your business, mannie?'

'I was led to think that I would get a situation,' I said, looking as modest as I could.

'What?' cries the carter, in so sharp a note that his very horse started; and then, 'Well, mannie,' he added, 'it's nane of my affairs; but ye seem a decent-spoken lad; and if ye'll take a word from me, ye'll keep clear of the Shaws.'

The next person I came across was a dapper little man in a beautiful white wig, whom I saw to be a barber on his rounds; and knowing well that barbers were great gossips, I asked him plainly what sort of a man was Mr Balfour of the Shaws.

'Hoot, hoot, hoot,' said the barber, 'nae kind of a man, nae kind of a man at all'; and began to ask me very shrewdly what my business was; but I was more than a match for him at that, and he went on to his next customer no wiser than he came.

I cannot well describe the blow this dealt to my illusions. The more indistinct the accusations were, the less I liked them, for they left the wider field to fancy. What kind of a great house was this, that all the parish should start and stare to be asked the way to it? or what sort of a gentleman, that his ill-fame should be thus current on the wayside? If an hour's walking would have brought me back to Essendean, I had left my adventure then and there, and returned to Mr Campbell's. But when I had come so far a way already, mere shame would not suffer me to desist till I had put the matter to the touch of proof; I was bound, out of mere self-respect, to carry it through; and little as I liked the sound of what I heard, and slow as I began to travel, I still kept asking my way and still kept advancing.

It was drawing on to sundown when I met a stout, dark, sour-looking woman coming trudging down a hill; and she, when I had put my usual question, turned sharp about, accompanied me back to the summit she had just left, and pointed to a great bulk of building standing very bare upon a green in the bottom of the next valley. The country was pleasant round about, running in low hills, pleasantly watered and wooded, and the crops, to my eyes, wonderfully good; but the house itself appeared to be a kind of ruin; no road led up to it; no smoke arose from any of the chimneys; nor was there any semblance of a garden. My heart sank. 'That!' I cried.

The woman's face lit up with a malignant anger. 'That is the house of Shaws!' she cried. 'Blood built it; blood stopped the building of it; blood shall bring it down. See here!' she cried again – 'I spit upon the ground, and crack my thumb at it! Black be its fall! If ye see the laird, tell him what ye hear; tell him this makes the twelve hunner and nineteen time that Jennet Clouston has called down the curse on him and his house, byre, and stable, man, guest, and master, wife, miss, or bairn – black, black be their fall!'

And the woman, whose voice had risen to a kind of eldritch sing-song, turned with a skip, and was gone. I stood where she left me, with my hair on end. In those days folk still believed in witches and trembled at a curse; and this one, falling so pat, like a wayside omen, to arrest me ere I carried out my purpose, took the pith out of my legs.

I sat me down and stared at the house of Shaws. The more I looked, the pleasanter that countryside appeared; being all set with hawthorn bushes full of flowers; the fields dotted with sheep; a fine flight of rooks in the sky; and every sign of a kind soil and climate; and yet the bar-rack in the midst of it went sore against my fancy.

Country folk went by from the fields as I sat there on the side of the ditch, but I lacked the spirit to give them a good-e'en. At last the sun went down, and then, right up against the yellow sky, I saw a scroll of smoke go mounting, not much thicker, as it seemed to me, than the smoke of a candle; but still there it was, and meant a fire, and warmth, and cookery, and some living inhabitant that must have lit it; and this comforted my heart wonderfully – more, I feel sure, than a whole flask of the lily of the valley water that Mrs Campbell set so great a store by.

So I set forward by a little faint track in the grass that led in my direction. It was very faint indeed to be the only way to a place of habitation; yet I saw no other. Presently it brought me to stone uprights, with an unroofed lodge beside them, and coats of arms upon the top. A main entrance, it was plainly meant to be, but never finished; instead of gates of wrought iron, a pair of hurdles were tied across with a straw rope; and as there were no park walls, nor any sign of avenue, the track that I was following passed on the right hand of the pillars, and went wandering on toward the house.

The nearer I got to that, the drearier it appeared. It seemed like the one wing of a house that had never been finished. What should have been the inner end stood open on the upper floors, and showed against the sky with steps and stairs of uncompleted masonry. Many of the windows were unglazed, and bats flew in and out like doves out of a dovecote.

The night had begun to fall as I got close; and in three of the lower windows, which were very high up, and narrow, and well barred, the changing light of a little fire began to glimmer.

Was this the palace I had been coming to? Was it within these walls that I was to seek new friends and begin great fortunes? Why, in my father's house on Essen-Waterside, the fire and the bright lights would show a mile away, and the door open to a beggar's knock.

I came forward cautiously, and giving ear as I came, heard someone rattling with dishes, and a little dry, eager cough that came in fits; but there was no sound of speech, and not a dog barked.

The door, as well as I could see it in the dim light, was a great piece of wood all studded with nails; and I lifted my hand with a faint heart under my jacket, and knocked once. Then I stood and waited. The house had fallen into a dead silence; a whole minute passed away, and nothing stirred but the bats overhead. I knocked again, and hearkened again. By this time my ears had grown so accustomed to the quiet, that I could hear the ticking of the clock inside as it slowly counted out the seconds; but whoever was in that house kept deadly still, and must have held his breath.

I was in two minds whether to run away; but anger got the upper hand, and I began instead to rain kicks and buffets on the door, and to shout out aloud for Mr Balfour. I was in full career, when I heard the cough right overhead, and jumping back and looking up, beheld a man's head in a tall nightcap, and the bell mouth of a blunderbuss, at one of the first storey windows.

'It's loaded,' said a voice.

'I have come here with a letter,' I said, 'to Mr Ebenezer Balfour of Shaws. Is he here?'

'From whom is it?' asked the man with the blunderbuss.

'That is neither here nor there,' said I, for I was growing very wroth.

'Well,' was the reply, 'ye can put it down upon the doorstep, and be off with ye.'

'I will do no such thing,' I cried. 'I will deliver it into Mr Balfour's hands, as it was meant I should. It is a letter of introduction.'

'A what?' cried the voice sharply.

I repeated what I had said.

'Who are ye, yourself?' was the next question, after a considerable pause.

'I am not ashamed of my name,' said I. 'They call me David Balfour.'

At that, I made sure the man started, for I heard the blunderbuss rattle on the window-sill; and it was after quite a long pause, and with a curious change of voice, that the next question followed:

'Is your father dead?'

I was so much surprised at this, that I could find no voice to answer, but stood staring.

'Ay,' the man resumed, 'he'll be dead, no doubt; and that'll be what brings ye chapping to my door.' Another pause, and then, defiantly, 'Well, man,' he said, 'I'll let ye in'; and he disappeared from the window.

THREE

I Make Acquaintance of My Uncle

PRESENTLY THERE CAME A great rattling of chains and bolts, and the door was cautiously opened, and shut to again behind me as soon as I had passed.

'Go into the kitchen and touch naething,' said the voice; and while the person of the house set himself to replacing the defences of the door, I gropped my way forward and entered the kitchen.

The fire had burned up fairly bright, and showed me the barest room I think I ever put my eyes on. Half-a-dozen dishes stood upon the shelves; the table was laid for supper with a bowl of porridge, a horn spoon, and a cup of small beer. Besides what I have named, there was not another thing in that great, stone-vaulted, empty chamber but lockfast chests arranged along the wall and a corner cupboard with a padlock.

As soon as the last chain was up, the man rejoined me. He was a mean, stooping, narrow-shouldered, clay-faced creature; and his age might have been anything between fifty and seventy. His nightcap was of flannel, and so was the nightgown that he wore, instead of coat and waistcoat, over his ragged shirt. He was long unshaved; but what most distressed and even daunted me, he would neither take his eyes away from me nor look me fairly in the face. What he was, whether by trade or birth, was more than I could fathom; but he seemed most like an old, unprofitable serving-man, who should have been left in charge of that big house upon board wages.

'Are ye sharp-set?' he asked, glancing at about the level of my knee. 'Ye can eat that drop parritch.'

I said I feared it was his own supper.

'Oh,' said he, 'I can do fine wanting it. I'll take the ale, though, for it slockens* my cough.' He drank the cup about half out, still keeping an eye upon me as he drank; and then suddenly held out his hand. 'Let's see the letter,' said he.

I told him the letter was for Mr Balfour; not for him.

'And who do you think I am?' says he. 'Give me Alexander's letter!'

'You know my father's name?'

'It would be strange if I didnae,' he returned, 'for he was my born brother; and little as ye seem to like either me or my house, or my good parritch, I'm your born uncle, Davie, my man, and you my born nephew. So give us the letter, and sit down and fill your kyte.'

If I had been some years younger, what with shame, weariness, and disappointment, I believe I had burst into tears. As it was, I could find no words, neither black nor white, but handed him the letter, and sat down to the porridge with as little appetite for meat as ever a young man had.

Meanwhile, my uncle, stooping over the fire, turned the letter over and over in his hands.

'Do ye ken what's in it?' he asked, suddenly.

*Moistens.

'You see for yourself, sir,' said I, 'that the seal has not been broken.'

'Aye,' said he, 'but what brought you here?'

'To give the letter,' said I.

'No,' says he, cunningly, 'but ye'll have had some hopes, nae doubt?'

'I confess, sir,' said I, 'when I was told that I had kinsfolk well-to-do, I did indeed indulge the hope that they might help me in my life. But I am no beggar; I look for no favours at your hands, and I want none that are not freely given. For as poor as I appear, I have friends of my own that will be blithe to help me.'

'Hoot-toot' said Uncle Ebenezer, 'dinnae fly up in the snuff at me. We'll agree fine yet. And, Davie, my man, if you're done with that bit parritch, I could just take a sup of it myself. Ay,' he continued, as soon as he had ousted me from the stool and spoon, 'they're fine, halesome food – they're grand food, parritch.' He murmured a little grace to himself and fell to. 'Your father was very fond of his meat, I mind; he was a hearty, if not a great eater; but as for me, I could never do mair than pyke at food.' He took a pull at the small beer, which probably reminded him of hospitable duties; for his next speech ran thus: 'If ye're dry, ye'll find water behind the door.'

To this I returned no answer, standing stiffly on my two feet, and looking down upon my uncle with a mighty angry heart. He, on his part, continued to eat like a man under some pressure of time, and to throw out little darting glances now at my shoes and now at my homespun stockings. Once only, when he had ventured to look a little higher, our eyes met; and no thief taken with a hand in a man's pocket could have shown more lively signals of distress. This set me in a muse, whether his timidity arose from too long a disuse of any human company; and whether perhaps, upon a little trial, it might pass off, and my uncle change into an altogether different man. From this I was awakened by his sharp voice.

'Your father's been long dead?,' he asked.

'Three weeks sir,' said I.

'He was a secret man, Alexander – a secret, silent man,' he continued. 'He never said muckle when he was young. He'll never have spoken muckle of me?'

'I never knew, sir, till you told it me yourself, that he had any brother.'

'Dear me, dear me!' said Ebenezer. 'Nor yet of Shaws, I dare say?'

'Not so much as the name, sir,' said I.

'To think o' that!' said he. 'A strange nature of a man!' For all that, he seemed singularly satisfied, but whether with himself, or me, or with this conduct of my father's, was more than I could read. Certainly, however, he seemed to be outgrowing that distaste, or ill-will, that he had conceived at first against my person; for presently he jumped up, came across the room behind me, and hit me a smack upon the shoulder. 'We'll agree fine yet!' he cried. 'I'm just as glad I let you in. And now come awa' to your bed.'

To my surprise, he lit no lamp or candle, but set forth into the dark passage, groped his way, breathing deeply, up a flight of steps, and paused before a door, which he unlocked. I was close upon his heels, having stumbled after him as best I might; and he bade me go in, for that was my chamber. I did as he bid, but paused after a few steps, and begged a light to go to bed with.

'Hoot-toot!' said Uncle Ebenezer, 'there's a fine room.'

'Neither moon nor star, sir, and pit-mirk*,' said I. 'I cannae see the bed.'

'Hoot-toot, hoot-toot' said he. 'Lights in a house is a thing I dinnae agree with. I'm unco feared of fires. Good night to ye, Davie, my man.' And before I had time to add a further protest, he pulled the door to, and I heard him lock me in from the outside.

I did not know whether to laugh or cry. The room was as cold as a well, and the bed, when I found had my way to it, as damp as a peat-hag; but by good fortune I had caught up my bundle and my plaid, and rolling myself in the latter, I lay down upon the floor under lee of the big bedstead, and fell speedily asleep.

With the first peep of day I opened my eyes, to find myself in a great chamber, hung with stamped leather, furnished with fine embroidered furniture, and lit by three fair windows. Ten years ago, or perhaps twenty, it must have been as pleasant a room to lie down or to awake in, as a man could wish; but damp, dirt, disuse, and the mice and spiders had done their worst since then. Many of the window-panes, besides, were broken; and indeed this was so common a feature in that house, that I believe my uncle must at some time have stood a siege from his indignant neighbours – perhaps with Jennet Clouston at their head.

Meanwhile the sun was shining outside; and being very cold in that miserable room, I knocked and shouted till my gaoler came and let me out. He carried me to the back of the house, where was a draw-well, and told me to 'wash my face there, if I wanted'; and when that was done, I made the best of my own way back to the kitchen, where he had lit the fire and was making the porridge. The table was laid with two bowls and two horn spoons, but the same single measure of small beer. Perhaps my eye rested on this particular with some surprise, and perhaps

*Dark as the pit.

my uncle observed it; for he spoke up as if in answer to my thought, asking me if I would like to drink ale – for so he called it.

I told him such was my habit, but not to put himself about.

'Na, na,' said he; 'I'll deny you nothing in reason.'

He fetched another cup from the shelf; and then, to my great surprise, instead of drawing more beer, he poured an accurate half from one cup to the other. There was a kind of nobleness in this that took my breath away; if my uncle was certainly a miser, he was one of that thorough breed that goes near to make the vice respectable.

When we had made an end of our meal, my uncle Ebenezer unlocked a drawer, and drew out of it a clay pipe and a lump of tobacco, from which he cut one fill before he locked it up again. Then he sat down in the sun at one of the windows and silently smoked. From time to time his eyes came coasting round to me, and he shot out one of his questions. Once it was, 'And your mother?' And when I had told him that she, too, was dead, 'Ay, she was a bonnie lassie!' Then, after another long pause, 'Whae were these friends o' yours?'

I told him they were different gentlemen of the name of Campbell; though, indeed, there was only one, and that the minister, that had ever taken the least note of me; but I began to think my uncle made too light of my position, and finding myself all alone with him, I did not wish him to suppose me helpless.

He seemed to turn this over in his mind; and then, 'Davie, my man,' said he, 'ye've come to the right bit when ye came to your Uncle Ebenezer. I've a great notion of the family, and I mean to do the right by you; but while I'm taking a bit think to mysel' of what's the best thing to put you to – whether the law, or the meenistry, or maybe the army, whilk is what boys are fondest of – I wouldnae like the Balfours to be humbled before a wheen Hieland Campbells, and I'll ask you to keep your tongue within your teeth. Nae letters; nae messages; no kind of word to onybody; or else – there's my door.'

'Uncle Ebenezer,' said I, 'I've no manner of reason to suppose you mean anything but well by me. For all that, I would have you to know that I have a pride of my own. It was by no will of mine that I came seeking you; and if you show me your door again, I'll take you at the word.'

He seemed grievously put out. 'Hoots-toots,' said he, 'ca' cannie, man – ca' cannie! Bide a day or two. I'm nae warlock, to find a fortune for you in the bottom of a parritch bowl; but just you give me a day or two, and say naething to naebody, and as sure as sure, I'll do the right by you.'

'Very well,' said I, 'enough said. If you want to help me, there's no doubt but I'll be glad of it, and none but I'll be grateful.'

It seemed to me (too soon, I daresay) that I was getting the upper hand of my uncle; and I began next to say that I must have the bed and bedclothes aired and put to sun-dry; for nothing would make me sleep in such a pickle.

'Is this my house or yours?' said he, in his keen voice, and then all of a sudden broke off. 'Na, na,' said he, 'I dinnae mean that. What's mine is yours, Davie, my man, and what's yours is mine. Blood's thicker than water; and there's naebody but you and me that ought the name.' And then on he rambled about the family, and its ancient greatness, and his father that began to enlarge the house, and himself that stopped the building as a sinful waste; and this put it in my head to give him Jennet Clouston's message.

'The limmer!' he cried. 'Twelve hunner and fifteen – that's every day since I had the limmer rowpit*! Dod, David, I'll have her roasted on red peats before I'm by with it! A witch – a proclaimed witch! I'll aff and see the session clerk.'

And with that he opened a chest, and got out a very old and well-preserved blue coat and waistcoat, and a good enough beaver hat, both without lace. These he threw on anyway, and taking a staff from the cupboard, locked all up again, and was for setting out, when a thought arrested him.

'I cannae leave you by yoursel' in the house,' said he. 'I'll have to lock you out.'

The blood came into my face. 'if you lock me out,' I said, 'it'll be the last you see of me in friendship.'

He turned very pale, and sucked his mouth in. 'This is no the way,' said he, looking wickedly at a corner of the floor – 'this is no the way to win my favour, David.'

'Sir,' says I, 'with a proper reverence for your age and our common blood, I do not value your favour at a boddle's purchase. I was brought up to have a good conceit of myself; and if you were all the uncle, and all the family, I had in the world ten times over, I wouldn't buy your liking at such prices.'

Uncle Ebenezer went and looked out of the window for a while. I could see him all trembling and twitching, like a man with palsy. But when he turned round, he had a smile upon his face.

'Well, well,' said he, 'we must bear and forbear. I'll no go; that's all that's to be said of it.'

*Sold up.

'Uncle Ebenezer,' I said, 'I can make nothing out of this. You use me like a thief; you hate to have me in this house; you let me see it, every word and every minute; it's not possible that you can like me; and as for me, I've spoken to you as I never thought to speak to any man. Why do you seek to help me, then? Let me gang back – let me gang back to the friends I have, and that like me!'

'Na, na; na, na,' he said, very earnestly. 'I like you fine; we'll agree fine yet; and for the honour of the house I couldnae let you leave the way ye came. Bide here quiet, there's a good lad; just you bide here quiet a bittie, and ye'll find that we agree.'

'Well, sir,' said I, after I had thought the matter out in silence, 'I'll stay a while. It's more just I should be helped by my own blood than strangers; and if we don't agree, I'll do my best it shall be through no fault of mine.'

FOUR

I Run a Great Danger in the House of Shaws

FOR A DAY THAT WAS BEGUN so ill, the day passed fairly well. We had the porridge cold again at noon, and hot porridge at night; porridge and small beer was my uncle's diet. He spoke but little, and that in the same way as before, shooting a question at me after a long silence; and when I sought to lead him in talk about my future, slipped out of it again. In a room next door to the kitchen, where he suffered me to go, I found a great number of books, both Latin and English, in which I took great pleasure all the afternoon. Indeed the time passed so lightly in this good company, that I began to be almost reconciled to my residence at Shaws; and nothing but the sight of my uncle, and his eyes playing hide and seek with mine, revived the force of my distrust.

One thing I discovered, which put me in some doubt. This was an entry on the fly-leaf of a chapbook (one of Patrick Walker's) plainly written in my father's hand and thus conceived: To my brother Ebenezer on his fifth birthday.' Now, what puzzled me was this: That as my father was of course the younger brother, he must either have made some strange error, or he must have written, before he was yet five, an excellent, clear, manly hand of writing.

I tried to get this out of my head; but though I took down many interesting authors, old and new, history, poetry, and story-book, this notion of my father's hand of writing stuck to me; and when at length I went back into the kitchen, and sat down once more to porridge and small beer, the first thing I said to Uncle Ebenezer was to ask him if my father had not been very quick at his book.

'Alexander? No him!' was the reply. 'I was far quicker mysel'; I was a clever chappie when I was young. Why, I could read as soon as he could.'

This puzzled me yet more: and a thought coming into my head, I asked if he and my father had been twins.

He jumped upon his stool, and the horn spoon fell out of his hand upon the floor. 'What gars ye ask that?' he said, and caught me by the breast of the jacket, and looked this time straight into my eyes; his own, which were little and light, and bright like a bird's blinking and winking strangely.

'What do you mean?' I asked, very calmly, for I was far stronger than he, and not easily frightened. 'Take your hand from my jacket. This is no way to behave.'

My uncle seemed to make a great effort upon himself. 'Dod, man David,' he said, 'ye shouldnae speak to me about your father. That's where the mistake is.' He sat a while and shook, blinking in his plate; 'He was all the brother that ever I had,' he added, but with no heart in his voice; and then he caught his spoon and fell to supper again, but still shaking.

Now this last passage, this laying of hands upon my person and sudden profession of love for my dead father, went so clean beyond my comprehension that it put me into both fear and hope. On the one hand, I began to think my uncle was perhaps insane and might be dangerous; on the other, there came up into my mind (quite unbidden by me and even discouraged) a story like some ballad I had heard folk singing, of a poor lad that was a rightful heir and a wicked kinsman that tried to keep him from his own. For why should my uncle play a part with a relative that came, almost a beggar, to his door, unless in his heart he had some cause to fear him?

With this notion, all unacknowledged, but nevertheless getting firmly settled in my head, I now began to imitate his covert looks; so that we sat at table like a cat and a mouse, each stealthily observing the other. Not another word had he to say to me, black or white, but was busy turning something secretly over in his mind; and the longer we sat and the more I looked at him, the more certain I became that the something was unfriendly to myself.

When he had cleared the platter, he got out a single pipeful of tobacco, just as in the morning, turned round a stool into the chimney corner, and sat a while smoking, with his back to me.

'Davie,' he said at length, 'I've been thinking'; then he paused, and said it again. 'There's a wee bit siller that I half promised ye before ye were born,' he continued; 'promised it to your father. Oh, naething legal, ye understand; just gentlemen daffing at their wine. Well I keepit that bit money separate – it was a great expense, but a promise is a promise – and it has grown by now to be a maitter of just precisely – just exactly' – and here he paused and stumbled – 'of just exactly forty pounds!' This last he rapped out with a sidelong glance over his shoulder; and the next moment added, almost with a scream, 'Scots!'

The pound Scots being the same thing as an English shilling, the difference made by this second thought was considerable; I could see, besides, that the whole story was a lie, invented with some end which it puzzled me to guess; and I made no attempt to conceal the tone of raillery in which I answered—

'Oh, think again, sir! Pounds sterling, I believe!'

'That's what I said,' returned my uncle: 'pounds sterling! And if you'll step out-by to the door a minute, just to see what kind of a night it is, I'll git it out to ye and call ye in again.'

I did his will, smiling to myself in my contempt that he should think I was so easily to be deceived. It was a dark night, with a few stars low down; and as I stood just outside the door, I heard a hollow moaning of wind far off among the hills. I said to myself there was something thundery and changeful in the weather, and little knew of what a vast importance that should prove to me before the evening passed.

When I was called in again, my uncle counted out into my hand seven and thirty golden guinea pieces; the rest was in his hand, in small gold and silver; but his heart failed him there, and he crammed the change into his pocket.

'There,' said he, 'that'll show you! I'm a queer man, and strange wi' strangers; but my word is my bond, and there's the proof of it.'

Now, my uncle seemed so miserly that I was struck dumb by this sudden generosity, and could find no words in which to thank him.

'No a word!' said he. 'Nae thanks: I want nae thanks. I do my duty; I'm no saying that everybody would have done it; but for my part (though I'm a careful body, too) it's a pleasure to me to do the right by my brother's son; and it's a pleasure to me to think that now we'll agree as such near friends should.'

I spoke him in return as handsomely as I was able; but all the while I was wondering what would come next, and why he had parted with his precious guineas; for as to the reason he had given, a baby would have refused it.

Presently, he looked towards me sideways.

'And see here,' says he, 'tit for tat.'

I told him I was ready to prove my gratitude in any reasonable degree, and then waited, looking for some monstrous demand. And yet, when at last he plucked up courage to speak, it was only to tell me (very properly, as I thought) that he was growing old and a little broken, and that he would expect me to help him with the house and the bit garden.

I answered, and expressed my readiness to serve.

'Well,' he said, 'let's begin.' He pulled out of his pocket a rusty key. 'There,' says he, 'there's the key of the stairtower at the far end of the house. Ye can only win into it from the outside, for that part of the house is no finished. Gang ye in there, and up the stairs, and bring me down the chest that's at the top. There's papers in't,' he added.

'Can I have a light, sir?' said I.

'Na,' said he, very cunningly, 'Nae lights in my house.'

'Very well, sir,' said I. 'Are the stairs good?'

'They're grand,' said he; and then as I was going, 'Keep to the wall,' he added; 'there's nae banisters. But the stairs are grand under foot.'

Out I went into the night. The wind was still moaning in the distance, though never a breath of it came near the house of Shaws. It had fallen blacker then ever; and I was glad to feel along the wall, till I came the length of the stairtower door at the far end of the unfinished wing. I had got the key into the keyhole and had just turned it, when all upon a sudden, without sound of wind or thunder, the whole sky lighted up with wild fire and went black again. I had to put my hand over my eyes to get back to the colour of the darkness; and indeed I was already half blinded when I stepped into the tower.

It was so dark inside, it seemed a body could scarce breathe; but I pushed out with foot and hand, and presently struck the wall with the one and the lowermost round of the stair with the other. The wall, by the touch, was of fine hewn stone; the steps too, though somewhat steep and narrow, were of polished mason-work, and regular and solid under foot. Minding my uncle's word about the banisters, I kept close to the tower side, and felt my way in the pitch darkness with a beating heart.

The house of Shaws stood some five full storeys high, not counting lofts. Well, as I advanced, it seemed to me the stair grew airier and a thought more lightsome; and I was wondering what might be the cause of this change, when a second blink of the summer lightning came and went. If I did not cry out, it was because fear had me by the throat; and if I did not fall, it was more by Heaven's mercy than my own strength. It was not only that the flash shone in on every side through breaches in the wall, so that I seemed to be clambering aloft upon an open scaffold, but the same passing brightness showed me the steps were of unequal length, and that one of my feet rested that moment within two inches of the well.

This was the grand stair! I thought; and with the thought, a gust of a kind of angry courage came into my heart. My uncle had sent me here, certainly to run great risks, perhaps to die. I swore I would settle that 'perhaps', if I should break my neck for it; got me down upon my hands and knees; and as slowly as a snail, feeling before me every inch, and testing the solidity of every stone, I continued to ascend the stair. The darkness, by contrast with the flash, appeared to have redoubled; nor was that all, for my ears were now troubled and my mind confounded by a great stir of bats in the top part of the tower, and the foul beasts, flying downwards, sometimes beat about my face and body.

The tower, I should have said, was square; and in every corner the step was made of a great stone of a different shape, to join the flights. Well, I had come close to one of these turns, when, feeling forward as usual, my hand slipped upon an edge and found nothing but emptiness beyond it. The stair had been carried no higher: to set a stranger mounting it in the darkness was to send him straight to his death; and (although, thanks to the lightning and my own precautions, I was safe enough) the mere thought of the peril in which I might have stood, and the dreadful height I might have fallen brought out the sweat upon my body and relaxed my joints.

But I knew what I wanted now, and turned and groped my way down again, with a wonderful anger in my heart. About half-way down, the wind sprang up in a clap and shook the tower, and died again; the rain followed; and before I had reached the ground level it fell in buckets. I put out my head into the storm, and looked along towards the kitchen. The door, which I had shut behind me when I left, now stood open, and shed a little glimmer of light; and I thought I could see a figure standing in the rain, quite still, like a man hearkening. And then there came a blinding flash, which showed me my uncle plainly, just where I had fancied him to stand; and hard upon the heels of it, a great tow-row of thunder.

Now, whether my uncle thought the crash to be the sound of my fall, or whether he heard in it God's voice denouncing murder, I will leave you to guess. Certain it is, at least, that he was seized on by a kind of panic fear, and that he ran into the house and left the door open behind him. I followed as softly as I could, and coming unheard into the kitchen, stood and watched him.

He had found time to open the corner cupboard and bring out a great case bottle of aqua vitae, and now sat with his back towards me at the table. Ever and again he would be seized with a fit of deadly shuddering and groan aloud, and carrying the bottle to his lips, drink down the raw spirits by the mouthful.

I stepped forward, came close behind him where he sat, and suddenly clapping my two hands down upon his shoulders – 'Ah!' cried I.

My uncle gave a kind of broken cry like a sheep's bleat, flung up his arms, and tumbled to the floor like a dead man. I was somewhat shocked at this; but I had myself to look to first of all, and did not hesitate to let him lie as he had fallen. The keys were hanging in the cupboard; and it was my design to furnish myself with arms before my uncle should come again to his senses and the power of devising evil. In the cupboard were a few bottles, some apparently of medicine; a great many bills and other papers, which I should willingly enough have rummaged, had I had the time; and a few necessaries, that were nothing to my purpose. Thence I turned to the chests. The first was full of meal; the second of money-bags and papers tied into sheaves; in the third, with many other things (and these for the most part clothes), I found a rusty, ugly-looking Highland dirk without the scabbard. This, then, I concealed inside my waistcoat, and turned to my uncle.

He lay as he had fallen, all huddled, with one knee up and one arm sprawling abroad; his face had a strange colour of blue, and he seemed to have ceased breathing. Fear came on me that he was dead; then I got water and dashed it in his face; and with that he seemed to come a little to himself, working his mouth and fluttering his eyelids. At last he looked up and saw me, and there came into his eyes a terror that was not of this world.

'Come, come,' said I, 'sit up.'

'Are ye alive?' he sobbed. 'O man, are ye alive?'

'That am I,' said I. 'Small thanks to you!'

He had begun to seek for his breath with deep sighs. 'The blue phial,' said he – 'in the aumry – the blue phial.' His breath came slower still.

I ran to the cupboard, and, sure enough, found there a blue phial of medicine, with the dose written on it on a paper, and this I administered to him with what speed I might.

'It's the trouble,' said he, reviving a little; 'I have a trouble, Davie. It's my heart.'

I set him on a chair and looked at him. It is true I felt some pity for a man that looked so sick, but I was full besides of righteous anger; and I numbered over before him the points on which I wanted explanation: why he lied to me at every word; why he feared that I should leave him; why he disliked it to be hinted that he and my father were twins – 'Is that because it is true?' I asked; why he had given me money to which I was convinced I had no claim; and, last of all, why he had tried to kill me. He heard me all through in silence; and then, in a broken voice, begged me to let him go to bed.

'I'll tell ye the morn,' he said; 'as sure as death I will.'

And so weak was he that I could do nothing but consent. I locked him into his room, however, and pocketed the key; and then returning to the kitchen, made up such a blaze as had not shone there for many a long year, and wrapping myself in my plaid, lay down upon the chests and fell asleep.

FIVE

❧ I Go to the Queen's Ferry ❧

MUCH RAIN FELL IN THE night; and the next morning there blew a bitter wintry wind out of the north-west, driving scattered clouds. For all that, and before the sun began to peep or the last of the stars had vanished, I made my way to the side of the burn, and had a plunge in a deep whirling pool. All aglow from my bath, I sat down once more beside the fire, which I replenished, and began gravely to consider my position.

There was now no doubt about my uncle's enmity; there was no doubt I carried my life in my hand, and he would leave no stone unturned that he might compass my destruction. But I was young and spirited, and like most lads that have been country-bred, I had a great opinion of my shrewdness. I had come to his door no better than a beggar and little more than a child; he had met me with treachery and violence; it would be a fine consummation to take the upper hand, and drive him like a herd of sheep.

I sat there nursing my knee and smiling at the fire; and I saw myself in fancy smell out his secrets one after another, and grow to be that man's king and ruler. The warlock of Essendean, they say, had made a mirror in which men could read the future; it must have been of other stuff than burning coal; for in all the shapes and pictures that I sat and gazed at, there was never a ship, never a seaman with a hairy cap, never a big bludgeon for my silly head, or the least sign of all those tribulations that were ripe to fall on me.

Presently, all swollen with conceit, I went upstairs and gave my prisoner his liberty. He gave me good morning civilly; and I gave the same to him, smiling down upon him from the heights of my sufficiency. Soon we were set to breakfast, as it might have been the day before.

'Well, sir,' said I, with a jeering tone, 'have you nothing more to say to me?' And then, as he made no articulate reply, 'It will be time, I think, to understand each other,' I continued. 'You took me for a country Johnnie Raw, with no more mother-wit or courage than a porridge-stick. I took you for a good man, or no worse than others at the least. It seems we were both wrong. What cause you have to fear me, to cheat me, and to attempt my life—'

He murmured something about a jest, and that he liked a bit of fun; and then, seeing me smile, changed his tone, and assured me he would make all clear as soon as we had breakfasted. I saw by his face that he had no lie ready for me, though he was hard at work preparing one; and I think I was about to tell him so, when we were interrupted by a knocking at the door.

Bidding my uncle sit where he was, I went to open it, and found on the doorstep a half-grown boy in sea-clothes. He had no sooner seen me that he began to dance some steps of the sea-hornpipe (which I had never before heard of, far less seen), snapping his fingers in the air and footing it right cleverly. For all that, he was blue with the cold; and there was something in his face, a look between tears and laughter, that was highly pathetic and consisted ill with this gaity of manner.

'What cheer, mate?' says he, with a cracked voice.

I asked him soberly to name his business.

'Oh, pleasure!' says he; and then began to sing:

> 'For it's my delight, of a shiny night,
> In the season of the year.'

'Well,' said I, 'If you have no business at all, I will even be so unmannerly as to shut you out.'

'Stay brother!' he cried. 'Have you no fun about you? or do you want to get me thrashed? I've brought a letter from old Heasy-oasy to Mr Belflower.' He showed me a letter as he spoke. 'And I say, mate,' he added, 'I'm mortal hungry.'

'Well,' said I, 'come into the house, and you shall have a bite if I go empty for it.'

With that I brought him in and set him down to my own place, where he fell-to greedily on the remains of breakfast, winking to me between whiles, and making many faces which I think the poor soul considered manly. Meanwhile, my uncle had read the letter and sat thinking; then, suddenly, he got to his feet with a great air of liveliness, and pulled me apart into the farthest corner of the room.

'Read that,' said he, and put the letter in my hand.

Here it is, lying before me as I write:

> *The Hawes Inn, at the Queen's Ferry.*
> SIR. – I lie here with my hawser up and down, and send my cabin-boy to informe. If you have any further commands for over-seas, to-day will be the last occasion, as the wind will serve us well out of the firth. I will not seek to deny that I have had crosses with your doer*, Mr Rankeillor; of which, if not speedily redd up, you may looke to see some losses follow. I have drawn a bill upon you, as per margin, and am, sir, your most obedt, humble servant,
>
> ELIAS HOSEASON

'You see, Davie,' resumed my uncle, as soon as he saw that I had done, 'I have a venture with this man Hoseason, the captain of a trading brig, the *Covenant*, of Dysart. Now, if you and me was to walk over with yon lad, I could see the captain at the Hawes, or maybe on board the *Covenant*, if there was papers to be signed; and so far from a loss of time, we can jog on to the lawyer, Mr Rankeillor's. After a' that's come and gone, ye would be swiert† to believe me upon my naked word; but ye'll believe Rankeillor. He's factor to half the gentry in these parts; an auld man, forby: highly respeckit; and he kenned your father.'

I stood awhile and thought. I was going to some place of shipping, which was doubtless populous, and where my uncle durst attempt no violence, and, indeed, even the society of the cabin-boy so far protected me. Once there, I believed I could force on the visit to the lawyer, even if my uncle were now insincere in proposing it; and perhaps, in the bottom of my heart, I wished a nearer view of the sea and ships. You are to remember I had lived all my life in the inland hills, and just two days before had my first sight of the firth lying like a blue floor, and the sailed ships moving on the face of it, no bigger than toys. One thing with another, I made up my mind.

'Very well,' says I, 'let us go to the Ferry.'

*Agent.
†Unwilling.

My uncle got into his hat and coat, and buckled an old rusty cutlass on; and then we trod the fire out, locked the door, and set forth upon our walk.

The wind, being in that cold quarter, the north-west, blew nearly in our faces as we went. It was the month of June; the grass was all white with daisies and the trees with blossom; but, to judge by our blue nails and aching wrists, the time might have been winter and the whiteness a December frost.

Uncle Ebenezer trudged in the ditch, jogging from side to side like an old ploughman coming home from work. He never said a word the whole way; and I was thrown for talk on the cabin-boy. He told me his name was Ransome, and that he had followed the sea since he was nine, but could not say how old he was, as he had lost his reckoning. He showed me tattoo marks, baring his breast in the teeth of the wind and in spite of my remonstrances, for I thought it was enough to kill him; he swore horribly whenever he remembered, but more like a silly schoolboy than a man; and boasted of many wild and bad things that he had done: stelthy thefts, false accusations, ay, and even murder; but all with such a dearth of likelihood in the details, and such a weak and crazy swagger in the delivery, as disposed me rather to pity than to believe him.

I asked him of the brig (which he declared was the finest ship that sailed) and of Captain Hoseason, in whose praise he was equally loud. Heasy-oasy (for so he still named the skipper) was a man, by his account, that minded for nothing either in heaven or earth; one that, as people said, would 'crack on all sail into the day of judgement'; rough, fierce, unscrupulous, and brutal; and all this my poor cabin-boy had taught himself to admire as something seamanlike and manly. He would only admit one flaw in his idol. 'He ain't no seaman,' he admitted. 'That's Mr Shuan that navigates the brig; he's the finest seaman in the trade, only for drink; and I tell you I believe it! Why, look 'ere'; and turning down his stocking, he showed me a great, raw, red wound that made my blood run cold. 'He done that – Mr Shuan done it,' he said, with an air of pride.

'What!' I cried, 'do you take such savage usage at his hands? Why, you are no slave, to be so handled!'

'No,' said the poor moon-calf, changing his tune at once, 'and so he'll find! See 'ere'; and he showed me a great case-knife, which he told me was stolen. 'Oh,' says he, 'let me see him try; I dare him to; I'll do for him! Oh, he ain't the first!' And he confirmed it with a poor, silly, ugly oath.

I have never felt such pity for anyone in this wide world as I felt for that halfwitted creature; and it began to come over me that the brig

Covenant (for all her pious name) was little better than a hell upon the seas.

'Have you no friends?' said I.

He said he had a father in some English seaport, I forgot which. 'He was a fine man, too,' he said; 'but he's dead.'

'In Heaven's name,' cried I, 'can you find no reputable life on shore?'

'Oh, no,' says he, winking and looking very sly; 'they would put me to a trade. I know a trick worth two of that, I do!'

I asked him what trade could be so dreadful as the one he followed, where he ran the continual peril of his life, not alone from wind and sea, but by the horrid cruelty of those who were his masters. He said it was very true; and then began to praise the life, and tell what a pleasure it was to get on shore with money in his pocket, and spend it like a man, and buy apples, and swagger, and surprise what he called stick-in-the-mud boys. 'And then it's not all so bad as that,' says he; 'there's worse off than me: there's the twenty-pounders. Oh, laws! you should see them taking on. Why, I've seen a man as old as you, I dessay' – (to him I seemed old) – 'ah, and he had a beard too, – well, and as soon as we cleared out of the river, and he had the drug out of his head – my how he cried and carried on! I made a fine fool of him, I tell you! And then there's little uns, too; oh, little by me! I tell you, I keep them in order. When we carry little uns, I have a rope's end of my own to wollop 'em.'

And so he ran on, until it came in on me that what he meant by twenty-pounders were those unhappy criminals who were sent overseas to slavery in North America, or the still more unhappy innocents who were kidnapped or trepanned (as the word went) for private interest or vengeance.

Just then we came to the top of the hill, and looked down on the Ferry and the Hope. The Firth of Forth (as is very well known) narrows at this point to the width of a good-sized river, which makes a convenient ferry going north, and turns the upper reach into a land-locked haven for all manner of ships. Right in the midst of the narrows lies an islet with some ruins; on the south shore they have built a pier for the service of the Ferry; and at the end of the pier, on the other side of the road, and backed against a pretty garden of holly-trees and hawthorns, I could see the building which they call the Hawes Inn.

The town of Queensferry lies farther west, and the neighbourhood of the inn looked pretty lonely at that time of day, for the boat had just gone north with passengers. A skiff, however, lay beside the pier, with some seamen sleeping on the thwarts; This, as Ransome told me, was the brig's boat waiting for the captain; and about half a mile off, and all alone in the anchorage, he showed me the *Covenant* herself. There was a sea-going bustle on board; yards were swinging into place; and as the wind blew from that quarter, I could hear the song of the sailors as they pulled upon the ropes. After all I had listened to upon the way, I looked at that ship with an extreme abhorrence; and from the bottom of my heart I pitied all poor souls that were condemned to sail in her.

We had all three pulled up on the brow of the hill; and now I marched across the road and addressed my uncle. 'I think it right to tell you, sir,' says I 'there's nothing that will bring me on board that *Covenant*.'

He seemed to waken from a dream. 'Eh?' he said. 'What's that?'

I told him over again.

'Well, well,' he said, 'we'll have to please ye, I suppose. But what are we standing here for? It's perishing cold; and if I'm no mistaken, they're busking the *Covenant* for sea.'

SIX

What Befell at the Queen's Ferry

As soon as we came to the inn, Ransome led us up the stair to a small room, with a bed in it, and heated like an oven by a great fire of coal. At a table hard by the chimney, a tall, dark, sober-looking man sat writing. In spite of the heat of the room, he wore a thick sea-jacket, buttoned to the neck, and a tall hairy cap drawn down over his ears; yet I never saw any man, not even a judge upon the bench, look cooler, or more studious and self-possessed, than this ship-captain.

He got to his feet at once, and coming forward, offered his large hand to Ebenezer. 'I am proud to see you, Mr Balfour,' said he, in a fine deep voice, 'and glad that ye are here in time. The wind's fair, and the tide upon the turn; we'll see the old coal-bucket burning on the Isle of May before tonight.'

'Captain Hoseason,' returned my uncle, 'you keep your room unco hot.'

'It's a habit I have, Mr Balfour,' said the skipper. 'I'm a cold-rife man by my nature; I have a cold blood, sir. There's neither fur, nor flannel – no, sir, nor hot rum, will warm up what they call the temperature. Sir, it's the same with most men that have been carbonadoed, as they call it, in the tropic seas.'

'Well, well, captain,' replied my uncle, 'we must all be the way we're made.'

But it chanced that this fancy of the captain's had a great share in my misfortunes. For though I had promised myself not to let my kinsman out of sight, I was both so impatient for a nearer look at the sea, and so sickened by the closeness of the room, that when he told me to 'run downstairs and play myself awhile', I was fool enough to take him at his word.

Away I went, therefore, leaving the two men sitting down to a bottle and a great mass of papers; and crossing the road in front of the inn, walked down upon the beach. With the wind in that quarter, only little wavelets, not much bigger than I had seen upon a lake, beat upon the shore. But the weeds were new to me – some green, some brown and long, and some with little bladders that cracked between my fingers. Even so far up the firth, the smell of the sea water was exceedingly salt and stirring; the *Covenant*, besides, was beginning to shake out her sails, which hung upon the yards in clusters; and the spirit of all that I beheld put me in thoughts of far voyages and foreign places.

I looked, too, at the seamen with the skiff – big brown fellows, some in shirts, some with jackets, some with coloured handkerchiefs about their throats, one with a brace of pistols stuck into his pockets, two or three with knotty bludgeons, and all with their case-knives. I passed the time of day with one that looked less desperate than his fellows, and asked him of the sailing of the brig. He said they would get under way as soon as the ebb set, and expressed his gladness to be out of port where there were no taverns and fiddlers; but all with such horrifying oaths, that I made haste to get away from him.

This threw me back on Ransome, who seemed the least wicked of that gang, and who soon came out of the inn and ran to me, crying for a bowl of punch. I told him I would give him no such thing, for neither he nor I was of an age for such indulgences. 'But a glass of ale you may have, and welcome,' said I. He mopped and mowed at me, and called me names; but he was glad to get the ale, for all that; and presently we were set down at a table in the front room of the inn, and both eating and drinking with a good appetite.

Here it occurred to me that, as the landlord was a man of that county, I might do well to make a friend of him. I offered him a share, as was much the custom in these days; and he was far too great a man to sit with such poor customers as Ransome and myself, and he was leaving the room, when I called him back to ask if he knew Mr Rankeillor.

'Hoot, ay,' says he, 'and a very honest man. And, oh, by the by,' says he, 'was it you that came in with Ebenezer?' And when I had told him yes, 'Ye'll be no friend of his?' he asked, meaning, in the Scottish way, that I would be no relative.

I told him no, none.

'I thought not,' said he, 'and yet ye have a kind of gliff* of Mr Alexander.'

I said it seemed that Ebenezer was ill-seen in the country.

'Nae doubt,' said the landlord. 'He's a wicked auld man, and there's many would like to see him girning in a tow†: Jennet Clouston and mony mair that he has harried out of house and hame. And yet he was ance a fine young fellow, too. But that was before the sought‡ gaed abroad about Mr Alexander; that was like the death of him.'

'And what was it?' I asked.

'Ou, just that he had killed him,' said the landlord. 'Did ye never hear that?'

'And what would he kill him for?' said I.

'And what for, but just to get the place,' said he.

'The place?' said I, 'The Shaws?'

'Nae other place that I ken,' said he.

'Ay, man?' said I. 'Is that so? Was my – was Alexander the eldest son?'

''Deed was he,' said the landlord. 'What else would he have killed him for?'

And with that he went away, as he had been impatient to do from the beginning.

Of course, I had guessed it a long while ago; but it is one thing to guess, another to know; and I sat stunned with my good fortune, and could scarce grow to believe that the same poor lad who had trudged in the dust from Ettrick Forest not two days ago, was now one of the rich of the earth, and had a house and broad lands, and if he but knew how to ride, might mount his horse tomorrow. All these pleasant things, and a thousand others, crowded into my mind, as I sat staring before me out of the inn window, and paying no heed to what I saw; only I remember that my eye lighted on Captain Hoseason down on the pier among his seamen, and speaking with some authority. And presently he came marching back towards the house, with no mark of a sailor's clumsiness, but carrying his fine, tall figure with a manly bearing, and still with the same sober, grave expression on his face. I wondered if it was possible that Ransome's stories could be true, and half disbelieved them; they

*Look.
†Rope.
‡Report.

fitted so ill with the man's looks. But indeed, he was neither so good as I supposed him, nor quite so bad as Ransome did; for, in fact, he was two men, and left the better one behind as soon as he set foot on board his vessel.

The next thing, I heard my uncle calling me, and found the pair in the road together. It was the captain who addressed me, and that with an air (very flattering to a young lad) of grave equality.

'Sir,' said he, 'Mr Balfour tells me great things of you; and for my own part, I like your looks. I wish I was for longer here, that we might make the better friends; but we'll make the most of what we have. Ye shall come on board my brig for half an hour, till the ebb sets, and drink a bowl with me.'

Now, I longed to see the inside of a ship more than words can tell; but I was not going to put myself in jeopardy, and I told him my uncle and I had an appointment with a lawyer.

'Ay, ay,' said he, 'he passed me word of that. But, ye see, the boat'll set ye ashore at the town pier, and that's but a penny stonecast from Rankeillor's house.' And here he suddenly leaned down and whispered in my ear: 'Take care of the old tod*; he means mischief. Come aboard till I can get a word with ye.' And then, passing his arm through mine, he continued aloud, as he set off towards his boat: 'But come, what can I bring ye from the Carolinas? Any friend of Mr Balfour's can command. A roll of tobacco? Indian featherwork? a skin of a wild beast? a stone pipe? the mocking-bird that mews for all the world like a cat? the cardinal bird that is as red as blood? – take your pick and say your pleasure.'

By this time we were at the boat-side, and he was handing me in. I did not dream of hanging back; I thought (the poor fool!) that I had found a good friend and helper, and I was rejoiced to see the ship. As soon as we were all set in our places, the boat was thrust off from the pier and began to move over the waters; and what with my pleasure in this new movement and my surprise at our low position, and the appearance of the shores, and the growing bigness of the brig as we drew near to it, I could hardly understand what the captain said, and must have answered him at random.

As soon as we were alongside (where I sat fairly gaping at the ship's height, the strong humming of the tide against its sides, and the pleasant cries of the seamen at their work) Hoseason, declaring that he and I must be the first aboard, ordered a tackle to be sent down from the mainyard. In this I was whipped into the air and set down again on the deck, where the captain stood ready waiting for me, and instantly slipped back his

*Fox.

arm under mine. There I stood some while, a little dizzy with the unsteadiness of all around me, perhaps a little afraid, and yet vastly pleased with these strange sights; the captain meanwhile pointing out the strangest, and telling me their names and uses.

'But where is my uncle?' said I, suddenly.

'Ay,' said Hoseason, with a sudden grimness, 'that's the point.'

I felt I was lost. With all my strength, I plucked myself clear of him and ran to the bulwarks. Sure enough, there was the boat pulling for the town, with my uncle sitting in the stern. I gave a piercing cry – 'Help, help! Murder!' – so that both sides of the anchorage rang with it, and my uncle turned round where he was sitting, and showed me a face full of cruelty and terror.

It was the last I saw. Already strong hands had been plucking me back from the ship's side; and now a thunderbolt seemed to strike me; I saw a great flash of fire, and fell senseless.

SEVEN

I Go to Sea in the Brig Covenant of Dysart

I CAME TO MYSELF IN darkness, in great pain, bound hand and foot, and deafened by many unfamiliar noises. There sounded in my ears a roaring of water as of a huge milldam; the thrashing of heavy sprays, the thundering of the sails, and the shrill cries of seamen. The whole world now heaved giddily up, and now rushed giddily downward; and so sick and hurt was I in body, and my mind so much confounded, that it took me a long while, chasing my thoughts up and down, and ever stunned again by a fresh stab of pain, to realize that I must be lying somewhere bound in the belly of that unlucky ship, and that the wind must have strengthened to a gale. With the clear perception of my plight, there fell upon me a blackness of despair, a horror of remorse at my own folly, and a passion of anger at my uncle, that once more bereft me of my senses.

When I returned again to life, the same uproar, the same confused and violent movements, shook and deafened me; and presently, to my other pains and distresses, there was added the sickness of an unused landsman on the sea. In that time of my adventurous youth, I suffered many hardships; but none that was so crushing to my mind and body, or lit by so few hopes, as these first hours on board the brig.

I heard a gun fire, and supposed the storm had proved too strong for us, and we were firing signals of distress. The thought of deliverance, even by death in the deep sea, was welcome to me. Yet it was no such matter; but (as I was afterwards told) a common habit of the captain's, which I here set down to show that even the worst man have his kindlier sides. We were then passing, it appeared, within some miles of Dysart, where the brig was built, and where old Mrs Hoseason, the captain's mother, had come some years before to live; and whether outward or inward bound, the *Covenant* was never suffered to go by that place by day without a gun fired and colours shown.

I had no measure of time; day and night were alike in that ill-smelling cavern of the ship's bowels where I lay; and the misery of my situation drew out the hours to double. How long, therefore, I lay waiting to hear the ship split upon some rock, or to feel her reel head foremost into the depths of the sea, I have not the means of computation. But sleep at length stole from me the consciousness of sorrow.

I was awakened by the light of a hand-lantern shining in my face. A small man of about thirty, with green eyes and a tangle of fair hair, stood looking down at me.

'Well,' said he, 'how goes it?'

I answered by a sob; and my visitor then felt my pulse and temples and set himself to wash and dress the wound upon my scalp.

'Ay,' said he, 'a sore dunt*. What, man? Cheer up! The world's no done; you've made a bad start of it, but you'll make a better. Have you had any meat?'

I said I could not look at it; and thereupon he gave me some brandy and water in a tin pannikin, and left me once more to myself.

The next time he came to see me, I was lying betwixt sleep and waking, my eyes wide open in the darkness, the sickness quite departed, but succeeded by a horrid giddiness and swimming that was almost worse to bear. I ached besides, in every limb, and the cords that bound me seemed to be on fire. The smell of the hole in which I lay seemed to have become a part of me; and during the long interval since his last visit I had suffered tortures of fear, now from the scurrying of the ship's rats, that sometimes pattered on my very face, and now from the dismal imaginings that haunt the bed of fever.

The glimmer of the lantern, as a trap opened, shone in like the heaven's

*Stroke.

34

sunlight; and though it only showed me the strong, dark beams of this ship that was my prison, I could have cried aloud for gladness. The man with the green eyes was the first to descend the ladder, and I noticed that he came somewhat unsteadily. He was followed by the captain. Neither said a word; but the first set to and examined me, and dressed my wound as before, while Hoseason looked me in my face with an odd, black look.

'Now, sir, you see for yourself,' said the first: 'a high fever, no appetite, no light, no meat, you see for yourself what that means.'

'I am no conjurer, Mr Riach,' said the captain.

'Give me leave sir,' said Riach; 'you've a good head upon your shoulders, and a good Scotch tongue to ask with; but I will leave you no manner of excuse; I want that boy taken out of this hole and put in the forecastle.'

'What ye may want, sir, is a matter of concern to nobody but yoursel',' returned the captain; 'but I can tell ye that which is to be. Here he is; here he shall bide.'

'Admitting that you have been paid in a proportion,' said the other, 'I will crave leave humbly to say that I have not. Paid I am, and none too much, to be the second officer of this old tub; and you ken very well if I do my best to earn it. But I was paid for nothing more.'

'If ye could hold back your hand from the tin-pan, Mr Riach, I would have no complaint to make of ye,' returned the skipper; 'and instead of asking riddles, I make bold to say that ye would keep your breath to cool your porridge. We'll be required on deck,' he added, in a sharper note, and set one foot upon the ladder.

But Mr Riach caught him by the sleeve.

'Admitting that you have been paid to do a murder—' he began.

Hoseason turned upon him with flash.

'What's that?' he cried. 'What kind of talk is that?'

'It seems it is the talk that you can understand,' said Mr Riach, looking him steadily in the face.

'Mr Riach I have sailed with ye three cruises,' replied the captain. 'In all that time, sir, ye should have learned to know me; I'm a stiff man, and a dour man; but for what ye say now – fie, fie – it comes from a bad heart and a black conscience. If ye say the lad will die—'

'Ay, will he!' said Mr Riach.

'Well, sir, is not that enough?' said Hoseason. 'Flit him where ye please!'

Thereupon the captain ascended the ladder; and I, who had lain silent throughout this strange conversation, beheld Mr Riach turn after him and bow as low as to his knees in what was plainly a spirit of derision.

Even in my then state of sickness, I perceived two things; that the mate was touched with liquor, as the captain hinted, and that (drunk or sober) he was like to prove a valuable friend.

Five minutes afterwards my bonds were cut, I was hoisted on a man's back, carried up to the forecastle, and laid in a bunk on some sea-blankets; where the first thing that I did was to lose my senses.

It was a blessed thing indeed to open my eyes again upon the daylight, and to find myself in the society of men. The forecastle was a roomy place enough, set all about with berths, in which the men of the watch below were seated smoking, or lying down asleep. The day being calm and the wind fair, the scuttle was open, and not only the good daylight, but from time to time (as the ship rolled) a dusty beam of sunlight shone in, and dazzled and delighted me. I had no sooner moved, moreover, than one of the men brought me a drink of something healing which Mr Riach had prepared, and bade me lie still and I should soon be well again. There were no bones broken, he explained: 'A clour* on the head was naething. Man,' said he, 'it was me that gave it ye!'

Here I lay for the space of many days a close prisoner, and not only got my health again, but come to know my companions. They were a rough lot indeed, as sailors mostly are; being men rooted out of all the kindly parts of life, and condemned to toss together on the rough seas, with masters no less cruel. There were some among them that had sailed with the pirates and seen things it would be a shame even to speak of; some were men that had run from the king's ships, and went with a halter round their necks, of which they made no secret; and all, as the saying goes, were 'at a word and a blow' with their best friends. Yet I had not been many days shut up with them before I began to be ashamed of my first judgement, when I had drawn away from them at the Ferry pier, as though they had been unclean beasts. No class of man is altogether bad; but each has its own faults and virtues; and these shipmates of mine were no exception to the rule. Rough they were, sure enough; and bad, I suppose; but they had many virtues. They were kind when it occurred to them, simple even beyond the simplicity of a country lad like me, and had some glimmerings of honesty.

There was one man of maybe forty, that would sit on my berthside for hours, and tell me of his wife and child. He was a fisher that had lost his boat, and thus been driven to the deep-sea voyaging. Well, it is years ago now: but I have never forgotten him. His wife (who was 'young by him', as he often told me) waited in vain to see her man return; he would never again make the fire for her in the morning, nor yet keep the bairn

*Blow.

when she was sick. Indeed, many of these poor fellows (as the event proved) were upon their last cruise; the deep seas and cannibal fish received them; and it is a thankless business to speak ill of the dead.

Among other good deeds that they did, they returned my money, which had been shared among them; and though it was about a third short, I was very glad to get it, and hoped great good from it in the land I was going to. The ship was bound for the Carolinas; and you must not suppose that I was going to that place merely as an exile. The trade was even then much depressed; since that, and with the rebellion of the colonies and the formation of the United States, it has, of course, come to an end; but in these days of my youth, white men were still sold into slavery on the plantations, and that was the destiny to which my wicked uncle had condemned me.

The cabin-boy Ransome (from whom I had first heard of these atrocities) came in at times from the round-house, where he berthed and served, now nursing a bruised limb in silent agony, now raving against the cruelty of Mr Shuan. It made my heart bleed; but the men had a great respect for the chief mate, who was, as they said, 'the only seaman of the whole jing-bang, and none such a bad man when he was sober.' Indeed, I found there was a strange peculiarity about our two mates: that Mr Riach was sullen, unkind, and harsh when he was sober, and Mr Shuan would not hurt a fly except when he was drinking. I asked about the captain: but I was told drink made no difference upon that man of iron.

I did my best in the small time allowed me to make something like a man, or rather I should say something like a boy, of the poor creature, Ransome. But his mind was scarce truly human. He could remember nothing of the time before he came to sea; only that his father had made clocks, and had a starling in the parlour, which could whistle 'The North Countrie'; all else had been blotted out in these years of hardship and cruelties. He had a strange notion of the dry land, picked up from sailors' stories: that it was a place where lads were put to some kind of slavery called a trade, and where apprentices were continually lashed and clapped into foul prisons. In a town, he thought every second person a decoy, and every third house a place in which seamen would be drugged and murdered. To be sure, I could tell him how kindly I had myself been used upon that dry land he was so much afraid of, and how well fed and carefully taught both by my friends and my parents: and if he had been recently hurt, he would weep bitterly and swear to run away; but if he was in his usual crackbrain humour or (still more) if he had had a glass of spirits in the round-house, he would deride the notion.

It was Mr Riach (Heaven forgive him!) who gave the boy drink; and it was, doubtless, kindly meant; but besides that it was ruin to his health, it was the pitifullest thing in life to see this unhappy, unfriended creature staggering, and dancing, and talking he knew not what. Some of the men laughed, but not all; others would grow as black as thunder (thinking, perhaps, of their own childhood or their own children) and bid him stop that nonsense, and think what he was doing. As for me, I felt ashamed to look at him, and the poor child still comes about me in my dreams.

All this time, you should know, the *Covenant* was meeting continuous headwinds and tumbling up and down against head-seas, so that the scuttle was almost constantly shut, and the forecastle lighted only by a swinging lantern on a beam. There was constant labour for all hands; the sails had to be made and shortened every hour; the strain told on the men's temper; there was a growl of quarrelling all day long from berth to berth; and as I was never allowed to set my foot on deck, you can picture to yourselves how weary of my life I grew to be, and how impaitent for a change.

And a change I was to get, as you shall hear; but I must first tell of a conversation I had with Mr Riach, which put a little heart in me to bear my troubles. Getting him in a favourable stage of drink (for indeed he never looked near me when he was sober) I pledged him to secrecy, and told him my whole story.

He declared it was like a ballad; that he would do his best to help me; that I should have paper, pen, and ink, and write one line to Mr Campbell and another to Mr Rankeillor; and that if I told the truth, ten to one he would be able (with their help) to pull me through and set me in my rights.

'And in the meantime,' says he, 'keep your heart up. You're not the only one, I'll tell you that. There's many a man hoeing tobacco over-seas that should be mounting his horse at his own door at home; many and many! And life is all a variorum, at the best. Look at me: I'm a laird's son and more than half a doctor, and here I am, man-Jack to Hoseason!'

I thought it would be civil to ask him for his story.

He whistled loud.

'Never had one,' said he. 'I liked fun, that's all.' And he skipped out of the forecastle.

EIGHT

❖ The Round-House ❖

ONE NIGHT, ABOUT NINE o'clock, a man of Mr Riach's watch (which was on deck) came down for his jacket; and instantly there began to go a whisper about the forecastle that 'Shuan had done for him at last'. There was no need of a name; we all knew who was meant; but we had scarce time to get the idea rightly in our heads, far less to speak of it, when the scuttle was again flung open, and Captain Hoseason came down the ladder. He looked sharply round the bunks in the tossing light of the lanter; and then walking straight up to me, he addressed me, to my surprise, in tones of kindness.

'My man,' said he, 'we want ye to serve in the round-house. You and Ransome are to change berths. Run away aft with ye.'

Even as he spoke, two seamen appeared in the scuttle, carrying Ransome in their arms; and the ship at that moment giving a great sheer into the sea, and the lantern swinging, the light fell direct on the boy's face. It was as white as wax, and had a look upon it like a dreadful smile. The blood in me ran cold, and I drew in my breath as if I had been struck.

'Run away aft; run away aft with ye!' cried Hoseason.

And at that I brushed by the sailors and the boy (who neither spoke nor moved), and ran up the ladder on deck.

The brig was sheering swiftly and giddily through a long, cresting swell. She was on the starboard tack, and on the left hand, under the arched foot of the foresail, I could see the sunset still quite bright. This, at such an hour of the night, surprised me greatly; but I was too ignorant to draw the true conclusion – that we were going north-about round Scotland, and were now on the high sea between the Orkney and the Shetland Islands, having avoided the dangerous currents of the Pentland Firth. For my part, who had been so long shut in the dark and knew nothing of head-winds, I thought we might be half-way or more across the Atlantic. And indeed (beyond that I wondered a little at the lateness of the sunset light) I gave no heed to it, and pushed on across the decks, running between the seas, catching at ropes, and only saved from going overboard by one of the hands on deck, who had been always kind to me.

The round-house, for which I was bound, and where I was now to sleep and serve, stood some six feet above the decks, and considering the size of the brig, was of good dimensions. Inside were a fixed table and bench, and two berths, one for the captain and the other for the two mates, turn and turn about. It was all fitted with lockers from top to bottom, so as to stow away the officers' belongings and a part of the ship's stores; there was a second storeroom underneath, which you entered by a hatchway in the middle of the deck; indeed, all the best of the meat and drink and the whole of the powder were collected in this place; and all the firearms, except the two pieces of brass ordnance, were set in a rack in the aftermost wall of the round-house. The most of the cutlasses were in another place.

A small window with a shutter on each side, and a skylight in the roof, gave it light by day; and after dark, there was a lamp always burning. It was burning when I entered, not brightly, but enough to show Mr Shuan sitting at the table, with the brandy bottle and a tin pannikin in front of him. He was a tall man, strongly made and very black; and he stared before him on the table like one stupid.

He took no notice of my coming in; nor did he move when the captain followed and leant on the berth beside me, looking darkly at the mate. I stood in great fear of Hoseason, and had my reasons for it; but something told me I need not be afraid of him just then; and I whispered in his ear, 'How is he?' He shook his head like one that does not know and does not wish to think, and his face was very stern.

Presently Mr Riach came in. He gave the captain a glance that meant the boy was dead as plain as speaking, and took his place like the rest of us; so that we all three stood without a word, staring down at Mr Shuan, and Mr Shuan (on his side) sat without a word, looking hard upon the table.

All of a sudden he put out his hand to take the bottle; and at that Mr Riach started forward and caught it away from him, rather by surprise than violence, crying out, with an oath, that there had been too much of this work altogether, and that a judgement would fall upon the ship. And as he spoke (the weather sliding-doors standing open) he tossed the bottle into the sea.

Mr Shuan was on his feet in a trice; he still looked dazed, but he meant murder, ay, and would have done it, for the second time that night, had not the captain stepped in between him and his victim.

'Sit down!' roars the captain. 'Ye sot and swine, do ye know what ye've done? Ye've murdered the boy!'

Mr Shuan seemed to understand; for he sat down again and put up his hand to his brow.

'Well,' he said, 'he brought me a dirty pannikin!'

At that word, the captain and I and Mr Riach all looked at each other for a second with a kind of frightened look; and then Hoseason walked up to his chief officer, took him by the shoulder, led him across to his bunk, and bade him lie down and go to sleep, as you might speak to a bad child. The murderer cried a little, but he took off his sea-boots and obeyed.

'Ah!' cried Mr Riach, with a dreadful voice, 'ye should have interfered long syne. It's too late now.'

'Mr Riach,' said the captain, 'this night's work must never be kennt in Dysart. The boy went overboard, sir; that's what the story is; and I would give five pounds out of my pocket it was true!' He turned to the table. 'What made ye throw the good bottle away?' he added. 'There was nae sense in that, sir. Here, David, draw me another. They're in the bottom locker'; and he tossed me a key. 'Ye'll need a glass yourself, sir,' he added, to Riach. 'Yon was an ugly thing to see.'

So the pair sat down and hob-a-nobbed; and while they did so, the murderer, who had been lying and whimpering in his berth, raised himself upon his elbow and looked at them and at me.

That was the first night of my new duties; and in the course of the next day I had got well into the run of them. I had to serve at the meals, which the captain took at regular hours, sitting down with the officer who was off duty; all the day through I would be running with a dram to one or other of my three masters; and at night I slept on a blanket thrown on the deck boards at the aftermost end of the round-house, and right in the draught of the two doors. It was a hard and a cold bed; nor was I suffered to sleep without interruption; for some one would be always coming in from deck to get a dram, and when a fresh watch was to be set, two and sometimes all three would sit down and brew a bowl together. How they kept their health, I know not, any more than how I kept my own.

And yet in other ways it was an easy service. There was no cloth to lay; the meals were either of oatmeal porridge or salt junk, except twice a week, when there was duff; and though I was clumsy enough and (not being firm on my sea-legs) sometimes fell with what I was bringing them, both Mr Riach and the captain were singularly patient. I could not but fancy they were making up lee-way with their consciences, and that they would scarce have been so good with me if they had not been worse with Ransome.

As for Mr Shuan, the drink, or his crime, or the two together, had certainly troubled his mind. I cannot say I ever saw him in his proper wits. He never grew used to my being there, stared at me continually (sometimes, I could have thought, with terror) and more than once drew back from my hand when I was serving him. I was pretty sure from the first that he had no clear mind of what he had done, and on my second day in the round-house I had proof of it. We were alone, and he had been staring at me a long time, when, all at once, up he got, as pale as death, and came close up to me, to my great terror. But I had no cause to be afraid of him.

'You were not here before?' he asked.

'No sir,' said I.

'There was another boy?' he asked again; and when I had answered him, 'Ah!' says he, 'I thought that,' and went and sat down, without another word, except to call for brandy.

You may think it strange, but for all the horror I had, I was still sorry for him. He was a married man, with a wife in Leith; but whether or no he had a family, I have now forgotten; I hope not.

Altogether it was no very hard life for the time it lasted, which (as you are to hear) was not long. I was as well fed as the best of them; even their pickles, which were the great dainty, I was allowed my share of; and had I liked, I might have been drunk from morning to night, like Mr Shuan. I had company, too, and good company of its sort. Mr Riach, who had been to the college, spoke to me like a friend when he was not sulking, and told me many curious things, and some that were informing; and even the captain, though he kept me at the stick's end the most part of the time, would sometimes unbuckle a bit, and tell me of the fine countries he had visited.

The shadow of poor Ransome, to be sure, lay on all four of us, and on me and Mr Shuan, in particular, most heavily. And then I had another trouble of my own. Here I was, doing dirty work for three men that I looked down upon, and one of whom, at least, should have hung upon a gallows; that was for the present; and as for the future, I could only see myself slaving alongside of negroes in the tobacco field. Mr Riach, perhaps from caution, would never suffer me to say another word about my story; the captain, whom I tried to approach, rebuffed me like a dog and would not hear a word; and as the days came and went, my heart sank lower and lower, till I was even glad of the work which kept me from thinking.

NINE

The Man with the Belt of Gold

❖ ❖

MORE THAN A WEEK WENT BY, in which the ill-luck that had hitherto pursued the *Covenant* upon this voyage grew yet more strongly marked. Some days she made a little way; others, she was driven actually back. At last we were beaten so far to the south that we tossed and tacked to and fro the whole of the ninth day, within sight of Cape Wrath and the wild, rocky coast on either hand of it. There followed on that a council of the officers, and some decision which I did not rightly understand, seeing only the result: that we had made a fair wind of a foul one and were running south.

The tenth afternoon, there was a falling swell and a thick, wet, white fog that hid one end of the brig from the other. All afternoon, when I went on deck, I saw men and officers listening hard over the bulwarks – 'for breakers', they said; and though I did not so much as understand the word, I felt danger in the air, and was excited.

Maybe about ten at night, I was serving Mr Riach and the captain at their supper, when the ship struck something with a great sound, and we heard voices singing out. My two masters leaped to their feet.

'She's struck,' said Mr Riach.

'No, sir,' said the captain. 'We've only run a boat down.'

And they hurried out.

The captain was in the right of it. We had run down a boat in the fog, and she had parted in the midst and gone to the bottom with all her crew, but one. This man (as I heard afterwards) had been sitting in the stern as a passenger, while the rest were on the benches rowing. At the moment of the blow, the stern had been thrown into the air, and the man (having his hands free, and for all he was encumbered with a frieze overcoat that came below his knees) had leaped up and caught hold of the brig's bow-sprit. It showed he had luck and much agility and unusual strength, that he should have thus saved himself from such a pass. And yet, when the captain brought him into the round-house, and I set eyes on him for the first time, he looked as cool as I did.

He was smallish in stature, but well set and as nimble as a goat; his face was of a good open expression, but sunburnt very dark, and heavily freckled and pitted with the smallpox; his eyes were unusually light and had a kind of dancing madness in them, that was both engaging and alarming; and when he took off his great-coat, he laid a pair of fine, silver-mounted pistols on the table, and I saw that he was belted with a great sword. His manners, besides, were elegant, and he pledged the captain handsomely. Altogether I thought of him, at the first sight, that here was a man I would rather call my friend than my enemy.

The captain, too, was taking his observations, but rather of the man's clothes than his person. And to be sure, as soon as he had taken off the great-coat, he showed forth mighty fine for the round-house of a merchant brig; having a hat with feathers, a red waistcoat, breeches of black plush, and a blue coat with silver buttons and handsome silver lace; costly clothes, though somewhat spoiled with the fog and being slept in.

'I'm vexed sir, about the boat,' says the captain.

'There are some pretty men gone to the bottom,' said the stranger, 'that I would rather see on the dry land again than half a score of boats.'

'Friends of yours?' said Hoseason.

'You have none such friends in your country,' was the reply. 'They would have died for me like dogs.'

'Well, sir,' said the captain, still watching him, 'there are more men in the world than boats to put them in.'

'And that's true too,' cried the other, 'and ye seem to be a gentleman of great penetration.'

'I have been in France, sir,' says the captain, so that it was plain he meant more by the words than showed upon the face of them.

'Well, sir,' says the other, 'and so has many a pretty man, for the matter of that.'

'No doubt, sir,' says the captain, 'and fine coats.'

'Oho!' says the stranger, 'is that how the wind sets?' And he laid his hand quickly on his pistols.

'Don't be hasty,' said the captain. 'Don't do a mischief, before ye see the need for it. Ye've a French soldier's coat upon your back and a Scotch tongue in your head, to be sure; but so has many an honest fellow in these days, and I dare say none the worse of it.'

'So?' said the gentleman in the fine coat: 'are ye of the honest party?' (meaning, Was he a Jacobite? for each side, in these sort of civil broils, takes the name of honesty for its own).

'Why, sir,' replied the captain, 'I am a true-blue Protestant, and I thank God for it.' (It was the first word of any religion I had ever heard from him, but I learnt afterwards he was a great church-goer while on shore.)

'But, for all that,' says he, 'I can be sorry to see another man with his back to the wall.'

'Can ye so, indeed?' asked the Jacobite. 'Well, sir, to be quite plain with ye, I am one of those honest gentlemen that were in trouble about the years forty-five and six; and (to be still quite plain with ye) if I got into the hands of any of the red-coated gentry, it's like it would go hard with me. Now, sir, I was for France; and there was a French ship cruising here to pick me up; but she gave us the go-by in the fog – as I wish from the heart that ye had done yoursel'! And the best that I can say is this: If ye can set me ashore where I was going, I have that upon me will reward you highly for your trouble.'

'In France?' says the captain. 'No, sir; that I cannot do. But where ye come from – we might talk of that.'

And then, unhappily, he observed me standing in my corner, and packed me off to the galley to get supper for the gentleman. I lost no time, I promise you; and when I came back into the round-house, I found the gentleman had taken a money-belt from about his waist, and poured out a guinea or two upon the table. The captain was looking at the guineas, and then at the belt, and then at the gentleman's face; and I thought he seemed excited.

'Half of it,' he cried, 'and I'm your man!'

The other swept back the guineas into the belt, and put it on again under his waistcoat. 'I have told ye, sir,' said he, 'that not one doit of it belongs to me. It belongs to my chieftain' – and here he touched his hat – 'and while I would be but a silly messenger to grudge some of it that the rest might come safe, I should show myself a hound indeed if I bought my own carcase any too dear. Thirty guineas on the seaside, or sixty if ye set me on the Linnhe loch. Take it, if ye will; if not, ye can do your worst.'

'Ay,' said Hoseason. 'And if I give ye over to the soldiers?'

'Ye would make a fool's bargain,' said the other. 'My chief, let me tell you, sir, is forfeited, like every honest man in Scotland. His estate is in the hands of the man they call King George; and it is his officers that collect the rents, or try to collect them. But for the honour of Scotland, the poor tenant bodies take a thought upon their chief lying in exile; and this money is a part of that very rent for which King George is looking. Now, sir, ye seem to me to be a man that understands things: bring this money within the reach of Government, and how much of it'll come to you?'

'Little enough, to be sure,' said Hoseason; and then, 'If they knew,' he added, dryly. 'But I think, if I was to try, that I could hold my tongue about it.'

'Ah, but I'll begowk* ye there!' cried the gentleman. 'Play me false, and I'll play you cunning. If a hand's laid upon me, they shall ken what money it is.'

'Well,' returned the captain, 'what must be must. Sixty guineas, and done. Here's my hand upon it.'

'And here's mine,' said the other.

And thereupon the captain went out (rather hurriedly, I thought), and left me alone in the round-house with the stranger.

At that period (so soon after the forty-five) there were many exiled gentlemen coming back at the peril of their lives, either to see their friends or to collect a little money; and as for the Highland chiefs that had been forfeited, it was a common matter of talk how their tenants would stint themselves to send them money, and their clansmen outface the soldiery to get it in, and run the gauntlet of our great navy to carry it across. All this I had, of course, heard tell of; and now I had a man under my eyes whose life was forfeit on all these counts and upon one more; for he was not only a rebel and a smuggler of rents, but had taken service with King Louis of France. And as if all this were not enough, he had a belt full of golden guineas round his loins. Whatever my opinions, I could not look on such a man without a lively interest.

'And so you're a Jacobite?' said I, as I set meat before him.

'Ay,' said he, beginning to eat. 'And you, by your long face, should be a Whig?'†

'Betwixt and between,' said I, not to annoy him; for indeed I was as good a Whig as Mr Campbell could make me.

'And that's naething,' said he. 'But I'm saying, Mr Betwixt-and-Between,' he added, 'this bottle of yours is dry; and it's hard if I'm to pay sixty guineas and be grudged a dram upon the back of it.'

'I'll go and ask for the key,' said I, and stepped on deck.

The fog was as close as ever, but the swell almost down. They had laid the brig to, not knowing precisely where they were, and the wind (what little there was of it) not serving well for their true course. Some of the hands were still hearkening for breakers; but the captain and the two officers were in the waist with their heads together. It struck me, I don't know why, that they were after no good; and the first word I heard, as I drew softly near, more than confirmed me.

It was Mr Riach, crying out as if upon a sudden thought:

'Couldn't we wile him out of the round-house?'

'He's better where he is,' returned Hoseason; 'he hasn't room to use his sword.'

*Befool.
†Whig or Whigamore was the cant name for those who were loyal to King George.

'Well, that's true,' said Riach; 'but he's hard to come at.'

'Hut!' said Hoseason. 'We can get the man in talk, one upon each side, and spin him by the two arms; or if that'll not hold, sir, we can make a run by both the doors and get him under hand before he has the time to draw.'

At this hearing, I was seized with both fear and anger at these treacherous greedy, bloody men that I sailed with. My first mind was to run away; my second was bolder.

'Captain,' said I, 'the gentleman is seeking a dram, and the bottle's out. Will you give me the key?'

They all started and turned about.

'Why, here's our chance to get the firearms!' Riach cried, and then to me: 'Hark ye, David,' he said, 'do ye ken where the pistols are?'

'Ay, ay,' put in Hoseason. 'David kens; David's a good lad. Ye see, David my man, yon wild Hielandman is a danger to the ship, besides being a rank foe to King George, God bless him!'

I had never been so be-Davided since I came on board; but I said yes, as if all I heard were quite natural.

'The trouble is,' resumed the captain, 'that all our firelocks, great and little, are in the round-house under this man's nose; likewise the powder. Now if I, or one of the officers, was to go in and take them, he would fall to thinking. But a lad like you, David, might snap up a horn and a pistol or two without remark. And if ye can do it cleverly, I'll bear in mind when it'll be good for you to have friends; and that's when we come to Carolina.'

Here Mr Riach whispered him a little.

'Very right, sir,' said the captain; and then to myself: 'And see here, David, yon man has a beltful of gold, and I give you my word that you shall have your fingers in it.'

I told him I would do as he wished, though indeed I had scarce breath to speak with; and upon that he gave me the key of the spirit locker, and I began to go slowly back to the round-house. What was I to do? They were dogs and thieves; they had stolen me from my own country; they had killed poor Ransome; and was I to hold the candle to another murder? But then, upon the other hand, there was the fear of death very plain before me; for what could a boy and a man, if they were as brave as lions, against a whole ship's company?

I was still arguing it back and forth, and getting no great clearness, when I came into the round-house and saw the Jacobite eating his supper under the lamp; and at that my mind was made up all in a moment. I have no credit by it; it was by no choice of mine, but as if by compulsion, that I walked right up to the table and put my hand on his shoulder.

'Do you want to be killed?' said I.

He sprang to his feet, and looked a question at me as clear as if he had spoken.

'Oh!' cried I, 'they're all murderers here; it's a ship full of them! They've murdered a boy already. Now it's you.'

'Ay, ay,' said he; 'but they haven't got me yet,' And then looking at me curiously, 'Will ye stand with me?'

'That will I!' said I, 'I am no thief, nor yet murderer. I'll stand by you.'

'Why, then,' said he, 'what's your name?'

'David Balfour,' said I; and then thinking that a man with so fine a coat must like fine people, I added for the first time 'of Shaws'.

It never occurred to him to doubt me, for a Highlander is used to see great gentlefolk in great poverty; but as he had no estate of his own, my words nettled a very childish vanity he had.

'My name is Stewart,' he said, drawing himself up. 'Alan Breck, they call me. A king's name is good enough for me, though I bear it plain and have the name of no farm-midden to clap to the hind-end of it.'

And having administered this rebuke, as though it were something of a chief importance, he turned to examine our defences.

The round-house was built very strong, to support the breaching of the seas. Of its five apertures, only the skylight and the two doors were large enough for the passage of a man. The doors, besides, could be drawn close: they were of stout oak, and ran in grooves, and were fitted with hooks to keep them either shut or open, as the need arose. The one that was already shut, I secured in this fashion; but when I was proceeding to slide to the other, Alan stopped me.

'David,' said he – 'for I cannae bring to mind the name of your landed estate, and so will make so bold as to call you David – that door, being open, is the best part of my defences.'

'It would be yet better shut,' says I.

'Not so, David,' says he, 'Ye see, I have but one face; but so long as that door is open and my face to it, the best part of my enemies will be in front of me, where I would aye wish to find them.'

Then he gave me from the rack a cutlass (of which there were a few besides the firearms), choosing it with great care, shaking his head and saying he had never in all his life seen poorer weapons; and next he set me down to the table with a powder-horn, a bag of bullets, and all the pistols, which he bade me charge.

'And that will be better work, let me tell you,' said he, 'for a gentleman of decent birth, than scraping plates and raxing* drams to a wheen tarry sailors.'

Thereupon he stood up in the midst with his face to the door, and drawing his great sword, made trial of the room he had to wield it in.

'I must stick to the point,' he said, shaking his head; 'and that's a pity, too. It doesn't set my genius, which is all for the upper guard. And now,' said he, 'do you keep on charging the pistols, and give heed to me.'

I told him I would listen closely. My chest was tight, my mouth dry, the light dark to my eyes; the thought of the numbers that were soon to leap in upon us kept my heart in a flutter; and the sea, which I heard washing round the brig, and where I thought my dead body would be cast ere morning, ran in my mind strangely.

'First of all,' said he, 'how many are against us?'

I reckoned them up; and such was the hurry of my mind, I had to cast the numbers twice, 'Fifteen,' said I.

Alan whistled. 'well,' said he, 'that can't be cured. And now follow me. It is my part to keep this door, where I look for the main battle. In that, ye have no hand. And mind and dinnae fire to this side unless they get me down; for I would rather have ten foes in front of me than one friend like you cracking pistols at my back.'

I told him, indeed I was no great shot.

'And that's very bravely said,' he cried, in a great admiration of my candour. 'There's many a pretty gentleman that wouldnae dare to say it.'

'But then, sir,' said I, 'there is the door behind you, which they may perhaps break in.'

'Ay,' said he, 'and that is a part of your work. No sooner the pistols charged, then ye must climb up into yon bed where ye're handy at the window; and if they lift hand against the door, ye're to shoot. But that's not all. Let's make a bit of a soldier of ye, David. What else have ye to guard?'

'There's the skylight,' said I. 'But indeed, Mr Stewart, I would need to have eyes upon both sides to keep the two of them; for when my face is at the one, my back is to the other.'

'And that's very true,' said Alan. 'But have ye no ears to your head?'

'To be sure!' cried I. 'I must hear the bursting of the glass!'

'Ye have some rudiments of sense,' said Alan, grimly.

*Reaching.

TEN

⚜ The Siege of the Round-house ⚜

BUT NOW OUR TIME OF TRUCE was come to an end. Those on deck had waited for my coming till they grew impatient; and scarce had Alan spoken, when the captain showed face in the open door.

'Stand!' cried Alan, and pointed his sword at him.

The captain stood, indeed; but he neither winced nor drew back a foot.

'A naked sword?' says he. 'This is a strange return for hospitality.'

'Do ye see me?' said Alan. 'I am come of kings; I bear a king's name. My badge is the oak. Do ye see my sword? It has slashed the heads off mair Whigamores than you have toes upon your feet. Call up your vermin to your back, sir, and fall on! The sooner the clash begins, the sooner ye'll taste this steel throughout your vitals.'

The captain said nothing to Alan, but he looked over at me with an ugly look. 'David,' said he, 'I'll mind this'; and the sound of his voice went through me with a jar.

Next moment he was gone.

'And now,' said Alan, 'let yur hand keep your head, for the grip is coming.'

Alan drew a dirk, which he held in his left hand in case they should run in under his sword. I, on my part, clambered up into the berth with an armful of pistols and something of a heavy heart, and set open the window where I was to watch. It was a small part of the deck that I could overlook, but enough for our purpose. The sea had gone down, and the wind was steady and kept the sails quiet; so that there was a great stillness in the ship, in which I made sure I heard the sound of muttering voices. A little after, and there came a clash of steel upon the deck, by which I knew they were dealing out the cutlasses and one had been left fall: and after that, silence again.

I do not know if I was what you call afraid; but my heart beat like a bird's, both quick and little; and there was a dimness came before my eyes which I continually rubbed away, and which continually returned. As for hope, I had none; but only a darkness of despair and a sort of anger against all the world that made me long to sell my life as dear as I was able. I tried to pray, I remember, but that same hurry of my mind, like a man running, would not suffer me to think upon the words, and my chief wish was to have the thing begin and be done with it.

It came all of a sudden when it did, with a rush of feet and a roar, and then a shout from Alan, and a sound of blows and someone crying out as if hurt. I looked back over my shoulder, and saw Mr Shuan in the doorway, crossing blades with Alan.

'That's him that killed the boy!' I cried.

'Look to your window!' said Alan; and as I turned back to my place, I saw him pass his sword through the mate's body.

It was none too soon for me to look to my own part; for my head was scarce back at the window, before five men carrying a spare yard for a battering-ram, ran past me and took post to drive the door in. I had never fired with a pistol in my life, and not often with a gun; far less against a fellow-creature. But it was now or never; and just as they swung the yard, I cried out, 'Take that!' and shot into their midst.

I must have hit one of them, for he sang out and gave back a step, and the rest stopped as if a little disconcerted. Before they had time to recover, I sent another ball over their heads; and at my third shot (which went as wide as the second) the whole party threw down the yard and ran for it.

Then I looked round again into the deck-house. The whole place was full of the smoke of my own firing, just as my ears seemed to be burst with the noise of the shots. But there was Alan, standing as before; only now his sword was running blood to the hilt, and himself swelled with triumph and fallen into so fine an attitude, that he looked to be invincible. Right before him on the floor was Mr Shuan, on his hands and knees; the blood was pouring from his mouth, and he was sinking slowly lower, with a terrible, white face, and just as I looked, some of those from behind caught hold of him by the heels and dragged him bodily out of the round-house. I believe he died as they were doing it.

'There's one of your Whigs for ye!' cried Alan; and then turning to me, he asked if I had done much execution.

I told him I had winged one, and thought it was the captain.

'And I've settled two,' says he. 'No, there's not enough blood let; they'll be back again. To your watch, David. This was but a dram before meat.'

I settled back to my place, re-charging the three pistols I had fired, and keeping watch with both eye and ear.

Our enemies were disputing not far off upon the deck, and that so loudly that I could hear a word or two above the washing of the seas.

'It was Shuan bauchled* it,' I heard one say.

And another answered him with a 'Wheesht, man! He's paid the piper.'

After that the voices fell again into the same muttering as before. Only now, one person spoke most of the time, as though laying down a plan, and first one and then another answered him briefly, like men taking orders. By this, I made sure they were coming on again, and told Alan.

'It's what we have to pray for,' said he. 'Unless we can give them a good distaste of us, and done with it, there'll be nae sleep for either you or me. But this time, mind, they'll be in earnest.'

By this, my pistols were ready, and there was nothing to do but listen and wait. While the brush lasted, I had not the time to think if I was frightened; but now, when all was still again, my mind ran upon nothing else. The thought of the sharp swords and the cold steel was strong in me; and presently, when I began to hear stealthy steps and a brushing of men's clothes against the roundhouse wall, and knew they were taking their places in the dark, I could have found it in my mind to cry out aloud.

All this was upon Alan's side; and I had begun to think my share of the fight was at an end, when I heard someone drop softly on the roof above me.

Then there came a single call on the sea-pipe, and that was the signal. A knot of them made one rush of it, cutlass in hand, against the door; and at the same moment, the glass of the skylight was dashed in a thousand pieces, and a man leaped through and landed on the floor. Before he got his feet, I had clapped a pistol to his back, and might have shot him, too; only at the touch of him (and him alive) my whole flesh misgave me, and I could no more pull the trigger than I could have flown.

He had dropped his cutlass as he jumped, and when he felt the pistol, whipped straight round and laid hold of me, roaring out an oath; and at that either my courage came again, or I grew so much afraid as came to the same thing; for I gave a shriek and shot him in the midst of the body. He gave the most horrible, ugly groan and fell to the floor. The foot of a second fellow, whose legs were dangling through the skylight, struck me at the same time upon the head; and at that I snatched another pistol and shot this one through the thigh, so that he slipped through and tumbled in a lump on his companion's body. There was no talk of missing, any more than there was time to aim; I clapped the muzzle to the very place and fired.

*Bungled.

I might have stood and stared at them for long, but I heard Alan shout as if for help, and that brought me to my senses.

He had kept the dorr so long; but one of the seamen, while he was engaged with others, had run in under his guard and caught him about the body. Alan was dirking him with his left hand, but the fellow clung like a leech. Another had broken in and had his cutlass raised. The door was thronged with their faces. I thought we were lost, and catching up my cutlass, fell on them in flank.

But I had not time to be of help. The wrestler dropped at last; and Alan, leaping back to get his distance, ran upon the others like a bull, roaring as he went. They broke before him like water, turning, and running, and falling one against another in their haste. The sword in his hands flashed like quicksilver into the huddle of our fleeing enemies; and at every flash there came the scream of a man hurt. I was still thinking we were lost, when lo! they were all gone, and Alan was driving them along the deck as a sheepdog chases sheep.

Yet he was no sooner out than he was back again, being as cautious as he was brave; and meanwhile the seamen continued running and crying out as if he was still behind them; and we heard them tumble one upon another into the forecastle, and clap-to the hatch upon the top.

The round-house was like a shambles; three were dead inside, another lay in his death agony across the threshold; and there were Alan and I victorious and unhurt.

He came to me with open arms. 'Come to my arms!' he cried, and embraced and kissed me hard upon both cheeks. 'David,' said he, 'I love you like a brother. And oh, man,' he cried in a kind of ecstasy, 'am I no a bonny fighter?'

Thereupon he turned to the four enemies, passed his sword clean through each of them, and tumbled them out of doors one after the other. As he did so, he keep humming and singing and whistling to himself, like a man trying to recall an air; only what *he* was trying, was to make one. All the while, the flush was in his face, and his eyes were as bright as a five-year-old child's with a new toy. And presently he sat down upon the table, sword in hand; the air that he was making all the time began to run a little clearer, and then clearer still; and then out he burst with a great voice into a Gaelic song.

I have translated it here, not in verse (of which I have no skill) but at least in the king's English. He sang it often afterwards, and the thing became popular; so that I have heard it, and had it explained to me, many's the time.

This is the song of the sword of Alan:
The smith made it,
The fire set it
Now it shines in the hand of Alan Breck.

Their eyes were many and bright,
Swift were they to behold,
Many the hands they guided:
The sword was alone.

The dun deer troop over the hill,
They are many, the hill is one:
The dun deer vanish,
The hill remains.

Come to me from the hills of heather,
Come from the isles of the sea.
O far-beholding eagles,
Here is your meat.

Now this song which he made (both words and music) in the hour of our victory, is something less than just to me, who stood beside him in the tussle. Mr Shuan and five more were either killed outright or thoroughly disabled; but of these, two fell by my hand, the two that came by the skylight. Four more were hurt, and of that number, one (and he not the least important) got his hurt from me. So that, altogether, I did my fair share both of the killing, and the wounding, and might have claimed a place in Alan's verses. But poets (as a very wise man once told me) have to think upon their rhymes; and in good prose talk, Alan always did me more than justice.

In the meanwhile, I was innocent of any wrong being done me. For not only I knew no word of the Gaelic; but what with the long suspense of the waiting, and the scurry and strain of our two spirts of fighting, and, more than all, the horror I had of some of my own share in it, the thing was no sooner over than I was glad to stagger to a seat. There was that tightness on my chest that I could hardly breathe; the thought of the two men I had shot sat upon me like a nightmare; and all upon a sudden, and before I had a guess of what was coming, I began to sob and cry like any child.

Alan clapped my shoulder, and said I was a brave lad and wanted nothing but a sleep.

'I'll take the first watch,' said he. 'Ye've done well by me, David, first and last; and I wouldn't lose you for all Appin – no, nor for Breadalbane.'

So he made up my bed on the floor, and took the first spell, pistol in hand and sword on knee; three hours by the captain's watch upon the wall. Then he roused me up, and I took my turn of three hours; before the end of which it was broad day, and a very quiet morning, with a smooth, rolling sea that tossed the ship and made the blood run to and fro on the round-house floor, and a heavy rain that drummed upon the roof. All my watch there was nothing stirring; and by the banging of the helm, I knew they had even no one at the tiller. Indeed (as I learned afterwards) they were so many of them hurt or dead, and the rest in so ill a temper, that Mr Riach and the captain had to take turn and turn like Alan and me, or the brig might have gone ashore and nobody the wiser. It was a mercy the night had fallen so still, for the wind had gone down as soon as the rain began. Even as it was, I judged by the wailing of a great number of gulls that went crying and fishing round the ship, that she must have drifted near pretty the coast or one of the islands of the Hebrides; and at last, looking out of the door of the round-house, I saw the great stone hills of Skye on the right hand, and, a little more astern, the strange isle of Rum.

ELEVEN

❖ The Captain Knuckles Under ❖

ALAN AND I SAT DOWN TO breakfast about six of the clock. The floor was covered with broken glass and in a horrid mess of blood, which took away my hunger. In all other ways we were in a situation not only agreeable but merry; having ousted the officers from their own cabin, and having at command all the drink in the ship – both wine and spirits and all the dainty part of what was eatable, such as the pickles and a fine sort of biscuit. This, of itself, was enough to set us in good humour; but the richest part of it was this, that the two thirstiest men that ever came out of Scotland (Mr Shuan being dead) were now shut in the fore-part of the ship and condemned to what they hated most – cold water.

'And depend upon it,' Alan said, 'we shall hear more of them ere long. Ye may keep a man from the fighting but never from his bottle.'

We made good company for each other. Alan, indeed, expressed himself most lovingly; and taking a knife from the table, cut me off one of the silver buttons from his coat.

'I had them,' says he, 'from my father, Duncan Stewart; and now give ye one of them to be a keepsake for last night's work. And wherever ye go and show that button, the friends of Alan Breck will come around you.'

He said this as if he had been Charlemagne, and commanded armies; and indeed, much as I admired his courage, I was always in danger of smiling at his vanity: in danger, I say, for had I not kept my countenance, I would be afraid to think what a quarrel might have followed.

As soon as we were through with our meal, he rummaged in the captain's locker till he found a clothes-brush; and then taking off his coat, began to visit his suit and brush away the stains, with such care and labour as I supposed to have been only usual with women. To be sure, he had no other; and, besides (as he said) it belonged to a King and so behoved to be royally looked after.

For all that, when I saw what care he took to pluck out the threads where the button had been cut away, I put a higher value on his gift.

He was still so engaged, when we were hailed by Mr Riach from the deck, asking for a parley; and I, climbing through the skylight and sitting on the edge of it, pistol in hand and with a bold front, though inwardly in fear of broken glass, hailed him back again and bade him speak out. He came to the edge of the round-house, and stood on a coil of rope, so that his chin was on a level with the roof; and we looked at each other a while in silence. Mr Riach, as I do not think he had been very forward in the battle, so he had got off with nothing worse than a blow upon the cheek; but he looked out of heart and very weary, having been all night afoot, either standing watch or doctoring the wounded.

'This is a bad job,' said he at last, shaking his head.

'It was none of our choosing,' said I.

'The captain,' says he, 'would like to speak with your friend. They might speak at the window.'

'And how do we know what treachery he means?' cried I.

'He means none, David,' returned Mr Riach; 'and if he did, I'll tell ye the honest truth, we couldnae get the men to follow.'

'Is that so?' said I.

'I'll tell ye more than that,' said he. 'it's not only the men; it's me. I'm frich'ened, Davie.' And he smiled across at me. 'No,' he continued, 'what we want is to be shut of him.'

Thereupon I consulted with Alan, and the parley was agreed to and parole given upon either side; but this was not the whole of Mr Riach's business, and he now begged me for a dram with such instancy and such reminders of his former kindness, that at last I handed him a pannikin with about a gill of brandy. He drank a part, and then carried the rest down uon the deck, to share it (I suppose) with his superior.

A little after, the captain came (as was agreed) to one of the windows, and stood there in the rain, with his arm in a sling, and looking stern and pale, and so old that my heart smote me for having fired upon him.

Alan at once held a pistol in his face.

'Put that thing up!' said the captain. 'Have I not passed my word, sir? or do ye seek to affront me?'

'Captain,' says Alan, 'I doubt your word is a breakable. Last night ye haggled and argle-bargled like an apple-wife; and then passed me your word, and gave me your hand to back it; and ye ken very well what was the upshot. Be damned to your word!' says he.

'Well, well, sir,' said the captain, 'ye'll get little good by swearing.' (And truly that was a fault of which the captain was quite free.) 'But we have other things to speak,' he continued, bitterly. 'Ye've made a sore hash of my brig; I haven't hands enough left to work her; and my first officer (whom I could ill spare) has got your sword throughout his vitals, and passed without speech. There is nothing left me, sir, but to put back into the port of Glasgow after hands; and there (by your leave) ye will find them that are better able to talk to you.'

'Ay?' said Alan; 'and faith, I'll have a talk with them mysel'! Unless there's naebody speaks English in that town, I have a bonny tale for them. Fifteen tarry sailors upon the one side, and a man and a halfling boy upon the other! Oh, man, it's peetiful!'

Hoseason flushed red.

'No,' continued Alan, 'that'll no do. Ye'll just have to set me ashore as we agreed.'

'Ay,' said Hoseason, 'but my first officer is dead – ye ken best how. There's none of the rest of us acquaint with this coast, sir; and it's one very dangerous to ships.'

'I give ye your choice,' says Alan. 'Set me on dry ground in Appin, or Ardgour, or in Morven, or Arisaig, or Morar; or, in brief where ye please, within thirty miles of my own country; except in a country of the Campbells. That's a broad target. If ye miss that, ye must be as feckless at the sailoring as I have found ye at the fighting. Why, my poor country people in their bit cobles* pass from island to island in all weathers, ay, and by night too, for the matter of that.'

'A coble's not a ship sir.' said the captain. 'It has nae draught of water.'

---

*Coble: a small boat used in fishing.

'Well, then, to Glasgow if ye list' says Alan. 'We'll have the laugh of ye at the least.'

'My mind runs little upon laughing,' said the captain. 'But all this will cost money sir.'

'Well, sir,' says Alan, 'I am nae weathercock. Thirty guineas, if ye land me on the sea-side; and sixty, if ye put me in the Linnhe lock.'

'But see, sir, where we lie, we are but a few hours' sail from Ardnamurchan,' said Hoseason. 'Give me sixty, and I'll set ye there.'

'And I'm to wear my brogues and run jeopardy of the red coats to please you?' cries Alan. 'No, sir, if ye want sixty guineas, earn them, and set me in my own country.'

'It's to risk the brig, sir,' said the captain, 'and your own lives along with her.'

'Take it or want it,' says Alan.

'Could ye pilot us at all?' asked the captain, who was frowning to himself.

'Well it's doubtful,' said Alan. 'I'm more of a fighting man (as ye have seen for yoursel') than a sailorman. But I have been often enough picked up and set down upon this coast, and should ken something of the lie of it.'

The captain shook his head, still frowning.

'If I had lost less money on this unchancy cruise,' says he, 'I would see you in a rope's-end before I risked my brig, sir. But be it as ye will. As soon as I get a slant of wind (and there's some coming, or I'm the more mistaken) I'll put it in hand. But there's one thing more. We may meet in with a king's ship and she may lay us aboard sir, with no blame of mine: they keep the cruisers thick upon this coast, ye ken who for. Now, sir, if that was to befall, ye might leave the money.'

'Captain,' says Alan, 'if ye see a pennant, it shall be your part to run away. And now, as I hear you're a little short of brandy in the forepart, I'll offer ye a change: a bottle of brandy against two buckets of water.'

That was the last clause of the treaty, and was duly executed on both sides; so that Alan and I could at last wash out the round-house and be quit of the memorials of those whom we had slain, and the captain and Mr Riach could be happy again in their own way, the name of which was drink.

TWELVE

❖ I Hear of the Red Fox ❖

BEFORE WE HAD DONE cleaning out the round-house, a breeze sprang up from a little to the east of north. This blew off the rain and brought out the sun.

And here I must explain; and the reader would do well to look at the map. On the day when the fog fell and we ran down Alan's boat, we had been running through the Little Minch. At dawn after the battle, we lay becalmed to the east of the Isle of Canna or between that and the Isle Eriska in the chain of the Long Islands. Now to get from there to the Linnhe Loch, the straight course was through the narrows of the Sound of Mull. But the captain had no chart; he was afraid to trust his brig so deep among the islands; and the wind serving well, he preferred to go by west of Tiree and come up under the southern coast of the great Isle of Mull.

All day the breeze held in the same point, and rather freshened then died down; and towards afternoon, a swell began to set in from round the outer Hebrides. Our course, to go round about the inner isles, was to the west of south, so that at first we had this swell upon our beam, and were much rolled about. But after nightfall, when we had turned the end of Tiree and began to head more to the east, the sea came right astern.

Meanwhile, the early part of the day, before the swell came up, was very pleasant; sailing, as we were, in a bright sunshine and with many mountainous islands upon different sides. Alan and I sat in the round-house with the doors open on each side (the wind being straight astern) and smoked a pipe or two of the captain's fine tobacco. It was at this time we heard each other's stories, which was the more important to me, as I gained some knowledge of that wild Highland country, on which I was so soon to land. In those days, so close on the back of the great rebellion, it was needful a man should know what he was doing when he went upon the heather.

It was I that showed the example, telling him all my misfortune; which he heard with great good nature. Only, when I came to mention that good friend of mine, Mr Campbell the minister, Alan fired up and cried out that he hated all that were of that name.

59

'Why,' said I, 'he is a man you should be proud to give your hand to.'

'I know nothing I would help a Campbell to,' says he, 'unless it was a leaden bullet. I would hunt all of that name like blackcocks. If I lay dying, I would crawl upon my knees to my chamber window for a shot at one.'

'Why, Alan,' I cried, 'what ails ye at the Campbells?'

'Well,' says he, 'ye ken very well that I am an Appin Stewart, and the Campbells have long harried and wasted those of my name; ay, and got lands of us by treachery – but never with the sword,' he cried loudly, and with the word brought down his fist upon the table. But I paid the less attention to this, for I knew it was usually said by those who have the under hand. 'There's more than that,' he continued, 'and all in the same story: lying words, lying papers, tricks fit for a peddler, and the show of what's legal over all, to make a man the more angry.'

'You that are so wasteful of your buttons,' said I, 'I can hardly think you would be a good judge of business.'

'Ah!' says he, falling again to smiling, 'I got my wastefulness from the same man I got the buttons from; and that was my poor father, Duncan Stewart, grace be to him! He was the prettiest man of his kindred; and the best swordsman in the Hielands, David, and that is the same as to say, in all the world. I should ken, for it was him that taught me. He was in the Black Watch, when first it was mustered; and like other gentlemen privates, had a gillie at his back to carry his firelock for him on the march. Well, the King, it appears, was wishful to see Hieland swordsmanship; and my father and three more were chosen out and sent to London town, to let him see it at the best. So they were had into the palace and showed the whole art of the sword for two hours at a stretch, before King George and Queen Carline, and the Butcher Cumberland, and many more of whom I have nae mind. And when they were through, the King (for all he was a rank usurper) spoke them fair and gave each man three guineas in his hand. Now, as they were going out of the palace, they had a porter's lodge to go by; and it came in on my father, as he was perhaps the first private Hieland gentleman that had ever gone by that door, it was right he should give the poor porter a proper notion of their quality. So he gives the King's three guineas into the man's hand, as if it was his common custom; the three others that came behind him did the same; and there they were on the street, never a peny the better for their pains. Some say it was one, that was the first to fee the King's porter; and some say it was another; but the truth of it is, that it was Duncan Stewart, as I am willing to prove with either sword or pistol. And that was the father that I had, God rest him!'

'I think he was not the man to leave you rich,' said I.

'And that's true,' said Alan. 'He left me my breeks to cover me, and little besides. And that was how I came to enlist, which was a black spot upon my character at the best of times, and would still be a sore job for me if I fell among the red-coats.'

'What,' cried I, 'were you in the English army?'

'That was I,' said Alan. 'But I deserted to the right side at Preston Pans – and that's some comfort.'

I could scarcely share this view: holding desertion under arms for an unpardonable fault in honour. But for all I was so young, I was wiser than say my thought. 'Dear, dear,' says I, 'the punishment is death.'

'Ay,' said he, 'if they got hands on me, it would be a short shrift and a long tow for Alan! But I have the King of France's commission in my pocket, which would aye be some protection.'

'I misdoubt it much,' said I.

'I have doubts mysel',' said Alan, drily.

'And, good heaven, man,' cried I, 'you that are a condemned rebel, and a deserter, and a man of the French King's – what tempts ye back into this country? It's a braving of Providence.'

'Tut!' says Alan, 'I have been back every year since forty-six!'

'And what brings ye, man?' cried I.

'Well, ye see, I weary for my friends and country,' said he. 'France is a braw place, nae doubt; but I weary for the heather and the deer. And then I have bit things that I attend to. Whiles I pick up a few lads to serve the King of France: recruits, ye see; and that's aye a little money. But the heart of the matter is the business of my chief, Ardshiel.'

'I thought they called your chief Appin,' said I.

'Ay, but Ardshiel is the captain of the clan,' said he, which scarcely cleared my mind. 'Ye see, David, he that was all his life so great a man, and come of the blood and bearing the name of kings, is now brought down to live in a French town like a poor and private person. He that had four hundred swords at his whistle, I have seen, with these eyes of mine, buying butter in the market-place, and taking it home in a kale-leaf. This is not only a pain but a disgrace to us of his family and clan. There are the bairns forby, the children and the hope of Appin, that must be learned their letters and how to hold a sword, in that far country. Now, the tenants of Appin have to pay a rent to King George; but their hearts are staunch, they are true to their chief; and what with love and a bit of pressure, and maybe a threat or two, the poor folk scrape up a second rent for Ardshiel. Well, David, I'm the hand that carries it.' And he struck the belt about his body, so that the guineas rang.

'Do they pay both?' cried I.

'Ay, David, both,' says he.

'What? two rents?' I repeated.

'Ay, David,' said he. 'I told a different tale to yon captain man; but this is the truth of it. And it's wonderful to me how little pressure is needed. But that's the handiwork of my good kinsman and my father's friend, James of the Glens; James Stewart, that is: Ardshiel's half-brother. He it is that gets the money in, and goes the management.'

This was the first time I heard the name of that James Stewart, who was afterwards so famous at the time of his hanging. But I took little heed at the moment, for all my mind was occupied with the generosity of these poor Highlanders.

'I call it noble,' I cried. 'I'm a Whig, or little better; but I call it noble.'

'Ay,' said he, 'ye're a Whig, but ye're a gentleman; and that's what does it. Now, if ye were one of the cursed race of Campbell, ye would gnash your teeth to hear tell of it. If ye were the Red Fox,' . . . And at that name, his teeth shut together, and he ceased speaking. I have seen many a grim face, but never a grimmer than Alan's when he had named the Red Fox.

'And who is the Red Fox?' I asked, daunted, but still curious.

'Who is he?' cried Alan. 'Well, and I'll tell you that. When the men of the clans were broken at Culloden, and the good cause went down, and the horses rode over the fetlocks in the best blood of the north, Ardshiel had to flee like a poor deer upon the mountains – he and his lady and his bairns. A sair job we had of it before we got him shipped; and while he still lay in the heather, the English rogues, that couldnae come at his life, were striking at his rights. They stripped him of his powers; they stripped him of his lands; they plucked the weapons from the hands of his clansmen, that had borne arms for thirty centuries; ay, and the very clothes off their backs – so that it's now a sin to wear a tartan plaid, and a man may be cast into a gaol if he has but a kilt about his legs. One thing they couldnae kill. That was the love the clansmen bore their chief. These guineas are the proof of it. And now, in there steps a man, a Campbell, red-headed Colin of Glenure—'

'Is that him you call the Red Fox?' said I.

'Will ye bring me his brush?' cries Alan, fiercely. 'Ay, that's the man. In he steps, and gets papers from King George, to be so-called King's factor on the lands of Appin. And at first he sings small, and is hail-fellow-well-met with Sheamus – that's James of the Glens, my chieftain's agent. But by and by, that came to his ears that I have just told you; how the poor commons of Appin, the farmers and the crofters and the boumen, were wringing their very plaids to get a second rent, and send it over-seas for Ardshiel and his poor bairns. What was it ye called it, when I told ye?'

'I called it noble, Alan,' said I.

'And you little better than a common Whig' cries Alan. 'But when it came to Colin Roy, the black Campbell blood in him ran wild. He sat gnashing his teeth at the wine table. What! should a Stewart get a bite of bread, and him not be able to prevent it? Ah! Red Fox, if ever I hold you at a gun's end, the Lord have pity upon ye!' (Alan stopped to swallow down his anger.) 'Well, David, what does he do? He declares all the farms to let. And thinks he, in his black heart, I'll soon get other tenants that'll overbid these Stewarts, and Maccolls, and Macrobs (for these are all names in my clan, David), "and then," thinks he, "Ardshiel will have to hold his bonnet on a French roadside." '

'Well,' said I, 'what followed?'

Alan laid down his pipe, which he had long since suffered to go out, and set his hands upon his knees.

'Ay,' said he, 'ye'll never guess that! For these same Stewarts, and Maccolls, and Macrobs (that had two rents to pay, one to King George by stark force, and one to Ardshiel by natural kindness), offered him a better price than any Campbell in all broad Scotland; and far he sent seeking them – as far as to the sides of Clyde and the cross of Edinburgh – seeking, and fleeching, and begging them to come, where there was a Stewart to be starved and a red-headed hound of a Campbell to be pleasured!'

'Well, Alan,' said I, 'that is a strange story, and a fine one, too. And Whig as I may be, I am glad the man was beaten.'

'Him beaten?' echoed Alan. 'It's little ye ken of Campbells and less of the Red Fox. Him beaten? No: nor will be, till his blood's on the hillside! But if the day comes, David man, that I can find time and leisure for a bit of hunting, there grows not enough heather in all Scotland to hide him from my vengeance!'

'Man Alan,' said I, 'ye are neither very wise nor very Christian to blow off so many words of anger. They will do the man ye call the Fox no harm, and yourself no good. Tell me your tale plainly out. What did he next?'

'And that's a good observe, David,' said Alan. 'Troth and indeed, they will do him no harm; the more's the pity! And barring that about Christianity (of which my opinion is quite otherwise, or I would be nae Christian) I am much of your mind.'

'Opinion here or opinion there,' said I, 'it's a kennt thing that Christianity forbids revenge.'

'Ay,' said he, 'it's well seen it was a Campbell taught ye! It would be a convenient world for them and their sort, if there was no such a thing as a lad and a gun behind a heather bush! But that's nothing to the point. This is what he did.'

'Ay,' said I, 'come to that.'

'Well, David,' said he, 'since he couldnae be rid of the loyal commons by fair means, he swore he would be rid of them by foul. Ardshiel was to starve: that was the thing he aimed at. And since them that fed him in his exile wouldnae be bought out – right or wrong, he would drive them out. Therefore he sent for lawyers, and papers, and red-coats to stand at his back. And the kindly folk of that country must all pack and tramp, every father's son out of his father's house, and out of the place where he was bred and fed, and played when he was a callant. And who are to succeed them? Bare-leggit beggars! King George is to whistle for his rents; he maun dow with less; he can spread his butter thinner: what cares Red Colin? If he can hurt Ardshiel, he has his wish; if he can pluck the meat from my chieftain's table, and the bit toys out of his children's hands, he will gang hame singing to Glenure!'

'Let me have a word,' said I. 'Be sure, if they take less rents, be sure Government has a finger in the pie. It's not this Campbell's fault, man – it's his orders. And if ye killed this Colin tomorrow, what better would ye be? There would be another factor in his shoes, as fast as spur can drive.'

'Ye're a good lad in a fight,' said Alan; 'but man! ye have Whig blood in ye!'

He spoke kindly enough, but there was so much anger under his contempt that I thought it was wise to change the conversation. I expressed my wonder how, with the Highlands covered with troops and guarded like a city in a siege, a man in his situation could come and go without arrest.

'It's easier than ye would think,' said Alan. 'A bare hillside (ye see) is like all one road; if there's a sentry at one place, ye just go by another. And then heather's a great help. And everywhere there are friends' houses and friends' byres and haystacks. And besides, when folk talk of a country covered with troops, it's but a kind of a byword at the best. A soldier covers nae mair of it than his bootsoles. I have fished a water with a sentry on the other side of the brae, and killed a fine trout; and I have sat in a heather bush within six feet of another, and learned a real bonny tune from his whistling. This was it,' said he, and whistled me the air.

'And then, besides,' he continued, 'it's no sae bad now as it was in forty-six. The Hielands are what they call pacified. Small wonder, with

never a gun or a sword left from Cantyre to Cape Wrath, but what tenty*
folk have hidden in their thatch! But what I would like to ken, David, is
just how long? Not long, ye would think, with men like Ardshiel in exile
and men like the Red Fox sitting birling the wine and oppressing the
poor at home. But it's a kittle thing to decide what folk'll bear, and what
they will not. Or why would Red Colin be riding his horse all over my
poor country of Appin, and never a pretty lad to put a bullet in him?'

And with this Alan fell into a muse, and for a long time sate very sad
and silent.

I will add the rest of what I have to say about my friend, that he was
skilled in all kinds of music, but principally pipe-music; was a well-
considered poet in his own tongue; had read several books both in French
and English; was a dead shot, a good angler, and an excellent fencer
with the small sword as well as with his own particular weapon. For his
faults, they were on his face, and I now knew them all. But the worst of
them, his childish propensity to take offence and to pick quarrels, he
greatly laid aside in my case, out of regard for the battle of the round-
house. But whether it was because I had done well myself, or because I
had been a witness of his own much greater prowess, is more than I can
tell. For though he had a great taste for courage in other men, yet he
admired it most in Alan Breck.

THIRTEEN

✦ The Loss of the Brig ✦

IT WAS ALREADY LATE AT night, and as dark as it ever would be at that
season of the year (and that is to say, it was still pretty bright), when
Hoseason clapped his head into the round-house door.

'Here,' said he, 'come out and see if ye can pilot.'

'Is this one of your tricks?' asked Alan.

'Do I look like tricks?' cried the captain. 'I have other things to think
of – my brig's in danger!' .

By the concerned look of his face, and, above all, by the sharp tones
in which he spoke of his brig, it was plain to both of us he was in deadly

*Careful.

earnest; and so Alan and I, with no great fear of treachery, stepped on deck.

The sky was clear; it blew hard, and was bitter cold; a great deal of daylight lingered; and the moon, which was nearly full, shone brightly. The brig was close hauled, so as to round the south-west corner of the Island of Mull, the hills of which (and Ben More above them all, with a wisp of mist upon the top of it) lay full upon the larboard bow. Though it was no good point of sailing for the *Covenant*, she tore through the seas at a great rate, pitching and straining, and pursued by the westerly swell.

Altogether it was no such ill night to keep the seas in; and I had begun to wonder what it was that sat so heavily upon the captain, when the brig rising suddenly on the top of a high swell, he pointed and cried to us to look. Away on the lee bow, a thing like a fountain rose out of the moonlit sea, and immediately after we heard a low sound of roaring.

'What do ye call that?' asked the captain, gloomily.

'The sea breaking on a reef,' said Alan. 'And now ye ken where it is; and what better would ye have?'

'Ay,' said Hoseason, 'if it was the only one.'

And sure enough just as he spoke there came a second fountain further to the south.

'There!' said Hoseason. 'Ye see for yourself. If I had kent of these reefs, if I had had a chart, or if Shuan had been spared, it's not sixty guineas, no, nor six hundred, would have made me risk my brig in sic a stoneyard! But you, sir, that was to pilot us, have ye never a word?'

'I'm thinking,' said Alan, 'these'll be what they call the Torran Rocks.'

'Are there many of them?' says the captain.

'Truly, sir, I am nae pilot,' said Alan; 'but it sticks in my mind there are ten miles of them.'

Mr Riach and the captain looked at each other.

'There's a way through them, I suppose?' said the captain.

'Doubtless,' said Alan; 'but where? But it somehow runs in my mind once more, that it is clearer under the land.'

'So?' said Hoseason. 'We'll have to haul our wind then, Mr Riach; we'll have to come as near in about the end of Mull as we can take her, sir; and even then we'll have the land to kep the wind off us, and that stoneyard on our lee. Well, we're in for it now, and may as well crack on.'

With that he gave an order to the steersman, and sent Riach to the foretop. There were only five men on deck, counting the officers; these were all that were fit (or, at least, both fit and willing) for their work; and two of these were hurt. So, as I say, it fell to Mr Riach to go aloft, and he sat there looking out and hailing the deck with news of all he saw.

'The sea to the south is thick,' he cried; and then, after a while, 'It does seem clearer in by the land.'

'Well, sir,' said Horseason to Alan, 'we'll try your way of it. But I think I might as well trust to a blind fiddler. Pray God you're right.'

'Pray God I am!' says Alan to me. 'But where did I hear it? Well, well, it will be as it must.'

As we got nearer to the turn of the land the reefs began to be sown here and there on our very path; and Mr Riach sometimes cried down to us to change the course. Sometimes, indeed, none too soon; for one reef was so close on the brig's weather board that when a sea burst upon it the lighter sprays fell upon her deck and wetted us like rain.

The brightness of the night showed us these perils as clearly as by day, which was, perhaps, the more alarming. It showed me, too, the face of the captain as he stood by the steersman, now on one foot, now on the other, and sometimes blowing in his hands, but still listening and looking and as steady as steel. Neither he nor Mr Riach had shown well in the fighting; but I saw they were brave in their own trade, and admired them all the more because I found Alan very white.

'Ochone, David,' says he, 'this is no the kind of death I fancy.'

'What, Alan!' I cried, 'you're not afraid?'

'No,' said he, wetting his lips, 'but you'll allow yourself it's a cold ending.'

By this time, now and then sheering to one side or the other to avoid a reef, but still hugging the wind and the land, we had got round Iona and begun to come alongside Mull. The tide at the tail of the land ran very strong, and threw the brig about. Two hands were put to the helm, and Hoseason himself would sometimes lend a help; and it was strange to see three strong men throw their weight upon the tiller, and it (like a living thing) struggle against and drive them back. This would have been the greater danger, had not the sea been for some while free of obstacles. Mr Riach, besides, announced from the top that he saw clear water ahead.

'Ye were right,' said Hoseason to Alan. 'Ye have saved the brig, sir; I'll mind that when we come to clear accounts.' And I believe he not only meant what he said, but would have done it; so high a place did the *Covenant* hold in his affections.

But this is matter only for conjecture, things having gone otherwise than he forecast.

'Keep her away a point,' sings out Mr Riach. 'Reef to windward!'

And just at the same time the tide caught the brig, and threw the wind out of her sails. She came round into the wind like a top, and the next moment struck the reef with such a dunch as threw us all flat upon the deck, and came near to shake Mr Riach from his place upon the mast.

I was on my feet in a minute. The reef on which we had struck was close in under the south-west end of Mull, off a little isle they called Earraid, which lay low and black upon the larboard. Sometimes the swell broke clean over us; sometimes it only ground the poor brig upon the reef, so that we could hear her beat herself to pieces; and what with the great noise of the sails, and the singing of the wind, and the flying of the spray in the moonlight, and the sense of danger, I think my head must have been partly turned, for I could scarcely understand the things I saw.

Presently I observed Mr Riach and the seamen busy round the skiff; and still in the same blank, ran over to assist them; and as soon as I set my hand to work, my mind came clear again. It was no very easy task, for the skiff lay amidships and was full of hamper, and the breaking of the heavier seas continually forced us to give over and hold on; but we all wrought like horses while we could.

Meanwhile such of the wounded as could move came clambering out of the fore-scuttle and began to help; while the rest that lay helpless in their bunks harrowed me with screaming and begging to be saved.

The captain took no part. It seemed he was struck stupid. He stood holding by the shrouds, talking to himself and groaning out aloud whenever the ship hammered on the rock. His brig was like wife and child to him; he had looked on, day by day, at the mishandling of poor Ransome; but when it came to the brig, he seemed to suffer along with her.

All the time of our working at the boat, I remember only one other thing; that I asked Alan, looking across at the shore, what country it was; and he answered, it was the worst possible for him, for it was a land of the Campbells.

We had one of the wounded men told off to keep a watch upon the seas and cry us warning. Well, we had the boat about ready to be launched, when this man sang out pretty shrill: 'For God's sake, hold on!' We knew by his tone that it was something more than ordinary; and sure enough, there followed a sea so huge that it lifted the brig right up and canted her over on her beam. Whether the cry came too late or my hold was too weak, I know not; but at the sudden tilting of the ship I was cast clean over the bulwarks into the sea.

I went down, and drank my fill; and then came up, and got a blink of the moon; and then down again. They say a man sinks the third time for good. I cannot be made like other folk, then; for I would not like to write how often I went down or how often I came up again. All the while, I was being hurled along, and beaten upon and choked, and then swallowed whole; and the thing was so distracting to my wits, that I was neither sorry nor afraid.

Presently, I found I was holding to a spar, which helped me somewhat. And then all of a sudden I was in quiet water, and began to come to myself.

It was the spare yard I had got hold of, and I was amazed to see how far I had travelled from the brig. I hailed her, indeed; but it was plain she was already out of cry. She was still holding together; but whether or not they had yet launched the boat, I was too far off and too low down to see.

While I was hailing the brig, I spied a tract of water lying between us, where no great waves came, but which yet boiled white all over and bristled in the moon with rings and bubbles. Sometimes the whole tract swung to one side, like the tail of a live serpent; sometimes, for a glimpse, it all would disappear and then boil up again. What it was I had no guess, which for the time increased my fear of it; but I now know it must have been the roost or tide race, which had carried me away so fast and tumbled me about so cruelly, and at last, as if tired of that play, had flung out me and the spare yard upon its landward margin.

I now lay quite becalmed, and began to feel that a man can die of cold as well as of drowning. The shores of Earraid were close in; I could see in the moonlight the dots of heather and the sparkling of the mica in the rocks.

'Well,' thought I to myself, 'if I cannot get as far as that, it's strange!'

I had no skill of swimming, Essen Water being small in our neighbourhood; but when I laid hold upon the yard with both arms, and kicked out with both feet, I soon began to find that I was moving. Hard work it was, and mortally slow; but in about an hour of kicking and splashing, I had got well in between the points of a sandy bay surrounded by low hills.

The sea was here quite quiet; there was no sound of any surf; the moon shone clear; and I thought in my heart I had never seen a place so desert and desolate. But it was dry land; and when at last it grew so shallow that I could leave the yard and wade ashore upon my feet, I cannot tell if I was more tired or more grateful. Both at least, I was; tired as I never was before that night; and grateful to God as I trust I have been often, though never with more cause.

FOURTEEN

❖ The Islet ❖

WITH MY STEPPING ASHORE I began the most unhappy part of my adventures. It was half past twelve in the morning, and though the wind was broken by the land, it was a cold night. I dared not sit down (for I thought I should have frozen), but took off my shoes and walked to and fro upon the sand, barefoot, and beating my breast, with infinite weariness. There was no sound of man or cattle; not a cock crew, though it was about the hour of their first waking; only the surf broke outside in the distance, which put me in mind of my perils and those of my friend. To walk by the sea at that hour of the morning, and in a place so desert-like and lonesome, struck me with a kind of fear.

As soon as the day began to break I put on my shoes and climbed a hill – the ruggedest scramble I ever undertook – falling, the whole way, between big blocks of granite or leaping from one to another. When I got to the top the dawn was come. There was no sign of the brig, which must have lifted from the reef and sunk. The boat, too, was nowhere to be seen. There was never a sail upon the ocean; and in what I could see of the land, was neither house nor man.

I was afraid to think what had befallen my shipmates, and afraid to look longer at so empty a scene. What with my wet clothes and weariness, and my belly that now began to ache with hunger, I had enough to trouble me without that. So I set off eastward along the south coast, hoping to find a house where I might warm myself, and perhaps get news of those I had lost. And at the worst, I considered the sun would soon rise and dry my clothes.

After a little, my way was stopped by a creek or inlet of the sea, which seemed to run pretty deep into the land; and as I had no means to get across, I must needs change my direction to go about the end of it. It was still the roughest kind of walking; indeed the whole, not only of Earraid, but of the neighbouring part of Mull (which they call the Ross) is nothing but a jumble of granite rocks with heather in among. At first the creek kept narrowing as I had looked to see; but presently to my surprise it began to widen out again. At this I scratched my head, but had still no notion of the truth; until at last I came to a rising ground, and it burst upon me all in a moment that I was cast upon a little, barren isle, and cut off on every side by the salt seas.

Instead of the sun rising to dry me, it came on to rain, with a thick mist; so that my case was lamentable.

I stood in the rain, and shivered, and wondered what to do, till it occurred to me that perhaps the creek was fordable. Back I went to the narrowest point and waded in. But not three yards from shore, I plumped in head over ears; and if ever I was heard of more it was rather by God's grace than my own prudence. I was no wetter (for that could hardly be) but I was all the colder for this mishap; and having lost another hope, was the more unhappy.

And now, all at once, the yard came in my head. What had carried me through the roost, would surely serve me to cross this little quiet creek in safety. With that I set off, undaunted, across the top of the isle, to fetch and carry it back. It was a weary tramp in all ways, and if hope had not buoyed me up, I must have cast myself down and given up. Whether with the sea salt, or because I was growing fevered, I was distressed with thirst, and had to stop, as I went, and drink the peaty water out of the hags.

I came to the bay at last, more dead than alive; and at the first glance, I thought the yard was something further out than when I left it. In I went, for the third time, into the sea. The sand was smooth and firm and shelved gradually down; so that I could wade out till the water was almost to my neck and the little waves splashed into my face. But at that depth my feet began to leave me and I durst venture in no further. As for the yard, I saw it bobbing very quietly some twenty feet in front of me.

I had borne up well until this last disappointment; but at that I came ashore, and flung myself down upon the sands and wept.

The time I spent upon the island is still so horrible a thought to me, that I must pass it lightly over. In all the books I have read of people cast away, they had either their pockets full of tools, or a chest of things would be thrown upon the beach along with them, as if on purpose. My case was very different. I had nothing in my pockets but money and Alan's silver button; and being inland bred, I was as much short of knowledge as of means.

I knew indeed that shell-fish were counted good to eat; and among the rocks of the isle I found a great plenty of limpets, which at first I could scarcely strike from their places, not knowing quickness to be needful. There were, besides, some of the little shells that we call buckies; I think periwinkle is the English name. Of these two I made my whole diet, devouring them cold and raw as I found them; and so hungry was I, that at first they seemed to me delicious.

Perhaps they were out of season, or perhaps there was something wrong in the sea about my island. But at least I had no sooner eaten my first meal than I was seized with giddiness and retching, and lay for a long time no better than dead. A second trial of the same food (indeed I had no other) did better with me and I revived my strength. But as long as I was on the island, I never knew what to expect when I had eaten; sometimes all was well, and sometimes I was thrown into a miserable sickness; nor could I ever distinguish what particular fish it was that hurt me.

All day it streamed rain; the island ran like a sop; there was no dry spot to be found; and when I lay down that night, between two boulders that made a kind of roof, my feet were in a bog.

The second day I crossed the island to all sides. There was no one part of it better than another; it was all desolate and rocky; nothing living on it but game birds which I lacked the means to kill, and the gulls which haunted the outlying rocks in a prodigious number. But the creek, or straits, that cut off the isle from the main land of the Ross, opened out on the north into a bay, and the bay again opened into the sound of Iona; and it was the neighbourhood of this place that I chose to be my home; though if I had thought upon the very name of home in such a spot, I must have burst out weeping.

I had good reasons for my choice. There was in this part of the isle a little hut of a house like a pig's hut, where fishers used to sleep when they came there upon their business; but the turf roof of it had fallen entirely in; so that the hut was of no use to me, and gave me less shelter than my rocks. What was more important, the shell-fish on which I lived grew there in great plenty; when the tide was out I could gather a peck at a time; and this was doubtless a convenience. But the other reason went deeper. I had become in no way used to the horrid solitude of the isle, but still looked round me on all sides (like a man that was hunted) between fear and hope that I might see some human creature coming. Now, from a little up the hillside over the bay, I could catch a sight of the great, ancient church and the roofs of the people's houses in Iona. And on the other hand, over the low country of the Ross, I saw smoke go up, morning and evening, as if from a homestead in a hollow of the land.

I used to watch this smoke, when I was wet and cold, and had my head half turned with loneliness; and think of the fireside and the company, till my heart burned. It was the same with the roofs of Iona. Altogether, this sight I had of men's homes and comfortable lives, although it put a point on my own sufferings, yet it kept hope alive, and helped me to eat my raw shell-fish (which had soon grown to be a disgust) and saved me from the sense of horror I had whenever I was quite alone with dead rocks, and fowls, and the rain, and the cold sea.

I say it kept hope alive; and indeed it seemed impossible that I should be left to die on the shores of my own country, and within view of a church tower and the smoke of men's houses. But the second day passed; and though as long as the light lasted I kept a bright look-out for boats on the Sound or men passing on the Ross, no help came near me. It still rained; and I turned in to sleep, as wet as ever and with a cruel sore throat, but a little comforted, perhaps, by having said good night to my next neighbours, the people of Iona.

Charles the Second declared a man could stay outdoors more days in the year in the climate of England than in any other. This was very like a king with a palace at his back and changes of dry clothes. But he must have had better luck on his flight from Worcester than I had on that miserable isle. It was the height of the summer; yet it rained for more than twenty-four hours, and did not clear until the afternoon of the third day.

This was the day of incidents. In the morning I saw a red deer, a buck with a fine spread of antlers, standing in the rain on the top of the island; but he had scarce seen me rise from under my rock, before he trotted off upon the other side. I supposed he must have swum the straits; though what should bring any creature to Earraid, was more than I could fancy.

A little after, as I was jumping about after my limpets, I was startled by a guinea-piece, which fell upon a rock in front of me and glanced off into the sea. When the sailors gave me my money again, they kept back not only about a third of the whole sum, but my father's leather purse; so that from that day out, I carried my gold loose in a pocket with a button. I now saw there must be a hole, and clapped my hand to the place in a great hurry. But this was to lock the stable door after the steed was stolen. I had left the shore at Queensferry with near on fifty pounds; now I found no more than two guinea pieces and a silver shilling.

It is true I picked up a third guinea a little after, where it lay shining on a piece of turf. That made a fortune of three pounds and four shillings, English money, for a lad, the rightful heir of an estate, and now starving on an isle at the extreme end of the wild Highlands.

This state of my affairs dashed me still further; and indeed my plight on that third morning was truly pitiful. My clothes were beginning to rot; my stockings in particular were quite worn through, so that my shanks went naked; my hands had grown quite soft with the continual soaking; my throat was very sore, my strength had much abated, and my heart so turned against the horrid stuff I was condemned to eat, that the very sight of it came near to sicken me.

And yet the worst was not yet come.

There is a pretty high rock on the north-west of Earraid, which (because it had a flat top and overlooked the Sound) I was much in the habit of frequenting; not that ever I stayed in one place, save when asleep, my misery giving me no rest. Indeed I wore myself down with continual and aimless goings and comings in the rain.

As soon, however, as the sun came out, I lay down on the top of that rock to dry myself. The comfort of the sunshine is a thing I cannot tell. It set me thinking hopefully of the deliverance, of which I had begun to despair, and I scanned the sea and the Ross with a fresh interest. On the south of my rock, a part of the island jutted out and hid the open ocean, so that a boat could thus come quite near me upon that side, and I be none the wiser.

Well, all of a sudden, a coble with a brown sail and a pair of fishers aboard of it, came flying round that corner of the isle, bound for Iona. I shouted out, and then fell on my knees on the rock and reached up my hands and prayed to them. They were near enough to hear – I could even see the colour of their hair; and there was no doubt but they observed me, for they cried out in the Gaelic tongue, and laughed. But the boat never turned aside, and flew on, right before my eyes, for Iona.

I could not believe such wickedness, and ran along the shore from rock to rock, crying on them piteously; even after they were out of reach of my voice, I still cried and waved to them; and when they were quite gone, I thought my heart would have burst. All the time of my troubles I wept only twice. Once, when I could not reach the yard; and now, the second time, when these fishers turned a deaf ear to my cries. But this time I wept and roared like a wicked child, tearing up the turf with my nails and grinding my face in the earth. If a wish would kill men, those two fishers would never have seen morning, and I should likely have died upon my island.

When I was a little over my anger, I must eat again, but with such loathing of the mess as I could now scarce control. Sure enough, I should have done as well to fast, for my fishes poisoned me again. I had all my first pains; my throat was so sore I could scarce swallow; I had a fit of strong shuddering, which clucked my teeth together; and there came on me that dreadful sense of illness, which we have no name for either in Scotch or English. I thought I should have died, and made my peace with God, forgiving all men, even my uncle and the fishers; and as soon as I had thus made up my mind to the worst, clearness came upon me: I observed the night was falling dry; my clothes were dried a good deal;

truly, I was in a better case than ever before, since I had landed on the isle; and so I got to sleep at last, with a thought of gratitude.

The next day (which was the fourth of this horrible life of mine) I found my bodily strength run very low. But the sun shone, the air was sweet, and what I managed to eat of the shell-fish agreed well with me and revived my courage.

I was scarce back on my rock (where I went always the first thing after I had eaten) before I observed a boat coming down the Sound, and with her head, as I thought, in my direction.

I began at once to hope and fear exceedingly; for I thought these men might have thought better of their cruelty and be coming back to my assistance. But another disappointment, such as yesterday's, was more than I could bear. I turned my back, accordingly, upon the sea, and did not look again till I had counted many hundreds. The boat was still heading for the island. The next time I counted the full thousand, as slowly as I could, my heart beating so as to hurt me. And then it was out of all question. She was coming straight to Earraid.

I could no longer hold myself back, but ran to the sea side and out, from one rock to another, as far as I could go. It is a marvel I was not drowned; for when I was brought to a stand at last, my legs shook under me, and my mouth was so dry, I must wet it with sea-water before I was able to shout.

All this time the boat was coming on; and now I was able to perceive it was the same boat and the same two men as yesterday. This I knew by their hair, which the one had of a bright yellow and the other black. But now there was a third man along with them, who looked to be of a better class.

As soon as they were come within easy speech, they let down their sail and lay quiet. In spite of my supplications, they drew no nearer in, and what frightened me most of all, the new man tee-hee'd with laughter as he talked and looked at me.

Then he stood up in the boat and addressed me a long while, speaking fast and with many wavings of his hand. I told him I had no Gaelic; and at this he became very angry, and I began to suspect he thought he was talking English. Listening very close, I caught the word 'whateffer' several times; but all the rest was Gaelic, and might have been Greek and Hebrew for me.

'Whatever,' said I, to show him I had caught a word.

'Yes, yes – yes, yes,' says he, and then he looked at the other men, as much as to say, 'I told you I spoke English', and began again as hard as ever in the Gaelic.

This time I picked out another word, 'tide'. Then I had a flash of hope.

I remembered he was always waving his hand towards the mainland of the Ross.

'Do you mean when the tide is out—?' I cried, and could not finish.

'Yes, yes,' said he. 'Tide.'

At that I turned tail upon their boat (where my adviser had once more begun to tee-hee with laughter), leaped back the way I had come, from one stone to another, and set off running across the isle as I had never run before. In about half an hour I came out upon the shores of the creek; and, sure enough, it was shrunk into a little trickle of water, through which I dashed, not above my knees, and landed with a shout on the main island.

A sea-bred boy would not have stayed a day on Earraid; which is only what they call a tidal islet, and except in the bottom of the neaps, can be entered and left twice in every twenty-four hours, either dry-shod, or at the most by wading. Even I, who had the tide going out and in before me in the bay, and even watched for the ebbs, the better to get my shell-fish – even I (I say), if I had sat down to think, instead of raging at my fate, must have soon guessed the secret, and got free. It was no wonder the fishers had not understood me. The wonder was rather that they had ever guessed my pitiful illusion, and taken the trouble to come back. I had starved with cold and hunger on that island for close upon one hundred hours. But for the fishers, I might have left my bones there, in pure folly. And even as it was, I had paid for it pretty dear, not only in past sufferings, but in my present case; being clothed like a beggar-man, scarce able to walk, and in great pain of my sore throat.

I have seen wicked men and fools, a great many of both; and I believe they both get paid in the end; but the fools first.

FIFTEEN

The Lad with the Silver Button: Through the Isle of Mull

THE ROSS OF MULL, WHICH I had now got upon, was rugged and trackless, like the isle I had just left; being all bog, and briar, and big stone. There may be roads for them that know that country well; but for my part I had no better guide than my own nose, and no other landmark than Ben More.

I aimed as well as I could for the smoke I had seen so often from the island; and with all my great weariness and the difficulty of the way, came upon the house in the bottom of a little hollow, about five or six at night. It was low and longish, roofed with turf and built of unmortared stones; and on a mound in front of it, an old gentleman sat smoking his pipe in the sun.

With what little English he had, he gave me to understand that my shipmates had got safe ashore, and had broken bread in that very house on the day after.

'Was there one,' I asked, 'dressed like a gentleman?'

He said they all wore rough great-coats; but to be sure, the first of them, the one that came alone, wore breeches and stockings, while the rest had sailors' trousers.

'Ah,' said I, 'and he would have a feathered hat?'

He told me, no, that he was bare-headed like myself.

At first I thought Alan might have lost his hat; and then the rain came in my mind, and I judged it more likely he had it out of harm's way under his great coat. This set me smiling, partly because my friend was sage, partly to think of his vanity in dress.

And then the old gentleman clapped his hand to his brow, and cried out that I must be the lad with the silver button.

'Why, yes!' said I, in some wonder.

'Well, then,' said the old gentleman, 'I have a word for you that you are to follow your friend to his country, by Torosay.'

He then asked me how I had fared, and I told him my tale. A south-country man would certainly have laughed; but this old gentleman (I call him so because of his manners, for his clothes were dropping off his back) heard me all through with nothing but gravity and pity. When I had done, he took me by the hand, led me into his hut (it was no better) and presented me before his wife, as if she had been the Queen and I a duke.

The good woman set oat-bread before me and a cold grouse, patting my shoulder and smiling to me all the time, for she had no English; and the old gentleman (not to be behind) brewed me a strong punch out of their country spirit. All the time I was eating, and after that when I was drinking the punch, I could scarce come to believe in my good fortune; and the house, though it was thick with the peat-smoke and as full of holes as a colander, seemed like a palace.

The punch threw me in a strong sweat and a deep slumber; the good people let me lie; and it was near noon of the next day before I took the road, my throat already easier and my spirits restored by good fare and good news. The old gentleman, although I pressed him hard, would take no money, and gave me an old bonnet for my head; though I am free to own I was no sooner out of view of the house, than I very jealously washed this gift of his in a wayside fountain.

Thought I to myself: 'If these are the wild Highlanders, I could wish my own folk wilder.'

I not only started late, but I must have wandered nearly half the time. True, I met plenty of people grubbing in little miserable fields that would not keep a cat, or herding little kine about the bigness of asses. The Highland dress being forbidden by law since the rebellion, and the people condemned to the lowland habit, which they much disliked, it was strange to see the variety of their array. Some went bare, only for a hanging cloak or great-coat, and carried their trousers on their backs like a useless burthen; some had made an imitation of the tartan with little parti-coloured stripes patched together like an old wife's quilt; others, again, still wore the highland philabeg, but by putting a few stitches between the legs, transformed it into a pair of trousers like a Dutchman's. All those makeshifts were condemned and punished, for the law was harshly applied, in hopes to break up the clan spirit; but in that out-of-the-way, seabound isle, there were few to make remarks and fewer to tell tales.

They seemed in great poverty; which was no doubt natural, now that rapine was put down, and the chiefs kept no longer an open house; and the roads (even such a wandering, country by-track as the one I followed) were infested with beggars. And here again I marked a difference from my own part of the country. For our lowland beggars – even the gownsmen themselves, who beg by patent – had a louting, flattering way with them, and if you gave them a plack and asked change, would very civilly return you a boddle. But these Highland beggars stood on their dignity, asked alms only to buy snuff (by their account) and would give no change.

To be sure, this was no concern of mine, except in so far as it entertained me by the way. What was much more to the purpose, few had any English, and these few (unless they were of the brotherhood of beggars) not very anxious to place it at my service. I knew Torosay to be my destination, and repeated the name to them and pointed; but instead of simply pointing in reply, they would give me a screed of the Gaelic that set me foolish; so it was small wonder if I went out of my road as often as I stayed in it.

At last, about eight at night and already very weary, I came to a lone house, where I asked admittance, and was refused, until I bethought me of the power of money in so poor a country, and held up one of my guineas in my finger and thumb. Thereupon, the man of the house, who had hitherto pretended to have no English, and driven me from his door by signals, suddenly began to speak as clearly as was needful, and agreed for five shillings to give me a night's lodging and guide me the next day to Torosay.

I slept uneasily that night, fearing I should be robbed; but I might have spared myself the pain; for my host was no robber, only miserably poor and a great cheat. He was not alone in his poverty; for the next morning, we must go five miles about to the house of what he called a rich man to have one of my guineas changed. This was perhaps a rich man for Mull; he would have scarce been thought so in the south; for it took all he had, the whole house was turned upside down, and a neighbour brought under contribution, before he could scrape together twenty shillings in silver. The odd shilling he kept for himself, protesting he could ill afford to have so great a sum of money lying 'locked up'. For all that he was very courteous and well spoken, made us both sit down with his family to dinner, and brewed punch in a fine china bowl, over which my rascal guide grew so merry that he refused to start.

I was for getting angry, and appealed to the rich man (Hector Maclean was his name) who had been a witness to our bargain and to my payment of the five shillings. But Maclean had taken his share of the punch, and vowed that no gentleman should leave his table after the bowl was brewed; so there was nothing for it but to sit and hear Jacobite toasts and Gaelic songs, till all were tipsy and staggered off to bed or the barn for their night's rest.

Next day (the fourth of my travels) we were up before five upon the clock; but my rascal guide got to the bottle at once, and it was three hours before I had him clear of the house, and then (as you shall hear) only for a worse disappointment.

As long as we went down a heathery valley that lay before Mr Maclean's house, all went well; only my guide looked constantly over his shoulder, and when I asked him the cause, only grinned at me. No sooner, however, had we crossed the back of a hill, and got out of sight of the house windows, than he told me Torosay lay right in front, and that a hill-top (which he pointed out) was my best landmark.

'I care very little for that,' said I, 'since you are going with me.'

The impudent cheat answered me in the Gaelic that he had no English.

'My fine fellow,' I said, 'I know very well your English comes and goes. Tell me what will bring it back? It is more money you wish?'

'Five shillings mair,' said he, 'and hersel' will bring ye there.'

I reflected a while and then offered him two, which he accepted greedily, and insisted on having in his hands at once – 'for luck', as he said, but I think it was rather for my misfortune.

The two shillings carried him not quite as many miles; at the end of which distance, he sat down upon the wayside and took off his brogues from his feet, like a man about to rest.

I was now red-hot. 'Ha!' said I, 'have you no more English?'

He said impudently, 'no'.

At that I boiled over and lifted my hand to strike him; and he, drawing a knife from his rags, squatted back and grinned at me like a wild-cat. At that, forgetting everything but my anger, I ran in upon him, put aside his knife with my left and struck him in the mouth with the right. I was a strong lad and very angry, and he but a little man; and he went down before me heavily. By good luck, his knife flew out of hand as he fell.

I picked up both that and his brogues, wished him a good morning, set off upon my way, leaving him bare-foot and disarmed. I chuckled to myself as I went, being sure I was done with that rogue, for a variety of reasons. First, he knew he could have no more of my money; next, the brogues were worth in that country only a few pence; and lastly the knife, which was really a dagger, it was against the law for him to carry.

In about half-an-hour of walk, I overtook a great, ragged man, moving pretty fast but feeling before him with a staff. He was quite blind, and told me he was a catechist, which should have put me at my ease. But his face went against me; it seemed dark and dangerous and secret; and presently, as we began to go on alongside, I saw the steel butt of a pistol sticking from under the flap of his coat-pocket. To carry such a thing meant a fine of fifteen pounds sterling upon a first offence, and transportation to the colonies upon a second. Nor could I quite see why a religious teacher should go armed, or what a blind man could be doing with a pistol.

I told him about my guide, for I was proud of what I had done, and my vanity for once got the heels of my prudence. At the mention of the five shillings he cried out so loud that I made up my mind I should say nothing of the other two, and was glad he could not see my blushes.

'Was it too much?' I asked, a little faltering.

'Too much!' cries he. 'Why, I will guide you to Torosay myself for a dram of brandy. And give you the great pleasure of my company (me that is a man of some learning) in the bargain.'

I said I did not see how a blind man could be a guide: but at that he laughed aloud, and said his stick was eyes enough for an eagle.

'In the Isle of Mull, at least,' says he, 'where I knew every stone and heather-bush by mark of head. See, now,' he said, striking right and left, as if to make sure, 'down there a burn is running; and at the head of it there stands a bit of a small hill with a stone cocked upon the top of that; and it's hard at the foot of the hill, that the way runs by to Torosay; and the way here, being for droves, is plainly trodden, and will show grassy through the heather.'

I had to own he was right in every feature, and told my wonder.

'Ha!' says he, 'that's nothing. Would ye believe me now, that before the Act came out, and when there were weapons in this country, I could shoot? Ay, could I!' cries he, and then with a leer: 'If ye had such a thing as a pistol here to try with, I would show ye how it's done.'

I told him I had nothing of the sort, and gave him a wider berth. If he had known, his pistol stuck at that time quite plainly out of his pocket, and I could see the sun twinkle on the steel of the butt. But by the better luck for me, he knew nothing, thought all was covered, and lied on in the dark.

He then began to question me cunningly, where I came from, whether I was rich, whether I could change a five-shilling piece for him (which he declared he had that moment in his sporran) and all the time he kept edging up to me and I avoiding him. We were now upon a sort of green cattle-track which crossed the hills towards Torosay, and we kept changing sides upon that like dancers in a reel. I had so plainly the upper-hand that my spirits rose, and indeed I took a pleasure in this game of blind-man's buff; but the catechist grew angrier and angrier, and at last began to swear in Gaelic and to strike for my legs with his staff.

Then I told him that, sure enough, I had a pistol in my pocket as well as he, and if he did not strike across the hill due south I would even blow his brains out.

He became at once very polite; and after trying to soften me for some time, but quite in vain, he cursed me once more in the Gaelic and took himself off. I watched him striding along, through bog and brier, tapping with his stick, until he turned the end of a hill and disappeared in the next hollow. Then I struck on again for Torosay, much better pleased to be alone than to travel with that man of learning. This was an unlucky day; and these two, of whom I had just rid myself one after the other, were the two worst men I met with in the Highlands.

At Torosay, on the Sound of Mull, and looking over to the mainland of Morven, there was an inn with an innkeeper, who was a Maclean, it appeared, of a very high family; for to keep an inn is thought even more genteel in the Highlands than it is with us, perhaps as partaking of hospitality, or perhaps because the trade is idle and drunken. He spoke good English, and finding me to be something of a scholar, tried me first in French, where he easily beat me, and then in the Latin, in which I don't know which of us did best. This pleasant rivalry put us at once upon friendly terms; and I sat up and drank punch with him (or to be more correct, sat up and watched him drink it) until he was so tipsy that he wept upon my shoulder.

I tried him, as if by accident, with a sight of Alan's button; but it was plain he had never seen or heard of it. Indeed, he bore some grudge against the family and friends of Ardshiel, and before he was drunk he read me a lampoon, in very good Latin, but with a very ill meaning, which he had made in elegiac verses upon a person of that house.

When I told him of my catechist, he shook his head, and said I was lucky to have got clear off. 'That is a very dangerous man,' he said; 'Duncan Mackiegh is his name; he can shoot by the ear at several yards, and has been often accused of highway robberies, and once of murder.'

'The cream of it is,' says I, 'that he called himself a catechist.'

'And why should he not?' says he, 'when that is what he is? It was Maclean of Duart gave it to him because he was blind. But, perhaps, it was a peety,' says my host, 'for he is always on the road, going from one place to another to hear the yound folk say their religion; and doubtless, that is a great temptation to the poor man.'

At last, when my landlord could drink no more, he showed me to a bed, and I lay down in very good spirits; having travelled the greater part of that big and crooked Island of Mull, from Earraid to Torosay, fifty miles as the crow flies and (with my wanderings) much nearer a hundred, in four days and with little fatigue. Indeed I was by far in better heart and health of body at the end of that long tramp than I had been at the beginning.

SIXTEEN

The Lad with the Silver Button: Across Morven

THERE IS A REGULAR FERRY from Torosay to Kinlochaline on the mainland. Both shores of the Sound are in the country of the strong clan of the Macleans, and the people that passed the ferry with me were almost all of that clan. The skipper of the boat, on the other hand, was called Neil Roy Macrob; and since Macrob was one of the names of Alan's clansmen, and Alan himself had sent me to that ferry, I was eager to come to private speech of Neil Roy.

In the crowded boat this was of course impossible, and the passage was a very slow affair. There was no wind, and as the boat was wretchedly equipped, we could pull but two oars on one side, and one on the other. The men gave way, however, with a good will, the passengers taking spells to help them, and the whole company giving the time in Gaelic boat-songs. And what with the songs, and the sea air, and the good nature and spirit of all concerned, and the bright weather, the passage was a pretty thing to have seen.

But there was one melancholy part. In the mouth of Loch Aline we found a great sea-going ship at anchor; and this I supposed at first to be one of the King's cruisers which were kept along that coast, both summer and winter, to prevent communication with the French. As we got a little nearer, it became plain she was a ship of merchandise; and what still puzzled me, not only her decks, but the sea-beach also, were quite black with people, and skiffs were continually plying to and fro between them. Yet nearer, and there began to come to our ears a great sound of mourning, the people on board and those on the shore crying and lamenting one to another so as to pierce the heart.

Then I understood this was an emigrant ship bound for the American colonies.

We put the ferry-boat alongside, and the exiles leaned over the bulwarks, weeping and reaching out their hands to my fellow-passengers, among whom they counted some near friends. How long this might have gone on I do not know, for they seemed to have no sense of time; but at last the captain of the ship, who seemed near beside himself (and no great wonder) in the midst of this crying and confusion, came to the side and begged us to depart.

Thereupon Neil sheered off; and the chief singer in our boat struck into a melancholy air, which was presently taken up both by the emigrants and their friends upon the beach, so that it sounded from all sides like a lament for the dying. I saw the tears run down the cheeks of the men and women in the boat, even as they bent at the oars; and the circumstances and the music of the song (which is one called 'Lochaber no more') were highly affecting even to myself.

At Kinlochaline I got Neil Roy upon one side on the beach, and said I made sure he was one of Appin's men.

'And what for no?' said he.

'I am seeking somebody,' said I; 'and it comes in my mind that you will have news of him. Alan Breck Stewart is his name.' And very foolishly, instead of showing him the button, I sought to pass a shilling in his hand.

At this he drew back. 'I am very much affronted,' he said; 'and this is not the way that one shentleman should behave to another at all. The man you ask for is in France; but if he was in my sporran,' says he, 'and your belly full of shillings, I would not hurt a hair upon his body.'

I saw I had gone the wrong way to work, and without wasting time upon apologies, showed him the button lying in the hollow of my palm.

'Aweel, aweel,' said Neil; 'and I think ye might have begun with that end of the stick, whatever! But if ye are the lad with the silver button, all is well, and I have the word to see that ye come safe. But if ye will pardon me to speak plainly,' says he, 'there is a name that you should never take into your mouth, and that is the name of Alan Breck; and there is a thing that ye would never do, and that is to offer your dirty money to a Hieland shentleman.'

It was not very easy to apologize; for I could scarce tell him (what was the truth) that I had never dreamed he would set up to be a gentleman until he told me so. Neil on his part had no wish to prolong his dealings with me, only to fulfil his orders and be done with it; and he made haste to give me my route. This was to lie the night in Kinlochaline in the public inn; to cross Morven the next day to Ardgour, and lie the night in the house of one John of the Claymore, who was warned that I might come; the third day, to be set across one loch at Corran and another at Balachulish, and then ask my way to the house of James of the Glens, at Aucharn in Duror of Appin. There was a good deal of ferrying, as you hear; the sea in all this part running deep into the mountains and winding about their roots. It makes the country strong to hold and difficult to travel, but full of prodigious wild and dreadful prospects.

I had some other advice from Neil: to speak with no one by the way, to avoid Whigs, Campbells, and the 'red-soldiers'; to leave the road and lie in a bush, if I saw any of the latter coming 'for it was never chancy to meet in with them'; and in brief, to conduct myself like a robber or a Jacobite agent, as perhaps Neil thought me.

The inn at Kinlochaline was the most beggarly vile place that ever pigs were styed in, full of smoke, vermin, and silent Highlanders. I was not only discontented with my lodging, but with myself for my mismanagement of Neil, and thought I could hardly be worse off. But very wrongly, as I was soon to see; for I had not been half an hour at the inn (standing in the door most of the time, to ease my eyes from the peat smoke) when a thunderstorm came close by, the springs broke in a little hill on which the inn stood, and one end of the house became a running water. Places of public entertainment were bad enough all over Scotland in those days; yet is was a wonder to myself, when I had to go from the fireside to the bed in which I slept, wading over the shoes.

Early in my next day's journey I overtook a little, stout, solemn man, walking very slowly with his toes turned out, sometimes reading in a book and sometimes marking the place with his finger, and dressed decently and plainly in something of a clerical style.

This I found to be another catechist, but of a different order from the blind man of Mull: being indeed one of those sent out by the Edinburgh Society for Propagating Christian Knowledge, to evangelize the more savage places of the Highlands. His name was Henderland; he spoke with the broad south-country tongue, which I was beginning to weary for the sound of; and besides common countryship, we soon found we had a more particular bond of interest. For my good friend, the minister of Essendean, had translated into the Gaelic in his by-time a number of hymns and pious books, which Henderland used in his work, and held in great esteem. Indeed it was one of these he was carrying and reading when we met.

We fell in company at once, our ways lying together as far as to Kingairloch. As we went, he stopped and spoke with all the wayfarers and workers that we met or passed; and though of course I could not tell what they discoursed about, yet I judged Mr Henderland must be well liked in the countryside, for I observed many of them to bring out their mulls and share a pinch of snuff with him.

I told him as far in my affairs as I judged wise; as far, that is, as they were none of Alan's; and gave Balachulish as the place I was travelling to, to meet a friend; for I thought Aucharn, or even Duror, would be too particular and might put him on the scent.

On his part he told me much of his work and the people he worked among, the hiding priests and Jacobites, the Disarming Act, the dress, and many other curiosities of the time and place. He seemed moderate; blaming Parliament in several points, and especially because they had framed the Act more severely against those who wore the dress than against those who carried weapons.

This moderation put it in my mind to question him of the Red Fox and the Appin tenants; questions which, I thought, would seem natural enough in the mouth of one travelling to that country.

He said it was a bad business. 'It's wonderful,' said he, 'where the tenants find the money, for their life is mere starvation. (Ye don't carry such a thing as snuff, do ye, Mr Balfour? No, Well, I'm better wanting it.) But these tenants (as I was saying) are doubtless partly driven to it.

James Stewart in Duror (that's him they call James of the Glens) is half-brother to Ardshiel, the captain of the clan; and he is a man much looked up to, and drives very hard. And then there's one they call Alan Breck—'

'Ah!' cried I, 'what of him?'

'What of the wind that bloweth where it listeth?' said Henderland. 'He's here and awa; here today and gone tomorrow: a fair heather-cat. He might be glowering at the two of us out of yon whin-bush, and I wouldnae wonder! Ye'll no carry such a thing as snuff, will ye?'

I told him no, and that he had asked the same thing more than once.

'It's highly possible,' said he sighing. 'But it seems strange ye should-nae carry it. However, as I was saying, this Alan Breck is a bold, desperate customer, and well kent to be James's right hand. His life is forfeit already; he would boggle at naething; and maybe, if a tenant-body was to hang back, he would get a dirk in his wame.'

'You make a poor story of it all, Mr Henderland,' said I. 'If it is all fear upon both sides, I care to hear no more of it.'

'Na,' said Mr Henderland, 'but there's love too, and self-denial that should put the like of you and me to shame. There's something fine about it; no perhaps Christian, but humanly fine. Even Alan Breck, by all that I hear, is a chield to be respected. There's many a lying sneck-draw sits close in kirk in our own part of the country, and stands well in the world's eye, and maybe is a far worse man, Mr Balfour, that yon misguided shedder of man's blood. Ay, ay, we might take a lesson by them. – Ye'll perhaps think I've been too long in the Hielands?' he added, smiling to me.

I told him not at all; that I had seen much to admire among the Highlanders; and if he came to that, Mr Campbell himself was a High-lander.

'Ay,' said he, 'that's true. It's a fine blood.'

'And what is the King's agent about?' I asked.

'Colin Campbell?' says Henderland. 'Putting his head in a bees' byke!'

'He is to turn the tenants out by force, I hear?' said I.

'Yes,' says he, 'but the business has gone back and forth, as folk say. First, James of the Glens rode to Edinburgh and got some lawyer (a Stewart, nae doubt – they all hing together like bats in a steeple) and had the proceedings stayed. And then Colin Campbell cam' in again, and had the upper-hand before the Barons of Exchequer. And now they tell me the first of the tenants are to flit tomorrow. It's to begin at Duror under James's very windows, which doesnae seem wise by my humble way of it.'

'Do you think they'll fight?' I asked.

'Well,' says Henderland, 'they're disarmed – or supposed to be – for there's still a good deal of cold iron lying by in quiet places. And then Colin Campbell has the sogers coming. But for all that, if I was his lady wife, I wouldnae be well pleased till I got him home again. They're queer customers, the Appin Stewarts.'

I asked if they were worse than their neighbours.

'No they,' said he. 'And that's the worst part of it. For if Colin Roy can get his business in Appin, he has it all to begin again in the next country, which they call Mamore, and which is one of the countries of the Camerons. He's King's Factor upon both, and from both he has to drive out the tenant; and indeed, Mr Balfour (to be open with ye), it's my belief that if he escapes the one lot, he'll get his death by the other.'

So we continued talking and walking the great part of the day; until at last, Mr Henderland, after expressing his delight in my company, and satisfaction at meeting with a friend of Mr Campbell's ('whom,' says he, 'I will make bold to call that sweet singer of our convenanted Zion') proposed that I should make a short stage, and lie the night in his house a little beyond Kingairloch. To say truth, I was overjoyed; for I had no great desire for John of the Claymore, and since my double misadventure, first with the guide and next with the gentleman skipper, I stood in some fear of any Highland stranger. Accordingly we shook hands upon the bargain, and came in the afternoon to a small house, standing alone by the shore of the Linnhe Loch. The sun was already gone from desert mountains of Ardgour upon the hither side, but shone on those of Appin on the farther; the loch lay as still as a lake, only the gulls were crying round the sides of it; and the whole place seemed solemn and uncouth.

We had no sooner come to the door of Mr Henderland's dwelling, than to my great surprise (for I was now used to the politeness of Highlanders) he burst rudely past me, dashed into the room, caught up a jar and a small horn spoon, and began ladling snuff into his nose in most excessive quantities. Then he had a hearty fit of sneezing, and looked round upon me with a rather silly smile.

'It's a vow I took,' says he. 'I took a vow upon me that I wouldnae carry it. Doubtless it's a great privation; but when I think upon the martyrs, not only to the Scottish Covenant but to other points of Christianity, I think shame to mind it.'

As soon as we had eaten (and porridge and whey was the best of the good man's diet) he took a grave face and said he had a duty to perform by Mr Campbell, and that was to inquire into my state of mind towards God. I was inclined to smile at him, since the business of the snuff; but he had not spoken long before he brought the tears into my eyes. There are two things that men should never weary of, goodness and humility; we get none too much of them in this rough world among cold, proud people; but Mr Henderland had their very speech upon his tongue. And though I was a good deal puffed up with my adventures and with having come off, as the saying is, with flying colours; yet he soon had me on my knees beside a simple, poor old man, and both proud and glad to be there.

Before we went to bed he offered me sixpence to help me on my way, out of a scanty store he kept in the turf wall of his house; at which excess of goodness I knew not what to do. But at last he was so earnest with me, that I thought it the more mannerly part to let him have his way, and so left him poorer than myself.

SEVENTEEN

✦ The Death of the Red Fox ✦

THE NEXT DAY MR HENDERLAND found for me a man who had a boat of his own and was to cross the Linnhe Loch that afternoon into Appin, fishing. Him he prevailed on to take me, for he was one of his flock; and in this way I saved a long day's travel and the price of the two public ferries I must otherwise have passed.

It was near noon before we set out; a dark sky, with clouds, and the sun shining upon little patches. The sea was here very deep and still, and had scarce a wave upon it; so that I must put the water to my lips before I could believe it to be truly salt. The mountains on either side were high, rough and barren, very black and gloomy in the shadow of the clouds, but all silver-laced with little watercourses where the sun shone upon them. It seemed a hard country, this of Appin, for people to care as much about as Alan did.

There was but one thing to mention. A little after we had started, the sun shone upon a little moving clump of scarlet close in along the waterside to the north. It was much of the same red as soldiers' coats; every now and then, too, there came little sparks and lightnings, as though the sun had struck upon bright steel.

I asked my boatman what it should be; and he answered he supposed it was some of the red soldiers coming from Fort William into Appin, against the poor tenantry of the country. Well, it was a sad sight to me; and whether it was because of my thoughts of Alan, or from something prophetic in my bosom, although this was but the second time I had seen King George's troops, I had no good will to them.

At last we came so near the point of land at the entering in of Loch Leven that I beddged to be set on shore. My boatman (who was an honest fellow and mindful of his promise to the catechist) would fain have carried me on to Balachulish; but as this was to take me farther from my secret destination, I insisted, and was set on shore at last under the wood of Lettermore (or Lettervore, for I have heard it both ways) in Alan's country of Appin.

This was a wood of birches, growing on a steep, craggy side of a mountain that overhung the loch. It had many openings and ferny dells; and a road or bridle track ran north and south through the midst of it, by the edge of which, where was a spring, I sat down to eat some oatbread of Mr Henderland's, and think upon my situation.

Here I was not only troubled by a cloud of stinging midges, but far more by the doubts of my mind. What I ought to do, why I was going to join my self with an outlaw and a would-be murderer like Alan, whether I should not be acting more like a man of sense to tramp back to the south country direct, by my own guidance and at my own charges, and what Mr Campbell or even Mr Henderland would think of me if they should ever learn my folly and presumption; these were the doubts that now began to come in on me stronger than ever.

As I was sitting and thinking, a sound of men and horses came to me through the wood; and presently after, at a turning of the road, I saw four travellers come into view. The way was in this part so rough and narrow that they came single and led their horses by the reins. The first was a great, red-headed gentleman, of an imperious and flushed face, who carried his hat in his hand and fanned himself, for he was in a breathing heat. The second, by his decent black garb and white wig, I correctly took to be a lawyer. The third was a servant, and wore some part of his clothes in tartan, which showed that his master was of a Highland family, and either an outlaw or else in singular good odour with the Government, since the wearing of tartan was against the Act. If I had been better versed in these things, I would have known the tartan to be of the Argyle (or Campbell) colours. This servant had a good-sized portmanteau strapped on his horse, and a net of lemons (to brew punch with) hanging at the saddle-bow; as was often enough the custom with luxurious travellers in that part of the country.

As for the fourth, who brought up the tail, I had seen his like before, and knew him at once to be a sheriff's officer.

I had no sooner seen these people coming than I made up my mind (for no reason that I can tell) to go through with my adventure; and when the first came alongside of me, I rose up from the bracken and asked him the way to Aucharn.

He stopped and looked at me, as I thought, a little oddly; and then, turning to the lawyer, 'Mungo,' said he, 'there's many a man would think this more of a warning than two pyats. Here am I on the road to Duror on the job ye ken; and here is a young lad starts up out of the bracken, and speers if I am on the way to Aucharn.'

'Glenure,' said the other, 'this is an ill subject for jesting.'

These two had now drawn close up and were gazing at me, while the two followers had halted about a stone-cast in the rear.

'And what seek ye in Aucharn?' said Colin Roy Campbell of Glenure; him they called the Red Fox; for he it was that I had stopped.

'The man that lives there,' said I.

'James of the Glens,' says Glenure, musingly; and then to the lawyer: 'Is he gathering his people, think ye?'

'Anyway,' says the lawyer, 'we shall do better to bide where we are, and let the soldiers rally us.'

'If you are concerned for me,' said I, 'I am neither of his people nor yours, but an honest subject of King George, owing no man and fearing no man.'

'Why, very well said,' replies the Factor. 'But if I may make so bold as ask, what does this honest man so far from his country? and why does he come seeking the brother of Ardshiel? I have power here, I must tell you. I am King's Factor upon several of these estates, and have twelve files of soldiers at my back.'

'I have heard a waif word in the country,' said I, a little nettled, 'that you were a hard man to drive.'

He still kept looking at me, as if in doubt.

'Well,' said he, at last, 'your tongue is bold; but I am no unfriend to plainness. If ye had asked me the way to the door of James Stewart on any other day but this, I would have set ye right and bidden ye God speed. But today – eh, Mungo?' And he turned again to look at the lawyer.

But just as he turned there came the shot of a firelock from higher up the hill; and with the very sound of it Glenure fell upon the road.

'Oh, I am dead!' he cried, several times over.

The lawyer had caught him up and held him in his arms, the servant standing over and clasping his hands. And now the wounded man looked from one to another with scared eyes, and there was a change in his voice that went to the heart.

'Take care of yourselves,' says he. 'I am dead.'

He tried to open his clothes as if to look for the wound, but his fingers slipped on the buttons. With that he gave a great sigh, his head rolled on his shoulder, and he passed away.

The lawyer said never a word, but his face was as sharp as a pen and as white as the dead man's; the servant broke out into a great noise of crying and weeping, like a child; and I, on my side, stood staring at them in a kind of horror. The sheriff's officer had run back at the first sound of the shot, to hasten the coming of the soldiers.

At last the lawyer laid down the dead man in his blood upon the road, and got to his own feet with a kind of stagger.

I believe it was his movement that brought me to my senses, for he had no sooner done so than I began to scramble up the hill, crying out, 'The murderer! the murderer!'

So little a time had elapsed, that when I got to the top of the first steepness, and could see some part of the open mountain, the murderer was still moving away at no great distance. He was a big man, in a black coat, with metal buttons, and carried a long fowling-piece.

'Here!' I cried, 'I see him!'

At that the murderer gave a little, quick look over his shoulder, and began to run. The next moment he was lost in a fringe of birches; then he came out again on the upper side, where I could see him climbing like a jackanapes, for that part was again very steep; and then he dipped behind a shoulder, and I saw him no more.

All this time I had been running on my side, and had got a good way up, when a voice cried upon me to stand.

I was at the edge of the upper wood, and so now, when I halted and looked back, I saw all the open part of the hill below me.

The lawyer and the sheriff's officer were standing just above the road, crying and waving on me to come back; and on their left, the red-coats, musket in hand, were beginning to struggle singly out of the lower wood.

'Why should I come back?' I cried. 'Come you on!'

'Ten pounds if ye take that lad!' cried the lawyer. 'He's an accomplice. He was posted here to hold us in talk.'

At that word (which I could hear quite plainly, though it was to the soldiers and not to me that he was crying it) my heart came into my mouth with quite a new kind of terror. Indeed, it is one thing to stand the danger of your life, and quite another to run the peril of both life and character. The thing, besides, had come so suddenly, like thunder out of a clear sky, that I was all amazed and helpless.

The soldiers began to spread, some of them to run, and others to put up their pieces and cover me; and still I stood.

'Jouk* in here among the trees,' said a voice, close by.

Indeed, I scarce knew what I was doing, but I obeyed; and as I did so, I heard the firelocks bang and the balls whistle in the birches.

Just inside the shelter of the trees I found Alan Breck standing, with a fishing-rod. He gave me no salutation; indeed it was no time for civilities; only 'Come!' says he, and set off running along the side of the mountain towards Balachulish; and I, like a sheep, to follow him.

Now we ran among the birches, now stooping behind low humps upon the mountain side; now crawling on all fours among the heather. The pace was deadly; my heart seemed bursting against my ribs; and I had neither time to think nor breath to speak with. Only I remembered seeing with wonder that Alan every now and then would straighten himself to his full height and look back; and every time he did so, there came a great far-away cheering and crying of the soldiers.

Quarter of an hour later, Alan stopped, clapped down flat in the heather, and turned to me.

'Now,' said he, 'it's earnest. Do as I do for your life.'

And at the same speed, but now with infinitely more precaution, we traced back again across the mountain side by the same way that we had come, only perhaps higher; till at last Alan threw himself down in the upper wood of Lettermore, where I had found him at the first, and lay, with his face in the bracken, panting like a dog.

My own sides so ached, my head so swam, my tongue so hung out of my mouth with heat and dryness, that I lay beside him like one dead.

EIGHTEEN

I Talk with Alan in the Wood of Lettermore

ALAN WAS THE FIRST TO COME round. He rose, went to the border of the wood, peered out a little, and then returned and sat down.

'Well,' said he, 'yon was a hot burst, David.'

I said nothing, nor so much as lifted my face. I had seen murder done, and a great, ruddy, jovial gentleman struck out of life in a moment; the

*Duck.

pity of that sight was still sore within me, and yet that was but a part of my concern. Here was murder done upon the man Alan hated; here was Alan skulking in the trees and running from the troops; and whether his was the hand that fired or only the head that ordered, signified but little. By my way of it, my only friend in that wild country was blood-guilty in the first degree; I held him in horror; I could not look upon his face; I would have rather lain alone in the rain on my cold isle, than in that warm wood beside a murderer.

'Are ye still wearied?' he asked again.

'No,' said I, still with my face in the bracken; 'no, I am not wearied now, and I can speak. You and me must twine*,' I said. 'I liked you very well, Alan; but your ways are not mine, and they're not God's; and the short and the long of it is just that we must twine.'

'I will hardly twine from ye, David, without some kind of reason for the same,' said Alan, mighty gravely. 'If ye ken anything against my reputation, it's the least thing that ye should do, for old acquaintance sake, to let me hear the name of it; and if ye have only taken a distaste to my society, it will be proper for me to judge if I'm insulted.'

'Alan,' said I, 'what is the sense of this? Ye ken very well yon Campbell-man lies in his blood upon the road.'

He was silent for a little; then says he, 'Did ever ye hear tell of the story of the Man and the Good People?' – by which he meant the fairies.

'No,' said I, 'nor do I want to hear it.'

'With your permission, Mr Balfour, I will tell it you, whatever,' says Alan. 'The man, ye should ken, was cast upon a rock in the sea, where it appears the Good People were in use to come and rest as they went through to Ireland. The name of this rock is called the Skerryvore, and it's not far from where we suffered shipwreck. Well, it seems the man cried so sore, if he could just see his little bairn before he died! that at last the king of the Good People took peety upon him, and sent one flying that brought back the bairn in a poke† and laid it down beside the man where he lay sleeping. So when the man woke, there was a poke beside him and something into the inside of it that moved. Well, it seems he was one of these gentry that think aye the worst of things; and for greater security, he stuck his dirk throughout that poke before he opened it, and there was his bairn dead. I am thinking to myself, Mr Balfour, that you and the man are very much alike.'

'Do you mean you had no hand in it?' cried I, sitting up.

'I will tell you first of all, Mr Balfour of Shaws, as one friend to another,' said Alan, 'that if I were going to kill a gentleman, it would

*Part.
†Bag.

93

not be in my own country, to bring trouble on my clan; and I would not go wanting sword and gun, and with a long fishing-rod upon my back.'

'Well,' said I, 'that's true!'

'And now,' continued Alan, taking out his dirk and laying his hand upon it in a certain manner, 'I swear upon the Holy Iron I had neither art nor part, act nor thought in it.'

'I thank God for that!' cried I, and offered him my hand.

He did not appear to see it.

'And here is a great deal of work about a Campbell!' said he. 'They are not so scarce, that I ken!'

'At least,' said I, 'you cannot justly blame me, for you know very well what you told me in the brig. But the temptation and act are different, I thank God again for that. We may all be tempted; but to take a life in cold blood, Alan!' And I could say no more for the moment. 'And do you know who did it?' I added. 'Do you know that man in the black coat?'

'I have nae clear mind about his coat,' said Alan, cunningly; 'but it sticks in my head that it was blue.'

'Blue or black, did ye know him?' said I.

'I couldnae just conscientiously swear to him,' says Alan. 'He gaed very close by me, to be sure, but it's a strange thing that I should just have been tying my brogues.'

'Can you swear that you don't know him, Alan?' I cried, half angered, half in a mind to laugh at his evasions.

'Not yet,' says he; 'but I've a grand memory for forgetting, David.'

'And yet there was one thing I saw clearly,' said I; 'and that was, that you exposed yourself and me to draw the soldiers.'

'It's very likely,' said Alan; 'and so would any gentleman. You and me were innocent of that transaction.'

'The better reason, since we were falsely suspected, that we should get clear,' I cried. 'The innocent should surely come before the guilty.'

'Why, David,' said he, 'the innocent have aye a chance to get assoiled in court; but for the lad that shot the bullet, I think the best place for him will be the heather. Them that havenae dipped their hands in any little difficulty, should be very mindful of the case of them that have. And that is the good Christianity. For if it was the other way round about, and the lad whom I couldnae just clearly see had been in our shoes, and we in his (as might very well have been) I think we would be a good deal obliged to him oursel's if he would draw the soldiers.'

When it came to this, I gave Alan up. But he looked so innocent all the time, and was in such clear good faith in what he said, and so ready to sacrifice himself for what he deemed his duty, that my mouth was closed. Mr Henderland's words came back to me: that we ourselves might take a lesson by these wild Highlanders. Well, here I had taken mine. Alan's morals were all tail-first; but he was ready to give his life for them, such as they were.

'Alan,' said I, 'I'll not say it's the good Christianity as I understand it, but it's good enough. And here I offer ye my hand for the second time.'

Whereupon he gave me both of his, saying surely I had cast a spell upon him, for he could forgive me anything. Then he grew very grave, and said we had not much time to throw away, but must both flee that country; he, because he was a deserter, and the whole Appin would now be searched like a chamber, and every one obliged to give a good account of himself; and I, because I was certainly involved in the murder.

'Oh!' says I, willing to give him a little lesson, 'I have no fear of the justice of my country.'

'As if this was your country!' said he. 'Or as if ye would be tried here, in a country of Stewarts!'

'It's all Scotland,' said I.

'Man, I whiles wonder at ye,' said Alan. 'This is a Campbell that's been killed. Well, it'll be tried in Inverara, the Campbells' head place; with fifteen Campbells in the jurybox, and the biggest Campbell of all (and that's the Duke) sitting cocking on the bench. Justice, David? The same justice, by all the world, as Glenure found a while ago at the roadside.'

This frightened me a little, I confess, and would have frighted me more if I had known how nearly exact were Alan's predictions; indeed it was but in one point that he exaggerated, there being but eleven Campbells on the jury; though as the other four were equally in the Duke's dependence, it mattered less than might appear. Still, I cried out that he was unjust to the Duke of Argyle who (for all he was a Whig), was yet a wise and honest nobleman.

'Hoot!' cried Alan, 'the man's a Whig, nae doubt; but I would never deny he was a good chieftain to his clan. And what would the clan think if there a Campbell shot, and naebody hanged, and their own chief the Justice General? But I have often observed,' says Alan, 'that you Low-country bodies have no clear idea of what's right and wrong.'

At this I did at last laugh out aloud; when to my surprise, Alan joined in and laughed as merrily as myself.

'Na, na,' said he, 'we're in the Hielands, David; and when I tell ye to run, take my word and run. Nae doubt it's a hard thing to skulk and starve in the heather, but it's harder yet to lie shackled in a red-coat prison.'

I asked him whither we should flee; and as he told me 'to the Lowlands', I was a little better inclined to go with him; for indeed I was growing impatient to get back and have the upper hand of my uncle. Besides, Alan made so sure there would be no question of justice in the matter, that I began to be afraid he might be right. Of all deaths, I would truly like least to die by the gallows; and the picture of that uncanny instrument came into my head with extraordinary clearness (as I had once seen it engraved at the top of a pedlar's ballad) and took away my appetite for courts of justice.

'I'll chance it, Alan,' said I. 'I'll go with you.'

'But mind you,' said Alan, 'it's no small thing. Ye maun lie bare and hard, and brook many an empty belly. Your bed shall be the moorcock's, and your life shall be like the hunted deer's, and ye shall sleep with your hand upon your weapons. Ay, man, ye shall taigle many a weary foot, or we get clear! I tell ye this at the start, for it's a life that I ken well. But if ye ask what other chance ye have, I answer: Nane. Either take to the heather with me, or else hang.'

'And that's a choice very easily made,' said I; and we shook hands upon it.

'And now let's take another keek at the red-coats,' says Alan, and he led me to the north-eastern fringe of the wood.

Looking out between the trees, we could see a great side of mountain, running down exceeding steep into the waters of the loch. It was a rough part, all hanging stone, and heather, and bit scrags of birchwood; and away at the far end towards Balachulish, little wee red soldiers were dipping up and down over hill and howe, and growing smaller every minute. There was no cheering now, for I think they had other uses for what breath was left them; but they still stuck to the trail, and doubtless thought that we were close in front of them.

Alan watched them, smiling to himself.

'Ay,' said he, 'they'll be gey weary before they've got to the end of that employ! And so you and me, David, can sit down and eat a bite, and breathe a bit longer, and take a dram from my bottle. Then we'll strike for Aucharn, the house of my kinsman, James of the Glens, where I must get my clothes, and my arms, and money to carry us along; and then David, we'll cry "Forth, Fortune!" and take a cast among the heather.'

So we sat again and ate and drank, in a place whence we could see the sun going down into a field of great, wild, and houseless mountains, such as I was now condemned to wander in with my companion. Partly as we so sat, and partly afterwards, on the way to Aucharn, each of us narrated his adventures; and I shall here set down so much of Alan's as seems either curious or needful.

It appears he ran to the bulwarks as soon as the wave was passed; saw me, and lost me, and saw me again, as I tumbled in the roost; and at last had one glimpse of me clinging on the yard. It was this that put him in some hope I would maybe get to land after all, and made him leave those clues and messages which had brought me (for my sins) to that unlucky country of Appin.

In the meanwhile, those still on the brig had got the skiff launched, and one or two were on board of her already, when there came a second wave greater than the first, and heaved the brig out of her place, and would certainly have sent her to the bottom, had she not struck and caught on some projection of the reef. When she had struck first, it had been bows-on, so that the stern had hitherto been lowest. But now her stern was thrown in the air, and the bows plunged under the sea; and with that, the water began to pour into the forescuttle like the pouring of a mill-dam.

It took the colour out of Alan's face, even to tell what followed. For there were still two men lying impotent in their bunks; and these, seeing the water pour in and thinking the ship had foundered, began to cry out aloud, and that with such harrowing cries that all who were on deck tumbled one after another into the skiff and fell to their oars. They were not two hundred yards away, when there came a third great sea; and at that the brig lifted clean over the reef; her canvas filled for a moment, and she seemed to sail in chase of them, but settling all the while; and presently she drew down and down, as if a hand was drawing her; and the sea closed over the *Covenant* of Dysart.

Never a word they spoke as they pulled ashore, being stunned with the horror of that screaming; but they had scarce set foot upon the beach when Hoseason woke up, as if out of a muse, and bade them lay hands upon Alan. They hung back indeed, having little taste for the employment; but Hoseason was like a fiend; crying that Alan was alone, that he had a great sum about him, that he had been the means of losing the brig and drowning all their comrades, and that here was both revenge and wealth upon a single cast. It was seven against one; in that part of the shore there was no rock that Alan could set his back to; and the sailors began to spread out and come behind him.

'And then,' said Alan, 'the little man with the red head – I havenae mind of the name that he is called.'

'Riach,' said I.

'Ay,' said Alan, 'Riach! Well, it was him that took up the clubs for me, asked the men if they werenae feared of a judgement, and says he, "Dod, I'll put my back to the Hielandman's mysel'," That's none such an entirely bad little man, yon little man with the red head,' said Alan. 'He had some spunks of decency.'

'Well,' said I, 'he was kind to me in his way.'

'And so he was to Alan,' said he; 'and by my troth, I found his way a very good one! But ye see, David, the loss of the ship and the cries of these poor lads sat very ill upon the man; and I'm thinking that would be the cause of it.'

'Well, I would think so,' says I; 'for he was as keen as any of the rest at the beginning. But how did Hoseason take it?'

'It sticks in my mind that he would take it very ill,' says Alan. 'But the little man cried to me to run, and indeed I thought it was a good observe, and ran. The last that I saw they were all in a knot upon the beach, like folk that were not agreeing very well together.'

'What do you mean by that?' said I.

'Well, the fists were going,' said Alan; 'and I saw one man go down like a pair of breeks. But I thought it would be better no to wait. Ye see there's a strip of Campbells in that end of Mull, which is no good company for a gentleman like me. If it hadnae been for that I would have waited aand looked for ye mysel', let alone giving a hand to the little man.' (It was droll how Alan dwelt on Mr Riach's stature, for, to say the truth, the one was not much smaller than the other). 'So,' says he, continuing, 'I set my best foot forward, and whenever I met in with anyone I cried out there was a wreck ashore. Man, they didnae stop to fash with me! Ye should have seen them linking for the beach! And when they got there they found they had had the pleasure of a run, which is aye good for a Campbell. I'm thinking it was a judgement on the clan that the brig went down in the lump and didnae break. But it was a very unlucky thing for you, that same; for if any wreck had come ashore they would have hunted high and low, and would soon have found ye.'

NINETEEN

✦ The House of Fear ✦

NIGHT FELL AS WE WERE walking, and the clouds, which had brocken up in the afternoon, settled in and thickened, so that it fell, for the season of the year, extremely dark. The way we went was over rough mountain sides; and though Alan pushed on with an assured manner, I could by no means see how he directed himself.

At last, about half past ten of the clock, we came to the top of a brae, and saw lights below us. It seemed a house door stood open and let out a beam of fire and candlelight; and all round the house and steading five or six persons were moving hurriedly about, each carrying a lighted brand.

'James must have tint his wits,' said Alan. 'If this was the soldiers instead of you and me, he would be in a bonny mess. But I dare say he'll have a sentry on the road, and he would ken well enough no soldiers would find the way that we came.'

Hereupon he whistled three times, in a particular manner. It was strange to see how, at the first sound of it, all the moving torches came to a stand, as if the bearers were affrighted; and how, at the third, the bustle began again as before.

Having thus set folks' minds at rest, we came down the brae, and were met at the yard gate (for this place was like a well-doing farm) by a tall, handsome man of more than fifty, who cried out to Alan in the Gaelic.

'James Stewart,' said Alan. 'I will ask ye to speak in Scotch, for here is a young gentleman with me that has nane of the other. This is him,' he added, putting his arm through mine, 'a young gentleman of the lowlands, and a laird in his country too, but I am thinking it will be the better for his health if we give his name the go-by.'

James of the Glens turned to me for a moment, and greeted me courteously enough; the next he had turned to Alan.

'This has been a dreadful accident,' he cried. 'It will bring trouble on the country.' And he wrung his hands.

'Hoots!' said Alan, 'ye must take the sour with the sweet, man. Colin Roy is dead, and be thankful for that!'

'Ay,' said James, 'and by my troth, I wish he was alive again! It's all very fine to blow and boast beforehand; but now it's done, Alan; and who's to bear the wyte* of it? The accident fell out in Appin – mind ye that, Alan; it's Appin that must pay; and I am a man that has a family.'

While this was going on I looked about me at the servants. Some were on ladders, digging in the thatch of the house or the farm buildings, from which they brought out guns, swords, and different weapons of war; others carried them away; and by the sound of mattock blows from somewhere further down the brae, I suppose they buried them. Though they were all so busy, there prevailed no kind of order in their efforts;

*Blame.

men struggled together for the same gun and ran into each other with their burning torches; and James was continually turning about from his talk with Alan, to cry out orders which were apparently never understood. The faces in the torchlight were like those of people overborne with hurry and panic; and though none spoke above his breath, their speech sounded both anxious and angry.

It was about this time that a lassie came out of the house carrying a pack or bundle; and it has often made me smile to think how Alan's instinct awoke at the mere sight of it.

'What's that the lassie has?' he asked.

'We're just setting the house in order, Alan,' said James, in his frightened and somewhat fawning way. 'They'll search Appin with candles, and we must have all things straight. We're digging the bit guns and swords into the moss, ye see; and these, I am thinking, will be your ain French clothes.'

'Bury my French clothes!' cried Alan. 'Troth, no!' And he laid hold upon the packet and retired into the barn to shift himself, recommending me in the meanwhile to his kinsman.

James carried me accordingly into the kitchen, and sat down with me at table, smiling and talking at first in a very hospitable manner. But presently the gloom returned upon him; he sat frowning, and biting his fingers; only remembered me from time to time; and then gave me but a word or two and a poor smile, and back into his private terrors. His wife sat by the fire and wept, with her face in her hands; his eldest son was crouched upon the floor, running over a great mass of papers and now and again setting one alight and burning it to the bitter end; all the while a servant with a red face was rummaging about the room, in a blind hurry of fear, and whimpering as she went: and every now and again one of the men would thrust in his face from the yard, and cry for orders.

At last James could keep his seat no longer, and begged my permission to be so unmannerly as walk about. 'I am but poor company altogether, sir,' says he, 'but I can think of nothing but this dreadful accident, and the trouble it is like to bring upon quite innocent persons.'

A little after he observed his son burning a paper, which he thought should have been kept; and at that his excitement burst out so that it was painful to witness. He struck the lad repeatedly.

'Are you gone gyte*?' he cried. 'Do you wish to hang your father?' and forgetful of my presence, carried on at him a long time together in the Gaelic, the young man answering nothing; only the wife, at the name

*Mad.

of hanging, throwing her apron over her face and sobbing out louder than before.

This was all wretched for a stranger like myself to hear and see; and I was right glad when Alan returned, looking like himself in his fine French clothes, though (to be sure) they were now grown almost too battered and withered to deserve the name of fine. I was then taken out in my turn by another of the sons, and given that change of clothing of which I had stood so long in need, and a pair of Highland brogues made of deer-leather, rather strange at first, but after a little practice very east to the feet.

By the time I came back Alan must have told his story; for it seemed understood that I was to fly with him, and they were all busy upon our equipment. They gave us each a sword and pistols, though I professed my inability to use the former; and with these, and some ammunition, a bag of oatmeal, an iron pan, and a bottle of right French brandy, we were ready for the heather. Money, indeed, was lacking. I had about two guineas left; Alan's belt having been despatched by another hand, that trusty messenger had no more than seventeen-pence to his whole fortune; and as for James, it appears he had brought himself so low with journeys to Edinburgh and legal expenses on behalf of the tenants, that he could only scrape together three-and-five-pence-halfpenny, the most of it in coppers.

'This'll no do,' said Alan.

'Ye must find a safe bit somewhere near by,' said James, 'and get word sent to me. Ye see, ye'll have to get this business prettily off, Alan. This is no time to be stayed for a guinea or two. They're sure to get wind of ye, sure to seek ye, and by my word of it, sure to lay on ye the wyte of this day's accident. If it falls on you, it falls on me that am your near kinsman and harboured ye while ye were in the country. And if it comes on me—' he paused, and bit his fingers, with a white face. 'It would be a painful thing for our friends if I was to hang,' said he.

'It would be an ill day for Appin,' says Alan.

'It's a day that sticks in my throat,' said James, 'Oh man, man, man – man Alan! you and me have spoken like two fools!' he cried, striking his hand upon the wall so that the house rang again.

'Well, and that's true, too,' said Alan; 'and my friend from the lowlands here' (nodding at me) 'gave me a good word upon that head, if I would only have listened to him.'

'But see here,' said James, returning to his former manner, 'if they lay me by the heels, Alan, it's then that you'll be needing the money. For with all that I have said and that you have said, it will look very black against the two of us; do ye mark that? Well, follow me cut, and ye'll see that I'll have to get a paper out against ye mysel'; I'll have to offer a reward for ye; ay, will I! It's a sore thing to do between such near friends; but if I get the dirdum* of this dreadful accident, I'll have to fend for myself, man. Do ye see that?'

He spoke with a pleading earnestness, taking Alan by the breast of the coat.

'Ay,' said Alan, 'I see that.'

'And ye'll have to be clear of the country, Alan – ay, and clear of Scotland – you and your friend from the lowlands, too. For I'll have to paper your friend from the lowlands. Ye see that, Alan – say that ye see that!'

I thought Alan flushed a bit. 'This is unco hard on me that brought him here, James,' said he, throwing his head back. 'It's like making me a traitor!'

'Now, Alan, man!' cried James. 'Look things in the face! He'll be papered anyway; Mungo Campbell'll be sure to paper him; what matters if I paper him too? And then, Alan, I am a man that has a family.' And then, after a little pause on both sides: 'And, Alan, it'll be a jury of Campbells,' said he.

'There's one thing,' said Alan, musingly, 'that naebody kens his name.'

'Nor yet they shallnae, Alan! There's my hand on that,' cried James, for all the world as if he had really known my name and was forgoing some advantage. 'But just the habit he was in, and what he looked like, and his age, and the like? I couldnae well do less.'

'I wonder at your father's son,' cried Alan, sternly. 'Would ye sell the lad with a gift? would ye change his clothes and then betray him?'

'No, no, Alan,' said James, 'No, no: the habit he took off – the habit Mungo saw him in.' But I thought he seemed crestfallen; indeed, he was clutching at every straw, and all the time, I dare say, saw the faces of his hereditary foes on the bench and in the jury-box, and the gallows in the background.

'Well, sir,' says Alan, turning to me, 'what say ye to that? Ye are here under the safeguard of my honour; and it's my part to see nothing done but what shall please you.'

'I have but one word to say,' said I; 'for to all this dispute I am a perfect stranger. But the plain common sense is to set the blame where it belongs, and that is on the man that fired the shot. Paper him, as ye call it, set the hunt on him; and let honest, innocent folk show their faces in safety.'

But at this both Alan and James cried out in horror; bidding me hold

*Blame.

my tongue, for that was not to be thought of; and asking me 'What the Camerons would think?' (which confirmed me, it must have been a Cameron from Mamore that did the act) and if I did not see that the lad might be caught? 'Ye havenae surely though of that?' said they, with such innocent earnestness, that my hands dropped at my side and I despaired of argument.

'Very well, then,' said I, 'paper me, if you please, paper Alan, paper King George! We're all three innocent, and that seems to be what's wanted! But at least, sir,' said I to James, recovering from my little fit of annoyance, 'I am Alan's friend, and if I can be helpful to friends of his, I will not stumble at the risk.'

I thought it best to put a fair face on my consent, for I saw Alan troubled; and besides (thinks I to myself) as soon as my back is turned, they will paper me, as they call it, whether I consent or not. But in this I saw I was wrong; for I had no sooner said the words, than Mrs Stewart leaped out of her chair, came running over to us, and wept first upon my neck and then on Alan's, blessing God for our goodness to her family.

'As for you, Alan, it was no more than your bounden duty,' she said. 'But for this lad that has come here and seen us at our worst, and seen the goodman fleeching like a suitor, him that by rights should give his commands like any king – as for you, my lad,' she says, 'my heart is wae not to have your name, but I have your face; and as long as my heart beats under my bosom, I will keep it, and think of it, and bless it.' And with that she kissed me, and burst once more into such sobbing, that I stood abashed.

'Hoot, hoot,' said Alan, looking mighty silly. 'The day comes unco soon in this month of July; and tomorrow there'll be a fine to-do in Appin, a fine riding of dragoons, and crying of "Cruachan!"* and running of red-coats; and it behoves you and me to be the sooner gone.'

Thereupon we said farewell, and set out again, bending somewhat eastward, in a fine mild dark night, and over much the same broken country as before.

*The rallying-word of the Campbells.

The Flight in the Heather: the Rocks

SOMETIMES WE WALKED, sometimes ran; and as it drew on to morning, walked ever the less and ran the more. Though, upon its face, that country appeared to be a desert, yet there were huts and houses of the people, of which we must have passed more than twenty, hidden in quiet places of the hills. When we came to one of these, Alan would leave me in the way, and go himself and rap upon the side of the house and speak a while at the window with some sleeper awakened. This was to pass the news; which, in that country, was so much of a duty that Alan must pause to attend to it even while fleeing for his life; and so well attended to by others, that in more than half of the houses where we called they had heard already of the murder. In the others, as well as I could make out (standing back at a distance and hearing a strange tongue) the news was received with more of consternation than surprise.

For all our hurry, day began to come in while we were still far from any shelter. It found us in a prodigious valley, strewn with rocks and where ran a foaming river. Wild mountains stood around it; there grew there neither grass nor trees; and I have sometimes thought since then, that it may have been the valley called Glencoe, where the massacre was in the time of King William. But for the details of our itinerary, I am all to seek; our way lying now by short cuts, now by great detours; our pace beging so hurried; our time of journeying usually by night; and the names of such places as I asked and heard, being in the Gaelic tongue and the more easily forgotten.

The first peep of morning, then, showed us this horrible place, and I could see Alan knit his brow.

'This is no fit place for you and me,' he said. 'This is a place they're bound to watch.'

And with that he ran harder than ever down to the water side, in a part where the river was split in two among three rocks. It went through with a horrid thundering that made my belly quake; and there hung over the lynn a little mist of spray. Alan looked neither to the right nor to the left, but jumped clean upon the middle rock and fell there on his hands and knees to check himself, for that rock was small and he might have pitched over on the far side. I had scarce time to measure the distance or to understand the peril, before I had followed him, and he had caught and stopped me.

So there we stood side by side upon a small rock slippery with spray, a far broader leap in front of us, and the river dinning upon all sides. When I saw where I was, there came on me a deadly sickness of fear, and I put my hand over my eyes. Alan took me and shook me; I saw he was speaking, but the roaring of the falls and the trouble of my mind prevented me from hearing; only I saw his face was red with anger, and that he stamped upon the rock. The same look showed me the water raging by, and the mist hanging in the air; and with that, I covered my eyes again and shuddered.

The next minute Alan had set the brandy bottle to my lips, and forced me to drink about a gill, which sent the blood into my head again. Then, putting his hands to his mouth and his mouth to my ear, he shouted, 'Hang or drown!' and turning his back upon me, leaped over the farther branch of the stream, and landed safe.

I was now alone upon the rock, which gave me the more room; the brandy was singing in my ears; I had this good example fresh before me, and just wit enough to see that if I did not leap at once, I should never leap at all. I bent low on my knees and flung myself forth, with that kind of anger of despair that has sometimes stood me in stead of courage. Sure enough, it was but my hands that reached the full length; these slipped, caught again, slipped again; and I was sliddering back into the lynn, when Alan seized me, first by the hair, then by the collar, and with a great strain dragged me into safety.

Never a word he said, but set off running again for his life, and I must stagger to my feet and run after him. I had been weary before, but now I was sick and bruised, and partly drunken, with the brandy; I kept stumbling as I ran, I had a stitch that came near to overmaster me; and when at last Alan paused under a great rock that stood there among a number of others, it was none too soon for David Balfour.

A great rock, I have said; but by rights it was two rocks leaning together at the top, both some twenty feet high, and at first sight inaccessible. Even Alan (though you may say he had as good as four hands) failed twice in an attempt to climb them; and it was only at the third trial, and then by standing on my shoulders and leaping up with such force as I thought must have broken my collar-bone, that he secured a lodgement. Once there, he let down his leathern girdle; and with the aid of that and a pair of shallow footholds in the rocks, I scrambled up beside him.

Then I saw why he had come there; for the two rocks, being both somewhat hollow on the top and sloping one to the other, made a kind of dish or saucer, where as many as three or four men might have lain hidden.

All this while Alan had not said a word, and had run and climbed with such a savage, silent frenzy of hurry, that I knew he was in mortal fear of some miscarriage. Even now we were on the rock he said nothing, nor so much as relaxed the frowning look upon his face; but clapped flat down, and keeping only one eye above the edge of our place of shelter, scouted all round the compass. The dawn had come quite clear; we could see the stony sides of the valley, and its bottom, which was bestrewed with rocks, and the river, which went from one side to another, and made white falls; but nowhere the smoke of a house, nor any living creature but some eagles screaming round a cliff.

Then at last Alan smiled.

'Ay,' said he, 'now we have a chance'; and then looking at me with some amusement, 'Ye're no very gleg* at the jumping,' said he.

At this I suppose I coloured with mortification, for he added at once, 'Hoots! small blame to ye! To be feared of a thing and yet to do it, is what makes the prettiest kind of a man. And then there was water there, and water's a thing that dauntons even me. No, no,' said Alan, 'it's no you that's to blame, it's me.'

I asked him why.

'Why,' said he, 'I have proved myself a gomeral this night. For first of all I take a wrong road, and that in my own country of Appin; so that the day has caught us where we should never have been; and thanks to that, we lie here in some danger and mair discomfort. And next (which is the worst of the two, for a man that has been so much among the heather as myself) I have come wanting a water-bottle, and here we lie for a long summer's day with naething but neat spirit. Ye may think that a small matter; but before it comes night, David, ye'll give me news of it.'

I was anxious to redeem my character, and offered, if he would pour out the brandy, to run down and fill the bottle at the river.

'I wouldnae waste the good spirit either,' says he. 'It's been a good friend to you this night; or in my poor opinion, ye would still be cocking on yon stone. And what's mair,' says he, 'ye may have observed (you that's a man of so much penetration) that Alan Breck Stewart was perhaps walking quicker than his ordinar'.'

'You!' I cried, 'you were running fit to burst.'

'Was I so?' said he. 'Well, then, ye may depend upon it, there was nae

*Brisk.

time to be lost. And now here is enough said; gang you to your sleep, lad, and I'll watch.'

Accordingly, I lay down to sleep; a little peaty earth had drifted in between the top of the two rocks, and some bracken grew there, to be a bed to me; the last thing I heard was still the crying of the eagles.

I dare say it would be nine in the morning when I was roughly awakened, and found Alan's hand pressed upon my mouth.

'Wheesht!' he whispered. 'Ye were snoring.'

'Well,' said I, surprised at his anxious and dark face, 'and why not?'

He peered over the edge of the rock, and signed to me to do the like. It was now high day, cloudless, and very hot. The valley was as clear as in a picture. About half a mile up the water was a camp of red-coats; a big fire blazed in their midst, at which some were cooking; and near by, on the top of a rock about as high as ours, there stood a sentry, with the sun sparkling on his arms. All the way down along the riverside were posted other sentries; here near together, there widelier scattered; some planted like the first, on places of command, some on the ground level and marching and counter-marching, so as to meet half way. Higher up the glen, where the ground was more open, the chain of posts was continued by horse-soldiers, whom we could see in the distance riding to and fro. Lower down, the infantry continued; but as the stream was suddenly swelled by the confluence of a considerable burn, they were more widely set, and only watched the fords and stepping-stones.

I took but one look at them, and ducked again into my place. It was strange indeed to see this valley, which had lain so solitary in the hour of dawn, bristling with arms and dotted with the red coats and breeches.

'Ye see,' said Alan, 'this was what I was afraid of, Davie: that they would watch the burn-side. They began to come in about two hours ago, and, man! but ye're a grand hand at the sleeping! We're in a narrow place. If they get up the sides of the hill, they could easy spy us with a glass; but if they'll only keep in the foot of the valley, we'll do yet. The posts are thinner down the water; and, come night, we'll try our hand at getting by them.'

'And what are we to do till night?' I asked.

'Lie here,' says he, 'and birstle.'

That one good Scotch word, 'birstle,' was indeed the most of the story of the day that we had now to pass. You are to remember that we lay on the bare top of a rock, like scones upon a girdle; the sun beat upon us cruelly; the rock grew so heated, a man could scarce endure the touch of it; and the little patch of earth and fern, which kept cooler, was only large enough for one at a time. We took turn about to lie on the naked rock, which was indeed like the position of that saint that was martyred

107

on a gridiron; and it ran in my mind how strange it was, that in the same climate and at only a few days' distance, I should have suffered so cruelly, first from cold upon my island, and now from heat upon this rock.

All the while we had no water, only a raw brandy for a drink, which was worse than nothing; but we kept the bottle as cool as we could, burying it in the earth, and got some relief by bathing our breasts and temples.

The soldiers kept stirring all day in the bottom of the valley, now changing guard, now in patrolling parties hunting among the rocks. These lay round in so great a number, that to look for men among them was like looking for a needle in a bottle of hay; and being so hopeless a task, it was gone about with the less care. Yet we could see the soldiers pike their bayonets among the heather, which sent a cold thrill into my vitals; and they would sometimes hang about our rock, so that we scarce dared to breathe.

It was in this way that I first heard the right English speech; one fellow as he went by actually clapping his hand upon the sunny face of the rock on which we lay, and plucking it off again with an oath.

'I tell you it's 'ot,' says he; and I was amazed at the clipping tones and the odd sing-song in which he spoke, and no less at that strange trick of dropping out the letter h. To be sure, I had heard Ransome; but he had taken his ways from all sorts of people, and spoke so imperfectly at the best, that I set down the most of it to childishness. My surprise was all the greater to hear that manner of speaking in the mouth of a grown man; and indeed I have never grown used to it; nor yet altogether with the English grammar, as perhaps a very critical eye might here and there spy out even in these memoirs.

The tediousness and pain of these hours upon the rock grew only the greater as the day went on; the rock getting still the hotter and the sun fiercer. There were giddiness, and sickness, and sharp pangs like rheumatism, to be supported. I minded then, and have often minded since, on the lines in our Scotch psalm:

> The moon by night thee shall not smite,
> Nor yet the sun by day;

and indeed it was only by God's blessing that we were neither of us sun-smitten.

At last, about two, it was beyond men's bearing, and there was now temptation to resist, as well as pain to thole. For the sun being now got a little into the west, there came a patch of shade on the east side of our rock, which was the side sheltered from the soldiers.

'As well one death as another,' said Alan, and slipped over the edge and dropped on the ground on the shadowy side.

I followed him at once, and instantly fell all my length, so weak was I and so giddy with that long exposure. Here, then, we lay for an hour or two, aching from head to foot, as weak as water, and lying quite naked to the eye of any soldier who should have strolled that way. None came, however, all passing by on the other side; so that our rock continued to be our shield even in this new position.

Presently we began again to get a little strength; and as the soldiers were now lying closer along the riverside, Alan proposed that we should try a start. I was by this time afraid of but one thing in the world; and that was to be set back upon the rock; anything else was welcome to me; so we got ourselves at once in marching order, and began to slip from rock to rock one after the other, now crawling flat on our bellies in the shade, now making a run for it, heart in mouth.

The soldiers, having searched this side of the valley after a fashion, and being perhaps somewhat sleepy with the sultriness of the afternoon, had now laid by much of their vigilance, and stood dozing at their posts or only kept a lookout along the banks of the river; so that in this way, keeping down the valley and at the same time towards the mountains we drew steadily away from their neighbourhood. But the business was the most wearing I had ever taken part in. A man had need of a hundred eyes in every part of him, to keep concealed in that uneven country and within cry of so many and scattered sentries. When we must pass an open place, quickness was not all, but a swift judgement not only of the lie of the whole country, but of the solidity of every stone on which we must set foot; for the afternoon was now fallen so breathless that the rolling of a pebble sounded abroad like a pistol shot, and would start the echo calling among the hills and cliffs.

By sundown we had made some distance, even by our slow rate of progress, though to be sure the sentry on the rock was still plainly in our view. But now we came on something that put all fears out of season; and that was a deep rushing burn, that tore down, in that part, to join the glen river. At the sight of this we cast ourselves on the ground and plunged head and shoulders in the water; and I cannot tell which was the more pleasant, the great shock as the cool stream went over us, or the greed with which we drank of it.

We lay there (for the banks hid us), drank again and again, bathed our chests, let our wrists trail in the running water till they ached with the chill; and at last, being wonderfully renewed, we got out the meal-bag and made drammach in the iron pan. This, though it is but cold water mingled with oatmeal, yet makes a good enough dish for a hungry man; and where there are no means of making fire, or (as in our case) good reason for not making one, it is the chief stand-by of those who have taken to the heather.

As soon as the shadow of the night had fallen, we set forth again, at first with the same caution, but presently with more boldness, standing our full height and stepping out at a good pace of walking. The way was very intricate, lying up the steep sides of mountains and along the brows of cliffs; clouds had come in with the sunset, and the night was dark and cool; so that I walked without much fatigue, but in continual fear of falling and rolling down the mountains, and with no guess at our direction.

The moon rose at last and found us still on the road; it was in its last quarter and was long beset with clouds; but after a while shone out, and showed me many dark heads of mountains, and was reflected far underneath us on the narrow arm of a sea-loch.

At this sight we both paused: I struck with wonder to find myself so high and walking (as it seemed to me, upon clouds): Alan to make sure of his direction.

Seemingly he was well pleased, and he must certainly have judged us out of ear-shot of all our enemies; for throughout the rest of our night-march he beguiled the way with whistling of many tunes, warlike, merry, plaintive; reel tunes that made the foot go faster; tunes of my own south country that made me fain to be home from my adventures; and all these, on the great, dark, desert mountains, making company upon the way.

TWENTY-ONE

The Flight in the Heather: ❧ the Heugh of Corrynakiegh ❧

EARLY AS DAY COMES IN THE beginning of July, it was still dark when we reached our destination, a cleft in the head of a great mountain, with a water running through the midst, and upon the one hand a shallow cave in a rock. Birches grew there in a thin, pretty wood, which a little farther on was changed into a wood of pines. The burn was full of trout; the wood of cushat-doves; on the open side of the mountain beyond, whaups would be always whistling, and cuckoos were plentiful. From the mouth of the cleft we looked down upon a part of Mamore, and on the sea-loch that divides that country from Appin; and this from so great a height, as made it my continual wonder and pleasure to sit and behold them.

The name of the cleft was the Heugh of Corrynakiegh; and although from its height and being so near upon the sea, it was often beset with clouds, yet it was on the whole a pleasant place, and the five days we lived in it went happily.

We slept in the cave, making our bed of heather bushes which we cut for that purpose, and covering ourselves with Alan's great-coat. There was a low concealed place, in a turning of the glen, where we were so bold as to make fire; so that we could warm ourselves when the clouds set in, and cook hot porridge, and grill the little trouts that we caught with our hands under the stones and overhanging banks of the burn. This was indeed our chief pleasure and business; and not only to save our meal against worse times, but with a rivalry that much amused us, we spent a great part of our days at the water side, stripped to the waist and groping about or (as they say) guddling for these fish. The largest we got might have been a quarter of a pound; but they were of good flesh and flavour, and when broiled upon the coals, lacked only a little salt to be delicious.

In any by-time Alan must teach me to use my sword, for my ignorance had much distressed him; and I think besides, as I had sometimes the upper hand of him in the fishing, he was not sorry to turn to an exercise where he had so much the upper hand of me. He made it somewhat more of a pain than need have been, for he stormed at me all through the lessons in a very violent manner of scolding, and would push me so close that I made sure he must run me through the body. I was often tempted to turn tail, but held my ground for all that, and got some profit of my lessons; if it was but to stand on guard with an assured countenance, which is often all that is required. So, though I could never in the least please my master, I was not altogether displeased with myself.

In the meantime, you are not to suppose that we neglected our chief business, which was to get away.

'It will be many a long day,' Alan said to me on our first morning, 'before the red-coats think upon seeking Corrynakiegh; so now we must get word sent to James, and he must find the siller for us.'

'And how shall we sent that word?' says I. 'We are here in a desert place, which yet we dare not leave; and unless ye get the fowls of the air to be your messengers, I see not what we shall be able to do.'

'Ay?' said Alan. 'Ye're a man of small contrivance, David.'

Thereupon he fell in a muse, looking in the embers of the fire; and presently, getting a piece of wood, he fashioned it in a cross, the four ends of which he blackened on the coals. Then he looked at me a little shyly.

'Could ye lend me my button?' says he. 'It seems a strange thing to ask a gift again, but I own I am laith to cut another.'

I gave him the button; whereupon he strung it on a strip of his great coat which he had used to bind the cross; and tying in a little sprig of birch and another of fir, he looked upon his work with satisfaction.

'Now,' said he, 'there is a little clachan' (what is called a hamlet in the English) 'not very far from Corrynakiegh, and it has the name of Koalisnacoan. There, there are living many friends of mine whom I could trust with my life, and some that I am not just so sure of. Ye see, David, there will be money set upon our heads; James himsel' is to set money on them; and as for the Campbells, they would never spare siller where there was a Stewart to be hurt. If it was otherwise, I would go down to Koalisnacoan whatever, and trust my life into these people's hands as lightly as I would trust another with my glove.'

'But being so?' said I.

'Being so,' said he, 'I would as lief they didnae see me. There's bad folk everywhere, and what's far worse, weak ones. So when it comes dark again, I will steal down into that clachan, and set this that I have been making in the window of a good friend of mine, John Breck Maccoll, a bouman* of Appin's.'

'With all my heart,' says I; 'and if he finds it, what is he to think?'

'Well,' says Alan, 'I wish he was a man of more penetration, for by my troth I am afraid he will make little enough of it! But this is what I have in my mind. This cross is something in the nature of the crosstarrie, or fiery cross, which is the signal of gathering in our clans; yet he will know well enough the clan is not to rise, for there it is standing in his window, and no word with it. So he will say to himsel', *The clan is not to rise, but there is something*. Then he will see my button, and that was Duncan Stewart's. And then he will say to himsel', *The son of Duncan is in the heather, and has need of me*.'

'Well,' said I, 'it may be. But even supposing so, there is a good deal of heather between here and the Forth.'

'And that is a very true word,' says Alan. 'But then John Breck will

---

*A bouman is a tenant who takes stock from the landlord and shares with him the increase.

see the sprig of birch and the sprig of pine; and he will say to himsel' (if he is a man of any penetration at all, which I misdoubt) *Alan will be lying in a wood which is both of pines and birches*. Then he will think to himsel', *That is not so very rife hereabout*; and then he will come and give us a look up in Corrynakiegh. And if he does not, David, the devil may fly away with him, for what I care; for he will no be worth the salt to his porridge.'

'Eh, man,' said I, drolling with him a little, 'you're very ingenious! But would it not be simpler for you to write him a few words in black-and-white?'

'And that is an excellent observe, Mr Balfour of Shaws,' says Alan, drolling with me; 'and it would certainly be much simpler for me to write to him, but it would be a sore job for John Breck to read it. He would have to go to the school for two-three years; and its possible we might be wearied waiting for him.'

So that night Alan carried down his fiery cross and set it in the bouman's window. He was troubled when he came back; for the dogs had barked and the folk run out from their houses; and he thought he had heard a clatter of arms and seen a red-coat come to one of the doors. On all accounts we lay the next day in the borders of the wood and kept a close look-out; so that if it was John Breck that came, we might be ready to guide him, and if it was the red-coats, we should have time to get away.

About noon a man was to be spied, straggling up the open side of the mountain in the sun, and looking round him as he came, from under his hand. No sooner had Alan seen him than he whistled; the man turned and came a little towards us; then Alan would give another 'peep!' and the man would come still nearer; and so by the sound of whistling, he was guided to the spot where we lay.

He was a ragged, wild, bearded man, about forty, grossly disfigured with the smallpox, and looked both dull and savage. Although his English was very bad and broken, yet Alan (according to his very handsome use, whenever I was by) would suffer him to speak no Gaelic. Perhaps the strange language made him appear more backward than he really was; but I thought he had little good-will to serve us, and what he had was the child of terror.

Alan would have had him carry a message to James; but the bouman would hear of no message. 'She was forget it,' he said in his screaming voice; and would either have a letter or wash his hands of us.

I thought Alan would be gravelled at that, for we lacked the means of writing in that desert, But he was a man of more resources than I knew; searched the wood until he found the quill of a cushat-dove, which he shaped into a pen; made himself a kind of ink with gunpowder from his horn and water from the running stream; and tearing a corner from his French Military commission (which he carried in his pocket, like a talisman to keep him from the gallows) he sat down and wrote as follows:

DEAR KINSMAN, – Please send the money by the bearer to the place he kens of. – Your affectionate cousin,

A.S.

This he entrusted to the bouman, who promised to make what manner of speed he best could, and carried it off with him down the hill.

He was three full days gone, but about five in the evening of the third, we heard a whistling in the wood, which Alan answered; and presently the bouman came up the waterside, looking for us, right and left. He seemed less sulky than before, and indeed he was no doubt well pleased to have got to the end of such a dangerous commission.

He gave us the news of the country; that it was alive with red-coats; that arms were being found, and poor folk brought in trouble daily; and that James and some of his servants were already clapped in prison at Fort William, under strong suspicion of complicity. It seemed, it was noised on all sides that Alan Breck had fired the shot; and there was a bill issued for both him and me, with one hundred pounds reward.

This was all as bad as could be; and the little note the bouman had carried us from Mrs Stewart was of a miserable sadness. In it she besought Alan not to let himself be captured, assuring him, if he fell in the hands of the troops, both he and James were no better than dead men. The money she had sent was all that she could beg or borrow, and she prayed heaven we could be doing with it. Lastly, she said she enclosed us one of the bills in which we were described.

This we looked upon with great curiosity and not a little fear, partly as a man may look in a mirror, partly as he might look into the barrel of an enemy's gun to judge if it be truly aimed. Alan was advertised as 'a small, pock-marked, active man of thirty-five or thereby, dressed in a feathered hat, a French side-coat of blue with silver buttons and lace a great deal tarnished, a red waistcoat and breeches of black shag'; and I as 'a tall strong lad of about eighteen, wearing an old blue coat, very ragged, an old Highland bonnet, a long homespun waistcoat, blue breeches; his legs bare; low-country shoes, wanting the toes; speaks like a low-lander, and has no beard.'

Alan was well enough pleased to see his finery so fully remembered and set down; only when he came to the word tarnish, he looked upon his lace like one a little mortified. As for myself, I thought I cut a miserable figure in the bill; and yet was well enough pleased too, for since I had changed these rags, the description had ceased to be a danger and become a source of safety.

'Alan,' said I, 'you should change your clothes.'

'Na, troth!' said Alan, 'I have nae others. A fine sight I would be, if I went back to France in a bonnet!'

This put a second reflection in my mind: that if I were to separate from Alan and his tell-tale clothes I should be safe against arrest, and might go openly about my business. Nor was this all; for suppose I was arrested when I was alone, there was little against me; but suppose I was taken in company with the reputed murderer, my case would begin to be grave. For generosity's sake, I dare not speak my mind upon this head; but I thought of it none the less.

I thought of it all the more, too, when the bouman brought out a green purse with four guineas in gold, and the best part of another in small change. True, it was more than I had. But then Alan, with less than five guineas, had to get as far as France; I, with my less than two, not beyond Queensferry; so that, taking things in their proportion, Alan's society was not only a peril to my life but a burden on my purse.

But there was no thought of the sort in the honest head of my companion. He believed he was serving, helping, and protecting me. And what could I do but hold my peace, and chafe, and take my chance of it?

'It's little enough,' said Alan, putting the purse in his pocket, 'but it'll do my business. And now John Breck, if ye will hand me over my button, this gentleman and me will be for taking the road.'

But the bouman, after feeling about in a hairy purse that hung in front of him in the Highland manner (though he wore otherwise the lowland habit, with sea-trousers) began to roll his eyes strangely, and at last said, 'Her nainsel will loss it', meaning he thought he had lost it.

'What!' cried Alan, 'you will lose my button, that was my father's before me? Now, I will tell you what is in my mind, John Breck: it is in my mind this is the worst day's work that ever ye did since ye were born.'

And as Alan spoke, he set his hands on his knees and looked at the bouman with a smiling mouth, and that dancing light in his eyes that meant mischief to his enemies.

Perhaps the bouman was honest enough; perhaps he had meant to cheat and then, finding himself alone with two of us in a desert place, cast back to honesty as being safer; at least, and all at once, he seemed to find that button and handed it to Alan.

'Well, and it is a good thing for the honour of the Maccolls,' said Alan, and then to me, 'Here is my button back again, and I thank you for parting with it, which is of a piece with all your friendships to me.' Then he took the warmest parting of the bouman. 'For,' says he, 'ye have done very well by me, and set your neck at a venture, and I will always give you the name of a good man.'

Lastly, the bouman took himself off by one way; and Alan and I (getting our chattels together) struck into another to resume our flight.

TWENTY-TWO

The Flight in the Heather:
⚜ ⚜
The Moor

MORE THAN ELEVEN HOURS OF incessant, hard travelling brought us early in the morning to the end of a range of mountains. In front of us there lay a piece of low, broken, desert land, which we must now cross. The sun was not long up, and shone straight in our eyes; a little, thin mist went up from the face of the moorland like a smoke; so that (as Alan said) there might have been twenty squadron of dragoons there and we none the wiser.

We sat down, therefore, in a howe of the hillside till the mist should have risen, and made ourselves a dish of drammach, and held a council of war.

'David,' said Alan, 'this is the kettle bit. Shall we lie here till it comes night, or shall we risk it and stave on ahead?'

'Well,' said I, 'I am tired indeed, but I could walk as far again, if that was all.'

'Ay, but it isnae,' said Alan, 'nor yet the half. This is how we stand: Appin's fair death to us. To the south it's all Campbells, and no to be thought of. To the north; well, there's no muckle to be gained by going north; neither for you, that wants to get to Queensferry, nor yet for me, that wants to get to France. Well, then, we'll can strike east.'

'East be it!' says I, quite cheerily; but I was thinking, in to myself: 'Oh, man, if you would only take one point of the compass and let me take any other, it would be the best for both of us.'

'Well, then, east, ye see, we have the muirs,' said Alan. 'Once there, David, it's mere pitch-and-toss. Out on yon bald, naked, flat place, where can a body turn to? Let the red-coats come over a hill, they can spy you miles away, and the sorrow's in their horses' heels, they would soon ride you down. It's no good place, David; and I'm free to say, it's worse by daylight than by dark.'

'Alan,' said I, 'hear my way of it. Appin's death for us; we have none too much money, nor yet meal; the longer they seek, the nearer they may guess where we are; it's all a risk; and I give my word to go ahead until we drop.'

Alan was delighted. 'There are whiles,' said he, 'when ye are altogether too canny and Whiggish to be company for a gentleman like me; but there come other whiles when ye show yoursel' a mettle spark; and it's then, David, that I love ye like a brother.'

The mist rose and died away, and showed us that country lying as waste as the sea; only the moorfowl and the peewees crying upon it, and far over to the east, a herd of deer, moving like dots. Much of it was red with heather; much of the rest broken up with bogs and hags and peaty pools; some had been burnt black in a heath fire; and in another place there was quite a forest of dead firs, standing like skeletons. A wearier looking desert man never saw; but at least it was clear of troops, which was our point.

We went down accordingly into the waste, and began to make our toilsome and devious travel towards the eastern verge. There were the tops of mountains all round (you are to remember) from whence we might be spied at any moment; so it behoved us to keep in the hollow parts of the moor, and when these turned aside from our direction, to move upon its naked face with infinite care. Sometimes, for half an hour together, we must crawl from one heather bush to another, as hunters do when they are hard upon the deer. It was a clear day again, with a blazing sun; the water in the brandy bottle was soon gone; and altogether, if I had guessed what it would be to crawl half the time upon my belly and to walk much of the rest stooping nearly to the knees, I should certainly have held back from such a killing enterprise.

Toiling and resting and toiling again, we wore away the morning; and about noon lay down in a thick bush of heather to sleep. Alan took the first watch; and it seemed to me I had scarce closed my eyes before I was shaken up to take the second. We had no clock to go by; and Alan stuck a sprig of heath in the ground to serve instead; so that as soon as the shadow of the bush should fall so far to the east, I might know to rouse him. But I was by this time so weary that I could have slept twelve hours at a stretch; I had the taste of sleep in my throat; my joints slept even when my mind was waking; the hot smell of the heather, and the drone of the wild bees, were like possets to me; and every now and again I would give a jump and find I had been dozing.

The last time I woke I seemed to come back from farther away, and thought the sun had taken a great start in the heavens. I looked at the sprig of heather, and at that I could have cried aloud; for I saw I had betrayed my trust. My head was nearly turned with fear and shame; and at what I saw, when I looked out around me on the moor, my heart was like dying in my body. For sure enough a body of horse-soldiers had come down during my sleep, and were drawing near to us from the south-east, spread out in shape of a fan and riding their horses to and fro in the deep parts of the heather.

When I waked Alan, he glanced first at the soldiers, then at the mark and the position of the sun, and knitted his brows with a sudden, quick look, both ugly and anxious, which was all the reproach I had of him.

'What are we to do now?' I asked.

'We'll have to play at being hares,' said he. 'Do ye see yon mountain?' pointing to one on the north-eastern sky.

'Ay,' said I.

'Well, then,' says he, 'let us strike for that. Its name is Ben Alder; it is a wild, desert mountain full of hills and hollows, and if we can win to it before the morn, we may do yet.'

'But, Alan,' cried I, 'that will take us across the very coming of the soldiers!'

'I ken that fine,' said he; 'but if we are driven back on Appin, we are two dead men. So now, David man, be brisk!'

With that he began to run forward on his hands and knees with an incredible quickness, as though it were his natural way of going. All the time, too, he kept winding in and out in the lower parts of the moorland where we were the best concealed. Some of these had been burned or at least scathed with fire; and there rose in our faces (which were close to the ground) a blinding, choking dust as fine as smoke. The water was long out; and this posture of running on the hands and knees brings an overmastering weakness and weariness, so that the joints ache and the wrists faint under your weight.

Now and then, indeed, where was a big bush of heather we lay a while, and panted, and putting aside the leaves, looked back at the dragoons. They had not spied us, for they held straight on; a half-troop, I think, covering about two miles of ground, and beating it mighty thoroughly as they went. I had awakened just in time; a little later, and we must have fled in front of them, instead of escaping on one side. Even as it was, the least misfortune might betray us; and now and again, when a grouse rose out of the heather with a clap of wings, we lay as still as the dead and were afraid to breathe.

The aching and faintness of my body, the labouring of my heart, the soreness of my hands, and the smarting of my throat and eyes in the continual smoke of dust and ashes, had soon grown to be so unbearable that I would gladly have given up. Nothing but the fear of Alan lent me enough of a false kind of courage to continue. As for himself (and you are to bear in mind that he was cumbered with a great coat), he had first turned crimson, but as time went on, the redness began to be mingled with patches of white; his breath cried and whistled as it came; and his voice, when he whispered his observations in my ear during our halts, sounded like nothing human. Yet he seemed in no way dashed in spirits, nor did he at all abate in his activity; so that I was driven to marvel at the man's endurance.

At length, in the first gloaming of the night, we heard a trumpet sound, and looking back from among the heather, saw the troops beginning to collect. A little after, they had built a fire and camped for the night, about the middle of the waste.

At this I begged and besought that we might lie down and sleep.

'There shall be no sleep the night!' said Alan. 'From now on, these weary dragoons of yours will keep the crown of the muirland, and none will get out of Appin but winged fowls. We got through in the nick of time, and shall we jeopard what we've gained? Na, na, when the day comes, it shall find you and me in a fast place on Ben Alder.'

'Alan,' I said, 'it's not the want of will: it's the strength that I want, if I could, I would; but as sure as I'm alive I cannot.'

'Very well, then,' said Alan. 'I'll carry ye.'

I looked to see if he were jesting; but no, the little man was in dead earnest; and the sight of so much resolution shamed me.

'Lead away!' said I, 'I'll follow.'

He gave me one look, as much as to say 'Well done, David!' and off he set again at his top speed.

It grew cooler and even a little darker (but not much) with the coming of the night. The sky was cloudless; it was still early in July, and pretty far north; in the darkest part of that night, you would have needed pretty good eyes to read, but for all that, I have often seen it darker in a winter midday. Heavy dew fell and drenched the moor like rain; and this refreshed me for a while. When we stopped to breathe, and I had time to see all about me, the clearness and sweetness of the night, the shapes of the hills like things asleep, and the fire dwindling away behind us, like a bright spot in the midst of the moor, anger would come upon me in a clap that I must still drag myself in agony and eat the dust like a worm.

By what I have read in books, I think few that have held a pen were ever really wearied, or they would write of it more strongly. I had no care of my life, neither past nor future, and I scarce remembered there was such a lad as David Balfour. I did not think of myself, but just of each fresh step which I was sure would be my last, with despair – and of Alan, who was the cause of it, with hatred. Alan was in the right trade as a soldier; this is the officer's part to make men continue to do things, they know not wherefore, and when, if the choice was offered, they would lie down where they were and be killed. And I dare say I would have made a good enough private; for in these last hours, it never occurred to me that I had any choice, but just to obey as long as I was able, and die obeying.

Day began to come in, after years, I thought; and by that time we were past the greatest danger, and could walk upon our feet like men, instead of crawling like brutes. But, dear heart have mercy! what a pair we must have made, going double like old grandfathers, stumbling like babes, and as white as dead folk. Never a word passed between us; each set his mouth and kept his eyes in front of him, and lifted up his foot and set it down again, like people lifting weights at a country play*; all the while, with the moorfowl crying 'peep!' in the heather, and the light coming slowly clearer in the east.

I say Alan did as I did. Not that ever I looked at him, for I had enough to keep my feet; but because it is plain he must have been as stupid with weariness as myself, and looked as little where we were going, or we should not have walked into an ambush like blind men.

It fell in this way. We were going down a heathery brae, Alan leading and I following a pace or two behind, like a fiddler and his wife; when upon a sudden the heather gave a rustle, three or four ragged men leaped out, and the next moment we were lying on our backs, each with a dirk at his throat.

I don't think I cared; the pain of this rough handling was quite swallowed up by the pains of which I was already full; and I was too glad to have stopped walking to mind about a dirk. I lay looking up in the face of the man that held me; and I mind his face was black with the sun and his eyes very light, but I was not afraid of him. I heard Alan and another whispering in the Gaelic; and what they said was all one to me.

Then the dirks were put up, our weapons were taken away, and we were set face to face, sitting in the heather.

*Village fair.

'They are Cluny's men,' said Alan. 'We couldnae have fallen better. We're just to bide here with these, which are his out-sentries, till they can get word to the chief of my arrival.'

Now Cluny Macpherson, the chief of the clan Vourich, had been one of the leaders of the great rebellion six years before; there was a price on his life; and I had supposed him long ago in France, with the rest of the heads of that desperate party. Even tired as I was, the surprise of what I heard half wakened me.

'What?' I cried, 'Is Cluny still here?'

'Ay is he so!' said Alan, 'Still in his own country and kept by his own clan. King George can do no more.'

I think I would have asked further, but Alan gave me the put-off. 'I am rather wearied,' he said, 'and I would like fine to get a sleep.' And without more words, he rolled on his face in a deep heather bush, and seemed to sleep at once.

There was no such thing possible for me. You have heard grasshoppers whirring in the grass in the summer time? Well, I had no sooner closed my eyes, than my body and above all my head, belly, and wrists, seemed to be filled with whirring grasshoppers; and I must open my eyes again at once, and tumble and toss, and sit up and lie down; and look at the sky which dazzled me, or at Cluny's wild and dirty sentries, peering out over the top of the brae and chattering to each other in the Gaelic.

That was all the rest I had, until the messenger returned; when, as it appeared that Cluny would be glad to receive us, we must get once more upon our feet and set forward. Alan was in excellent good spirits, much refreshed by his sleep, very hungry, and looking pleasantly forward to a dram and a dish of hot collops, of which, it seems, the messenger had brought him word. For my part, it made me sick to hear of eating. I had been dead-heavy before, and now I felt a kind of dreadful lightness, which would not suffer me to walk. I drifted like a gossamer; the ground seemed to me a cloud, the hills a feather-weight, the air to have a current, like a running bum, which carried me to and fro. With all that, a sort of horror of despair set on my mind, so that I could have wept at my own helplessness.

I saw Alan knitting his brows at me, and supposed it was in anger; and that gave me a pang of light-headed fear, like what a child may have. I remember, too, that I was smiling, and could not stop smiling, hard as I tried; for I thought it was out of place at such a time. But my good companion had nothing in his mind but kindness; and the next moment, two of the gillies had me by the arms, and I began to be carried forward with great swiftness (or so it appeared to me, although I dare say it was slowly enough in truth) through a labyrinth of dreary glens and hollows and into the heart of that dismal mountain of Ben Alder.

TWENTY-THREE

❖ Cluny's Cage ❖

WE CAME AT LAST TO THE FOOT of an exceeding steep wood, which scrambled up a craggy hillside, and was crowned by a naked precipice.

'It's here,' said one of the guides, and we struck up hill.

The trees clung upon the slope, like sailors on the shrouds of a ship; and their trunks were like the rounds of a ladder, by which we mounted.

Quite at the top, and just before the rocky face of the cliff sprang above the foliage, we found that strange house which was known in the country as 'Cluny's Cage'. The trunks of several trees had been wattled across, the intervals strengthened with stakes, and the ground behind this barricade levelled up with earth to make the floor. A tree, which grew out from the hillside, was the living centre beam of the roof. The walls were of wattle and covered with moss. The whole house had something of an egg shape; and it half hung, half stood in that steep, hillside thicket, like a wasps' nest in a green hawthorn.

Within, it was large enough to shelter five or six persons with some comfort. A projection of the cliff had been cunningly employed to be the fireplace; and the smoke rising against the face of the rock, and being not dissimilar in colour, readily escaped notice from below.

This was but one of Cluny's hiding places; he had caves, besides, and underground chambers in several parts of his country; and following the reports of his scouts, he moved from one to another as the soldiers drew near or moved away. By this manner of living, and thanks to the affection of his clan, he had not only stayed all this time in safety, while so many others had fled or been taken and slain; but stayed four or five years longer, and only went to France at last by the express command of his master. There he soon died; and it is strange to reflect that he may have regretted his Cage upon Ben Alder.

When we came to the door he was seated by his rock chimney, watching a gillie about some cookery. He was mighty plainly habited, with a knitted nightcap drawn over his ears, and smoked a foul cutty pipe. For all that he had the manners of a king, and it was quite a sight to see him rise out of his place to welcome us.

'Well, Mr Stewart, come awa' sir!' said he, 'and bring in your friend that as yet I dinna ken the name of.'

'And how is yourself, Cluny?' said Alan. 'I hope ye do brawly, sir. And I am proud to see ye, and to present to ye my friend the Laird of Shaws, Mr David Balfour.'

Alan never referred to my estate without a touch of a sneer, when we were alone; but with strangers, he rang the words out like a herald.

'Step in by, the both of ye, gentlemen,' said Cluny. 'I make ye welcome to my house, which is a queer, rude place for certain, but one where I have entertained a royal personage, Mr Stewart – ye doubtless ken the personage I have in my eye. We'll take a drain for luck, and as soon as this handless man of mine has the collops ready, we'll dine and take a hand at the cartes as gentlemen should. My life is a bit driegh,' says he, pouring out the brandy; 'I see little company, and sit and twirl my thumbs, and mind upon a great day that is gone by, and weary for another great day that we all hope will be upon the road. And so here's a toast to ye: The Restoration!'

Thereupon we all touched glasses and drank. I am sure I wished no ill to King George; and if he had been there himself in proper person, it's like he would have done as I did. No sooner had I taken out the dram than I felt hugely better, and could look on and listen, still a little mistily perhaps, but no longer with the same groundless horror and distress of mind.

It was certainly a strange place, and we had a strange host. In his long hiding, Cluny had grown to have all manner of precise habits, like those of an old maid. He had a particular place, where no one else must sit; the Cage was arranged in a particular way, which none must disturb; cookery was one of his chief fancies, and even while he was greeting us in, he kept an eye to the collops.

It appears, he sometimes visited or received visits from his wife and one or two of his nearest friends, under the cover of night; but for the most part lived quite alone, and communicated only with his sentinels and the gillies that waited on him in the Cage. The first thing in the morning, one of them, who was a barber, came and shaved him, and gave him the news of the country, of which he was immoderately greedy. There was no end to his questions; he put them as earnestly as a child; and at some of the answers, laughed out of all bounds of reason, and would break out again laughing at the mere memory, hours after the barber was gone.

To be sure, there might have been a purpose in his questions; for though he was thus sequestered, and like the other landed gentlemen of Scotland, stripped by the late Act of Parliament of legal powers, he still exercised a patriarchal justice in his clan. Disputes were brought to him in his hiding-hole to be decided; and the men of his country, who would have snapped their fingers at the Court of Session, laid aside revenge and paid down money at the bare word of this forfeited and hunted outlaw. When he was angered, which was often enough, he gave his commands and breathed threats of punishment like any king; and his gillies trembled and crouched away from him like children before a hasty father. With each of them, as he entered, he ceremoniously shook hands, both parties touching their bonnets at the same time in a military manner. Altogether, I had a fair chance to see some of the inner workings of a Highland clan; and this was a proscribed, fugitive chief; his country conquered; the troops riding upon all sides in quest of him, sometimes within a mile of where he lay; and when the least of the ragged fellows whom he rated and threatened, could have made a fortune by betraying him.

On that first day as soon as the collops were ready, Cluny gave them with his own hand a squeeze of a lemon (for he was well supplied with luxuries) and bade us draw in to our meal.

'They', said he, meaning the collops, 'are such as I gave His Royal Highness in this very house; bating the lemon juice, for at that time we were glad to get the meat and never fashed for kitchen*. Indeed, there were mair dragoons than lemons in my country in the year forty-six.'

I do not know if the collops were truly very good, but my heart rose against the sight of them, and I could eat but little. All the while Cluny entertained us with stories of Prince Charlie's stay in the Cage, giving us the very words of the speakers, and rising from his place to show us where they stood. By these, I gathered the Prince was a gracious, spirited boy, like the son of a race of polite kings, but not so wise as Solomon. I gathered, too, that while he was in the Cage, he was often drunk; so the fault that has since, by all accounts, made such a wreck of him, had even then begun to show itself.

We were no sooner done eating than Cluny brought out an old thumbed, greasy pack of cards, such as you may find in a mean inn; and his eys brightened in his face as he proposed that we should fall to playing.

Now this was one of the things I had been brought up to eschew like disgrace; it being held by my father neither the part of a Christian nor yet a gentleman, to set his own livelihood and fish for that of others, on

*Condiment.

the cast of painted pasteboard. To be sure, I might have pleaded my fatigue, which was excuse enough; but I thought it behoved that I should bear a testimony. I must have got very red in the face, but I spoke steadily, and told them I had no call to be a judge of others, but for my own part, it was a matter in which I had no clearness.

Cluny stopped mingling the cards. 'What in deil's name is this?' says he. 'What kind of Whiggish, canting talk is this, for the house of Cluny Macpherson?'

'I will put my hand in the fire for Mr Balfour,' says Alan. 'He is an honest and a mettle gentleman, and I would have ye bear in mind who says it. I bear a king's name,' says he, cocking his hat; 'and I and any that I call friend are company for the best. But the gentleman is tired, and should sleep; if he had no mind to the cartes, it will never hinder you and me. And I'm fit and willing, sir, to play ye any game that ye can name.'

'Sir,' says Cluny, 'in this poor house of mine I would have you ken that any gentleman may follow his pleasure. If your friend would like to stand on his head, he is welcome. And if either he, or you, or any other man, is not preceesely satisfied, I will be proud to step outside with him.'

I had no will that these two friends should cut their throats for my sake.

'Sir,' said I, 'I am very wearied, as Alan says; and what's more, as you are a man that likely has sons of your own, I may tell you it was a promise to my father.'

'Say nae mair, say nae mair,' said Cluny, and pointed me to a bed of heather in a corner of the Cage. For all that he was displeased enough, looked at me askance, and grumbled when he looked. And indeed it must be owned that both my scruples and the words in which I declared them, smacked somewhat of the Covenanter, and were little in their place among wild Highland Jacobites.

What with the brandy and the venison, a strange heaviness had come over me; and I had scarce lain down upon the bed before I fell into a kind of trance, in which I continued almost the whole time of our stay in the Cage. Sometimes I was broad awake and understood what passed; sometimes I only heard voices or men snoring, like the voice of a silly river; and the plaids upon the wall dwindled down and swelled out again, like firelight shadows on the roof. I must sometimes have spoken or cried out, for I remember I was now and then amazed at being answered; yet I was conscious of no particular nightmare, only of a general, black, abiding horror – a horror of the place I was in, and the bed I lay in, and the plaids on the wall, and the voices, and the fire, and myself.

The barber-gillie, who was a doctor too, was called in to prescribe for me; but as he spoke in the Gaelic, I understood not a word of his opinion, and was too sick even to ask for a translation. I knew well enough I was ill, and that was all I cared about.

I paid little heed while I lay in this poor pass. But Alan and Cluny were most of the time at the cards, and I am clear that Alan must have begun by winning; for I remember sitting up, and seeing them hard at it, and a great glittering pile of as much as sixty or a hundred guineas on the table. It looked strange enough, to see all this wealth in a nest upon a cliff-side, wattled about growing trees. And even then, I thought it seemed deep water for Alan to be riding, who had no better battle-horse than a green purse and a matter of five pounds.

The luck, it seems, changed on the second day. About noon I was awakened as usual for dinner, and as usual refused to eat, and was given a dram with some bitter infusion which the barber had prescribed. The sun was shining in at the open door of the Cage, and this dazzled and offended me. Cluny sat at the table, biting the pack of cards. Alan had stooped over the bed, and had his face close to my eyes; to which, troubled as they were with the fever, it seemed of the most shocking bigness.

He asked me for a loan of my money.

'What for?' said I.

'Oh, just for a loan,' said he.

'But why?' I repeated. 'I don't see.'

'Hut, David!' said Alan, 'ye wouldnae grudge me a loan?'

I would though, if I had my senses. But all I thought of then was to get his face away, and I handed him my money.

On the morning of the third day, when we had been forty-eight hours in the Cage, I awoke with a great relief of spirits, very weak and weary indeed, but seeing things of the right size and with their honest, everyday appearance. I had a mind to eat, moreover; rose from bed of my own movement; and as soon as we had breakfasted, stepped to the entry of the Cage and sat down outside in the top of the wood. It was a grey day with a cold, mild air: and I sat in a dream all morning, only disturbed by the passing by of Cluny's scouts and servants coming with provisions and reports; for as the coast was at that time clear, you might almost say he held court openly.

When I returned, he and Alan had laid the cards aside, and were questioning a gillie; and the chief turned about and spoke to me in the Gaelic.

'I have no Gaelic, sir,' said I.

Now since the card question, everything I said or did had the power of annoying Cluny. 'Your name has more sense than yourself then,' said he, angrily; 'for it's good Gaelic. But the point is this. My scout reports all clear in the south, and the question is have ye the strength to go?'

I saw cards on the table, but no gold; only a heap of little written papers, and these all on Cluny's side. Alan, besides, had an odd look, like man not very well content; and I began to have a strong misgiving.

'I do not know if I am as well as I should be,' said I, looking at Alan; 'but the little money we have has a long way to carry us.'

Alan took his under-lip into his mouth, and looked upon the ground. 'David,' says he, at last, 'I've lost it; there's the naked truth.'

'My money too?' said I.

'Your money too,' says Alan, with a groan. 'Ye shouldnae have given it me. I'm daft when I get to the cartes.'

'Hoot-toot, hoot-toot,' said Cluny. 'It was all daffing; it's all nonsense. Of course, ye'll have your money back again, and the double of it, if ye'll make so free with me. It would be a singular thing for me to keep it. It's not to be supposed that I would be any hindrance to gentlemen in your situation; that would be a singular thing!' cries he, and began to pull gold out of his pocket, with a mighty red face.

Alan said nothing, only looked on the ground.

'Will you step to the door with me, sir?' said I.

Cluny said he would be very glad, and followed me readily enough, but he looked flustered and put out.

'And now sir,' says I, 'I must first acknowledge your generosity.'

'Nonsensical nonsense!' cries Cluny. 'Where's the generosity? This is just most unfortunate affair; but what would ye have me do – boxed up in this beeskep of a cage of mine – but just set my friends to the cartes, when I can get them? And if they lose, of course, it's not to be supposed—' And here he came to a pause.

'Yes,' said I, 'if they lose, you give them back their money; and if they win, they carry away yours in their pouches! I have said before that I grant your generosity; but to me, sir, it's a very painful thing to be placed in this position.'

There was a little silence, in which Cluny seemed always as if he was about to speak, but said nothing. All the time he grew redder and redder in the face.

'I am a young man,' said I, 'and I ask your advice. Advise me as you would your son. My friend fairly lost this money, after having fairly gained a far greater sum of yours; can I accept it back again? would that be the right part for me to play? Whatever I do, you can see for yourself it must be hard upon a man of any pride.'

'It's rather hard on me, too, Mr Balfour,' said Cluny, 'and ye give me very much the look of a man that has entrapped poor people to their hurt. I wouldnae have my friends come to any house of mine to accept affronts; no,' he cried, with a sudden heat of anger, 'nor yet to give them!'

'And so you see, sir,' said I, 'there is something to be said upon my side; and this gambling is a very poor employ for gentlefolks. But I am still waiting your opinion.'

I am sure if ever Cluny hated any man it was David Balfour. He looked me all over with a warlike eye, and I saw the challenge at his lips. But either my youth disarmed him, or perhaps his own sense of justice. Certainly it was a mortifying matter for all concerned, and not least for Cluny; the more credit that he took it as he did.

'Mr Balfour,' said he, 'I think you are too nice and covenanting, but for all that you have the spirit of a very pretty gentleman. Upon my honest word, ye may take this money – it's what I would tell my son – and here's my hand along with it!'

TWENTY-FOUR

The Flight in the Heather: the Quarrel

ALAN AND I WERE PUT ACROSS Loch Errocht under cloud of night, and went down its eastern shore to another hiding place near the head of Loch Rannoch, whither we were led by one of the gillies from the Cage. This fellow carried all our luggage and Alan's great-coat in the bargain, trotting along under the burden, far less than the half of which used to weigh me to the ground, like a stout hill pony with a feather; yet he was a man that, in plain contest, I could have broken on my knee.

Doubtless it was a great relief to walk disencumbered; and perhaps without that relief, and the consequent sense of liberty and lightness, I could not have walked at all. I was but new risen from a bed of sickness; and there was nothing in the state of our affairs to hearten me for much exertion; travelling, as we did, over the most dismal deserts in Scotland, under a cloudy heaven, and with divided hearts among the travellers.

For long, we said nothing, marching alongside or one behind the other, each with a set countenance; I, angry and proud, and drawing what strength I had from these two violent and sinful feelings: Alan angry and ashamed, ashamed that he had lost my money, angry that I should take it so ill.

The thought of a separation ran always the stronger in my mind; and the more I approved of it, the more ashamed I grew of my approval. It would be a fine, handsome, generous thing, indeed, for Alan to turn round and say to me: 'Go, I am in the most danger, and my company only increases yours.' But for me to turn to the friend who certainly loved me, and say to him: 'You are in great danger, I am in but little; your friendship is a burden; go take your risks and bear your hardships alone' – no, that was impossible; and even to think of it privily to myself, made my cheeks to burn.

And yet Alan had behaved like a child and (what is worse) a treacherous child. Wheedling my money from me while I lay half-conscious, was scarce better than theft; and yet here he was trudging by my side, without a penny to his name, and by what I could see, quite blithe to sponge upon the money he had driven me to beg. True, I was ready to share it with him; but it made me rage to see him count upon my readiness.

These were the two things uppermost in my mind; and I could open my mouth upon neither without black ungenerosity. So I did the next worst, and said nothing, nor so much as looked once at my companion, save with the tail of my eye.

At last, upon the other side of Loch Errocht, going over a smooth, rushy place, where the walking was easy, he could bear it no longer, and came close to me.

'David,' says he, 'this is no way for two friends to take a small accident. I have to say that I'm sorry; and so that's said. And now if you have anything, ye'd better say it.'

'Oh,' says I, 'I have nothing.'

He seemed disconcerted; at which I was meanly pleased.

'No,' said he, with rather a trembling voice, 'but when I say I was to blame?'

'Why, of course, ye were to blame,' said I, coolly; 'and you will bear me out that I have never reproached you.'

'Never,' says he; 'but ye ken very well that ye've done worse. Are we to part? Ye said so once before. Are ye to say it again? There's hills and heather enough between here and the two seas, David; and I will own I'm no very keen to stay where I'm no wanted.'

This pierced me like a sword, and seemed to lay bare my private disloyalty.

'Alan Breck!' I cried; and then: 'Do you think I am one to turn my back on you in your chief need? You dursn't say it to my face. My whole conduct's there to give the lie to it. It's true, I fell asleep upon the muir; but that was from weariness, and you do wrong to cast it up to me—'

'Which is what I never did,' said Alan.

'But aside from that,' I continued, 'what have I done that you should even me to dogs by such a supposition? I never yet failed a friend, and it's not likely I'll begin with you. There are things between us that I can never forget, even if you can.'

'I will only say this to ye, David,' said Alan, very quietly, 'that I have long been owing ye my life, and now I owe ye money. Ye should try to make that burden light for me.'

This ought to have touched me, and in a manner it did, but the wrong manner. I felt I was having badly; and was now not only angry with Alan, but angry with myself in the bargain; and it made me the more cruel.

'You asked me to speak,' said I. 'Well, then, I will. You own yourself that you have done me a disservice; I have had to swallow an affront: I have never reproached you, I never named the thing till you did. And now you blame me,' cried I, 'because I cannae laugh and sing as if I was glad to be affronted. The next thing will be that I'm to go down upon my knees and thank you for it! Ye should think more of others, Alan Breck. If ye thought more of others, ye would perhaps speak less about yourself; and when a friend that likes you very well, has passed over an offence without a word, you would be blithe to let it lie, instead of making it a stick to break his back with. By your own way of it, it was you that was to blame; then it shouldnae be you to seek the quarrel.'

'Aweel,' said Alan, 'say nae mair.'

And we fell back into our former silence; and came to our journey's end, and supped, and lay down to sleep, without another word.

The gillie put us across Loch Rannoch in the dusk of the next day, and gave us his opinion as to our best route. This was to get us up at once into the tops of the mountains: to go round by a circuit, turning the heads of Glen Lyon, Glen Lochay, and Glen Dochart, and come down upon the lowlands by Kippen and the upper waters of the Forth. Alan was little pleased with a route which led us through the country of his blood-foe, the Glenorchy Campbells. He objected that by turning to the east, we should come almost at once among the Athole Stewarts, a race of his own name and lineage although following a different chief, and come besides by a far easier and swifter way to the place whither we were bound. But the gillie, who was indeed the chief man of Cluny's scouts, had good reasons to give him on all hands, naming the force of troops in every district, and alleging finally (as well as I could understand) that we should nowhere be so little troubled as in a country of the Campbells.

Alan gave way at last, but with only half a heart. 'It's one of the dowiest countries in Scotland,' said he. 'There's naething there that I ken, but heath and crows, and Campbells. But I see that ye're a man of some penetration; and be it as ye please!'

We set forth accordingly by this itinerary; and for the best part of three nights travelled on eerie mountains and among the well-heads of wild rivers; often buried in mist, almost continually blown and rained upon, and not once cheered by any glimpse of sunshine. By day, we lay and slept in the drenching heather; by night, incessantly clambered upon breakneck hills and among rude crags. We often wandered; we were often so involved in fog, that we must lie quiet till it lightened. A fire was never to be thought of. Our only food was drammach and a portion of cold meat that we had carried from the Cage; and as for drink, Heaven knows we had no want of water.

This was a dreadful time, rendered the more dreadful by the gloom of the weather and the country. I was never warm; my teeth chattered in my head; I was troubled with a very sore throat, such as I had on the isle; I had a painful stitch in my side, which never left me; and when I slept in my wet bed, with the rain beating above and the mud oozing below me, it was to live over again in fancy the worst part of my adventures – to see the tower of Shaws lit by lightning, Ransome carried below on the men's backs, Shuan dying on the round-house floor, or Colin Campbell grasping at the bosom of his coat. From such broken slumbers, I would be aroused in the gloaming, to sit up in the smae puddle where I had slept, and sup cold drammach; the rain driving sharp in my face or running down my back in icy trickles; the mist enfolding us like as in a gloomy chamber – or perhaps, if the wind blew, falling suddenly apart and showing us the gulf of some dark valley where the streams were crying aloud.

The sound of an infinite number of rivers came up from all round. In this steady rain the springs of the mountain were broken up; every glen gushed water like a cistern; every stream was in high spate, and had filled and overflowed its channel. During our night tramps, it was solemn to hear the voice of them below in the valleys, now booming like thunder, now with an angry cry. I could well understand the story of the Water Kelie, that demon of the streams, who is fabled to keep wailing and roaring at the ford until the coming of the doomed traveller. Alan I saw believed it, or half believed it; and when the cry of the river rose more than usually sharp, I was little surprised (though, of course, I would still be shocked) to see him cross himself in the manner of the Catholics.

During all these horrid wanderings we had no familiarity, scarcely even that of speech. The truth is that I was sickening for my grave, which is my best excuse. But besides that I was of an unforgiving disposition from my birth, slow to take offence, slower to forget it, and now incensed both against my companion and myself. For the best part of two days he was unweariedly kind; silent, indeed, but always ready to help, and always hoping (as I could very well see) that my displeasure would blow by. For the same length of time I stayed in myself, nursing my anger, roughly refusing his services, and passing him over with my eyes as if he had been a bush or a stone.

The second night, or rather the peep of the third day, found us upon a very open hill, so that we could not follow our usual plan and lie down immediately to eat and sleep. Before we had reached a place of shelter, the grey had come pretty clear, for though it still rained, the clouds ran higher; and Alan, looking in my face, showed some marks of concern.

'Ye had better let me take your pack,' said he, for perhaps the ninth time since we had parted from the scout beside Loch Rannoch.

'I do very well, I thank you,' said I, as cold as ice.

Alan flushed darkly. 'I'll not offer it again,' he said. 'I'm not a patient man, David.'

'I never said you were,' said I, which was exactly the rude, silly speech of a boy of ten.

Alan made no answer at the time, but his conduct answered for him. Henceforth, it is to be thought, he quite forgave himself for the affair at Cluny's; cocked his hat again, walked jauntily, whistled airs, and looked at me upon one side with a provoking smile.

The third night we were to pass through the western end of the country of Balquidder. It came clear and cold, with a touch in the air like frost, and a northerly wind that blew the clouds away and made the stars bright. The streams were full, of course, and still made a great noise among the hills; but I observed that Alan thought no more upon the Kelpie, and was in high good spirits. As for me, the change of weather came too late; I had lain in the mire so long that (as the Bible has it) my very clothes 'abhorred me'; I was dead weary, deadly sick, and full of pains and shiverings; the chill of the wind went through me, and the sound of it confused my ears. In this poor state I had to bear from my companion something in the nature of a persecution. He spoke a good deal, and never without a taunt. 'Whig' was the best name he had to give me. 'Here,' he would say, 'here's a dub for ye to jump, my Whiggie! I ken you're a fine jumper!' And so on; all the time with a gibing voice and face.

I knew it was my own doing, and no one else's; but I was too miserable to repent. I felt I could drag myself but little farther; pretty soon, I must lie down and die on these wet mountains like a sheep or a fox, and my bones must whiten there like the bones of a beast. My head was light, perhaps; but I began to love the prospect, I began to glory in the thought of such a death, alone in the desert, with the wild eagles besieging my last moments. Alan would repent then, I thought; he would remember, when I was dead, how much he owed me, and the remembrance would be torture. So I went like a sick, silly, and bad-hearted schoolboy, feeding my anger against a fellow-man, when I would have been better on my knees, crying on God for mercy. And at each of Alan's taunts, I hugged myself. 'Ah!' thinks I to myself, 'I have a better taunt in readiness; when I lie down and die, you will feel it like a buffet in your face; ah, what a revenge! ah, how you will regret your ingratitude and cruelty!'

All the while, I was growing worse and worse. Once I had fallen, my legs simply doubling under me, and this had struck Alan for the moment; but I was afoot so briskly, and set off again with such a natural manner, that he soon forgot the incident. Flushes of heat went over me, and then spasms of shuddering. The stitch in my side was hardly bearable. At last I began to feel that I could trail myself no farther; and with that, there came on me all at once the wish to have it out with Alan, let my anger blaze, and be done with my life in a more sudden manner. He had just called me 'Whig'. I stopped.

'Mr Stewart,' said I, in a voice that quivered like a fiddlestring, 'you are older than I am, and should know your manners. Do you think it either very wise or very witty to cast my politics in my teeth? I thought, where folk differed, it was the part of gentlemen to differ civilly; and if I did not, I may tell you I could find a better taunt than some of yours.'

Alan had stopped opposite to me, his hat cocked, his hands in his breeches pockets, his head a little to one side. He listened, smiling evilly, as I could see by the starlight; and when I had done he began to whistle a Jacobite air. It was the air made in mockery of General Cope's defeat at Preston Pans:

> Hey, Johnnie Cope, are ye waukin' yet?
> And are your drums a-beatin' yet?

And it came in my mind that Alan, on the day of that battle, had been engaged upon the royal side.

'Why do ye take that air, Mr Stewart?' said I. 'Is that to remind me you have been beaten on both sides?'

The air stopped on Alan's lips. 'David!' said he.

'But it's time these manners ceased,' I continued; 'and I mean you shall henceforth speak civilly of my King and my good friends the Campbells.'

'I am a Stewart—' began Alan.

'Oh,' says I, 'I ken ye bear a king's name. But you are to remember, since I have been in the Highlands, I have seen a good many of those that bear it; and the best I can say of them is this, that they would be none the worse of washing.'

'Do you know that you insult me?' said Alan, very low.

'I am sorry for that,' said I, 'for I am not done; and if you distaste the sermon, I doubt the pirliecue* will please you as little. You have been chased in the field by the grown men of my party; it seems a poor kind of pleasure to outface a boy. Both the Campbells and the Whigs have beaten you; you have run before them like a hare. It behoves you to speak of them as of your betters.'

Alan stood quite still, the tails of his great-coat clapping behind him in the wind.

'This is a pity,' he said at last. 'There are things said that cannot be passed over.'

'I never asked you to,' said I. 'I am as ready as yourself.'

'Ready?' said he.

'Ready,' I repeated. 'I am no blower and boaster like some that I could name. Come on!' And drawing my sword, I fell on guard as Alan himself had taught me.

'David!' he cried. 'Are ye daft? I cannae draw upon ye, David. It's fair murder.'

'That was your look-out when you insulted me,' said I.

'It's the truth!' cried Alan, and he stood for a moment, wringing his mouth in his hand like a man in sore perplexity. 'It's the bare truth,' he said, and drew his sword. But before I could touch his blade with mine, he had thrown it from him and fallen to the ground. 'Na, na,' he kept saying, 'na, na – I cannae, I cannae.'

At this the last of my anger oozed all out of me; and I found myself only sick, and sorry, and blank, and wondering at myself. I would have given the world to take back what I had said; but a word once spoken, who can recapture it? I minded me of all Alan's kindness and courage in the past, how he had helped and cheered and borne with me in our

*A second sermon.

evil days; and then recalled my own insults, and saw that I had lost for ever that doughty friend. At the same time, the sickness that hung upon me seemed to redouble, and the pang in my side was like a sword for sharpness. I thought I must have swooned where I stood.

This it was that gave me a thought. No apology could blot out what I had said; it was needless to think of one, none could cover the offence; but where an apology was vain, a mere cry for help might bring Alan back to my side. I put my pride away from me. 'Alan!' I said; 'if you cannae help me, I must just die here.'

He started up sitting, and looked at me.

'It's true,' said I. 'I'm by with it. Oh, let me get into the bield of a house – I'll can die there easier.' I had no need to pretent; whether I chose or not, I spoke in a weeping voice that would have melted a heart of stone.

'Can ye walk?' asked Alan.

'No,' said I, 'not without help. This last hour, my legs have been fainting under me; I've a stitch in my side like a red-hot iron; I cannae breathe right. If I die, Ye'll can forgive me, Alan? In my heart, I liked ye fine – even when I was the angriest.'

'Wheesht, wheesht!' cried Alan. 'Dinnae say that! David man, ye ken—' He shut his mouth upon a sob. 'Let me get my arm about ye,' he continued; 'that's the way! Now lean upon me hard. Gude kens where there's a house! We're in Balwhidder, too; there should be no want of houses, no, nor friends' houses here. Do ye gang easier so, Davie?'

'Ay,' said I, 'I can be doing this way'; and I pressed his arm with my hand.

Again he came near sobbing. 'Davie,' said he, 'I'm no a right man at all; I have neither sense nor kindness; I couldnae remember ye were just a bairn, I couldnae see ye were dying on your feet; Davie, ye'll have to try and forgive me.'

'Oh, man, let's say no more about it!' said I. 'We're neither one of us to mend the other – that's the truth! We must just bear and forbear, man Alan! Oh, but my stitch is sore! Is there nae house?'

'I'll find a house to ye, David,' he said, stoutly. 'We'll follow down the burn, where there's bound to be houses. My poor man, will ye no be better on my back?'

'Oh, Alan,' says I, 'and me a good twelve inches taller?'

'Ye're no such a thing,' cried Alan, with a start. 'There may be a trifling matter of an inch or two; I'm no saying I'm just exactly what ye would call a tall man, whatever; and dare say,' he added, his voice trailing off in a laughable manner, 'now when I come to think of it, I dare say ye'll be just about right. Ay, it'll be a foot, or near hand; or may be even mair!'

It was sweet and laughable to hear Alan eat his words up in the fear of some fresh quarrel. I could have laughed, had not my stitch caught me so hard; but if I had laughed, I think I must have wept too.

'Alan,' cried I, 'what makes ye so good to me? What makes ye care for such a thankless fellow?'

'Deed, and I don't know,' said Alan. 'For just precisely what I thought I liked about ye, was that ye never quarrelled; – and now I like ye better!'

TWENTY-FIVE

✣ In Balquhidder ✣

AT THE DOOR OF THE FIRST house we came to, Alan knocked, which was no very safe enterprise in such a part of the Highlands as the Braes of Balquidder. No great clan held rule there; it was filled and disputed by small septs, and broken remnants, and what they call 'chiefless folk', driven into the wild country about the springs of Forth and Teith by the advance of the Campbells. Here were Stewarts and Maclarens, which came to the same thing, for the Maclarens followed Alan's chief in war, and made but one clan with Appin. Here, too, were many of that old, proscribed, nameless, red-handed clan of the Macgregors. They had always been ill considered, and now worse than ever, having credit with no side or party in the whole country of Scotland. Their chief, Macgregor of Macgregor, was in exile; the more immediate leader of that part of them about Balquhidder, James More, Rob Roy's eldest son, lay waiting his trial in Edinburgh Castle; they were in ill-blood with Highlander and Lowlander, with the Grahames, the Maclarens and the Stewarts; and Alan, who took up the quarrel of any friend however distant, was extremely wishful to avoid them.

Chance served us very well; for it was a household of Maclarens that we found, where Alan was not only welcome for his name's sake but known by reputation. Here then I was got to bed without delay, and a doctor fetched, who found me in a sorry plight. But whether because he was a very good doctor, or I a very young, strong man, I lay bed-ridden for no more than a week, and before a month I was able to make the road again with a good heart.

All this time Alan would not leave me; though I often pressed him, and indeed his foolhardiness in staying was a common subject of outcry with the two or three friends that were let into the secret. He hid by day in a hole of the braes under a little wood; and at night when the coast was clear, would come into the house to visit me. I need not say if I was pleased to see him; Mrs Maclaren, our hostess, thought nothing good enough for such a guest; and as Duncan Dhu (which was the name of our host) had a pair of pipes in his house and was much of a lover of music, the time of my recovery was quite a festival, and we commonly turned night into day.

The soldiers let us be; although once a party of two companies and some dragoons went by in the bottom of the valley, where I could see them through the windows as I lay in bed. What was much more astonishing, no magistrate came near me, and there was no question put of whence I came or whither I was going; and in that time of excitement, I was as free of all inquiry as though I had lain in a desert. Yet my presence was known before I left to all the people in Balquidder and the adjacent parts; many coming about the house on visits and these (after the custom of the country) spreading the news among their neighbours. The bills, too, had now been printed. There was one pinned near the foot of my bed, where I could read my own not very flattering portrait and, in larger characters, the amount of the blood money that had been set upon my life. Duncan Dhu and the rest that knew that I had come there in Alan's company, could have entertained no doubt of who I was; and many others must have had their guess. For though I had changed my clothes, I could not change my age or person; and lowland boys of eighteen were not so rife in these parts of the world, and above all about that time, that they could fail to put one thing with another and connect me with the bill. So it was, at least. Other folk keep a secret among two or three near friends, and somehow it leaks out; but among these clansmen, it is told to a whole countryside, and they will keep it for a century.

There was but one thing happened worth narrating; and that is the visit I had of Robin Oig, one of the sons of the notorious Rob Roy. He was sought upon all sides on a charge of carrying a young woman from Balfron and marrying her (as was alleged) by force; yet he stepped about Balquidder like a gentleman in his own walled policy. It was he who had shot James Maclaren at the plough stilts, a quarrel never satisfied; yet he walked into the house of his blood enemies as a rider* might into a public inn.

Duncan had time to pass me word of who it was; and we looked at one another in concern. You should understand, it was then close upon

*Commercial traveller.

the time of Alan's coming; the two were little likely to agree; and yet if we sent word or sought to make a signal, it was sure to arouse suspicion in a man under so dark a cloud as the Macgregor.

He came in with a great show of civility, but like a man among inferiors; took off his bonnet to Mrs Maclaren, but clapped it on his head again to speak to Duncan; and having thus set himself (as he would have thought) in a proper light, came to my bedside and bowed.

'I am given to know, sir,' says he, 'that your name is Balfour.'

'They call me David Balfour,' said I, 'at your service.'

'I would give ye my name in return sir,' he replied, 'but it's one somewhat blown upon of late days; and it's perhaps suffice if I tell ye that I am own brother to James More Drummond or Macgregor, of whom ye will scarce have failed to hear.'

'No, sir,' said I, a little alarmed; 'nor yet of your father, Macgregor-Campbell.' And I sat up and bowed in bed; for I thought to compliment him, in case he was proud of having had an outlaw to his father.

He bowed in return. 'But what I am come to say, sir,' he went on, 'is this. In the year '45, my brother raised a part of the "Gregara", and marched six companies to strike a stroke for the good side; and the surgeon that marched with our clan and cured my brother's leg when it was broken in the brush at Preston Pans, was a gentleman of the same name precisely as yourself. He was brother to Balfour of Baith; and if you are in any reasonable degree of nearness one of the genetleman's kin, I have come to put myself and my people at your command.'

You are to remember that I knew no more of my descent than any cadger's dog; my uncle, to be sure, had prated of some of our high connexions, but nothing to the present purpose; and there was nothing left me but that bitter disgrace of owning that I could not tell.

Robin told me shortly he was sorry he had put himself about, turned his back upon me without a sign of salutation, and as he went towards the door, I could hear him telling Duncan that I was 'only some kinless loon that didn't know his own father'. Angry as I was at these words and ashamed of my own ignorance, I could scarce keep from smiling that a man who was under the lash of the law (and was indeed hanged some three years later) should be so nice as to the descent of his acquaintances.

Just in the door, he met Alan coming in; and the two drew back and looked at each other like strange dogs. They were neigher of them big men, but they seemed fairly to swell out with pride. Each wore a sword, and by a movement of his haunch, thrust clear the hilt of it, so that it might be the more readily grasped and the blade drawn.

'Mr Stewart, I am thinking,' says Robin.

'Troth, Mr Macgregor, it's not a name to be ashamed of,' answered Alan.

'I did not know ye were in my country, sir,' says Robin.

'It sticks in my mind that I am in the country of my friends the Maclarens,' says Alan.

'That's a kittle point,' returned the other. 'There may be two words to say to that. But I think I will have heard that you are a man of your sword?'

'Unless ye were born deaf, Mr Macgregor, ye will have heard a good deal more than that,' says Alan. 'I am not the only man that can draw steel in Appin; and when my kinsman and captain, Ardshiel, had a talk with a gentleman of your name, not so may years back, I could never hear that the Macgregor had the best of it.'

'Do ye mean my father, sir,' says Robin.

'Well, I wouldnae wonder,' said Alan. 'The gentleman I have in my mind had the ill-taste to clap Campbell to his name.'

'My father was an old man,' returned Robin. 'The match was unequal. You and me would make a better pair, sir.'

'I was thinking that,' said Alan.

I was half out of bed, and Duncan had been hanging at the elbow of these fighting cocks, ready to intervene upon the least occasion. But when the word was uttered, it was a case of now or never; and Duncan, with something of a white face to be sure, thrust himself between.

'Gentlemen,' said he, 'I will have been thinking of a very different matter, whateffer. Here are my pipes, and here are you two gentlemen who are baith acclaimed pipers. It's an auld dispute which one of ye's the best. Here will be a braw chance to settle it.'

'Why, sir,' said Alan, still addressing Robin, from whom indeed he had not so much as shifted his eyes, nor yet Robin from him, 'why, sir,' says Alan, 'I think I will have heard some sough of the sort. Have ye music, as folk say? Are ye a bit of a piper?'

'I can pipe like a Macrimmon!' cries Robin.

'And that is a very bold word,' quoth Alan.

'I have made bolder words good before now,' returned Robin, 'and that against better adversaries.'

'It is easy to try that,' says Alan.

Duncan Dhu made haste to bring out the pair of pipes that was his principal possession, and to set before his guests a mutton-ham and a bottle of that drink which the call Athole brose, and which is made of old whiskey, strained honey, and sweet cream, slowly beaten together in the right order and porportion. The two enemies were still on the very breach of a quarrel; but down they sat, one upon each side of the peat fire, with a mighty show of politeness. Maclaren pressed them to taste his mutton-ham and 'the wife's brose', reminding them the wife was out of Athole and had a name far and wide for her skill in that confection. But Robin put aside these hospitalities as bad for the breath.

'I would have ye to remark, sir,' said Alan, 'that I havenae broken bread for near upon ten hours, which will be worse for the breath than any brose in Scotland.'

'I will take no advantages, Mr Stewart,' replied Robin. 'Eat and drink; I'll follow you.'

Each ate a small portion of the ham and drank a glass of the brose to Mrs Maclaren; and then after a great number of civilities, Robin took the pipes and played a little spring in a very ranting manner.

'Ay, ye can blow,' said Alan; and taking the instrument from his rival, he first played the same spring in a manner identical with Robin's; and then wandered into variations, which, as he went on, he decorated with a perfect flight of grace-notes, such as pipers love, and call the 'warblers'.

I had been pleased with Robin's playing, Alan's ravished me.

'That's not very bad, Mr Stewart,' said the rival, 'but ye show a poor device in your warblers.'

'Me!' cried Alan, the blood starting to his face. 'I give ye the lie.'

'Do ye own yourself beaten at the pipes, then,' said Robin, 'that ye seek to change them for the sword?'

'And that's very well said, Mr Macgregor,' returned Alan; 'and in the meantime' (laying a strong accent on the word) 'I take back the lie. I appeal to Duncan.'

'Indeed, ye need appeal to naebody,' said Robin. 'Ye're a far better judge than any Maclaren in Balquidder: for it's a God's truth that you're a very creditable piper for a Stewart. Hand me the pipes.'

Alan did as he asked; and Robin proceeded to imitate and correct some part of Alan's variations, which it seemed that he remembered perfectly.

'Ay, ye have music,' said Alan, gloomily.

'And now be the judge yourself, Mr Stewart,' said Robin; and taking up the variations from the beginning, he worked them throughout to so new a purpose, with some ingenuity and sentiment, and with so odd a fancy and so quick a knack in the grace-notes, that I was amazed to hear him.

As for Alan, his face grew dark and hot, and he sat and gnawed his fingers, like a man under some deep affront. 'Enough!' he cried. 'Ye can blow the pipes – make the most of that.' And he made as if to rise.

But Robin only held out his hand as if to ask for silence, and struck into the slow measure of a pibroch. It was a fine piece of music in itself, and nobly played; but it seems besides it was a piece peculiar to the Appin Stewarts and a chief favourite with Alan. The first notes were scarce out, before there came a change in his face; when the time quickened, he seemed to grow restless in his seat; and long before that piece was at an end, the last signs of his anger died from him, and he had no thought but for the music.

'Robin Oig,' he said, when it was done, 'ye are a great piper. I am not fit to blow in the same kingdom with ye. Body of me! ye have mair music in your sporran that I have in my head! And though it still sticks in my mind that I could maybe show ye another of it with the cold steel, I warn ye beforehand – it'll no be fair! It would go against my heart to haggle a man that can blow the pipes as you can!'

Thereupon the quarrel was made up; all night long the brose was going and the pipes changing hands; and the day had come pretty bright, and the three men were none the better for what they had been taking, before Robin as much as thought upon the road.

It was the last I saw of him, for I was in the Low Countries at the University of Leyden, when he stood his trial, and was hanged in the Grassmarket. And I have told this at so great length, partly because it was the last incident of any note that befell me on the wrong side of the Highland Line, and partly because (as the man came to be hanged) it's in a manner history.

TWENTY-SIX

End of the Flight: we Pass the Forth

THE MONTH, AS I HAVE SAID, was not yet out, but it was already far through August, and beautiful warm weather, with every sign of an early and great harvest, when I was pronounced able for my journey. Our money was now run to so low an ebb that we must think first of all on speed; for if we came not soon to Mr Rankeillor's, or if when we came there he should fail to help me, we must surely starve. In Alan's view, besides, the hunt must have now greatly slackened; and the line of the Forth and even Stirling Bridge, which is the main pass over that river, would be watched with little interest.

'It's a chief principle in military affairs,' said he, 'to go where ye are least expected. Forth is our trouble; ye ken the saying, "Forth bridles the wild Hielandman". Well, if we seek to creep round about the head of that river and come down by Kippen or Balfron, it's just precisely there that they'll bo looking to lay hands on us. But if we stave on straight to the auld Brig of Stirling, I'll lay my sword they let us pass unchallenged.'

The first night, accordingly, we pushed to the house of a Maclaren in Strathire, a friend of Duncan's, where we slept the twenty-first of the month, and whence we set forth again about the fall of night to make another easy stage. The twenty-second we lay in a heather bush on a hillside in Uam Var, within view of a herd of deer, the happiest ten hours of sleep in a fine, breathing sunshine and on bone-dry ground, that I have ever tasted. That night we struck Allan Water, and followed it down; and coming to the edge of the hills saw the whole Carse of Stirling underfoot, as flat as a pancake, with the town and castle on a hill in the midst of it, and the moon shining on the Links of Forth.

'Now,' said Alan, 'I kenna if ye care, but ye're in your own land again. We passed the Hieland Line in the first hour; and now if we could but pass yon crooked water, we might cast our bonnets in the air.'

In Allan Water, near by where it falls into the Forth, we found a little sandy islet, overgrown with burdock, butterbur, and the like low plants, that would just cover us if we lay flat. Here it was we made our camp, within plain view of Stirling Castle, whence we could hear the drums beat as some part of the garrison paraded. Shearers worked all day in a field on one side of the river, and we could hear the stones going on the hooks and the voices and even the words of the men talking. It behoved to lie close and keep silent. But the sand of the little isle was sun-warm, the green plants gave us shelter for our heads, we had food and drink in plenty; and to crown all, we were within sight of safety.

As soon as the shearers quit their work and the dusk began to fall, we waded ashore and struck for the Bridge of Stirling, keeping to the fields and under the field fences.

The bridge is close under the castle hill, an old high, narrow bridge with pinnacles along the parapet; and you may conceive with how much interest I looked upon it, not only as a place famous in history, but as the very doors of salvation to Alan and myself. The moon was not yet up when we came there; a few lights shone along the front of the fortress, and lower down a few lighted windows in the town; but it was all mighty still, and there seemed to be no guard upon the passage.

I was for pushing straight across; but Alan was more wary.

'It looks unco' quiet,' said he; 'but for all that we'll lie down here cannily behind a dyke, and make sure.'

So we lay for about a quarter of an hour, whiles whispering, whiles lying still and hearing nothing earthly but the washing of the water on the pier. At last there came by an old, hobbling woman with a crutch stick; who first stopped a little, close to where we lay, and bemoaned herself and the long way she had travelled; and then set forth again up the steep spring of the bridge. The woman was so little, and the night still so dark, that we soon lost sight of her; only heard the sound of her steps, and her stick and a cough that she had by fits, draw slowly farther away.

'She's bound to be across now,' I whispered.

'Na,' said Alan, 'her foot still sounds boss* upon the bridge.'

And just then – 'Who goes?' cried a voice, and we heard the butt of a musket rattle on the stones. I must suppose the sentry had been sleeping, so that had we tried, we might have passed unseen; but he was awake now, and the chance forfeited.

'This'll never do,' said Alan. 'This'll never, never do for us, David.'

And without another word, he began to crawl away through the fields; and a little after, being well out of eyeshot, got to his feet again, and struck along a road that led to the eastward. I could not conceive what he was doing; and indeed I was so sharply cut by the disappointment, that I was little likely to be pleased with anything. A moment back, and I had seen myself knocking at Mr Rankeillor's door to claim my inheritance, like a hero in a ballad; and here was I back again, a wandering, hunted blackguard, on the wrong side of Forth.

'Well?' said I.

'Well,' said Alan, 'what would ye have? They're none such fools as I took them for. We have still the Forth to pass, Davie – weary fall the rains that fed the hillsides that guided it!'

'And why go east?' said I.

'Ou, just upon the chance!' said he, 'If we cannae pass the river, we'll have to see what can do for the firth.'

'There are fords upon the river, and none upon the firth,' said I.

'To be sure there are fords, and a bridge forby,' quoth Alan: 'and of what service, when they are watched?'

'Well,' said I, 'but a river can be swum.'

'By them that have the skill of it,' returned he; 'But I have yet to hear that either you or me is much of a hand as that exercise; and for my own part, I swim like a stone.'

*Hollow.

'I'm not up to you in talking back, Alan,' I said; 'but I can see we're making bad worse. If it's hard to pass a river, it stands to reason it must be worse to pass a sea.'

'But there's such a thing as a boat,' says Alan, 'or I'm the more deceived.'

'Ay, and such a thing as money,' says I. 'But for us that have neither one nor other, they might just as well not have been invented.'

'Ye think so?' said Alan.

'I do that,' said I.

'David,' says he, 'ye're a man of small invention and less faith. But let me set my wits upon the hone, and if I cannae beg, borrow, nor yet steal a boat, I'll make one!'

'I think I see ye!' said I. 'And what's more than all that: if ye pass a bridge, it can tell no tales; but if we pass the firth, there's the boat on the wrong side – somebody must have brought it – the countryside will all be in a bizz—'

'Man!' cried Alan, 'if I make a boat, I'll make a body to take it back again! So deave me with no more of your nonsense, but walk (for that's what you've got to do) – and let Alan think for ye.'

All night, then, we walked through the north side of the Carse under the high line of the Ochil mountains; and by Alloa and Clackmannan and Culross, all of which we avoided; and about ten in the morning, mighty hungry and tired, came to the little clachan of Limekilns. This is a place that sits near in by the waterside, and looks across the Hope to the town of the Queensferry. Smoke went up from both of these, and from other villages and farms upon all hands. The fields were being reaped; two ships lay anchored and boats were coming and going on the Hope. It was altogether a right pleasant sight to me; and I could not take my fill of gazing at these comfortable, green, cultivated hills and the busy people both of the field and sea.

For all that, there was Mr Rankeillor's house on the south shore, where I had no doubt wealth awaited me; and here was I upon the north, clad in poor enough attire of an outlandish fashion, with three silver shillings left to me of all my fortune, a price set upon my head, and an outlawed man for my sole company.

'O, Alan!' said I, 'to think of it! Over there, there's all that heart could want waiting me; and the birds go over, and the boats go over – all that please can go, but just me only! O, man, but it's a heartbreak!'

In Limekilns we entered a small change-house, which we only knew to be a public by the wand over the door, and bought some bread and cheese from a good-looking lass that was the servant. This we carried with us in a bundle, meaning to sit and eat it in a bush of wood on the seashore, that we saw some third part of a mile in front. As we went, I kept looking across the water and sighing to myself; and though I took no heed of it, Alan had fallen into a muse. At last he stopped in the way.

'Did ye take heed of the lass we bought this of?' says he, tapping on the bread and cheese.

'To be sure,' said I, 'and a bonny lass she was.'

'Ye thought that?' cried he. 'Man David, that's good news.'

'In the name of all that's wonderful, why so?' says I, 'What good can that do?'

'Well,' said Alan, with one of his droll looks, 'I was rather in hopes it would maybe get us that boat.'

'If it were the other way about, it would be liker it,' said I.

'That's all that you ken, ye see,' said Alan. 'I don't want the lass to fall in love with ye, I want her to be sorry for ye, David; to which end, there is no manner of need that she should take you for a beauty. Let me see' (looking me curiously over). 'I wish ye were a wee thing paler; but apart from that ye'll do fine for my purpose – ye have a fine, hang-dog, rag-and-tatter, clappermaclaw kind of a look to ye, as I ye had stolen the coat from a potato-bogle. Come; right about, and back to the change-house for that boat of ours.'

I followed him laughing.

'David Balfour,' said he, 'ye're a very funny gentleman by your way of it, and this is a very funny employ for ye, no doubt. For all that, if ye have any affection for my neck (to say nothing of your own) ye will perhaps be kind enough to take this matter responsibly. I am going to do a bit of play-acting, the bottom ground of which is just exactly as serious as the gallows for the pair of us. So bear it, if ye please, in mind, and conduct yourself according.'

'Well, well,' said I, 'have it as you will.'

As we got near the clachan, he made me take his arm and hang upon it like one almost helpless with weariness; and by the time he pushed open the change-house door, he seemed to be half carrying me. The maid appeared surprised (as well she might be) at our speedy return; but Alan had no words to spare for her in explanation, helped me to a chair, called for a tass of brandy with which he fed me in little sips, and then breaking up the bread and cheese helped me to eat it like a nursery-lass; the whole with that grave, concerned, affectionate countenance, that might have imposed upon a judge. It was small wonder if the maid were taken with the picture we presented, of a poor sick, overwrought lad and his most tender comrade. She drew quite near, and stood leaning with her back on the next table.

'What's like wrong with him?' said she at last.

Alan turned upon her, to my great wonder, with a kind of fury. 'Wrong?' cries he. 'He's walked more hundreds of miles than he has hairs upon his chin, and slept oftener in wet heather than dry sheets. Wrong, quo' she! Wrong enough, I would think! Wrong indeed!' and he kept grumbling to himself, as he fed me, like a man ill-pleased.

'He's young for the like of that,' said the maid.

'Ower young,' said Alan, with his back to her.

'He would be better riding,' says she.

'And where could I get a horse to him?' cried Alan turning on her with the same appearance of fury. 'Would ye have me steal?'

I thought this roughness would have sent her off in dudgeon, as indeed it closed her mouth for the time. But my companion knew very well what he was doing; and for as simple as he was in some things of life, had a great fund of roguishness in such affairs as these.

'Ye neednae tell me,' she said at last – 'ye're gentry.'

'Well,' said Alan, softened a little (I believe against his will) by this artless comment, 'and suppose we were? Did ever you hear that gentrice put money in folk's pockets?'

She sighed at this, as if she were herself some disinherited great lady. 'No,' says she, 'that's true indeed.'

I was all this while chafing at the part I played, and sitting tongue-tied between shame and merriment; but somehow at this I could hold in no longer, and bade Alan let me be, for I was better already. My voice struck in my throat, for I ever hated to take part in lies; but my very embarrassment helped on the plot, for the lass no doubt set down my husky voice to sickness and fatigue.

'Has he nae friends?' said she, in a tearful voice.

'That has he so!' cried Alan, 'if we could but win to them! – friends and rich friends, beds to lie in, food to eat, doctors to see to him – and here he must tramp in the dubs and sleep in the heather like a beggarman.'

'And why that?' says the lass.

'My dear,' says Alan, 'I cannae very safely say; but I'll tell ye what I'll do instead,' says he, 'I'll whistle ye a bit tune.' And with that he leaned pretty far over the table, and in a mere breath of a whistle, but with a wonderful pretty sentiment, gave her a few bars of 'Charlie is my darling'.

'Wheesht,' says she, and looked over her shoulder to the door.

'That's it,' said Alan.

'And him so young!' cried the lass.

'He's old enough to—' and Alan struck his forefinger on the back part of his neck, meaning that I was old enough to lose my head.

'It would be a black shame,' she cried, flushing high.

'It's what will be, though,' said Alan, 'unless we manage the better.'

At this the lass turned and ran out of that part of the house, leaving us alone together, Alan in high good humour at the furthering of his schemes, and I in bitter dudgeon at being called a Jacobite and treated like a child.

'Alan,' I cried, 'I can stand no more of this.'

'Ye'll have to sit it then, Davie,' said he. 'For if ye upset the pot now, ye may scrape your own life out of the fire, but Alan Breck is a dead man.'

This was so true that I could only groan; and even my groan served Alan's purpose, for it was overheard by the lass as she came flying in again with a dish of white puddings and a bottle of strong ale.

'Poor lamb!' says she, and had no sooner set the meat before us, than she touched me on the shoulder with a little friendly touch, as much as to bid me cheer up. Then she told us to fall to, and there would be no more to pay; for the inn was her own, or at least her father's, and he was gone for the day to Pittencrieff. We waited for no second bidding, for bread and cheese is but cold comfort and the puddings smelt excellently well; and while we sat and ate, she took up that same place by the next table, looking on, and thinking, and frowning to herself, and drawing the string of her apron through her hand.

'I'm thinking ye have rather a long tongue,' she said at last to Alan.

'Ay,' said Alan; 'but ye see I ken the folk I speak to.'

'I would never betray ye,' said she, 'if ye mean that.'

'No,' said he, 'ye're not that kind. But I'll tell ye what ye would do, ye would help.'

'I couldnae,' said she, shaking her head. 'Na, I couldnae.'

'No,' said he, 'but if ye could?'

She answered him nothing.

'Look here my lass,' said Alan, 'there are boats in the kingdom of Fife, for I saw two (no less) upon the beach, as I came in by your town's end. Now if we could have the use of a boat to pass under cloud of night into Lothian, and some secret, decent kind of a man to bring that both back again and keep his counsel, there would be two souls saved – mine to all likelihood – his to a dead surety. If we lack that boat, we have but three shillings left in this wide world; and where to go, and how to do, and what other place there is for us except the chains of a gibbet – I give you my naked word, I kenna! Shall we go wanting, lassie? Are ye to lie in your warm bed and think upon us, when the wind gowls in the chimney and the rain tirls on the roof? Are ye to eat your meat by the cheeks of a red fire, and think upon this poor sick lad of mine, biting his finger ends on a blae muir for cauld and hunger? Sick or sound, he must aye be moving; with the death grapple at his throat he must aye be trailing in the rain on the lang roads; and when he gants his last on a rickle of cauld stanes, there will be nae friends near him but only me and God.'

At this appeal, I could see the lass was in great trouble of mind, being tempted to help us, and yet in some fear she might be helping malefactors; and so now I determined to step in myself and to allay her scruples with a portion of the truth.

'Did ever you hear,' said I, 'of Mr Rankeillor of the Ferry?'

'Rankeillor the writer?' said she. 'I daursay that!'

'Well,' said I, 'it's to his door that I am bound, so you may judge by that if I am an ill-doer; and I will tell you more, that though I am indeed, by a dreadful error, in some peril of my life, King George has no truer friend in all Scotland than myself.'

Her face cleared up mightily at this, although Alan's darkened.

'That's more than I would ask,' said she. 'Mr Rankeillor is a kennt man.' And she bade us finish our meat, get clear of the clachan as soon as might be, and lie close in the bit wood on the sea beach. 'And ye can trust me,' says she, 'I'll find some means to put you over.'

At this we waited for no more, but shook hands with her upon the bargain, made short work of the puddings, and set forth again from Limekilns as far as to the wood. It was a small piece of perhaps a score of elders and hawthorns and a few young ashes, not thick enough to veil us from passers-by upon the road or beach. Here we must lie, however, making the best of the brave warm weather and the good hopes we now had of a deliverance, and planning more particularly what remained for us to do.

We had but one trouble all day; when a strolling piper came and sat in the same wood with us; a red-nosed, blear-eyed, drunken dog, with a great bottle of whisky in his pocket, and a long story of wrongs that had been done him by all sorts of persons, from the Lord President of the Court of Session who had denied him justice, down to the Baillies of Inverkeithing who had given him more of it than he desired. It was impossible but he should conceive some suspicion of two men lying all day concealed in a thicket and having no business to allege. As long as he stayed there he kept us in hot water with prying questions; and after he was gone, as he was a man not very likely to hold his tongue, we were in the greater impatience to be gone ourselves.

The day came to an end with the same brightness; the night fell quiet and clear; lights came out in houses and hamlets and then, one after another, began to be put out; but it was past eleven, and we were long since strangely tortured with anxieties, before we heard the grinding of oars upon the rowing pins. At that, we looked out and saw the lass herself comig rowing to us in a boat. She had trusted no one with our affairs, not even her sweetheart, if she had one; but as soon as her father was asleep, had left the house by a window, stolen a neighbour's boat, and come to our assistance single-handed.

I was abashed how to find expression for my thanks; but she was no less abashed at the thought of hearing them; begged us to lose no time and to hold our peace, saying (very properly) that the heart of our matter was in haste and silence; and so, what with one thing and another, she had set us on the Lothian shore not far from Carriden, had shaken hands with us, and was out again at sea and rowing for Limekilns, before there was one word said either of her service or our gratitude.

Even after she was gone, we had nothing to say, as indeed nothing was enough for such a kindness. Only Alan stood a great while upon the shore shaking his head.

'It is a very fine lass,' he said at last. 'David, it is a very fine lass.' And a matter of an hour later, as we were lying in a den on the seashore and I had been already dozing, he broke out again in commendations of her character. For my part, I could say nothing, she was so simple a creature that my heart smote me both with remorse and fear; remorse because we had traded upon her ignorance; and fear lest we should have anyway involved her in the dangers of our situation.

TWENTY-SEVEN

✧ I Come to Mr Rankeillor ✧

THE NEXT DAY IT WAS AGREED that Alan should fend for himself till sunset; but as soon as it began to grow dark, he should lie in the fields by the roadside near to Newhalls, and stir for naught until he heard me whistling. At first I proposed I should give him for a signal the 'Bonnie House of Airlie', which was a favourite of mine; but he objected that as the piece was very commonly known, any ploughman might whistle it by accident; and taught me instead a little fragment of a Highland air, which has run in my head from that day to this, and will likely run in my head when I lie dying. Every time it comes to me, it takes me off to that last day of my uncertainty, with Alan sitting up in the bottom of the den, whistling and beating the measure with a finger, and the grey of the dawn coming on his face.

I was in the long street of Queensferry before the sun was up. It was a fairly built burgh, the houses of good stone, many slated; the town-hall not so fine, I thought, as that of Peebles, nor yet the street so noble; but take it altogether, it put me to shame for my foul tatters.

As the morning went on, and the fires began to be kindled, and the windows to open, and the people to appear out of the houses, my concern and despondency grew ever the blacker. I saw now that I had no grounds to stand upon; and no clear proof of my rights, nor so much as of my own identity. If it was all a bubble, I was indeed sorely cheated and left in a sore pass. Even if things were as I conceived, it would in all likelihood take time to establish my contentions; and what time had I to spare with less than three shillings in my pocket, and a condemned, hunted man upon my hands to ship out of the country? Truly, if my hope broke with me, it might come to the gallows yet for both of us. And as I continued to walk up and down, and saw people looking askance at me upon the street or out of windows, and nudging or speaking one to another with smiles, I began to take a fresh apprehension; that it might be no easy matter even to come to speech of the lawyer, far less to convince him of my story.

For the life of me I could not muster up the courage to address any of these reputable burghers; I thought shame even to speak with them in such a pickle of rags and dirt; and if I had asked for the house of such a man as Mr Rankeillor, I supposed they would have burst out laughing in my face. So I went up and down, and through the street, and down to the harbour-side, like a dog that has lost its master, with a strange gnawing in my inwards, and every now and then a movement of despair. It grew to be high day at last, perhaps nine in the forenoon; and I was worn with these wanderings, and chanced to have stopped in front of a very good house on the landward side, a house with beautiful, clear glass windows, flowering knots upon the sills, the walls new-harled,* and a chase-dog sitting yawning on the step like one that was at home. Well, I was even envying this dumb brute, when the door fell open and there issued forth a shrewd, ruddy, kindly, consequential man in a well-powered wig and spectacles. I was in such a plight that no one set eyes on me once, but he looked at me again; and this gentleman, as it proved, was so much struck with my poor appearance that he came straight up to me and asked me what I did.

*Newly rough-cast.

I told him I was come to the Queensferry on business, and taking heart of grace, asked him to direct me to the house of Mr Rankeillor.

'Why,' said he, 'that is his house that I have just come out of; and for a rather singular chance, I am that very man.'

'Then, sir,' said I, 'I have to beg the favour of an interview.'

'I do not know your name,' said he, 'nor yet your face.'

'My name is David Balfour,' said I.

'David Balfour?' he repeated, in rather a high tone, like one surprised. 'And where have you come from, Mr David Balfour?' he asked, looking me pretty drily in the face.

'I have come from a great many strange places, sir,' said I; 'but I think it would be as well to tell you where and how in a more private manner.'

He seemed to muse awhile, holding his lip in his hand, and looking now at me and now upon the causeway of the street.

'Yes,' says he, 'that will be the best, no doubt,' And he led me back with him into his house, cried out to someone whom I could not see that he would be engaged all morning, and brought me into a little dusty chamber full of books and documents. Here he sat down, and bade me be seated; though I thought he looked a little ruefully from his clean chair to my muddy rags. 'And now,' says he, 'if you have any business, pray be brief and come swiftly to the point. *Nec gemino bellum Trojanum orditur ab ovo* – do you understand that?' says he, with a keen look.

'I will even do as Horace says, sir,' I answered, smiling, 'and carry you *in medias res*.' He nodded as if he was well pleased, and indeed his scrap of Latin had been set to test me. For all that, and though I was somewhat encouraged, the blood came in my face when I added I have reason to believe myself some rights on the estate of Shaws.'

He got a paper book out of a drawer and set it before him open. 'Well?' said he.

But I had shot my bolt and sat speechless.

'Come, come, Mr Balfour,' said he, 'you must continue. Where were you born?'

'In Essendean, sir,' said I, 'the year 1734, the 12th of March.'

He seemed to follow this statement in his paper book; but what that meant I knew not. 'Your father and mother?' said he.

'My father was Alexander Balfour, schoolmaster of that place,' said I, 'and my mother Grace Pitarrow; I think her people were from Angus.'

'Have you any papers proving your identity?' asked Mr Rankeillor.

'No, sir,' said I, 'but they are in the hands of Mr Campbell, the minister, and could be readily produced. Mr Campbell, too, would give me his word; and for that matter, I do not think my uncle would deny me.'

'Meaning Mr Ebenezer Balfour?' says he.

'The same,' said I.

'Whom you have seen?' he asked.

'By whom I was received into his own house,' I answered.

'Did you ever meet a man of the name of Hoseason?' asked Mr Rankeillor.

'I did so, sir, for my sins,' said I; 'for it was by his means and the procurement of my uncle, that I was kidnapped within sight of this town, carried to sea, suffered shipwreck and a hundred other hardships, and stand before you today in this poor accoutrement.'

'You say you were shipwrecked,' said Rankeillor; 'where was that?'

'Off the south end of the Isle of Mull,' said I. 'The name of the isle on which I was cast up is the Island Earraid.'

'Ah!' says he, smiling, 'you are deeper than me in the geography. But so far, I may tell you, this agrees pretty exactly with other information that I hold. But you say you were kidnapped; in what sense?'

'In the plain meaning of the word, sir,' said I. 'I was on my way to your house, when I was trepanned on board the brig, cruelly struck down, thrown below, and knew no more of anything till we were far at sea. I was destined for the plantations; a fate that, in God's providence, I have escaped.'

'The brig was lost on June the 27th,' says he, looking in his book, 'and we are now at August the 24th. Here is a considerable hiatus, Mr Balfour, of near upon two months. It has already caused a vast amount of trouble to your friends; and I own I shall not be very well contented until it is set right.'

'Indeed, sir,' said I, 'these months are very easily filled up; but yet before I told my story, I would be glad to know that I was talking to a friend.'

'This is to argue in a circle,' said the lawyer. 'I cannot be convinced till I have heard you. I cannot be your friend till I am properly informed. If you were more trustful, it would better befit your time of life. And you know, Mr Balfour, we have a proverb in the country that evil-doers are aye evil-dreaders.'

'You are not to forget, sir,' said I, 'that I have already suffered by my trustfulness; and was shipped off to be a slave by the very man that (if I rightly understand) is your employer.'

All this while, I had been gaining ground with Mr Rankeillor, and in proportion as I gained ground, gaining confidence. But at this sally, which I made with something of a smile myself, he fairly laughed aloud.

'No, no,' said he, 'it is not so bad as that. *Fui, non sum. I was* indeed your uncle's man of business; but while you (*imberbis juvenis custode remoto*) were gallivanting in the west, a good deal of water has run under the bridge; and if your ears did not sing, it was not for lack of being talked about. On the very day of your sea disaster, Mr Campbell stalked into my office, demanding you from all the winds. I had never heard of your existence; but I had known your father; and from matters in my competence (to be touched upon hereafter) I was disposed to fear the worst. Mr Ebenezer admitted having seen you; declared (what seemed improbable) that he had given you considerable sums; and that you had started for the continent of Europe, intending to fulfil your education, which was probable and praiseworthy. Interrogated how you had come to send no word to Mr Campbell, he deponed that you had expressed a great desire to break with your past life. Further interrogated where you now were, protested ignorance, but believed you were in Leyden. That is a close sum of his replies. I am not exactly sure that anyone believed him,' continued Mr Rankeillor with a smile; 'and in particular he so much disrelished some expressions of mine that (in a word) he showed me to the door. We were then at a full stand; for whatever shrewd suspicions we might entertain, we had no shadow of probation. In the very article, comes Captain Hoseason with the story of your drowning; whereupon all fell through; with no consequence but concern to Mr Campbell, injury to my pocket, and another blot upon your uncle's character, which could very ill afford it. And now, Mr Balfour,' said he, 'you understand the whole process of these matters, and can judge for yourself to what extent I may be trusted.'

Indeed he was more pedantic than I can represent him, and placed more scraps of Latin in his speech; but it was all uttered with a fine geniality of eye and manner which went far to conquer my distrust. Moreover, I could see he now treated me as if I was myself beyond a doubt; so that first point of my identity seemed fully granted.

'Sir,' said I, 'if I tell you my story, I must commit a friend's life to your discretion. Pass me your word it shall be sacred; and for what touches myself, I will ask no better guarantee than just your face.'

He passed me his word very seriously. 'But,' said he, 'these are rather alarming prolocutions; and if there are in your story any little jostles to the law, I would beg you to bear in mind that I am a lawyer, and pass lightly.'

Thereupon I told him my story from the first, he listening with his spectacles thrust up and his eyes closed, so that I sometimes feared he was asleep. But no such matter! he heard every word (as I found afterwards) with such quickness of hearing and precision of memory as often surprised me. Even strange, outlandish Gaelic names, heard for that time only, he remembered and would remind me of, years after. Yet when I called Alan Breck in full, we had an odd scene. The name of

Alan had of course rung through Scotland, with the news of the Appin murder and the offer of the reward; and it had no sooner escaped me than the lawyer moved in his seat and opened his eyes.

'I would name no unnecessary names, Mr Balfour,' said he; 'above all of Highlanders, many of whom are obnoxious to the law.'

'Well, it might have been better not,' said I; 'but since I have let it slip, I may as well continue.'

'Not at all,' said Mr Rankeillor. 'I am somewhat dull of hearing, as you may have remarked; and I am far from sure I caught the name exactly. We will call your friend, if you please, Mr Thomson – that there may be no reflections. And in future, I would take some such way with any Highlander that you may have to mention – dead or alive.'

By this, I saw he must have heard the name all too clearly and had already guessed I might be coming to the murder. If he chose to play this part of ignorance, it was no matter of mine; so I smiled, said it was no very Highland sounding name, and consented. Through all the rest of my story Alan was Mr Thomson; which amused me the more, as it was a piece of policy after his own heart. James Stewart, in like manner, was mentioned under the style of Mr Thomson's kinsman; Colin Campbell passed as a Mr Glen; and to Cluny, when I came to that part of my tale, I gave the name of 'Mr Jameson, a Highland chief'. It was truly the most open farce, and I wondered that the lawyer should care to keep it up; but after all it was quite in the taste of that age, when there were two parties in the state, and quiet persons, with no very high opinions of their own, sought out every cranny to avoid offence to either.

'Well, well,' said the lawyer, when I had quite done, 'this is a great epic, a great Odyssey of yours. You must tell it, sir, in a sound Latinity when your scholarship is riper; or in English if you please, though for my part I prefer the stronger tongue. You have rolled much; *quae regio in terris* – what parish in Scotland (to make a homely translation) has not been filled with your wanderings? You have shown, besides, a singular aptitude for getting into false positions; and, yes, upon the whole, for behaving well in them. This Mr Thomson seems to me a gentleman of some choice qualities, though perhaps a trifle bloody-minded. It would please me none the worse, if (with all his merits) he were soused in the North Sea; for the man, Mr David, is a sore embarrassment. But you are doubtless quite right to adhere to him; indubitably, he adhered to you. *It comes* – we may say – he was your true companion; nor less, *paribus curis vestigia figit*, for I dare say you would both take an orra thought upon the gallows. Well, well, these days are fortunately by; and I think (speaking humanly) that you are near the end of your troubles.'

As he thus moralized on my adventures, he looked upon me with so much humour and benignity that I could scarce contain my satisfaction. I had been so long wandering with lawless people, and making my bed upon the hills and under the bare sky, that to sit once more in a clean, covered house, and to talk amicably with a gentleman in broadcloth, seemed mighty elevations. Even as I thought so, my eye fell on my unseemly tatters, and I was once more plunged in confusion. But the lawyer saw and understood me. He rose, called over the stair to lay another plate, for Mr Balfour would stay to dinner, and led me into a bedroom in the upper part of the house. Here he set before me water and soap and a comb; and laid out some clothes that belonged to his son; and here, with another apposite tag, he left me to my toilet.

TWENTY-EIGHT

⚜ I Go in Quest of My Inheritance ⚜

I MADE WHAT CHANGE I COULD in my appearance; and blithe was I to look in the glass and find the beggar-man a thing of the past, and David Balfour come to life again. And yet I was ashamed of the change too, and above all, of the borrowed clothes. When I had done, Mr Rankeillor caught me on the stair, made me his compliments, and had me again into the cabinet.

'Sit ye down, Mr David,' said he, 'and now that you are looking a little more like yourself, let me see if I can find you any news. You will be wondering, no doubt, about your father and your uncle? To be sure it is a singular tale; and the explanation is one that I blush to have to offer you. For,' says he, really with embarrassment, 'the matter hinges on a love affair.'

'Truly,' said I, 'I cannot very well join that notion with my uncle.'

'But your uncle, Mr David, was not always old,' replied the lawyer, 'and what may perhaps surprise you more, not always ugly. He had a fine gallant air; people stood in their doors to look after him, as he went by upon a mettle horse. I have seen it with these eyes, and I ingenuously confess, not altogether without envy; for I was a plain lad myself and a plain man's son; and in those days, it was a case of *Odi te, qui bellus es, Sabelle.*'

'It sounds like a dream,' said I.

'Ay, ay,' said the lawyer, 'that is how it is with youth and age. Nor was that all, but he had a spirit of his own that seemed to promise great things in the future. In 1715, what must he do but run away to join the rebels? It was your father that pursued him, found him in a ditch, and brought him back *multum gementem*; to the mirth of the whole country. However, *majora canamus* – the two lads fell in love, and that with the same lady. Mr Ebenezer, who was the admired and the beloved, and the spoiled one, made, no doubt, mighty certain of the victory; and when he found he had deceived himself, screamed like a peacock. The whole county heard of it; now he lay sick at home, with his silly family standing round the bed in tears; now he rode from public house to public house, and shouted his sorrows into the lug of Tom, Dick, and Harry. Your father, Mr David, was a kind gentleman; but he was weak, dolefully weak; took all this folly with a long countenance; and one day – by your leave – resigned the lady. She was no such fool, however; its from her you must inherit your excellent good sense; and she refused to be bandied from one to another. Both got upon their knees to her; and the upshot of the matter for that while, was that she showed both of them the door. That was in August; dear me! the same year I came from college. The scene must have been highly farcial.'

I thought myself it was a silly business, but I could not forget my father had a hand in it. 'Surely, sir, it had some note of tragedy,' said I.

'Why, no, sir, not at all,' returned the lawyer. 'For tragedy implies some ponderable matter in dispute, some *dignus vindice nodus*; and this piece of work was all about the petulance of a young ass that had been spoiled, and wanted nothing so much as to be tied up and soundly belted. However, that was not your father's view; and the end of it was, that from concession to concession on your father's part, and from one height to another of squalling, sentimental selfishness upon your uncle's, they came at last to drive a sort of bargain, from whose ill-results you have recently been smarting. The one man took the lady, the other the estate. Now, Mr David, they talk a great deal of charity and generosity; but in this disputable state of life, I often think the happiest consequences seem to flow when a gentleman consults his lawyers and takes all the law allows him. Anyhow, this piece of quixotry upon your father's part, as it was unjust in itself, has brought forth a monstrous family of injustices. Your father and mother lived and died poor folk; you were poorly reared; and in the meanwhile, what a time it has been for the tenants on the estate of Shaws! And I might add (if it was a matter I cared much about) what a time for Mr Ebenezer!'

'And yet that is certainly the strangest part of all,' said I, 'that a man's nature should thus change.'

'True,' said Mr Rankeillor. 'And yet I imagine it was natural enough. He could not think that he had played a handsome part. Those who knew the story gave him the cold shoulder; those who knew it not, seeing one brother disappear, and the other succeed in the estate, raised a cry of murder; so that upon all sides, he found himself evited. Money was all he got by his bargain; well, he came to think the more of money. He was selfish when he was young, he is selfish now that he is old; and the latter end of all these pretty manners and fine feelings, you have seen for yourself.'

'Well, sir,' said I, 'and in all this, what is my position?'

'The estate is yours beyond a doubt,' replied the lawyer. 'It matters nothing what your father signed, you are the heir of entail. But your uncle is a man to fight the indefensible; and it would be likely your identity that he would call in question. A lawsuit is always expensive, and a family lawsuit always scandalous; besides which, if any of your doings with your friend Mr Thomson were to come out, we might find that we had burned our fingers. The kidnapping, to be sure, would be a court card upon our side, if we could only prove it. But it may be difficult to prove; and my advice (upon the whole) is to make a very easy bargain with your uncle, perhaps even leaving him at Shaws where he has taken root for a quarter of a century, and contenting yourself in the meanwhile with a fair provision.'

I told him I was very willing to be easy, and that to carry family concerns before the public was a step from which I was naturally much averse. In the meantime (thinking to myself) I began to see the outlines of that scheme on which we afterwards acted.

'The great affair,' I asked, 'is to bring home to him the kidnapping?'

'Surely,' said Mr Rankeillor, 'and if possible, out of court. For mark you here, Mr David; we could no doubt find some men of the *Covenant* who would swear to your reclusion; but once they were in the box, we could no longer check their testimony, and some word of your friend Mr Thomson must certainly crop out. Which (from what you have let fall) I cannot think to be desirable.'

'Well sir,' said I, 'here is my way of it.' And I opened my plot to him.

'But this would seem to involve my meeting the man Thomson?' says he, when I had done.

'I think so, indeed, sir,' said I.

'Dear doctor!' cries he, rubbing his brow. 'Dear doctor! No, Mr David, I am afraid your scheme is inadmissible. I say nothing against your friend Mr Thomson; I know nothing against him; and if I did – mark this, Mr David! – it would be my duty to lay hands on him. Now I put it to you: is it wise to meet? He may have matters to his charge. He may not have told you all. His name may not be even Thomson!' cries the lawyer, twinkling; 'for some of these fellows will pick up names by the roadside as another would gather haws.'

'You must be the judge, sir,' said I.

But it was clear my plan had taken hold upon his fancy, for he kept musing to himself till we were called to dinner and the company of Mrs Rankeillor; and that lady had scarce left us again to ourselves and a bottle of wine, ere he was back harping on my proposal. When and where was I to meet my friend Mr Thomson; was I sure of Mr T's discretion; supposing we could catch the old fox tripping, would I consent to such and such a term of an agreement – these and the like questions he kept asking at long intervals, while he thoughtfully rolled his wine upon his tongue. When I had answered all of them, seemingly to his contentment, he fell into a still deeper muse, even the claret being now forgotten. Then he got a sheet of paper and a pencil, and set to work writing and weighing every word; and at last touched a bell and had his clerk into the chamber.

'Torrance,' said he, 'I must have this written out fair against tonight; and when it is done, you will be so kind as to put on your hat and be ready to come along with this gentleman and me, for you will probably be wanted as a witness.'

'What, sir,' cried I, as soon as the clerk was gone, 'are you to venture it?'

'Why, so it would appear,' says he, filling his glass. 'But let us speak no more of business. The very sight of Torrance brings in my head a little, droll matter of some years ago, when I had made a tryst with the poor oaf at the cross of Edinburgh. Each had gone his proper errand; and when it came four o'clock, Torrance had been taking a glass and did not know his master, and I, who had forgot my spectacles, was so blind without them, that I give you my word I did not know my own clerk.' And thereupon he laughed heartily.

I said it was an odd chance, and smiled out of politeness; but what held me all the afternoon in wonder, he kept returning and dwelling on this story, and telling it again with fresh details and laughter; so that I began at last to be quite put out of countenance and feel ashamed for my friend's folly.

Towards the time I had appointed with Alan, we set out from the house, Mr Rankeillor and I arm in arm, and Torrance following behind with the deed in his pocket and a covered basket in his hand. All through the town, the lawyer was bowing right and left, and continually being button-holed by gentlemen on matters of burgh or private business; and I could see he was greatly looked up to in the county. At last we were clear of the houses, and began to go along the side of the haven and towards the Hawes Inn and the ferry pier, the scene of my misfortune. I could not look upon the place without emotion, recalling how many that had been there with me that day were now no more: Ransome taken, I could hope, from the evil to come; Shuan passed where I dared not follow him; and the poor souls that had gone down with the brig in her last plunge. All these, and the brig herself, I had out-lived; and come through these hardships and fearful perils without scathe. My only thought should have been of gratitude; and yet I could not behold the place without sorrow for others and a chill of recollected fear.

I was so thinking when, upon a sudden, Mr Rankeillor cried out, clapped his hand to his pockets, and began to laugh.

'Why,' he cries, 'if this be not a farcical adventure! After all that I said, I have forgotten my glasses!'

At that, of course, I understood the purpose of his anecdote, and knew that if he had left his spectacles at home, it had been done on purpose, so that he might have the benefit of Alan's help without the awkwardness of recognizing him. And indeed it was well thought upon; for now (suppose things to go the very worst) how could Rankeillor swear to my friend's identity, or how be made to bear damaging evidence against myself? For all that, he had been a long while of finding out his want, and had spoken to and recognized a good few persons as we came through the town; and I had little doubt myself that he saw reasonably well.

As soon as we were past the Hawes (where I recognized the landlord smoking his pipe in the door, and was amazed to see him look no older) Mr Rankeillor changed the order of march, walking behind with Torrance and sending me forward in the manner of a scout. I went up the hill, whistling from time to time my Gaelic air; and at length I had the pleasure to hear it answered and to see Alan rise from behind a bush, he was somewhat dashed in spirits, having passed a long day along skulking in the country, and made but a poor meal in an alehouse near Dundas. But at the mere sight of my clothes, he began to brighten up; and as soon as I had told him in what a forward state our matters were, and the part I looked to him to play in what remained, he sprang into a new man.

'And that is a very good notion of yours,' says he; 'and I dare say that you could lay your hands upon no better man to put it through, than Alan Breck. It is not a thing (mark ye) that anyone could do, but takes a gentleman of penetration. But it sticks in my head your lawyer-man will be somewhat wearying to see me,' says Alan.

Accordingly I cried and waved on Mr Rankeillor, who came up alone and was presented to my friend, Mr Thomson.

'Mr Thomson, I am pleased to meet you,' said he. 'But I have forgotten my glasses; and our friend, Mr David here' (clapping me on the shoulder) 'will tell you that I am little better than blind, and that you must not be surprised if I pass you by tomorrow.'

This he said, thinking that Alan would be pleased; but the Highlandman's vanity was ready to startle at a less matter than that.

'Why, sir,' said he, stiffly, 'I would say it mattered the less as we are met here for a particular end, to see justice done to Mr Balfour; and by what I can see, not very likely to have much else in common. But I accept your apology, which was a very proper one to make.'

'And that is more than I could look for, Mr Thomson,' said Rankeillor, heartily. 'And now as you and I are the chief actors in this enterprise, I think we should come into a nice agreement; to which end, I porpose that you should lend me your arm, for (what with the dusk and the want of my glasses) I am not very clear as to the path; and as for you, Mr David, you will find Torrance a pleasant kind of body to speak with. Only let me remind you, it's quite needless he should hear more of your adventures or those of ahem – Mr Thomson.'

Accordingly these two went on ahead in very close talk, and Torrance and I brought up the rear.

Night was quite come when we came in view of the house of Shaws. Ten had been gone some time; it was dark and mild, with a pleasant, rustling wind in the south-west that covered the sound of our approach; and as we drew near we saw no glimmer of light in any portion of the building. It seemed my uncle was already in bed, which was indeed the best thing for our arrangements. We made our last whispered consultations some fifty yards away; and then the lawyer and Torrance and I crept quietly up and crouched down beside the corner of the house; and as soon as we were in our places, Alan strode to the door without concealment and began to knock.

❧ I Come into My Kingdom ❧

FOR SOME TIME ALAN VOLLEYED upon the door, and his knocking only roused the echoes of the house and neighbourhood. At last however, I could hear the noise of a window gently thrust up, and knew that my uncle had come to his observatory. By what light there was he would see Alan standing, like a dark shadow, on the steps; the three witnesses were hidden quite out of his view; so that there was nothing to alarm an honest man in his own house. For all that, he studied his visitor awhile in silence, and when he spoke his voice had a quaver of misgiving.

'What's this?' says he. 'This is nae kind of time of night for decent folk; and I hae nae trokings* wi' nighthawks. What brings ye here? I have a blunderbush.'

'Is that yoursel', Mr Balfour?' returned Alan, stepping back and looking up into the darkness. 'have a care of that blunderbuss; they're nasty things to burst.'

'What brings ye here? and whae are ye?' says my uncle, angrily.

'I have no manner of inclination to rowt out my name to the country-side,' said Alan; 'but what brings me here is another story, being more of your affairs than mine; and if ye're sure it's what ye would like, I'll set it to a tune and sing it to you.'

'And what isn't?' asked my uncle.

'David,' says Alan.

'What was that?' cried my uncle, in a mighty changed voice.

'Shall I give ye the rest of the name, then?' said Alan.

There was a pause; and then, 'I'm thinking I'll better let ye in,' says my uncle, doubtfully.

'I dare say that,' said Alan; 'but the point is, Would I go? Now I will tell you what I am thinking. I am thinking that it is here upon this doorstep that we must confer upon this business; and it shall be here or nowhere at all whatever; for I would have you to understand that I am as stiff-necked as yoursel', and a gentleman of better family.'

This change of note disconcerted Ebenezer; he was a little while digesting it; and then says he, 'Weel, weel, what must be must,' and shut the

*Dealings.

window. But it took him a long time to get downstairs, and a still longer to undo the fastenings, repenting (I dare say) and taken with fresh claps of fear at every second step and every bolt and bar. At last, however, we heard the creak of the hinges, and it seems my uncle slipped gingerly out and (seeing that Alan had stepped back a pace or two) sate him down on the top doorstep with the blunderbuss ready in his hands.

'And now,' says he, 'mind I have my blunderbush, and if ye take a step nearer y're as good as deid.'

'And a very civil speech,' said Alan, 'to be sure.'

'Na,' says my uncle, 'but this is no a very chancy kind of a proceeding, and I'm bound to be prepared. And now that we understand each other, ye'll can name your business.'

'Why,' says Alan, 'you that are a man of so much understanding, will doubtless have perceived that I am a Hieland gentleman. My name has nae business in my story; but the county of my friends is no very far from the Isle of Mull, of which ye will have heard. It seems there was a ship lost in those parts; and the next day a gentleman of my family was seeking wreckwood for his fire among the hands, when he came upon a lad that was half drowned. Well, he brought him to; and he and some other gentlemen took and clapped him in an auld, ruined castle, where from that day to this he has been a great expense to my friends. My friends are a wee wild-like, and not so particular about the law as some that I could name; and finding that the lad owned some decent folk, and was your born nephew, Mr Balfour, they asked me to give ye a bit call and to confer upon the matter. And I may tell ye at the off-go, unless we can agree upon some terms, ye are little likely to set eyes upon him. For my friends,' added Alan, simply, 'are no very well off,'

My uncle cleared his throat. 'I'm no very caring,' says he. 'He wasnae a good lad at the best of it, and I've nae call to interfere.'

'Ay, ay,' said Alan, 'I see what ye would be at: pretending ye don't care, to make the ransome smaller.'

'Na,' said my uncle, 'it's the mere truth. I take nae manner of interest in the lad, and I'll pay nae ransom, and ye can make a kirk and a mill of him for what I care.'

'Hoot, sir,' says Alan, 'Blood's thicker than water, in the deil's name! Ye cannae desert your brother's son for the fair shame of it; and if ye did, and it came to be kennt, ye wouldnae by very popular in your countryside, or I'm the more deceived.'

'I'm no just very popular the way it is,' returned Ebenezer, 'and I dinnae see how it would come to be kennt. No by me, onyway; nor by you or your friends. So that's idle talk, my buckie,' says he.

'Then it'll have to be David that tells it,' said Alan.

'How that?' says my uncle, sharply.

'Ou, just this way,' says Alan. 'My friends would doubtless keep your nephew as long as there was any likelihood of siller to be made of it, but if there was nane, I am clearly of opinion they would let him gang where he pleased, and be damned to him.'

'Ay, but I'm no very caring about that either,' said my uncle. 'I would-nae be muckle made up with that.'

'I was thinking that,' said Alan.

'And what for why?' asked Ebenezer.

'Why, Mr Balfour,' replied Alan, 'by all that I could hear, there were two ways of it: either ye liked David and would pay to get him back; or else ye had very good reasons for not wanting him, and would pay for us to keep him. It seems it's not the first; well then, it's the second; and blythe am I to ken it, for it should be a pretty penny in my pocket and the pockets of my friends.'

'I dinnae follow ye there,' said my uncle.

'No?' said Alan. 'Well, see here; you dinnae want the lad back; well, what do ye want down with him, and how much will ye pay?'

My uncle made no answer, but shifted uneasily on his seat.

'Come, sir,' cried Alan. 'I would have ye ken that I am a gentleman; I bear a king's name; I am nae rider to kick my shanks at your hall door. Either give me an answer in civility, and that out of hand; or by the top of Glencoe, I will ram three feet of iron through your vitals.'

'Eh, man,' cried my uncle, scrambling to his feet, 'give me a meenit! What's like wrong with ye? I'm just a plain man, and nae dancing master; and I'm trying to be as ceevil as it's morally possible. As for that wild talk, it's fair disrepitable. Vitals, says you! And where would I be with my blunderbush?' he snarled.

'Power and your auld hands are but as the snail to the swallow against the bright stell in the hands of Alan,' said the other. 'Before your jottering finger could find the trigger, the hilt would dirl on your breast bane.'

'Eh, man, whae's denying it?' said my uncle. 'Pit it as ye please, hae't your ain way; I'll do naething to cross ye. Just tell me what like ye'll be wanting, and ye'll see that we'll can agree fine.'

'Troth, sir,' said Alan, 'I ask for nothing but plain dealing. In two words: do ye want the lad killed or kept?'

'O, sirs!' cried Ebenezer. 'O, sirs, me! that's no kind of language!'

'Killed or kept?' repeated Alan.

'Oh, keepit, keepit!' wailed my uncle. 'We'll have nae bloodshed, if you please.'

'Well,' says Alan, 'as ye please; that'll be the dearer.'

'The dearer?' cries Ebenezer. 'Would ye fyle your hands wi' crime?'

'Hoot!' said Alan, 'they're baith crime, whatever! And the killing's easier, and quicker, and surer. Keeping the lad'll be a fashious* job, a fashious, kittle business.'

'I'll have him keepit, though,' returned my uncle. 'I never had naething to do with onything morally wrong; and I'm no gaun to begin to pleasure a wild Hielandman.'

'Ye're unco scrupulous,' sneered Alan.

'I'm a man o' principle,' said Ebenezer simply; 'and if I have to pay for it, I'll have to pay for it. And besides,' says he, 'ye forget the lad's my brother's son.'

'Well, well,' said Alan, 'and now about the price. It's no very easy for me to set a name upon it; I would first have to ken some small matters. I would have to ken, for instance, what ye gave Hoseason at the first off-go?'

'Hoseason?' cries my uncle, struck aback. 'What for?'

'For kidnapping David,' says Alan.

'It's a lee, it's a black lee!' cried my uncle. 'He was never kidnapped. He leed in his throat that tauld ye that. Kidnapped? He never was!'

'That's no fault of mine or yet of yours,' said Alan; 'nor yet of Hoseason's, if he's a man that can be trusted.'

'What do ye mean?' cried Ebenezer. 'Did Hoseason tell ye?'

'Why, ye donnered auld runt, how else would I ken?' cried Alan. 'Hoseason and I are partners; we gang shares; so ye can see for yoursel', what good ye can do leeing. And I must plainly say ye drove a fool's bargain when ye let a man like the sailor-man so far forward in your private matters. But that's past praying for; and ye must lie on your bed the way ye made it. And the point in hand is just this what did ye pay him?'

'Has he tauld ye himsel',' asked my uncle.

'That's my concern,' said Alan.

'Weel,' said my uncle, 'I dinnae care what he said, he leed, and the solemn God's truth is this, that I gave him twenty pound. But I'll be perfec'ly honest with ye: forby that, he was to have the selling of the lad in Caroliny, whilk would be as muckle mair, but no from my pocket, ye see.'

'Thank you, Mr Thomson. That will do excellently well,' said the lawyer, stepping forward; and then mighty civilly, 'Good evening, Mr Balfour,' said he.

And, 'Good evening, Uncle Ebenezer,' said I.

And, 'It's a braw nicht, Mr Balfour,' added Torrance.

*Troublesome.

164

Never a word said my uncle, neither black nor white; but just sat where he was on the top doorstep and stared upon us like a man turned to stone. Alan filched away his blunderbuss; and the lawyer, taking him by the arm, plucked him up from the doorstep, led him into the kitchen, whither we all followed, and set him down in a chair beside the hearth, where the fire was out and only a rush-light burning.

There we all looked upon him for a while, exulting greatly in our success, but yet with a sort of pity for the man's shame.

'Come, come, Mr Ebenezer,' said the lawyer, 'you must not be down-hearted, for I promise you we shall make easy terms. In the meanwhile give us the cellar key, and Torrance shall draw us a bottle of your father's wine in honour of the event.' Then, turning to me and taking me by the hand, 'Mr David,' says he, 'I wish you all joy in your good fortune, which I believe to be deserved.' And then to Alan, with a spice of drollery, 'Mr Thomson, I pay you my compliment; it was most artfully conducted; but in one point you somewhat outran my comprehension. Do I understand your name to be James? or Charles? or is it George perhaps?'

'And why should it be any of the three, sir?' quoth Alan, drawing himself up like one who smelt an offence.

'Only, sir, that you mentioned a king's name,' replied Rankeillor; 'and as there has never yet been a King Thomson, or his fame at least has never come my way, I judged you must refer to that you had in baptism.'

This was just the stab that Alan would feel keenest, and I am free to confess he took it very ill. Not a word would he answer, but stept off to the far end of the kitchen, and sat down and sulked; and it was not till I stepped after him, and gave him my hand, and thanked him by title as the chief spring of my success, that he began to smile a bit, and was at last prevailed upon to join our party.

By that time we had the fire lighted, and a bottle of wine uncorked; a good supper came out of the basket, to which Torrance and I and Alan set ourselves down; while the lawyer and my uncle passed into the next chamber to consult. They stayed there closeted about an hour; at the end of which period there had come to a good understanding, and my uncle and I set our hands to the agreement in a formal manner. By the terms of this, my uncle bound himself to satisfy Rankeillor as to his intro-missions, and to pay me two thirds of the yearly income of Shaws.

So the beggar in the ballad had come home; and when I lay down that night on the kitchen chests, I was a man of means and had a name in the country. Alan and Torrance and Rankeillor slept and snored on their hard beds; but for me, who had lain out under heaven and upon dirt and stones, so many days and nights, and often with an empty belly, and in fear of death, this good change in my case unmanned me more than any of the former evil ones; and I lay till dawn, looking at the fire on the roof and planning the future.

THIRTY

❖ Good-Bye ❖

So FAR AS I WAS CONCERNED myself, I had come to port; but I had still Alan, to whom I was so much beholden, on my hands; and I felt besides a heavy charge in the matter of the murder and James of the Glens. On both these heads I unbosomed to Rankeillor the next morning, walking to and fro about six of the clock before the house of Shaws, and with nothing in view but the fields and woods that had been my ancestors' and were now mine. Even as I spoke on these grave subjects, my eye would take a glad bit of a run over the prospect, and my heart jump with pride.

About my clear duty to my friend, the lawyer had no doubt; I must help him out of the county at whatever risk; but in the case of James, he was of a different mind.

'Mr Thomson,' says he, 'is one thing, Mr Thomson's kinsman quite another. I know little of the facts; but I gather that a great noble (whom we will call, if you like, the D. of A.*) has some concern and is even supposed to feel some animosity in the matter. The D. of A. is doubtless an excellent nobleman; but, Mr David, *timeo qui nocuere deos*. If you interfere to baulk his vengeance, you should remember there is one way to shut your testimony out; and that is to put you in the dock. There, you would be in the same pickle as Mr Thomson's kinsman. You will object that you are innocent; well, but so is he. And to be tried for your life before a Highland jury, on a Highland quarrel, and with a Highland judge upon the bench, would be a brief transition to the gallows.'

Now I had made all these reasonings before and found no very good reply to them; so I put on all the simplicity I could. 'In that case, sir,' said I, 'I would just have to be hanged – would I not?'

'My dear boy,' cries he, 'go in God's name, and do what you think is

*The Duke of Argyle.

right. It is a poor thought that at my time of life I should be advising you to choose the safe and shameful; and I take it back with an apology. Go and do your duty; and be hanged, if you must, like a gentleman. There are worse things in the world than to be hanged.'

'Not many, sir,' said I, smiling.

'Why, yes, yes, sir,' he cried, 'very many. And it would be ten times better for your uncle (to go no farther afield) if he were dangling decently upon a gibbet.'

Thereupon he turned into the house (still in a great fervour of mind, so that I saw I had pleased him heartily) and there he wrote me two letters, making his comments on them as he wrote.

'This,' says he, 'is to my bankers, the British Linen Company, placing a credit to your name. Consult Mr Thomson; he will know of ways; and you, with this credit, can supply the means. I trust you will be a good husband of your money; but in the affairs of a friend like Mr Thomson, I would be even prodigal. Then, for his kinsman, there is no better way than that you should seek the Advocate, tell him your tale, and offer testimony; whether he may ask it or not, is quite another matter, and will turn on the D. of A. Now that you may reach the Lord Advocate well recommended, I give you here a letter to a namesake of your own the learned Mr Balfour of Pilrig, a man whom I esteem. It will look better that you should be presented by one of your own name; and the laird of Pilrig is much looked up to in the Faculty and stands well with the Lord Advocate Grant. I would not trouble him, if I were you, with any particulars; and (do you know?) I think it would be needless to refer to Mr Thomson. Form yourself upon the laird, he is a good model; when you deal with the Advocate, be discreet; and in all these matters, may the Lord guide you, Mr David!'

Thereupon he took his farewell, and set out with Torrance for the Ferry, while Alan and I turned our faces for the city of Edinburgh. As we went by the footpath and beside the gateposts and the unfinished lodge, we kept looking back at the house of my fathers. It stood there, bare and great and smokeless, like a place not lived in; only in one of the top windows, there was the peak of a nightcap bobbing up and down and back and forward, like the head of a rabbit from a burrow. I had little welcome when I came, and less kindness while I stayed; but at least I was watched as I went away.

Alan and I went slowly forward upon our way, having little heart either to walk or speak. The same thought was uppermost in both, that we were near the time of our parting; and remembrance of all the bygone days sate upon us sorely. We talked indeed of what should be done; and it was resolved that Alan should keep to the country, biding now here, now there, but coming once in the day to a particular place where I might be able to communicate with him, either in my own person or by messenger. In the meanwhile, I was to seek out a lawyer, who was an Appin Stewart, and a man therefore to be wholly trusted; and it should be his part to find a ship and to arrange for Alan's safe embarkation. No sooner was this business done, than the words seemed to leave us; and though I would seek to jest with Alan under the name of Mr Thomson, and he with me on my new clothes and my estate, you could feel very well that we were nearer tears than laughter.

We came the by-way over the hill of Corstorphine; and when we got near to the place called Rest-and-be-Thankful, and looked down on Corstorphine bogs and over to the city and the castle on the hill, we both stopped, for we both knew without a word said, that we had come to where our ways parted. Here he repeated to me once again what had been agreed upon between us; the address of the lawyer, the daily hour at which Alan might be found, and the signals that were to be made by any that came seeking him. Then I gave what money I had (a guinea or two of Rankeillor's) so that he should not starve in the meanwhile; and then we stood a space, and looked over at Edinburgh in silence.

'Well, good-bye,' said Alan, and held out his left hand.

'Good-bye,' said I, and gave the hand a little grasp, and went off down hill.

Neither one of us looked the other in the face, nor so long as he was in my view did I take one back glance at the friend I was leaving. But as I went on my way to the city, I felt so lost and lonesome, that I could have found it in my heart to sit down by the dyke, and cry and weep like any baby.

It was coming near noon when I passed in by the West Kirk and the Grassmarket into the streets of the capital. The huge height of the buildings, running up to ten and fifteen storeys, the narrow arched entries that continually vomited passengers, the wares of the merchants in their windows, the hubbub and endless stir, the foul smells and the fine clothes, and a hundred other particulars too small to mention, struck me into a kind of stupor of surprise, so that I let the crowd carry me to and fro; and yet all the time what I was thinking of was Alan at Rest-and-be-Thankful; and all the time (although you would think I would not choose but be delighted with these braws and novelties) there was a cold gnawing in my inside like a remorse for something wrong.

The hand of Providence brought me in my drifting to the very doors of the British Linen Company's bank.

[Just there, with his hand upon his fortune, the present editor inclines for the time to say farewell to David. How Alan escapes, and what was done about the murder, with a variety of other delectable particulars, may be some day set forth. That is a thing however, that hinges on the public fancy. The editor has a great kindness for both Alan and David, and would gladly spend much of his life in their society; but in this he may find himself to stand alone. In the fear of which, and lest any one should complain of scurvy usage, he hastens to protest that all went well with both, in the limited and human sense of the word 'well'; that whatever befell them, it was not dishonour, and whatever failed them, they were not found wanting to themselves.]

THE MASTER
OF BALLANTRAE

TO

SIR PERCY FLORENCE AND LADY SHELLEY

HERE IS A TALE WHICH extends over many years and travels into many countries. By a peculiar fitness of circumstance the writer began, continued it, and concluded it among distant and diverse scenes. Above all, he was much upon the sea. The character and fortune of the fraternal enemies, the hall and shrubbery of Durrisdeer, the problem of Mackellar's homespun and how to shape it for superior flights; these were his company on deck in many star-reflecting harbours, ran often in his mind at sea to the tune of slatting canvas, and were dismissed (something of the suddenest) on the approach of squalls. It is my hope that these surroundings of its manufacture may to some degree find favour for my story with seafarers and sea-lovers like yourselves.

And at least here is a dedication from a great way off: written by the loud shores of a subtropical island near upon ten thousand miles from Boscombe Chine and Manor: scenes which rise before me as I write, along with the faces and voices of my friends.

Well, I am for the sea once more; no doubt Sir Percy also. Let us make the signal B.R.D.!

R.L.S.

WAIKIKI, *May 17, 1889.*

❖ Preface ❖

ALTHOUGH AN OLD, CONSISTENT exile, the editor of the following pages revisits now and again the city of which he exults to be a native; and there are few things more strange, more painful, or more salutary, than such revisitations. Outside, in foreign spots, he comes by surprise and awakens more attention than he had expected; in his own city, the relation is reversed, and he stands amazed to be so little recollected. Elsewhere he is refreshed to see attractive faces, to remark possible friends; there he scouts the long streets, with a pang at heart, for the faces and friends that are no more. Elsewhere he is delighted with the presence of what is new, there tormented by the absence of what is old. Elsewhere he is content to be his present self; there he is smitten with an equal regret for what he once was and for what he once hoped to be.

He was feeling all this dimly, as he drove from the station, on his last visit; he was feeling it still as he alighted at the door of his friend Mr Johnstone Thomson, W.S., with whom he was to stay. A hearty welcome, a face not altogether changed, a few words that sounded of old days, a laugh provoked and shared, a glimpse in passing of the snowy cloth and bright decanters and the Piranesis on the dining-room wall, brought him to his bedroom with a somewhat lightened cheer, and when he and Mr Thomson sat down a few minutes later, cheek by jowl, and pledged the past in a preliminary bumper, he was already almost consoled, he had already almost forgiven himself his two unpardonable errors, that he should ever have left his native city, or ever returned to it.

'I have something quite in your way,' said Mr Thomson. 'I wished to do honour to your arrival; because, my dear fellow, it is my own youth that comes back along with you; in a very tattered and withered state, to be sure, but – well! – all that's left of it.'

'A great deal better than nothing,' said the editor. 'But what is this which is quite in my way?'

'I was coming to that,' said Mr Thomson: 'Fate has put it in my power to honour your arrival with something really original by way of dessert. A mystery.'

'A mystery?' I repeated.

'Yes,' said his friend, 'a mystery. It may prove to be nothing, and it may prove to be a great deal. But in the meanwhile it is truly mysterious, no eye having looked on it for near a hundred years; it is highly genteel, for it treats of a titled family; and it ought to be melodramatic, for (according to the superscription) it is concerned with death.'

'I think I rarely heard a more obscure or a more promising annunciation,' the other remarked. 'But what is It?'

'You remember my predecessor's, old Peter M'Brair's business?'

'I remember him acutely; he could not look at me without a pang of reprobation, and he could not feel the pang without betraying it. He was to me a man of a great historical interest, but the interest was not returned.'

'Ah well, we go beyond him,' said Mr Thomson. 'I dare say old Peter knew as little about this as I do. You see, I succeeded to a prodigious accumulation of old law-papers and old tin boxes, some of them of Peter's hoarding, some of his father's, John, first of the dynasty, a great man in his day. Among other collections were all the papers of the Durrisdeers.'

'The Durrisdeers!' cried I. 'My dear fellow, these may be of the greatest interest. One of them was out in the '45; one had some strange passages with the devil – you will find a note of it in Law's *Memorials*, I think; and there was an unexplained tragedy, I know not what, much later, about a hundred years ago—'

'More than a hundred years ago,' said Mr Thomson. 'In 1783.'

'How do you know that? I mean some death.'

'Yes, the lamentable deaths of my lord Durrisdeer and his brother, the Master of Ballantrae (attainted in the troubles),' said Mr Thomson with something the tone of a man quoting. 'Is that it?'

'To say truth,' said I, 'I have only seen some dim reference to the things in memoirs; and heard some traditions dimmer still, through my uncle (whom I think you knew). My uncle lived when he was a boy in the neighbourhood of St Bride's; he has often told me of the avenue closed up and grown over with grass, the great gates never opened, the last lord and his old maid sister who lived in the back parts of the house, a quiet, plain poor, humdrum couple it would seem – but pathetic too, as the last of that stirring and brave house – and, to the country folk, faintly terrible from some deformed traditions.'

'Yes,' said Mr Thomson. 'Henry Graeme Durie, the last lord, died in 1820; his sister, the Honourable Miss Katherine Durie, in '27; so much I know; and by what I have been going over the last few days, they were what you say, decent, quiet people and not rich. To say truth, it was a letter of my lord's that put me on the search for the packet we are going to open this evening. Some papers could not be found; and he wrote to Jack M'Brair suggesting they might be among those sealed up by a Mr Mackellar. M'Brair answered, that the papers in question were all in Mackellar's own hand, all (as the writer understood) of a purely narrative character; and besides, said he, 'I am bound not to open them before the year 1889.' You may fancy if these words struck me: I instituted a hunt through all the M'Brair repositories; and at last hit upon that packet which (if you have had enough wine) I propose to show you at once.'

In the smoking-room, to which my host now led me, was a packet, fastened with many seals and enclosed in a single sheet of strong paper thus endorsed:

Papers relating to the lives and lamentable deaths of the late Lord Durisdeer, and his elder brother James, commonly called Master of Ballantrae, attainted in the troubles: entrusted into the hands of John M'Brair in the Lawnmarket of Edinburgh, W.S.; this 20th day of September Anno Domini 1789; by him to be kept secret until the revolution of one hundred years complete, or until the 20th day of September 1889: the same compiled and written by me,

EPHRAIM MACKELLAR,
For near forty years Land Steward on the
estates of His Lordship.

As Mr Thomson is a married man, I will not say what hour had struck when we laid down the last of the following pages; but I will give a few words of what ensued.

'Here,' said Mr Thomson, 'is a novel ready to your hand: all you have to do is to work up the scenery, develop the characters, and improve the style.'

'My dear fellow,' said I, 'they are just the three things that I would rather die than set my hand to. It shall be published as it stands.'

'But it's so bald,' objected Mr Thomson.

'I believe there is nothing so noble as baldness,' replied I, 'and I am sure there is nothing so interesting. I would have all literature bald, and all authors (if you like) but one.'

'Well, well,' said Mr Thomson, 'we shall see.'

ONE

❧ Summary of events during ❧ the Master's wanderings

THE FULL TRUTH OF THIS ODD matter is what the world has long been looking for, and public curiosity is sure to welcome. It so befell that I was intimately mingled with the last years and history of the house; and there does not live one man so able as myself to make these matters plain, or so desirous to narrate them faithfully. I knew the Master; on many secret steps of his career I have an authentic memoir in my hand; I sailed with him on his last voyage almost alone; I made one upon that winter's journey of which so many tales have gone abroad; and I was there at the man's death. As for my late Lord Durrisdeer, I served him and loved him near twenty years; and thought more of him the more I knew of him. Altogether, I think it not fit that so much evidence should perish; the truth is a debt I owe my lord's memory; and I think my old years will flow more smoothly, and my white hair lie quieter on the pillow, when the debt is paid.

The Duries of Durrisdeer and Ballantrae were a strong family in the south-west from the days of David First. A rhyme still current in the countryside

> Kittle folk are the Durrisdeers,
> They ride wi' ower mony spears

bears the mark of its antiquity; and the name appears in another, which common report attributes to Thomas of Ercildoune himself – I cannot say how truly, and which some have applied – I dare not say with how much justice – to the events of this narration:

> Twa Duries in Durrisdeer,
>   Ane to tie and ane to ride,
> An ill day for the groom
>   And a waur day for the bride.

Authentic history besides is filled with their exploits, which (to our modern eyes) seem not very commendable: and the family suffers its full share of those ups and downs to which the great houses of Scotland have been ever liable. But all these I pass over, to come to that memorable year 1745, when the foundations of this tragedy were laid.

At that time there dwelt a family of four persons in the house of Durrisdeer, near St Bride's, on the Solway shore; a chief hold of their race since the Reformation. My old lord, eighth of the name, was not old in years, but he suffered prematurely from the disabilities of age; his place was at the chimneyside; there he sat reading, in a lined gown, with few words for any man, and wry words for none: the model of an old retired housekeeper; and yet his mind very well nourished with study, and reputed in the country to be more cunning than he seemed. The Master of Ballantrae, James in baptism, took from his father the love of serious reading; some of his tact perhaps as well, but that which was only policy in the father became black dissimulation in the son. The face of his behaviour was merely popular and wild: he sat late at wine, later at the cards; had the name in the country of 'an unco man for the lasses'; and was ever in the front of broils. But for all he was the first to go in, yet it was observed he was invariably the best to come off; and his partners in mischief were usually alone to pay the piper. This luck or dexterity got him several ill-wishers, but with the rest of the country, enhanced his reputation; so that great things were looked for in his future, when he should have gained more gravity. One very black mark he had to his name; but the matter was hushed up at the time, and so defaced by legends before I came into those parts, that I scruple to set it down. If it was true, it was a horrid fact in one so young; and if false, it was a horrid calumny. I think it notable that he had always vaunted himself quite implacable, and was taken at his word; so that he had the addition among his neighbours of 'an ill man to cross.' Here was altogether a young nobleman (not yet twenty-four in the year '45) who had made a figure in the country beyond his time of life. The less marvel if there were little heard of the second son, Mr Henry (my late Lord Durrisdeer), who was neither very bad nor yet very able, but an honest, solid sort of lad like many of his neighbours. Little heard, I say; but indeed it was a case of little spoken. He was known among the salmon fishers in the firth, for that was a sport that he assiduously followed; he was an excellent good horse-doctor besides; and took a chief hand, almost from a boy, in the management of the estates. How hard a part that was, in the situation of that family, none knows better than myself; nor yet with how little colour of justice a man may there acquire the reputation of a tyrant and a miser. The fourth person in the house was Miss Alison Graeme, a near kinswoman, an orphan, and the heir to a considerable fortune which her father had acquired in trade. This money was loudly called for by my lord's necessities; indeed the land was deeply mortgaged; and Miss Alison was designed accordingly to be the Master's wife, gladly enough on her side; with how much good-will on his, is another matter. She was a comely girl, and in those days very spirited and self-willed; for the old lord having no daughter of his own, and my lady being long dead, she had grown up as best she might.

To these four came the news of Prince Charlie's landing, and set them presently by the ears. My lord, like the chimney-keeper that he was, was all for temporizing. Miss Alison held the other side, because it appeared romantical; and the Master (though I have heard they did not agree often) was for this once of her opinion. The adventure tempted him, as I conceive; he was tempted by the oppotunity to raise the fortunes of the house, and not less by the hope of paying off his private liabilities, which were heavy beyond all opinion. As for Mr Henry, it appears he said little enough at first; his part came later on. It took the three a whole day's disputation before they agreed to steer a middle course, one son going forth to strike a blow for King James, my lord and the other staying at home to keep in favour with King George. Doubtless this was my lord's decision; and, as is well known, it was the part played by many considerable families. But the one dispute settled, another opened. For my lord, Miss Alison, and Mr Henry all held the one view: that it was the cadet's part to go out; and the Master, what with restlessness and vanity, would at no rate consent to stay at home. My lord pleaded, Miss Alison wept, Mr Henry was very plain spoken: all was of no avail.

'It is the direct heir of Durrisdeer that should ride by his King's bridle,' says the Master.

'If we were playing a manly part,' says Mr Henry, 'there might be sense in such talk. But what are we doing? Cheating at cards!'

'We are saving the house of Durrisdeer, Henry,' his father said.

'And see, James,' said Mr Henry, 'if I go, and the Prince has the upper hand, it will be easy to make your peace with King James. But if you go, and the expedition fails, we divide the right and the title. And what shall I be then?'

'You will be Lord Durrisdeer,' said the Master. 'I put all I have upon the table.'

'I play at no such game,' cries Mr Henry. 'I shall be left in such a situation as no man of sense and honour could endure. I shall be neither fish nor flesh!' he cried. And a little after he had another expression, plainer perhaps than he intended. 'It is your duty to be here with my father,' said he. 'You know well enough you are the favourite.'

'Ay?' said the Master. 'And there spoke Envy! Would you trip up my heels – Jacob?' said he, and dwelled upon the name maliciously.

Mr Henry went and walked at the low end of the hall without reply; for he had an excellent gift of silence. Presently he came back.

'I am the cadet and I *should* go,' said he. 'And my lord here is the master, and he says I *shall* go. What say ye to that, my brother?'

'I say this, Harry,' returned the Master, 'that when very obstinate folk are met, there are only two ways out: Blows – and I think none of us could care to go so far; or the arbitrament of chance – and here is a guinea piece. Will you stand by the toss of the coin?'

'I will stand and fall by it,' said Mr Henry. 'Heads, I go; shield, I stay.'

The coin was spun, and it fell shield. 'So there is a lesson for Jacob,' says the Master.

'We shall live to repent of this,' says Mr Henry, and flung out of the hall.

As for Miss Alison, she caught up that piece of gold which had just sent her lover to the wars, and flung it clean through the family shield in the great painted window.

'If you loved me as well as I love you, you would have stayed,' cried she.

'I could not love you, dear, so well, loved I not honour more,' sang the Master.

'Oh!' she cried, 'you have no heart – I hope you may be killed!' and she ran from the room, and in tears, to her own chamber.

It seems the Master turned to my lord with his most comical manner, and says he, 'This looks like a devil of a wife.'

'I think you are a devil of a son to me,' cried his father, 'you that have always been the favourite, to my shame be it spoken. Never a good hour have I gotten of you, since you were born; no, never one good hour,' and repeated it again the third time. Whether it was the Master's levity, or his insubordination, or Mr Henry's word about the favourite son, that had so much disturbed my lord, I do not know; but I incline to think it was the last, for I have it by all accounts that Mr Henry was more made up to from that hour.

Altogether it was in pretty ill blood with his family that the Master rode to the North; which was the more sorrowful for others to remember when it seemed too late. By fear and favour he had scraped together near upon a dozen men, principally tenants' sons; they were all pretty full when they set forth, and rode up the hill by the old abbey, roaring and singing, the white cockade in every hat. It was a desperate venture for so small a company to cross the most of Scotland unsupported; and (what made folk think so the more) even as that poor dozen was clattering up the hill, a great ship of the king's navy, that could have brought them under with a single boat, lay with her broad ensign streaming in the bay. The next afternoon, having given the Master a fair start, it was Mr Henry's turn; and he rode off, all by himself, to offer his sword and carry letters from his father to King George's Government. Miss Alison was shut in her room, and did little but weep, till both were gone; only she stitched the cockade upon the Master's hat, and (as John Paul told me) it was wetted with tears when he carried it down to him.

In all that followed, Mr Henry and my old lord were true to their bargain. That ever they accomplished anything is more than I could learn; and that they were anyway strong on the king's side, more than I believe. But they kept the letter of loyalty, corresponded with my Lord President, sat still at home, and had little or no commerce with the Master while that business lasted. Nor was he, on his side, more communicative. Miss Alison, indeed, was always sending him expresses, but I do not know if she had many answers. Macconochie rode for her once, and found the Highlanders before Carlisle, and the Master riding by the Prince's side in high favour; he took the letter (so Macconochie tells), opened it, glanced it through with a mouth like a man whistling, and stuck it in his belt, whence, on his horse passaging, it fell unregarded to the ground. It was Macconochie who picked it up; and he still kept it, and indeed I have seen it in his hands. News came to Durrisdeer of course, by the common report, as it goes travelling through a country, a thing always wonderful to me. By that means the family learned more of the Master's favour with the Prince, and the ground it was said to stand on: for by a strange condescension in a man so proud – only that he was a man still more ambitious – he was said to have crept into notability by truckling to the Irish. Sir Thomas Sullivan, Colonel Burke, and the rest, were his daily comrades, by which course he withdrew himself from his own country-folk. All the small intrigues he had a hand in fomenting; thwarted my Lord George upon a thousand points; was always for the advice that seemed palatable to the Prince, no matter if it was good or bad; and seems upon the whole (like the gambler he was all through life) to have had less regard to the chances of the campaign than to the greatness of favour he might aspire to, if, by any luck, it should succeed. For the rest, he did very well in the field; no one questioned that; for he was no coward.

The next was the news of Culloden, which was brought to Durrisdeer by one of the tenants' sons – the only survivor, he declared, of all those that had gone singing up the hill. By an unfortunate chance John Paul and Macconochie had that very morning found the guinea piece – which was the root of all the evil – sticking in a holly bush; they had been 'up the gait,' as the servants say at Durrisdeer, to the change-house; and if they had left of the guinea, they had less of their wits. What must John Paul do but burst into the hall where the family sat at dinner, and cry the news to them that 'Tam Macmorland was but new lichtit at the door, and – wirra, wirra – there were nane to come behind him'?

They took the word in silence like folk condemned; only Mr Henry carrying his palm to his face, and Miss Alison laying her head outright upon her hands. As for my lord, he was like ashes.

'I have still one son,' says he. 'And, Henry, I will do you this justice – it is the kinder that is left.'

It was a strange thing to say in such a moment; but my lord had never forgotten Mr Henry's speech, and he had years of injustice on his conscience. Still it was a strange thing, and more than Miss Alison could let pass. She broke out and blamed my lord for his unnatural words, and Mr Henry because he was sitting there in safety when his brother lay dead, and herself because she had given her sweetheart ill words at his departure, calling him the flower of the flock, wringing her hands, protesting her love, and crying on him by his name – so that the servants stood astonished.

Mr Henry got to his feet, and stood holding his chair. It was he that was like ashes now.

'Oh!' he burst out suddenly, 'I know you loved him.'

'The world knows that, glory be to God!' cries she; and then to Mr Henry: 'There is none but me to know one thing – that you were a traitor to him in your heart.'

'God knows,' groans he, 'it was lost love on both sides.'

Time went by in the house after that without much change; only they were now three instead of four, which was a perpetual reminder of their loss. Miss Alison's money, you are to bear in mind, was highly needful for the estates; and the one brother being dead, my lord soon set his heart upon her marrying the other. Day in, day out, he would work upon her, sitting by the chimney-side with his finger in his Latin book, and his eyes set upon her face with a kind of pleasant intentness that became the old gentleman very well. If she wept, he would condole with her like an ancient man that has seen worse times and begins to think lightly even of sorrow; if she raged, he would fall to reading again in his Latin book, but always with some civil excuse; if she offered, as she often did, to let them have her money in a gift, he would show her how little it consisted with his honour, and remind her, even if he should consent, that Mr Henry would certainly refuse. *Non vi sed saepe cadendo* was a favourite word of his; and no doubt this quiet persecution wore away much of her resolve; no doubt, besides, he had a great influence on the girl, having stood in the place of both her parents; and, for that matter, she was herself filled with the spirit of the Duries, and would have gone a great way for the glory of Durrisdeer; but not so far, I think, as to marry my poor patron, had it not been – strangely enough – for the circumstance of his extreme unpopularity.

This was the work of Tam Macmorland. There was not much harm in Tam; but he had that grievous weakness, a long tongue; and as the only man in that country who had been out – or, rather who had come in again – he was sure of listeners. Those that have the underhand in any fighting, I have observed, are ever anxious to persuade themselves they were betrayed. By Tam's account of it, the rebels had been betrayed at every turn and by every officer they had; they had been betrayed at Derby, and betrayed at Falkirk; the night march was a step of treachery of my Lord George's; and Culloden was lost by the treachery of the Macdonalds. This habit of imputing treason grew upon the fool, till at last he must have in Mr Henry also. Mr Henry (by his account) had betrayed the lads of Durrisdeer; he had promised to follow with more men, and instead of that he had ridden to King George. 'Ay, and the next day!' Tam would cry. 'The puir bonnie Master, and the puir, kind lads that rade wi' him, were hardly ower the scaur, or he was aff – the Judis! – Ay, weel – he has his way o't: he's to be my lord, nae less, and there's mony a cold corp amang the Hieland heather!' And at this, if Tam had been drinking, he would begin to weep.

Let anyone speak long enough, he will get believers. This view of Mr Henry's behaviour crept about the country by little and little; it was talked upon by folk that knew the contrary, but were short of topics; and it was heard and believed and given out for gospel by the ignorant and the ill-willing. Mr Henry began to be shunned; yet awhile, and the commons began to murmur as he went by, and the women (who are always the most bold because they are the most safe) to cry out their reproaches to his face. The Master was cried up for a saint. It was remembered how he had never any hand in pressing the tenants; as, indeed, no more he had, except to spend the money. He was a little wild perhaps, the folk said; but how much better was a natural wild lad that would soon have settled down, than a skinflint and a sneck-draw, sitting, with his nose in an account book, to persecute poor tenants! One trollop, who had had a child to the Master, and by all accounts been very badly used, yet made herself a kind of champion of his memory. She flung a stone one day at Mr Henry.

'Whaur's the bonnie lad that trustit ye?' she cried.

Mr Henry reined in his horse and looked upon her, the blood flowing from his lip. 'Ay, Jess?' says he. 'You, too? And yet ye should ken me better.' For it was he who had helped her with money.

The woman had another stone ready, which she made as if she would cast; and he, to ward himself, threw up the hand that held his riding-rod.

'What, would ye beat a lassie, ye ugly—?' cries she, and ran away screaming as though he had struck her.

Next day word went about the country like wildfire that Mr Henry had beaten Jessie Broun within an inch of her life. I give it as one instance of how this snowball grew, and one calumny brought another; until my poor patron was so perished in reputation that he began to keep the house like my lord. All this while, you may be very sure, he uttered no complaints at home; the very ground of the scandal was too sore a matter to be handled; and Mr Henry was very proud and strangely obstinate in silence. My old lord must have heard of it, by John Paul, if by no one else; and he must at least have remarked the altered habits of his son. Yet even he, it is probable, knew not how high the feeling ran; and as for Miss Alison, she was ever the last person to hear news, and the least interested when she heard them.

In the height of the ill-feeling (for it died away as it came, no man could say why) there was an election forward in the town of St Bride's, which is the next to Durrisdeer, standing on the Water of Swift; some grievance was fermenting, I forget what, if ever I heard; and it was currently said there would be broken heads ere night, and that the sheriff had sent as far as Dumfries for soldiers. My lord moved that Mr Henry should be present, assuring him it was necessary to appear, for the credit of the house. 'It will soon be reported,' said he, 'that we do not take the lead in our own country.'

'It is a strange lead that I can take,' said Mr Henry; and when they had pushed him further, 'I tell you the plain truth,' he said, 'I dare not show my face.'

'You are the first of the house that ever said so,' cried Miss Alison.

'We will go all three,' said my lord; and sure enough he got into his boots (the first time in four years – a sore business John Paul had to get them on), and Miss Alison into her riding-coat, and all three rode together to St Bride's.

The streets were full of the riff-raff of all the countryside, who had no sooner clapped eyes on Mr Henry than the hissing began, and the hooting, and the cries of 'Judas!' and 'Where was the Master?' and 'Where were the poor lads that rode with him?' Even a stone was cast; but the more part cried shame at that, for my old lord's sake, and Miss Alison's. It took not ten minutes to persuade my lord that Mr Henry had been right. He said never a word, but turned his horse about, and home again, with his chin upon his bosom. Never a word said Miss Alison; no doubt she thought the more; no doubt her pride was stung, for she was a bone-bred Durie; and no doubt her heart was touched to see her cousin so unjustly used. That night she was never in bed; I have often blamed my lady – when I call to mind that night, I readily forgive her all; and the first thing in the morning she came to the old lord in his usual seat.

'If Henry still wants me,' said she, 'he can have me now.' To himself she had a different speech: 'I bring you no love, Henry; but God knows, all the pity in the world.'

June the 1st, 1748, was the day of their marriage. It was December of the same year that first saw me alighting at the doors of the great house; and from there I take up the history of events as they befell under my own observation, like a witness in a court.

TWO

Summary of Events ⚜ ⚜ (continued)

I MADE THE LAST OF MY journey in the cold end of December, in a mighty dry day of frost, and who should be my guide but Patey Macmorland, brother of Tam! For a tow-headed, bare-legged brat of ten, he had more ill tales upon his tongue than ever I heard the match of; having drunken betimes in his brother's cup. I was still not so old myself; pride had not yet the upper hand of curiosity; and indeed it would have taken any man, that cold morning, to hear all the old clashes of the country, and be shown all the places by the way where strange things had fallen out. I had tales of Claverhouse as we came through the bogs, and tales of the devil as we came over the top of the scaur. As we came in by the abbey I heard somewhat of the old monks, and more of the freetraders, who use its ruins for a magazine, landing for that cause within a cannon-shot of Durrisdeer; and along all the road the Duries and poor Mr Henry were in the first rank of slander. My mind was thus highly prejudiced against the family I was about to serve, so that I was half surprised when I beheld Durrisdeer itself, lying in a pretty, sheltered bay, under the

Abbey Hill; the house most commodiously built in the French fashion, or perhaps Italianate, for I have no skill in these arts; and the place the most beautified with gardens, lawns, shrubberies, and trees I have ever seen. The money sunk here unproductively would have quite restored the family; but as it was, it cost a revenue to keep it up.

Mr Henry came himself to the door to welcome me; a tall dark young gentleman (the Duries are all black men) of a plain and not cheerful face, very strong in body, but not so strong in health: taking me by the hand without any pride, and putting me at home with plain kind speeches. He led me into the hall, booted as I was, to present me to my lord. It was still daylight; and the first thing I observed was a lozenge of clear glass in the midst of the shield in the painted window, which I remember thinking a blemish on a room otherwise so handsome, with its family portraits, and the pargeted ceiling with pendants, and the carved chimney, in one corner of which my old lord sat reading in his Livy. He was like Mr Henry, with much the same plain countenance, only more subtle and pleasant, and his talk a thousand times more entertaining. He had many questions to ask me, I remember, of Edinburgh College, where I had just received my mastership of arts, and of the various professors, with whom and their proficiency he seemed well acquainted; and thus, talking of things that I knew, I soon got liberty of speech in my new home.

In the midst of this came Mrs Henry into the room; she was very far gone, Miss Katharine being due in about six weeks, which made me think less of her beauty at the first sight; and she used me with more of condescension than the rest; so that upon all accounts, I kept her in the third place of my esteem.

It did not take long before all Patey Macmorland's tales were blotted out of my belief, and I was become, what I have ever since remained, a loving servant of the house of Durrisdeer. Mr Henry had the chief part of my affection. It was with him I worked; and I found him an exacting master, keeping all his kindness for those hours in which we were unemployed, and in the steward's office not only loading me with work, but viewing me with a shrewd supervision. At length one day he looked up from his paper with a kind of timidness, and says he, 'Mr Mackellar, I think I ought to tell you that you do very well.' That was my first word of commendation; and from that day his jealousy of my performance was relaxed; soon it was 'Mr Mackellar' here, and 'Mr Mackellar' there, with the whole family; and for much of my service at Durrisdeer, I have transacted everything at my own time, and to my own fancy, and never a farthing challenged. Even while he was driving me, I had begun to find my heart go out to Mr Henry; no doubt, partly in pity, he was a man so palpably unhappy. He would fall into a deep muse over our accounts, staring at the page or out of the window; and at those times the look of his face, and the sigh that would break from him, awoke in me strong feelings of curiosity and commiseration. One day, I remember, we were late upon some business in the steward's room. This room is in the top of the house, and has a view upon the bay, and over a little wooded cape, on the long sands; and there, right over against the sun, which was then dipping, we saw the freetraders, with a great force of men and horses, scouring on the beach. Mr Henry had been staring straight west, so that I marvelled he was not blinded by the sun; suddenly he frowns, rubs his hand upon his brow, and turns to me with a smile.

'You would not guess what I was thinking,' says he. 'I was thinking I would be a happier man if I could ride and run the danger of my life, with these lawless companions.'

I told him I had observed he did not enjoy good spirits; and that it was a common fancy to envy others and think we should be the better of some change; quoting Horace to the point, like a young man fresh from college.

'Why, just so,' said he. 'And with that we may get back to our accounts.'

It was not long before I began to get wind of the causes that so much depressed him. Indeed a blind man must have soon discovered there was a shadow on the house, the shadow of the Master of Ballantrae. Dead or alive (and he was then supposed to be dead) that man was his brother's rival: his rival abroad, where there was never a good word for Mr Henry, and nothing but regret and praise for the Master; and his rival at home, not only with his father and his wife, but with the very servants.

They were two old serving-men that were the leaders. John Paul, a little, bald, solemn, stomachy man, a great professor of piety and (take him for all in all) a pretty faithful servant, was the chief of the Master's faction. None durst go so far as John. He took a pleasure in disregarding Mr Henry publicly, often with a slighting comparison. My lord and Mrs Henry took him up, to be sure, but never so resolutely as they should; and he had only to pull his weeping face and begin his lamentations for the Master – 'his laddie,' as he called him – to have the whole condoned. As for Henry, he let these things pass in silence, sometimes with a sad and sometimes with a black look. There was no rivalling the dead, he knew that; and how to censure an old serving-man for a fault of loyalty, was more than he could see. His was not the tongue to do it.

Macconochie was chief upon the other side; an old, ill-spoken, swearing, ranting, drunken dog; and I have often thought it an odd circumstance in human nature that these two serving-men should each have been the champion of his contrary, and blackened their own faults and made light of their own virtues when they beheld them in a master. Macconochie had soon smelled out my secret inclination, took me much into his confidence, and would rant against the Master by the hour, so that even my work suffered. 'They're a' daft here,' he would cry, 'and be damned to them! The Master – the deil's in their thrapples that should call him sae! it's Mr Henry should be master now! They were nane sae fond o' the Master when they had him, I'll can tell ye that. Sorrow on his name! Never a guid word did I hear on his lips, nor naebody else, but just fleering and flyting and profane cursing – deil hae him! There's nane kent his wickedness: him a gentleman! Did ever ye hear tell, Mr Mackellar, o' Wully White the wabster? No? Aweel, Wully was an unco praying kind o' man; a dreigh body, nane o' my kind, I never could abide the sight o' him; onyway he was a great hand by his way of it, and he up and rebukit the Master for some of his on-goings. It was a grand thing for the Master o' Ball'ntrae to tak up a feud wi' a' wabster, was-nae't?' Macconochie would sneer; indeed, he never took the full name upon his lips but with a sort of a whine of hatred. 'But he did! A fine employ it was; chapping at the man's door, and crying 'boo' in his lum, and puttin' poother in his fire, and pee-oys* in his window; till the man thocht it was auld Hornie was come seekin' him. Weel, to make a lang story short, Wully gaed gyte. At the hinder end, they couldnae get him frae his knees, but he just roared and prayed and grat straucht on, till he got his release. It was fair murder, a'body said that. Ask John Paul – he was brawly ashamed o' that game, him that's sic a Christian man! Grand doin's for the Master o' Ball'ntrae!' I asked him what the Master had thought of it himself. 'How would I ken?' says he. 'He never said naething.' And on again in his usual manner of banning and swearing, with every now and again a 'Master of Ballantrae' sneered through his nose. It was in one of these confidences that he showed me the Carlisle letter, the print of the horse-shoe still stamped in the paper. Indeed, that was our last confidence; for he then expressed himself so ill-naturedly of Mrs Henry that I had to reprimand him sharply, and must thenceforth hold him at a distance.

My old lord was uniformly kind to Mr Henry; he had even pretty ways of gratitude, and would sometimes clap him on the shoulder and say, as if to the world at large: 'This is a very good son to me.' And grateful he was, no doubt, being a man of sense and justice. But I think that was all, and I am sure Mr Henry thought so. The love was all for the dead son. Not that this was often given breath to; indeed, with me

---

*A kind of firework made with damp powder.

but once. My lord had asked me one day how I got on with Mr Henry, and I had told him the truth.

'Ay,' said he, looking sideways on the burning fire, 'Henry is a good lad, a very good lad,' said he. 'You have heard, Mr Mackellar, that I had another son? I am afraid he was not so virtuous a lad as Mr Henry; but dear me, he's dead, Mr Mackellar! and while he lived we were all very proud of him, all very proud. If he was not all he should have been in some ways, well, perhaps we loved him better!' This last he said looking musingly in the fire; and then to me, with a great deal of briskness, 'But I am rejoiced you do so well with Mr Henry. You will find him a good master.' And with that he opened his book, which was the customary signal of dismission. But it would be little that he read, and less that he understood; Culloden field and the Master, these would be the burthen of his thought; and the burthen of mine was an unnatural jealousy of the dead man for Mr Henry's sake, that had even then begun to grow on me.

I am keeping Mrs Henry for the last, so that this exression of my sentiment may seem unwarrantably strong: the reader shall judge for himself when I have done. But I must first tell of another matter, which was the means of bringing me more intimate. I had not yet been six months at Durrisdeer when it chanced that John Paul fell sick and must keep his bed; drink was the root of his malady, in my poor thought; but he was tended, and indeed carried himself, like an afflicted saint; and the very minister, who came to visit him, professed himself edified when he went away. The third morning of his sickness, Mr Henry comes to me with something of a hang-dog look.

'Mackellar,' says he, 'I wish I could trouble you upon a little service. There is a pension we pay; it is John's part to carry it, and now that he is sick I know not to whom I should look unless it was yourself. The matter is very delicate; I could not carry it with my own hand for a sufficient reason; I dare not send Macconochie, who is a talker, and I am – I have – I am desirous this should not come to Mrs Henry's ears,' says he, and flushed to his neck as he said it.

To say truth, when I found I was to carry money to one Jessie Broun, who was no better than she should be, I supposed it was some trip of his own that Mr Henry was dissembling. I was the more impressed when the truth came out.

It was up a wynd off a side street in St Bride's that Jessie had her lodging. The place was very ill inhabited, mostly by the freetrading sort. There was a man with a broken head at the entry; half-way up, in a tavern, fellows were roaring and singing, though it was not yet nine in the day. Altogether, I had never seen a worse neighbourhood, even in the great city of Edinburgh, and I was in two minds to go back. Jessie's room was of a piece with her surroundings, and herself no better. She would not give me the receipt (which Mr Henry told me to demand, for he was very methodical) until she had sent out for spirits, and I had pledged her in a glass; and all the time she carried on in a light-headed, reckless way – now aping the manners of a lady, now breaking into unseemly mirth, now making coquettish advances that oppressed me to the ground. Of the money she spoke more tragically.

'It's blood money!' said she; 'I take it for that; blood money for the betrayed! See what I'm brought down to! Ah, if the bonnie lad were back again, it would be changed days. But he's deid – he's lyin' deid amang the Hieland hills – the bonnie lad, the bonnie lad!'

She had a rapt manner of crying on the bonnie lad, clasping her hands and casting up her eyes, that I think she must have learned of strolling players; and I thought her sorrow very much of an affectation, and that she dwelled upon the business because her shame was now all she had to be proud of. I will not say I did not pity her, but it was a loathing pity at the best; and her last change of manner wiped it out. This was when she had had enough of me for an audience, and had set her name at last to the receipt. 'There!' says she, and taking the most unwomanly oaths upon her tongue, bade me begone and carry it to the Judas who had sent me. It was the first time I had heard the name applied to Mr Henry; I was staggered besides at her sudden vehemence of word and manner, and got forth from the room, under this shower of curses, like a beaten dog. But even then I was not quit, for the vixen threw up her window, and, leaning forth, continued to revile me as I went up the wynd; the freetraders, coming to the tavern door, joined in the mockery, and one had even the inhumanity to set upon me a very savage small dog, which bit me in the ankle. This was a strong lesson, had I required one, to avoid ill company; and I rode home in much pain from the bite and considerable indignation of mind.

Mr Henry was in the steward's room, affecting employment, but I could see he was only impatient to hear of my errand.

'Well?' says he, as soon as I come in; and when I had told him something of what passed, and that Jessie seemed an undeserving woman and far from grateful: 'She is no friend to me,' said he; 'but, indeed, Mackellar, I have few friends to boast of, and Jessie has some cause to be unjust. I need not dissemble what all the country knows: she was not very well used by one of our family.' This was the first time I had heard him refer to the Master even distantly; and I think he found his tongue rebellious even for that much, but presently he resumed: 'This is why I would have nothing said. It would give pain to Mrs Henry ... and to my father,' he added with another flush.

'Mr Henry,' said I, 'if you will take a freedom at my hands, I would tell you to let that woman be. What service is your money to the like of her? She has no sobriety and no economy – as for gratitude, you will as soon get milk from a whin-stone; and if you will pretermit your bounty, it will make no change at all but just to save the ankles of your messengers.'

Mr Henry smiled. 'But I am grieved about your ankle,' said he, the next moment, with a proper gravity.

'And observe,' I continued, 'I give you this advice upon consideration; and yet my heart was touched for the woman in the beginning.'

'Why, there it is, you see!' said Mr Henry. 'And you are to remember that I knew her once a very decent lass. Besides which, although I speak little of my family, I think much of its repute.'

And with that he broke up the talk, which was the first we had together in such confidence. But the same afternoon I had the proof that his father was perfectly acquainted with the business, and that it was only from his wife that Mr Henry kept it secret.

'I fear you had a painful errand today,' says my lord to me, 'for which, as it enters in no way among your duties, I wish to thank you, and to remind you at the same time (in case Mr Henry should have neglected) how very desirable it is that no word of it should reach my daughter. Reflections on the dead, Mr Mackellar, are doubly painful.'

Anger glowed in my heart; and I could have told my lord to his face how little he had to do, bolstering up the image of the dead in Mrs Henry's heart, and how much better he were employed to shatter that false idol; for by this time I saw very well how the land lay between my patron and his wife.

My pen is clear enough to tell a plain tale; but to render the effect of an infinity of small things, not one great enough in itself to be narrated; and to translate the story of looks, and the message of voices when they are saying no great matter; and to put in half a page the essence of near eighteen months – this is what I despair to accomplish. The fault, to be very blunt, lay all in Mrs Henry. She felt it a merit to have consented to the marriage, and she took it like a martyrdom; in which my old lord, whether he knew it or not, fomented her. She made a merit, besides, of her constancy to the dead, though its name, to a nicer conscience, should have seemed rather disloyalty to the living; and here also my lord gave her his countenance. I suppose he was glad to talk of his loss, and ashamed to dwell on it with Mr Henry. Certainly, at least, he made a little coterie apart in that family of three, and it was the husband who was shut out. It seems it was an old custom when the family were alone in Durrisdeer, that my lord should take his wine to the chimney-side, and Miss Alison, instead of withdrawing, should bring a stool to his knee, and chatter to him privately; and after she had become my patron's wife the same manner of doing was continued. It should have been pleasant to behold this ancient gentleman so loving with his daughter, but I was too much a partisan of Mr Henry's to be anything but wroth at his exclusion. Many's the time I have seen him make an obvious resolve, quit the table, and go and join himself to his wife and my Lord Durrisdeer; and on their part, they were never backward to make him welcome, turned to him smilingly as to an intruding child, and took him into their talk with an effort so ill-concealed that he was soon back again me at the table, whence (so great is the hall of Durrisdeer) we could but hear the murmur of voices at the chimney. There he would sit and watch, and I along with him; and sometimes by my lord's head sorrowfully shaken, or his hand laid on Mrs Henry's head, or hers upon his knee as if in consolation, or sometimes by an exchange of tearful looks, we would draw our conclusion that the talk had gone to the old subject and the shadow of the dead was in the hall.

I have hours when I blame Mr Henry for taking all too patiently; yet we are to remember he was married in pity, and accepted his wife upon that term. And, indeed, he had small encouragement to make a stand. Once, I remember, he announced he had found a man to replace the pane of the stained window, which, as it was he that managed all the business, was a thing clearly within his attributions. But to the Master's fanciers, that pane was like a relic; and on the first word of any change, the blood flew to Mrs Henry's face.

'I wonder at you!' she cried.

'I wonder at myself,' says Mr Henry, with more of bitterness than I had ever heard him to express.

Thereupon my old lord stepped in with his smooth talk, so that before the meal was at an end all seemed forgotten; only that, after dinner, when the pair had withdrawn as usual to the chimney-side, we could see her weeping with her head upon his knee. Mr Henry kept up the talk with me upon some topic of the estates – he could speak of little else but business, and was never the best of company; but he kept it up that day with more continuity, his eye straying ever and again to the chimney, and his voice changing to another key, but without check of delivery. The pane, however, was not replaced; and I believe he counted it a great defeat.

Whether he was stout enough or no, God knows he was kind enough. Mrs Henry had a manner of condescension with him, such as (in a wife) would have pricked my vanity into an ulcer; he took it like a favour. She held him at the staff's end; forgot and then remembered and unbent to him, as we do to children; burthened him with cold kindness; reproved him with a change of colour and a bitten lip, like one shamed by his disgrace; ordered him with a look of the eye, when she was off her guard; when she was on the watch, pleaded with him for the most natural attentions, as though they were unheard-of favours. And to all this he replied with the most unwearied service; loving, as folks say, the very ground she trod on, and carrying that love in his eyes as bright as a lamp. When Miss Katharine was to be born, nothing would serve but he must stay in the room behind the head of the bed. There he sat, as white (they tell me) as a sheet, and the sweat dropping from his brow; and the handkerchief he had in his hand was crushed into a little ball no bigger than a musket-bullet. Nor could he bear the sight of Miss Katharine for many a day; indeed, I doubt if he was ever what he should have been to my young lady; for the which want of natural feeling he was loudly blamed.

Such was the state of this family down to the 7th April, 1749, when there befell the first of that series of events which were to break so many hearts and lose so many lives.

On that day I was sitting in my room a little before supper when John Paul burst open the door with no civility of knocking, and told me there was one below that wished to speak with the steward; sneering at the name of my office.

I asked what manner of man, and what his name was; and this disclosed the excuse of John's ill-humour, for it appeared the visitor refused to name himself except to me, a sore affront to the major-demo's consequence.

'Well,' said I, smiling a little, 'I will see what he wants.'

I found in the entrance hall a big man, very plainly habited, and wrapped in a sea-cloak, like one new landed, as indeed he was. Not far off Macconochie was standing, with his tongue out of his mouth and his hand upon his chin, like a dull fellow thinking hard; and the stranger, who had brought his cloak about his face, appeared uneasy. He had no sooner seen me coming than he went to meet me with an effusive manner.

'My dear man,' said he, 'a thousand apologies for disturbing you, but I'm in the most awkward position. And there's a son of a ramrod there that I should know the looks of, and more betoken I believe that he knows mine. Being in this family, sir, and in a place of some responsibility (which was the cause I took the liberty to send for you), you are doubtless of the honest party?'

'You may be sure at least,' says I, 'that all of that party are quite safe in Durrisdeer.'

'My dear man, it is my very thought,' says he. 'You see, I have just been set on shore here by a very honest man, whose name I cannot remember, and who is to stand off and on for me till morning, at some danger to himself; and, to be clear with you, I am a little concerned lest it should be at some to me. I have saved my life so often, Mr—, I forget your name, which is a very good one – that, faith, I would be very loath to lose it after all. And the son of a ramrod, whom I believe I saw before Carlisle . . .'

'Oh, sir,' said I, 'you can trust Macconochie until tomorrow.'

'Well, and it's a delight to hear you say so,' says the stranger. 'The truth is that my name is not a very suitable one in this country of Scotland. With a gentleman like you, my dear man, I would have no concealments, of course; and by your leave I'll just breathe it in your ear. They call me Francis Burke – Colonel Francis Burke; and I am here, at a most damnable risk to myself, to see your masters – if you'll excuse me, my good man, for giving them the name, for I'm sure it's a circumstance I would never have guessed from your appearance. And if you would just be so very obliging as to take my name to them, you might say that I come bearing letters which I am sure they will be very rejoiced to have the reading of.'

Colonel Francis Burke was one of the Prince's Irishmen, that did his cause such an infinity of hurt, and were so much distasted of the Scots at the time of the rebellion; and it came at once into my mind, how the Master of Ballantrae had astonished all men by going with that party. In the same moment a strong foreboding of the truth possessed my soul.

'If you will step in here,' said I, opening a chamber door, 'I will let my lord know.'

'And I am sure it's very good of you, Mr What's-your-name,' says the Colonel.

Up to the hall I went, slow-footed. There they were, all three – my old lord in his place, Mrs Henry at work by the window, Mr Henry (as was much his custom) pacing the low end. In the midst was the table laid for supper. I told them briefly what I had to say. My old lord lay back in his seat. Mrs Henry sprang up standing with a mechanical motion, and she and her husband stared at each other's eyes across the room: it was the strangest challenging look these two exchanged, and as they looked, the colour faded in their faces. Then Mr Henry turned to me; not to speak, only to sign with his finger; but that was enough, and I went down again for the Colonel.

When we returned these three were in much the same position I had left them in; I believe no word had passed.

'My Lord Durrisdeer, no doubt?' says the Colonel, bowing, and my lord bowed in answer. 'And this,' continues the Colonel, 'should be the Master of Ballantrae?'

'I have never taken that name,' said Mr Henry; 'but I am Henry Durie, at your service.'

Then the Colonel turns to Mrs Henry, bowing with his hat upon his heart and the most killing airs of gallantry. 'There can be no mistake about so fine a figure of a lady,' says he. 'I address the seductive Miss Alison, of whom I have so often heard?'

Once more husband and wife exchanged a look.

'I am Mrs Henry Durie,' she said; 'but before my marriage my name was Alison Graeme.'

Then my lord spoke up. 'I am an old man, Colonel Burke,' said he, 'and a frail one. It will be mercy on your part to be expeditious. Do you bring me news of—' he hesitated, and then the words broke from him with a singular change of voice – 'my son?'

'My dear lord, I will be round with you like a soldier,' said the Colonel. 'I do.'

My lord held out a wavering hand; he seemed to wave a signal, but whether it was to give him time or to speak on, was more than we could guess. At length he got out the one word, 'Good?'

'Why, the very best in the creation!' cries the Colonel. 'For my good friend and admired comrade is at this hour in the fine city of Paris, and as like as not, if I know anything of his habits, he will be drawing in his chair to a piece of dinner. – Bedad, I believe the lady's fainting.'

Mrs Henry was indeed the colour of death, and drooped against the windowframe. But when Mr Henry made a movement as if to run to her, she straightened with a sort of shiver. 'I am well,' she said, with her white lips.

Mr Henry stopped, and his face had a strong twitch of anger. The next moment he had turned to the Colonel. 'You must not blame yourself,' says he, 'for this effect on Mrs Durie. It is only natural; we were all brought up like brother and sister.'

Mrs Henry looked at her husband with something like relief or even gratitude. In my way of thinking, that speech was the first step he made in her good graces.

'You must try to forgive me, Mrs Durie, for indeed and I am just an Irish savage,' said the Colonel; 'and I deserve to be shot for not breaking the matter more artistically to a lady. But here are the Master's own letters; one for each of the three of you; and to be sure (if I know anything of my friend's genius) he will tell his own story with a better grace.'

He brought the three letters forth as he spoke, arranged them by their superscriptions, presented the first to my lord, who took it greedily, and advanced towards Mrs Henry holding out the second.

But the lady waved it back. 'To my husband,' says she, with a choked voice.

The Colonel was a quick man, but at this he was somewhat nonplussed. 'To be sure!' says he; 'how very dull of me! To be sure!' But he still held the letter.

At last Mr Henry reached forth his hand, and there was nothing to be done but give it up. Mr Henry took the letters (both hers and his own), and looked upon their outside, with his brows knit hard, as if he were thinking. He had surprised me all through by his excellent behaviour; but he was to excel himself now.

'Let me give you a hand to your room,' said he to his wife. 'This has come something of the suddenest; and, at any rate, you will wish to read your letter by yourself.'

Again she looked upon him with the same thought of wonder; but he gave her no time, coming straight to where she stood. 'It will be better so, believe me,' said he; 'and Colonel Burke is too considerate not to excuse you.' And with that he took her hand by the fingers, and led her from the hall.

Mrs Henry returned no more that night; and when Mr Henry went to visit her next morning, as I heard long afterwards, she gave him the letter again, still unopened.

'Oh, read it and be done!' he had cried.

'Spare me that,' said she.

And by these two speeches, to my way of thinking, each undid a great part of what they had previously done well. But the letter, sure enough, came into my hands, and by me was burned, unopened.

To be very exact as to the adventures of the Master after Culloden, I wrote not long ago to Colonel Burke, now a Chevalier of the Order of St Louis, begging him for some notes in writing, since I could scarce depend upon my memory at so great an interval. To confess the truth, I have been somewhat embarrassed by his response; for he sent me the complete memoirs of his life, touching only in places on the Master; running to a much greater length than my whole story, and not everywhere (as it seems to me) designed for edification. He begged in his letter, dated from Ettenheim, that I would find a publisher for the whole, after I had made what use of it I required; and I think I shall best answer my own purpose and fulfil his wishes by printing certain parts of it in full. In this way my readers will have a detailed and, I believe, a very genuine account of some essential matters; and if any publisher should take a fancy to the Chevalier's manner of narration, he knows where to apply for the rest, of which there is plenty at his service. I put in my first extract here, so that it may stand in the place of what the Chevalier told us over our wine in the hall of Durrisdeer; but you are to suppose it was not the brutal fact, but a very varnished version that he offered to my lord.

THREE

The Master's Wanderings From the Memoirs of the Chevalier de Burke

✣   ✣

... I LEFT RUTHVEN (it's hardly necessary to remark) with much greater satisfaction than I had come to it; but whether I missed my way in the deserts, or whether my companions failed me, I soon found myself alone. This was a predicament very disagreeable; for I never understood this horrid country or savage people, and the last stroke of the Prince's withdrawal had made us of the Irish more unpopular than ever. I was reflecting on my poor chances, when I saw another horseman on the hill, whom I supposed at first to have been a phantom, the news of his death in the very front at Culloden being current in the army generally. This was the Master of Ballantrae, my Lord Durrisdeer's son, a young nobleman of the rarest gallantry and parts, and equally designed by nature to adorn a Court and to reap laurels in the field. Our meeting was the more welcome to both, as he was one of the few Scots who had used the Irish with consideration, and as he might now be of very high utility in aiding my escape. Yet what founded our particular friendship was a circumstance by itself as romantic as any fable of King Arthur.

This was on the second day of our flight, after we had slept one night in the rain upon the inclination of a mountain. There was an Appin man,

Alan Black Stewart (or some such name,* but I have seen him since in France), who chanced to be passing the same way, and had a jealousy of my companion. Very uncivil expressions were exchanged; and Stewart calls upon the Master to alight and have it out.

'Why, Mr Stewart,' says the Master, 'I think at the present time I would prefer to run a race with you.' And with the word claps spurs to his horse.

Stewart ran after us, a childish thing to do, for more than a mile; and I could not help laughing, as I looked back at last and saw him on a hill, holding his hand to his side, and nearly burst with running.

'But, all the same,' I could not help saying to my companion, 'I would let no man run after me for any such proper purpose, and not give him his desire. It was a good jest, but it smells a trifle cowardly.'

He bent his brows at me. 'I do pretty well,' says he, 'when I saddle myself with the most unpopular man in Scotland, and let that suffice for courage.'

'O, bedad,' says I, 'I could show you a more unpopular with the naked eye. And if you like not my company, you can "saddle" yourself on someone else.'

'Colonel Burke,' says he, 'do not let us quarrel; and, to that effect, let me assure you I am the least patient man in the world.'

'I am as little patient as yourself,' said I. 'I care not who knows that.'

'At this rate,' says he, reining in, 'we shall not go very far. And I propose we do one of two things upon the instant: either quarrel and be done; or make a sure bargain to bear everything at each other's hands.'

'Like a pair of brothers?' said I.

'I said no such foolishness,' he replied. 'I have a brother of my own, and I think no more of him than of a colewort. But if we are to have our noses rubbed together in this course of flight, let us each dare to be ourselves like savages, and each swear that he will neither resent nor deprecate the other. I am a pretty bad fellow at bottom, and I find the pretence of virtues very irksome.'

'O, I am as bad as yourself,' said I. 'There is no skim milk in Francis Burke. But which is it to be? Fight or make friends?'

'Why,' says he, 'I think it will be the best manner to spin a coin for it.'

This proposition was too highly chivalrous not to take my fancy; and, strange as it may seem of two well-born gentlemen of today, we span a half-crown (like a pair of ancient paladins) whether we were to cut each other's throats or be sworn friends. A more romantic circumstance can rarely have occurred; and it is one of those points in my memoirs, by

*Note by Mr Mackellar. Should not this be Alan *Breck* Stewart, afterwards notorious as the Appin murderer? The Chevalier is sometimes very weak on names.

which we may see the old tales of Homer and the poets are equally true to-day – at least, of the noble and genteel. The coin fell for peace, and we shook hands upon our bargain. And then it was that my companion explained to me his thought in running away from Mr Stewart, which was certainly worthy of his political intellect. The report of his death, he said, was a great guard to him; Mr Stewart having recognized him had become a danger: and he had taken the briefest road to that gentleman's silence. 'For,' says he, 'Alan Black is too vain a man to narrate any such story of himself.'

Towards afternoon we came down to the shores of that loch for which we were heading; and there was the ship, but newly come to anchor. She was the *Sainte-Marie-des-Anges*, out of the port of Havre-de-Grace. The Master, after we had signalled for a boat, asked me if I knew the captain. I told him he was a countryman of mine, of the most unblemished integrity, but, I was afraid, a rather timorous man.

'No matter,' says he. 'For all that, he should certainly hear the truth.'

I asked him if he meant about the battle, for if the captain once knew the standard was down, he would certainly put to sea again at once.

'And even then!' said he; 'the arms are now of no sort of utility.'

'My dar man,' said I, 'who thinks of the arms? But, to be sure, we must remember our friends. They will be close upon our heels, perhaps the Prince himself, and if the ship be gone, a great number of valuable lives may be imperilled.'

'The captain and the crew have lives also, if you come to that,' says Ballantrae.

This I declared was but a quibble, and that I would not hear of the captain being told; and then it was that Ballantrae made me a witty answer, for the sake of which (and also because I have been blamed myself in this business of the *Sainte-Marie-des-Anges*) I have related the whole conversation as it passed.

'Frank,' says he, 'remember our bargain. I must not object to your holding your tongue, which I hereby even encourage you to do; but, by the same terms, you are not to resent my telling.'

I could not help laughing at this; though I still forewarned him what would come of it.

'The devil may come of it for what I care,' says the reckless fellow. 'I have always done exactly as I felt inclined.'

As is well known, my prediction came true. The captain had no sooner heard the news than he cut his cable and to sea again; and before morning broke, we were in the Great Minch.

The ship was very old; and the skipper, although the most honest of men (and Irish too), was one of the least capable. The wind blew very boisterous, and the sea raged extremely. All that day we had little heart whether to eat or drink; went early to rest in some concern of mind; and (as if to give us a lesson) in the night the wind chopped suddenly into the north-east, and blew a hurricane. We were awaked by the dreadful thunder of the tempest and the stamping of the mariners on deck; so that I supposed our last hour was certainly come; and the terror of my mind was increased out of all measure by Ballantrae, who mocked at my devotions. It is in hours like these that a man of any piety appears in his true light, and we find (what we are taught as babes) the small trust that can be set in worldly friends: I would be unworthy of my religion if I let this pass without particular remark. For three days we lay in the dark in the cabin, and had but a biscuit to nibble. On the fourth the wind fell, leaving the ship dismasted and heaving on vast billows. The captain had got a guess of whither we were blown; he was stark ignorant of his trade, and could do naught but bless the Holy Virgin; a very good thing, too, but scarce the whole of seamanship. It seemed our one hope was to be picked up by another vessel; and if that should prove to be an English ship, it might be no great blessing to the Master and myself.

The fifth and sixth days we tossed there helpless. The seventh some sail was got on her, but she was an unwieldy vessel at the best, and we made little but leeway. All the time, indeed, we had been drifting to the south and west, and during the tempest must have driven in that direction with unheard-of voilence. The ninth dawn was cold and black, with a great sea running, and every mark of foul weather. In this situation we were overjoyed to sight a small ship on the horizon, and to perceive her go about and head for the *Sainte-Marie*. But our gratification did not very long endure; for when she had laid to and lowered a boat, it was immediately filled with disorderly fellows, who sang and shouted as they pulled across to us, and swarmed in on our deck with bare cutlasses, cursing loudly. Their leader was a horrible villain, with his face blacked and his whiskers curled in ringlets; Teach, his name; a most notorious pirate. He stamped about the deck, raving and crying out that his name was Satan, and his ship was called Hell. There was something about him like a wicked child or a half-witted person, that daunted me beyond expression. I whispered in the ear of Ballantrae that I would not be the last to volunteer, and only prayed God they might be short of hands; he approved my purpose with a nod.

'Bedad,' said I to Master Teach, 'if you are Satan, here is a devil for ye.'

The word pleased him; and (not to dwell upon these shocking incidents) Ballantrae and I and two others were taken for recruits, while the skipper and all the rest were cast into the sea by the method of walking the plank. It was the first time I had seen this done; my heart died within me at the spectacle; and Master Teach or one of his acolytes (for my head was too much lost to be precise) remarked upon my pale face in a very alarming manner. I had the strength to cut a step or two of a jig, and cry out some ribaldry, which saved me for that time; but my legs were like water when I must get down into the skiff among these miscreants; and what with my horror of my company and fear of the monstrous billows, it was all I could do to keep an Irish tongue and break a jest or two as we were pulled aboard. By the blessing of God, there was a fiddle in the pirate ship, which I had no sooner seen than I fell upon; and in my quality of crowder I had the heavenly good luck to get favour in their eyes. *Crowding Pat* was the name they dubbed me with; and it was little I cared for a name so long as my skin was whole.

What kind of a pandemonium that vessel was, I cannot describe, but she was commanded by a lunatic, and might be called a floating Bedlam. Drinking, roaring, singing, quarrelling, dancing, they were never all sober at one time; and there were days together when, if a squall had supervened, it must have sent us to the bottom; or if a king's ship had come along, it would have found us quite helpless for defence. Once or twice we sighted a sail, and, if we were sober enough, overhauled her, God forgive us! and if we were all too drunk, she got away, and I would bless the saints under my breath. Teach ruled, if you can call that rule which brought no order, by the terror he created; and I observed the man was very vain of his position. I have known marshals of France – ay, and even Highland chieftains – that were less openly puffed up; which throws a singular light on the pursuit of honour and glory. Indeed, the longer we live, the more we perceive the sagacity of Aristotle and the other old philosophers; and though I have all my life been eager for legitimate distinctions, I can lay my hand upon my heart, at the end of my career, and declare there is not one – no, nor yet life itself – which is worth acquiring or preserving at the slightest cost of dignity.

It was long before I got private speech of Ballantrae; but at length one night we crept out upon the bowsprit, when the rest were better employed, but commiserated our position.

'None can deliver us but the saints,' said I.

'My mind is very different,' said Ballantrae; 'for I am going to deliver myself. This Teach is the poorest creature possible; we make no profit of him, and lie continually open to capture; and,' says he. 'I am not going to be a tarry pirate for nothing, nor yet to hang in chains if I can help it.' And he told me what was in his mind to better the state of the ship in the way of discipline, which would give us safety for the present, and a sooner hope of deliverance when they should have gained enough and should break up their company.

I confessed to him ingenuously that my nerve was quite shook amid these horrible surroundings, and I durst scarce tell him to count upon me.

'I am not very easy frightened,' said he, 'nor very easy beat.'

A few days after, there befell an accident which had nearly hanged us all; and offers the most extraordinary picture of the folly that ruled in our concerns. We were all pretty drunk: and some bedlamite spying a sail, Teach put the ship about in chase without a glance, and we began to bustle up the arms and boast of the horrors that should follow. I observed Ballantrae stood quiet in the bows, looking under the shade of his hand; but for my part, true to my policy among these savages, I was at work with the busiest and passing Irish jests for their diversion.

'Run up the colours,' cries Teach. 'Show the—s the Jolly Roger!'

It was the merest drunken braggadocio at such a stage, and might have lost us a valuable prize; but I thought it no part of mine to reason, and I ran up the black flag with my own hand.

Ballantrae steps presently aft with a smile upon his face.

'You may perhaps like to know, you drunken dog,' says he, 'that you are chasing a king's ship.'

Teach roared him the lie; but he ran at the same time to the bulwarks, and so did they all. I have never seen so many drunken men struck suddenly sober. The cruiser had gone about, upon our impudent display of colours; she was just then filling on the new tack; her ensign blew out quite plain to see; and even as we stared, there came a puff of smoke, and then a report, and a shot plunged in the waves a good way short of us. Some ran to the ropes, and got the *Sarah* round with an incredible swiftness. One fellow fell on the rum barrel, which stood broached upon the deck, and rolled it promptly overboard. On my part, I made for the Jolly Roger, struck it, tossed it in the sea; and could have flunged myself after, so vexed was I with our mismanagement. As for Teach, he grew as pale as death, and incontinently went down to his cabin. Only twice he came on deck that afternoon; went to the taffrail; took a long look at the king's ship, which was still on the horizon heading after us; and then, without speech, back to his cabin. You may say he deserted us; and if it had not been for one very capable sailor we had on board, and for the lightness of the airs that blew all day, we must certainly have gone to the yard-arm.

It is to be supposed Teach was humiliated, and perhaps alarmed for his position with the crew; and the way in which he set about regaining what he had lost, was highly characteristic of the man. Early next day we smelled him burning sulphur in his cabin and crying out of 'Hell, hell!' which was well understood among the crew, and filled their minds with apprehension. Presently he comes on deck, a perfect figure of fun, his face blacked, his hair and whiskers curled, his belt stuck full of pistols; chewing bits of glass so that the blood ran down his chin, and brandishing a dirk. I do not know if he had taken these manners from the Indians of America, where he was a native; but such was his way, and he would always thus announce that he was wound up to horrid deeds. The first that came near him was the fellow who had sent the rum overboard the day before; him he stabbed to the heart, damning him for a mutineer; and then capered about the body, raving and swearing and daring us to come on. It was the silliest exhibition; and yet dangerous too, for the cowardly fellow was plainly working himself up to another murder.

All of a sudden Ballantrae stepped forth. 'Have done with this play-acting,' says he. 'Do you think to frighten us with making faces? We saw nothing of you yesterday, when you were wanted; and we did well without you, let me tell you that.'

There was a murmur and a movement in the crew, of pleasure and alarm, I thought, in nearly equal parts. As for Teach, he gave a barbarous howl, and swung his dirk to fling it, an art in which (like many seamen) he was very expert.

'Knock that out of his hand!' says Ballantrae, so sudden and sharp that my arm obeyed him before my mind had understood.

Teach stood like one stupid, never thinking on his pistols.

'Go down to your cabin,' cries Ballantrae, 'and come on deck again when you are sober. Do you think we are going to hang for you, you black-faced, half-witted, drunken brute and butcher? Go down!' And he stamped his foot at him with such a sudden smartness that Teach fairly ran for it to the companion.

'And now, mates,' says Ballantrae, 'a word with you. I don't know if you are gentlemen of fortune for the fun of the thing, but I am not. I want to make money, and get ashore again, and spend it like a man. And on one thing my mind is made up: I will not hang if I can help it. Come: give me a hint; I'm only a beginner! Is there no way to get a little discipline and common sense about this business?'

One of the men spoke up: he said by rights they should have a quartermaster; and no sooner was the word out of his mouth than they were all of that opinion. The thing went by acclamation, Ballantrae was made quartermaster, the rum was put in his charge, laws were passed in imitation of those of a pirate by the name of Roberts, and the last proposal was to make an end of Teach. But Ballantrae was afraid of a more efficient captain, who might be a counterweight to himself, and he opposed this stoutly. Teach, he said, was good enough to board ships and to frighten fools with his blacked face and swearing; we could scarce get a better man than Teach for that; and besides, as the man was now disconsidered and as good as deposed, we might reduce his proportion of the plunder. This carried it; Teach's share was cut down to a mere derision, being actually less than mine; and there remained only two points: whether he would consent, and who was to announce to him this resolution.

'Do not let that stick you,' says Ballantrae, 'I will do that.'

And he stepped to the companion and down alone into the cabin to face that drunken savage.

'This is the man for us,' cries one of the hands. 'Three cheers for the quartermaster!' which were given with a will, my own voice among the loudest, and I dare say these plaudits had their effect on Master Teach in the cabin, as we have seen of late days how shouting in the streets may trouble even the minds of legislators.

What passed precisely was never known, though some of the heads of it came to the surface later on; and we were all amazed, as well as gratified, when Ballantrae came on deck with Teach upon his arm, and announced that all had been consented.

I pass swiftly over those twelve or fifteen months in which we continued to keep the sea in the North Atlantic, getting our food and water from the ships we overhauled, and doing on the whole a pretty fortunate business. Sure, no one could wish to read anything so ungenteel as the memoirs of a pirate, even an unwilling one like me! Things went extremely better with our designs, and Ballantrae kept his lead, to my admiration, from that day forth. I would be tempted to suppose that a gentleman must everywhere be first, even aboard a rover: but my birth is every whit as good as any Scottish lord's, and I am not ashamed to confess that I stayed Crowding Pat until the end, and was not much better than the crew's buffoon. Indeed, it was no scene to bring out my merits. My health suffered from a variety of reasons; I was more at home to the last on a horse's back than a ship's deck; and, to be ingenuous, the fear of the sea was constantly in my mind, battling with the fear of my companions. I need not cry myself up for courage; I have done well on many fields under the eyes of famous generals, and earned my late advancement by an act of the most distinguished valour before many witnesses. But when we must proceed on one of our abordages, the heart of Francis Burke was in his boots; the little egg-shell skiff in which we must set forth, the horrible heaving of the vast billows, the height of the ship that we must scale, the thought of how many there might be there in garrison upon their legitimate defence, the scowling heavens which (in that climate) so often looked darkly down upon our exploits, and the mere crying of the wind in my ears, were all considerations most unpalatable to my valour. Besides which, as I was always a creature of the nicest sensibility, the scenes that must follow on our success tempted me as little as the chances of defeat. Twice we found women on board; and though I have seen towns sacked, and of late days in France some very horrid public tumults, there was something in the smallness of the numbers engaged, and the bleak, dangerous sea-surroundings, that made these acts of piracy far the most revolting. I confess ingenuously I could never proceed unless I was three parts drunk; it was the same even with the crew; Teach himself was fit for no enterprise till he was full of rum; and it was one of the most difficult parts of Ballantrae's performance, to serve us with liquor in the proper quantities. Even this he did to admiration; being upon the whole the most capable man I ever met with, and the one of the most natural genius. He did not even scrape favour with the crew, as I did, by continual buffoonery made upon a very anxious heart; but preserved on most occasions a great deal of gravity and distance: so that he was like a parent among a family of young children, or a schoolmaster with his boys. What made his part the harder to perform, the men were most inveterate grumblers; Ballantrae's discipline, little as it was, was yet irksome to their love of licence; and what was worse, being kept sober they had time to think. Some of them accordingly would fall to repenting their abominable crimes; one in particular, who was a good Catholic, and with whom I would sometimes steal apart for prayer; above all in bad weather, fogs, lashing rain and the like, when we would be the less observed; and I am sure no two criminals in the cart have ever performed their devotions with more anxious sincerity. But the rest, having no such grounds of hope, fell to another pastime, that of computation. All day long they would be telling up their shares or glooming over the result. I have said we were pretty fortunate. But an observation falls to be made: that in this world, in no business that I have tried, do the profits rise to a man's expectations. We found many ships and took many; yet few of them contained much money, their goods were usually nothing to our purpose – what did we want with a cargo of ploughs, or even of tobacco? – and it is quite a painful reflection how many whole crews we have made to walk the plank for no more than a stock of biscuit or an anker or two of spritis.

In the meanwhile our ship was growing very foul, and it was high time we should make for our *port de carénage*, which was in the estuary of a river among swamps. It was openly understood that we should then break up and go and squander our proportions of the spoil; and this made every man greedy of a little more, so that our decision was delayed from day to day. What finally decided matters was a trifling accident, such as an ignorant person might suppose incidental to our way of life. But here I must explain: on only one of all the ships we boarded, the first on which we found women, did we meet with any genuine resistance. On that occasion we had two men killed and several injured, and if it had not been for the gallantry of Ballantrae, we had surely been beat back at last. Everywhere else the defence (where there was any at all) was what the worst troops in Europe would have laughed at; so that the most dangerous part of our employment was to clamber up the side of the ship; and I have even known the poor souls on board to cast us a line, so eager were they to volunteer instead of walking the plank. This constant immunity had made our fellows very soft, so that I understood how Teach had made so deep a mark upon their minds; for indeed the company of that lunatic was the chief danger in our way of life. The accident to which I have referred was this: – We had sighted a little full-rigged ship very close under our board in a haze; she sailed near as well as we did – I should be nearer truth if I said, near as ill; and we cleared the bow-chaser to see if we could bring a spar or two about their ears. The swell was exceedingly great; the motion of the ship beyond description; it was little wonder if our gunners should fire thrice and be still quite broad of what they aimed at. But in the meanwhile the chase had cleared a stern gun, the thickness of the air concealing them; and being better marksmen, their first shot struck us in the bows, knocked our two gunners into mincemeat, so that we were all sprinkled with the blood, and plunged through the deck into the forecastle where we slept. Ballantrae would have held on; indeed, there was nothing in this *contretemps* to affect the mind of any soldier; but he had a quick perception of the men's wishes, and it was plain this lucky shot had given them a sickener of their trade. In a moment they were all of one mind: the chase was drawing away from us, it was needless to hold on, the *Sarah* was too foul to overhaul a bottle, it was mere foolery to keep the sea with her; and on these pretended grounds her head was incontinently put about and the course laid for the river. It was strange to see what merriment fell on that ship's company, and how they stamped about the deck jesting, and each computing what increase had come to his share by the death of the two gunners.

We were nine days making our port, so light were the airs we had to sail on, so foul was the ship's bottom; but early on the tenth, before dawn, and in a light lifting haze, we passed the head. A little after, the haze lifted, and fell again, showing us a cruiser very close. This was a sore blow, happening so near our refuge. There was a great debate of whether she had seen us, and if so whether it was likely they had recognized the *Sarah*. We were very careful, by destroying every member of those crews we overhauled, to leave no evidence as to our own persons; but the appearance of the *Sarah* herself we could not keep so private; and above all of late, since she had been foul, and we had pursued many ships without success, it was plain that her description had been often published. I supposed this alert would have made us separate upon the instant. But here again that original genius of Ballantrae's had a surprise in store for me. He and Teach (and it was the most remarkable step of his success) had gone hand in hand since the first day of his appointment. I often questioned him upon the fact, and never got an answer but once, when he told me he and Teach had an understanding 'which would very much surprise the crew if they should hear of it, and would surprise himself a good deal if it was carried out.' Well, here again he and Teach were of a mind; and by their joint procurement the anchor was no sooner down than the whole crew went off upon a scene of drunkenness indescribable. By afternoon we were a mere shipful of lunatical persons, throwing of things overboard, howling of different songs at the same time, quarrelling and falling together, and then forgetting our quarrels to embrace. Ballantrae had bid me drink nothing, and feign drunkenness, as I valued my life; and I have never passed a day so wearisomely, lying the best part of the time upon the forecastle and watching the swamps and thickets by which our little basin was entirely surrounded for the eye. A little after dusk Ballantrae stumbled up to my side, feigned to fall, with a drunken laugh, and before he got his feet again, whispered me too 'reel down into the cabin and seem to fall asleep upon a locker, for there would be need of me soon.' I did as I was told, and coming into the cabin, where it was quite dark, let myself fall on the first locker. There was a man there already; by the way he stirred and threw me off, I could not think he was much in liquor; and yet when I had found another place, he seemed to continue to sleep on. My heart now beat very hard, for I saw some desperate matter was in act. Presently down came Ballantrae, lit the lamp, looked about the cabin, nodded as if pleased, and on deck again without a word. I peered out from between my fingers, and saw there were three of us slumbering, or feigning to slumber, on the lockers: myself, one Dutton, and one Gradey, both resolute men. On deck the rest were got to a pitch of revelry quite beyond the bounds of what is human; so that no reasonable name can describe the sounds they were now making. I have heard many a drunken bout in my time, many on board that very *Sarah*, but never anything the least like this, which made me early suppose the liquor had been tampered with. It was a long while before these yells and howls died out into a sort of miserable moaning, and then to silence; and it seemed a long while after that before Ballantrae came down again, this time with Teach upon his heels. The latter cursed at the sight of us three upon the lockers.

'Tut,' says Ballantrae, 'you might fire a pistol at their ears. You know what stuff they have been swallowing.'

There was a hatch in the cabin floor, and under that the richest part of the booty was stored against the day of division. It fastened with a ring and three padlocks, the keys (for greater security) being divided; one to Teach, one to Ballantrae, and one to the mate, a man called Hammond. Yet I was amazed to see they were now all in the one hand; and yet more amazed (still looking through my fingers) to observe Ballantrae and Teach bring up several packets, four of them in all, very carefully made up and with a loop for carriage.

'And now,' says Teach, 'let us be going.'

'One word,' says Ballantrae. 'I have discovered there is another man besides yourself who knows a private path across the swamp; and it seems it is shorter than yours.'

Teach cried out, in that case, they were undone.

'I do not know for that,' says Ballantrae. 'For there are several other circumstances with which I must acquaint you. First of all, there is no bullet in your pistols, which (if you remember) I was kind enough to load for both of us this morning. Secondly, as there is someone else who knows a passage, you must think it highly improbable I should saddle myself with a lunatic like you. Thirdly, these gentlemen (who need no longer pretend to be asleep) are those of my party, and will now proceed to gag and bind you to the mast; and when your men awaken (if they ever do awake after the drugs we have mingled in their liquor), I am sure they will be so obliging as to deliver you, and you will have no difficulty, I daresay, to explain the business of the keys.'

Not a word said Teach, but looked at us like a frightened baby as we gagged and bound him.

'Now you see, you moon-calf,' says Ballantrae, 'why we make four packets. Heretofore you have been called Captain Teach, but I think you are now rather Captain Learn.'

That was our last word on board the *Sarah*. We four, with our four packets, lowered ourselves softly into a skiff, and left that ship behind us as silent as the grave, only for the moaning of some of the drunkards. There was a fog about breast-high upon the waters; so that Dutton, who knew the passage, must stand on his feet to direct our rowing; and this, as it forced us to row gently, was the means of our deliverance. We were yet but a little way from the ship, when it began to come grey, and the birds to fly abroad upon the water. All of a sudden Dutton clapped down upon his hams, and whispered us to be silent for our lives, and hearken. Sure enough, we heard a little faint creak of oars upon one hand, and then again, and further off, a creak of oars upon the other. It was clear we had been sighted yesterday in the morning; here were the cruiser's boats to cut us out; here were we defenceless in their very midst. Sure, never were poor souls more perilously placed; and as we lay there on our oars, praying God the mist might hold, the sweat poured from my brow. Presently we heard one of the boats where we might have thrown a biscuit in her. 'Softly, men,' we heard an officer whisper; and I marvelled they could not hear the drumming of my heart.

'Never mind the path,' says Ballantrae; 'we must get shelter anyhow; let us pull straight ahead for the sides of the basin.'

This we did with the most anxious precaution, rowing, as best we could, upon our hands, and steering at a venture in the fog, which was (for all that) our only safety. But Heaven guided us; we touched ground at a thicket; scrambled ashore with our treasure; and having no other way of concealment, and the mist beginning already to lighten, hove down the skiff and let her sink. We were still but new under cover when the sun rose; and at the same time, from the midst of the basin, a great shouting of seamen sprang up, and we knew the *Sarah* was being boarded. I heard afterwards the officer that took her got great honour; and it's true the approach was creditably managed, but I think he had an easy capture when he came to board.*

I was still blessing the saints for my escape, when I became aware we were in trouble of another kind. We were here landed at random in a vast and dangerous swamp; and how to come at the path was a concern of doubt, fatigue, and peril. Dutton, indeed, was of opinion we should wait until the ship was gone, and fish up the skiff; for any delay would be more wise than to go blindly ahead in that morass. One went back accordingly to the basin-side and (peering through the thicket) saw the fog already quite drunk up, and English colours flying on the *Sarah*, but no movement made to get her under way. Our situation was now very doubtful. The swamp was an unhealthful place to linger in; we had been so greedy to bring treasures that we had brought but little food; it was highly desirable, besides, that we should get clear of the neighbourhood and into the settlements before the news of the capture went abroad; and

---

*Note by Mr Mackellar. This Teach of the *Sarah* must not be confused with the celebrated *Blackbeard*. The dates and facts by no means tally. It is possible the second Teach may have at once borrowed the name and imitated the more excessive part of his manners from the first. Even the Master of Ballantrae could make admirers.

against all these considerations, there was only the peril of the passage on the other side. I think it not wonderful we decided on the active part.

It was already blistering hot when we set forth to pass the marsh, or rather to strike the path, by compass. Dutton took the compass and one or other of us three carried his proportion of the treasure. I promise you he kept a sharp eye to his rear, for it was like the man's soul that he must trust us with. The thicket was as close as a bush; the ground very treacherous, so that we often sank in the most terrifying manner, and must go round about; the heat, besides, was stifling, the air singularly heavy, and the stinging insects abounded in such myriads that each of us walked under his own cloud. It has often been commented on, how much better gentlemen of birth endure fatigue than persons of the rabble; so that walking officers who must tramp in the dirt beside their men, shame them by their constancy. This was well to be observed in the present instance; for here were Ballantrae and I, two gentlemen of the highest breeding, on the one hand; and on the other Grady, a common mariner, and a man nearly a giant in physical strength. The case of Dutton is not in point, for I confess he did as well as any of us.* But as for Grady, he began early to lament his case, tailed in the rear, refused to carry Dutton's packet when it came his turn, clamoured continually for rum (of which we had too little), and at last even threatened us from behind with a cocked pistol, unless we should allow him rest. Ballantrae would have fought it out, I believe; but I prevailed with him the other way; and we made a stop and ate a meal. It seemed to benefit Grady little; he was in the rear again at once, growling and bemoaning his lot; and at last, by some carelessness, not having followed properly in our tracks, stumbled into a deep part of the slough where it was mostly water, gave some very dreadful screams, and before we could come to his aid had sunk along with his booty. His fate, and above all these screams of his, appalled us to the soul; yet it was, on the whole, a fortunate circumstance, and the means of our deliverance, for it moved Dutton to mount into a tree, whence he was able to perceive and to show me, who had climbed after him, a high piece of the wood, which was a landmark for the path. He went forward the more carelessly, I must suppose; for presently we saw him sink a little down, draw up his feet and sink again, and so twice. Then he turned his face to us, pretty white.

'Lend a hand,' said he, 'I am in a bad place.'

'I don't know about that,' said Ballantrae, standing still.

Dutton broke out into the most violent oaths, sinking a little lower as

---

*Note by Mr Mackellar. And is not this the whole explanation? since this Dutton, exactly like the officers, enjoyed the stimulus of some responsibility.

he did, so that the mud was nearly to his waist, and plucking a pistol from his belt, 'Help me,' he cries, 'or die and be damned to you!'

'Nay,' says Ballantrae, 'I did but jest. I am coming.' And he set down his own packet and Dutton's, which he was then carrying. 'Do not venture near till we see if you are needed,' said he to me, and went forward alone to where the man was bogged. He was quiet now, though he still held the pistol; and the marks of terror in his countenance were very moving to behold.

'For the Lord's sake,' says he, 'look sharp.'

Ballantrae was now got close up. 'Keep still,' says he, and seemed to consider; and then, 'Reach out both your hands!'

Dutton laid down his pistol, and so watery was the top surface that it went clear out of sight; with an oath he stooped to snatch it; and as he did so, Ballantrae leaned forth and stabbed him between the shoulders. Up went his hands over his head – I know not whether with the pain or to ward himself; and the next moment he doubled forward in the mud.

Ballantrae was already over the ankles; but he plucked himself out, and came back to me, where I stood with my knees smiting one another. 'The devil take you, Francis!' says he. 'I believe you are a half-hearted fellow, after all. I have only done justice on a pirate. And here we are quite clear of the *Sarah*! Who shall now say that we have dipped our hands in any irregularities?'

I assured him he did me injustice; but my sense of humanity was so much affected by the horridness of the fact that I could scarce find breath to answer with.

'Come,' said he, 'you must be more resolved. The need for this fellow ceased when he had shown you where the path ran; and you cannot deny I would have been daft to let slip so fair an opportunity.'

I could not deny but he was right in principle; nor yet could I refrain from shedding tears, of which I think no man of valour need have been ashamed; and it was not until I had a share of the rum that I was able to proceed. I repeat, I am far from ashamed of my generous emotion; mercy is honourable in the warrior; and yet I cannot altogether censure Ballantrae, whose step was really fortunate, as we struck the path without further misadventure, and the same night, about sundown, came to the edge of the morass.

We were too weary to seek far; on some dry sands, still warm with the day's sun, and close under a wood of pines, we lay down and were instantly plunged in sleep.

We awaked the next morning very early, and began with a sullen spirit a conversation that came near to end in blows. We were now cast on shore in the southern provinces, thousands of miles from any French settlement; a dreadful journey and a thousand perils lay in front of us; and sure, if there was ever need for amity, it was in such an hour. I must suppose that Ballantrae had suffered in his sense of what is truly polite; indeed, and there is nothing strange in the idea, after the seawolves we had consorted with so long; and as for myself, he fubbed me off unhandsomely, and any gentleman would have resented his behaviour.

I told him in what light I saw his conduct; he walked a little off, I following to upbraid him; and at last he stopped me with his hand.

'Frank,' says he, 'you know what we swore; and yet there is no oath invented would induce me to swallow such expressions, if I did not regard you with sincere affection. It is impossible you should doubt me there: I have given proofs. Dutton I had to take, because he knew the pass, and Grady because Dutton would not move without him; but what call was there to carry you along? You are a perpetual danger to me with your cursed Irish tongue. By rights you should now be in irons in the cruiser. And you quarrel with me like a baby for some trinkets!'

I considered this one of the most unhandsome speeches ever made; and indeed to this day I can scarce reconcile it to my notion of a gentleman that was my friend. I retorted upon him with his Scotch accent, of which he had not so much as some, but enough to be very barbarous and disgusting, as I told him plainly; and the affair would have gone to a great length, but for an alarming intervention.

We had got some way off upon the sand. The place where we had slept, with the packets lying undone and the money scattered openly, was now between us and the pines; and it was out of these the stranger must have come. There he was at least, a great hulking fellow of the country, with a broad axe on his shoulder, looking open-mouthed, now at the treasure, which was just at his feet, and now at our disputation, in which we had gone far enough to have weapons in our hands. We had no sooner observed him than he found his legs and made off again among the pines.

This was no scene to put our minds at rest; a couple of armed men in sea-clothes found quarrelling over a treasure, not many miles from where a pirate had been captured – here was enough to bring the whole country about our ears. The quarrel was not even made up; it was blotted from our minds; and we got our packets together in the twinkling of an eye, and made off, running with the best will in the world. But the trouble was, we did not know in what direction, and must continually return upon our steps. Ballantrae had indeed collected what he could from Dutton; but it's hard to travel upon hearsay; and the estuary, which spreads into a vast irregular harbour, turned us off upon every side with a new stretch of water.

We were near beside ourselves, and already quite spent with running, when, coming to the top of a dune, we saw we were again cut off by another ramification of the bay. This was a creek, however, very different from those that had arrested us before; being set in rocks, and so precipitously deep that a small vessel was able to lie alongside, made fast with a hawser; and her crew had laid a plank to the shore. Here they had lighted a fire, and were sitting at their meal. As for the vessel herself, she was one of those they build in the Bermudas.

The love of gold and the great hatred that everybody has to pirates were motives of the most influential, and would certainly raise the country in our pursuit. Besides, it was now plain we were on some sort of straggling peninsula, like the fingers of a hand; and the wrist, or passage to the mainland, which we should have taken at the first, was by this time not improbably secured. These considerations put us on a bolder counsel. For as long as we dared, looking every moment to hear sounds of the chase, we lay among some bushes on the top of the dune; and having by this means secured a little breath and recomposed our appearance, we strolled down at last, with a great affectation of carelessness, to the party by the fire.

It was a trader and his negroes, belonging to Albany, in the province of New York, and now on the way home from the Indies with a cargo; his name I cannot recall. We were amazed to learn he had put in here from terror of the *Sarah*; for we had no thought our exploits had been so notorious. As soon as the Albanian heard she had been taken the day before, he jumped to his feet, gave us a cup of spirits for our good news, and sent his negroes to get sail on the Bermudan. On our side, we profited by the dram to become more confidential, and at last offered ourselves as passengers. He looked askance at our tarry clothes and pistols, and replied civilly enough that he had scarce accommodation for himself; nor could either our prayers or our offers of money, in which we advanced pretty far, avail to shake him.

'I see, you think ill of us,' says Ballantrae, 'but I will show you how well we think of you by telling you the truth. We are Jacobite fugitives, and there is a price upon our heads.'

At this, the Albanian was plainly moved a little. He asked us many questions as to the Scotch war, which Ballantrae very patiently answered. And then, with a wink, in a vulgar manner, 'I guess you and your Prince Charlie got more than you cared about,' said he.

'Bedad, and that we did,' said I. 'And, my dear man, I wish you would set a new example and give us just that much.'

This I said in the Irish way, about which there is allowed to be something very engaging. It's a remarkable thing, and a testimony to the love with which our nation is regarded, that this address scarce ever fails in a handsome fellow. I cannot tell how often I have seen a private soldier escape the horse, or a beggar wheedle out a good alms by a touch of the brogue. And, indeed, as soon as the Albanian had laughed at me I was pretty much at rest. Even then, however, he made many conditions, and – for one thing – took away our arms, before he suffered us aboard; which was the signal to cast off; so that in a moment after, we were gliding down the bay with a good breeze, and blessing the name of God for our deliverance. Almost in the mouth of the estuary, we passed the cruiser, and a little after, the poor *Sarah* with her prize crew; and these were both sights to make us tremble. The Bermudan seemed a very safe place to be in, and our bold stroke to have been fortunately played, when we were thus reminded of the case of our companions. For all that, we had only exchanged traps, jumped out of the frying-pan into the fire, run from the yard-arm to the block, and escaped the open hostility of the man-of-war to lie at the mercy of the doubtful faith of our Albanian merchant.

From many circumstances, it chanced we were safer than we could have dared to hope. The town of Albany was at that time much concerned in contraband trade across the desert with the Indians and the French. This, as it was highly illegal, relaxed their loyalty, and as it brought them in relation with the politest people on the earth, divided even their sympathies. In short, they were like all the smugglers in the world, spies and agents ready-made for either party. Our Albanian, besides, was a very honest man indeed, and very greedy; and, to crown our luck, he conceived a great delight in our society. Before we had reached the town of New York we had come to a full agreement, that he should carry us as far as Albany upon his ship, and thence put us on a way to pass the boundaries and join the French. For all this we were to pay at a high rate; but beggars cannot be choosers, nor outlaws bargainers.

We sailed, then, up the Hudson River, which I protest is a very fine stream, and put at the 'King's Arms' in Albany. The town was full of the militia of the province, breathing slaughter against the French. Governor Clinton was there himself, a very busy man, and, by what I could learn, very near distracted by the factiousness of his Assembly. The Indians on both sides were on the war-path; we saw parties of them bringing in prisoners and (what was much worse) scalps, both male and female, for which they were paid at a fixed rate; and I assure you the sight was not encouraging. Altogether, we could scarce have come at a period more unsuitable for our designs; our position in the chief inn was dreadfully conspicuous; our Albanian fubbed us off with a thousand delays, and seemed upon the point of a retreat from his engagements; nothing but peril appeared to environ the poor fugitives, and for some time we drowned our concern in a very irregular course of living.

This too, proved to be fortunate; and it's one of the remarks that fall to be made upon our escape, how providentially our steps were conducted to the very end. What a humiliation to the dignity of man! My philosophy, the extraordinary genius of Ballantrae, our valour, in which I grant that we were equal – all these might have proved insufficient without the Divine blessing on our efforts. And how true it is, as the Church tells us, that the Truths of Religon are, after all, quite applicable even to daily affairs! At least, it was in the course of our revelry that we made the acquaintance of a spirited youth by the name of Chew. He was one of the most daring of the Indian traders, very well acquainted with the secret paths of the wilderness, needy, dissolute, and, by a last good fortune, in some disgrace with his family. Him we persuaded to come to our relief; he privately provided what was needful for our flight, and one day we slipped out of Albany, without a word to our former friend, and embarked, a little above, in a canoe.

To the toils and perils of this journey, it would require a pen more elegant than mine to do full justice. The reader must conceive for himself the dreadful wilderness which we had now to thread; its thickets, swamps, precipitous rocks, impetuous rivers, and amazing waterfalls. Among these barbarous scenes we must toil all day, now paddling, now carrying our canoe upon our shoulders; and at night we slept about a fire, surrounded by the howling of wolves and other savage animals. It was our design to mount the headwaters of the Hudson, to the neighbourhood of Crown Point, where the French had a strong place in the woods, upon Lake Champlain. But to have done this directly were too perilous; and it was accordingly gone upon by such a labyrinth of rivers, lakes, and portages as makes my head giddy to remember. These paths were in ordinary times entirely desert; but the country was now up, the tribes on the war-path, the woods full of Indian scouts. Again and again we came upon these parties when we least expected them; and one day, in particular, I shall never forget, how, as dawn was coming in, we were suddenly surrounded by five or six of these painted devils, uttering a very dreary sort of cry, and brandishing their hatchets. It passed off harmlessly, indeed, as did the rest of our encounters; for Chew was well known and highly valued among the different tribes. Indeed, he was a very gallant, respectable young man; but even with the advantage of his companionship, you must not think these meetings were without sensible peril. To prove friendship on our part, it was needful to draw upon our stock of rum – indeed, under whatever disguise, that is the true business of the Indian trader, to keep a travelling public-house in the forest; and when once the braves had got their bottle of *scaura* (as they call this beastly liquor), it behoved us to set forth and paddle for our scalps. Once they were a little drunk, good-bye to any sense or decency; they had but one thought, to get more *scaura*. They might easily take it in their heads to give us chase, and had we been overtaken, I had never written these memoirs.

We were come to the most critical portion of our course, where we might equally expect to fall into the hands of French or English, when a terrible calamity befell us. Chew was taken suddenly sick with symptoms like those of poison, and in the course of a few hours expired in the bottom of the canoe. We thus lost at once our guide, our interpreter, our boatman, and our passport, for he was all these in one; and found ourselves reduced, at a blow, to the most desperate and irremediable distress. Chew, who took a great pride in his knowledge, had indeed often lectured us on the geography; and Ballantrae, I believe, would listen. But for my part I have always found such information highly tedious; and beyond the fact that we were now in the country of the Adirondack Indians, and not so distant from our destination, could we but have found the way, I was entirely ignorant. The wisdom of my course was soon the more apparent; for with all his pains, Ballantrae was no further advanced than myself. He knew we must continue to go up one stream; then, by way of a portage, down another; and they up a third. But you are to consider in a mountain country, how many streams came rolling in from every hand. And how is a gentleman, who is a perfect stranger in that part of the world, to tell any one of them from any other? Nor was this our only trouble. We were great novices, besides, in handling a canoe; the portages were almost beyond our strength, so that I have seen us sit down in despair for half an hour at a time without one word; and the appearance of a single Indian, since we had now no means of speaking to them, would have been in all probability the means of our destruction. There is altogether some excuse if Ballantrae showed something of a glooming disposition; his habit of imputing blame to others, quite as capable as himself, was less tolerable, and his language it was not always easy to accept. Indeed, he had contracted on board the pirate ship a manner of address which was in a high degree unusual between gentlemen; and now, when you might say he was in a fever, it increased upon him hugely.

The third day of these wanderings, as we were carrying the canoe up a rocky portage, she fell, and was entirely bilged. The portage was between two lakes, both pretty extensive; the track, such as it was, opened at both ends upon the water, and on both hands was enclosed by the unbroken woods; and the sides of the lakes were quite impassable with bog: so that we beheld ourselves not only condemned to go without our boat and the greater part of our provisions, but to plunge at once into impenetrable thickets and to desert what little guidance we still had – the course of the river. Each stuck his pistols in his belt, shouldered an axe, made a pack of his treasure and as much food as he could stagger under; and deserting the rest of our possessions, even to our swords, which would have much embarrassed us among the woods, we set forth on this deplorable adventure. The labours of Hercules, so finely described by Homer, were a trifle to what we now underwent. Some parts of the forest were perfectly dense down to the ground, so that we must cut our way like mites in a cheese. In some the bottom was full of deep swamp, and the whole wood entirely rotten I have leapt on a great fallen log and sunk to the knees in touchwood; I have sought to stay myself, in falling, against what looked to be a solid trunk, and the whole thing has whiffed away at my touch like a sheet of paper. Stumbling, falling, bogging to the knees, hewing our way, our eyes almost put out with twigs and branches, our clothes plucked from our bodies, we laboured all day, and it is doubtful if we made two miles. What was worse, as we could rarely get a view of the country, and were perpetually justled from our path by obstacles, it was impossible even to have a guess in what direction we were moving.

A little before sundown, in an open place with a stream, and set about with barbarous mountains, Ballantrae threw down his pack. 'I will go no further,' said he, and bade me light the fire, damning my blood in terms not proper for a chairman.

I told him to try to forget he had ever been a pirate, and to remember he had been a gentleman.

'Are you mad?' he cried. 'Don't cross me here!' And then, shaking his fist at the hills, 'To think,' cries he, 'that I must leave my bones in this miserable wilderness! Would God I had died upon the scaffold like a gentleman!' This he said ranting like an actor; and then sat biting his fingers and staring on the ground, a most unchristian object.

I took a certain horror of the man, for I thought a soldier and a gentleman should confront his end with more philosophy. I made him no reply, therefore, in words; and presently the evening fell so chill that I was glad, for my own sake, to kindle a fire. And yet God knows, in such an open spot, and the country alive with savages, the act was little short of lunacy. Ballantrae seemed never to observe me; but at last, as I was about parching a little corn, he looked up.

'Have you ever a brother?' said he.

'By the blessing of Heaven,' said I, 'not less than five.'

'I have the one,' said he, with a strange voice; and then presently, 'He shall pay me for all this,' he added. And when I asked him what was his brother's part in our distress, 'What!' he cried, 'he sits in my place, he bears my name, he courts my wife; and I am here alone with a damned Irishman in this toothchattering desert! Oh, I have been a common gull!' he cried.

The explosion was in all ways so foreign to my friend's nature that I was daunted out of all my just susceptibility. Sure, an offensive expression, however vivacious, appears a wonderfully small affair in circumstances so extreme! But here there is a strange thing to be noted. He had only once before referred to the lady with whom he was contracted. That was when we came in view of the town of New York, when he had told me, if all had their rights, he was now in sight of his own property, for Miss Graeme enjoyed a large estate in the province. And this was certainly a natural occasion; but now here she was named a second time; and what is surely fit to be observed, in this very month, which was November, '47, and *I believe upon that very day as we sat among these barbarous mountains*, his brother and Miss Graeme were married. I am the least superstitious of men; but the hand of Providence is here displayed too openly not to be remarked.*

The next day, and the next, were passed in similar labours; Ballantrae often deciding on our course by the spinning of a coin; and once, when I expostulated on this childishness, he had an odd remark that I have never forgotten. 'I know no better way,' said he, 'to express my scorn of human reason.' I think it was the third day that we found the body of a Christian, scalped and most abominably mangled, and lying in a pudder of his blood; the birds of the desert screaming over him, as thick as flies. I cannot describe how dreadfully this sight affected us; but it robbed me of all strength and all hope for this world. The same day, and only a little after, we were scrambling over a part of the forest that had been burned, when Ballantrae, who was a little ahead, ducked suddenly behind a fallen trunk. I joined him in this shelter, whence we could look abroad without being seen ourselves; and in the bottom of the next vale, beheld a large war party of the savages going by across our line. There might be the value of a weak battalion present; all naked to the waist, blacked with grease and soot, and painted with white lead and vermilion, according to their beastly habits. They went one behind another like a string of geese, and at a quickish trot; so that they took but a little while to rattle by, and disappear again among the woods. Yet I suppose we endured a greater agony of hesitation and suspense in these few minutes than goes usually to a man's whole life. Whether they were French or

*Note by Mr Mackellar. A complete blunder: there was at this date no word of the marriage: see above in my own narration.

English Indians, whether they desired scalps or prisoners, whether we should declare ourselves upon the chance, or lie quiet and continue the heart-breaking business of our journey: sure, I think these were questions to have puzzled the brains of Aristotle himself. Ballantrae turned to me with a face all wrinkled up and his teeth showing in his mouth, like what I have read of people starving; he said no word, but his whole appearance was a kind of dreadful question.

'They may be of the English side,' I whispered; 'and think! the best we could then hope, is to begin this over again.'

'I know – I know,' he said. 'Yet it must come to a plunge at last.' And he suddenly plucked out his coin, shook it in his closed hands, looked at it, and then lay down with his face in the dust.

Addition by Mr Mackellar. – I drop the Chevalier's narration at this point because the couple quarrelled and separated the same day; and the Chevalier's account of the quarrel seems to me (I must confess) quite incompatible with the nature of either of the men. Henceforth they wandered alone, undergoing extraordinary sufferings; until first one and then the other was picked up by a party from Fort St Frederick. Only two things are to be noted. And first (as most important for my purpose) that the Master, in the course of his miseries, buried his treasure, at a point never since discovered, but of which he took a drawing in his own blood on the lining of his hat. And second, that on his coming thus penniless to the Fort, he was welcomed like a brother by the Chevalier, who thence paid his way to France. The simplicity of Mr Burke's character leads him at this point to praise the Master exceedingly; to an eye more worldly wise, it would seem it was the Chevalier alone that was to be commended. I have the more pleasure in pointing to this really very noble trait of my esteemed correspondent, as I fear I may have wounded him immediately before. I have refrained from comments on any of his extraordinary and (in my eyes) immoral opinions, for I know him to be jealous of respect. But his version of the quarrel is really more than I can reproduce; for I knew the Master myself, and a man more insusceptible of fear is not conceivable. I regret this oversight of the Chevalier's, and all the more because the tenor of his narrative (set aside a few flourishes) strikes me as highly ingenuous.

FOUR

Persutions Endured by
❖ Mr Henry ❖

YOU CAN GUESS ON WHAT PART of his adventures the Colonel principally dwelled. Indeed, if we had heard it all, it is to be thought the current of this business had been wholly altered; but the pirate ship was very gently touched upon. Nor did I heard the Colonel to an end even of that which he was willing to disclose; for Mr Henry, having for some while been plunged in a brown study, rose at last from his seat and (reminding the Colonel there were matters that he must attend to) bade me follow him immediately to the office.

Once there, he sought no longer to dissemble his concern, walking to and fro in the room with a contorted face, and passing his hand repeatedly upon his brow.

'We have some business,' he began at last; and there broke off, declared we must have wine, and sent for a magnum of the best. This was extremely foreign to his habitudes; and what was still more so, when the wine had come, he gulped down one glass upon another like a man careless of appearances. But the drink steadied him.

'You will scarce be surprised, Mackellar,' says he, 'when I tell you that my brother – whose safety we are all rejoiced to learn – stands in some need of money.'

I told him I had misdoubted as much; but the time was not very fortunate, as the stock was low.

'Not mine,' said he. 'There is the money for the mortgage.'

I reminded him it was Mrs Henry's.

'I will be answerable to my wife,' he cried violently.

'And then,' said I, 'there is the mortgage.'

'I know,' said he; 'it is on that I would consult you.'

I showed him how unfortunate a time it was to divert this money from its destination; and how, by so doing, we must lose the profit of our past economies, and plunge back the estate into the mire. I even took the liberty to plead with him; and when he still opposed me with a shake of the head and a bitter dogged smile, my zeal quite carried me beyond my place. 'This is midsummer madness,' cried I; 'and I for one will be no party to it.'

'You speak as though I did it for my pleasure,' says he. 'But I have a child now; and, besides, I love order; and to say the honest truth, Mackellar, I had begun to take a pride in the estates.' He gloomed for a moment. 'But what would you have?' he went on. 'Nothing is mine, nothing. This day's news has knocked the bottom out of my life. I have only the name and the shadow of things – only the shadow; there is no substance in my rights.'

'They will prove substantial enough before a court,' said I.

He looked at me with a burning eye, and seemed to repress the word upon his lips; and I repented what I had said, for I saw that while he spoke of the estate he had still a side-thought to his marriage. And then, of a sudden, he twitched the letter from his pocket, where it lay all crumpled, smoothed it violently on the table, and read these words to me with a trembling tongue: – ' "My dear Jacob" – This is how he begins!' cried he – ' "My dear Jacob, I once called you so, you may remember; and you have now done the business, and flung my heels as high as Criffel." What do you think of that, Mackellar,' says he, 'from an only brother? I declare to God I liked him very well; I was always staunch to him; and this is how he writes! But I will not sit down under the imputation' – walking to and fro – 'I am as good as he; I am a better man than he, I call on God to prove it! I cannot give him all the monstrous sum he asks; he knows the estate to be incompetent; but I will give him what I have, and it is more than he expects. I have borne all this too long. See what he writes further on; read it for yourself: "I know you are a niggardly dog." A niggardly dog! I niggardly? Is that true, Mackellar? You think it is?' I really thought he would have struck me at that. 'Oh, you all think so! Well, you shall see, and he shall see, and God shall see. If I ruin the estate and go barefoot, I shall stuff this bloodsucker. Let him ask all – all, and he shall have it! It is all his by rights. Ah!' he cried, 'and I foresaw all this, and worse, when he would not let me go.' He poured out another glass of wine, and was about to carry it to his lips, when I made so bold as to lay a finger on his arm. He stopped a moment. 'You are right,' said he, and flung glass and all in the fireplace. 'Come, let us count the money.'

I durst no longer oppose him; indeed, I was very much affected by the sight of so much disorder in a man usually so controlled; and we sat down together, counted the money, and made it up in packets for the greater ease of Colonel Burke, who was to be the bearer. This done, Mr Henry returned to the hall, where he and my old lords sat all night through with their guest.

A little before dawn I was called and set out with the Colonel. He would scarce have liked a less responsible convoy, for he was a man who valued himself; nor could we afford him one more dignified, for Mr Henry must not appear with the free-traders. It was a very bitter morning of wind, and as we went down through the long shrubbery the Colonel held himself muffled in his cloak.

'Sir,' said I, 'this is a great sum of money that your fiend requires. I must suppose his necessities to be very great.'

'We must suppose so,' says he, I thought drily, but perhaps it was the cloak about his mouth.

'I am only a servant of the family,' said I. 'You may deal openly with me. I think we are likely to get little good by him?'

'My dear man,' said the Colonel, 'Ballantrae is a gentleman of the most eminent natural abilities, and a man that I admire, and that I revere, to the very ground he treads on.' And then he seemed to me to pause like one in a difficulty.

'But for all that,' said I, 'we are likely to get little good by him?'

'Sure, and you can have it your own way, my dear man,' says the Colonel.

By this time we had come to the side of the creek, where the boat awaited him. 'Well,' said he, 'I am sure I am very much your debtor for your civility, Mr Whatever-your-name-is; and just as a last word, and since you show so much intelligent interest, I will mention a small circumstance that may be of use to the family. For I believe my friend omitted to mention that he has the largest pension on the Scots Fund of any refugee in Paris; and it's the more disgraceful, sir,' cries the Colonel, warming, 'because there's not one dirty penny for myself.'

He cocked his hat at me, as if I had been to blame for this partiality; then changed again into his usual swaggering civility, shook me by the hand, and set off down to the boat, with the money under his arms, and whistling as he went the pathetic air of *Shule Aroon*. It was the first time I had heard that tune; I was to hear it again, words and all, as you shall learn, but I remember how that little stave of it ran in my head after the freetraders had bade him 'Wheesht, in the deil's name,' and the grating of the oars had taken its place, and I stood and watched the dawn creeping on the sea, and the boat drawing away, and the lugger lying with her foresail backed awaiting it.

The gap made in our money was a sore embarrassment, and, among other consequences, it had this: that I must ride to Edinburgh, and there raise a new loan on very questionable terms to keep the old afloat;

and was thus, for close upon three weeks, absent from the house of Durrisdeer.

What passed in the interval I had none to tell me, but I found Mrs Henry, upon my return, much changed in her demeanour. The old talks with my lord for the most part pretermitted; a certain deprecation visible towards her husband, to whom I thought she addressed herself more often; and, for one thing, she was now greatly wrapped up in Miss Katharine. You would think the change was agreeable to Mr Henry; no such matter! To the contrary, every circumstance of alteration was a stab to him; he read in each the avowal of her truant fancies. That constancy to the Master of which she was proud while she supposed him dead, she had a blush for now she knew he was alive, and these blushes were the hated spring of her new conduct. I am to conceal no truth; and I will here say plainly, I think this was the period in which Mr Henry showed the worst. He contained himself, indeed, in public; but there was a deep-seated irritation visible underneath. With me, from whom he had less concealment, he was often grossly unjust, and even for his wife he would sometimes have a sharp retort: perhaps when she had ruffled him with some unwonted kindness; perhaps upon no tangible occasion, the mere habitual tenor of the man's annoyance bursting spontaneously forth. When he would thus forget himself (a thing so strangely out of keeping with the terms of their relation), there went a shock through the whole company, and the pair would look upon each other in a kind of pained amazement.

All the time, too, while he was injuring himself by this defect of temper, he was hurting his position by a silence, of which I scarce know whether to say it was the child of generosity or pride. The freetraders came again and again, bringing messengers from the Master, and none departed empty-handed. I never durst reason with Mr Henry; he gave what was asked of him in a kind of noble rage. Perhaps because he knew he was by nature inclining to the parsimonious, he took a back-foremost pleasure in the recklessness with which he supplied his brother's exigence. Perhaps the falsity of the position would have spurred a humbler man into the same excess. But the estate (if I may say so) groaned under it; our daily expenses were shorn lower and lower; the stables were emptied, all but four roadsters; servants were discharged, which raised a dreadful murmuring in the country, and heated up the old disfavour upon Mr Henry; and at last the yearly visit to Edinburgh must be discontinued.

This was in 1756. You are to suppose that for seven years this bloodsucker had been drawing the life's blood from Durrisdeer, and that all this time my patron had held his peace. It was an effect of devilish malice in the Master that he addressed Mr Henry alone upon the matter of his demands, and there was never a word to my lord. The family had looked on, wondering at our economies. They had lamented, I have no doubt, that my patron had become so great a miser – a fault always despicable, but in the young abhorrent, and Mr Henry was not yet thirty years off age. Still, he had managed the business of Durrisdeer almost from a boy; and they bore with these changes in a silence as proud and bitter as his own until the coping-stone of the Edinburgh visit.

At this time I believe my patron and his wife were rarely together, save at meals. Immediately on the back of Colonel Burke's announcement Mrs Henry made palpable advances; you might say she had paid a sort of timid court to her husband, different, indeed, from her former manner of unconcern and distance. I never had the heart to blame Mr Henry because he recoiled from these advances; nor yet to censure the wife, when she was cut to the quick by their rejection. But the result was an entire estrangement, so that (as I say) they rarely spoke, except at meals. Even the matter of the Edinburgh visit was first broached at table, and it chanced that Mrs Henry was that day ailing and querulous. She had no sooner understood her husband's meaning than the red flew in her face.

'At last,' she cried, 'this is too much! Heaven knows what pleasure I have in my life, that I should be denied my only consolation. These shameful proclivities must be trod down; we are already a mark and an eyesore in the neighbourhood. I will not endure this fresh insanity.'

'I cannot afford it,' says Mr Henry.

'Afford!' she cried. 'For shame! But I have money of my own.'

'That is all mine, madam, by marriage,' he snarled, and instantly left the room.

My old lord threw up his hands to Heaven, and he and his daughter, withdrawing to the chimney, gave me a broad hint to be gone. I found Mr Henry in his usual retreat, the steward's room, perched on the end of the table, and plunging his penknife in it with a very ugly countenance.

'Mr Henry,' said I, 'you do yourself too much injustice, and it is time this should cease.'

'Oh!' cries he, 'nobody minds here. They think it only natural. I have shameful proclivities. I am a niggardly dog,' and he drove his knife up to the hilt. 'But I will show that fellow,' he cried with an oath, 'I will show him which is the more generous.'

'This is no generosity,' said I; 'this is only pride.'

'Do you think I want morality?' he asked.

I thought he wanted help, and I should give it him, willy-nilly; and no sooner was Mrs Henry gone to her room than I presented myself at her door and sought admittance.

She openly showed her wonder. 'What do you want with me, Mr Mackellar?' said she.

'The Lord knows, madam,' says I, 'I have never troubled you before with any freedoms; but this thing lies too hard upon my conscience, and it will out. Is it possible that two people can be so blind as you and my lord? and have lived all these years with a noble gentleman like Mr Henry, and understand so little of his nature?'

'What does this mean?' she cried.

'Do you not know where his money goes to? his – and yours – and the money for the very wine he does not drink at table?' I went on. 'To Paris – to that man! Eight thousand pounds has he had of us in seven years, and my patron fool enough to keep it secret!'

'Eight thousand pounds!' she repeated. 'It is impossible; the estate is not sufficient.'

'God knows how we have sweated farthings to produce it,' said I. 'But eight thousand and sixty is the sum, beside odd shillings. And if you can think my patron miserly after that, this shall be my last interference.'

'You need say no more, Mr Mackellar,' said she. 'You have done most properly in what you too modestly call your interference. I am much to blame; you must think me indeed a very unobservant wife' (looking upon me with a strange smile), 'But I shall put this right at once. The Master was always of a very thoughtless nature; but his heart is excellent; he is the soul of generosity. I shall write to him myself. You cannot think how you have pained me by this communication.'

'Indeed, madam, I had hope to have pleased you,' said I, for I raged to see her still thinking of the Master.

'And pleased,' said she, 'and pleased me, of course.'

That same day (I will not say but what I watched) I had the satisfaction to see Mr Henry come from his wife's room in a state most unlike himself; for his face was all bloated with weeping, and yet he seemed to me to walk upon the air. By this, I was sure his wife had made him full amends for once. 'Ah,' thought I to myself, 'i have done a brave stroke this day.'

On the morrow, as I was seated at my books, Mr Henry came in softly behind me, took me by the shoulders, and shook me in a manner of playfulness. 'I find you are a faithless fellow after all,' says he, which was his only reference to my part; but the tone he spoke in was more to me than any eloquence of protestation. Nor was this all I had effected; for when the next messenger came (as he did not long afterwards) from the Master, he got nothing away with him but a letter. For some while back it had been I myself who had conducted these affairs; Mr Henry not setting pen to paper, and I only in the dryest and most formal terms. But this letter I did not even see; it would scarce be pleasant reading, for

Mr Henry felt he had his wife behind him for once, and I observed, on the day it was despatched, he had a very gratified expression.

Things went better now in the family, though it could scarce be pretended they went well. There was now at least no misconception; there was kindness upon all sides; and I believe my patron and his wife might again have drawn together if he could but have pocketed his pride, and she forgot (what was the ground of all) her brooding on another man. It is wonderful how a private thought leaks out; it is wonderful to me now how we should all have followed the current of her sentiments; and though she bore herself quietly, and had a very even disposition, yet we should have known whenever her fancy ran to Paris. And would not anyone have thought that my disclosure must have rooted up that idol? I think there is a devil in women: all these years passed, never a sight of the man, little enough kindness to remember (by all accounts) even while she had him, the notion of his death intervening, his heartless rapacity laid bare to her; that all should not do, and she must still keep the best place in her heart for this accursed fellow, is a thing to make a plain man rage. I had never much natural sympathy for the passion of love; but this unreason in my patron's wife disgusted me outright with the whole matter. I remember checking a maid because she sang some bairnly kickshaw while my mind was thus engaged; and my asperity brought about my ears the enmity of all the petticoats about the house; of which I recked very little, but it amused Mr Henry, who rallied me much upon our joint unpopularity. It is strange enough (for my own mother was certainly one of the salt of the earth, and my Aunt Dickson, who paid my fees at the University, a very notable woman), but I have never had much toleration for the female sex, possibly not much understanding; and being far from a bold man, I have ever shunned their company. Not only do I see no cause to regret this diffidence in myself, but have invariably remarked that most unhappy consequences follow those who were less wise. So much I thought proper to set down lest I show myself unjust to Mrs Henry. And, besides, the remark arose naturally, on a reperusal of the letter which was the next step in these affairs, and reached me, to my sincere astonishment, by a private hand, some week or so after the departure of the last messenger.

Letter from Colonel BURKE (*afterwards Chevalier*) *to*

MR MACKELLAR.
TROYES IN CHAMPAGNE,
July 12, 1756.

MY DEAR SIR, – You will doubtless be surprised to receive a communi-

cation from one so little known to you; but on the occasion I had the
good fortune to rencounter you at Durrisdeer, I remarked you for a
young man of a solid gravity of character: a qualification which I
profess I admire and revere next to natural genius or the bold chivalrous spirit of the soldier. I was, besides, interested in the noble family
which you have the honour to serve, or (to speak more by the book)
to be the humble and respected friend of; and a conversation I had the
pleasure to have with you very early in the morning has remained
much upon my mind.

Being the other day in Paris, on a visit from this famous city, where
I am in garrison, I took occasion to inquire your name (which I profess I had forgot) at my friend, the Master of B.; and a fair opportunity
occurring, I write to inform you of what's new.

The Master of B. (when we had last some talk of him together) was
in receipt, as I think I then told you, of a highly advantageous pension
on the Scots Fund. He next received a company, and was soon after
advanced to a regiment of his own. My dear sir, I do not offer to
explain this circumstance; any more than why I myself, who have rid
at the right hand of Princes, should be fubbed off with a pair of colours
and sent to rot in a hole at the bottom of the province. Accustomed as
I am to Courts, I cannot but feel it is no atmosphere for a plain soldier;
and I could never hope to advance by similar means, even could I
stoop to the endeavour. But our friend has a particular aptitude to
succeed by the means of ladies; and if all be true that I have heard, he
enjoyed a remarkable protection. It is like this turned against him; for
when I had the honour to shake him by the hand, he was but newly
released from the Bastile, where he had been cast on a sealed letter;
and, though now released, has both lost his regiment and his pension.
My dear sir, the loyalty of a plain Irishman will ultimately succeed in
the place of craft; as I am sure a gentleman of your probity will agree.

Now, sir, the Master is a man whose genius I admire beyond
expression, and, besides, he is my friend; but I thought a little word
of this revolution in his fortunes would not come amiss, for, in my
opinion, the man's desperate. He spoke, when I saw him, of an adventure upon India (whither I am myself in some hope of accompanying
my illustrious countryman, Mr Lally); but for this he would require
(as I understood) more money than was readily at this command. You
may have heard a military proverb: that it is a good thing to make a
bridge of gold to a flying enemy? I trust you will take my meaning,
and I subscribe myself, with proper respects to my Lord Durrisdeer,
to his son, and to the beauteous Mrs Durie,

My dear Sir,

Your obedient humble servant,

FRANCIS BURKE.

This missive I carried at once to Mr Henry; and I think there was but the one thought between the two of us: that it had come a week too late. I made haste to send an answer to Colonel Burke, in which I begged him, if he should see the Master, to assure him his next messenger would be attended to. But with all my haste I was not in time to avert what was impending; the arrow had been drawn, it must now fly. I could almost doubt the power of Providence (and certainly His will) to stay the issue of events; and it is a strange thought, how many of us had been storing up the elements of this catastrophe, for how long a time, and with how blind an ignorance of what we did.

From the coming of the Colonel's letter, I had a spy-glass in my room, began to drop questions to the tenant folk, and as there was no great secrecy observed, and the freetrade (in our part) went by force as much as stealth, I had soon got together a knowledge of the signals in use, and know pretty well to an hour when any messenger might be expected. I say, I questioned the tenants; for with the traders themselves, desperate blades that went habitually armed, I could never bring myself to meddle willingly. Indeed, by what proved in the sequel an unhappy chance, I was an object of scorn to some of these braggadocios; who had not only gratified me with a nickname, but catching me one night upon a by-path, and being all (as they would have said) somewhat merry, had caused me to dance for their diversion. The method employed was that of cruelly chipping at my toes with naked cutlasses, shouting at the same time 'Square Toes'; and though they did me no bodily mischief, I was none the less deplorably affected, and was indeed for several days confined to my bed: a scandal on the state of Scotland on which no comment is required.

It happened on the afternoon on November 7th, in this same unfortunate year, that I espied, during my walk, the smoke of a beacon fire upon the Muckleross. It was drawing near time for my return; but the uneasiness upon my spirits was that day so great that I must burst through the thicket to the edge of what they call the Craig Head. The sun was already down, but there was still a broad light in the west, which showed me some of the smugglers treading out their signal fire upon the Ross, and in the bay the lugger lying with her sails brailed up. She was plainly but new come to anchor, and yet the skiff was already lowered and pulling for the landing-place at the end of the long shrubbery. And this I knew could signify but one thing, the coming of a messenger for Durrisdeer.

I laid aside the remainder of my terrors, clambered down the brae – a place I had never ventured through before – and was hid among the shore-side thickets in time to see the boat touch. Captain Crail himself was steering, a thing not usual; by his side there sat a passenger; and the men gave way with difficulty, being hampered with near upon half a dozen portmanteaus, great and small. But the business of landing was briskly carried through; and presently the baggage was all tumbled on shore, the boat on its return voyage to the lugger, and the passenger standing alone upon the point of rock, a tall slender figure of a gentleman, habited in black, with a sword by his side and a walking-cane upon his wrist. As he so stood, he waved the cane to Captain Crail by way of salutation, with something both of grace and mockery that wrote the gesture deeply on my mind.

No sooner was the boat away with my sworn enemies than I took a sort of half-courage, came forth to the margin of the thicket, and there halted again, my mind being greatly pulled about between natural diffidence and a dark foreboding of the truth. Indeed, I might have stood there swithering all night, had not the stranger turned, spied me through the mists, which were beginning to fall, and waved and cried on me to draw near. I did so with a heart like lead.

'Here, my good man,' said he, in the English accent, 'here are some things for Durrisdeer.'

I was now near enough to see him, a very handsome figure and countenance, swarthy, lean, long, with a quick, alert, black look, as of one who was a fighter, and accustomed to command; upon one cheek he had a mole, not unbecoming; a large diamond sparkled on his hand; his clothes, although of the one hue, were of a French and foppish design; his ruffles, which he wore longer than common, of exquisite lace; and I wondered the more to see him in such a guise when he was but newly landed from a dirty smuggling lugger. At the same time he had a better look at me, toised me a second time sharply, and then smiled.

'I wager, my friend,' says he, 'that I know both your name and your nickname. I divined these very clothes upon your hand of writing, Mr Mackellar.'

At these words I fell to shaking.

'Oh,' says he, 'you need not be afraid of me. I bear no malice for your tedious letters; and it is my purpose to employ you a good deal. You may call me Mr Bally: it is the name I have assumed; or rather (since I am addressing so great a precisian) it is so I have curtailed my own. Come now, pick up that and that' – indicating two of the portmanteaus.

'That will be as much as you are fit to bear, and the rest can very well wait. Come, lose no time, if you please.'

His tone was so cutting that I managed to do as he bid by a sort of instinct, my mind being all the time quite lost. No sooner had I picked up the portmanteaus than he turned his back and marched off through the long shrubbery, where it began already to be dusk, for the wood is thick and evergreen. I followed behind, loaded almost to the dust, though I profess I was not conscious of the burthen; being swallowed up in the monstrosity of this return, and my mind flying like a weaver's shuttle.

On a sudden I set the portmanteaus to the ground and halted. He turned and looked back at me.

'Well?' said he.

'You are the Master of Ballantrae?'

'You will do me the justice to observe,' says he, 'that I have made no secret with the astute Mackellar.'

'And in the name of God,' cries I, 'what brings you here? Go back, while it is yet time.'

'I thank you,' said he. 'Your master has chosen his way, and not I; but since he has made the choice, he (and you also) must abide by the result. And now pick up these things of mine, which you have set down in a very boggy place, and attend to that which I have made your business.'

But I had no thought now of obedience; I came stright up to him. 'If nothing will move you to go back,' said I; 'though sure, under all the circumstances, any Christian or even any gentleman would scruple to go forward . . .'

'These are gratifying expressions,' he threw in.

'If nothing will move you to go back,' I continued, 'there are still some decencies to be observed. Wait here with your baggage, and I will go forward and prepare your family. Your father is an old man; and . . .' I stumbled . . . 'there are decencies to be observed.'

'Truly,' said he, 'this Mackellar improves upon acquaintance. But look you here, my man, and understand it once for all – you waste your breath upon me, and I go my own way with inevitable motion.'

'Ah!' says I. 'Is that so? We shall see then!'

And I turned and took to my heels for Durrisdeer. He clutched at me and cried out angrily, and then I believed I heard him laugh, and then I am certain he pursued me for a step or two, and (I supposee) desisted. One thing at least is sure, that I came but a few minutes later to the door of the great house, nearly strangled for the lack of breath, but quite alone. Straight up the stair I ran, and burst into the hall, and stopped before the family without the power of speech; but I must have carried my story in my looks, for they rose out of their places and stared on me like changelings.

'He has come,' I panted out at last.

'He?' said Mr Henry.

'Himself,' said I.

'My son?' cried my lord. 'Imprudent, imprudent boy! Oh, could he not stay where he was safe!'

Never a word says Mrs Henry; nor did I look at her, I scarce knew why.

'Well,' said Mr Henry, with a very deep breath, 'and where is he?'

'I left him in the long shrubbery,' said I.

'Take me to him,' said he.

So we went out together, he and I, without another word from anyone; and in the midst of the gravelled plot encountered the Master strolling up, whistling as he came, and beating the air with his cane. There was still light enough overhead to recognize, though not to read, a countenance.

'Ah! Jacob,' says the Master. 'So here is Esau back.'

'James,' says Mr Henry, 'for God's sake, call me by my name. I will not pretend that I am glad to see you; but I would fain make you as welcome as I can in the house of our fathers.'

'Or in *my* house? or *yours*?' says the Master. 'Which were you about to say? But this is an old sore, and we need not rub it. If you would not share with me in Paris, I hope you will yet scarce deny your elder brother a corner of the fire at Durrisdeer?'

'That is very idle speech,' replied Mr Henry. 'And you understand the power of your position excellently well.'

'Why, I believe I do,' said the other with a little laugh. And this, though they had never touched hands, was (as we may say) the end of the brothers' meeting; for at this the Master turned to me and bade me fetch his baggage.

I, on my side, turned to Mr Henry for a confirmation; perhaps with some defiance.

'As long as the Master is here, Mr Mackellar, you will very much oblige me by regarding his wishes as you would my own,' says Mr Henry. 'We are constantly troubling you: will you be so good as send one of the servants?' – with an accent on the word.

If this speech were anything at all, it was surely a well-deserved reproof upon the stranger; and yet, so devilish was his impudence, he twisted it the other way.

'And shall we be common enough to say "Sneck up"?' inquires he softly, looking upon me sideways.

Had a kingdom depended on the act, I could not have trusted myself in words; even to call a servant was beyond me; I had rather serve the man myself than speak; and I turned away in silence and went into the long shrubbery, with a heart full of anger and despair. It was dark under the trees, and I walked before me and forgot what business I was come upon, till I near broke my shin on the portmanteaus. Then it was that I remarked a strange particular; for whereas I had before carried both and scarce observed it, it was now as much as I could do to manage one. And this, as it forced me to make two journeys, kept me the longer from the hall.

When I got there, the business of welcome was over long ago; the company was already at supper; and, by an oversight that cut me to the quick, my place had been forgotten. I had seen one side of the Master's return; now I was to see the other. It was he who first remarked my coming in and standing back (as I did) in some annoyance. He jumped from his seat.

'And if I have not got the good Mackellar's place!' cries he. 'John, lay another for Mr Bally; I protest he will disturb no one, and your table is big enough for all.'

I could scarce credit my ears, nor yet my senses, when he took me by the shoulders and thrust me, laughing, into my own place – such an affectionate playfulness was in his voice. And while John laid the fresh place for him (a thing on which he still insisted), he went and leaned on his father's chair and looked down upon him, and the old man turned about and looked upwards on his son, with such a pleasant mutual tenderness that I could have carried my hand to my head in mere amazement.

Yet all was of a piece. Never a harsh word fell from him, never a sneer showed upon his lip. He had laid aside even his cutting English accent, and spoke with the kindly Scots tongue, that set a value on affectionate words; and though his manners had a graceful elegance mighty foreign to our ways in Durrisdeer, it was still a homely courtliness, that did not shame but flattered us. All that he did throughout the meal, indeed, drinking wine with me with a notable respect, turning about for a pleasant word with John, fondling his father's hand, breaking into little merry tales of his adventures, calling up the past with happy reference – all he did was so becoming, and himself so handsome, that I could scarce wonder if my lord and Mrs Henry sat about the board with radiant faces, or if John waited behind with dropping tears.

As soon as supper was over, Mrs Henry rose to withdraw.

'This was never your way, Alison,' said he.

'It is my way now,' she replied: which was notoriously false, 'and I will give you a good-night, James, and a welcome – from the dead,' said she, and her voice dropped and trembled.

Poor Mr Henry, who had made rather a heavy figure through the meal, was more concerned than ever; pleased to see his wife withdraw, and yet half displeased, as he thought upon the cause of it; and the next moment altogether dashed by the fervour of her speech.

On my part, I thought I was now one too many; and was stealing after Mrs Henry, when the Master saw me.

'Now, Mr Mackellar,' says he, 'I take this near on an unfriendliness. I cannot have you go: this is to make a stranger of the prodigal son; and let me remind you where – in his own father's house! Come, sit ye down, and drink another glass with Mr Bally.'

'Ay, ay, Mr Mackellar,' says my lord, 'we must not make a stranger either of him or you. I have been telling my son,' he added, his voice brightening as usual on the word, 'how much we valued all your friendly service.'

So I sat there, silent, till my usual hour; and might have been almost deceived in the man's nature but for one passage, in which his perfidy appeared too plain. Here was the passage; of which, after what he knows of the brothers' meeting, the reader shall consider for himself. Mr Henry sitting somewhat dully, in spite of his best endeavours to carry things before my lord, up jumps the Master, passes about the board, and claps his brother on the shoulder.

'Come, come, *Hairry lad*,' says he, with a broad accent such as they must have used together when they were boys, 'you must not be downcast because your brother has come home. All's yours, that's sure enough, and little I grudge it you. Neither must you grudge me my place beside my father's fire.'

'And that is too true, Henry,' says my old lord with a little frown, a thing rare with him. 'You have been the elder brother of the parable in the good sense; you must be careful of the other.'

'I am easily put in the wrong,' said Mr Henry.

'Who puts you in the wrong?' cried my lord, I thought very tartly for so mild a man. 'You have earned my gratitude and your brother's many thousand times: you may count on its endurance; and let that suffice.'

'Ay. Harry, that you may,' said the Master: and I thought Mr Henry looked at him with a kind of wildness in his eye.

On all the miserable business that now followed, I have four questions that I asked myself often at the time, and ask myself still: – Was the man moved by a particular sentiment against Mr Henry? or by what he thought to be his interest? or by a mere delight in cruelty such as cats display and theologians tell us of the devil? or by what he would have called love? My common opinion halts among the three first; but perhaps there lay at the spring of his behaviour an element of all. As thus: – Animosity to Mr Henry would explain his hateful usage of him when they were alone; the interests he came to serve would explain his very different attitude before my lord; that and some spice of a design of gallantry, his care to stand well with Mrs Henry; and the pleasure of malice for itself, the pains he was continually at to mingle and oppose these lines of conduct.

Partly because I was a very open friend to my patron, partly because in my letters to Paris I had often given myself some freedom of remonstrance, I was included in his diabolical amusement. When I was alone with him, he pursued me with sneers; before the family he used me with the extreme of friendly condescension. This was not only painful in itself; not only did it put me continually in the wrong; but there was in it an element of insult indescribable. That he should thus leave me out in his dissimulation, as though even my testimony were too despicable to be considered, galled me to the blood. But what it was to me is not worth notice. I make but memorandum of it here; and chiefly for this reason, that it had one good result, and gave me the quicker sense of Mr Henry's martydrom.

It was on him the burthen fell. How was he to respond to the public advances of one who never lost a chance of gibing him in private? How was he to smile back on the deceiver and the insulter? He was condemned to seem ungracious. He was condemned to silence. Had he been less proud, had he spoken, who would have credited the truth? The acted calumny had done its work; my lord and Mrs Henry were the daily witnesses of what went on; they could have sworn in court that the Master was a model of long-suffering good-nature, and Mr Henry a pattern of jealousy and thanklessness. And ugly enough as these must have appeared in anyone, they seemed tenfold uglier in Mr Henry; for who could forget that the Master lay in peril of his life, and that he had already lost his mistress, his title, his fortune?

'Henry, will you ride with me?' asks the Master one day.

And Mr Henry, who had been goaded by the man all morning, raps out: 'I will not.'

'I sometimes wish you would be kinder, Henry,' says the other, wistfully.

I give this for a specimen; but such scenes befell continually. Small wonder if Mr Henry was blamed; small wonder if I fretted myself into something near upon a bilous fever; nay, and at the mere recollection feel a bitterness in my blood.

Sure, never in this world was a more diabolical contrivance: so perfidious, so simple, so impossible to combat. And yet I think again, and I think always, Mrs Henry might have read between the lines; she might have had more knowledge of her husband's nature; after all these years of marriage she might have commanded or captured his confidence. And my old lord, too – that very watchful gentleman – where was all his observation? But, for one thing, the deceit was practised by a master hand, and might have gulled an angel. For another (in the case of Mrs Henry), I have observed there are no persons so far away as those who are both married and estranged, so that they seem out of earshot or to have no common tongue. For a third (in the case of both of these spectators), they were blinded by old ingrained predilection. And for a fourth, the risk the Master was supposed to stand in (supposed, I say – you will soon hear why) made it seem the more ungenerous to criticize; and keeping them in a perpetual tender solicitude about his life, blinded them the more effectually to his faults.

It was during this time that I perceived most clearly the effect of manner, and was led to lament most deeply the plainness of my own. Mr Henry had the essence of a gentleman; when he was moved, when there was any call of circumstance, he could play his part with dignity and spirit; but in the day's commerce (it is idle to deny it) he fell short of the ornamental. The Master (on the other hand) had never a movement but it commended him. So it befell that when the one appeared gracious and the other ungracious, every trick of their bodies seemed to call out confirmation. Not that alone: but the more deeply Mr Henry floundered in his brother's toils, the more clownish he grew; and the more the Master enjoyed his spiteful entertainment, the more engagingly, the more smilingly, he went! So that the plot, by its own scope and progress, furthered and confirmed itself.

It was one of the man's arts to use the peril in which (as I say) he was supposed to stand. He spoke of it to those who loved him with a gentle pleasantry, which made it the more touching. To Mr Henry he used it as a cruel weapon of offence. I remember his laying his finger on the clean lozenge of the painted window one day when we three were alone together in the hall. 'Here went your lucky guinea, Jacob,' said he. And when Mr Henry only looked upon him darkly, 'Oh!' he added, 'you need not look such impotent malice, my good fly. You can be rid of your spider when you please. How long, O Lord? When are you to be wrought to the point of a denunciation, scrupulous brother? It is one of my interests in this dreary hole. I ever loved experiment.' Still Mr Henry only stared upon him with a glooming brow and a changed colour; and at last the Master broke out in a laugh and clapped him on the shoulder, calling him a sulky dog. At this my patron leaped back with a gesture I thought very dangerous; and I must suppose the Master thought so too, for he looked the least in the world discountenanced, and I do not remember him again to have laid hands on Mr Henry.

But though he had his peril always on his lips in the one way or the other, I thought his conduct strangely incautious, and began to fancy the Government – who had set a price upon his head – was gone sound asleep. I will not deny I was tempted with the wish to denounce him; but two thoughts withheld me: one, that if he were thus to end his life upon an honourable scaffold, the man would be canonized for good in the minds of his father and my patron's wife; the other, that if I was anyway mingled in the matter, Mr Henry himself would scarce escape some glancings of suspicion. And in the meanwhile our enemy went in and out more than I could have thought possible, the fact that he was home again was buzzed about all the country-side, and yet he was never stirred. Of all these so-many and so-different persons who were acquainted with his presence, none had the least greed – as I used to say in my annoyance – or the least loyalty; and the man rode here and there – fully more welcome, considering the lees of old unpopularity, than Mr Henry – and considering the freetraders, far safer than myself.

Not but what he had a trouble of his own; and this, as it brought about the gravest consequences, I must now relate. The reader will scarce have forgotten Jessie Broun; her way of life was much among the smuggling party; Captain Crail himself was of her intimates; and she had early word of Mr Bally's presence at the house. In my opinion, she had long ceased to care two straws for the Master's person; but it was become her habit to connect herself continually with the Master's name; that was the ground of all her play-acting; and so now, when he was back, she thought she owed it to herself to grow a haunter of the neighbourhood of Durrisdeer. The Master could scarce go abroad but she was there in wait for him; a scandalous figure of a woman, not often sober; haling him wildly as 'her bonny laddie,' quoting pedlar's poetry, and, as I receive the story, even seeking to weep upon his neck. I own I rubbed my hands over this persecution; but the Master, who laid so much upon others, was himself the least patient of men. There were strange scenes enacted in the policies. Some say he took his cane to her, and Jessie fell back upon her former weapons – stones. It is certain at least that he made a motion to Captain Crail to have the woman trepanned, and that the Captain refused the proposition with uncommon vehemence. And the end of the matter was victory for Jessie. Money was got together; an interview took place, in which my proud gentleman must consent to be kissed and wept upon; and the woman was set up in a public of her own, somewhere on Solway side (but I forget where), and, by the only news I ever had of it, extremely ill-frequented.

This is to look forward. After Jessie had been but a little while upon his heels, the Master comes to me one day in the steward's office, and with more civility than usual, 'Mackellar,' says he, 'there is a damned crazy wench comes about here. I cannot well move in the matter myself, which brings me to you. Be so good as to see to it; the men must have a strict injunction to drive the wench away.'

'Sir,' said I, trembling a little, 'you can do your own dirty errands for yourself.'

He said not a word to that, and left the room.

Presently came Mr Henry. 'Here is news!' cried he. 'It seems all is not enough, and you must add to my wretchedness. It seems you have insulted Mr Bally.'

'Under your kind favour, Mr Henry,' said I, 'it was he that insulted me, and, as I think, grossly. But I may have been careless of your position when I spoke; and if you think so when you know all, my dear patron, you have but to say the word. For you I would obey in any point whatever, even to sin, God pardon me!' And thereupon I told him what had passed.

Mr Henry smiled to himself; a grimmer smile I never witnessed. 'You did exactly well,' said he. 'He shall drink his Jessie Broun to the dregs.' And then, spying the Master outside, he opened the window, and crying to him by the name of Mr Bally, asked him to step up and have a word.

'James,' said he, when our persecutor had come in and closed the door behind him, looking at me with a smile, as if he thought I was to be humbled, 'you brought me a complaint against Mr Mackellar, into which I have inquired. I need not tell you I would always take his word against yours; for we are alone, and I am going to use something of your own freedom. Mr Mackellar is a gentleman I value; and you must contrive, so long as you are under this roof, to bring yourself into no more collisions with one whom I will support at any possible cost to me or mine. As for the errand upon which you came to him, you must deliver yourself from the consequences of your own cruelty, and none of my servants shall be at all employed in such a case.'

'My father's servants, I believe,' says the Master.

'Go to him with this tale,' said Mr Henry.

The Master grew very white. He pointed at me with his finger. 'I want that man discharged,' he said.

'He shall not be,' said Mr Henry.

'You shall pay pretty dear for this,' says the Master.

'I have paid so dear already for a wicked brother,' said Mr Henry, 'that

I am bankrupt even of fears. You have no place left where you can strike me.'

'I will show you about that,' says the Master, and went softly away.

'What will he do next, Mackellar?' cries Mr Henry.

'Let me go away,' said I. 'My dear patron, let me go away; I am but the beginning of fresh sorrows.'

'Would you leave me quite alone?' said he.

We were not long in suspense as to the nature of the new assault. Up to that hour the Master had played a very close game with Mrs Henry; avoiding pointedly to be alone with her, which I took at the time for an effect of decency, but now think to be a most insidious art; meeting her, you may say, at meal-time only; and behaving, when he did so, like an affectionate brother. Up to that hour, you may say he had scarce directly interfered between Mr Henry and his wife; except in so far as he had manoeuvred the one quite forth from the good graces of the other. Now all that was to be changed; but whether really in revenge, or because he was wearying of Durrisdeer and looked about for some diversion, who but the devil shall decide?

From that hour, at least, began the siege of Mrs Henry; a thing so deftly carried on that I scarce know if she was aware of it herself, and that her husband must look on in silence. The first parallel was opened (as was made to appear) by accident. The talk fell, as it did often, on the exiles in France; so it glided to the matter of their songs.

'There is one,' says the Master, 'if you are curious in these matters, that has always seemed to me very moving. The poetry is harsh; and yet, perhaps because of my situation, it has always found the way to my heart. It is supposed to be sung, I should tell you, by an exile's sweetheart; and represents perhaps, not so much the truth of what she is thinking, as the truth of what he hopes of her, poor soul! in these far lands.' And here the Master sighed. 'I protest it is a pathetic sight when a score of rough Irish, all common sentinels, get to this song; and you may see, by their falling tears, how it strikes home to them. It goes thus, father,' says he, very adroitly taking my lord for his listener, 'and if I cannot get to the end of it, you must think it is a common case with us exiles.' And thereupon he struck up the same air as I had heard the Colonel whistle; but now to words, rustic indeed, yet most pathetically setting forth a poor girl's aspirations for an exiled lover; of which one verse indeed (or something like it) still sticks by me:

> O, I will dye my petticoat red,
> With my dear boy I'll beg my bread,

Though all my friends should wish me dead,
For Willie among the rushes, O!

He sang it well, even as a song; but he did better yet as a performer. I have heard famous actors, when there was not a dry eye in the Edinburgh theatre; a great wonder to behold; but no more wonderful than how the Master played upon that little ballad, and on those who heard him, like an instrument, and seemed now upon the point of failing, and now to conquer his distress, so that words and music seemed to pour out of his own heart and his own past, and to be aimed directly at Mrs Henry. And his art went further yet; for all was so delicately touched, it seemed impossible to suspect him of the least design; and so far from making a parade of emotion, you would have sworn he was striving to be calm. When it came to an end, we all sat silent for a time; he had chosen the dusk of the afternoon, so that none could see his neighbour's face; but it seemed as if we held our breathing; only my old lord cleared his throat. The first to move was the singer, who got to his feet suddenly and softly, and went and walked softly to and fro in the low end of the hall, Mr Henry's customary place. We were to suppose that he there struggled down the last of his emotion; for he presently returned and launched into a disquisition on the nature of the Irish (always so much miscalled, and whom he defended) in his natural voice; so that before the lights were brought, we were in the usual course of talk. But even then, methought Mrs Henry's face was a shade pale; and, for another thing, she withdrew almost at once.

The next sign was a friendship this insidious devil struck up with innocent Miss Katharine; so that they were always together, hand in hand, or she climbing on his knee, like a pair of children. Like all his diabolical acts, this cut in several ways. It was the last stroke to Mr Henry, to see his own babe debauched against him; it made him harsh with the poor innocent; which brought him still a peg lower in his wife's esteem; and (to conclude) it was a bond of union between the lady and the Master. Under this influence, their old reserve melted by daily stages. Presently there came walks in the long shrubbery, talks in the Belvedere, and I know not what tender familiarity. I am sure Mrs Henry was like many a good woman; she had a whole conscience, but perhaps by the means of a little winking. For even to so dull an observer as myself, it was plain her kindness was of a more moving nature than the sisterly. The tones of her voice appeared more numerous: she had a light softness in her eye; she was more gentle with all of us, even with Mr Henry, even with myself; methought she breathed of some quiet melancholy happiness.

To look on at this, what a torment it was for Mr Henry! And yet it brought our ultimate deliverance, as I am soon to tell.

The purport of the master's stay was no more noble (gild it as they might) than to wring money out. He had some design of a fortune in the French Indies, as the Chevalier wrote me; and it was the sum required for this that he came seeking. For the rest of the family it spelled ruin; but my lord, in his incredible partiality, pushed ever for the granting. The family was now so narrowed down (indeed, there were no more of them than just the father and the two sons) that it was possible to break the entail and alienate a piece of land. And to this, at first by hints, and then by open pressure, Mr Henry was brought to consent. He never would have done so, I am very well assured, but for the weight of the distress under which he laboured. But for his passionate eagerness to see his brother gone, he would not thus have broken with his own sentiment and the traditions of his house. And even so, he sold them his consent at a dear rate, speaking for once openly, and holding the business up in its own shameful colours.

'You will observe,' he said, 'this is an injustice to my son, if ever I have one.'

'But that you are not likely to have,' said my lord.

'God knows!' said Mr Henry. 'And considering the cruel falseness of the position in which I stand to my brother, and that you, my lord, are my father, and have a right to command me, I set my hand to this paper. But one thing I will say first: I have been ungenerously pushed, and when next, my lord, you are tempted to compare your sons, I call on you to remember what I have done and what he has done. Acts are the fair test.'

My lord was the most uneasy man I ever saw; even in his old face the blood came up. 'I think this is not a very wisely chosen moment, Henry, for complaints,' said he. 'This takes away from the merit of your generosity.'

'Do not deceive yourself, my lord,' said Mr Henry. 'This injustice is not done from generosity to him, but in obedience to yourself.'

'Before strangers ...' begins my lord, still more unhappily affected.

'There is no one but Mackellar here,' said Mr Henry; 'he is my friend. And, my lord, as you make him no stranger to your frequent blame, it were hard if I must keep him one to a thing so rare as my defence.'

Almost I believe my lord would have rescinded his decision; but the Master was on the watch.

'Ah! Henry, Henry,' says he, 'you are the best of us still. Rugged and true! Ah! man, I wish I was as good.'

And at that instance of his favourite's generosity, my lord desisted from his hesitation, and the deed was signed.

As soon as it could be brought about, the land of Ochterhall was sold for much below its value, and the money paid over to our leech and sent by some private carriage into France. And now here was all the man's business brought to a successful head, and his pockets once more bulging with our gold; and yet the point for which we had consented to this sacrifice was still denied us, and the visitor still lingered on at Durrisdeer. Whether in malice, or because the time was not yet come for his adventure to the Indies, or because he had hopes of his design on Mrs Henry, or from the orders of the Government, who shall say? but linger he did, and that for weeks.

You will observe I say: from the orders of Government; for about this time the man's disreputable secret trickled out.

The first hint I had was from a tenant, who commented on the Master's stay, and yet more on his security; for this tenant was a Jacobitish sympathizer, and had lost a son at Culloden, which gave him the more critical eye. 'There is one thing,' said he, 'that I cannot but think strange; and that is how he got to Cockermouth.'

'To Cockermouth?' said I, with a sudden memory of my first wonder on beholding the man disembark so point-de-vice after so long a voyage.

'Why, yes,' says the tenant, 'it was there he was picked up by Captain Crail. You thought he had come from France by sea? And so we all did.'

I turned this news a little in my head, and then carried it to Mr Henry. 'Here is an odd circumstance,' said I, and told him.

'What matters how he came, Mackellar, so long as he is here?' groans Mr Henry.

'No, no,' said I, 'but think again! Does not this smack a little of some Government connivance? You know how much we have wondered already at the man's security.'

'Stop,' said Mr Henry. 'Let me think of this.' And as he thought there came that grim smile upon his face that was a little like the Master's. 'Give me paper,' said he. And he sat without another word and wrote to a gentleman of his acquaintance – I will name no unnecessary names, but he was one in a high place. This letter I despatched by the only hand I could depend upon in such a case – Macconochie's; and the old man rode hard, for he was back with the reply before even my eagerness had ventured to expect him. Again, as he read it, Mr Henry had the same grim smile.

'This is the best you have done for me yet, Mackellar,' says he. 'With this in my hand I will give him a shog. Watch for us at dinner.'

At dinner accordingly Mr Henry proposed some very public appearance for the Master; and my lord, as he had hoped, objected to the danger of the course.

'Oh!' says Mr Henry, very easily, 'you need no longer keep this up with me. I am as much in the secret as yourself.'

'In the secret?' says my lord. 'What do you mean, Henry? I give you my word, I am in no secret from which you are exluded.'

The Master had changed countenance, and I saw he was struck in a joint of his harness.

'How?' says Mr Henry, turning to him with a huge appearance of surprise. 'I see you serve your masters very faithfully; but I had thought you would have been humane enough to set your father's mind at rest.'

'What are you talking of? I refuse to have my business publicly discussed. I order this to cease,' cries the Master, very foolishly and passionately, and indeed more like a child than a man.

'So much discretion was not looked for at your hands, I can assure you,' continued Mr Henry. 'For see what my correspondent writes' – unfolding the paper – ' "It is, of course, in the interests both of the Government and the gentleman whom we may perhaps best continue to call Mr Bally, to keep this understanding secret; but it was never meant his own family should continue to endure the suspense you paint so feelingly; and I am pleased mine should be the hand to set these fears at rest. Mr Bally is as safe in Great Britain as yourself." '

'Is this possible?' cries my lord, looking at his son, with a great deal of wonder and still more of suspicion in his face.

'My dear father,' says the Master, already much recovered, 'I am overjoyed that this may be disclosed. My own instructions, direct from London, bore a very contrary sense, and I was charged to keep the indulgence secret from everyone, yourself not excepted, and indeed yourself expressly named – as I can show in black and white unless I have destroyed the letter. They must have changed their mind very swiftly, for the whole matter is still quite fresh; or rather, Henry's correspondent must have misconceived that part, as he seems to have misconceived the rest. To tell you the truth, sir,' he continued, getting visibly more easy, 'I had supposed this unexplained favour to a rebel was the effect of some application from yourself; and the injunction to secrecy among my family the result of a desire on your part to conceal your kindness. Hence I was the more careful to obey orders. It remains now to guess by what other channel indulgence can have flowed on so notorious an offender as myself; for I do not think your son need defend himself from what seems hinted at in Henry's letter. I have never yet heard of a Durrisdeer who was a turncoat or a spy,' says he proudly.

And so it seemed he had swum out of this danger unharmed; but this was to reckon without a blunder he had made, and without the pertinacity of Mr Henry, who was now to show he had something of his brother's spirit.

'You say the matter is still fresh,' says Mr Henry.

'It is recent,' says the Master, with a fair show of stoutness and yet not without a quaver.

'Is it so recent as that?' asks Mr Henry, like a man a little puzzled, and spreading his letter forth again.

In all the letter there was no word as to the date; but how was the Master to know that?

'It seemed to come late enough for me,' says he, with a laugh. And at the sound of that laugh, which rang false, like a cracked bell, my lord looked at him again across the table, and I saw his old lips draw together close.

'No,' said Mr Henry, still glancing on his letter, 'But I remember your expression. You said it was very fresh.'

And here we had a proof of our victory, and the strongest instance yet of my lord's incredible indulgence; for what must he do but interfere to save his favourite from exposure!

'I think, Henry,' says he, with a kind of pitiful eagerness, 'I think we need dispute no more. We are all rejoiced at last to find your brother safe; we are all at one on that; and, as grateful subjects, we can do no less than drink to the king's health and bounty.'

Thus was the Master extricated; but at least he had been put to his defence, he had come lamely out, and the attraction of his personal danger was now publicly plucked away from him. My lord, in his heart of hearts, now knew his favourite to be a Government spy; and Mrs Henry (however she explained the tale) was notably cold in her behaviour to the discredited hero of romance. Thus in the best fabric of duplicity there is some weak point, if you can strike it, which will loosen all; and if, by this fortunate stroke, we had not shaken the idol, who can say how it might have gone with us at the catastrophe?

And yet at the time we seemed to have accomplished nothing. Before a day or two he had wiped off the ill-results of his discomfiture, and, to all appearance, stood as high as ever. As for my Lord Durrisdeer, he was sunk in parental partiality; it was not so much love, which should be an active quality, as an apathy and torpor of his other powers; and forgiveness (so to misapply a noble word) flowed from him in sheer weakness, like the tears of senility. Mrs Henry's was a different case; and Heaven alone knows what he found to say to her, or how he persuaded her from her contempt. It is one of the worst things of sentiment, that the voice grows to be more important than the words, and the speaker than that which is spoken. But some excuse the Master must have found, or perhaps he had even struck upon some art to wrest this exposure to his own advantage; for after a time of coldness, it seemed as if things went worse than ever between him and Mrs Henry. They were then constantly together. I would not be thought to cast one shadow of blame, beyond what is due to a half-wilful blindness, on that unfortunate lady; but I do think, in these last days, she was playing very near the fire; and whether I be wrong or not in that, one thing is sure and quite sufficient: Mr Henry thought so. The poor gentleman sat for days in my room, so great a · picture of distress that I could never venture to address him; yet it is to be thought he found some comfort even in my presence and the knowledge of my sympathy. There were times, too, when we talked, and a strange manner of talk it was; there was never a person named, nor an individual circumstance referred to; yet we had the same matter in our minds, and we were each aware of it. It is a strange art that can thus be practised; to talk for hours of a thing, and never name nor yet so much as hint at it. And I remember I wondered if it was by some such natural skill that the Master made love to Mrs Henry all day long (as he manifestly did), yet never startled her into reserve.

To show how far affairs had gone with Mr Henry, I will give some words of his, uttered (as I have cause not to forget) upon the 26th of February, 1757. It was unseasonable weather, a cast back into winter: windless, bitter cold, the world all white with rime, the sky low and grey: the sea black and silent like a quarry-hole. Mr Henry sat close by the fire and debated (as was now common with him) whether 'a man' should 'do things,' whether 'interference was wise,' and the like general propositions, which each of us particularly applied. I was by the window, looking out, when there passed below me the Master, Mrs Henry, and Miss Katharine, that now constant trio. The child was running to and fro, delighted with the frost; the Master spoke close in the lady's ear with what seemed (even from so far) a devilish grace of insinuation; and she on her part looked on the ground like a person lost in listening. I broke out of my reserve.

'If I were you, Mr Henry,' said I, 'I would deal openly with my lord.'

'Mackellar, Mackellar,' said he, 'you do not see the weakness of my ground. I can carry no such base thoughts to anyone – to my father least of all; that would be to fall into the bottom of his scorn. The weakness of my ground,' he continued, 'lies in myself, that I am not one who engages love. I have their gratitude, they all tell me that; I have a rich estate of it! But I am not present in their minds; they are moved neither to think with me nor to think for me. There is my loss!' He got to his feet and trod down the fire. 'But some method must be found, Mackellar,' said

245

he, looking at me suddenly over his shoulder; 'some way must be found. I am a man of a great deal of patience – far too much – far too much. I begin to despise myself. And yet, sure, never was a man involved in such a toil!' He fell back to his brooding.

'Cheer up,' said I. 'It will burst of itself.'

'I am far past anger now,' says he, which had so little coherency with my own observation that I let both fall.

FIVE

Account of all that passed on ❧ the night of February 27th, 1757 ❧

ON THE EVENING OF THE interview referred to, the Master went abroad; he was abroad a great deal of the next day also, that fatal 27th; but where he went, or what he did, we never concerned ourselves to ask until next day. If we had done so, and by any chance found out, it might have changed all. But as all we did was done in ignorance, and should be so judged, I shall so narrate these passages as they appeared to us in the moment of their birth, and reserve all that I since discovered for the time of its discovery. For I have now come to one of the dark parts of my narrative, and must engage the reader's indulgence for my patron.

All the 27th that rigorous weather endured: a stifling cold; the folk passing about like smoking chimneys; the wide hearth in the hall piled high with fuel; some of the spring birds that had already blundered north into our neighbourhood, besieging the windows of the house or trotting on the frozen turf like things distracted. About noon there came a blink of sunshine; showing a very pretty, wintry, frosty landscape of white hills and woods, with Crail's lugger waiting for a wind under the Craig Head, and the smoke mounting straight into the air from every farm and cottage. With the coming of night, the haze closed in overhead; it fell dark and still and starless, and exceeding cold: a night the most unseasonable, fit for strange events.

Mrs Henry withdrew, as was now her custom, very early. We had set ourselves of late to pass the evening with a game of cards; another mark that our visitor was wearying mightily of the life at Durrisdeer; and we had not been long at this when my old lord slipped from his place beside the fire, and was off without a word to seek the warmth of bed. The three thus left together had neither love nor courtesy to share; not one of us would have sat up one instant to oblige another; yet from the influence of custom, and as the cards had just been dealt, we continued the form of playing out the round. I should say we were late sitters; and though my lord had departed earlier than was his custom, twelve was already gone some time upon the clock, and the servants long ago in bed. Another thing I should say, that although I never saw the Master anyway affected with liquor, he had been drinking freely, and was perhaps (although he showed it not) a trifle heated.

Anyway, he now practised one of his transitions; and so soon as the door closed behind my lord, and without the smallest change of voice, shifted from ordinary civil talk into a stream of insult.

'My dear Henry, it is yours to play,' he had been saying, and now continued: 'it is a very strange thing how, even in so small a matter as a game of cards, you display your rusticity. You play, Jacob, like a bonnet laird, or a sailor in a tavern. The same dulness, the same petty greed, *cette lenteur d'hébété qui me fait rager*; it is strange I should have such a brother. Even Square-toes has a certain vivacity when his stake is imperilled; but the dreariness of a game with you I positively lack language to depict.'

Mr Henry continued to look at his cards, as though very maturely considering some play; but his mind was elsewhere.

'Dear God, will this never be done?' cries the Master. '*Quel loudeau!* But why do I trouble you with French expressions, which are lost on such an ignoramus? A *lourdeau*, my dear brother, is as we might say a bumpkin, a clown, a clodpole: a fellow without grace, lightness, quickness; any gift of pleasing, any natural brilliancy: such a one as you shall see, when you desire, by looking in the mirror. I tell you these things for your good, I assure you; and besides, Square-toes' (looking at me and stifling a yawn), 'it is one of my diversions in this very dreary spot to toast you and your master at the fire like chestnuts. I have great pleasure in your case, for I observe the nickname (rustic as it is) has always the power to make you writhe. But sometimes I have more trouble with this dear fellow here, who seems to have gone to sleep upon his cards. Do you not see the applicability of the epithet I have just explained, dear Henry? Let me show you. For instance, with all those solid qualities which I delight to recognize in you. I never knew a woman who did not prefer me – not, I think,' he continued, with the most silken deliberation, 'I think – who did not continue to prefer me.'

Mr Henry laid down his cards. He rose to his feet very softly, and seemed all the while like a person in deep thought. 'You coward!' he said gently, as if to himself. And then, with neither hurry nor any particular violence, he struck the Master in the mouth.

The Master sprang to his feet like one transfigured; I had never seen the man so beautiful. 'A blow!' he cried. 'I would not take a blow from God Almighty!'

'Lower your voice,' said Mr Henry. 'Do you wish my father to interfere for you again?'

'Gentlemen, gentlemen,' I cried, and sought to come between them.

The Master caught me by the shoulder, held me at arm's length, and still addressing his brother: 'Do you know what this means?' said he.

'It was the most deliberate act of my life,' said Mr Henry.

'I must have blood, I must have blood for this,' said the Master.

'Please God it shall be yours,' said Mr Henry; and he went to the wall and took down a pair of swords that hung there with others, naked. These he presented to the Master by the points. 'Mackellar shall see us play fair,' said Mr Henry. 'I think it very needful.'

'You need insult me no more,' said the Master, taking one of the swords at random. 'I have hated you all my life.'

'My father is but newly gone to bed,' said Mr Henry. 'We must go somewhere forth of the house.'

'There is an excellent place in the long shrubbery,' said the Master.

'Gentlemen,' said I, 'shame upon you both! Sons of the same mother, would you turn against the life she gave you?'

'Even so, Mackellar,' said Mr Henry, with the same perfect quietude of manner he had shown throughout.

'It is what I will prevent,' said I.

And now here is a blot upon my life. At these words of mine the Master turned his blade against my bosom; I saw the light run along the steel; and I threw up my arms and fell to my knees before him on the floor. 'No, no,' I cried, like a baby.

'We shall have no trouble with him,' said the Master. 'It is a good thing to have a coward in the house.'

'We must have light,' said Mr Henry, as though there had been no interruption.

'This trembler can bring a pair of candles,' said the Master.

To my shame be it said, I was still so blinded with the flashing of that bare sword that I volunteered to bring a lantern.

'We do not need a l-l-lantern,' says the Master, mocking me. 'There is no breath of air. Come, get to your feet, take a pair of lights, and go before. I am close behind with this' – making the blade glitter as he spoke.

I took up the candlesticks and went before them, steps that I would give my hand to recall; but a coward is a slave at the best; and even as I went, my teeth smote each other in my mouth. It was as he had said: there was no breath stirring; a windless stricture of frost had bound the air; and as we went forth in the shine of the candles, the blackness was like a roof over our heads. Never a word was said; there was never a sound but the creaking of our steps along the frozen path. The cold of the night fell about me like a bucket of water; I shook as I went with more than terror; but my companions, bare-headed like myself, and fresh from the warm hall, appeared not even conscious of the change.

'Here is the place,' said the Master. 'Set down the candles.' I did as he bid me, and presently the flames went up, as steady as in a chamber, in the midst of the frosted trees, and I beheld these two brothers take their places.

'The light is something in my eyes,' said the Master.

'I will give you every advantage,' replied Mr Henry, shifting his ground, 'for I think you are about to die.' He spoke rather sadly than otherwise, yet there was a ring in his voice.

'Henry Durie,' said the Master, 'two words before I begin. You are a fencer, you can hold a foil; you little know what a change it makes to hold a sword! And by that I know you are to fall. But see how strong is my situation! If you fall, I shift out of this country to where my money is before me. If I fall where are you? My father, your wife – who is in love with me, as you very well know – your child even, who prefers me to yourself: – how will these avenge me! Had you thought of that, dear Henry?' He looked at his brother with a smile; then made a fencing-room salute.

Never a word said Mr Henry, but saluted too, and the swords rang together.

I am no judge of the play; my head, besides, was gone with cold and fear and horror; but it seems that Mr Henry took and kept the upper hand from the engagement, crowding in upon his foe with a contained and glowing fury. Nearer and nearer he crept upon the man, till of a sudden the Master leaped back with a little sobbing oath; and I believe the movement brought the light once more against his eyes. To it they went again, on the fresh ground; but now methought closer, Mr Henry pressing more outrageously, the Master beyond doubt with shaken confidence. For it is beyond doubt he now recognized himself for lost, and had some taste of the cold agony of fear; or he had never attempted the foul stroke. I cannot say I followed it, my untrained eye was never quick enough to seize details, but it appears he caught his brother's blade with his left hand, a practice not permitted. Certainly Mr Henry only saved himself by leaping on one side; as certainly the Master, lunging in the air, stumbled on his knee, and before he could move the sword was through his body.

I cried out with a stifled scream, and ran in; but the body was already fallen to the ground, where it writhed a moment like a trodden worm, and then lay motionless.

'Look at his left hand,' said Mr Henry.

'It is all bloody,' said I.

'On the inside?' said he.

'It is cut on the inside,' said I.

'I thought so,' said he, and turned his back.

I opened the man's clothes; the heart was quite still, it gave not a flutter.

'God forgive us, Mr Henry!' said I. 'He is dead.'

'Dead?' he repeated, a little stupidly; and then with a rising tone, 'Dead? dead?' says he, and suddenly cast his bloody sword upon the ground.

'What must we do?' said I. 'Be yourself, sir. It is too late now: you must be yourself.'

He turned and stared at me. 'Oh, Mackellar!' says he, and put his face in his hands.

I plucked him by the coat. 'For God's sake, for all our sakes, be more courageous!' said I. 'What must we do?'

He showed me his face with the same stupid stare. 'Do?' says he. And with that his eye fell on the body, and 'Oh!' he cries out, with his hand to his brow, as if he had never remembered; and, turning from me, made off towards the house of Durrisdeer at a strange stumbling run.

I stood a moment mused; then it seemed to me my duty lay most plain on the side of the living; and I ran after him, leaving the candles on the frosty ground and the body lying in their light under the trees. But run as I pleased, he had the start of me, and was got into the house, and up to the hall, where I found him standing before the fire with his face once more in his hands, and as he so stood he visibly shuddered.

'Mr Henry, Mr Henry,' I said, 'this will be the ruin of us all.'

'What is this that I have done?' cries he, and then looking upon me with a countenance that I shall never forget, 'Who is to tell the old man?' he said.

The word knocked at my heart; but it was no time for weakness. I went and poured him out a glass of brandy. 'Drink that,' said I, 'drink it down.' I forced him to swallow it like a child; and, being still perished with the cold of the night, I followed his example.

'It has to be told, Mackellar,' said he. 'It must be told.' And he fell suddenly in a seat – my old lord's seat by the chimney-side – and was shaken with dry sobs.

Dismay came upon my soul: it was plain there was no help in Mr Henry.

'Well,' said I, 'sit there, and leave all to me.' And taking a candle in my hand, I set forth out of the room in the dark house. There was no movement; I must suppose that all had gone unobserved; and I was now to consider how to smuggle through the rest with the like secrecy. It was no hour for scruples; and I opened my lady's door without so much as a knock, and passed boldly in.

'There is some calamity happened,' she cried, sitting up in bed.

'Madam,' said I, 'I will go forth again into the passage; and do you get as quickly as you can into your clothes. There is much to be done.'

She troubled me with no questions, nor did she keep me waiting. Ere I had time to prepare a word of that which I must say to her, she was on the threshold singing me to enter.

'Madam,' said I, 'if you cannot be very brave, I must go elsewhere; for if no one helps me tonight, there is an end of the house of Durrisdeer.'

'I am very courageous,' said she; and she looked at me with a sort of smile, very painful to see, but very brave too.

'It has come to a duel,' said I.

'A duel?' she repeated. 'A duel! Henry and—'

'And the Master,' said I. 'Things have been borne so long, things of which you know nothing, which you would not believe if I should tell. But tonight it went too far, and when he insulted you—'

'Stop,' said she. 'He? Who?'

'Oh! madam,' cried I, my bitterness breaking forth, 'do you ask me such a question? Indeed, then, I may go elsewhere for help; there is none here!'

'I do not know in what I have offended you,' said she. 'Forgive me; put me out of this suspense.'

But I dared not tell her yet; I felt not sure of her; and at the doubt, and under the sense of impotence it brought with it, I turned on the poor woman with something near to anger.

'Madam,' said I, 'we are speaking of two men; one of them insulted you, and you ask me which. I will help you to the answer. With one of these men you have spent all your hours: has the other reproached you? To one you have been always kind; to the other, as God sees me and judges between us two, I think not always: has his love ever failed you? Tonight one of these two men told the other, in my hearing – the hearing of a hired stranger – that you were in love with him. Before I say one word, you shall answer your own question: Which was it? Nay, madam, you shall answer me another: If it has come to this dreadful end, whose fault is it?'

She stared at me like one dazzled. 'Good God!' she said once, in a kind of bursting exclamation; and then a second time in a whisper to herself: 'Great God! – In the name of mercy, Mackellar, what is wrong?' she cried. 'I am made up; I can hear all.'

'You are not fit to hear,' said I. 'Whatever it was, you shall say first it was your fault.'

'Oh!' she cried, with a gesture of wringing her hands, 'this man will drive me mad! Can you not put *me* out of your thoughts?'

'I think not once of you,' I cried. 'I think of none but my dear unhappy master.'

'Ah!' she cried, with her hand to her heart, 'is Henry dead!'

'Lower your voice,' said I. 'The other.'

I saw her sway like something stricken by the wind; and I know not whether in cowardice or misery, turned aside and looked upon the floor. 'These are dreadful tidings,' said I at length, when her silence began to put me in some fear; 'and you and I behove to be the more bold if the house is to be saved.' Still she answered nothing. 'There is Miss Katharine besides,' I added; 'unless we bring this matter through, her inheritance is like to be shame.'

I do not know if it was the thought of her child or the naked word shame that gave her deliverance; at least, I had no sooner spoken than a sound passed her lips, the like of it I never heard; it was as though she had lain buried under a hill and sought to move that burthen. And the next moment she had found a sort of voice.

'It was a fight,' she whispered. 'It was not—?' and she paused upon the word.

'It was a fair fight on my dear master's part,' said I. 'As for the other, he was slain in the very act of a foul stroke.'

'Not now!' she cried.

'Madam,' said I, 'hatred of that man glows in my bosom like a burning fire; ay, even now he is dead. God knows, I would have stopped the fighting, had I dared. It is my shame I did not. But when I saw him fall, if I could have spared one thought from pitying of my master, it had been to exult in that deliverance.'

I do not know if she marked; but her next words were, 'My lord?'

'That shall be my part,' said I.

'You will not speak to him as you have to me?' she asked.

'Madam,' said I, 'have you not someone else to think of? Leave my lord to me.'

'Someone else?' she repeated.

'Your husband,' said I. She looked at me with a countenance illegible. 'Are you going to turn your back on him?' I asked.

Still she looked at me; then her hand went to her heart again. 'No,' said she.

'God bless you for that word!' I said. 'Go to him now, where he sits in the hall; speak to him – it matters not what you say; give him your hand; say, "I know all"; – if God gives you grace enough, say, "Forgive me." '

'God strengthen you, and make you merciful,' said she. 'I will go to my husband.'

'Let me light you there,' said I, taking up the candle.

'I will find my way in the dark,' she said, with a shudder, and I think the shudder was at me.

So we separated – she down the stairs to where a little light glimmered in the hall-door, I along the passage to my lord's room. It seems hard to say why, but I could not burst in on the old man as I could on the young woman; with whatever reluctance, I must knock. But his old slumbers were light, or perhaps he slept not; and at the first summons I was bidden enter.

He, too, sat up in bed; very aged and bloodless he looked; and whereas he had a certain largeness of appearance when dressed for daylight, he now seemed frail and little, and his face (the wig being laid aside) not bigger than a child's. This daunted me; nor less, the haggard surmise of misfortune in his eye. Yet his voice was even peaceful as he inquired my errand. I set my candle down upon a chair, leaned on the bed-foot, and looked at him.

'Lord Durrisdeer,' said I, 'it is very well known to you that I am a partisan in your family.'

'I hope we are none of us partisans,' said he. 'That you love my son sincerely, I have always been glad to recognize.'

'Oh! my lord, we are past the hour of these civilities,' I replied. 'If we are to save anything out of the fire, we must look the face in its bare contenance. A partisan I am; partisans we have all been; it is as a partisan I am here in the middle of the night to plead before you. Hear me; before I go, I will tell you why.'

'I would always hear you, Mr Mackellar,' said he, 'and that at any hour, whether of the day or night, for I would be always sure you had a reason. You spoke once before to very proper purpose; I have not forgotten that.'

'I am here to plead the cause of my master,' said I. 'I need not tell you how he acts. You know how he is placed. You know with what generosity he has always met your other – met your wishes,' I corrected myself, stumbling at that name of son. 'You know – you must know – what he has suffered – what he has suffered about his wife.'

'Mr Mackellar!' cried my lord, rising in bed like a bearded lion.

'You said you would hear me,' I continued. 'What you do not know, what you should know, one of the things I am here to speak of, is the persecution he must bear in private. Your back is not turned before one whom I dare not name to you falls upon him with the most unfeeling taunts; twits him – pardon me, my lord – twits him with your partiality, calls him Jacob, calls him clown, pursues him with ungenerous raillery, not to be borne by man. And let but one of you appear, instantly he changes; and my master must smile and courtesy to the man who has been feeding him with insults; I know, for I have shared in some of it, and I tell you the life is insupportable. All these months it has endured; it began with the man's landing; it was by the name of Jacob that my master was greeted the first night.'

My lord made a movement as if to throw aside the clothes and rise. 'If there be any truth in this—' said he.

'Do I look like a man lying?' I interrupted, checking him with my hand.

'You should have told me at first,' he said.

'Ah, my lord! indeed I should, and you may well hate the face of this unfaithful servant!' I cried.

'I will take order,' said he, 'at once.' And again made the movement to rise.

Again I checked him. 'I have not done,' said I. 'Would God I had! All this my dear, unfortunate patron has endured without help or countenance. Your own best word, my lord, was only gratitude. Oh, but he was your son, too! He had no other father. He was hated in the country, God knows how unjustly. He had a loveless marriage. He stood on all hands without affection or support – dear, generous, ill-fated, noble heart!'

'Your tears do you much honour and me much shame,' says my lord, with a palsied trembling. 'But you do me some injustice. Henry has been ever dear to me, very dear. James (I do not deny it, Mr Mackellar), James is perhaps dearer; you have not seen my James in quite a favourable light; he has suffered under his misfortunes; and we can only remember how great and how unmerited these were. And even now his is the more affectionate nature. But I will not speak of him. All that you say of Henry is most true; I do not wonder, I know him to be very magnanimous; you will say I trade upon the knowledge? It is possible; there are dangerous virtues: virtues that tempt the encroacher. Mr Mackellar, I will make it up to him! I will take order with all this. I have been weak; and, what is worse, I have been dull.'

'I must not hear you blame yourself, my lord, with that which I have yet to tell upon my conscience,' I replied. 'You have not been weak; you have been abused by a devilish dissembler. You saw yourself how he had deceived you in the matter of his danger; he has deceived you throughout in every step of his career. I wish to pluck him from your heart; I wish to force your eyes upon your other son; ah, you have a son there!'

'No, no,' said he, 'two sons – I have two sons.'

I made some gesture of despair that struck him; he looked at me with a changed face. 'There is much worse behind?' he asked, his voice dying as it rose upon the question.

'Much worse,' I answered. 'This night he said these words to Mr Henry: "I have never known a woman who did not prefer me to you, and I think who did not continue to prefer me." '

'I will hear nothing against my daughter,' he cried; and from his readiness to stop me in this direction, I conclude his eyes were not so dull as I had fancied, and he had looked not without anxiety upon the siege of Mrs Henry.

'I think not of blaming her,' cried I. 'It is not that. These words were said in my hearing to Mr Henry; and if you find them not yet plain enough, these others but a little after: "Your wife, who is in love with me." '

'They have quarrelled?' he said.

I nodded.

'I must fly to them,' he said, beginning once again to leave his bed.

'No, no!' I cried, holding forth my hands.

'You do not know,' said he. 'These are dangerous words.'

'Will nothing make you understand, my lord?' said I.

His eyes besought me for the truth.

I flung myself on my knees by the bedside. 'Oh, my lord,' cried I, 'think on him you have left; think of this poor sinner whom you begot, whom your wife bore to you, whom we have none of us strengthened as we could; think of him, not of yourself; he is the other sufferer – think of him! That is the door for sorrow – Christ's door, God's door: oh! it stands open. Think of him, even as he thought of you. "*Who is to tell the old man?*" – these were his words: It was for that I came; that is why I am here pleading at your feet.'

'Let me get up,' he cried, thrusting me aside, and was on his feet before myself. His voice shook like a sail in the wind, yet he spoke with a good loudness; his face was like the snow, but his eyes were steady and dry. 'Here is too much speech,' said he. 'Where was it?'

'In the shrubbery,' said I.

'And Mr Henry?' he asked. And when I had told him he knotted his old face in thought.

'And Mr James?' says he.

'I have left him lying,' said I, 'beside the candles.'

'Candles?' he cried. And with that he ran to the window, opened it, and looked abroad. 'It might be spied from the road.'

'Where none goes by at such an hour,' I objected.

'It makes no matter,' he said. 'One might. Hark!' cries he. 'What is that?'

It was the sound of men very guardedly rowing in the bay; and I told him so.

'The freetraders,' said my lord. 'Run at once, Mackellar; put these candles out. I will dress in the meanwhile; and when you return we can debate on what is wisest.'

I groped my way downstairs, and out of the door. From quite a far way off a sheen was visible, making points of brightness in the shrubbery; in so black a night it might have been remarked for miles; and I blamed myself bitterly for my incaution. How much more sharply when I reached the place! One of the candlesticks was overthrown, and that taper quenched. The other burned steadily by itself, and made a broad space of light upon the frosted ground. All within that circle seemed, by the force of contrast and the overhanging blackness, brighter than by day. And there was the bloodstain in the midst; and a little farther off Mr Henry's sword, the pommel of which was of silver; but of the body, not a trace. My heart thumped upon my ribs, the hair stirred upon my scalp, as I stood there staring – so strange was the sight, so dire the fears it wakened. I looked right and left; the ground was so hard it told no story. I stood and listened till my ears ached, but the night was hollow about me like an empty church; not even a ripple stirred upon the shore; it seemed you might have heard a pin drop in the county.

I put the candle out, and the blackness fell about me groping dark; it was like a crowd surrounding me; and I went back to the house of Durrisdeer, with my chin upon my shoulder, startling, as I went, with craven suppositions. In the door a figure moved to meet me, and I had near screamed with terror ere I recognized Mrs Henry.

'Have you told him?' says she.

'It was he who sent me,' said I. 'It is gone. But why are you here?'

'It is gone!' she repeated. 'What is gone?'

'The body,' said I. 'Why are you not with your husband?'

'Gone?' said she. 'You cannot have looked. Come back.'

'There is no light now,' said I. 'I dare not.'

'I can see in the dark. I have been standing here so long – so long,' said she. 'Come give me your hand.'

We returned to the shrubbery hand in hand, and to the fatal place.

'Take care of the blood,' said I.

'Blood?' she cried, and started violently back.

'I suppose it will be,' said I. 'I am like a blind man.'

'No,' said she, 'nothing! Have you not dreamed?'

'Ah, would to God we had!' cried I.

She spied the sword, picked it up, and seeing the blood, let it fall again with her hands thrown wide. 'Ah!' she cried. And then, with an instant courage, handled it the second time. 'I will take it back and clean it properly,' says she, and again looked about her on all sides. 'It cannot be that he was dead?' she added.

'There was no flutter of his heart,' said I, and then remembering: 'Why are you not with your husband?'

'It is no use,' said she; 'he will not speak to me.'

'Not speak to you?' I repeated. 'Oh! you have not tried.'

'You have a right to doubt me,' she replied, with a gentle dignity.

At this, for the first time, I was seized with sorrow for her. 'God knows, madam,' I cried, 'God knows I am not so hard as I appear; on this dreadful night who can veneer his words? But I am a friend to all who are not Henry Durie's enemies.'

'It is hard, then, you should hesitate about his wife,' said she.

I saw all at once, like the rending of a veil, how nobly she had borne this unnatural calamity, and how generously my reproaches.

'We must go back and tell this to my lord,' said I.

'Him I cannot face,' she cried.

'You will find him the least moved of all of us,' said I.

'And yet I cannot face him,' said she.

'Well,' said I, 'you can return to Mr Henry: I will see my lord.'

As we walked back, I bearing the candlesticks, she the sword – a strange burthen for that woman – she had another thought. 'Should we tell Henry?' she asked.

'Let my lord decide,' said I.

My lord was nearly dressed when I came to his chamber. He heard me with a frown. 'The freetraders,' said he. 'But whether dead or alive?'

'I thought him—' said I, and paused, ashamed of the word.

'I know; but you may very well have been in error. Why should they remove him if not living?' he asked. 'Oh! here is a great door of hope. It must be given out that he departed – as he came – without any note of preparation. We must save all scandal.'

I saw he had fallen, like the rest of us, to think mainly of the house.

Now that all the living members of the family were plunged in irremedi-able sorrow, it was strange how we turned to the conjoint abstraction of the family itself, and sought to bolster up the airy nothing of its repu-tation: not the Duries only, but the hired steward himself.

'Are we to tell Mr Henry?' I asked him.

'I will see,' said he. 'I am going first to visit him; then I go forth with you to view the shrubbery and consider.'

We went downstairs into the hall. Mr Henry sat by the table with his head upon his hand, like a man of stone. His wife stood a little back from him, her hand at her mouth; it was plain she could not move him. My old lord walked very steadily to where his son was sitting; he had a steady countenance, too, but methought a little cold. When he was quite come up, he held out both his hands and said, 'My son!'

With a broken, strangled cry, Mr Henry leaped up and fell on his father's neck, crying and weeping, the most pitiful sight that ever a man witnessed. 'Oh! father,' he cried, 'you know I loved him; you know I loved him in the beginning; I could have died for him – you know that! I would have given my life for him and you. Oh! say you know that. Oh! say you can forgive me. O father, father, what have I done – what have I done? And we used to be bairns together!' and wept and sobbed, and fondled the old man, and clutched him about the neck, with the passion of a child in terror.

And then he caught sight of his wife (you would have thought for the first time), where she stood weeping to hear him, and in a moment had fallen at her knees. 'And O my lass,' he cried, 'you must forgive me too! Not your husband – I have only been the ruin of your life. But you knew me when I was a lad; there was no harm in Henry Durie then; he meant aye to be a friend to you. It's him – it's the old bairn that played with you – oh, can ye never, never forgive him?'

Throughout all this my lord was like a cold, kind spectator with his wits about him. At the first cry, which was indeed enough to call the house about us, he had said to me over his shoulder, 'Close the door.' And now he nodded to himself.

'We may leave him to his wife now,' says he. 'Bring a light, Mr Mackellar.'

Upon my going forth again with my lord, I was aware of a strange phenomenon; for though it was quite dark, and the night not yet old, methought I smelt the morning. At the same time there went a tossing through the branches of the evergreens, so that they sounded like a quiet sea, and the air puffed at times against our faces, and the flame of the candle shook. We made the more speed, I believe, being surrounded by this bustle; visited the scene of the duel, where my lord looked upon the blood with stoicism; and passing farther on toward the landing-place, came at last upon some evidences of the truth. For, first of all, where there was a pool across the path, the ice had been trodden in, plainly by more than one man's weight; next, and but a little farther, a young tree was broken, and down by the landing-place, where the traders' boats were usually beached, another stain of blood marked where the body must have been infallibly set down to rest the bearers.

This stain we set ourselves to wash away with the seawater, carrying it in my lord's hat; and as we were thus engaged there came a sudden moaning gust and left us instantly benighted.

'It will come to snow,' says my lord; 'and the best thing that we could hope. Let us go back now; we can do nothing in the dark.'

As we went houseward, the wind being again subsided, we were aware of a strong pattering noise about us in the night; and when we issued from the shelter of the trees, we found it raining smartly.

Throughout the whole of this my lord's clearness of mind, no less than his activity of body, had not ceased to minister to my amazement. He set the crown upon it in the council we held on our return. The freetraders had certainly secured the Master, though whether dead or alive we were still left to our conjectures; the rain would, long before day, wipe out all marks of the transaction; by this we must profit. The Master had unexpectedly come after the fall of night; it must now be given out he had as suddenly departed before the break of day; and, to make all this plausible, it now only remained for me to mount into the man's chamber, and pack and conceal his baggage. True, we still lay at the discretion of the traders; but that was the incurable weakness of our guilt.

I heard him, as I said, with wonder, and hastened to obey. Mr and Mrs Henry were gone from the hall; my lord, for warmth's sake, hurried to his bed; there was still no sign of stir among the servants, and as I went up the tower stair, and entered the dead man's room, a horror of solitude weighed upon my mind. To me extreme surprise, it was all in the disorder of departure. Of his three portmanteaus, two were already locked; the third lay open and near full. At once there flashed upon me some suspicion of the truth. The man had been going, after all; he had but waited upon Crail, as Crail waited upon the wind; early in the night the seamen had perceived the weather changing; the boat had come to give notice of the change and call the passenger aboard, and the boat's crew had stumbled on him lying in his blood. Nay, and there was more behind. This prearranged departure shed some light upon his inconceivable insult of the night before; it was a parting shot, hatred being no longer checked by policy. And, for another thing, the nature of that insult, and the conduct of Mrs Henry, pointed to one conclusion, which I have never verified, and can now never verify until the great assize – the conclusion that he had at last forgotten himself, had gone too far in his advances, and had been rebuffed. It can never be verified, as I say; but as I thought of it that morning among his baggage, the thought was sweet to me like honey.

Into the open portmanteau I dipped a little ere I closed it. The most beautiful lace and linen, many suits of those fine plain clothes in which he loved to appear; a book or two, and those of the best, Caesar's *Commentaries*, a volume of Mr Hobbes the *Henriade* of M. de Voltaire, a book upon the Indies, one on the mathematics, far beyond where I have studied: these were what I observed with very mingled feelings. But in the open portmanteau no papers of any description. This set me musing. It was possible the man was dead; but, since the traders had carried him away, not likely. It was possible that he might still die of his wound; but it was also possible he might not. And in this latter case I was determined to have the means of some defence.

One after another I carried his portmanteaus to a loft in the top of the house which we kept locked; went to my own room for my keys, and, returning to the loft, had the gratification to find two that fitted pretty well. In one of the portmanteaus there was a shagreen letter-case, which I cut open with my knife; and thenceforth (so far as any credit went) the man was at my mercy. Here was a vast deal of gallant correspondence, chiefly of his Paris days; and, what was more to the purpose, here were the copies of his own reports to the English Secretary, and the originals of the Secretary's answers: a most damning series: such as to publish would be to wreck the Master's honour and to set a price upon his life. I chuckled to myself as I ran through the documents; I rubbed my hands, I sang aloud in my glee. Day found me at the pleasing task; nor did I then remit my diligence, except in so far as I went to the window – looked out for a moment, to see the frost quite gone, the world turned black again, and the rain and the wind driving in the bay – and to assure myself that the lugger was gone from its anchorage, and the Master (whether dead or alive) now tumbling on the Irish Sea.

It is proper I should add in this place the very little I have subsequently angled out upon the doings of that night. It took me a long while to gather it: for we dared not openly ask, and the freetraders regarded me with enmity, if not with scorn. It was near six months before we even knew for certain that the man survived; and it was years before I learned from one of Crail's men, turned publican on his ill-gotten gain, some particulars which smack to me of truth. It seems the traders found the Master struggled on one elbow, and now staring round him, and now gazing at the candle or at his hand which was all bloodied, like a man stupid. Upon their coming, he would seem to have found his mind, bade them carry him aboard, and hold their tongues; and on the captain asking how he had come in such a pickle, replied with a burst of passionate swearing, and incontinently fainted. They held some debate, but they were momently looking for a wind, they were highly paid to smuggle him to France, and did not care to delay. Besides which, he was well enough liked by these abominable wretches: they supposed him under capital sentence, knew not in what mischief he might have got his wound, and judged it a piece of good nature to remove him out of the way of danger. So he was taken aboard, recovered on the passage over, and was set ashore a convalescent at the Havre de Grace. What is truly notable: he said not a word to anyone of the duel, and not a trader knows to this day in what quarrel, or by the hand of what adversary, he fell. With any other man I should have set this down to natural decency; with him, to pride. He could not bear to avow, perhaps even to himself, that he had been vanquished by one whom he had so much insulted and whom he so cruelly despised.

SIX

❖ Summary of Events during the Master's second absence ❖

OF THE HEAVY SICKNESS which declared itself next morning I can think with equanimity, as of the last unmingled trouble that befell my master; and even that was perhaps a mercy in disguise; for what pain of the body could equal the miseries of his mind? Mrs Henry and I had the watching by the bed. My old lord called from time to time to take the news, but would not usually pass the door. Once, I remember, when hope was nigh gone, he stepped to the bedside, looked awhile in his son's face, and turned away with a singular gesture of the head and hand thrown up, that remains upon my mind as something tragic; such grief and such a scorn of sublunary things were there expressed. But the most of the time Mrs Henry and I had the room to ourselves, taking turns by night, and bearing each other company by day, for it was dreary watching. Mr Henry, his shaven head bound in a napkin, tossed to and fro without remission, beating the bed with his hands. His tongue never lay; his voice ran continuously like a river, so that my heart was weary with the sound of it. It was notable, and to me inexpressibly mortifying, that he spoke all the while on matters of no import: comings and goings, horses – which he was ever calling to have saddled, thinking perhaps (the poor soul!) that he might ride away from his discomfort – matters of the garden, the salmon nets, and (what I particularly raged to hear) continually of his affairs, cyphering figures and holding disputation with the tenantry. Never a word of his father or his wife, nor of the Master, save only for a day or two, when his mind dwelled entirely in the past, and he supposed himself a boy again and upon some innocent child's play with his brother. What made this the more affecting: it appeared the Master had then run some peril of his life, for there was a cry – 'Oh! Jamie will be drowned – Oh, save Jamie!' which he came over and over with a great deal of passion.

This, I say, was affecting both to Mrs Henry and myself; but the balance of my master's wanderings did him little justice. It seemed he had set out to justify his brother's calumnies; as though he was bent to prove himself a man of a dry nature, immersed in money-getting. Had I been there alone, I would not have troubled my thumb; but all the while, as I listened, I was estimating the effect on the man's wife, and telling myself that he fell lower every day. I was the one person on the surface of the globe that comprehended him, and I was bound there should be yet another. Whether he was to die there and his virtues perish: or whether he should save his days and come back to that inheritance of sorrows, his right memory: I was bound he should be heartily lamented in the one case, and unaffectedly welcomed in the other, by the person he loved the most, his wife.

Finding no occasion of free speech, I bethought me at last of a kind of documentary disclosure; and for some nights, when I was off duty and should have been asleep, I gave my time to the preparation of that which I may call my budget. But this I found to be the easiest portion of my task, and that which remained – namely, the presentation to my lady – almost more than I had fortitude to overtake. Several days I went about with my papers under my arm, spying for some juncture of talk to serve as introduction. I will not deny but that some offered; only when they did my tongue clove to the roof of my mouth; and I think I might have been carrying about my packet till this day, had not a fortunate accident delivered me from all my hesitations. This was at night, when I was once more leaving the room, the thing not yet done, and myself in despair at my own cowardice.

'What do you carry about with you, Mr Mackellar?' she asked. 'These last days, I see you always coming in and out with the same armful.'

I returned upon my steps without a word, laid the papers before her on the table, and left her to her reading. Of what that was, I am now to give you some idea; and the best will be to reproduce a letter of my own which came first in the budget and of which (according to an excellent habitude) I have preserved the scroll. It will show, too, the moderation of my part in these affairs, a thing which some have called recklessly in question.

DURRISDEER,
1757.

HONOURED MADAM,

I trust I would not step out of my place without occasion; but I see how much evil has flowed in the past to all of your noble house from that unhappy and secretive fault of reticency, and the papers on which I venture to call your attention are family papers, and all highly worthy your acquaintance.

I append a schedule with some necessary observations,

And am,
Honoured Madam,
Your ladyship's obliged, obedient servant
EPHRAIM MACKELLAR.

Schedule of Papers

A. Scroll of ten letters from Ephraim Mackellar to the Hon James Durie, Esq., by courtesy Master of Ballantrae, during the latter's residence in Paris: under dates ... (*follow the dates*) ... *Nota:* to be read in connection with B. and C.

B. Seven original letters from the said Mr of Ballantrae to the said E. Mackellar, under dates ... (*follow the dates*).

C. Three original letters from the said Mr of Ballantrae to the Hon Henry Durie, Esq., under dates ... (*follow the dates*) ... *Nota:* given me by Mr Henry to answer: copies of my answers A4, A5 and A9 of these productions. The purport of Mr Henry's communications, of which I can find no scroll, may be gathered from those of his unnatural brother.

D. A correspondence, original and scroll, extending over a period of three years till January of the current year, between the said Mr of Ballantrae and—, Under Secretary of State; twenty-seven in all. *Nota:* found among the Master's papers.

*

Weary as I was with watching and distress of mind, it was impossible for me to sleep. All night long I walked in my chamber, revolving what should be the issue, and sometimes repenting the temerity of my immixture in affairs so private; and with the first peep of morning I was at the sick-room door. Mrs Henry had thrown open the shutters and even the window, for the temperature was mild. She looked steadfastly before her; where was nothing to see, or only the blue of the morning creeping among woods. Upon the stir of my entrance she did not so much as turn about her face: a circumstance from which I augured very ill.

'Madam,' I began; and then again, 'Madam'; but could make no more of it. Nor yet did Mrs Henry come to my assistance with a word. In this pass I began gathering up the papers where they lay scattered on the table; and the first thing that struck me, their bulk appeared to have diminished. Once I ran them through, and twice; but the correspondence with the Secretary of State, on which I had reckoned so much against the future, was nowhere to be found. I looked in the chimney; amid the smouldering embers, black ashes of papers fluttered in the draught; and at that my timidity vanished.

'Good God, madam,' cried I, in a voice not fitting for a sick-room. 'Good God, madam, what have you done with my papers?'

'I have burned them,' said Mrs Henry, turning about. 'It is enough, it is too much, that you and I have seen them.'

'This is a fine night's work that you have done!' cried I. 'And all to save the reputation of a man that ate bread by the shedding of his comrade's blood, as I do by the shedding of ink.'

'To save the reputation of that family in which you are a servant, Mr Mackellar,' she returned, 'and for which you have already done so much.'

'It is a family I will not serve much longer,' I cried, 'for I am driven desperate. You have stricken the sword out of my hands; you have left us all defenceless. I had always these letters I could shake over his head; and now – what is to do? We are so falsely situate we dare not show the man the door; the country would fly on fire against us; and I had this one hold upon him – and now it is gone – now he may come back tomorrow, and we must all sit down with him to dinner, go for a stroll with him on the terrace, or take a hand at cards, of all things, to divert his leisure! No, madam! God forgive you, if He can find it in His heart, for I cannot find it in mine.'

'I wonder to find you so simple, Mr Mackellar,' said Mrs Henry. 'What does this man value reputation? But he knows how high we prize it; he knows we would rather die than make these letters public; and do you suppose he would not trade upon the knowledge? What you call your sword, Mr Mackellar, and which had been one indeed against a man of any remnant of propriety, would have been but a sword of paper against him. He would smile in your face at such a threat. He stands upon his degradation, he makes that his strength: it is in vain to struggle with such characters.' She cried out this last a little desperately, and then with more quiet: 'No, Mr Mackellar; I have thought upon this matter all night, and there is no way out of it. Papers or no papers, the door of this house stands open for him; he is the rightful heir, forsooth! If we sought to exclude him, all would redound against poor Henry, and I should see him stoned again upon the streets. Ah! if Henry dies, it is a different matter! They have broke the entail for their own good purposes; the estate goes to my daughter; and I shall see who sets a foot upon it. But if Henry lives, my poor Mr Mackellar, and that man returns, we must suffer: only this time it will be together.'

On the whole I was well pleased with Mrs Henry's attitude of mind; nor could I even deny there was some cogency in that which she advanced about the papers.

'Let us say no more about it,' said I. 'I can only be sorry I trusted a lady with the originals, which was an unbusinesslike proceeding at the best. As for what I said of leaving the service of the family, it was spoken with the tongue only; and you may set your mind at rest. I belong to Durrisdeer, Mrs Henry, as if I had been born there.'

I must do her the justice to say she seemed perfectly relieved; so that we began this morning, as we were to continue for so many years, on a proper ground of mutual indulgence and respect.

The same day, which was certainly prededicate to joy, we observed the first signal of recovery in Mr Henry; and about three of the following afternoon he found his mind again, recognizing me by name with the strongest evidences of affection. Mrs Henry was also in the room, at the bed-foot; but it did not appear that he observed her. And indeed (the fever being gone) he was so weak that he made but the one effort and sank again into a lethargy. The course of his restoration was now slow, but equal; every day his appetite improved; every week we were able to remark an increase both of strength and flesh; and before the end of the month he was out of bed and had even begun to be carried in his chair upon the terrace.

It was perhaps at this time that Mrs Henry and I were the most uneasy in mind. Apprehension for his days was at an end; and a worse fear succeeded. Every day we drew consciously nearer to the day of reckoning; and the days passed on, and still there was nothing. Mr Henry bettered in strength, he held long talks with us on a great diversity of subjects, his father came and sat with him and went again; and still there was no reference to the late tragedy or to the former troubles which had brought it on. Did he remember, and conceal his dreadful knowledge? or was the whole blotted from his mind? This was the problem that kept us watching and trembling all day when we were in his company and held us awake at night when we were in our lonely beds. We knew not even which alternative to hope for, both appearing so unnatural and pointing so directly to an unsound brain. Once this fear offered, I observed his conduct with sedulous particularity. Something of the child he exhibited: a cheerfulness quite foreign to his previous character, an interest readily aroused, and then very tenacious, in small matters which he had heretofore despised. When he was stricken down, I was his only confidant, and I may say his only friend, and he was on terms of division with his wife; upon his recovery, all was changed, the past forgotten, the wife first and even single in his thoughts. He turned to her with all his emotions, like a child to its mother, and seemed secure of sympathy; called her in all his needs with something of that querulous familiarity that marks a certainty of indulgence; and I must say, in justice to the woman, he was never disappointed. To her, indeed, this changed behaviour was inexpressibly affecting; and I think she felt it secretly as a reproach; so that I have seen her, in early days, escape out of the room that she might indulge herself in weeping. But to me the change appeared not natural; and viewing it along with all the rest, I began to wonder, with many head-shakings, whether his reason was perfectly erect.

As this doubt stretched over many years, endured indeed until my master's death, and clouded all our subsequent relations, I may well consider of it more at large. When he was able to resume some charge of his affairs, I had many opportunities to try him with precision. There was no lack of understanding, nor yet of authority; but the old continuous interest had quite departed; he grew readily fatigued, and fell to yawning; and he carried into money relations, where it is certainly out of place, a facility that bordered upon slackness. True, since we had no longer the exactions of the Master to contend against, there was the less occasion to raise strictness into principle or do battle for a farthing. True, again, there was nothing excessive in these relaxations, or I would have been no party to them. But the whole thing marked a change, very slight yet very perceptible; and though no man could say my master had gone at all out of his mind, no man could deny that he had drifted from his character. It was the same to the end, with his manner and appearance. Some of the heat of the fever lingered in his veins: his movements a little hurried, his speech notably more voluble, yet neither truly amiss. His whole mind stood open to happy impressions, welcoming these and making much of them; but the smallest suggestion of trouble or sorrow he received with visible impatience and dismissed again with immediate relief. It was to this temper that he owed the felicity of his later days; and yet here it was, if anywhere, that you could call the man insane. A great part of this life consists in contemplating what we cannot cure; but Mr Henry, if he could not dismiss solicitude by an effort of the mind, must instantly and at whatever cost annihilate the cause of it; so that he played alternately the ostrich and the bull. It is to this strenuous coward-ice of pain that I have to set down all the unfortunate and excessive steps of his subsequent career. Certainly this was the reason of his beating M'Manus, the groom, a thing so much out of all his former practice, and which awakened so much comment at the time. It is to this, again, that I must lay the total loss of near upon two hundred pounds, more than the half of which I could have saved if his impatience would have suffered me. But he preferred loss or any desperate extreme to a continu-ance of mental suffering.

All this has led me far from our immediate trouble: whether he remem-bered or had forgotten his late dreadful act; and if he remembered, in what light he viewed it. The truth burst upon us suddenly, and was indeed one of the chief surprises of my life. He had been several times abroad, and was now beginning to walk a little with an arm, when it chanced I should be left alone with him upon the terrace. He turned to me with a singular furtive smile, such as schoolboys use when in fault; and says he, in a private whisper and without the least preface: 'Where have you buried him?'

I could not make one sound in answer.

'Where have you buried him?' he repeated. 'I want to see his grave.'

I conceived I had best take the bull by the horns. 'Mr Henry,' said I, 'I have news to give that will rejoice you exceedingly. In all human likeli-hood, your hands are clear of blood. I reason from certain indices; and by these it should appear your brother was not dead, but was carried in a swound on board the lugger. But now he may be perfectly recovered.'

What there was in his countenance I could not read. 'James?' he asked.

'Your brother James,' I answered. 'I would not raise a hope that may be found deceptive, but in my heart I think it very probable he is alive.'

'Ah!' says Mr Henry; and suddenly rising from his seat with more alacrity than he had yet discovered, set one finger on my breast, and cried at me in a kind of screaming whisper, 'Mackellar' – these were his words – 'nothing can kill that man. He is not mortal. He is bound upon my back to all eternity – to all God's eternity!' says he, and, sitting down again, fell upon a stubborn silence.

A day or two after, with the same secret smile, and first looking about as if to be sure we were alone, 'Mackellar,' said he, 'when you have any intelligence, be sure and let me know. We must keep an eye upon him, or he will take us when we least expect.'

'He will not show his face here again,' said I.

'Oh yes he will,' said Mr Henry. 'Wherever I am, there will he be.' And again he looked all about him.

'You must not dwell upon this thought, Mr Henry,' said I.

'No,' said he, 'that is a very good advice. We will never think of it, except when you have news. And we do not know yet,' he added; 'he may be dead.'

The manner of his saying this convinced me thoroughly of what I had scarce ventured to suspect: that, so far from suffering any penitence for the attempt, he did but lament his failure. This was a discovery I kept to myself, fearing it might do him a prejudice with his wife. But I might have saved myself the trouble; she had divined it for herself, and found the sentiment quite natural. Indeed, I could not but say that there were three of us, all of the same mind; nor could any news have reached Durrisdeer more generally welcome than tidings of the Master's death.

This brings me to speak of the exception, my old lord. As soon as my anxiety for my own master began to be relaxed, I was aware of a change in the old gentleman, his father, that seemed to threaten mortal consequences. His face was pale and swollen; as he sat in the chimneyside with his Latin, he would drop off sleeping and the book roll in the ashes; some days he would drag his foot, others stumble in speaking. The amenity of his behaviour appeared more extreme; full of excuses for the least trouble, very thoughtful for all; to myself, of a most flattering civility. One day, that he had sent for his lawyer and remained a long while private, he met me as he was crossing the hall with painful footsteps and took me kindly by the hand, 'Mr Mackellar,' said he, 'I have had many occasions to set a proper value on your services; and today, when I recast my will, I have taken the freedom to name you for one of my executors. I believe you bear love enough to our house to render me this service.' At that very time he passed the greater portion of his days in slumber, from which it was often difficult to rouse him; seemed to have lost all count of years, and had several times (particularly on waking) called for his wife and for an old servant whose very gravestone was now green with moss. If I had been put to my oath, I must have declared he was incapable of testing; and yet there was never a will drawn more sensible in every trait, or showing a more excellent judgment both of persons and affairs.

His dissolution, though it took not very long, proceeded by infinitesimal gradations. His faculties decayed together steadily; the power of his limbs was almost gone, he was extremely deaf, his speech had sunk into mere mumblings; and yet to the end he managed to discover something of his former courtesy and kindness, pressing the hand of any that helped him, presenting me with one of his Latin books, in which he had laboriously traced my name, and in a thousand ways reminding us of the greatness of that loss which it might almost be said we had already suffered. To the end, the power of articulation returned to him in flashes; it seemed he had only forgotten the art of speech as a child forgets his lesson, and at times he would call some part of it to mind. On the last night of his life he suddenly broke silence with these words from Virgil: 'Gnatique patrisque, alma, precor, miserere,' perfectly uttered, and with a fitting accent. At the sudden clear sound of it we started from our several occupations; but it was in vain we turned to him; he sat there silent, and, to all appearance, fatuous. A little later he was had to bed with more difficulty than ever before; and some time in the night, without any mortal violence, his spirit fled.

At a far later period I chanced to speak of these particulars with a doctor of medicine, a man of so high a reputation that I scruple to adduce his name. By his view of it father and son both suffered from the same affection: the father from the strain of his unnatural sorrows – the son perhaps in the excitation of the fever; each had ruptured a vessel in the brain, and there was probably (my doctor added) some predisposition in the family to accidents of that description. The father sank, the son recovered all the externals of a healthy man; but it is like there was some destruction in those delicate tissues where the soul resides and does her earthly business; her heavenly, I would fain hope, cannot be thus obstructed by material accidents. And yet, upon a more mature opinion, it matters not one jot; for He who shall pass judgment on the records of our life is the same that formed us in frailty.

The death of my old lord was the occasion of a fresh surprise to us who watched the behaviour of his successor. To any considering mind, the two sons had between them slain their father, and he who took the sword might be even said to have slain him with his hand; but no such thought appeared to trouble my new lord. He was becomingly grave; I could scarce say sorrowful, or only with a pleasant sorrow; talking of the dead with a regretful cheerfulness, relating old examples of his character, smiling at them with a good conscience; and when the day of the funderal came round, doing the honours with exact propriety. I could perceive, besides, that he found a solid gratification in his accession to the title: the which he was punctilious in exacting.

And now there came upon the scene a new character, and one that played his part, too, in the story; I mean the present lord, Alexander, whose birth (17th July, 1757) filled the cup of my poor master's happiness. There was nothing then left him to wish for; nor yet leisure to wish for it. Indeed, there never was a parent so fond and doting as he showed himself. He was continually uneasy in his son's absence. Was the child abroad? the father would be watching the clouds in case it rained. Was it night? he would rise out of his bed to observe its slumbers. His conversation grew even wearyful to strangers, since he talked of little but his son. In matters relating to the estate, all was designed with a particular eye to Alexander; and it would be: 'Let us put it in hand at once, that the wood may be grown against Alexander's majority'; or 'This will fall in again handsomely for Alexander's marriage.' Every day this absorption of the man's nature became more observable, with many touching and some very blame-worthy particulars. Soon the child could walk abroad with him, at first on the terrace, hand in hand, and afterwards at large about the policies; and this grew to be my lord's chief occupation. The sound of their two voices (audible a great way off, for they spoke loud) became familiar in the neighbourhood; and for my part I found it more agreeable than the sound of birds. It was pretty to see the pair returning, full of briers, and the father as flushed and sometimes as bemuddied as the child, for they were equal sharers in all sorts of boyish entertainment, digging in the beach, damming of streams, and what not; and I have seen them gaze through a fence at cattle with the same childish contemplation.

The mention of these rambles brings me to a strange scene of which I was a witness. There was one walk I never followed myself without emotion, so often had I gone there upon miserable errands, so much had there befallen against the house of Durrisdeer. But the path lay handy from all points beyond the Muckle Ross; and I was driven, although much against my will, to take my use of it perhaps once in the two months. It befell when Mr Alexander was of the age of six or seven, I had some business on the far side in the morning, and entered the shrubbery, on my homeward way, about nine of a bright forenoon. It was that time of year when the woods are all in their spring colours, the thorns all in flower, and the birds in the high season of their singing. In contrast to this merriment, the shrubbery was only the more sad, and I the more oppressed by its associations. In this situation of spirit it struck me disagreeably to hear voices a little way in front, and to recognize the tones of my lord and Mr Alexander. I pushed ahead, and came presently into their view. They stood together in the open space where the duel was, my lord with his hand on his son's shoulder, and speaking with some gravity. At least, as he raised his head upon my coming, I thought I could perceive his countenance to lighten.

'Ah!' says he, 'here comes the good Mackellar. I have just been telling Sandie the story of this place, and how there was a man whom the devil tried to kill, and how near he came to kill the devil instead.'

I had thought it strange enough he should bring the child into that scene; that he should actually be discoursing of his act, passed measure. But the worst was yet to come; for he added, turning to his son, – 'You can ask Mackellar; he was here and saw it.'

'Did you really see the devil?' asked the child.

'I have not heard the tale,' I replied; 'and I am in a press of business.' So far I said, sourly, fencing with the embarrassment of the position; and suddenly the bitterness of the past, and the terror of that scene by candlelight, rushed in upon my mind. I bethought me that, for a difference of a second's quickness in parade, the child before me might have never seen the day; and the emotion that always fluttered round my heart in that dark shrubbery burst forth in words. 'But so much is true,' I cried, 'that I have met the devil in these woods, and seen him foiled here. Blessed be God that we escaped with life – blessed be God that one stone yet stands upon another in the walls of Durrisdeer! And, oh! Mr Alexander, if every you come by this spot, thought it was a hundred years hence, and you came with the gayest and the highest in the land, I would step aside and remember a bit prayer.'

My lord bowed his head gravely. 'Ah!' says he, 'Mackellar is always in the right. Come, Alexander, take your bonnet off.' And with that he uncovered, and held out his hand. 'O Lord,' says he, 'I thank Thee, and my son thanks Thee, for Thy manifold great mercies. Let us have peace for a little; defend us from the evil man. Smite him, O Lord, upon the lying mouth!' The last broke out of him like a cry; and at that, whether remembered anger choked his utterance, or whether he perceived this was a singular sort of prayer, at least he suddenly came to a full stop; and, after a moment, set back his hat upon his head.

'I think you have forgot a word, my lord,' said I. ' "Forgive us our trespasses, as we forgive them that trespass against us. For thine is the kingdom, and the power, and the glory, for ever and ever. Amen." '

'Ah! that is easy saying,' said my lord. 'That is very easy saying, Mackellar. But for me to forgive! – I think I would cut a very silly figure if I had the affectation to pretend it.'

'The bairn, my lord!' said I, with some severity, for I thought his expressions little fitted for the ears of children.

'Why, very true,' said he. 'This is dull work for a bairn. Let's go nesting.'

I forget if it was the same day, but it was soon after, my lord, finding me alone, opened himself a little more on the same head.

'Mackellar,' he said, 'I am now a very happy man.'

'I think so indeed, my lord,' said I, 'and the sight of it gives me a light heart.'

'There is an obligation in happiness – do you not think so?' says he, musingly.

'I think so indeed,' says I, 'and one in sorrow, too. If we are not here to try to do the best, in my humble opinion the sooner we are away the better for all parties.'

'Ay, but if you were in my shoes, would you forgive him?' asks my lord.

The suddenness of the attack a little gravelled me. 'It is a duty laid upon us strictly,' said I.

'Hut!' said he. 'These are expressions! Do you forgive the man yourself?'

'Well – no!' said I. 'God forgive me, I do not.'

'Shake hands upon that!' cries my lord, with a kind of joviality.

'It is an ill sentiment to shake hands upon,' said I, 'for Christian people. I think I will give you mine on some more evangelical occasion.'

This I said, smiling a little; but as for my lord, he went from the room laughing aloud.

For my lord's slavery to the child, I can find no expression adequate. He lost himself in that continual thought: business, friends, and wife being all alike forgotten, or only remembered with a painful effort, like that of one struggling with a posset. It was most notable in the matter of his wife. Since I had known Durrisdeer, she had been the burthen of his thought and the loadstone of his eyes; and now she was quite cast out. I have seen him come to the door of a room, look round, and pass my lady over as though she were a dog before the fire. It would be Alexander he was seeking, and my lady knew it well. I have heard him speak to her so ruggedly that I nearly found it in my heart to intervene: the cause would still be the same, that she had in some way thwarted Alexander. Without doubt this was in the nature of a judgment upon my lady. Without doubt she had the tables turned upon her, as only Providence can do it; she who had been cold so many years to every mark of tenderness, it was her part now to be neglected.

An odd situation resulted: that we had once more two parties in the house, and that now I was of my lady's. Not that ever I lost the love I bore my master. But, for one thing, he had the less use for my society. For another, I could not but compare the case of Mr Alexander with that of Miss Katharine; for whom my lord had never found the least attention. And for a third, I was wounded by the change he discovered to his wife, which struck me in the nature of an infidelity. I could not but admire, besides, the constancy and kindness she displayed. Perhaps her sentiment to my lord, as it had been founded from the first in pity, was that rather of a mother than of a wife; perhaps it pleased her – if I may so say – to behold her two children so happy in each other; the more as one had suffered so unjustly in the past. But for all that, and though I could never trace in her one spark of jealousy, she must fall back for society on poor neglected Miss Katharine; and I, on my part, came to pass my spare hours more and more with the mother and daughter. It would be easy to make too much of this division, for it was a pleasant family, as families go; still the thing existed; whether my lord knew it or not, I am in doubt. I do not think he did; he was bound up so entirely in his son; but the rest of us knew it, and in a manner suffered from the knowledge.

What troubled us most, however, was the great and growing danger to the child. My lord was his father over again; it was to be feared the son would prove a second Master. Time has proved these fears to have been quite exaggerate. Certainly there is no more worthy gentleman today in Scotland than the seventh Lord Durrisdeer. Of my own exodus from his employment it does not become me to speak, above all in a memorandum written only to justify his father. . . .

[Editor's Note. Five pages of Mr Mackellar's MS are here omitted. I have gathered from their perusal an impression that Mr Mackellar, in his old age, was rather an exacting servant. Against the seventh Lord Durrisdeer (with whom, at any rate, we have no concern) nothing material is alleged. – R. L. S.]

. . . But our fear at the time was lest he should turn out, in the person of his son, a second edition of his brother. My lady had tried to interject some wholesome discipline; she had been glad to give that up, and now looked on with secret dismay; sometimes she even spoke of it by hints; and sometimes, when there was brought to her knowledge some monstrous instance of my lord's indulgence, she would betray herself in a gesture or perhaps an exclamation. As for myself, I was haunted by the thought both day and night: not so much for the child's sake as for the father's. The man had gone to sleep, he was dreaming a dream, and any rough wakening must infallibly prove mortal. That he should survive the child's death was inconceivable; and the fear of its dishonour made me cover my face.

It was this continual preoccupation that screwed me up at last to a remonstrance; a matter worthy to be narrated in detail. My lord and I sat one day at the same table upon some tedious business of detail; I have said that he had lost his former interest in such occupations; he was plainly itching to be gone, and he looked fretful, weary, and methought older than I had ever previously observed. I suppose it was the haggard face that put me suddenly upon my enterprise.

'My lord,' said I, with my head down, and feigning to continue my occupation – 'or, rather, let me call you again by the name of Mr Henry, for I fear your anger and want you to think upon old times—'

'My good Mackellar!' said he; and that in tones so kindly that I had near forsook my purpose. But I called to mind that I was speaking for his good, and stuck to my colours.

'Has it never come in upon your mind what you are doing?' I asked.

'What I am doing?' he repeated. 'I was never good at guessing riddles.'

'What you are doing with your son?' said I.

'Well,' said he, with some defiance in his tone, 'and what am I doing with my son?'

'Your father was a very good man,' says I, straying from the direct path. 'But do you think he was a wise father?'

There was a pause before he spoke, and then: 'I say nothing against him,' he replied. 'I had the most cause perhaps; but I say nothing.'

'Why, there it is,' said I. 'You had the cause at least. And yet your father was a good man; I never knew a better, save on the one point, nor yet a wiser. Where he stumbled, it is highly possible another man should fall. He had the two sons—'

My lord rapped suddenly and violently on the table.

'What is this?' cried he. 'Speak out!'

'I will, then,' said I, my voice almost strangled with the thumping of my heart. 'If you continue to indulge Mr Alexander, you are following in your father's footsteps. Beware, my lord, lest (when he grows up) your son should follow in the Master's.'

I had never meant to put the thing so crudely; but in the extreme of fear there comes a brutal kind of courage, the most brutal indeed of all; and I burnt my ships with that plain word. I never had the answer. When I lifted my head, my lord had risen to his feet, and the next moment he fell heavily on the floor. The fit or seizure endured not very long; he came to himself vacantly, put his hand to his head, which I was then supporting, and says he, in a broken voice: 'I have been ill,' and a little after: 'Help me.' I got him to his feet, and he stood pretty well, though he kept hold of the table. 'I have been ill, Mackellar,' he said again. 'Something broke, Mackellar – or was going to break, and then all swam away. I think I was very angry. Never mind, Mackellar; never you mind, my man. I wouldnae hurt a hair upon your head. Too much has come and gone. It's a certain thing between us two. But I think, Mackellar, I will go to Mrs Henry – I think I will go to Mrs Henry.' said he, and got pretty steadily from the room, leaving me overcome with penitence.

Presently the door flew open, and my lady swept in with flashing eyes. 'What is all this?' she cried. 'What have you done to my husband? Will nothing teach you your position in this house? Will you never cease from making and meddling?'

'My lady,' said I, 'since I have been in this house I have had plenty of hard words. For a while they were my daily diet, and I swallowed them all. As for today, you may call me what you please; you will never find the name hard enough for such a blunder. And yet I meant it for the best.'

I told her all with ingenuity, even as it is written here; and when she had heard me out she pondered, and I could see her animosity fall. 'Yes,' she said, 'you meant well indeed. I have had the same thought myself, or the same temptation rather, which makes me pardon you. But, dear God, can you not understand that he can bear no more? He can bear no more!' she cried. 'The cord is stretched to snapping. What matters the future if he have one or two good days?'

'Amen,' said I. 'I will meddle no more. I am pleased enough that you should recognize the kindness of my meaning.'

'Yes,' said my lady; 'but when it came to the point, I have to suppose your courage failed you; for what you said was said cruelly.' She paused, looking at me; then suddenly smiled a little and said a singular thing: 'Do you know what you are, Mr Mackellar? You are an old maid.'

No more incident of any note occurred in the family until the return of that ill-starred man the Master. But I have to place here a second extract from the memoirs of Chevalier Burke, interesting in itself, and highly necessary for my purpose. It is our only sight of the Master on his Indian travels; and the first word in these pages of Secundra Dass. One fact, it is to observe, appears here very clearly, which if we had known some twenty years ago, how many calamities and sorrows had been spared! – that Secundra Dass spoke English.

SEVEN

Adventure of Chevalier Burke in
 India Extracted from his Memoirs

... HERE WAS I, THEREFORE, on the street of that city, the name of which I cannot call to mind, while even then I was so ill-acquainted with its situation that I knew not whether to go south or north. The alert being sudden, I had run forth without shoes or stockings; my hat had been struck from my head in the mellay; my kit was in the hands of the English; I had no companion but the cipaye, no weapon but my sword, and the devil a coin in my pocket. In short, I was for all the world like one of those calendars with whom Mr Galland has made us acquainted in his elegant tales. These gentlemen, you will remember, were for ever falling in with extraordinary incidents; and I was myself upon the brink of one so astonishing that I protest I cannot explain it to this day.

The cipaye was a very honest man; he had served many years with the French colours, and would have let himself be cut to pieces for any of the brave countrymen of Mr Lally. It is the same fellow (his name has quite escaped me) of whom I have narrated already a surprising instance of generosity of mind – when he found Mr de Fessac and myself upon the ramparts, entirely overcome with liquor, and covered us with straw while the commandant was passing by. I consulted him, therefore, with perfect freedom. It was a fine question what to do; but we decided at last to escalade a garden wall, where we could certainly sleep in the shadow of the trees, and might perhaps find an occasion to get hold of a pair of slippers and a turban. In that part of the city we had only the difficulty of the choice, for it was a quarter consisting entirely of walled gardens, and the lanes which divided them were at that hour of the night deserted. I gave the cipaye a back, and we had soon dropped into a large enclosure full of trees. The place was soaking with dew, which, in that country is exceedingly unwholesome, above all to whites; yet my fatigue was so extreme that I was already half asleep, when the cipaye recalled me to my senses. In the far end of the enclosure a bright light had suddenly shone out, and continued to burn steadily among the leaves. It was a circumstance highly unusual in such a place and hour;

and, in our situation, it behoved us to proceed with some timidity. The cipaye was sent to reconnoitre, and pretty soon returned with the intelligence that we had fallen extremely amiss, for the house belonged to a white man, who was in all likelihood English.

'Faith,' says I, 'if there is a white man to be seen, I will have a look at him; for, the Lord be praised! there are more sorts than the one!'

The cipaye led me forward accordingly to a place from which I had a clear view upon the house. It was surrounded with a wide verandah; a lamp, very well trimmed, stood upon the floor of it, and on either side of the lamp there sat a man, crosslegged, after the Oriental manner. Both, besides, were bundled up in muslin like two natives; and yet one of them was not only a white man, but a man very well known to me and the reader, being indeed that very Master of Ballantrae of whose gallantry and genius I have had to speak so often. Word had reached me that he was come to the Indies, though we had never met at least, and I head little of his occupations. But, sure, I had no sooner recognized him, and found myself in the arms of so old a comrade, than I supposed my tribulations were quite done. I stepped plainly forth into the light of the moon, which shone exceeding strong, and hailing Ballantrae by name, made him in a few words master of my grievous situation. He turned, started the least thing in the world, looked me fair in the face while I was speaking, and when I had done addressed himself to his companion in the barbarous native dialect. The second person, who was of an extraordinary delicate appearance, with legs like walking canes and fingers like the stalk of a tobacco pipe,* now rose to his feet.

'The Sahib,' says he, 'understands no English language. I understand it myself, and I see you make some small mistake – oh! which may happen very often. But the Sahib would be glad to know how you come in a garden.'

'Ballantrae!' I cried, 'have you the damned impudence to deny me to my face.'

Ballantrae never moved a muscle, staring at me like an image in a pagoda.

'The Sahib understands no English language,' says the native, as glib as before. 'He be glad to know how you come in a garden.'

'Oh! the divil fetch him,' says I. 'He would be glad to know how I come in a garden, would he? Well, now, my dear man, just have the civility to tell the Sahib, with my kind love, that we are two soldiers here whom he never met and never heard of, but the cipaye is a broth of a boy, and I am a broth of a boy myself; and if we don't get a full meal of

*'Note by Mr Mackellar. – Plainly Secundra Dass. – E. McK.

277

meat, and a turban, and slippers, and the value of a gold mohur in small change as a matter of convenience, bedad, my friend, I could lay my finger on a garden where there is going to be trouble.'

They carried their comedy so far as to converse awhile in Hindustanee; and then says the Hindu, with the same smile, but sighing as if he were tired of the repetition, 'The Sahib would be glad to know how you come in a garden.'

'Is that the way of it?' says I, and laying my hand on my sword-hilt I bade the cipaye draw.

Ballantrae's Hindu, still smiling, pulled out a pistol from his bosom, and though Ballantrae himself never moved a muscle I knew him well enough to be sure he was prepared.

'The Sahib thinks you better go away,' says the Hindu.

Well, to be plain, it was what I was thinking myself; for the report of a pistol would have, under Providence, the means of hanging the pair of us.

'Tell the Sahib I consider him no gentleman,' says I, and turned away with a gesture of contempt.

I was not gone three steps when the voice of the Hindu called me back. 'The Sahib would be glad to know if you are a dam low Irishman,' says he; and at the words Ballantrae smiled and bowed very low.

'What is that?' says I.

'The Sahib say you ask your friend Mackellar,' says the Hindu. 'The Sahib he cry quits.'

'Tell the Sahib I will give him a cure for the Scots fiddle when next we meet,' cried I.

The pair were still smiling as I left.

There is little doubt some flaws may be picked in my own behaviour; and when a man, however gallant, appeals to posterity with an account of his exploits, he must almost certainly expect to share the fate of Caesar and Alexander, and to meet with some detractors. But there is one thing that can never be laid at the door of Francis Burke: he never turned his back on a friend. . . .

(Here follows a passage which the Chevalier Burke has been at the pains to delete before sending me his manuscript. Doubtless it was some very natural complaint of what he supposed to be an indiscretion on my part; though, indeed, I can call none to mind. Perhaps Mr Henry was less guarded; or it is just possible the Master found the means to examine my correspondence, and himself read the letter from Troyes: in revenge for which this cruel jest was perpetrated on Mr Burke in his extreme necessity. The Master, for all his wickedness, was not without some natural affection; I believe he was sincerely attached to Mr Burke in the beginning; but the thought of treachery dried up the springs of his very shallow friendship, and his detestable nature appeared naked. – E. McK.)

EIGHT

❖ The Enemy in the House ❖

IT IS A STRANGE THING THAT I should be at a stick for a date – the date, besides, of an incident that changed the very nature of my life, and sent us all into foreign lands. But the truth is, I was stricken out of all my habitudes, and find my journals very ill redd-up,* the day not indicated sometimes for a week or two together, and the whole fashion of the thing like that of a man near desperate. It was late in March at least, or early in April, 1764. I had slept heavily, and awakened with a premonition of some evil to befall. So strong was this upon my spirit that I hurried downstairs in my shirt and breeches, and my hand (I remember) shook upon the rail. It was a cold, sunny morning, with a thick white frost; the blackbirds sang exceeding sweet and loud about the house of Durrisdeer, and there was a noise of the sea in all the chambers. As I came by the doors of the hall, another sound arrested me – of voices talking. I drew nearer, and stood like a man dreaming. Here was certainly a human voice, and that in my own master's house, and yet I knew it not; certainly human speech, and that in my native land; and yet, listen as I pleased, I could not catch one syllable. An old tale started up in my mind of a fairy wife (or perhaps only a wandering stranger), that came to the place of my fathers some generations back, and stayed the matter of a week, talking often in a tongue that signified nothing to the hearers; and went again, as she had come, under cloud of night, leaving not so much as a name behind her. A little fear I had but more curiosity; and I opened the hall-door and entered.

The supper-things still lay upon the table; the shutters were still closed, although day peeped in the divisions; and the great room was lighted only with a single taper and the shining of the fire. Close in the chimney sat two men. The one that was wrapped in a cloak and wore boots, I knew at once: it was the bird of ill-omen back again. Of the other, who

*Ordered.

was set close to the red embers, and made up into a bundle like a mummy, I could but see that he was an alien, of a darker hue than any man of Europe, very frailly built, with a singular tall forehead, and a secret eye. Several bundles and a small valise were on the floor; and to judge by the smallness of this luggage, and by the condition of the Master's boots, grossly patched by some unscrupulous country cobbler, evil had not prospered.

He rose upon my entrance; our eyes crossed; and I know not why it should have been, but my courage rose like a lark on a May morning.

'Ha!' said I, 'is this you?' – and I was pleased with the unconcern of my own voice.

'It is even myself, worthy Mackellar,' says the Master.

'This time you have brought the black dog visibly upon your back,' I continued.

'Referring to Secundra Dass?' asked the Master. 'Let me present you. He is a native gentleman of India.'

'Hum!' said I. 'I am no great lover of you or your friends, Mr Bally. But I will let a little daylight in, and have a look at you.' And so saying, I undid the shutters of the eastern window.

By the light of the morning I could perceive the man was changed. Later, when we were all together, I was more struck to see how lightly time had dealt with him; but the first glance was otherwise.

'You are getting an old man,' said I.

A shade came upon his face. 'If you could see yourself,' said he, 'you would perhaps not dwell upon the topic.'

'Hut!' I returned, 'old age is nothing to me. I think I have been always old; and I am now, I thank God, better known and more respected. It is not everyone that can say that, Mr Bally! The lines in *your* brow are calamities: your life begins to close in upon you like a prison; death will soon be rapping at the door: and I see not from what source you are to draw your consolations.'

Here the Master addressed himself to Secundra Dass in Hindustanee, from which I gathered (I freely confess, with a high degree of pleasure) that my remarks annoyed him. All this while, you may be sure, my mind had been busy upon other matters, even while I rallied my enemy; and chiefly as to how I should communicate secretly and quickly with my lord. To this, in the breathing-space now given me, I turned all the forces of my mind; when, suddenly shifting my eyes, I was aware of the man himself standing in the doorway, and, to all appearance, quite composed. He had no sooner met my looks than he stepped across the threshold. The Master heard him coming, and advanced upon the other side; about four feet apart, these brothers came to a full pause, and stood exchanging steady looks, and then my lord smiled, bowed a little forward, and turned briskly away.

'Mackellar,' says he, 'we must see to breakfast for these travellers.'

It was plain the Master was a trifle disconcerted; but he assumed the more impudence of speech and manner. 'I am as hungry as a hawk,' says he. 'Let it be something good, Henry.'

My lord turned to him with the same hard smile. 'Lord Durrisdeer,' says he.

'Oh! never in the family,' returned the Master.

'Everyone in this house renders me my proper title,' says my lord. 'If it please you to make an exception, I will leave you to consider what appearance it will bear to strangers, and whether it may not be translated as an effect of impotent jealousy.'

I could have clapped my hands together with delight: the more so as my lord left no time for any answer, but bidding me with a sign to follow him, went straight out of the hall.

'Come quick,' says he; 'we have to sweep vermin from the house.' And he sped through the passages, with so swift a step that I could scarce keep up with him, straight to the door of John Paul, the which he opened without summons and walked in. John was, to all appearance, sound asleep, but my lord made no pretence of waking him.

'John Paul,' said he, speaking as quietly as ever I heard him, 'you served my father long, or I would pack you from the house like a dog. If in half an hour's time I find you gone, you shall continue to receive your wages in Edinburgh. If you linger here or in St Bride's – old man, old servant, and altogether – I shall find some very astonishing way to make you smart for your disloyalty. Up and begone. The door you let them in by will serve for your departure. I do not choose my son shall see your face again.'

'I am rejoiced to find you bear the thing so quietly,' said I, when we were forth again by ourselves.

'Quietly?' cries he, and put my hand suddenly against his heart, which struck upon his bosom like a sledge.

At this revelation I was filled with wonder and fear. There was no constitution could bear so violent a strain – his least of all, that was unhinged already; and I decided in my mind that we must bring this monstrous situation to an end.

'It would be well, I think, if I took word to my lady,' said I. Indeed, he should have gone himself, but I counted – not in vain – on his indifference.

'Ay,' says he, 'do. I will hurry breakfast: we must all appear at the table, even Alexander; it must appear we are untroubled.'

I ran to my lady's room, and with no preparatory cruelty disclosed my news.

'My mind was long ago made up,' said she. 'We must make our packets secretly today, and leave secretly tonight. Thank heaven, we have another house! The first ship that sails shall bear us to New York.'

'And what of him?' I asked.

'We leave him Durrisdeer,' she cried. 'Let him work his pleasure upon that.'

'Not so, by your leave,' said I. 'There shall be a dog at his heels that can hold fast. Bed he shall have, and board, and a horse to ride upon, if he behave himself; but the keys – if you think well of it, my lady – shall be left in the hands of one Mackellar. There will be good care taken; trust him for that.'

'Mr Mackellar,' she cried, 'I thank you for that thought. All shall be left in your hands. If we must go into a savage country, I bequeath it to you to take our vengeance. Send Macconochie to St Bride's to arrange privately for horses and to call the lawyer. My lord must leave procuration.'

At that moment my lord came to the door, and we opened our plan to him.

'I will never hear of it,' he cried; 'he would think I feared him. I will stay in my own house, please God, until I die. There lives not the man can beard me out of it. Once and for all, here I am, and here I stay, in spite of all the devils in hell.' I can give no idea of the vehemency of his words and utterance; but we both stood aghast, and I in particular, who had been a witness of his former self-restraint.

My lady looked at me with an appeal that went to my heart and recalled me to my wits. I made her a private sign to go, and when my lord and I were alone, went up to him where he was racing to and fro in one end of the room like a half-lunatic, and set my hand firmly on his shoulder.

'My lord,' says I, 'I am going to be the plain-dealer once more; if for the last time, so much the better, for I am grown weary of the part.'

'Nothing will change me,' he answered. 'God forbid I should refuse to hear you; but nothing will change me.' This he said firmly, with no signal of the former violence, which already raised my hopes.

'Very well,' said I. 'I can afford to waste my breath.' I pointed to a chair, and he sat down and looked at me. 'I can remember a time when my lady very much neglected you,' said I.

'I never spoke of it while it lasted,' returned my lord, with a high flush of colour; 'and it is all changed now.'

'Do you know how much?' I said. 'Do you know how much it is all changed? The tables are turned, my lord! It is my lady that now courts you for a word, a look – ay, and courts you in vain. Do you know with whom she passes her days while you are out gallivanting in the policies? My lord, she is glad to pass them with a certain dry old grieve* of the name of Ephraim Mackellar; and I think you may be able to remember what that means, for I am the more in a mistake or you were once driven to the same company yourself.'

'Mackellar!' cried my lord, getting to his feet. 'O my God, Mackellar!'

'It is neither the name of Mackellar nor the name of God that can change the truth,' said I; 'and I am telling you the fact. Now for you, that suffered so much, to deal out the same suffering to another, is that the part of any Christian? But you are so swallowed up in your new friend that the old are all forgotten. They are all clean vanished from your memory. And yet they stood by you at the darkest; my lady not the least. And does my lady ever cross your mind? Does it ever cross your mind what she went through that night? – or what manner of a wife she has been to you thenceforward? – or in what kind of a position she finds herself today? Never. It is your pride to stay and face him out, and she must stay along with you. Oh! my lord's pride – that's the great affair! And yet she is the woman, and you are a great hulking man! She is the woman that you swore to protect; and, more betoken, the own mother of that son of yours!'

'You are speaking very bitterly, Mackellar,' said he; 'but, the Lord knows, I fear you are speaking very true. I have not proved worthy of my happiness. Bring my lady back.'

My lady was waiting near at hand to learn the issue. When I brought her in, my lord took a hand of each of us, and laid them both upon his bosom. 'I have had two friends in my life,' said he. 'All the comfort ever I had, it came from one or other. When you two are in a mind, I think I would be an ungrateful dog—' He shut his mouth very hard, and looked on us with swimming eyes. 'Do what ye like with me,' says he, 'only don't think—' He stopped again. 'Do what ye please with me: God knows I love and honour you.' And dropping our two hands, he turned his back and went and gazed out of the window. But my lady ran after, calling his name, and threw herself upon his neck in a passion of weeping.

I went out and shut the door behind me, and stood and thanked God from the bottom of my heart.

At the breakfast board, according to my lord's design, we were all met.

*Land steward.

The Master had by that time plucked off his patched boots and made a toilet suitable to the hour; Secundra Dass was no longer bundled up in wrappers, but wore a decent plain black suit, which misbecame him strangely; and the pair were at the great window, looking forth, when the family entered. They turned; and the black man (as they had already named him in the house) bowed almost to his knees, but the Master was for running forward like one of the family. My lady stopped him, curtseying low from the far end of the hall, and keeping her children at her back. My lord was a little in front: so there were the three cousins of Durrisdeer face to face. The hand of time was very legible on all; I seemed to read in their changed faces a *memento mori*; and what affected me still more, it was the wicked man that bore his years the handsomest. My lady was quite transfigured into the matron, a becoming woman for the head of a great tableful of children and dependants. My lord was grown slack in his limbs; he stooped; he walked with a running motion, as though he had learned again from Mr Alexander; his face was drawn; it seemed a trifle longer than of old; and it wore at times a smile very singularly mingled, and which (in my eyes) appeared both bitter and pathetic. But the Master still bore himself erect, although perhaps with effort; his brow barred about the centre with imperious lines, his mouth set as for command. He had all the gravity and something of the splendour of Satan in the *Paradise Lost*. I could not help but see the man with admiration, and was only surprised that I saw him with so little fear.

But indeed (as long as we were at the table) it seemed as if his authority were quite vanished and his teeth all drawn. We had known him a magician that controlled the elements; and here he was, transformed into an ordinary gentleman, chatting like his neighbours at the breakfast-board. For now the father was dead, and my lord and lady reconciled, in what ear was he to pour his calumnies? It came upon me in a kind of vision how hugely I had overrated the man's subtlety. He had his malice still; he was false as ever; and, the occasion being gone that made his strength, he sat there impotent; he was still the viper, but now spent his venom on a file. Two more thoughts occurred to me while yet we sat at breakfast: the first, that he was abashed – I had almost said, distressed – to find his wickedness quite unavailing; the second, that perhaps my lord was in the right, and we did amiss to fly from our dismasted enemy. But my poor master's leaping heart came in my mind, and I remembered it was for his life we played the coward.

When the meal was over, the Master followed me to my room, and, taking a chair (which I had never offered him), asked me what was to be done with him.

'Why, Mr Bally,' said I, 'the house will still be open to you for a time.'

'For a time?' says he. 'I do not know if I quite take your meaning.'

'It is plain enough,' said I. 'We keep you for our reputation; as soon as you shall have publicly disgraced yourself by some of your misconduct, we shall pack you forth again.'

'You are become an impudent rogue,' said the Master, bending his brows at me dangerously.

'I learned in a good school,' I returned. 'And you must have perceived yourself that with my old lord's death your power is quite departed. I do not fear you now, Mr Bally; I think even – God forgive me – that I take a certain pleasure in your company.'

He broke out in a burst of laughter, which I clearly saw to be assumed.

'I have come with empty pockets,' says he, after a pause.

'I do not think there will be any money going,' I replied. 'I would advise you not to build on that.'

'I shall have something to say on the point,' he returned.

'Indeed?' said I. 'I have not a guess what it will be, then.'

'Oh! you affect confidence,' said the Master. 'I have still one strong position – that you people fear a scandal, and I enjoy it.'

'Pardon me, Mr Bally,' says I. 'We do not in the least fear a scandal against you.'

He laughed again. 'You have been studying repartee,' he said. 'But speech is very easy, and sometimes very deceptive. I warn you fairly: you will find me vitriol in the house. You would do wiser to pay money down and see my back.' And with that he waved his hand to me and left the room.

A little after, my lord came with the lawyer, Mr Carlyle; a bottle of old wine was brought, and we all had a glass before we fell to business. The necessary deeds were then prepared and executed, and the Scottish estates made over in trust to Mr Carlyle and myself.

'There is one point, Mr Carlyle,' said my lord, when these affairs had been adjusted, 'on which I wish that you would do us justice. This sudden departure coinciding with my brother's return will be certainly commented on. I wish you would discourage any conjunction of the two.'

'I will make a point of it, my lord,' said Mr Carlyle. 'The Mas – Mr Bally does not, then, accompany you?'

'It is a point I must approach,' said my lord. 'Mr Bally remains at Durrisdeer, under the care of Mr Mackellar; and I do not mean that he shall even know our destination.'

'Common report, however—' began the lawyer.

'Ah! but, Mr Carlyle, this is to be a secret quite among ourselves,' interrupted my lord. 'None but you and Mackellar are to be made acquainted with my movements.'

'And Mr Bally stays here? Quite so,' said Mr Carlyle. 'The powers you leave—' Then he broke off again. 'Mr Mackellar, we have a rather heavy weight upon us.'

'No doubt, sir,' said I.

'No doubt,' said he. 'Mr Bally will have no voice?'

'He will have no voice,' said my lord; 'and I hope no influence. Mr Bally is not a good adviser.'

'I see,' said the lawyer. 'By the way, has Mr Bally means?'

'I understand him to have nothing,' replied my lord. 'I give him table, fire, and candle in this house.'

'And in the matter of an allowance? If I am to share the responsibility, you will see how highly desirable it is that I should understand your views,' said the lawyer. 'On the question of an allowance?'

'There will be no allowance,' said my lord. 'I wish Mr Bally to live very private. We have not always been gratified with his behaviour.'

'And in the matter of money,' I added, 'he has shown himself an infamous bad husband. Glance your eye upon that docket, Mr Carlyle, where I have brought together the different sums the man has drawn from the estate in the last fifteen or twenty years. The total is petty.'

Mr Carlyle made the motion of whistling. 'I had no guess of this,' said he. 'Excuse me once more, my lord, if I appear to push you; but it is really desirable that I should penetrate your intentions. Mr Mackellar might die, when I should find myself alone upon this trust. Would it not be rather your lordship's preference that Mr Bally should – ahem – should leave the country?'

My lord looked at Mr Carlyle. 'Why do you ask that?' said he.

'I gather, my lord, that Mr Bally is not a comfort to his family,' says the lawyer with a smile.

My lord's face became suddenly knotted. 'I wish he was in hell!' cried he, and filled himself a glass of wine, but with a hand so tottering that he spilled the half into his bosom. This was the second time that, in the midst of the most regular and wise behaviour, his animosity had spurted out. It startled Mr Carlyle, who observed my lord thenceforth with covert curiosity, and to me it restored the certainty that we were acting for the best in view of my lord's health and reason.

Except for this explosion the interview was very successfully conducted. No doubt Mr Carlyle would talk, as lawyers do, little by little. We could thus feel we had laid the foundations of a better feeling in the country, and the man's own misconduct would certainly complete what we had begun. Indeed, before his departure, the lawyer showed us there had already gone abroad some glimmerings of the truth.

'I should perhaps explain to you, my lord,' said he, pausing, with his hat in his hand, 'that I have not been altogether surprised with your lordship's dispositions in the case of Mr Bally. Something of this nature oozed out when he was last in Durrisdeer. There was some talk of a woman at St Bride's, to whom you had behaved extremely handsome, and Mr Bally with no small degree of cruelty. There was the entail, again, which was much controverted. In short, there was no want of talk, back and forward; and some of our wiseacres took up a strong opinion. I remained in suspense, as became one of my cloth; but Mr Mackellar's docket here has finally opened my eyes. I do not think, Mr Mackellar, that you and I will give him that much rope.'

The rest of that important day passed prosperously through. It was our policy to keep the enemy in view, and I took my turn to be his watchman with the rest. I think his spirits rose as he perceived us to be so attentive, and I know that mine insensibly declined. What chiefly daunted me was the man's singular dexterity to worm himself into our troubles. You may have felt (after a horse accident) the hand of a bone-setter artfully divide and interrogate the muscles, and settle strongly on the injured place? It was so with the Master's tongue, that was so cunning to question; and his eyes, that were so quick to observe. I seemed to have said nothing, and yet to have let all out. Before I knew where I was the man was condoling with me on my lord's neglect of my lady and myself, and his hurtful indulgence to his son. On this last point I perceived him (with panic fear) to return repeatedly. The boy had displayed a certain shrinking from his uncle; it was strong in my mind that his father had been fool enough to indoctrinate the same, which was no wise beginning: and when I looked upon the man before me, still so handsome, so apt a speaker, with so great a variety of fortunes to relate, I saw he was the very personage to captivate a boyish fancy. John Paul had left only that morning; it was not to be supposed he had been altogether dumb upon his favourite subject: so that here would be Mr Alexander in the part of Dido, with a curiosity inflamed to hear; and there would be the Master, like a diabolical Aeneas, full of matter the most pleasing in the world to any youthful ear, such as battles, sea-disasters, flights, the forests of the West, and (since his later voyage) the ancient cities of the Indies. How cunningly these baits might be employed, and what an empire might be so founded, little by little, in the mind of any boy, stood obviously clear to me. There was no inhibition, so long as the man was in the house, that would be strong enough to hold these two apart; for if it be hard to charm serpents, it is no very difficult thing to cast a glamour on a little chip of manhood not very long in breeches. I recalled an ancient sailor-man who dwelt in a lone house beyond the Figgate Whins (I believe he called it after Portobello), and how the boys would troop out of Leith on a Saturday, and sit and listen to his swearing tales, as thick as crows about a carrion: a think I often remarked as I went by, a young student, on my own more meditative holiday diversion. Many of these boys went, no doubt, in the face of an express command; many feared and even hated the old brute of whom they made their hero; and I have seen them flee from him when he was tipsy, and stone him when he was drunk. And yet there they came each Saturday! How much more easily would a boy like Mr Alexander fall under the influence of a high-looking, high-spoken gentleman-adventurer, who should conceive the fancy to entrap him; and the influence gained, how easy to employ it for the child's perversion!

I doubt if our enemy had named Mr Alexander three times before I perceived which way his mind was aiming – all this train of thought and memory passed in one pulsation through my own – and you may say I started back as though an open hole had gaped across a pathway. Mr Alexander: there was the weak point, there was the Eve in our perishable paradise; and the serpent was already hissing on the trail.

I promise you, I went the more heartily about the preparations; my last scruple gone, the danger of delay written before me in huge characters. From that moment forth I seem not to have sat down or breathed. Now I would be at my post with the Master and his Indian; now in the garret buckling a valise; now sending forth Macconochie by the side postern and the wood-path to bear it to the trysting-place; and, again, snatching some words of counsel with my lady. This was the *verso* of our life in Durrisdeer that day; but on the *recto* all appeared quite settled, as of a family at home in its paternal seat; and what perturbation may have been observable, the Master would set down to the blow of his unlooked-for coming, and the fear he was accustomed to inspire.

Supper went creditably off, cold salutations passed, and the company trooped to their respective chambers. I attended the Master to the last. We had put him next door to his Indian, in the north wing; because that was the most distant and could be severed from the body of the house with doors. I saw he was a kind friend or good master (whichever it was) to his Secundra Dass – seeing to his comfort; mending the fire with his own hand, for the Indian complained of cold; inquiring as to the rice on which the stranger made his diet; talking with him pleasantly in the Hindustanee, while I stood by, my candle in my hand, and affected to be overcome with slumber. At length the Master observed my signals of distress. 'I perceive,' says he, 'that you have all your ancient habits: early to bed and early to rise. Yawn yourself away!'

Once in my own room, I made the customary motions of undressing, so that I might time myself; and when the cycle was complete, set my tinder-box ready, and blew out my taper. The matter of an hour afterward I made a light again, put on my shoes of list that I had worn by my lord's sick-bed, and set forth into the house to call the voyagers. All were dressed and waiting – my lord, my lady, Miss Katharine, Mr Alexander, my lady's woman Christie; and I observed the effect of secrecy even upon quite innocent persons, that one after another showed in the chink of the door a face as white as paper. We slipped out of the side postern into a night of darkness, scarce broken by a star or two; so that at first we groped and stumbled and fell among the bushes. A few hundred yards up the wood-path Macconochie was waiting us with a great lantern; so the rest of the way we went easy enough, but still in a kind of guilty silence. A little beyond the abbey the path debouched on the main road; and some quarter of a mile farther, at the place called Eagles, where the moors begin, we saw the lights of the two carriages stand shining by the wayside. Scarce a word or two was uttered at our parting, and these regarded business: a silent grasping of hands, a turning of faces aside, and the thing was over; the horses broke into a trot, the lamplight sped like Will-o'-the-Wisp upon the broken moorland, it dipped beyond Stony Brae; and there were Macconochie and I alone with our lantern on the road. There was one thing more to wait for, and that was the reappearance of the coach upon Cartmore. It seems they must have pulled up upon the summit, looked back for a last time, and seen our lantern not yet moved away from the place of separation. For a lamp was taken from a carriage, and waved three times up and down by way of a farewell. And then they were gone indeed, having looked their last on the kind roof of Durrisdeer, their faces towards a barbarous country. I never knew before the greatness of that vault of night in which we two poor serving-men – the one old, and the one elderly – stood for the first time deserted; I had never felt before my own dependency upon the countenance of others. The sense of isolation burned in my bowels like a fire. It seemed that we who remained at home were the true exiles, and that Durrisdeer and Solwayside, and all that made my country native, its air good to me, and its language welcome, had gone forth and was for over the sea with my old masters.

The remainder of that night I paced to and fro on the smooth highway, reflecting on the future and the past. My thoughts, which at first dwelled tenderly on those who were just gone, took a more manly temper as I considered what remained for me to do. Day came upon the inland mountain-tops, and the fowls began to cry, and the smoke of homesteads to arise in the brown bosom of the moors, before I turned my face homeward, and went down the path to where the roof of Durrisdeer shone in the morning by the sea.

At the customary hour I had the Master called, and awaited his coming in the hall with a quiet mind. He looked about him at the empty room and the three covers set.

'We are a small party,' said he. 'How comes that?'

'This is the party to which we must grow accustomed,' I replied.

He looked at me with a sudden sharpness. 'What is all this?' said he.

'You and I and your friend Mr Dass are now all the company,' I replied. 'My lord, my lady, and the children, are gone upon a voyage.'

'Upon my word!' said he. 'Can this be possible? I have indeed fluttered your Volscians in Corioli! But this is no reason why our breakfast should go cold. Sit down, Mr Mackellar, if you please' – taking, as he spoke, the head of the table, which I had designed to occupy myself – 'and as we eat, you can give me the details of this evasion.'

I could see he was more affected than his language carried, and I determined to equal him in coolness. 'I was about to ask you to take the head of the table,' said I; 'for though I am now thrust into the position of your host, I could never forget that you were, after all, a member of the family.'

For a while he played the part of entertainer, giving directions to Macconochie, who received them with an evil grace, and attending specially upon Secundra. 'And where has my good family withdrawn to?' he asked carelessly.

'Ah! Mr Bally, that is another point,' said I. 'I have no orders to communicate their destination.'

'To me,' he corrected.

'To anyone,' said I.

'It is the less pointed,' said the Master; '*c'est de bon ton*: my brother improves as he continues. And I, my dear Mr Mackellar?'

'You will have bed and board, Mr Bally,' said I. 'I am permitted to give you the run of the cellar, which is pretty reasonably stocked. You have only to keep well with me, which is no very difficult matter, and you shall want neither for wine nor for a saddle-horse.'

He made an excuse to send Macconochie from the room.

'And for money?' he inquired. 'Have I to keep well with my good friend Mackellar for my pocket-money also? This is a pleasing return to the principles of boyhood.'

'There was no allowance made,' said I; 'but I will take it on myself to see you are supplied in moderation.'

'In moderation?' he repeated. 'And you will take it on yourself?' He drew himself up, and looked about the hall at the dark rows of portraits. 'In the name of my ancestors, I thank you,' says he; and then, with a return to irony, 'But there must certainly be an allowance for Secundra Dass?' he said. 'It is not possible they have omitted that?'

'I will make a note of it, and ask instructions when I write,' said I.

And he, with a sudden change of manner and leaning forward with an elbow on the table, 'Do you think this entirely wise?'

'I execute my orders, Mr Bally,' said I.

'Profoundly modest,' said the Master; 'perhaps not equally ingenuous. You told me yesterday my power was fallen with my father's death. How comes it, then, that a peer of the realm flees under cloud of night out of a house in which his fathers have stood several sieges? that he conceals his address, which must be a matter of concern to his Gracious Majesty and to the whole republic? and that he should leave me in possession and under the paternal charge of his invaluable Mackellar? This smacks to me of a very considerable and genuine apprehension.'

I sought to interrupt him with some not very truthful denegation; but he waved me down and pursued his speech.

'I say it smacks of it,' he said; 'but I will go beyond that, for I think the apprehension grounded. I came to this house with some reluctancy. In view of the manner of my last departure, nothing but necessity could have induced me to return. Money, however, is that which I must have. You will not give with a good grace; well, I have the power to force it from you. Inside of a week, without leaving Durrisdeer, I will find out where these fools are fled to. I will follow; and when I have run my quarry down, I will drive a wedge into that family that shall once more burst it into shivers. I shall see then whether my Lord Durrisdeer' (said with indescribable scorn and rage) 'will choose to buy my absence; and you will all see whether, by that time, I decide for profit or revenge.'

I was amazed to hear the man so open. The truth is, he was consumed with anger at my lord's successful flight, felt himself to figure as a dupe, and was in no humour to weigh language.

'Do you consider *this* entirely wise?' said I, copying his words.

'These twenty years I have lived by my poor wisdom,' he answered, with a smile that seemed almost foolish in its vanity.

'And come out a beggar in the end,' said I, 'if beggar be a strong enough word for it.'

'I would have you to observe, Mr Mackellar,' cried he, with a sudden imperious heat, in which I could not but admire him, 'that I am scrupulously civil: copy me in that, and we shall be the better friends.'

Throughout this dialogue I had been incommoded by the observation of Secundra Dass. Not one of us, since the first word, had made a feint of eating: our eyes were in each other's faces – you might say, in each other's bosoms; and those of the Indian troubled me with a certain changing brightness, as of comprehension. But I brushed the fancy aside, telling myself once more he understood no English; only, from the gravity of both voices, and the occasional scorn and anger in the Master's, smelled out there was something of import in the wind.

For the matter of three weeks we continued to live together in the house of Durrisdeer: the beginning of that most singular chapter of my life – what I must call my intimacy with the Master. At first he was somewhat changeable in his behaviour: now civil, now returning to his old manner of flouting me to my face; and in both I met him half-way. Thanks be to Providence, I had now no measure to keep with the man; and I was never afraid of black brows, only of naked swords. So that I found a certain entertainment in these bouts of incivility, and was not always ill-inspired in my rejoinders. At last (it was at supper) I had a droll expression that entirely vanquished him. He laughed again and again; and 'Who would have guessed,' he cried, 'that this old wife had any wit under his petticoats?'

'It is no wit, Mr Bally,' said I: 'a dry Scot's humour, and something of the driest.' And, indeed, I never had the least pretension to be thought a wit.

From that hour he was never rude with me, but all passed between us in a manner of pleasantry. One of our chief times of daffing* was when he required a horse, another bottle, or some money. He would approach me then after the manner of a schoolboy and I would carry it on by way of being his father: on both sides, with infinity of mirth. I could not but perceive that he thought more of me, which tickled that poor part of mankind, the vanity. He dropped, besides (I must suppose unconsciously), into a manner that was not only familiar, but even friendly; and this on the part of one who had so long detested me, I found the more insidious. He went little abroad; sometimes even refusing invitations. 'No,' he would say, 'what do I care for these thick-headed bonnet-lairds? I will stay at home, Mackellar; and we shall share a bottle quietly, and have one of our good talks.' And, indeed, meal-time at Durrisdeer must have been a delight to anyone, by reason of the brilliancy

*Fooling.

292

of the discourse. He would often express wonder at his former indifference to my society. 'But you see,' he would add, 'we were upon opposite sides. And so we are today; but let us never speak of that. I would think much less of you if you were not staunch to your employer.' You are to consider he seemed to me quite impotent for any evil; and how it is a most engaging form of flattery when (after many years) tardy justice is done to a man's character and parts. But I have no thought to excuse myself. I was to blame; I let him cajole me, and, in short, I think the watch-dog was going sound asleep, when he was suddenly aroused.

I should say the Indian was continually travelling to and fro in the house. He never spoke, save in his own dialect and with the Master; walked without sound; and was always turning up where you would least expect him, fallen into a deep abstraction, from which he would start (upon your coming) to mock you with one of his grovelling obeisances. He seemed so quiet, so frail, and so wrapped in his own fancies, that I came to pass him over without much regard, or even to pity him for a harmless exile from his country. And yet without doubt the creature was still eavesdropping; and without doubt it was through his stealth and my security that our secret reached the Master.

It was one very wild night, after supper, and when we had been making more than usually merry, that the blow fell on me.

'This is all very fine,' says the Master, 'but we should do better to be buckling our valise.'

'Why so?' I cried. 'Are you leaving?'

'We are all leaving tomorrow in the morning,' said he. 'For the port of Glasgow first, thence for the province of New York.'

I suppose I must have groaned aloud.

'Yes,' he continued, 'I boasted; I said a week, and it has taken me twenty days. But never mind; I shall make it up; I will go the faster.'

'Have you the money for this voyage?' I asked.

'Dear and ingenuous personage, I have,' said he. 'Blame me, if you choose, for my duplicity; but while I have been wringing shillings from my daddy, I had a stock of my own put by against a rainy day. You will pay for your own passage, if you choose to accompany us on our flank march; I have enough for Secundra and myself, but not more – enough to be dangerous, not enough to be generous. There is, however, an outside seat upon the chaise which I will let you have upon a moderate commutation; so that the whole menagerie can go together – the house-dog, the monkey, and the tiger.'

'I go with you,' said I.

'I count upon it,' said the Master. 'You have seen me foiled; I mean you shall see me victorious. To gain that I will risk wetting you like a sop in this wild weather.'

'And at least,' I added, 'you know very well you could not throw me off.'

'Not easily,' said he. 'You put your finger on the point with your usual excellent good sense. I never fight with the inevitable.'

'I suppose it is useless to appeal to you?' said I.

'Believe me, perfectly,' said he.

'And yet, if you would give me time, I could write—' I began.

'And what would be my Lord Durrisdeer's answer?' asks he.

'Ay,' said I, 'That is the rub.'

'And, at any rate, how much more expeditions that I should go myself!' says he. 'But all this is quite a waste of breath. At seven tomorrow the chaise will be at the door. For I start from the door, Mackellar; I do not skulk through woods and take my chaise upon the wayside – shall we say, at Eagles?'

My mind was now thoroughly made up. 'Can you spare me a quarter of an hour at St Brides?' said I. 'I have a little necessary business with Carlyle.'

'An hour, if you prefer,' said he. 'I do not seek to deny that the money for your seat is an object to me; and you could always get the first to Glasgow with saddle-horses.'

'Well,' said I, 'I never thought to leave old Scotland.'

'It will brisken you up,' says he.

'This will be an ill journey for someone,' I said. 'I think, sir, for you. Something speaks in my bosom; and so much it says plain – that this is an ill-omened journey.'

'If you take to prophecy,' says he, 'listen to that.'

There came up a violent squall off the open Solway, and the rain was dashed on the great windows.

'Do you ken what that bodes, warlock?' said he, in a broad accent: 'that there'll be a man Mackellar unco' sick at sea.'

When I got to my chamber, I sat there under a painful excitation, hearkening to the turmoil of the gale, which struck full upon that gable of the house. What with the pressure on my spiritis, the eldritch cries of the wind among the turret-tops, and the perpetual trepidation of the masoned house, sleep fled my eyelids utterly. I sat by my taper, looking on the black panes of the window, where the storm appeared continually on the point of bursting in its entrance; and upon that empty field I beheld a perspective of consequences that made the hair to rise upon my scalp. The child corrupted, the home broken up, my master dead or worse than dead, my mistress plunged in desolation – all these I saw before me painted brightly on the darkness; and the outcry of the wind appeared to knock at my inaction.

NINE

Mr Mackellar's Journey with the Master

THE CHAISE CAME TO THE DOOR in a strong drenching mist. We took our leave in silence: the house of Durrisdeer standing with dropping gutters and windows closed, like a place dedicated to melancholy. I observed the Master kept his head out, looking back on these splashed walls and glimmering roofs, till they were suddenly swallowed in the mist; and I must suppose some natural sadness fell upon the man at this departure; or was it some pre-vision of the end? At least, upon our mounting the long brae from Durrisdeer, as we walked side by side in the wet, he began first to whistle and then to sing the saddest of our country tunes, which sets folk weeping in a tavern, *Wandering Willie*. The set of words he used with it I have not heard elsewhere, and could never come by any copy; but some of them which were the most appropriate to our departure linger in my memory. One verse began.

> Home was home then, my dear, full of kindly faces;
> Home was home then, my dear, happy for the child.

And ended somewhat thus:

> Now, when day dawns on the brow of the moorland,
> Lone stands the house, and the chimney-stone is cold.
> Lone let it stand, now the folks are all departed,
> The kind hearts, the true hearts, that loved the place of old.

I could never be a judge of the merit of these verses; they were so hallowed by the melancholy of the air, and were sung (or rather 'soothed') to me by a master-singer at a time so fitting. He looked in my face when he had done, and saw that my eyes watered.

'Ah! Mackellar,' said he, 'do you think I have never a regret?'

'I do not think you could be so bad a man,' said I, 'if you had not all the machinery to be a good one.'

'No, not all,' says he: 'not all. You are there in error. The malady of not wanting, my evangelist.' But methought he sighed as he mounted again into the chaise.

All day long we journeyed in the same miserable weather: the mist besetting us closely, the heavens incessantly weeping on my head. The road lay over moorish hills, where was no sound but the crying of moorfowl in the wet weather and the pouring of the swollen burns. Sometimes I would doze off in slumber, when I would find myself plunged at once in some foul and ominous nightmare, from the which I would awake strangling. Sometimes, if the way was steep and the wheels turning slowly, I would overhear the voices from within, talking in that tropical tongue which was to me as inarticulate as the piping of the fowls. Sometimes, at a longer ascent, the Master would set foot to ground and walk by my side, mostly without speech. And all the time, sleeping or waking, I beheld the same black perspective of approaching ruin; and the same pictures rose in my view, only they were now painted upon hillside mist. One, I remember, stood before me with the colours of a true illusion. It showed me my lord seated at a table in a small room; his head, which was at first buried in his hands, he slowly raised, and turned upon me a countenance from which hope had fled. I saw it first on the black window-panes, my last night in Durrisdeer; it haunted and returned upon me half the voyage through; and yet it was no effect of lunacy, for I have come to a ripe old age with no decay of my intelligence; nor yet (as I was then tempted to suppose) a heaven-sent warning of the future, for all manner of calamities befell, not that calamity – and I saw many pitiful sights, but never that one.

It was decided we should travel on all night; and it was singular, once the dusk had fallen, my spirits somewhat rose. The bright lamps, shining forth into the mist and on the smoking horses and the hodding post-boy, gave me perhaps an outlook intrinsically more cheerful than what day had shown; or perhaps my mind had become wearied of its melancholy. At least, I spent some waking hours, not without satisfaction in my thoughts, although wet and weary in my body; and fell at last into a natural slumber without dreams. Yet I must have been at work even in the deepest of my sleep; and at work with at least a measure of intelligence. For I started broad awake, in the very act of crying out to myself:

HOME WAS HOME THEN, MY DEAR, HAPPY FOR THE CHILD,

stricken to find in it an appropriateness, which I had not yesterday observed, to the Master's detestable purpose in the present journey.

We were then close upon the city of Glasgow, where we were soon breakfasting together at an inn, and where (as the devil would have it) we found a ship in the very article of sailing. We took our places in the cabin; and, two days after, carried our effects on board. Her name was the *Nonesuch*, a very ancient ship and very happily named. By all accounts this should be her last voyage; people shook their heads upon the quays, and I had several warnings offered me by strangers in the street to the effect that she was rotten as a cheese, too deeply loaden, and must infallibly founder if we met a gale. From this it fell out we were the only passengers; the Captain, McMurtrie, was a silent, absorbed man, with the Glasgow or Gaelic accent; the mates ignorant rough seafarers, come in through the hawsehole; and the Master and I were cast upon each other's company.

The *Nonesuch* carried a fair wind out of the Clyde, and for near upon a week we enjoyed bright weather and a sense of progress. I found myself (to my wonder) a born seaman, in so far at least as I was never sick; yet I was far from tasting the usual serenity of my health. Whether it was the motion of the ship on the billows, the confinement, the salted food, or all of these together, I suffered from a blackness of spirit and a painful strain upon my temper. The nature of my errand on that ship perhaps contributed; I think it did no more; the malady (whatever it was) sprang from my environment; and if the ship were not to blame, then it was the Master. Hatred and fear are ill bedfellows; but (to my shame be it spoken) I have tasted those in other places, lain down and got up with them, and eaten and drunk with them, and yet never before, nor after, have I been so poisoned through and through, in soul and body, as I was on board the *Nonesuch*. I freely confess my enemy set me a fair example of forbearance; in our worst days displayed the most patient geniality, holding me in conversation as long as I would suffer, and when I had rebuffed his civility, stretching himself on deck to read. The book he had on board with him was Mr Richardson's famous *Clarissa*; and among other small attentions he would read me passages aloud; nor could any elocutionist have given with greater potency the pathetic portions of that work. I would retort upon him with passages out of the Bible, which was all my library – and very fresh to me, my religious duties (I grieve to say it) being always and even to this day extremely neglected. He tasted the merits of the work like the connoisseur he was; and would sometimes take it from my hand, turn the leaves over like a man that knew his way, and give me, with his fine declamation, a Roland for my Oliver. But it was singular how little he applied his reading to himself; it passed high above his head like summer thunder: Lovelace and Clarissa, the tales of David's generosity, the psalms of his penitence, the solemn questions of the Book of Job, the touching poetry of Isaiah – they were to him a source of entertainment only, like the scraping of a fiddle in a change-house. This outer sensibility and inner toughness set me against him; it seemed of a piece with that impudent grossness which I knew to underlie the veneer of his fine manners; and sometimes my gorge rose against him as though he were deformed – and sometimes I would draw away as though from something partly spectral. I had moments when I thought of him as of a man of pasteboard – as though, if one should strike smartly through the buckram of his countenance, there would be found a mere vacuity within. This horror (not merely fanciful, I think) vastly increased my detestation of his neighbourhood; I began to feel something shiver within me on his drawing near; I had at times a longing to cry out; there were days when I thought I could have struck him. This frame of mind was doubtless helped by shame, because I had dropped during our last days at Durrisdeer into a certain toleration of the man; and if anyone had then told me I should drop into it again, I must have laughed in his face. It is possible he remained unconscious of these extreme fever of my resentment; yet I think he was too quick; and rather that he had fallen, in a long life of idleness, into a positive need of company, which obliged him to confront and tolerate my unconcealed aversion. Certain, at least, that he loved the note of his own tongue, as, indeed, he entirely loved all the parts and properties of himself; a sort of imbecility which almost necessarily attends on wickedness. I have seen him driven, when I proved recalcitrant, to long discourses with the skipper; and this, although the man plainly testified his weariness, fiddling miserably with both hand and foot, and replying only with a grunt.

After the first week out we fell in with foul winds and heavy weather. The sea was high. The *Nonesuch*, being an old-fashioned ship and badly loaden, rolled beyond belief; so that the skipper trembled for his masts, and I for my life. We made no progress on our course. An unbearable ill-humour settled on the ship: men, mates, and master girding at one another all day long. A saucy word on the one hand, and a blow on the other, made a daily incident. There were times when the whole crew refused their duty; and we of the afterguard were twice got under arms – being the first time that ever I bore weapons – in the fear of mutiny.

In the midst of our evil season sprang up a hurricane of wind; so that all supposed she must go down. I was shut in the cabin from noon of one day till sundown of the next; the Master was somewhere lashed on deck. Secundra had eaten of some drug and lay insensible; so you may say I passed these hours in an unbroken solitude. At first I was terrified beyond motion, and almost beyond thought, my mind appearing to be frozen. Presently there stole in on me a ray of comfort. If the *Nonesuch* foundered, she would carry down with her into the deeps of that unsounded sea the creature whom we all so feared and hated; there would be no more Master of Ballantrae, the fish would sport among his ribs; his schemes all brought to nothing, his harmless enemies at peace. At first, I have said, it was but a ray of comfort; but it had soon grown to be broad sunshine. The thought of the man's death, of his deletion from this world, which he embittered for so many, took possession of my mind. I hugged it, I found it sweet in my belly. I conceived the ship's last plunge, the sea bursting upon all sides into the cabin, the brief mortal conflict there, all by myself, in that closed place; I numbered the horrors, I had almost said with satisfaction; I felt I could bear all and more, if the *Nonesuch* carried down with her, overtook by the same ruin, the enemy of my poor master's house. Towards noon of the second day the screaming of the wind abated; the ship lay not so perilously over, and it began to be clear to me that we were past the height of the tempest. As I hope for mercy, I was singly disappointed. In the selfishness of that vile, absorbing passion of hatred, I forgot the case of our innocent shipmates, and thought but of myself and my enemy. For myself, I was already old; I had never been young, I was not formed for the world's pleasures, I had few affections; it mattered not the toss of a silver tester whether I was drowned there and then in the Atlantic, or dribbled out a few more years, to die, perhaps no less terribly, in a deserted sick-bed. Down I went upon my knees – holding on by the locker, or else I had been instantly dashed across the tossing cabin – and, lifting up my voice in the midst of that clamour of the abating hurricane, impiously prayed for my own death. 'O God!' I cried, 'I would be liker a man if I rose and struck this creature down; but Thou madest me a coward from my mother's womb. O Lord, Thou madest me so, Thou knowest my weakness, Thou knowest that any face of death will set me shaking in my shoes. But, lo! here is Thy servant ready, his mortal weakness laid aside. Let me give my life for this creature's; take the two of them, Lord! take the two, and have mercy on the innocent!' In some such words as these, only yet more irreverent and with more sacred adjurations, I continued to pour forth my spirit. God heard me not, I must suppose in mercy; and I was still absorbed in my agony of supplication when someone, removing the tarpaulin cover, let the light of the sunset pour into the cabin. I stumbled to my feet ashamed, and was seized with surprise to find myself totter and ache like one that had been stretched upon the rack. Secundra Dass, who had slept off the effects of his drug, stood in a corner not far off, gazing at me with wild eyes; and from the open skylight the captain thanked me for my supplications.

'It's you that's saved the ship, Mr Mackellar,' says he. 'There is no craft of seamanship that could have kept her floating: well may we say "Except the Lord the city keep, the watchmen watch in vain"!'

I was abashed by the captain's error; abashed, also, by the surprise and fear with which the Indian regarded me at first, and the obsequious civilities with which he soon began to cumber me. I know now that he must have overheard and comprehended the peculiar nature of my prayers. It is certain, of course, that he at once disclosed the matter to his patron; and looking back with greater knowledge, I can now understand what so much puzzled me at the moment, those singular and (so to speak) approving smiles with which the Master honoured me. Similarly, I can understand a word that I remember to have fallen from him in conversation that same night; when, holding up his hand and smiling, 'Ah! Mackellar,' said he, 'not every man is so great a coward as he thinks he is – nor yet so good a Christian.' He did not guess how true he spoke! For the fact is, the thoughts which had come to me in the violence of the storm retained their hold upon my spirit; and the words that rose to my lips unbidden in the instancy of prayer continued to sound in my ears: with what shameful consequences it is fitting I should honestly relate; for I could not support a part of such disloyalty as to describe the sins of others and conceal my own.

The wind fell, but the sea hove ever the higher. All night the *Nonesuch* rolled outrageously; the next day dawned, and the next, and brought no change. To cross the cabin was scarce possible; old experienced seamen were cast down upon the deck, and one cruelly mauled in the concussion; every board and block in the old ship cried out aloud; and the great bell by the anchor-bitts continually and dolefully rang. One of these days the Master and I sate alone together at the break of the poop. I should say the *Nonesuch* carried a high-raised poop. About the top of it ran considerable bulwarks, which made the ship unweatherly; and these, as they approached the front on each side, ran down in a fine, old-fashioned, carven scroll to join the bulwarks of the waist. From this disposition, which seems designed rather for ornament than use, it followed there was a discontinuance of protection: and that, besides, at the very margin of the elevated part where (in certain movements of the ship) it might be the most needful. It was here we were sitting: our feet hanging down, the Master betwixt me and the side, and I holding on with both hands to the grating of the cabin skylight; for it struck me it was a dangerous position, the more so as I had continually before my eyes a measure of our evolutions in the person of the Master, which stood out in the break of the bulwarks against the sun. Now his head would be in the zenith and his shadow fall quite beyond the *Nonesuch* on the farther side; and now he would swing down till he was underneath my feet, and the line of the sea leaped high above him like the ceiling of a room. I looked on upon this with a growing fascination, as birds are said to look on snakes. My mind, besides, was troubled with an astonishing diversity of noises; for now that we had all sails spread in the vain hope to bring her to the sea, the ship sounded like a factory with their reverberations. We spoke first of the mutiny with which we had been threatened; this led us on to the topic of assassination; and that offered a temptation to the Master more strong than he was able to resist. He must tell me a tale, and show me at the same time how clever he was and how wicked. It was a thing he did always with affectation and display; generally with a good effect. But this tale, told in a high key in the midst of so great a tumult, and by a narrator who was one moment looking down at me from the skies and the next peering up from under the soles of my feet – this particular tale, I say, took hold upon me in a degree quite singular.

'My friend the count,' it was thus that he began his story, 'had for an enemy a certain German baron, a stranger in Rome. It matters not what was the ground of the count's enmity; but as he had a firm design to be revenged, and that with safety to himself, he kept it secret even from the baron. Indeed, that is the first principle of vengeance; and hatred betrayed is hatred impotent. The count was a man of a curious, searching mind; he had something of the artist; if anything fell for him to do, it must always be done with an exact perfection, not only as to the result, but in the very means and instruments, or he thought the thing miscarried. It chanced he was one day riding in the outer suburbs, when he came to a disused by-road branching off into the moor which lies about Rome. On the one hand was an ancient Roman tomb; on the other a deserted house in a garden of evergreen trees. This road brought him presently into a field of ruins, in the midst of which, in the side of a hill, he saw an open door, and, not far off, a single stunted pine no greater than a currant-bush. The place was desert and very secret; a voice spoke in the count's bosom that there was something here to his advantage. He tied his horse to the pine-tree, took his flint and steel in his hand to make a light and entered into the hill. The doorway opened on a passage of old Roman masonry, which shortly after branched in two. The count took the turning to the right, and followed it, groping forward in the dark, till he was brought up by a kind of fence, about elbow high, which extended quite across the passage. Sounding forward with his foot, he found an edge of polished stone, and then vacancy. All his curiosity was now awakened, and, getting some rotten sticks that lay about the floor, he made a fire. In front of him was a profound well; doubtless some neighbouring peasant had once used it for his water, and it was he that had set up the fence. A long while the count stood leaning on the rail and looking down into the pit. It was of Roman foundation, and, like all that nation set their hands to, built as for eternity; the sides were still straight, and the joints smooth; to a man who should fall in no escape was possible. 'Now,' the count was thinking, 'a strong impulsion brought me to this place. What for? what have I gained? why should I be sent to gaze into this well?' when the rail of the fence gave suddenly under his weight, and he came within an ace of falling headlong in. Leaping back to save himself, he trod out the last flicker of his fire, which gave him thenceforth no more light, only an incommoding smoke. 'Was I sent here to my death?' says he, and shook from head to foot. And then a thought flashed in his mind. He crept forth on hands and knees to the brink of the pit, and felt above him in the air. The rail had been fast to a pair of uprights; it had only broken from the one, and still depended from the other. The count set it back again as he had found it, so that the place meant death to the first comer, and groped out of the catacomb like a sick man. The next day, riding in the Corso with the baron, he purposely betrayed a strong preoccupation. The other (as he had designed) inquired into the cause; and he, after some fencing, admitted that his spirits had been dashed by an unusual dream. This was calculated to draw on the baron – a superstitious man, who affected the scorn of superstition. Some rallying followed, and then the count, as if suddenly carried away, called on his friend to beware, for it was of him that he had dreamed. You know enough of human nature, my excellent Mackellar, to be certain of one thing: I mean that the baron did not rest till he had heard the dream. The count, sure that he would never desist, kept him in play till his curiosity was highly inflamed, and then suffered himself, with seeming reluctance, to be overborne. 'I warn you,' says he, 'evil will come of it; something tells me so. But since there is to be no peace either for you or me except on this condition, the blame be on your own head! This was the dream: I beheld you riding, I know not where, yet I think it must have been near Rome, for on your one hand was an ancient tomb, and on the other a garden of evergreen trees. Methought I cried and cried upon you to come back in a very agony of terror; whether you heard me I know not, but you went doggedly on. The road brought you to a desert place among ruins, where was a door in a hillside, and hard by the door a misbegotten pine. Here you dismounted (I still crying on you to beware), tied your horse to the pine-tree, and entered resolutely in by the door. Within, it was dark; but in my dream I could still see you and still besought you to hold back. You felt your way along the right-hand wall, took a branching passage to the right, and came to a little chamber, where was a well with a railing. At this – I know not why – my alarm for you increased a thousandfold, so that I seemed to scream myself hoarse with warnings, crying it was still time, and bidding you begone at once from that vestibule. Such was the word I used in my dream, and it seemed then to have a clear significancy; but today, and awake, I profess I know not what it means. To all my outcry you rendered not the least attention, leaning the while upon the rail and looking down intently in the water. And then there was made to you a communication; I do not think I even gathered what it was, but the fear of it plucked me clean out of my slumber, and I awoke shaking and sobbing. And now,' continues the count, 'I thank you from my heart for your insistency. This dream lay on me like a load; and now I have told it in plain words and in the broad daylight, it seems no great matter.' – 'I do not know,' says the baron. 'It is in some points strange. A communication, did you say? Oh, it is an odd dream. It will make a story to amuse our friends.' – 'I am not so sure,' says the count. 'I am sensible of some reluctancy. Let us rather forget it.' – 'By all means,' says the baron. And (in fact) the dream was not again referred to. Some days after, the count proposed a ride in the fields, which the baron (since they were daily growing faster friends) very readily accepted. On the way back to Rome, the count led them insensibly by a particular route. Presently he reined in his horse, clapped his hand before his eyes, and cried out aloud. Then he showed his face again (which was now quite white, for he was a consummate actor), and stared upon the baron. 'What ails you?' cries the baron. 'What is wrong with you?' – 'Nothing,' cries the count. 'It is nothing. A seizure, I know not what. Let us hurry back to Rome.' But in the meanwhile the baron had looked about him; and there, on the left-hand side of the way as they went back to Rome, he saw a dusty by-road with a tomb upon the one hand and a garden of evergreen trees upon the other. – 'Yes,' says he, with a changed voice. 'Let us by all means hurry back to Rome. I fear you are not well in health.' – 'Oh, for God's sake!' cries the count, shuddering, 'back to Rome and let me get to bed.' They made their return with scarce a word; and the count, who should by rights have gone into society, took to his bed and gave out he had a touch of country fever. The next day the baron's horse was found tied to the pine, but himself was never heard of from that hour. – And, now, was that a murder?' says the Master, breaking sharply off.

'Are you sure he was a count?' I asked.

'I am not certain of the title,' said he, 'but he was a gentleman of family: and the Lord deliver you, Mackellar, from an enemy so subtile!'

These last words he spoke down at me, smiling, from high above; the next, he was under my feet. I continued to follow his evolutions with a childish fixity; they made me giddy and vacant, and I spoke as in a dream.

'He hated the baron with a great hatred?' I asked.

'His belly moved when the man came near him,' said the Master.

'I have felt that same,' said I.

'Verily!' cries the Master. 'Here is news indeed! I wonder – do I flatter myself? or am I the cause of these ventral perturbations?'

He was quite capable of choosing out a graceful posture, even with no one to behold him but myself, and all the more if there were any element of peril. He sat now with one knee flung across the other, his arms on his bosom, fitting the swing of the ship with an exquisite balance, such as a featherweight might overthrow. All at once I had the vision of my lord at the table, with his head upon his hands: only now, when he showed me his countenance, it was heavy with reproach. The words of my own prayer – *I were liker a man if I struck this creature down* – shot at the same time into my memory. I called my energies together, and (the ship then heeling downward toward my enemy) thrust at him swiftly with my foot. It was written I should have the guilt of this attempt without the profit. Whether from my own uncertainty or his incredible quickness, he escaped the thrust, leaping to his feet and catching hold at the same moment of a stay.

I do not know how long a time passed by: I lying where I was upon the deck, overcome with terror and remorse and shame: he standing with the stay in his hand, backed against the bulwarks, and regarding me with an expression singularly mingled. At last he spoke.

'Mackellar,' said he, 'I make no reproaches, but I offer you a bargain. On your side, I do not suppose you desire to have this exploit made public; on mine, I own to you freely I do not care to draw my breath in a perpetual terror of assassination by the man I sit at meat with. Promise me – but no,' says he, breaking off, 'you are not yet in the quiet possession of your mind; you might think I had extorted the promise from your weakness; and I would leave no door open for casuistry to come in – that dishonesty of the conscientious. Take time to meditate.'

With that he made off up the sliding deck like a squirrel, and plunged into the cabin. About half an hour later he returned – I still lying as he had left me.

'Now,' says he, 'will you give me your troth as a Christian, and a faithful servant of my brother's, that I shall have no more to fear from your attempts?'

'I give it you,' said I.

'I shall require your hand upon it,' says he.

'You have the right to make conditions,' I replied, and we shook hands. He sat down at once in the same place and the old perilous attitude.

'Hold on!' cried I, covering my eyes. 'I cannot bear to see you in that posture. The least irregularity of the sea might plunge you overboard.'

'You are highly inconsistent,' he replied, smiling, but doing as I asked. 'For all that, Mackellar, I would have you to know you have risen forty feet in my esteem. You think I cannot set a price upon fidelity? But why do you suppose I carry that Secundra Dass about the world with me? Because he would die or do murder for me tomorrow; and I love him for it. Well, you may think it odd, but I like you the better for this afternoon's performance. I thought you were magnetized with the Ten Commandments; but no – God damn my soul!' – he cries, 'the old wife has blood in his body after all! Which does not change the fact,' he continued, smiling again, 'that you have done well to give your promise; for I doubt if you would ever shine in your new trade.'

'I suppose,' said I, 'I should ask your pardon and God's for my attempt. At any rate, I have passed my word, which I will keep faithfully. But when I think of those you persecute—' I paused.

'Life is a singular thing,' said he, 'and mankind a very singular people. You suppose yourself to love my brother. I assure you, it is merely custom. Interrogate your memory; and when first you came to Durrisdeer, you will find you considered him a dull, ordinary youth. He is as dull and ordinary now, though not so young. Had you instead fallen in with me, you would today be as strong upon my side.'

'I would never say you were ordinary, Mr Bally,' I returned; 'but here you prove yourself dull. You have just shown your reliance on my word. In other terms, that is my conscience – the same which starts instinctively back from you, like the eye from a strong light.'

'Ah!' says he, 'but I mean otherwise. I mean, had I met you in my youth. You are to consider I was not always as I am today; nor (had I met in with a friend of your description) should I have ever been so.'

'But, Mr Bally,' says I, 'you would have made a mock of me; you would never have spent ten civil words on such a Square-toes.'

But he was now fairly started on his new course of justification, with which he wearied me throughout the remainder of the passage. No doubt in the past he had taken pleasure to paint himself unnecessarily black, and made a vaunt of his wickedness, bearing it for a coat-of-arms. Nor was he so illogical as to abate one item of his old confessions. 'But now that I know you are a human being,' he would say, 'I can take the trouble to explain myself. For I assure you I am human, too, and have my virtues, like my neighbours.' I say, he wearied me, for I had only the one word to say in answer: twenty times I must have said it: 'Give up your present purpose and return with me to Durrisdeer; then I will believe you.'

Thereupon he would shake his head at me. 'Ah! Mackellar, you might live a thousand years and never understand my nature,' he would say. 'This battle is now committed, the hour of reflection quite past, the hour for mercy not yet come. It began between us when we span a coin in the hall of Durrisdeer, now twenty years ago; we have had our ups and downs, but never either of us dreamed of giving in; and as for me, when my glove is cast, life and honour go with it.'

'A fig for your honour!' I would say. 'And by your leave, these warlike similitudes are something too high-sounding for the matter in hand. You want some dirty money; there is the bottom of your contention; and as for your means, what are they? to stir up sorrow in a family that never harmed you, to debauch (if you can) your own nephew, and to wring the heart of your born brother! A footpad that kills an old granny in a woollen mutch with a dirty bludgeon, and that for a shilling-piece and a paper of snuff – there is all the warrior that you are.'

When I would attack him thus (or somewhat thus) he would smile, and sigh like a man misunderstood. Once, I remember, he defended himself more at large, and had some curious sophistries, worth repeating, for a light upon his character.

'You are very like a civilian to think war consists in drums and banners,' said he. 'War (as the ancients said very wisely) is *ultima ratio*. When we take our advantage unrelentingly, then we make war. Ah! Mackellar, you are a devil of a soldier in the steward's room at Durrisdeer, or the tenants do you sad injustice!'

'I think little of what war is or is not,' I replied. 'But you weary me with claiming my respect. Your brother is a good man, and you are a bad one – neither more nor less.'

'Had I been Alexander—' he began.

'It is so we all dupe ourselves,' I cried. 'Had I been St Paul, it would have been all one; I would have made the same hash of that career that you now see me making of my own.'

'I tell you,' he cried, bearing down my interruption; 'had I been the least petty chieftain in the Highlands, had I been the least king of naked negroes in the African desert, my people would have adored me. A bad man, am I? Ah! but I was born for a good tyrant! Ask Secundra Dass; he will tell you I treat him like a son. Cast in your lot with me tomorrow, become my slave, my chattel, a thing I can command as I command the powers of my own limbs and spirit – you will see no more that dark side that I turn upon the world in anger. I must have all or none. But where all is given, I give it back with usury. I have a kingly nature: there is my loss!'

'It has been hitherto rather the loss of others,' I remarked, 'which seems a little on the hither side of royalty.'

'Tilly-vally!' cried he. 'Even now, I tell you, I would spare that family in which you take so great an interest: yes, even now – tomorrow I would leave them to their petty warfare, and disappear in that forest of cut-throats and thimble-riggers that we call the world. I would do it tomorrow!' says he. 'Only – only—'

'Only what?' I asked.

'Only they must beg it on their bended knees. I think in public, too,' he added, smiling. 'Indeed, Mackellar, I doubt if there be a hall big enough to serve my purpose for that act of reparation.'

'Vanity, vanity!' I moralized. 'To think that this great force for evil should be swayed by the same sentiment that sets a lassie mincing to her glass!'

'Oh! there are double words for everything: the word that swells, the word that belittles; you cannot fight me with a word!' said he. 'You said the other day that I relied on your conscience: were I in your humour of detraction, I might say I built upon your vanity. It is your pretension to be *un homme de parole*; 'tis mine not to accept defeat. Call it vanity, call it virtue, call it greatness of soul – what signifies the expression? But recognize in each of us a common strain: that we both live for an idea.'

It will be gathered from so much familiar talk, and so much patience on both sides, that we now lived together upon excellent terms. Such was again the fact, and this time more seriously than before. Apart from disputations such as that which I have tried to reproduce, not only consideration reigned, but, I am tempted to say, even kindness. When I fell sick (as I did shortly after our great storm), he sat by my berth to entertain me with his conversation, and treated me with excellent remedies, which I accepted with security. Himself commented on the circumstance. 'You see,' says he, 'you begin to know me better. A very little while ago, upon this lonely ship, where no one but myself has any smattering of science, you would have made sure I had designs upon your life. And, observe, it is since I found you had designs upon my own, that I have shown you most respect. You will tell me if this speaks of a small mind.' I found little to reply. In so far as regarded myself, I believed him to mean well; I am, perhaps, the more a dupe of his dissimulation, but I believed (and I still believe) that he regarded me with genuine kindness. Singular and sad fact! so soon as this change began, my animosity abated, and these haunting visions of my master passed utterly away. So that, perhaps, there was truth in the man's last vaunting word to me, uttered on the twenty-second day of July, when our long voyage was at last brought almost to an end, and we lay becalmed at the sea end of the vast harbour of New York, in a gasping heat, which was presently exchanged for a surprising waterfall of rain. I stood on the poop, regarding the green shores near at hand, and now and then the light smoke of the little town, our destination. And as I was even then devising how to steal a march on a familiar enemy, I was conscious of a shade of embarrassment when he approached me with his hand extended.

'I am now to bid you farewell,' said he, 'and that for ever. For now you go among my enemies, where all your former prejudices will revive. I never yet failed to charm a person when I wanted; even you, my good friend – to call you so for once – even you have now a very different portrait of me in your memory, and one that you will never quite forget. The voyage has not lasted long enough, or I should have wrote the impression deeper. But now all is at an end, and we are again at war. Judge by this little interlude how dangerous I am; and tell those fools' – pointing with his finger to the town – 'to think twice and thrice before they set me at defiance.'

TEN

✢ Passages at New York ✢

I HAVE MENTIONED I WAS resolved to steal a march upon the Master; and this, with the complicity of Captain M'Murtrie, was mighty easily effected: a boat being partly loaded on the one side of our ship and the Master placed on board of it, the while a skiff put off from the other, carrying me alone. I had no more trouble in finding a direction to my lord's house, whither I went at top speed, and which I found to be on the outskirts of the place, a very suitable mansion, in a fine garden, with an extraordinary large barn, byre, and stable, all in one. It was here my lord was walking when I arrived; indeed, it had become his chief place of frequentation, and his mind was now filled with farming. I burst in upon him breathless, and gave him my news: which was, indeed, no news at all, several ships having outsailed the *Nonesuch* in the interval.

'We have been expecting you long,' said my lord: 'and indeed, of late days, ceased to expect you any more. I am glad to take your hand again, Mackellar. I thought you had been at the bottom of the sea.'

'Ah! my lord, would God I had!' cried I. 'Things would have been better for yourself.'

'Not in the least,' says he, grimly. 'I could not ask better. There is a long score to pay, and now – at last – I can begin to pay it.'

I cried out against his security.

'Oh!' says he, 'this is not Durrisdeer, and I have taken my precautions. His reputation awaits him; I have prepared a welcome for my brother. Indeed, fortune has served me; for I found here a merchant of Albany who knew him after the '45 and had mighty convenient suspicions of a murder: someone of the name of Chew it was, another Albanian. No one here will be surprised if I deny him my door; he will not be suffered to address my children, nor even to salute my wife: as for myself, I make so much exception for a brother that he may speak to me. I should lose my pleasure else,' says my lord, rubbing his palms.

Presently he bethought himself, and set men off running with billets, to summon the magnates of the province. I cannot recall what pretext he employed; at least, it was successful; and when our ancient enemy appeared upon the scene, he found my lord pacing in front of his house under some trees of shade, with the Governor upon one hand, and various notables upon the other. My lady, who was seated in the verandah, rose with a very pinched expression and carried her children into the house.

The Master, well dressed and with an elegant walking-sword, bowed to the company in a handsome manner and nodded to my lord with familiarity. My lord did not accept the salutation, but looked upon his brother with bended brows.

'Well, sir,' says he, at last, 'what ill wind brings you hither of all places, where (to our common disgrace) your reputation has preceded you?'

'Your lordship is pleased to be civil,' cries the Master, with a fine start.

'I am pleased to be very plain,' returned my lord; 'because it is needful you should clearly understand your situation. At home, where you were so little known, it was still possible to keep appearances; that would be quite vain in this province; and I have to tell you that I am quite resolved to wash my hands of you. You have already ruined me almost to the door, as you ruined my father before me – whose heart you also broke. Your crimes escape the law; but my friend the Governor has promised protection to my family. Have a care, sir!' cries my lord, shaking his cane at him; 'if you are observed to utter two words to any of my innocent household, the law shall be stretched to make you smart for it.'

'Ah!' says the Master, very slowly. 'And so this is the advantage of a foreign land! These gentlemen are unacquainted with our story, I perceive. They do not know that I am the true Lord Durrisdeer; they do not know you are my younger brother, sitting in my place under a sworn family compact; they do not know (or they would not be seen with you in familiar correspondence) that every acre is mine before God Almighty – and every doit of the money you withhold from me, you do it as a thief, a perjurer, and a disloyal brother!'

'General Clinton,' I cried, 'do not listen to his lies. I am the steward of the estate, and there is not one word of truth in it. The man is a forfeited rebel turned into a hired spy: there is his story in two words.'

It was thus that (in the heat of the moment) I let slip his infamy.

'Fellow,' said the Governor, turning his face sternly on the Master, 'I know more of you than you think for. We have some broken ends of your adventures in the provinces, which you will do very well not to drive me to investigate. There is the disappearance of Mr Jacob Chew with all his merchandise; there is the matter of where you came ashore from with so much money and jewels, when you were picked up by a Bermudan out of Albany. Believe me, if I let these matters lie, it is in commiseration for your family, and out of respect for my valued friend, Lord Durrisdeer.'

There was a murmur of applause from the provincials.

'I should have remembered how a title would shine out in such a hole as this,' says the Master, white as a sheet: 'no matter how unjustly come by. It remains for me, then, to die at my lord's door, where my dead body will form a very cheerful ornament.'

'Away with your affectations!' cries my lord. 'You know very well I have no such meaning; only to protect myself from calumny, and my home from your intrusion. I offer you a choice. Either I shall pay your passage home on the first ship, when you may perhaps be able to resume your occupations under Government, although God knows I would rather see you on the highway! Or, if that likes you not, stay here and welcome! I have inquired the least sum on which body and soul can be decently kept together in New York; so much you shall have, paid weekly; and if you cannot labour with your hands to better it, high time you should betake yourself to learn. The condition is – that you speak with no member of my family except myself,' he added.

I do not think I have ever seen any man so pale as was the Master; but he was erect and his mouth firm.

'I have been met here with some very unmerited insults,' said he, 'from which I have certainly no idea to take refuge by flight. Give me your pittance; I take it without shame, for it is mine already – like the shirt upon your back; and I choose to stay until these gentlemen shall understand me better. Already they must spy the cloven hoof, since with all your pretended eagerness for the family honour, you take a pleasure to degrade it in my person.'

'This is all very fine,' says my lord; 'but to us who know you of old, you must be sure it signifies nothing. You take that alternative out of which you think that you can make the most. Take it, if you can, in silence; it will serve you better in the long run, you may believe me, than this ostentation of ingratitude.'

'Oh, gratitude, my lord,' cries the Master, with a mounting intonation and his forefinger very conspicuously lifted up. 'Be at rest: it will not fail you. It now remains that I should salute these gentlemen whom we have wearied with our family affairs.'

And he bowed to each in succession, settled his walking-sword, and took himself off, leaving everyone amazed at his behaviour, and me not less so at my lord's.

We were now to enter on a changed phase of this family division. The Master was by no manner of means so helpless as my lord supposed, having at his hand, and entirely devoted to his service, an excellent artist in all sorts of goldsmith work. With my lord's allowance, which was not so scanty as he had described it, the pair could support life; and all the earning of Secundra Dass might be laid upon one side for any future purpose. That this was done, I have no doubt. It was in all likelihood the Master's design to gather a sufficiency, and then proceed in quest of that treasure which he had buried long before among the mountains; to which, if he had confined himself, he would have been more happily inspired. But unfortunately for himself and all of us, he took counsel of his anger. The public disgrace of his arrival – which I sometimes wonder he could manage to survive – rankled in his bones; he was in that humour when a man – in the words of the old adage – will cut off his nose to spite his face; and he must make himself a public spectacle in the hopes that some of the disgrace might spatter on my lord.

He chose, in a poor quarter of the town, a lonely, small house of boards, overhung with some acacias. It was furnished in front with a sort of hutch opening, like that of a dog's kennel, but about as high as a table from the ground, in which the poor man that built it had formerly displayed some wares; and it was this which took the Master's fancy and possibly suggested his proceedings. It appears, on board the pirate ship he had acquired some quickness with the needle – enough, at least, to play the part of tailor in the public eye; which was all that was required by the nature of his vengeance. A placard was hung above the hutch, bearing these words in something of the following disposition:

James Durie
formerly MASTER of BALLANTRAE
Clothes Neatly Clouted

SECUNDRA DASS,
Decayed Gentleman of India
Fine Goldsmith work

Underneath this, when he had a job, my gentleman sat withinside tailor-wise and busily stitching. I say, when he had a job; but such customers as came were rather for Secundra and the Master's sewing would be more in the manner of Penelope's. He could never have designed to gain even butter to his bread by such a means of livelihood: enough for him that there was the name of Durie dragged in the dirt on the placard, and the sometime heir of that proud family set up cross-legged in public for a reproach upon his brother's meanness. And in so far his device succeeded that there was murmuring in the town and a party formed highly inimical to my lord. My lord's favour with the Governor laid him more open on the other side; my lady (who was never so well received in the colony) met with painful innuendoes; in a party of women, where it would be the topic most natural to introduce, she was almost debarred from the naming of needlework; and I have seen her return with a flushed countenance and vow that she would go abroad no more.

In the meantime my lord dwelled in his decent mansion, immersed in farming; a popular man with his intimates, and careless or unconscious of the rest. He laid on flesh; had a bright, busy face; even the heat seemed to prosper with him; and my lady – in despite of her own annoyances – daily blessed Heaven her father should have left her such a paradise. She had looked on from a window upon the Master's humiliation; and from that hour appeared to feel at ease. I was not so sure myself; as time went on there seemed to me a something not quite wholesome in my lord's condition. Happy he was, beyond a doubt, but the grounds of this felicity were secret; even in the bosom of his family he brooded with manifest delight upon some private thought; and I conceived at last the suspicion (quite unworthy of us both) that he kept a mistress somewhere in the town. Yet he went little abroad, and his day was very fully occupied; indeed, there was but a single period, and that pretty early in the morning, while Mr Alexander was at his lesson-book, of which I was not certain of the disposition. It should be borne in mind, in the defence of that which I now did, that I was always in some fear my lord was not quite justly in his reason; and with our enemy sitting so still in the same town with us, I did well to be upon my guard. Accordingly I made a pretext, had the hour changed at which I taught Mr Alexander the foundation of cyphering and the mathematic, and set myself instead to dog my master's footsteps.

Every morning, fair or foul, he took his gold-headed cane, set his hat on the back of his head – a recent habitude, which I thought to indicate a burning brow – and betook himself to make a certain circuit. At the first his way was among pleasant trees and beside a graveyard, where he would sit awhile, if the day were fine, in meditation. Presently the path turned down to the waterside, and came back along the harbour-front and past the Master's booth. As he approached this second part of his circuit, my Lord Durrisdeer began to pace more leisurely, like a man delighted with the air and scene; and before the booth, half-way between that and the water's edge, would pause a little, leaning on his staff. It was the hour when the Master sate within upon his board and plied his needle. So these two brothers would gaze upon each other with hard faces; and then my lord moved on again, smiling to himself.

It was but twice that I must stoop to that ungrateful necessity of playing spy. I was then certain of my lord's purpose in his rambles and of the secret source of his delight. Here was his mistress: it was hatred and not love that gave him healthful colours. Some moralists might have been relieved by the discovery; I confess that I was dismayed. I found this situation of two brethren not only odious in itself, but big with possibilities of further evil; and I made it my practice, in so far as many occupations would allow, to go by a shorter path and be secretly present at their meeting. Coming down one day a little late, after I had been near a week prevented, I was struck with surprise to find a new develop-ment. I should say there was a bench against the Master's house, where customers might sit to parley with the shopman; and here I found my lord seated, nursing his cane and looking pleasantly forth upon the bay. Not three feet from him sate the Master, stitching. Neither spoke; nor (in this new situation) did my lord so much as cast a glance upon his enemy. He tasted his neighbourhood, I must suppose, less indirectly in the bare proximity of person; and, without doubt, drank deep of hateful pleasures.

He had no sooner come away than I openly joined him.

'My lord, my lord,' said I, 'this is no manner of behaviour.'

'I grow fat upon it,' he replied; and not merely the words, which were strange enough, but the whole character of his expression shocked me.

'I warn you, my lord, against this indulgency of evil feeling,' said I. 'I know not to which it is more perilous, the soul or the reason; but you go the way to murder both.'

'You cannot understand,' said he. 'You had never such mountains of bitterness upon your heart.'

'And if it were no more,' I added, 'you will surely goad the man to some extremity.'

'To the contrary; I am breaking his spirit,' says my lord.

Every morning for hard upon a week my lord took this same place upon the bench. It was a pleasant place, under the green acacias, with a sight upon the bay and shipping, and a sound (from some way off) of mariners singing at their employ. Here the two sate without speech or any external movement, beyond that of the needle or the Master biting off a thread, for he still clung to his pretence of industry; and here I made a point to join them wondering at myself and my companions. If any of my lord's friends went by, he would hail them cheerfully, and cry out he was there to give some good advice to his brother, who was now (to his delight) grown quite industrious. And even this the Master accepted with a steady countenance; what was in his mind, God knows, or perhaps Satan only.

All of a sudden, on a still day of what they call the Indian Summer, when the woods were changed into gold and pink and scarlet, the Master laid down his needle and burst into a fit of merriment. I think he must have been preparing it a long while in silence, for the note in itself was pretty naturally pitched; but breaking suddenly from so extreme a silence, and in circumstances so averse from mirth, it sounded ominously on my ear.

'Henry,' said he, 'I have for once made a false step, and for once you have had the wit to profit by it. The farce of the cobbler ends today; and I confess to you (with my compliments) that you have had the best of it. Blood will out; and you have certainly a choice idea of how to make yourself unpleasant.'

Never a word said my lord; it was just as though the Master had not broken silence.

'Come,' resumed the Master, 'do not be sulky; it will spoil your attitude. You can now afford (believe me) to be a little gracious; for I have not merely a defeat to accept. I had meant to continue this performance till I had gathered enough money for a certain purpose; I confess ingenuously, I have not the courage. You naturally desire my absence from this town; I have come round by another way to the same idea. And I have a proposition to make; or, if your lordship prefers, a favour to ask.'

'Ask it,' says my lord.

'You may have heard that I had once in this country a considerable treasure,' returned the Master; 'it matters not whether or no – such is the fact; and I was obliged to bury it in a spot of which I have sufficient indications. To the recovery of this has my ambition now come down; and, as it is my own, you will not grudge it me.'

'Go and get it,' says my lord. 'I make no opposition.'

'Yes,' said the Master; 'but to do so, I must find men and carriage. The way is long and rough, and the country infested with wild Indians. Advance me only so much as shall be needful: either as a lump sum, in lieu of my allowance; or, if you prefer it, as a loan, which I shall repay on my return. And then, if you so decide, you may have seen the last of me.'

My lord stared him steadily in the eyes; there was a hard smile upon his face, but he uttered nothing.

'Henry,' said the Master, with a formidable quietness, and drawing at the same time somewhat back – 'Henry, I had the honour to address you.'

'Let us be stepping homeward,' says my lord to me, who was plucking at his sleeve; and with that he rose, stretched himself, settled his hat, and still without a syllable of response, began to walk steadily along the shore.

I hesitated awhile between the two brothers, so serious a climax did we seem to have reached. But the Master had resumed his occupation, his eyes lowered, his hand seemingly as deft as ever; and I decided to pursue my lord.

'Are you mad?' I cried, so soon as I had overtook him. 'Would you cast away so fair an opportunity?'

'Is it possible you should still believe in him?' inquired my lord, almost with a sneer.

'I wish him forth of this town!' I cried. 'I wish him anywhere and anyhow but as he is.'

'I have said my say,' returned my lord, 'and you have said yours. There let it rest.'

But I was bent on dislodging the Master. That sight of him patiently returning to his needlework was more than my imagination could digest. There was never a man made, and the Master the least of any, that could accept so long a series of insults. The air smelt blood to me. And I vowed there should be no neglect of mine if, through any chink of possibility, crime could be yet turned aside. That same day, therefore, I came to my lord in his business room, where he sat upon some trivial occupation.

'My lord,' said I, 'I have found a suitable investment for my small economies. But these are unhappily in Scotland; it will take some time to lift them, and the affair presses. Could your lordship see his way to advance me the amount against my note?'

He read me awhile with keen eyes. 'I have never inquired into the state of your affairs, Mackellar,' says he. 'Beyond the amount of your caution, you may not be worth a farthing, for what I know.'

'I have been a long while in your service, and never told a lie, nor yet asked a favour for myself,' said I, 'until today.'

'A favour for the Master,' he returned, quietly. 'Do you take me for a fool, Mackellar? Understand it once and for all, I treat this beast in my own way; fear nor favour shall not move me; and before I am hoodwinked, it will require a trickster less transparent than yourself. I ask service, loyal service; not that you should make and mar behind my back, and steal my own money to defeat me.'

'My lord,' said I, 'these are very unpardonable expressions.'

'Think once more, Mackellar,' he replied; 'and you will see they fit the fact. It is your own subterfuge that is unpardonable. Deny (if you can) that you designed this money to evade my orders with, and I will ask your pardon freely. If you cannot, you must have the resolution to hear your conduct go by its own name.'

'If you think I had any design but to save you—' I began.

'Oh! my old friend,' said he, 'you know very well what I think! Here is my hand to you with all my heart; but of money, not one rap.'

Defeated upon this side, I went straight to my room, wrote a letter, ran with it to the harbour, for I knew a ship was on the point of sailing; and came to the Master's door a little before dusk. Entering without the form of any knock, I found him sitting with his Indian at a simple meal of maize porridge with some milk. The house within was clean and poor; only a few books upon a shelf distinguished it, and (in one corner) Secundra's little bench.

'Mr Bally,' said I, 'I have near five hundred pounds laid by in Scotland, the economies of a hard life. A letter goes by yon ship to have it lifted. Have so much patience till the return ship comes in, and it is all yours, upon the same condition you offered to my lord this morning.'

He rose from the table, came forward, took me by the shoulders, and looked me in the face, smiling.

'And yet you are very fond of money!' said he. 'And yet you love money beyond all things else, except my brother!'

'I fear old age and poverty,' said I, 'which is another matter.'

'I will never quarrel for a name. Call it so,' he replied. 'Ah, Mackellar, Mackellar, if this were done from any love to me, how gladly would I close upon your offer!'

'And yet,' I eagerly answered – 'I say it to my shame, but I cannot see you in this poor place without compunction. It is not my single thought, nor my first; and yet it's there! I would gladly see you delivered. I do not offer it in love, and far from that; but, as God judges me – and I wonder at it too! – quite without enmity.'

'Ah!' says he, still holding my shoulders, and now gently shaking me, 'you think of me more than you suppose. "And I wonder at it too," ' he added, repeating my expression and, I suppose, something of my voice. 'You are an honest man, and for that cause I spare you.'

'Spare me?' I cried.

'Spare you,' he repeated, letting me go and turning away. And then fronting me once more: 'You little know what I would do with it, Mackellar! Did you think I had swallowed my defeat indeed? Listen: my life has been a series of unmerited cast-backs. That fool, Prince Charlie, mismanaged a most promising affair: there fell my first fortune. In Paris I had my foot once more high up on the ladder: that time it was an accident: a letter came to the wrong hand, and I was bare again. A third time I found my opportunity; I built up a place for myself in India with an infinite patience; and then Clive came, my rajah was swallowed up, and I escaped out of the convulsion, like another Aeneas, with Secundra Dass upon my back. Three times I have had my hand upon the highest station: and I am not yet three-and-forty. I know the world as few men know it when they come to die – Court and camp, the East and the West; I know where to go, I see a thousand openings. I am now at the height of my resources, sound of health, of inordinate ambition. Well, all this I resign; I care not if I die and the world never hear of me; I care only for one thing, and that I will have. Mind yourself; lest, when the roof falls, you, too, should be crushed under the ruins.'

As I came out of his house, all hope of intervention quite destroyed, I was aware of a stir on the harbour side, and, raising my eyes, there was a great ship newly come to anchor. It seems strange I could have looked upon her with so much indifference, for she brought death to the brothers of Durrisdeer. After all the desperate episodes of this contention, the insults, the opposing interests, the fraternal duel in the shrubbery, it was reserved for some poor devil in Grub Street, scribbling for his dinner, and not caring what he scribbled, to cast a spell across four thousand miles of the salt sea, and send forth both these brothers into savage and wintry deserts, there to die. But such a thought was distant from my mind; and while all the provincials were fluttered about me by the unusual animation of their port, I passed throughout their midst on my return homeward, quite absorbed in the recollection of my visit and the Master's speech.

The same night there was brought to us from the ship a little packet of pamphlets. The next day my lord was under engagement to go with the Governor upon some party of pleasure; the time was nearly due, and I left him for a moment alone in his room and skimming through the pamphlets. When I returned, his head had fallen upon the table, his arms lying abroad amongst the crumpled papers.

'My lord, my lord!' I cried as I ran forward, for I supposed he was in some fit.

He sprang up like a figure upon wires, his countenance deformed with fury, so that in a strange place I should scarce have known him. His hand at the same time flew above his head, as though to strike me down. 'Leave me alone!' he screeched, and I fled, as fast as my shaking legs would bear me, for my lady. She, too, lost no time; but when we returned, he had the door locked within, and only cried to us from the other side to leave him be. We looked in each other's faces, very white – each supposing the blow had come at last.

'I will write to the Governor to excuse him,' says she. 'We must keep our strong friends.' But when she took up the pen, it flew out of her fingers. 'I cannot write,' said she. 'Can you?'

'I will make a shift, my lady,' said I.

She looked over me as I wrote. 'That will do,' she said, when I had done. 'Thank God, Mackellar, I have you to lean upon! But what can it be now? What, what can it be?'

In my own mind, I believed there was no explanation possible, and none required; it was my fear that the man's madness had now simply burst forth its way, like the long-smothered flames of a volcano; but to this (in mere mercy to my lady) I durst not give expression.

'It is more to the purpose to consider our own behaviour,' said I. 'Must we leave him there alone?'

'I do not dare disturb him,' she replied. 'Nature may know best; it may be Nature that cries to be alone; and we grope in the dark. Oh yes, I would leave him as he is.'

'I will, then, despatch this letter, my lady, and return here, if you please, to sit with you,' said I.

'Pray do,' cries my lady.

All afternoon we sat together, mostly in silence, watching my lord's door. My own mind was busy with the scene that had just passed, and its singular resemblance to my vision. I must say a word upon this, for the story has gone abroad with great exaggeration, and I have even seen it printed, and my own name referred to for particulars. So much was the same: here was my lord in a room, with his head upon the table, and when he raised his face, it wore such an expression as distressed me to the soul. But the room was different, my lord's attitude at the table not at all the same, and his face, when he disclosed it, expressed a painful degree of fury instead of that haunting despair which had always (except once, already referred to) characterized it in the vision. There is the whole truth at last before the public; and if the differences be great, the coincidence was yet enough to fill me with uneasiness. All afternoon, as I say, I sat and pondered upon this quite to myself; for my lady had trouble of her own, and it was my last thought to vex her with fancies. About the midst of our time of waiting, she conceived an ingenious scheme, had Mr Alexander fetched, and bid him knock at his father's door. My lord sent the boy about his business, but without the least violence, whether of manner or expression; so that I began to entertain a hope the fit was over.

At last, as the night fell and I was lighting a lamp that stood there trimmed, the door opened and my lord stood within upon the threshold. The light was not so strong that we could read his countenance; when he spoke, methought his voice a little altered but yet perfectly, steady.

'Mackellar,' said he, 'carry this note to its destination with your own hand. It is highly private. Find the person alone when you deliver it.'

'Henry,' says my lady, 'you are not ill?'

'No, no,' says he, querulously, 'I am occupied. Not at all; I am only occupied. It is a singular thing a man must be supposed to be ill when he has any business! Send me supper to this room, and a basket of wine: I expect the visit of a friend. Otherwise I am not to be disturbed.'

And with that he once more shut himself in.

The note was addressed to one Captain Harris, at a tavern on the portside. I knew Harris (by reputation) for a dangerous adventurer, highly suspected of piracy in the past, and now following the rude business of an Indian trader. What my lord should have to say to him, or he to my lord, it passed my imagination to conceive: or yet how my lord had heard of him, unless by a disgraceful trial from which the man was recently escaped. Altogether I went upon the errand with reluctance, and from the little I saw of the Captain, returned from it with sorrow. I found him in a foul-smelling chamber, sitting by a guttering candle and an empty bottle; he had the remains of a military carriage, or rather perhaps it was an affectation, for his manners were low.

'Tell my lord, with my service, that I will wait upon his lordship in the inside of half an hour,' says he, when he had read the note; and then had the servility, pointing to his empty bottle, to propose that I should buy him liquor.

Although I returned with my best speed, the Captain followed close upon my heels, and he stayed late into the night. The cock was crowing a second time when I saw (from my chamber window) my lord lighting him to the gate, both men very much affected with their potations, and sometimes leaning one upon the other to confabulate. Yet the next morning my lord was abroad again early with a hundred pounds of money in his pocket. I never supposed that he returned with it; and yet I was quite sure it did not find its way to the Master, for I lingered all morning within view of the booth. That was the last time my Lord Durrisdeer passed his own enclosure till we left New York; he walked in his barn, or sat and talked with his family, all much as usual; but the town saw nothing of him, and his daily visits to the Master seemed forgotten. Nor yet did Harris reappear; or not until the end.

I was now much oppressed with a sense of the mysteries in which we had begun to move. It was plain, if only from his change of habitude, my lord had something on his mind of a grave nature; but what it was, whence it sprang, or why he should now keep the house and garden, I could make no guess at. It was clear, even to probation, the pamphlets had some share in this revolution; I read all I could find, and they were all extremely insignificant, and of the usual kind of party scurrility; even to a high politician, I could spy out no particular matter of offence, and my lord was a man rather indifferent on public questions. The truth is, the pamphlet which was the spring of this affair, lay all the time on my lord's bosom. There it was that I found it at last, after he was dead, in the midst of the north wilderness: in such a place, in such dismal circumstances, I was to read for the first time these idle, lying words of a Whig pamphleteer declaiming against indulgency to Jacobites: 'Another notorious Rebel, the M—r of B—e, is to have his Title restored,' the passage ran. 'This Business has been long in hand, since he rendered some very disgraceful Services in Scotland and France. His Brother, L—d D—r, is known to be no better than himself in Inclination; and the supposed Heir, who is now to be set aside, was bred up in the most detestable Principles. In the old Phrase, it is *six of the one and half a dozen of the other*; but the Favour of such a Reposition is too extreme to be passed over.' A man in his right wits could not have cared two straws for a tale so manifestly false; that Government should ever entertain the notion, was inconceivable to any reasoning creature, unless possibly the fool that penned it; and my lord, though never brilliant, was ever remarkable for sense. That he should credit such a rodomontade, and carry the pamphlet on his bosom and the words in his heart, is the clear proof of the man's lunacy. Doubtless the mere mention of Mr Alexander, and the threat directly held out against the child's succession, precipitated that which had so long impended. Or else my master had been truly mad for a long time, and we were too dull or too much used to him, and did not perceive the extent of his infirmity.

About a week after the day of the pamphlets I was late upon the harbour-side, and took a turn towards the Master's, as I often did. The door opened, a flood of light came forth upon the road, and I beheld a man taking his departure with friendly salutations. I cannot say how singularly I was shaken to recognize the adventurer Harris. I could not but conclude it was the hand of my lord that had brought him there; and prolonged my walk in very serious and apprehensive thought. It was late when I came home, and there was my lord making up his portmanteau for a voyage.

'Why do you come so late?' he cried. 'We leave tomorrow for Albany, you and I together; and it is high time you were about your preparations.'

'For Albany, my lord?' I cried. 'And for what earthly purpose?'

'Change of scene,' said he.

And my lady, who appeared to have been weeping, gave me the signal to obey without more parley. She told me a little later (when we found occasion to exchange some words) that he had suddenly announced his intention after a visit from Captain Harris, and her best endeavours, whether to dissuade him from the journey, or to elicit some explanation of its purpose, had alike proved unavailing.

ELEVEN

❧ The Journey in the Wilderness ❧

WE MADE A PROSPEROUS VOYAGE up that fine river of the Hudson, the weather grateful, the hills singularly beautified with the colours of the autumn. At Albany we had our residence at an inn, where I was not so blind and my lord not so cunning but what I could see he had some design to hold me prisoner. The work he found for me to do was not so pressing that we should transact it apart from necessary papers in the chamber of an inn; nor was it of such importance that I should be set upon as many as four or five scrolls of the same document. I submitted in appearance; but I took private measures on my own side, and had the news of the town communicated to me daily by the politeness of our host. In this way I received at last a piece of intelligence for which, I may say, I had been waiting. Captain Harris (I was told) with 'Mr Mountain, the trader,' had gone up the river in a boat. I would have feared the landlord's eye, so strong the sense of some complicity upon my master's part oppressed me. But I made out to say I had some knowledge of the Captain, although none of Mr Mountain, and to inquire who else was of the party. My informant knew not; Mr Mountain had come ashore upon some needful purchases; had gone round the town buying, drinking, and prating; and it seemed the party went upon some likely venture, for he had spoken much of great things he would do when he returned. No more was known, for none of the rest had come ashore, and it seemed they were pressed for time to reach a certain spot before the snow should fall.

And sure enough, the next day, there fell a sprinkle even in Albany; but it passed as it came, and was but a reminder of what lay before us. I thought of it lightly then, knowing so little as I did of that inclement province: the retrospect is different; and I wonder at times if some of the horror of these events which I must now rehearse flowed not from the foul skies and savage winds to which we were exposed, and the agony of cold that we must suffer.

The boat having passed by, I thought at first we should have left the town. But no such matter. My lord continued his stay in Albany, where he had no ostensible affairs, and kept me by him, far from my due employment, and making a pretence of occupation. It is upon this passage I expect, and perhaps deserve, censure. I was not so dull but what I had my own thoughts. I could not see the Master entrust himself into the hands of Harris, and not expect some underhand contrivance. Harris bore a villainous reputation, and he had been tampered with in private by my lord; Mountain, the trader, proved, upon inquiry, to be another of the same kidney; the errand they were all gone upon being the recovery of ill-gotten treasures, offered in itself a very strong incentive to foul play; and the character of the country where they journeyed promised impunity to deeds of blood. Well: it is true I had all these thoughts and fears, and guesses of the Master's fate. But you are to consider I was the same man that sought to dash him from the bulwarks of a ship in the mid-sea; the same that, a little before, very impiously but sincerely offered God a bargain, seeking to hire God to be my bravo. It is true again that I had a good deal melted towards our enemy. But this I always thought of as a weakness of the flesh and even culpable; my mind remaining steady and quite bent against him. True, yet again, that it was one thing to assume on my own shoulders the guilt and danger of a criminal attempt, and another to stand by and see my lord imperil and besmirch himself. But this was the very ground of my inaction. For (should I anyway stir in the business) I might fail indeed to save the Master, but I could not miss to make a byword of my lord.

Thus it was that I did nothing; and upon the same reasons, I am still strong to justify my course. My lord had carried with him several introductions to chief people of the town and neighbourhood; others he had before encountered in New York: with this consequence, that he went much abroad, and I am sorry to say was altogether too convivial in his habits. I was often in bed, but never asleep, when he returned; and there was scarce a night when he did not betray the influence of liquor. By day he would still lay upon me endless tasks, which he showed considerable ingenuity to fish up and renew, in the manner of Penelope's web. I never refused, as I say, for I was hired to do his bidding; but I took no pains to keep my penetration under a bushel, and would sometimes smile in his face.

'I think I must be the devil and you Michael Scott,' I said to him one day. 'I have bridged the Tweed and split the Eildons; and now you set me to the rope of sand.'

He looked at me with shining eyes, and looked away again, his jaw chewing, but without words.

'Well, well, my lord,' said I, 'your will is my pleasure. I will do this thing for the fourth time; but I would beg of you to invent another task against tomorrow, for by my troth, I am weary of this one.'

'You do not know what you are saying,' returned my lord, putting on his hat and turning back to me. 'It is a strange thing you should take a pleasure to annoy me. A friend – but that is a different affair. It is a strange thing. I am a man that has had ill-fortune all my life through. I am still surrounded by contrivances. I am always treading in plots,' he burst out. 'The whole world is banded against me.'

'I would not talk wicked nonsense if I were you,' said I: 'but I will tell you what I *would* do – I would put my head in cold water, for you had more last night than you could carry.'

'Do ye think that?' said he, with a manner of interest highly awakened. 'Would that be good for me? It's a thing I never tried.'

'I mind the days when you had no call to try, and I wish, my lord, that they were back again,' said I. 'But the plain truth is, if you continue to exceed, you will do yourself a mischief.'

'I don't appear to carry drink the way I used to,' said my lord. 'I get overtaken, Mackellar. But I will be more upon my guard.'

'That is what I would ask of you,' I replied. 'You are to bear in mind that you are Mr Alexander's father: give the bairn a chance to carry his name with some responsibility.'

'Ay, ay,' said he. 'Ye're a very sensible man, Mackellar, and have been long in my employ. But I think, if you have nothing more to say to me, I will be stepping. If you have nothing more to say?' he added, with that burning, childish eagerness that was now so common with the man.

'No, my lord, I have nothing more,' said I, dryly enough.

'Then I think I will be stepping,' says my lord, and stood and looked at me, fidgeting with his hat, which he had taken off again. 'I suppose you will have no errands. No? I am to meet Sir William Johnson, but I will be more upon my guard.' He was silent for a time, and then, smiling: 'Do you call to mind a place, Mackellar – it's a little below Eagles – where the burn runs very deep under a wood of rowans. I mind being there when I was a lad – dear, it comes over me like an old song! – I was after the fishing, and I made a bonny cast. Eh, but I was happy. I wonder, Mackellar, why I am never happy now?'

'My lord,' said I, 'if you would drink with more moderation you would have the better chance. It is an old byword that the bottle is a false consoler.'

'No doubt,' said he, 'no doubt. Well, I think I will be going.'

'Good-morning, my lord,' said I.

'Good-morning, good-morning,' said he, and so got himself at last from the apartment.

I give that for a fair specimen of my lord in the morning; and I must have described my patron very ill if the reader does not perceive a notable falling off. To behold the man thus fallen: to know him accepted among his companions for a poor, muddled toper, welcome (if he were welcome at all) for the bare consideration of his title; and to recall the virtues he had once displayed against such odds of fortune; was not this a thing at once to rage and to be humbled at?

In his cups he was more excessive. I will give but the one scene, close upon the end, which is strongly marked upon my memory to this day, and at the time affected me almost with horror.

I was in bed, lying there awake, when I heard him stumbling on the stair and singing. My lord had no gift of music, his brother had all the graces of the family, so that when I say singing, you are to understand a manner of high, carolling utterance, which was truly neither speech nor song. Something not unlike is to be heard upon the lips of children, ere they learn shame; from those of a man grown elderly, it had a strange effect. He opened the door with noisy precaution; peered in, shading his candle; conceived me to slumber; entered, set his light upon the table, and took off his hat. I saw him very plain; a high feverish exultation appeared to boil in his veins, and he stood and smiled and smirked upon the candle. Presently he lifted up his arm, snapped his fingers, and fell to undress. As he did so, having once more forgot my presence, he took back to his singing; and now I could hear the words, which were those from the old song of the *Twa Corbies* endlessly repeated:

> And over his banes when they are bare
> The wind sall blaw for evermair!

324

I have said there was no music in the man. His strains had no logical succession except in so far as they inclined a little to the minor mode; but they exercised a rude potency upon the feelings, and followed the words, and signified the feelings of the singer with barbaric fitness. He took it first in the time and manner of a rant; presently this ill-favoured gleefulness abated, he began to dwell upon the notes more feelingly, and sank at last into a degree of maudlin pathos that was to me scarce bearable. By equal steps, the original briskness of his acts declined; and when he was stripped to his breeches, he sat on the bedside and fell to whimpering. I know nothing less respectable than the tears of drunkenness, and turned my back impatiently on this poor sight.

But he had started himself (I am to suppose) on that slippery descent of self-pity; on the which, to a man unstrung by old sorrows and recent potations, there is no arrest except exhaustion. His tears continued to flow, and the man to sit there, three parts naked, in the cold air of the chamber. I twitted myself alternately with inhumanity and sentimental weakness, now half rising in my bed to interfere, now reading myself lessons of indifference and courting slumber, until, upon a sudden, the *quantum mutatus ab illo* shot into my mind; and calling to remembrance his old wisdom, constancy, and patience, I was overborne with a pity almost approaching the passionate, not for my master alone but for the sons of man.

At this I leaped from my place, went over to his side and laid a hand on his bare shoulder, which was cold as stone. He uncovered his face and showed it me all swollen and begrutten* like a child's; and at the sight my impatience partially revived.

'Think shame to yourself,' said I. 'This is bairnly conduct. I might have been snivelling myself, if I had cared to swill my belly with wine. But I went to my bed sober like a man. Come: get into yours, and have done with this pitiable exhibition.'

'Oh, Mackellar,' said he, 'my heart is wae!'

'Wae?' cried I. 'For a good cause, I think. What words were these you sang as you came in? Show pity to others, we then can talk of pity to yourself. You can be the one thing or the other, but I will be no party to halfway houses. If you're a striker, strike, and if you're a bleater, bleat!'

'Ay!' cries he, with a burst, 'that's it – strike! that's talking! Man, I've stood it all too long. But when they laid a hand upon the child, when the child's threatened' – his momentary vigour whimpering off – 'my child, my Alexander!' – and he was at his tears again.

I took him by the shoulder and shook him. 'Alexander!' said I. 'Do

*Tear-marked.

you ever think of him? Not you! Look yourself in the face like a brave man, and you'll find you're but a self-deceiver. The wife, the friend, the child, they're all equally forgot, and you sunk in a mere bog of selfishness.'

'Mackellar,' said he, with a wonderful return to his old manner and appearance, 'you may say what you will of me, but one thing I never was – I was never selfish.'

'I will open your eyes in your despite,' said I. 'How long have we been here? and how often have you written to your family? I think this is the first time you were ever separate: have you written at all? Do they know if you are dead or living?'

I had caught him here too openly; it braced his better nature; there was no more weeping, he thanked me very penitently, got to bed and was soon fast asleep; and the first thing he did the next morning was to sit down and begin a letter to my lady: a very tender letter it was too, though it was never finished. Indeed all communication with New York was transacted by myself; and it will be judged I had a thankless task of it. What to tell my lady and in what words, and how far to be false and how far cruel, was a thing that kept me often from my slumber.

All this while, no doubt, my lord waited with growing impatiency for news of his accomplices. Harris, it is to be thought, had promised a high degree of expedition; the time was already overpast when word was to be looked for; and suspense was a very evil counsellor to a man of an impared intelligence. My lord's mind throughout this interval dwelled almost wholly in the Wilderness, following that party with whose deeds he had so much concern. He continually conjured up their camps and progresses, the fashion of the country, the perpetration in a thousand different manners of the same horrid fact, and that consequent spectacle of the Master's bones lying scattered in the wind. These private guilty considerations I would continually observe to peep forth in the man's talk, like rabbits from a hill. And it is the less wonder if the scene of his meditations began to draw him bodily.

It is well known what pretext he took. Sir William Johnson had a diplomatic errand in these parts; and my lord and I (from curiosity, as was given out) went in his company. Sir William was well attended and liberally supplied. Hunters brought us venison, fish was taken for us daily in the streams, and brandy ran like water. We proceeded by day and encamped by night in the military style; sentinels were set and changed; every man had his named duty; and Sir William was the spring of all. There was much in this that might at times have entertained me; but, for our misfortune, the weather was extremely harsh, the days were in the beginning open, but the nights frosty from the first. A painful keen wind blew most of the time, so that we sat in the boat with flue fingers, and at night, as we scorched our faces at the fire, the clothes upon our back appeared to be of paper. A dreadful solitude surrounded our steps; the land was quite dispeopled, there was no smoke of fires, and save for a single boat of merchants on the second day, we met no travellers. The season was indeed late, but this desertion of the water-ways impressed Sir William himself; and I have heard him more than once express a sense of intimidation. 'I have come too late, I fear; they must have dug up the hatchet,' he said; and the future proved how justly he had reasoned.

I could never depict the blackness of my soul upon this journey. I have none of those minds that are in love with the unusual; to see the winter coming and to lie in the field so far from any house, oppressed me like a nightmare; it seemed, indeed, a kind of awful braving of God's power; and this thought, which I daresay only writes me down a coward, was greatly exaggerated by my private knowledge of the errand we were come upon. I was besides encumbered by my duties to Sir William, whom it fell upon me to entertain; for my lord was quite sunk into a state bordering on *pervigilium*, watching the woods with a rapt eye, sleeping scarce at all, and speaking sometimes not twenty words in a whole day. That which he said was still coherent; but it turned almost invariably upon the party for whom he kept his crazy look-out. He would tell Sir William often, and always as if it were a new communication, that he had 'a brother somewhere in the woods,' and beg that the sentinels should be directed 'to inquire for him.' 'I am anxious for news of my brother,' he would say. And sometimes, when we were under way, he would fancy he spied a canoe far off upon the water or a camp on the shore, and exhibit painful agitation. It was impossible but Sir William should be struck with these singularities; and at last he led me aside, and hinted his uneasiness. I touched my head and shook it; quite rejoiced to prepare a little testimony against possible disclosures.

'But in that case,' cries Sir William, 'is it wise to let him go at large?'

'Those that know him best,' said I, 'are persuaded that he should be humoured.'

'Well, well,' replied Sir William, 'it is none of my affairs. But if I had understood, you would never have been here.'

Our advance into this savage country had thus uneventfully proceeded for about a week, when we encamped for a night at a place where the river ran among considerable mountains clothed in wood. The fires were lighted in a level space at the water's edge; and we supped and lay down to sleep in the customary fashion. It chanced the night fell murderously cold; the stringency of the frost seized and bit me through my coverings, so that pain kept me wakeful; and I was afoot again before the peep of day, crouching by the fires or trotting to and fro at the stream's edge, to combat the aching of my limbs. At last dawn began to break upon hoar woods and mountains, the sleepers rolled in their robes, and the boisterous river dashing among spears of ice. I stood looking about me, swaddled in my stiff coat of a bull's fur, and the breath smoking from my scorched nostrils, when, upon a sudden, a singular, eager cry rang from the borders of the wood. The sentries answered it, the sleepers sprang to their feet, one pointed, the rest followed his direction with their eyes, and there, upon the edge of the forest and betwixt two trees we beheld the figure of a man reaching forth his hands like one in ecstasy. The next moment he ran forward, fell on his knees at the side of the camp, and burst in tears.

This was John Mountain, the trader, escaped from the most horrid perils; and his first word, when he got speech, was to ask if we had seen Secundra Dass.

'Seen what?' cries Sir William.

'No,' said I, 'we have seen nothing of him. Why?'

'Nothing?' says Mountain. 'Then I was right after all.' With that he struck his palm upon his brow. 'But what takes him back?' he cried. 'What takes the man back among dead bodies? There is some damned mystery here.'

This was a word which highly aroused our curiosity, but I shall be more perspicacious, if I narrate these incidents in their true order. Here follows a narrative which I have compiled out of three sources, not very consistent in all points:

First, a written statement by Mountain, in which everything criminal is cleverly smuggled out of view;

Second, two conversations with Secundra Dass; and

Third, many conversations with Mountain himself, in which he was pleased to be entirely plain; for the truth is he regarded me as an accomplice.

NARRATIVE OF THE TRADER, MOUNTAIN

The crew that went up the river under the joint command of Captain Harris and the Master numbered in all nine persons, of whom (if I except Secundra Dass) there was not one that had not merited the gallows. From Harris downwards the voyagers were notorious in that colony for desperate, bloody-minded miscreants; some were reputed pirates, the most hawkers of rum; all ranters and drinkers; all fit associates, embarking together without remorse upon this treacherous and murderous design. I could not hear there was much discipline or any set captain in the gang; but Harris and four others, Mountain himself, two Scotsmen – Pinkerton and Hastie – and a man of the name of Hicks, a drunken shoemaker, put their heads together and agreed upon the course. In a material sense, they were well enough provided, and the Master in particular brought with him a tent where he might enjoy some privacy and shelter.

Even this small indulgence told against him in the minds of his companions. But indeed he was in a position so entirely false (and even ridiculous) that all his habit of command and arts of pleasing were here thrown away. In the eyes of all, except Secundra Dass, he figured as a common gull and designated victim; going unconsciously to death; yet he could not but suppose himself the contriver and the leader of the expedition; he could scarce help but so conduct himself; and at the least hint of authority or condescension, his deceivers would be laughing in their sleeves. I was so used to see and to conceive him in a high authoritative attitude, that when I had conceived his position on this journey, I was pained and could have blushed. How soon he may have entertained a first surmise, we cannot know; but it was long, and the party had advanced into the Wilderness beyond the reach of any help, ere he was fully awakened to the truth.

It fell thus. Harris and some others had drawn apart into the woods for consultation, when they were startled by a rustling in the brush. They were accustomed to the arts of Indian warfare, and Mountain had not only lived and hunted, but fought and earned some reputation, with the savages. He could move in the woods without noise, and follow a trail like a hound; and upon the emergence of this alert, he was deputed by the rest to plunge into the thicket for intelligence. He was soon convinced there was a man in his close neighbourhood, moving with precaution but without art among the leaves and branches; and coming shortly to a place of advantage, he was able observe Secundra Dass crawling briskly off with many backward glances. At this he knew not whether to laugh or cry; and his accomplices, when he had returned and reported, were in much the same dubiety. There was now no danger of an Indian onslaught; but on the other hand, since Secundra Dass was at the pains to spy upon them, it was highly probable he knew English, and if he knew English it was certain the whole of their design was in the Master's knowledge. There was one singularity in the position. If Secundra Dass knew and concealed his knowledge of English, Harris was a proficient in several of the tongues of India, and as his career in that part of the world had been a great deal worse than profligate, he had not thought proper to remark upon the circumstance. Each side had thus a spy-hole on the counsels of the other. The plotters, so soon as this advantage was explained, returned to camp; Harris, hearing the Hindustani was once more closeted with his master, crept to the side of the tent; and the rest, sitting about the fire with their tobacco, awaited his report with impatience. When he came at last, his face was very black. He had overheard enough to confirm the worst of his suspicions. Secundra Dass was a good English scholar; he had been some days creeping and listening, the Master was now fully informed of the conspiracy, and the pair proposed on the morrow to fall out of line at a carrying place and plunge at a venture in the woods: preferring the full risk of famine, savage beasts, and savage men to their position in the midst of traitors.

What, then, was to be done? Some were for killing the Master on the spot; but Harris assured them that would be a crime without profit, since the secret of the treasure must die along with him that buried it. Others were for desisting at once from the whole enterprise and making for New York; but the appetizing name of treasure, and the thought of the long way they had already travelled, dissuaded the majority. I imagine they were dull fellows for the most part. Harris, indeed, had some acquirements, Mountain was no fool, Hastie was an educated man; but even these had manifestly failed in life, and the rest were the dregs of colonial rascality. The conclusion they reached, at least, was more the offspring of greed and hope, than reason. It was to temporize, to be wary and watch the Master, to be silent and supply no further aliment to his suspicions, and to depend entirely (as well as I make out) on the chance that their victim was as greedy, hopeful, and irrational as themselves, and might, after all, betray his life and treasure.

Twice in the course of the next day Secundra and the Master must have appeared to themselves to have escaped; and twice they were circumvented. The Master, save that the second time he grew a little pale, displayed no sign of disappointment, apologized for the stupidity with which he had fallen aside, thanked his recapturers as for a service, and rejoined the caravan with all his usual gallantry and cheerfulness of mien and bearing. But it is certain he had smelled a rat; for from thenceforth he and Secundra spoke only in each other's ear, and Harris listened and shivered by the tent in vain. The same night it was announced they were to leave the boats and proceed by foot, a circumstance which (as it put an end to the confusion of the portages) greatly lessened the chances of escape.

And now there began between the two sides a silent contest, for life on the one hand, for riches on the other. They were now near that quarter of the desert in which the Master himself must begin to play the part of the guide; and using this for a pretext of persecution, Harris and his men sat with him every night about the fire, and laboured to entrap him into some admission. If he let slip his secret, he knew well it was the warrant for his death; on the other hand, he durst not refuse their questions, and must appear to help them to the best of his capacity, or he practically published his mistrust. And yet Mountain assures me the man's brow was never ruffled. He sat in the midst of these jackals, his life depending by a thread, like some easy, witty householder at home by his own fire; an answer he had for everything – as often as not a jesting answer; avoided threats, evaded insults; talked, laughed, and listened with an open countenance; and, in short, conducted himself in such a manner as must have disarmed suspicion, and went near to stagger knowledge. Indeed, Mountain confessed to me they would soon have disbelieved the Captain's story, and supposed their designated victim still quite innocent of their designs; but for the fact that he continued (however ingeniously) to give the slip to questions, and the yet stronger confirmation of his repeated efforts to escape. The last of these, which brought things to a head, I am now to relate. And first I should say that by this time the temper of Harris's companions was utterly worn out; civility was scarce pretended; and, for one very significant circumstance, the Master and Secundra had been (on some pretext) deprived of weapons. On their side, however, the threatened pair kept up the parade of friendship handsomely; Secundra was all bows, the Master all smiles; and on the last night of the truce he had even gone so far as to sing for the diversion of the company. It was observed that he had also eaten with unusual heartiness and drank deep, doubtless from design.

At least, about three in the morning, he came out of the tent into the open air, audibly mourning and complaining, with all the manner of a sufferer from surfeit. For some while, Secundra publicly attended on his patron, who at last became more easy and fell asleep on the frosty ground behind the tent, the Indian returning within. Some time after, the sentry was changed; had the Master pointed out to him, where he lay in what is called a robe of buffalo: and thenceforth kept an eye upon him (he declared) without remission. With the first of the dawn, a draught of wind came suddenly and blew open one side the corner of the robe; and with the same puff, the Master's hat whirled in the air and fell some yards away. The sentry thinking it remarkable the sleeper should not awaken, thereupon drew near; and the next moment, with a great shout, informed the camp their prisoner was escaped. He had left behind his Indian, who (in the first vicacity of the surprise) came near to pay the forfeit of his life, and was, in fact, inhumanly mishandled; but Secundra, in the midst of threats and cruelties, stuck to it with extraordinary loyalty, that he was quite ignorant of his master's plans, which might indeed be true, and of the manner of his escape, which was demonstrably false. Nothing was therefore left to the conspirators but to rely entirely on the skill of Mountain. The night had been frosty, the ground quite hard; and the sun was no sooner up than a strong thaw set in. It was Mountain's boast that few men could have followed that trail, and still fewer (even of the native Indians) found it. The Master had thus a long start before his pursuers had the scent, and he must have travelled with surprising energy for a pedestrian so unused, since it was near noon before Mountain had a view of him. At this conjuncture the trader was alone, all his companions following, at his own request, several hundred yards in the rear; he knew the Master was unarmed; his heart was besides heated with the exercise and lust of hunting; and seeing the quarry so close, so defenceless, and seeming so fatigued, he vaingloriously determined to effect the capture with his single hand. A step or two farther brought him to one margin of a little clearing; on the other, with his arms folded and his back to a huge stone, the Master sat. It is possible Mountain may have made a rustle, it is certain, at least, the Master raised his head and gazed directly at that quarter of the thicket where his hunter lay; 'I could not be sure he saw me,' Mountain said; 'he just looked my way like a man with his mind made up, and all the courage ran out of me like rum out of a bottle.' And presently, when the Master looked away again, and appeared to resume those meditations in which he had sat immersed before the trader's coming, Mountain slunk stealthily back and returned to seek the help of his companions.

And now began the chapter of surprises, for the scout had scarce informed the others of his discovery, and they were yet preparing their weapons for a rush upon the fugitive, when the man himself appeared in their midst, walking openly and quietly, with his hands behind his back.

'Ah, men!' says he, on his beholding them. 'Here is a fortunate encounter. Let us get back to camp.'

Mountain had not mentioned his own weakness or the Master's disconcerting gaze upon the thicket, so that (with all the rest) his return appeared spontaneous. For all that, a hubbub arose; oaths flew, fists were shaken, and guns pointed.

'Let us get back to camp,' said the Master. 'I have an explanation to make, but it must be laid before you all. And in the meanwhile I would put up these weapons, one of which might very easily go off and blow away your hopes of treasure. I would not kill,' says he, smiling, 'the goose with the golden eggs.'

The charm of his superiority once more triumphed; and the party, in no particular order, set off on their return. By the way, he found occasion to get a word or two apart with Mountain.

'You are a clever fellow and bold,' says he, 'but I am not so sure that you are doing yourself justice. I would have you to consider whether you would not do better, ay, and safer, to serve me instead of serving so commonplace a rascal as Mr Harris. Consider of it,' he concluded, dealing the man a gentle tap upon the shoulder, 'and don't be in haste. Dead or alive, you will find me an ill man to quarrel with.'

When they were come back to the camp where Harris and Pinkerton stood guard over Secundra, these two ran upon the Master like viragoes, and were amazed out of measure when they were bidden by the comrades to 'stand back and hear what the gentleman had to say.' The Master had not flinched before their onslaught; nor, at this proof of the ground he had gained, did he betray the least sufficiency.

'Do not let us be in haste,' says he. 'Meat first and public speaking after.'

With that they made a hasty meal; and as soon as it was done, the Master, leaning on one elbow, began his speech. He spoke long, addressing himself to each except Harris, finding for each (with the same exception) some particular flattery. He called them 'bold, honest blades,' declared he had never seen a more jovial company, work better done, or pains more merrily supported. 'Well, then,' says he, 'someone asks me, Why the devil I ran away? But that is scarce worth answer, for I think you all know pretty well. But you know only pretty well: that is a point I shall arrive at presently, and be you ready to remark it when it comes. There is a traitor here: a double traitor: I will give you his name before I am done; and let that suffice for now. But here comes some other gentleman and asks me, "Why, in the devil, I came back?" Well, before I answer that question, I have one to put to you. It was this cur here, this Harris, that speaks Hindustani?' cries he, rising on one knee and pointing fair at the man's face, with a gesture indescribably menacing; and when he had been answered in the affirmative, 'Ah!' says he, 'then are all my suspicions verified, and I did rightly to come back. Now, men, hear the truth for the first time.' Thereupon he launched forth in a long story, told with extraordinary skill, how he had long suspected Harris, how he had found the confirmation of his fears, and how Harris must have misrepresented what passed between Secundra and himself. At this point he made a bold stroke with excellent effect. 'I suppose,' says he, 'you think you are going shares with Harris, I suppose you think you will see to that yourselves; you would naturally not think so flat a rogue could cozen you. But have a care! These half-idiots have a sort of cunning, as the skunk has its stench; and it may be news to you that Harris has taken care of himself already. Yes, for him the treasure is all money in the bargain. You must find it or go starve. But he has been paid beforehand; my brother paid him to destroy me; look at him, if you doubt – look at him, grinning and gulping, a detected thief!' Thence, having made this happy impression, he explained how he had escaped and thought better of it, and at last concluded to come back, lay the truth before the company, and take his chance with them once more: persuaded as he was, they would instantly depose Harris and elect some other leader. 'There is the whole truth,' said he: 'and with one exception, I put myself entirely in your hands. What is the exception? There he sits,' he cried, pointing once more to Harris; 'a man that has to die! Weapons and conditions are all one to me; put me face to face with him, and if you give me nothing but a stick, in five minutes I will show you a sop of broken carrion, fit for dogs to roll in.'

It was dark night when he made an end; they had listened in almost perfect silence; but the firelight scarce permitted anyone to judge, from the look of his neighbours, with what result of persuasion or conviction. Indeed, the Master had set himself in the brightest place, and kept his face there, to be the centre of men's eyes: doubtless on a profound calculation. Silence followed for a while, and presently the whole party became involved in disputation: the Master lying on his back, with his hands knit under his head and one knee flung across the other, like a person unconcerned in the result. And here, I daresay, his bravado carried him too far and prejudiced his case. At least, after a cast or two back and forward, opinion settled finally against him. It's possible he hoped to repeat the business of the pirate ship, and be himself, perhaps, on hard enough conditions, elected leader; and things went so far that way, that Mountain actually threw out the proposition. But the rock he split upon was Hastie. This fellow was not well liked, being sour and slow, with an ugly, glowering disposition, but he had studied some time for the Church at Edinburgh College, before ill conduct had destroyed his prospects, and he now remembered and applied what he had learned. Indeed he had not proceeded very far, when the Master rolled carelessly upon one side, which was done (in Mountain's opinion) to conceal the beginnings of despair upon his countenance. Hastie dismissed the most of what they had heard as nothing to the matter: what they wanted was the treasure. All that was said of Harris might be true, and they would have to see to that in time. But what had that to do with the treasure? They had heard a vast of words; but the truth was just this, that Mr Durie was damnably frightened and had several times run off. Here he was – whether caught or come back was all one to Hastie: the point was to make an end of the business. As for the talk of deposing and electing captains, he hoped they were all free men and could attend their own affairs. That was dust flung in their eyes, and so was the proposal to fight Harris. 'He shall fight no one in this camp, I can tell him that,' said Hastie. 'We had trouble enough to get his arms away from him, and we should look pretty fools to give them back again. But it it's excitement the gentleman is after, I can supply him with more than perhaps he cares about. For I have no intention to spend the remainder of my life in these mountains; already I have been too long; and I propose that he should immediately tell us where that treasure is, or else immediately be shot. And there,' says he, producing his weapon, 'there is the pistol that I mean to use.'

'Come, I call you a man,' cries the Master, sitting up and looking at the speaker with an air of admiration.

'I didn't ask you to call me anything,' returned Hastie; 'which is it to be?'

'That's an idle question,' said the Master. 'Needs must when the devil drives. The truth is we are within easy walk of the place, and I will show it you tomorrow.'

With that, as if all were quite settled, and settled exactly to his mind, he walked off to his tent, whither Secundra had preceded him.

I cannot think of these last turns and wriggles of my old enemy except with admiration; scarce even pity is mingled with the sentiment, so strongly the man supported, so boldly resisted his misfortunes. Even at that hour, when he perceived himself quite lost, when he saw he had but effected an exchange of enemies, and overthrown Harris to set Hastie up, no sign of weakness appeared in his behaviour, and he withdrew to his tent, already determined (I must suppose) upon affronting the incredible hazard of his last expedient, with the same easy, assured, genteel expression and demeanour as he might have left a theatre withal to join a supper of the wits. But doubtless within, if we could see there, his soul trembled.

Early in the night, word went about the camp that he was sick; and the first thing the next morning he called Hastie to his side, and inquired most anxiously if he had any skill in medicine. As a matter of fact, this was a vanity of that fallen divinity student's, to which he had cunningly addressed himself. Hastie examined him; and being flattered, ignorant, and highly suspicious, knew not in the least whether the man was sick or malingering. In this state he went forth again to his companions; and (as the thing which would give himself most consequence either way) announced that the patient was in a fair way to die.

'For all that,' he added with an oath, 'and if he bursts by the wayside, he must bring us this morning to the treasure.'

But there were several in the camp (Mountain among the number) whom this brutality revolted. They would have seen the Master pistolled, or pistolled him themselves, without the smallest sentiment of pity; but they seemed to have been touched by his gallant fight and unequivocal defeat the night before; perhaps, too, they were even already beginning to oppose themselves to their new leader; at least, they now declared that (if the man was sick) he should have a day's rest in spite of Hastie's teeth.

The next morning he was manifestly worse, and Hastie himself began to display something of humane concern, so easily does even the pretence of doctoring awaken sympathy. The third the Master called Mountain and Hastie to the tent, announced himself to be dying, gave them full particulars as to the position of the cache, and begged them to set out incontinently on the quest, so that they might see if he deceived them, and (if they were at first unsuccessful) he should be able to correct their error.

But here arose a difficulty on which he doubtless counted. None of these men would trust another, none would consent to stay behind. On the other hand, although the Master seemed extremely low, spoke scarce above a whisper, and lay much of the time insensible, it was still possible it was a fraudulent sickness; and if all went treasure-hunting, it might prove they had gone upon a wild-goose chase, and return to find their prisoner flown. They concluded, therefore, to hang idling round the camp, alleging sympathy to their reason; and certainly, so mingled are our dispositions, several were sincerely (if not very deeply) affected by the natural peril of the man whom they callously designed to murder. In the afternoon Hastie was called to the bedside to pray: the which (incredible as it must appear) he did with unction; about eight at night, the wailing of Secundra announced that all was over; and before ten, the Indian, with a link stuck in the ground, was toiling at the grave. Sunrise of next day beheld the Master's burial, all hands attending with great decency of demeanour; and the body was laid in the earth, wrapped in a fur robe, with only the face uncovered; which last was of a waxy whiteness, and had the nostrils plugged according to some Oriental habit of Secundra's. No sooner was the grave filled than the lamentations of the Indian once more struck concern to every heart; and it appears this gang of murderers, so far from resenting his outcries, although both distressful and (in such a country) perilous to their own safety, roughly but kindly endeavoured to console him.

But if human nature is even in the worst of men occasionally kind, it is still, and before all things, greedy; and they soon turned from the mourner to their own concerns. The cache of the treasure being hard by, although yet unidentified, it was concluded not to break camp; and the day passed, on the part of the voyagers, in unavailing exploration of the woods, Secundra the while lying on his master's grave. That night they placed no sentinel, but lay together about the fire in the customary woodman fashion, the heads outward, like the spokes of a wheel. Morning found them in the same disposition; only Pinkerton, who lay on Mountain's right, between him and Hastie, had (in the hours of darkness) been secretly butchered, and there lay, still wrapped as to his body in his mantle, but offering above that ungodly and horrific spectacle of the scalped head. The gang were that morning as pale as a company of phantoms, for the pertinacity of Indian war (or to speak more correctly, Indian murder) was well known to all. But they laid the chief blame on their unsentinelled posture; and fired with the neighbourhood of the treasure, determined to continue where they were. Pinkerton was buried hard by the Master; the survivors again passed the day in exploration, and returned in a mingled humour of anxiety and hope, being partly certain they were now close on the discovery of what they sought, and on the other hand (with the return of darkness) infected with the fear of Indians. Mountain was the first sentry; he declares he neither slept nor yet sat down, but kept his watch with a perpetual and straining vigilance, and it was even with unconcern that (when he saw by the stars his time was up) he drew near the fire to awaken his successor. This man (it was Hicks the shoemaker) slept on the lee side of the circle, something farther off in consequence than those to windward, and in a place darkened by the blowing smoke. Mountain stooped and took him by the shoulder; his hand was at once smeared by some adhesive wetness; and (the wind at the moment veering) the firelight shone upon the sleeper, and showed him, like Pinkerton, dead and scalped.

It was clear they had fallen in the hands of one of those matchless Indian bravos, that will sometimes follow a party for days, and in spite of indefatigable travel, and unsleeping watch, continue to keep up with their advance, and steal a scalp at every resting-place. Upon this discovery, the treasure-seekers, already reduced to a poor half-dozen, fell into mere dismay, seized a few necessaries, and deserting the remainder of their goods, fled outright into the forest. Their fire they left still burning, and their dead comrade unburied. All day they ceased not to flee, eating by the way, from hand to mouth; and since they feared to sleep, continued to advance at random even in the hours of darkness. But the limit of man's endurance is soon reached; when they rested at last it was to sleep profoundly; and when they woke, it was to find that the enemy was still upon their heels, and death and mutilation had once more lessened and deformed their company.

By this they had become light-headed, they had quite missed their path in the wilderness, their stores were already running low. With the further horrors, it is superfluous that I should swell this narrative, already too prolonged. Suffice it to say that when at length a night passed by innocuous, and they might breathe again in the hope that the murderer had at last desisted from pursuit, Mountain and Secundra were alone. The trader is firmly persuaded their unseen enemy was some warrior of his own acquaintance, and that he himself was spared by favour. The mercy extended to Secundra he explains on the ground that the East Indian was thought to be insane; partly from the fact that, through all the horrors of the flight and while others were casting away their food and weapons, Secundra continued to stagger forward with a mattock on his shoulder, and partly because, in the last days and with a great degree of heat and fluency, he perpetually spoke with himself in his own language. But he was sane enough when it came to English.

'You think he will be gone quite away?' he asked, upon their blest awakening in safety.

'I pray God so, I believe so, I dare to believe so,' Mountain had replied almost with incoherence, as he described the scene to me.

And indeed he was so much distempered that until he met us, the next morning, he could scarce be certain whether he had dreamed or whether it was a fact, that Secundra had thereupon turned directly about and returned without a word upon their footprints, setting his face for these wintry and hungry solitudes, along a path whose every stage was mile-stoned with a mutilated corpse.

TWELVE

The Journey in the Wilderness
(continued)

MOUNTAIN'S STORY, AS IT WAS laid before Sir William Johnson and my lord, was shorn, of course, of all the earlier particulars, and the expedition described to have proceeded uneventfully, until the Master sickened. But the latter part was very forcibly related, the speaker visibly thrilling to his recollections; and our then situation, on the fringe of the same desert, and the private interests of each, gave him an audience prepared to share in his emotions. For Mountain's intelligence not only changed the world for my Lord Durrisdeer, but materially affected the designs of Sir William Johnson.

These I find I must lay more at length before the reader. Word had reached Albany of dubious import; it had been rumoured some hostility was to be put in act; and the Indian diplomatist had, thereupon, sped into the wilderness, even at the approach of winter, to nip that mischief in the bud. Here, on the borders, he learned that he was come too late; and a difficult choice was thus presented to a man (upon the whole) not any more bold than prudent. His standing with the painted braves may be compared to that of my Lord President Culloden among the chiefs of our own Highlanders at the 'Forty-five; that is as much as to say, he was, to these men, reason's only speaking-trumpet, and counsels of peace and moderation, if they were to prevail at all, must prevail singly through his influence. If, then, he should return, the province must lie open to all the abominable tragedies of Indian war – the houses blaze, the wayfarer be cut off, and the men of the woods collect their usual disgusting spoil of human scalps. On the other side, to go farther north, to risk so small a party deeper in the desert, to carry words of peace among warlike savages already rejoicing to return to war; here was an extremity from which it was easy to perceive his mind revolted.

'I have come too late,' he said more than once, and would fall into a deep consideration, his head bowed in his hands, his foot patting the ground.

At length he raised his face and looked upon us, that is to say upon my lord, Mountain, and myself, sitting close round a small fire, which had been made for privacy in one corner of the camp.

'My lord, to be quite frank with you, I find myself in two minds,' said he. 'I think it very needful I should go on, but not at all proper I should any longer enjoy the pleasure of your company. We are here still upon the water side; and I think the risk to southward no great matter. Will not yourself and Mr Mackellar take a single boat's crew and return to Albany?'

My lord, I should say, had listened to Mountain's narrative, regarding him throughout with a painful intensity of gaze; and since the tale concluded, had sat as in a dream. There was something very daunting in his look; something to my eyes not rightly human; the face, lean, and dark, and aged, the mouth painful, the teeth disclosed in a perpetual rictus; the eyeball swimming clear of the lids upon a field of blood-shot white. I could not behold him myself without a jarring irritation, such as, I believe, is too frequently the uppermost feeling on the sickness of those dear to us. Others, I could not but remark, were scarce able to support his neighbourhood – Sir William eviting to be near him, Mountain dodging his eye, and, when he met it, blenching and halting in his story. At this appeal, however, my lord appeared to recover his command upon himself.

'To Albany?' said he, with a good voice.

'Not short of it, at least,' replied Sir William. 'There is no safety nearer hand.'

'I would be very sweir* to return,' says my lord. 'I am not fraid – of Indians,' he added, with a jerk.

'I wish that I could say so much,' returned Sir William, smiling; 'although, if any man durst say it, it should be myself. But you are to keep in view my responsibility, and that as the voyage has now become highly dangerous, and your business – if you ever had any,' says he – 'brought quite to a conclusion by the distressing family intelligence you have received, I should be hardly justified if I even suffered you to proceed, and run the risk of some obloquy if anything regrettable should follow.'

My lord turned to Mountain. 'What did he pretend he died of?' he asked.

'I don't think I understand your honour,' said the trader, pausing, like a man very much affected, in the dressing of some cruel frostbites.

For a moment my lord seemed at a full stop: and then, with some irritation, 'I ask you what he died of. Surely that's a plain question,' said he.

'Oh! I don't know,' said Mountain. 'Hastie even never knew. He seemed to sicken natural, and just pass away.'

'There it is, you see!' concluded my lord, turning to Sir William.

'Your lordship is too deep for me,' replied Sir William.

'Why,' says my lord, 'this is a matter of succession; my son's title may be called in doubt; and the man being supposed to be dead of nobody can tell what, a great deal of suspicion would be naturally roused.'

'But, God damn me, the man's buried!' cried Sir William.

'I will never believe that,' returned my lord, painfully trembling. 'I'll never believe it!' he cried again, and jumped to his feet. 'Did he look dead?' he asked of Mountain.

'Look dead?' repeated the trader. 'He looked white. Why, what would he be at? I tell you, I put the sods upon him.'

My lord caught Sir William by the coat with a hooked hand. 'This man

*Unwilling.

340

has the name of my brother,' says he, 'but it's well understood that he was never canny.'

'Canny?' says Sir William. 'What is that?'

'He's not of this world,' whispered my lord, 'neither him nor the black deil that serves him. I have struck my sword throughout his vitals,' he cried; 'I have felt the hilt dirl* on his breastbone, and the hot blood spirt in my very face, time and again, time and again!' he repeated, with a gesture indescribable. 'But he was never dead for that,' said he, and sighed aloud. 'Why should I think he was dead now? No, not till I see him rotting,' says he.

Sir William looked across at me with a long face. Mountain forgot his wounds, staring and gaping.

'My lord,' said I, 'I wish you would collect your spirits.' But my throat was so dry, and my own wits so scattered, I could add no more.

'No,' says my lord, 'it's not to be supposed that he would understand me. Mackellar does, for he kens all, and has seen him buried before now. This is a very good servant to me, Sir William, this man Mackellar; he buried him with his own hands – he and my father – by the light of two siller candlesticks. The other man is a familiar spirit; he brought him from Coromandel. I would have told ye this long syne, Sir William, only it was in the family,' These last remarks he made with a kind of melancholy composure, and his time of aberration seemed to pass away. 'You can ask yourself what it all means,' he proceeded. 'My brother falls sick, and dies, and is buried, or so they say; and all seems very plain. But why did the familiar go back? I think ye must see for yourself it's a point that wants some clearing.'

'I will be at your service, my lord, in half a minute,' said Sir William, rising. 'Mr Mackellar, two words with you'; and he led me without the camp, the frost crunching in our steps, the trees standing at our elbow, hoar with frost, even as on that night in the Long Shrubbery. 'Of course, this is midsummer madness,' said Sir William, as soon as we were gotten out of hearing.

'Why, certainly,' said I. 'The man is mad. I think that manifest.'

'Shall I seize and bind him?' asked Sir William. 'I will upon your authority. If these are all ravings, that should certainly be done.'

I looked down upon the ground, back at the camp, with its bright fires and the folk watching us, and about me on the woods and mountains; there was just the one way that I could not look, and that was in Sir William's face.

'Sir William,' said I at last, 'I think my lord not sane, and have long

*Ring.

thought him so. But there are degrees in madness; and whether he should be brought under restraint – Sir William, I am no fit judge,' I concluded.

'I will be the judge,' said he. 'I ask for facts. Was there, in all that jargon, any word of truth or sanity? Do you hesitate?' he asked. 'Am I to understand you have buried this gentleman before?'

'Not buried,' said I; and then, taking up courage at last, 'Sir William,' said I, 'unless I were to tell you a long story, which much concerns a noble family (and myself not in the least), it would be impossible to make this matter clear to you. Say the word, and I will do it, right or wrong. And, at any rate I will say so much, that my lord is not so crazy as he seems. This is a strange matter, into the tail of which you are unhappily drifted.'

'I desire none of your secrets,' replied Sir William; 'but I will be plain at the risk of incivility, and confess that I take little pleasure in my present company.'

'I would be the last to blame you,' said I, 'for that.'

'I have not asked either for your censure or your praise, sir,' returned Sir William. 'I desire simply to be quit of you: and to that effect I put a boat and complement of men at your disposal.'

'This is fairly offered,' said I, after reflection. 'But you must suffer me to say a word upon the other side. We have a natural curiosity to learn the truth of this affair; I have some of it myself; my lord (it is very plain) has but too much. The matter of the Indian's return is enigmatical.'

'I think so myself,' Sir William interrupted, 'and I propose (since I go in that direction) to probe it to the bottom. Whether or not the man has gone like a dog to die upon his master's grave, his life, at least, is in great danger, and I propose, if I can, to save it. There is nothing against his character?'

'Nothing, Sir William,' I replied.

'And the other?' he said. 'I have heard my lord, of course; but, from the circumstances of his servant's loyalty, I must suppose he had some noble qualities.'

'You must not ask that!' I cried. 'Hell may have noble flames. I have known him a score of years, and always hated, and always admired, and always slavishly feared him.'

'I appear to intrude again upon your secrets,' and Sir William, 'believe me, inadvertently. Enough that I will see the grave, and (if possible) rescue the Indian. Upon these terms, can you persuade your master to return to Albany?'

'Sir William,' said I, 'I will tell you how it is. You do not see my lord to advantage; it will seem even strange to you that I should love him; but I do, and I am not alone. If he goes back to Albany, it must be by force, and it will be the death-warrant of his reason, and perhaps his life. That is my sincere belief; but I am in your hands, and ready to obey, if you will assume so much responsibility as to command.'

'I will have no shred or responsibility; it is my single endeavour to avoid the same,' cried Sir William. 'You insist upon following this journey up; and be it so! I wash my hands of the whole matter.'

With which word, he turned upon his heel and gave the order to break camp; and my lord, who had been hovering near by, came instantly to my side.

'Which is it to be?' said he.

'You are to have your way,' I answered. 'You shall see the grave.'

The situation of the master's grave was, between guides, easily described; it lay, indeed, beside a chief landmark of the wilderness, a certain range of peaks, conspicuous by their design and altitude, and the source of many brawling tributaries to that inland sea, Lake Champlain. It was therefore possible to strike for it direct, instead of following back the blood-stained trail of the fugitives, and to cover, in some sixteen hours of march, a distance which their perturbed wanderings had extended over more than sixty. Our boats we left under a guard upon the river; it was, indeed, probable we should return to find them frozen fast; and the small equipment with which we set forth upon the expedition included not only an infinity of furs to protect us from the cold, but an arsenal of snow-shoes to render travel possible, when the inevitable snow should fall. Considerable alarm was manifested at our departure; the march was conducted with soldierly precaution, the camp at night sedulously chosen and patrolled; and it was a consideration of this sort that arrested us, the second day, within not many hundred yards of our destination – the night being already imminent, the spot in which we stood well qualified to be a strong camp for a party of our numbers; and Sir William, therefore, on a sudden thought, arresting our advance.

Before us was the high range of mountains toward which we had been all day deviously drawing near. From the first light of the dawn, their silver peaks had been the goal of our advance across a tumbled lowland forest, thrid with rough streams, and strewn with monstrous boulders; the peaks (as I say) silver, for already at the higher altitudes the snow fell nightly; but the woods and the low ground only breathed upon with frost. All day heaven had been charged with ugly vapours in the which the sun swam and glimmered like a shilling piece; all day the wind blew on our left cheek barbarous cold, but very pure to breathe. With the end of the afternoon, however, the wind fell; the clouds, being no longer reinforced, were scattered or drunk up; the sun set behind us with some wintry splendour, and the white brow of the mountains shared its dying glow.

It was dark ere we had supper; we ate in silence, and the meal was scarce despatched before my lord slunk from the fireside to the margin of the camp; whither I made haste to follow him. The camp was on high ground, overlooking a frozen lake, perhaps a mile in its longest measurement; all about us, the forest lay in heights and hollows; above rose the white mountains; and higher yet, the moon rode in a fair sky. There was no breath of air; nowhere a twig creaked; and the sounds of our own camp were hushed and swallowed up in the surrounding stillness. Now that the sun and the wind were both gone down, it appeared almost warm, like a night of July; a singular illusion of the sense, when earth, air, and water were strained to bursting with the extremity of frost.

My lord (or what I still continued to call by his loved name) stood with his elbow in one hand, and his chin sunk in the other, gazing before him on the surface of the wood. My eyes followed his, and rested almost pleasantly upon the frosted contexture of the pines, rising in moonlit hillocks, or sinking in the shadow of small glens. Hard by, I told myself, was the grave of our enemy, now gone where the wicked cease from troubling, the earth heaped for ever on his once so active limbs. I could not but think of him as somehow fortunate to be thus done with man's anxiety and weariness, the daily expense of spirit, and that daily river of circumstance to be swum through, at any hazard, under the penalty of shame or death. I could not but think how good was the end of that long travel; and with that, my mind swung at a tangent to my lord. For was not my lord dead also? a maimed soldier, looking vainly for discharge, lingering derided in the line of battle? A kind man, I remembered him; wise, with a decent pride, a son perhaps too dutiful, a husband only too loving, one that could suffer and be silent, one whose hand I loved to press. Of a sudden, pity caught in my windpipe with a sob; I could have wept aloud to remember and behold him; and standing thus by his elbow, under the broad moon, I prayed fervently either that he should be released, or I strengthened to persist in my affection.

'Oh God,' said I, 'this was the best man to me and to himself, and now I shrink from him. He did no wrong, or not till he was broke with sorrows; these are but his honourable wounds that we begin to shrink from. Oh, cover them up, oh, take him away, before we hate him!'

I was still so engaged in my own bosom, when a sound broke suddenly upon the night. It was neither very loud, nor very near; yet, bursting as it did from so profound and so prolonged a silence, it startled the camp like an alarm of trumpets. Ere I had taken breath, Sir William was beside me, the main part of the voyagers clustered at his back, intently giving ear. Methought, as I glanced at them across my shoulder, there was a whiteness, other than moonlight, on their cheeks; and the rays of the moon reflected with a sparkle on the eyes of some, and the shadows lying black under the brows of others (according as they raised or bowed the head to listen) gave to the group a strange air of animation and anxiety. My lord was to the front, crouching a little forth, his hand raised as for silence: a man turned to stone. And still the sounds continued, breathlessly renewed with a precipitate rhythm.

Suddenly Mountain spoke in a loud, broken whisper, as of a man relieved. 'I have it now,' he said; and, as we all turned to hear him, 'the Indian must have known the cache,' he added. 'That is he – he is digging out the treasure.'

'Why, to be sure!' exclaimed Sir William. 'We were geese not to have supposed so much.'

'The only thing is,' Mountain resumed, 'the sound is very close to our old camp. And, again, I do not see how he is there before us, unless the man had wings!'

'Greed and fear are wings,' remarked Sir William. 'But this rogue has given us an alert, and I have a notion to return the compliment. What say you, gentlemen, shall we have a moonlight hunt?'

It was so agreed; dispositions were made to surround Secundra at his task; some of Sir William's Indians hastened in advance; and a strong guard being left at our headquarters, we set forth along the uneven bottom of the forest; frost crackling, ice sometimes loudly splitting under foot; and overhead the blackness of pine-woods, and the broken brightness of the moon. Our way led down into a hollow of the land; and as we descended, the sounds diminished and had almost died away. Upon the other slope it was more open, only dotted with a few pines, and several vast and scattered rocks that made inky shadows in the moonlight. Here the sounds began to reach us more distinctly; we could now perceive the ring of iron, and more exactly estimate the furious degree of haste with which the digger plied his instrument. As we neared the top of the ascent, a bird or two winged aloft and hovered darkly in the moonlight; and the next moment we were gazing through a fringe of trees upon a singular picture.

A narrow plateau, overlooked by the white mountains, and encompassed nearer hand by woods, lay bare to the strong radiance of the moon. Rough goods, such as make the wealth of foresters, were sprinkled here and there upon the ground in meaningless disarray. About the midst, a tent stood, silvered with frost: the door open, gaping on the black interior. At the one end of this small stage lay what seemed the tattered remnants of a man. Without doubt we had arrived upon the scene of Harris's encampment; there were the goods scattered in the panic of flight; it was in yon tent the Master breathed his last; and the frozen carrion that lay before us was the body of the drunken shoemaker. It was always moving to come upon the theatre of any tragic incident; to come upon it after so many days, and to find it (in the seclusion of a desert) still unchanged, must have impressed the mind of the most careless. And yet it was not that which struck us into pillars of stone; but the sight (which yet we had been half expecting) of Secundra ankle deep in the grave of his late Master. He had cast the main part of his raiment by, yet his frail arms and shoulders glistened in the moonlight with a copious sweat; his face was contracted with anxiety and expectation; his blows resounded on the grave, as thick as sobs; and behind him, strangely deformed and ink-black upon the frosty ground, the creature's shadow repeated and parodied his swift gesticulations. Some night birds arose from the boughs upon our coming, and then settled back; but Secundra, absorbed in his toil, heard or heeded not at all.

I heard Mountain whisper to Sir William, 'Good God! it's the grave! He's digging him up!' It was what we had all guessed, and yet to hear it put in language thrilled me. Sir William violently started.

'You damned sacrilegious hound!' he cried. 'What's this?'

Secundar leaped in the air, a little breathless cry escaped him, the tool flew from his grasp, and he stood one instant staring at the speaker. The next, swift as an arrow, he sped for the woods upon the farther side; and the next again, throwing up his hands with a violent gesture of resolution, he had begun already to retrace his steps.

'Well, then, you come, you help—' he was saying. But by now my lord had stepped beside Sir William; the moon shone fair upon his face, and the words were still upon Secundra's lips, when he beheld and recognized his master's enemy. 'Him!' he screamed, clasping his hands, and shrinking on himself.

'Come, come!' said Sir William. 'There is none here to do you harm, if you be innocent; and if you be guilty, your escape is quite cut off. Speak, what do you here among the graves of the dead and the remains of the unburied?'

'You no murderer?' inquired Secundra. 'You true man? You see me safe?'

'I will see you safe, if you be innocent,' returned Sir William. 'I have said the thing, and I see not wherefore you should doubt it.'

'These all murderers,' cried Secundra, 'that is why! He kill – murderer,' pointing to Mountain; 'there two hire-murderers,' pointing to my lord and myself – 'all gallows-murderers! Ah! I see you all swing in a rope.

Now I go save the sahib; he see you swing in a rope. The sahib,' he continued, pointing to the grave, 'he not dead. He bury, he not dead.'

My lord uttered a little noise, moved nearer to the grave, and stood and stared in it.

'Buried and not dead?' exclaimed Sir William. 'What kind of rant is this?'

'See, sahib,' said Secundra. 'The sahib and I alone with murderers; try all way to escape, no way good. Then try this way: good way in warm climate good way in India; here, in this dam cold place, who can tell? I tell you pretty good hurry: you help, you light a fire, help rub.'

'What is the creature talking of?' cried Sir William. 'My head goes round.'

'I tell you I bury him alive,' said Secundra. 'I teach him swallow his tongue. Now dig him up pretty good hurry, and he not much worse. You light a fire.'

Sir William turned to the nearest of his men. 'Light a fire,' said he. 'My lot seems to be cast with the insane.'

'You good man,' returned Secundra. 'Now I go dig the sahib up.'

He returned as he spoke to the grave, and resumed his former toil. My lord stood rooted, and I at my lord's side, fearing I knew not what.

The frost was not yet very deep, and presently the Indian threw aside his tool, and began to scoop the dirt by handfuls. Then he disengaged a corner of a buffalo robe; and then I saw hair catch among his fingers: yet a moment more, and the moon shone on something white. A while Secundra crouched upon his knees, scraping with delicate fingers, breathing with puffed lips; and when he moved aside I beheld the face of the Master wholly disengaged. It was deadly white, the eyes closed, the ears and nostrils plugged, the cheeks fallen, the nose sharp as if in death; but for all he had lain so many days under the sod, corruption had not approached him, and (what strangely affected all of us) his lips and chin were mantled with a swarthy beard.

'My God!' cried Mountain, 'he was as smooth as a baby when we laid him there!'

'They say hair grows upon the dead,' observed Sir William, but his voice was thick and weak.

Secundra paid no heed to our remarks, digging swift as a terrier in the loose earth. Every moment the form of the Master, swathed in his buffalo robe, grew more distinct in the bottom of that shallow trough; the moon shining strong, and the shadows of the standers-by, as they drew forward and back, falling and flitting over his emergent countenance. The sight held us with a horror not before experienced. I dared not look my lord in the face; but for as long as it lasted, I never observed him to draw breath; and a little in the background one of the men (I know not whom) burst into a kind of sobbing.

'Now,' said Secundra, 'you help me lift him out.'

Of the flight of time, I have no idea; it may have been three hours, and it may have been five, that the Indian laboured to reanimate his master's body. One thing only I know, that it was still night, and the moon was not yet set, although it had sunk low, and now barred the plateau with long shadows, when Secundra uttered a small cry of satisfaction; and, leaning swiftly forth, I thought I could myself perceive a change upon the icy countenance of the unburied. The next moment I beheld his eyelids flutter; the next they rose entirely, and the week-old corpse looked me for a moment in the face.

So much display of life I can myself swear to. I have heard from others that he visibly strove to speak, that his teach showed in his beard, and that his brow was contorted as with an agony of pain aand effort. And this may have been; I know not, I was otherwise engaged. For at that first disclosure of the dead man's eyes, my Lord Durrisdeer fell to the ground, and when I raised him up, he was a corpse.

Day came, and still Secundra could not be persuaded to desist from his unavailing efforts. Sir William, leaving a small party under my command, proceeded on his embassy with the first light; and still the Indian rubbed the limbs and breathed in the mouth of the dead body. You would think such labours might have vitalized a stone; but, except for that one moment (which was my lord's death), the black spirit of the Master held aloof from its discarded clay; and by about the hour of noon, even the faithful servant was at length convinced. He took it with unshaken quietude.

'Too cold,' said he, 'good way in India, no good here.' And, asking for some food, which he ravenously devoured as soon as it was set before him, he drew near the fire and took his place at my elbow. In the same spot, as soon as he had eaten, he stretched himself out, and fell into a childlike slumber, from which I must arouse him, some hours afterwards, to take his part as one of the mourners at the double funeral. It was the same throughout; he seemed to have outlived at once, and with the same effort, his grief for his master and his terror of myself and Mountain.

One of the men left with me was skilled in stone-cutting; and before Sir William returned to pick us up, I had chiselled on a boulder this inscription, with a copy of which I may fitly bring my narrative to a close:

J. D.,

HEIR TO A SCOTTISH TITLE,

A MASTER OF THE ARTS AND GRACES,

ADMIRED IN EUROPE, ASIA, AMERICA,

IN WAR AND PEACE,

IN THE TENTS OF SAVAGE HUNTERS AND THE

CITADELS OF KINGS, AFTER SO MUCH

ACQUIRED, ACCOMPLISHED, AND

ENDURED,

LIES HERE FORGOTTEN.

—

H. D.,

HIS BROTHER,

AFTER A LIFE OF UNMERITED DISTRESS,

BRAVELY SUPPORTED,

DIED ALMOST IN THE SAME HOUR,

AND SLEEPS IN THE SAME GRAVE

WITH HIS FRATERNAL ENEMY.

—

THE PIETY OF HIS WIFE AND ONE OLD

SERVANT RAISED THIS STONE

TO BOTH.

THE STRANGE CASE
OF
DR JEKYLL
AND MR HYDE

To
KATHARINE DE MATTOS

It's ill to loose the bands that God decreed to bind;
Still will we be the children of the heather and the wind;
Far away from home, O it's still for you and me
That the broom is blowing bonnie in the north countrie.

ONE

⚜ Story of the Door ⚜

MR UTTERSON THE LAWYER was a man of a rugged countenance, that was never lighted by a smile; cold, scanty and embarrassed in discourse; backward in sentiment; lean, long, dusty, dreary, and yet somehow lovable. At friendly meetings, and when the wine was to his taste, something eminently human beaconed from his eye; something indeed which never found its way into his talk, but which spoke not only in these silent symbols of the after-dinner face, but more often and loudly in the acts of his life. He was austere with himself; drank gin when he was alone, to mortify a taste for vintages; and though he enjoyed the theatre, had not crossed the doors of one for twenty years. But he had an approved tolerance for others; sometimes wondering, almost with envy, at the high pressure of spirits involved in their misdeeds; and in any extremity inclined to help rather than to reprove. 'I incline to Cain's heresy,' he used to say quaintly: 'I let my brother go to the devil in his own way.' In this character it was frequently his fortune to be the last reputable acquaintance and the last good influence in the lives of down-going men. And to such as these, so long as they came about his chambers, he never marked a shade of change in his demeanour.

No doubt the feat was easy to Mr Utterson; for he was undemonstrative at the best, and even his friendships seemed to be founded in a similar catholicity of good-nature. It is the mark of a modest man to accept his friendly circle ready made from the hands of opportunity; and that was the lawyer's way. His friends were those of his own blood, or those whom he had known the longest; his affections, like ivy, were the growth of time, they implied no aptness in the object. Hence, no doubt, the bond that united him to Mr Richard Enfield, his distant kinsman, the well-known man about town. It was a nut to crack for many, what these two could see in each other, or what subject they could find in common. It was reported by those who encountered them in their Sunday walks, that they said nothing, looking singularly dull, and would hail with obvious relief the appearance of a friend. For all that, the two men put the greatest store by these excursions, counted them the chief jewel of each week, and not only set aside occasions of pleasure, but even resisted the calls of business, that they might enjoy them uninterrupted.

It chanced on one of these rambles that their way led them down a by-street in a busy quarter of London. The street was small and what is called quiet, but it drove a thriving trade on the week-days. The inhabitants were all doing well, it seemed, and all emulously hoping to do better still, and laying out the surplus of their gains in coquetry; so that the shop fronts stood along that thoroughfare with an air of invitation, like rows of smiling saleswomen. Even on Sunday, when it veiled its more florid charms and lay comparatively empty of passage, the street shone out in contrast to its dingy neighbourhood, like a fire in a forest; and with its freshly painted shutters, well-polished brasses, and general cleanliness and gaiety of note, instantly caught and pleased the eye of the passenger.

Two doors from one corner, on the left hand going east, the line was broken by the entry of a court; and just at that point, a certain sinister block of building thrust forward its gable on the street. It was two storeys high; showed no window, nothing but a door on the lower storey and a blind forehead of discoloured wall on the upper; and bore in every feature the marks of prolonged and sordid negligence. The door, which was equipped with neither bell nor knocker, was blistered and distained. Tramps slouched into the recess and struck matches on the panels; children kept shop upon the steps; the schoolboy had tried his knife on the mouldings; and for close on a generation no one had appeared to drive away these random visitors or to repair their ravages.

Mr Enfield and the lawyer were on the other side of the by-street; but when they came abreast of the entry, the former lifted up his cane and pointed.

'Did you ever remark that door?' he asked; and when his companion had replied in the affirmative, 'It is connected in my mind,' added he, 'with a very odd story.'

'Indeed!' said Mr Utterson, with a slight change of voice, 'and what was that?'

'Well, it was this way,' returned Mr Enfield: 'I was coming home from some place at the end of the world, about three o'clock of a black winter morning, and my way lay through a part of town where there was literally nothing to be seen but lamps. Street after street, and all the folks asleep – street after street, all lighted up as if for a procession, and all as empty as a church – till at last I got into that state of mind when a man listens and listens and begins to long for the sight of a policeman. All at once, I saw two figures: one a little man who was stumping along eastward at a good walk, and the other a girl of maybe eight or ten who was running as hard as she was able down a cross-street. Well, sir, the two ran into one another naturally enough at the corner; and then came the horrible part of the thing; for the man trampled calmly over the child's body and left her screaming on the ground. It sounds nothing to hear, but it was hellish to see. It wasn't like a man; it was like some damned Juggernaut. I gave a view halloa, took to my heels, collared my gentleman, and brought him back to where there was already quite a group about the screaming child. He was perfectly cool and made no resistance, but gave me one look, so ugly that it brought the sweat on me like running. The people who had turned out were the girl's own family; and pretty soon the doctor, for whom she had been sent, put in his appearance. Well, the child was not much the worse, more frightened, according to the Sawbones; and there you might have supposed would be an end to it. But there was one curious circumstance. I had taken a loathing to my gentleman at first sight. So had the child's family, which was only natural. But the doctor's case was what struck me. He was the usual cut-and-dry apothecary, of no particular age and colour, with a strong Edinburgh accent, and about as emotional as a bagpipe. Well, sir, he was like the rest of us: every time he looked at my prisoner, I saw that Sawbones turned sick and white with the desire to kill him. I knew what was in his mind, just as he knew what was in mine; and killing being out of the question, we did the next best. We told the man we could and would make such a scandal out of this, as should make his name stink from one end of London to the other. If he had any friends or any credit, we undertook that he should lose them. And all the time, as we were pitching it in red hot, we were keeping the women off him as best we could, for they were as wild as harpies. I never saw a circle of such hateful faces; and there was the man in the middle, with a kind of black sneering coolness – frightened, too, I could see that – but carrying it off, sir, really like Satan. "If you choose to make capital out of this accident," said he, "I am naturally helpless. No gentleman but wishes to avoid a scene," says he. "Name your figure." Well, we screwed him up to a hundred pounds for the child's family; he would have clearly liked to stick out; but there was something about the lot of us that means mischief, and at last he struck. The next thing was to get the money; and where do you think he carried us but to that place with the door? – whipped out a key, went in, and presently came back with the matter of ten pounds in gold and a cheque for the balance on Coutts's, drawn payable to bearer, and signed with a name that I can't mention, though it's one of the points of my story, but it was a name at least very well known and often printed. The figure was stiff; but the signature was good for more than that, if it was only genuine. I took the liberty of pointing out to my gentleman that the whole business looked apocryphal; and that a man does not, in real life, walk into a cellar door at four in the morning and come out of it with another man's cheque for close upon a hundred pounds. But he was quite easy and sneering. "Set your mind at rest," says he; "I will stay with you till the banks open, and cash the cheque myself." So we all set off, the doctor, and the child's father, and our friend and myself, and passed the rest of the night in my chambers; and next day, when we had breakfasted, went in a body to the bank. I gave in the cheque myself, and said I had every reason to believe it was a forgery. Not a bit of it. The cheque was genuine.'

'Tut-tut!' said Mr Utterston.

'I see you feel as I do,' said Mr Enfield. 'Yes, it's a bad story. For my man was a fellow that nobody could have to do with, a really damnable man; and the person that drew the cheque is the very pink of the properties, celebrated too, and (what makes it worse) one of your fellows who do what they call good. Blackmail, I suppose; an honest man paying through the nose for some of the capers of his youth. Blackmail House is what I call that place with the door, in consequence. Though even that, you know, is far from explaining all,' he added; and with the words fell into a vein of musing.

From this he was recalled by Mr Utterson asking rather suddenly: 'And you don't know if the drawer of the cheque lives there?'

'A likely place, isn't it?' returned Mr Enfield. 'But I happened to have noticed his address; he lives in some square or other.'

'And you never asked about – the place with the door?' said Mr Utterson.

'No, sir: I had a delicacy,' was the reply. 'I feel very strongly about putting questions; it partakes too much of the style of the day of judgment. You start a question, and it's like starting a stone. You sit quietly on the top of a hill; and away the stone goes, starting others; and presently some bland old bird (the last you would have thought of) is knocked on the head in his own back garden, and the family have to change their name. No, sir, I make it a rule of mine: the more it looks like Queer Street, the less I ask.'

'A very good rule, too,' said the lawyer.

'But I have studied the place for myself,' continued Mr Enfield. 'It seems scarcely a house. There is no other door, and nobody goes in or out of that one, but, once in a great while, the gentleman of my adventure. There are three windows looking on the court on the first floor; none below; the windows are always shut, but they're clean. And then there is a chimney, which is generally smoking; so somebody must live there. And yet it's not so sure; for the buildings are so packed together about that court, that it's hard to say where one ends and another begins.'

The pair walked on again for a while in silence; and then – 'Enfield,' said Mr Utterson, 'that's a good rule of yours.'

'Yes, I think it is,' returned Enfield.

'But for all that,' continued the lawyer, 'there's one point I want to ask: I want to ask the name of that man who walked over the child.'

'Well,' said Mr Enfield, 'I can't see what harm it would do. It was a man of the name of Hyde.'

'Hm,' said Mr Utterson. 'What sort of a man is he to see?'

'He is not easy to describe. There is something wrong with his appearance; something displeasing, something downright detestable. I never saw a man I so disliked, and yet I scarce know why. He must be deformed somewhere; he gives a strong feeling of deformity, although I couldn't specify the point. He's an extraordinary-looking man, and yet I really can name nothing out of the way. No, sir; I can make no hand of it; I can't describe him. And it's not want of memory; for I declare I can see him this moment.'

Mr Utterson again walked some way in silence, and obviously under a weight of consideration. 'You are sure he used a key?' he inquired at last.

'My dear sir . . .' began Enfield, surprised out of himself.

'Yes, I know,' said Utterson; 'I know it must seem strange. The fact is, if I do not ask you the name of the other party, it is because I know it already. You see, Richard, your tale has gone home. If you have been inexact in any point, you had better correct it.'

'I think you might have warned me,' returned the other, with a touch of sullenness. 'But I have been pedantically exact, as you call it. The fellow had a key; and, what's more, he has it still. I saw him use it, not a week ago.'

Mr Utterson sighed deeply, but said never a word; and the young man presently resumed. 'Here is another lesson to say nothing,' said he. 'I am ashamed of my long tongue. Let us make a bargain never to refer to this again.'

'With all my heart,' said the lawyer. 'I shake hands on that, Richard.'

TWO

❖ Search for Mr Hyde ❖

THAT EVENING MR UTTERSON came home to his bachelor house in sombre spirits, and sat down to dinner without relish. It was his custom on a Sunday, when this meal was over, to sit close by the fire, a volume of some dry divinity on his reading-desk, until the clock of the neighbouring church rang out the hour of twelve, when he would go soberly and gratefully to bed. On this night, however, as soon as the cloth was taken away, he took up a candle and went into his business room. There he opened his safe, took from the most private part of it a document endorsed on the envelope as Dr Jekyll's Will, and sat down with a clouded brow to study its contents. The will was holograph; for Mr Utterson, though he took charge of it now that it was made, had refused to lend the least assistance in the making of it; it provided not only that, in case of the decease of Henry Jekyll, M.D., D.C.L., LL.D., F.R.S., &c., all his possessions were to pass into the hands of his 'friend and benefactor Edward Hyde'; but that in case of Dr Jekyll's 'disappearance or unexplained absence for any period exceeding three calendar months,' the said Edward Hyde should step into the said Henry Jekyll's shoes without further delay, and free from any burden or obligation, beyond the payment of a few small sums to the member's of the doctor's household. This document had long been the lawyer's eyesore. It offended him both as a lawyer and as a lover of the sane and customary sides of life, to whom the fanciful was the immodest. And hitherto it was his ignorance of Mr Hyde that had swelled his indignation; now, by a sudden turn, it was his knowledge. It was already bad enough when the name was but a name of which he could learn no more. It was worse when it began to be clothed upon with detestable attributes; and out of the shifting, insubstantial mists that had so long baffled his eye, there leaped up the sudden, definite presentment of a fiend.

'I thought it was madness,' he said, as he replaced the obnoxious paper in the safe; 'and now I begin to fear it is disgrace.'

With that he blew out his candle, put on a great-coat, and set forth in the direction of Cavendish Square, that citadel of medicine, where his friend the great Dr Lanyon, had his house and received his crowding patients. 'If any one knows, it will be Lanyon,' he had thought.

The solemn butler knew and welcomed him; he was subjected to no stage of delay, but ushered direct from the door to the dining-room, where Dr Lanyon sat alone over his wine. This was a hearty, healthy, dapper, red-faced gentleman, with a shock of hair prematurely white, and a boisterous and decided manner. At sight of Mr Utterson, he sprang up from his chair and welcomed him with both hands. The geniality, as was the way of the man, was somewhat theatrical to the eye; but it reposed on genuine feeling. For these two were old friends, old mates both at school and college, both thorough respecters of themselves and of each other, and, what does not always follow, men who thoroughly enjoyed each other's company.

After a little rambling talk, the lawyer led up to the subject which so disagreeably preoccupied his mind.

'I suppose, Lanyon,' he said, 'you and I must be the two oldest friends that Henry Jekyll has?'

'I wish the friends were younger,' chuckled Dr Lanyon. 'But I suppose we are. And what of that? I see little of him now.'

'Indeed!' said Utterson. 'I thought you had a bond of common interest.'

'We had,' was his reply. 'But it is more than ten years since Henry Jekyll became too fanciful for me. He began to go wrong, wrong in mind; and though, of course, I continue to take an interest in him for old sake's sake as they say, I see and I have seen devilish little of the man. Such unscientific balderdash,' added the doctor, flushing suddenly purple, 'would have estranged Damon and Pythias.'

This little spirit of temper was somewhat of a relief to Mr Utterson. 'They have only differed on some point of science,' he thought; and being a man of no scientific passions (except in the matter of conveyancing), he even added: 'It is nothing worse than that!' He gave his friend a few seconds to recover his composure, and then approached the question he had come to put.

'Did you ever come across a *protegé* of his – one Hyde?' he asked.

'Hyde?' repeated Lanyon. 'No. Never heard of him. Since my time.'

That was the amount of information that the lawyer carried back with him to the great, dark bed on which he tossed to and fro until the small hours of the morning began to grow large. It was a night of little ease to his toiling mind, toiling in mere darkness and besieged by questions.

Six o'clock struck on the bells of the church that was so conveniently near to Mr Utterson's dwelling, and still he was digging at the problem. Hitherto it had touched him on the intellectual side alone; but now his imagination also was engaged, or rather enslaved; and as he lay and tossed in the gross darkness of the night and the curtained room, Mr Enfield's tale went by before his mind in a scroll of lighted pictures. He would be aware of the great field of lamps of a nocturnal city; then of the figure of a man walking swiftly; then of a child running from the doctor's; and then these met, and that human Juggernaut trod the child down and passed on regardless of her screams. Or else he would see a room in a rich house, where his friend lay asleep, dreaming and smiling at his dreams; and then the door of that room would be opened, the curtains of the bed plucked apart, the sleeper recalled, and, lo! there would stand by his side a figure to whom power was given, and even at that dead hour he must rise and do its bidding. The figure in these two phases haunted the lawyer all night; and if at any time he dozed over, it was but to see it glide more stealthily through sleeping houses, or move the more swiftly, and still the more swiftly, even to dizziness, through wider labyrinths of lamp-lighted city, and at every street corner crush a child and leave her screaming. And still the figure had no face by which he might know it; even in his dreams it had no face, or one that baffled him and melted before his eyes; and thus it was that there sprang up and grew apace in the lawyer's mind a singularly strong, almost an inordinate, curiosity to behold the features of the real Mr Hyde. If he could but once set eyes on him, he thought the mystery would lighten and perhaps roll altogether away, as was the habit of mysterious things when well examined. He might see a reason for his friend's strange preference or bondage (call it which you please), and even for the startling clauses of the will. And at least it would be a face worth seeing: the face of a man who was without bowels of mercy: a face which had but to show itself to raise up, in the mind of the unimpressionable Enfield, a spirit of enduring hatred.

From that time forward, Mr Utterson began to haunt the door in the by-street of shops. In the morning before office hours, at noon when business was plenty and time scarce, at night under the face of the fogged city moon, by all lights and at all hours of solitude or concourse, the lawyer was to be found on his chosen post.

'If he be Mr Hyde,' he had thought, 'I shall be Mr Seek.'

And at last his patience was rewarded. It was a fine dry night; frost in the air; the streets as clean as a ballroom floor; the lamps, unshaken by any wind, drawing a regular pattern of light and shadow. By ten o'clock, when the shops were closed, the by-street was very solitary, and, in spite of the low growl of London from all round, very silent. Small sounds carried far; domestic sounds out of the houses were clearly audible on either side of the roadway; and the rumour of the approach of any passenger preceded him by a long time. Mr Utterson had been some minutes at his post when he was aware of an odd light footstep drawing near. In the course of his nightly patrols he had long grown accustomed to the quaint effect with which the footfalls of a single person, while he is still a great way off, suddenly spring out distinct from the vast hum and clatter of the city. Yet his attention had never before been so sharply and decisively arrested; and it was with a strong, superstitious prevision of success that he withdrew into the entry of the court.

The steps drew swiftly nearer, and swelled out suddenly louder as they turned the end of the street. The lawyer, looking forth from the entry of the court, could soon see what manner of man he had to deal with. He was small, and very plainly dressed; and the look of him, even at that distance, went somehow strongly against the watcher's inclination. But he made straight for the door, crossing the roadway to save time; and as he came, he drew a key from his pocket, like one approaching home.

Mr Utterson stepped out and touched him on the shoulder as he passed. 'Mr Hyde, I think?'

Mr Hyde shrank back with a hissing intake of the breath. But his fear was only momentary; and though he did not look the lawyer in the face, he answered coolly enough: 'That is my name. What do you want?'

'I see you are going in,' returned the lawyer. 'I am an old friend of Dr Jekyll's – Mr Utterson, of Gaunt Street – you must have heard my name; and meeting you so conveniently, I thought you might admit me.'

'You will not find Dr Jekyll; he is from home,' replied Mr Hyde, blowing in the key. And then suddenly, but still without looking up, 'How did you know me?' he asked.

'On your side,' said Mr Utterson, 'will you do me a favour?'

'With pleasure,' replied the other. 'What shall it be?'

'Will you let me see your face?' asked the lawyer.

Mr Hyde appeared to hesitate; and then, as if upon some sudden reflection, fronted about with an air of defiance; and the pair stared at each other pretty fixedly for a few seconds. 'Now I shall know you again,' said Mr Utterson. 'It may be useful.'

'Yes,' returned Mr Hyde, 'it is as well we have met; and *à propos*, you should have my address.' And he gave a number of a street in Soho.

'Good God!' thought Mr Utterson, 'can he too have been thinking of the will?' But he kept his feelings to himself, and only grunted in acknowledgment of the address.

'And now,' said the other, 'how did you know me?'

'By description,' was the reply.

'Whose description?'

'We have common friends,' said Mr Utterson.

'Common friends!' echoed Mr Hyde, a little hoarsely. 'Who are they?'

'Jekyll, for instance,' said the lawyer.

'He never told you,' cried Mr Hyde, with a flush of anger. 'I did not think you would have lied.'

'Come,' said Mr Utterson, 'that is not fitting language.'

The other snarled aloud into a savage laugh; and the next moment, with extraordinary quickness, he had unlocked the door and disappeared into the house.

The lawyer stood awhile when Mr Hyde had left him, the picture of disquietude. Then he began slowly to mount the street, pausing every step or two, and putting his hand to his brow like a man in mental perplexity. The problem he was thus debating as he walked was one of a class that is rarely solved. Mr Hyde was pale and dwarfish; he gave an impression of deformity without any namable malformation, he had a displeasing smile, he had borne himself to the lawyer with a sort of murderous mixture of timidity and boldness, and he spoke with a husky, whispering and somewhat broken voice, – all these were points against him; but not all of these together could explain the hitherto unknown disgust, loathing and fear with which Mr Utterson regarded him. 'There must be something else,' said the perplexed gentleman. 'There *is* something more, if I could find a name for it. God bless me, the man seems hardly human! Something troglodytic, shall we say? or can it be the old story of Dr Fell? or is it the mere radiance of a foul soul that thus transpires through, and transfigures, its clay continent? The last, I think; for, O my poor old Harry Jekyll, if ever I read Satan's signature upon a face, it is on that of your new friend!'

Round the corner from the by-street there was a square of ancient, handsome houses, now for the most part decayed from their high estate, and let in flats and chambers to all sorts and conditions of men: map-engravers, architects, shady lawyers, and the agents of obscure enterprises. One house, however, second from the corner, was still occupied entire; and at the door of this, which wore a great air of wealth and comfort, though it was now plunged in darkness except for the fanlight, Mr Utterson stopped and knocked. A well-dressed, elderly servant opened the door.

'Is Dr Jekyll at home, Poole?' asked the lawyer.

'I will see, Mr Utterson,' said Poole, admitting the visitor, as he spoke, into a large, low-roofed, comfortable hall, paved with flags, warmed (after the fashion of a country house) by a bright, open fire, and furnished with costly cabinets of oak. 'Will you wait here by the fire, sir? or shall I give you a light in the dining-room?'

'Here, thank you,' said the lawyer; and he drew near and leaned on the tall fender. This hall, in which he was now left alone, was a pet fancy of his friend the doctor's; and Utterson himself was wont to speak of it as the pleasantest room in London. But tonight there was a shudder in his blood; the face of Hyde sat heavy on his memory; he felt (what was rare with him) a nausea and distaste of life; and in the gloom of his spirits, he seemed to read a menace in the flickering of the firelight on the polished cabinets and the uneasy starting of the shadow on the roof. He was ashamed of his relief when Poole presently returned to announce that Dr Jekyll was gone out.

'I saw Mr Hyde go in by the old dissecting-room door, Poole,' he said. 'Is that right, when Dr Jekyll is from home?'

'Quite right, Mr Utterson, sir,' replied the servant. 'Mr Hyde has a key.'

'Your master seems to repose a great deal of trust in that young man, Poole,' resumed the other, musingly.

'Yes, sir, he do indeed,' said Poole. 'We have all orders to obey him.'

'I do not think I ever met Mr Hyde?' asked Utterson.

'O dear no, sir. He never *dines* here,' replied the butler. 'Indeed, we see very little of him on this side of the house; he mostly comes and goes by the laboratory.'

'Well, good-night, Poole.'

'Good-night, Mr Utterson.'

And the lawyer set out homeward with a very heavy heart. 'Poor Harry Jekyll,' he thought, 'my mind misgives me he is in deep waters! He was wild when he was young; a long while ago, to be sure; but in the law of God there is no statute of limitations. Ah, it must be that; the ghost of some old sin, the cancer of some concealed disgrace; punishment coming, *pede claudo*, years after memory has forgotten and self-love condoned the fault.' And the lawyer, scared by the thought, brooded awhile on his own past, groping in all the corners of memory, lest by chance some Jack-in-the-Box of an old iniquity should leap to light there. His past was fairly blameless; few men could read the rolls of their life with less apprehension; yet he was humbled to the dust by the many ill things he had done, and raised up again into a sober and fearful gratitude by the many that he had come so near to doing, yet avoided. And then by a return on his former subject, he conceived a spark of hope. 'This Master Hyde, if he were studied,' thought he, 'must have secrets of his own: black secrets, by the look of him; secrets compared to which poor Jekyll's worst would be like sunshine. Things cannot continue as they are. It turns me cold to think of this creature stealing like a thief to Harry's bedside; poor Harry, what a wakening! And the danger of it! for if this Hyde suspects the existence of the will, he may grow impatient to inherit. Ay, I must put my shoulder to the wheel – if Jekyll will but let me,' he added, 'if Jekyll will only let me.' For once more he saw before his mind's eye, as clear as a transparency, the strange clauses of the will.

THREE

✤ Dr Jekyll Was Quite at Ease ✤

A FORTNIGHT LATER, by excellent good fortune, the doctor gave one of his pleasant dinners to some five or six old cronies, all intelligent reputable men, and all judges of good wine; and Mr Utterson so contrived that he remained behind after the others had departed. This was no new arrangement, but a thing that had befallen many scores of times. Where Utterson was liked, he was liked well. Hosts loved to detain the dry lawyer, when the light-hearted and the loose-tongued had already their foot on the threshold; they liked to sit awhile in his unobtrusive company, practising for solitude, sobering their minds in the man's rich silence, after the expense and strain of gaiety. To this rule Dr Jekyll was no exception; and as he now sat on the opposite side of the fire – a large, well-made, smooth-faced man of fifty, with something of a slyish cast perhaps, but every mark of capacity and kindness – you could see by his looks that he cherished for Mr Utterson a sincere and warm affection.

'I have been wanting to speak to you, Jekyll,' began the latter. 'You know that will of yours?'

A close observer might have gathered that the topic was distasteful; but the doctor carried it off gaily. 'My poor Utterson,' said he, 'you are unfortunate in such a client. I never saw a man so distressed as you were by my will; unless it were that hide-bound pedant, Lanyon, at what he called my scientific heresies. O, I know he's a good fellow – you needn't frown – an excellent fellow, and I always mean to see more of him; but a hide-bound pedant for all that; an ignorant, blatant pedant. I was never more disappointed in any man than Lanyon.'

'You know I never approved of it,' pursued Utterson, ruthlessly disregarding the fresh topic.

'My will? Yes, certainly, I know that,' said the doctor, a trifle sharply. 'You have told me so.'

'Well, I tell you so again,' continued the lawyer. 'I have been learning something of young Hyde.'

The large handsome face of Dr Jekyll grew pale to the very lips, and there came a blackness about his eyes. 'I do not care to hear more,' said he. 'This is a matter I thought we had agreed to drop.'

'What I heard was abominable,' said Utterson.

'It can make no change. You do not understand my position,' returned the doctor, with a certain incoherency of manner. 'I am painfully situated, Utterson; my position is a very strange – a very strange one. It is one of those affairs that cannot be mended by talking.'

'Jekyll,' said Utterson, 'You know me: I am a man to be trusted. Make a clean breast of this in confidence; and I make no doubt I can get you out of it.'

'My good Utterson,' said the doctor, 'this is very good of you, this is downright good of you, and I cannot find words to thank you in. I believe you fully; I would trust you before any man alive, ay, before myself, if I could make the choice; but indeed it isn't what you fancy; it is not so bad as that; and just to put your good heart at rest, I will tell you one thing: the moment I choose, I can be rid of Mr Hyde. I give you my hand upon that; and I thank you again and again; and I will just add one little word, Utterson, that I'm sure you'll take in good part: this is a private matter, and I beg of you to let it sleep.'

Utterson reflected a little, looking in the fire.

'I have no doubt you are perfectly right,' he said at last, getting to his feet.

'Well, but since we have touched upon this business, and for the last time, I hope,' continued the doctor, 'there is one point I should like you to understand. I have really a very great interest in poor Hyde. I know you have seen him; he told me so; and I fear he was rude. But I do sincerely take a great, a very great interest in that young man; and if I am taken away, Utterson, I wish you to promise me that you will bear with him and get his rights for him. I think you would, if you knew all; and it would be a weight off my mind if you would promise.'

'I can't pretend that I shall ever like him,' said the lawyer.

'I don't ask that,' pleaded Jekyll, laying his hand upon the other's arm; 'I only ask for justice; I only ask you to help him for my sake, when I am no longer here.'

Utterson heaved an irrepressible sigh. 'Well,' said he, 'I promise.'

FOUR

⚜ The Carew Murder Case ⚜

NEARLY A YEAR LATER, in the month of October, 18—, London was startled by a crime of singular ferocity, and rendered all the more notable by the high position of the victim. The details were few and startling. A maidservant living alone in a house not far from the river had gone upstairs to bed about eleven. Although a fog rolled over the city in the small hours, the early part of the night was cloudless, and the lane, which the maid's window overlooked, was brilliantly lit by the full moon. It seems she was romantically given; for she sat down upon her box, which stood immediately under the window, and fell into a dream of musing. Never (she used to say, with streaming tears, when she narrated that experience), never had she felt more at peace with all men or thought more kindly of the world. And as she so sat she became aware of an aged and beautiful gentleman with white hair drawing near along the lane; and advancing to meet him, another and very small gentleman, to whom at first she paid less attention. When they had come within speech (which was just under the maid's eyes) the older man bowed and accosted the other with a very pretty manner of politeness. It did not seem as if the subject of his address were of great importance; indeed, from his pointing, it sometimes appeared as if he were only inquiring his way; but the moon shone on his face as he spoke, and the girl was pleased to watch it, it seemed to breathe such an innocent and old-world kindness of disposition, yet with something high too, as of a well-founded self-content. Presently her eye wandered to the other, and she was surprised to recognize in him a certain Mr Hyde, who had once visited her master, and from whom she had conveived a dislike. He had in his hand a heavy cane, with which he was trifling; but he answered never a word, and seemed to listen with an ill-contained impatience. And then all of a sudden he broke out in a great flame of anger, stamping with his foot, brandishing the cane, and carrying on (as the maid described it) like a madman. The gentleman took a step back, with the air of one very much surprised and a trifle hurt; and at that Mr Hyde broke out of all bounds, and clubbed him to the earth. And next moment, with ape-like fury, he was trampling his victim under foot, and hailing down a storm of blows, under which the bones were audibly shattered and the body jumped upon the roadway. At the horror of these sights and sounds the maid fainted.

It was two o'clock when she came to herself and called for the police. The murderer was gone long ago; but there lay his victim in the middle of the lane, incredibly mangled. The stick with which the deed had been done, although it was of some rare and very tough and heavy wood, had broken in the middle under the stress of this insensate cruelty; and one splindered half had rolled in the neighbouring gutter – the other, without doubt, had been carried away by the murderer. A purse and a gold watch were found upon the victim; but no cards or papers, except a sealed and stamped envelope. Which he had been probably carrying to the post, and which bore the name and address of Mr Utterson.

This was brought to the lawyer the next morning, before he was out of bed; and he had no sooner seen it, and been told the circumstances, than he shot out a solemn lip. 'I shall say nothing till I have seen the body,' said he; 'this may be very serious. Have the kindness to wait while I dress.' And with the same grave countenance he hurried through his breakfast and drove to the police station, whither the body had been carried. As soon as he came into the cell, he nodded.

'Yes,' said he, 'I recognize him. I am sorry to say that this is Sir Danvers Carew.'

'Good God, sir!' exclaimed the officer, 'is it possible?' And the next moment his eye lighted up with professional ambition. 'This will make a deal of noise,' he said. 'And perhaps you can help us to the man.' And he briefly narrated what the maid had seen and showed the broken stick.

Mr Utterson had already quailed at the name of Hyde; but when the stick was laid before him, he could doubt no longer: broken and battered as it was, he recognized it for one that he had himself presented many years before to Henry Jekyll.

'Is this Mr Hyde a person of small stature?' he inquired.

'Particularly small and particularly wicked-looking, is what the maid calls him,' said the officer.

Mr Utterson reflected; and then, raising his head, 'If you will come with me in my cab,' he said, 'I think I can take you to his house.'

It was by this time about nine in the morning, and the first fog of the season. A great chocolate-coloured pall lowered over heaven, but the wind was continually charging and routing these embattled vapours; so that as the cab crawled from street to street, Mr Utterson beheld a marvellous number of degrees and hues of twilight; for here it would be dark like the back-end of evening; and there would be a glow of a rich, lurid brown, like the light of some strange conflagration; and here, for a moment, the fog would be quite broken up, and a haggard shaft of daylight would glance in between the swirling wreaths. The dismal quarter of Soho seen under these changing glimpses, with its muddy ways, and slatternly passengers, and its lamps, which had never been extinguished or had been kindled afresh to combat this mournful reinvasion of darkness, seemed, in the lawyer's eyes, like a district of some city in a nightmare. The thoughts of his mind, besides, were of the gloomiest dye; and when he glanced at the companion of his drive, he was conscious of some touch of that terror of the law and the law's officers which may at times assail the most honest.

As the cab drew up before the address indicated, the fog lifted a little and showed him a dingy street, a gin palace, a low French eating-house, a shop for the retail of penny numbers and twopenny salads, many ragged children huddled in the doorways, and many women of many different nationalities passing out, key in hand, to have a morning glass; and the next moment the fog settled down again upon that part, as brown as umber, and cut him off from his blackguardly surroundings. This was the home of Henry Jekyll's favourite; of a man who was heir to a quarter of a million sterling.

An ivory-faced and silvery-haired old woman opened the door. She had an evil face, smoothed by hypocrisy; but her manners were excellent. Yes, she said, this was Mr Hyde's, but he was not at home; he had been in that night very late, but had gone away again in less than an hour: there was nothing strange in that; his habits were very irregular, and he was often absent; for instance, it was nearly two months since she had seen him till yesterday.

'Very well then, we wish to see his rooms,' said the lawyer; and when the woman began to declare it was impossible, 'I had better tell you who this person is,' he added. 'This is Inspector Newcomen, of Scotland Yard.'

A flash of odious joy appeared upon the woman's face. 'Ah!' said she, 'he is in trouble! What has he done?'

Mr Utterson and the inspector exchanged glances. 'He don't seem a very popular character,' observed the latter. 'And now, my good woman, just let me and this gentleman have a look about us.'

In the whole extent of the house, which but for the old woman remained otherwise empty, Mr Hyde had only used a couple of rooms; but these were furnished with luxury and good taste. A closet was filled with wine; the plate was of silver, the napery elegant; a good picture hung upon the walls, a gift (as Utterson supposed) from Henry Jekyll, who was much of a connoisseur; and the carpets were of many plies and agreeable in colour. At this moment, however, the rooms bore every mark of having been recently and hurriedly ransacked; clothes lay about the floor, with their pockets inside out; lockfast drawers stood open; and on the hearth there lay a pile of gray ashes, as though many papers had been burned. From these embers the inspector disinterred the butt end of a green cheque book which had resisted the action of the fire; the other half of the stick was found behind the door; and as this clinched his suspicions, the officer declared himself delighted. A visit to the bank, where several thousand pounds were found to be lying to the murderer's credit, completed his gratification.

'Yoy may depend upon it, sir,' he told Mr Utterson: 'I have him in my hand. He must have lost his head, or he never would have left the stick, or, above all, burned the cheque book. Why, money's life to the man. We have nothing to do but wait for him at the bank, and get out the handbills.'

This last, however, was not so easy of accomplishment; for Mr Hyde had numbered few familiars – even the master of the servant-maid had only seen him twice; his family could nowhere be traced; he had never been photographed; and the few who could describe him differed widely, as common observers will. Only on one point were they agreed; and that was the haunting sense of unexpressed deformity with which the fugitive impressed his beholders.

FIVE

✤ Incident of the Letter ✤

IT WAS LATE IN THE AFTERNOON when Mr Utterson found his way to Dr Jekyll's door, where he was at once admitted by Poole, and carried down by the kitchen offices and across a yard which had once been a garden, to the building which was indifferently known as the laboratory or the dissecting-rooms. The doctor had bought the house from the heirs of a celebrated surgeon; and his own tastes being rather chemical than anatomical, had changed the destination of the block at the bottom of the garden. It was the first time that the lawyer had been received in that part of his friend's quarters; and he eyed the dingy windowless structure with curiosity, and gazed round with a distasteful sense of strangeness as he crossed the theatre, once crowded with eager students and now lying gaunt and silent, the tables laden with chemical apparatus, the floor strewn with crates and littered with packing straw, and the light falling dimly through the foggy cupola. At the further end, a flight of stairs mounted to a door covered with red baize; and through this Mr Utterson was at last received into the doctor's cabinet. It was a large room, fitted round with glass presses, furnished, among other things, with a cheval-glass and a business table, and looking out upon the court by three dusty windows barred with iron. The fire burned in the grate; a lamp was set lighted on the chimney-shelf, for even in the houses the fog began to lie thickly; and there, close up to the warmth, sat Dr Jekyll, looking deadly sick. He did not rise to meet his visitor, but held out a cold hand, and bade him welcome in a changed voice.

'And now,' said Mr Utterson, as soon as Poole had left them, 'you have heard the news?'

The doctor shuddered. 'They were crying it in the square,' he said. 'I heard them in my dining-room.'

'One word,' said the lawyer. 'Carew was my client, but so are you; and I want to know what I am doing. You have not been mad enough to hide this fellow?'

'Utterson, I swear to God,' cried the doctor, 'I swear to God I will never set eyes on him again. I bind my honour to you that I am done with him in this world. It is all at an end. And indeed he does not want my help; you do not know him as I do; he is safe, he is quite safe; mark my words, he will never more be heard of.'

The lawyer listened gloomily; he did not like his friend's feverish manner. 'You seem pretty sure of him,' said he; 'and for your sake, I hope you may be right. If it came to a trial, your name might appear.'

'I am quite sure of him,' replied Jekyll; 'I have grounds for certainty that I cannot share with any one. But there is one thing on which you may advise me. I have – I have received a letter; and I am at a loss whether I should show it to the police. I should like to leave it in your hands, Utterson; you would judge wisely, I am sure; I have so great a trust in you.'

'You fear, I suppose, that it might lead to his detection?' asked the lawyer.

'No,' said the other. 'I cannot say that I care what becomes of Hyde; I am quite done with him. I was thinking of my own character, which this hateful business has rather exposed.'

Utterson ruminated awhile; he was surprised at his friend's selfishness, and yet relieved by it 'Well,' said he, at last, 'let me see the letter.'

The letter was written in an odd, upright hand, and signed 'Edward Hyde'; and it signified, briefly enough, that the writer's benefactor, Dr Jekyll, whom he had long so unworthily repaid for a thousand generosities, need labour under no alarm for his safety, as he had means of escape on which he placed a sure dependence. The lawyer liked this letter well enough: it put a better colour on the intimacy than he had looked for; and he blamed himself for some of his past suspicions.

'Have you the envelope?' he asked.

'I burned it,' replied Jekyll, 'before I thought what I was about. But it bore no postmark. The note was handed in.'

'Shall I keep this and sleep upon it?' asked Utterson.

'I wish you to judge for me entirely,' was the reply. 'I have lost confidence in myself.'

'Well, I shall consider,' returned the lawyer. 'And now one word more: it was Hyde who dictated the terms in your will about that disappearance?'

The doctor seemed seized with a qualm of faintness; he shut his mouth tight and nodded.

'I knew it,' said Utterson. 'He meant to murder you. You have had a fine escape.'

'I have had what is far more to the purpose,' returned the doctor solemnly: 'I have had a lesson – O God, Utterson, what a lesson I have had!' And he covered his face for a moment with his hands.

On his way out, the lawyer stopped and had a word or two with Poole. 'By the by,' said he, 'there was a letter handed in today: what was the messenger like?' But Poole was positive nothing had come except by post; 'and only circulars by that,' he added.

This news sent off the visitor with his fears renewed. Plainly the letter had come by the laboratory door; possibly, indeed, it had been written in the cabinet; and, if that were so, it must be differently judged, and handled with the more caution. The news-boys, as he went, were crying themselves hoarse along the footways. 'Special edition. Shocking murder of an M. P.' That was the funeral oration of one friend and client; and he could not help a certain apprehension lest the good name of another should be sucked down in the eddy of the scandal. It was, at least, a ticklish decision that he had to make; and, self-reliant as he was by habit, he began to cherish a longing for advice. It was not to be had directly; but perhaps, he thought, it might be fished for.

Presently after, he sat on one side of his own hearth, with Mr Guest, his head clerk, upon the other, and midway between, at a nicely calculated distance from the fire, a bottle of a particular old wine that had long dwelt unsunned in the foundations of his house. The fog still slept on the wing above the drowned city, where the lamps glimmered like carbuncles; and through the muffle and smother of these fallen clouds, the procession of the town's life was still rolling in through the great arteries with a sound as of a mighty wind. But the room was gay with firelight. In the bottle the acids were long ago resolved; the imperial dye had softened with time, as the colour grows richer in stained windows; and the glow of hot autumn afternoons on hillside vineyards was ready to be set free and to disperse the fogs of London. Insensibly the lawyer melted. There was no man from whom he kept fewer secrets than Mr Guest; and he was not always sure that he kept as many as he meant. Guest had often been on business to the doctor's: he knew Poole; he could scarce have failed to hear of Mr Hyde's familiarity about the house; he might draw conclusions: was it not as well, then, that he should see a letter which put that mystery to rights? and, above all, since Guest, being a great student and critic of handwriting, would consider the step natural and obliging? The clerk, besides, was a man of counsel; he would scarce read so strange a document without dropping a remark; and by that remark Mr Utterson might shape his future course.

'This is a sad business about Sir Danvers,' he said.

'Yes, sir, indeed. It has elicited a great deal of public feeling,' returned Guest. 'The man, of course, was mad.'

'I should like to hear your views on that,' replied Utterson. 'I have a document here in his handwriting; it is between ourselves, for I scarce know what to do about it; it is an ugly business at the best. But there it is; quite in your way: a murderer's autograph.'

Guest's eyes brightened, and he sat down at once and studied it with passion. 'No, sir,' he said; 'not mad; but it is an odd hand.'

'And by all accounts a very odd writer,' added the lawyer.

Just then the servant entered with a note.

'Is that from Dr Jekyll, sir?' inquired the clerk. 'I thought I knew the writing. Anything private, Mr Utterson?'

'Only an invitation to dinner. Why? do you want to see it?'

'One moment. I thank you, sir'; and the clerk laid the two sheets of paper alongside and sedulously compared their contents. 'Thank you, sir,' he said at last, returning both; 'it's a very interesting autograph.'

There was a pause, during which Mr Utterson struggled with himself. 'Why did you compare them, Guest?' he inquired suddenly.

'Well, sir,' returned the clerk, 'there's a rather singular resemblance; the two hands are in many points identical; only differently sloped.'

'Rather quaint,' said Utterson.

'It is, as you say, rather quaint,' returned Guest.

'I wouldn't speak of this note, you know,' said the master.

'No, sir,' said the clerk. 'I understand.'

But no sooner was Mr Utterson alone that night than he locked the note into his safe, where it reposed from that time forward. 'What!' he thought. 'Henry Jekyll forge for a murderer!' And his blood ran cold in his veins.

SIX

Remarkable Incident of Dr Lanyon

TIME RAN ON; THOUSANDS of pounds were offered in reward, for the death of Sir Danvers was resented as a public injury; but Mr Hyde had disappeared out of the ken of the police as though he had never existed. Much of his past was unearthed, indeed, and all disreputable: tales came out of the man's cruelty, at once so callous and violent, of his vile life, of his strange associates, of the hatred that seemed to have surrounded his career; but of his present whereabouts, not a whisper. From the time he had left the house in Soho on the morning of the murder, he was simply blotted out; and gradually, as time drew on, Mr Utterson began to recover from the hotness of his alarm, and to grow more at quiet with himself. The death of Sir Danvers was, to his way of thinking, more than paid for by the disappearance of Mr Hyde. Now that evil influence had been withdrawn, a new life began for Dr Jekyll. He came out of his seclusion, renewed relations with his friends, became once more their familiar guest and entertainer; and whilst he had always been known for charities, he was now no less distinguished for religion. He was busy, he was much in the open air, he did good; his face seemed to open and brighten, as if with an inward consciousness of service; and for more than two months the doctor was at peace.

On the 8th of January Utterson had dined at the doctor's with a small party; Lanyon had been there; and the face of the host had looked from one to the other as in the old days when the trio were inseparable friends. On the 12th, and again on the 14th, the door was shut against the lawyer. 'the doctor was confined to the house,' Poole said, 'and saw no one.' On the 15th he tried again, and was again refused; and having now been used for the last two months to see his friend almost daily, he found this return of solitude to weigh upon his spirits. The fifth night he had in Guest to dine with him; and the sixth he betook himself to Dr Lanyon's.

There at least he was not denied admittance; but when he came in, he was shocked at the change which had taken place in the doctor's appearance. He had his death-warrant written legibly upon his face. The rosy man had grown pale; his flesh had fallen away; he was visibly balder and older; and yet it was not so much these tokens of a swift physical decay that arrested the lawyer's notice, as a look in the eye and quality of manner that seemed to testify to some deepseated terror of the mind. It was unlikely that the doctor should fear death; and yet that was what Utterson was tempted to suspect. 'Yes,' he thought; 'he is a doctor, he must know his own state and that his days are counted; and the knowledge is more than he can bear.' And yet when Utterson remarked on his ill looks, it was with an air of great firmness that Lanyon declared himself a doomed man.

'I have had a shock,' he said, 'and I shall never recover. It is a question of weeks. Well, life has been pleasant; I liked it; yes, sir, I used to like it. I sometimes think if we knew all, we should be more glad to get away.'

'Jekyll is ill, too,' observed Utterson. 'Have you seen him?'

But Lanyon's face changed, and he held up a trembling hand. 'I wish to see or hear no more of Dr Jekyll,' he said, in a loud, unsteady voice. 'I am quite done with that person; and I beg that you will spare me any allusion to one whom I regard as dead.'

'Tut, tut!' said Mr Utterson; and then, after a considerable pause, 'Can't I do anything?' he inquired. 'We are three very old friends, Lanyon; we shall not live to make others.'

'Nothing can be done,' returned Lanyon; 'ask himself.'

'He will not see me,' said the lawyer.

'I am not surprised at that,' was the reply. 'Some day, Utterson, after I am dead, you may perhaps come to learn the right and wrong of this. I cannot tell you. And in the meantime, if you can sit and talk with me of other things, for God's sake, stay and do so; but if you cannot keep clear of this accursed topic, then, in God's name, go, for I cannot bear it.'

As soon as he got home, Utterson sat down and wrote to Jekyll, complaining of his exclusion from his house, and asking the cause of this unhappy break with Lanyon; and the next day brought him a long answer, often very pathetically worded, and sometimes darkly mysterious in drift. The quarrel with Lanyon was incurable. 'I do not blame our old friend,' Jekyll wrote, 'but I share his view that we must never meet. I mean from henceforth to lead a life of extreme seclusion; you must not be surprised, nor must you doubt my friendship, if my door is often shut even to you. You must suffer me to go my own dark way. I have brought on myself a punishment and a danger that I cannot name. If I am the chief of sinners, I am the chief of sufferers also. I could not think that this earth contained a place for sufferings and terrors so unmanning; and you can do but one thing, Utterson, to lighten this destiny, and that is to respect my silence.' Utterson was amazed; the dark influence of Hyde had been withdrawn, the doctor had returned to his old tasks and amities; a week ago, the prospect had smiled with every promise of a cheerful and an honoured age; and now in a moment, friendship and peace of mind and the whole tenor of his life were wrecked. So great and unprepared a change pointed to madness; but in view of Lanyon's manner and words, there must lie for it some deeper ground.

A week afterwards Dr Lanyon took to his bed, and in something less than a fortnight he was dead. The night after the funeral, at which he had been sadly affected, Utterson locked the door of his business room, and sitting there by the light of a melancholy candle, drew out and set before him an envelope addressed by the hand and sealed with the seal of his dead friend. 'PRIVATE: for the hands of J.G. Utterson ALONE, and in case of his predecease *to be destroyed unread*,' so it was emphatically superscribed; and the lawyer dreaded to behold the contents. 'I have buried one friend today,' he thought: 'what if this should cost me another?' And then he condemned the fear as a disloyalty, and broke the seal. Within there was another enclosure, likewise sealed, and marked upon the cover as 'not to be opened till the death or disappearance of Dr Henry Jekyll.' Utterson could not trust his eyes. Yes, it was disappearance; here again, as in the mad will, which he had long ago restored to its author, here again were the idea of a disappearance and the name of Henry Jekyll bracketed. But in the will, that idea had sprung from the sinister suggestion of the man Hyde; it was set there with a purpose all too plain and horrible. Written by the hand of Lanyon, what should it mean? A great curiosity came to the trustee, to disregard the prohibition and dive at once to the bottom of these mysteries; but professional honour and faith to his dead friend were stringent obligations; and the packet slept in the inmost corner of his private safe.

It is one thing to mortify curiosity, another to conquer it; and it may be doubted if, from that day forth, Utterson desired the society of his surviving friend with the same eagerness. He thought of him kindly; but his thoughts were disquieted and fearful. He went to call indeed; but he was perhaps relieved to be denied admittance; perhaps, in his heart, he preferred to speak with Poole upon the doorstep, and surrounded by the air and sounds of the open city, rather than to be admitted into that house of voluntary bondage, and to sit and speak with its inscrutable recluse. Poole had, indeed, no very pleasant news to communicate. The doctor, it appeared, now more than ever confined himself to the cabinet over the laboratory, where he would sometimes even sleep: he was out of spirits, he had grown very silent, he did not read; it seemed as if he had something on his mind. Utterson became so used to the unvarying character of these reports, that he fell off little by little in the frequency of his visits.

SEVEN

✤ Incident at the Window ✤

IT CHANCED ON SUNDAY, WHEN Mr Utterson was on his usual walk with Mr Enfield, that their way lay once again through the by-street; and that when they came in front of the door, both stopped to gaze on it.

'Well,' said Enfield, 'that story's at an end, at least. We shall never see more of Mr Hyde.'

'I hope not,' said Utterson. 'Did I ever tell you that I once saw him, and shared your feeling of repulsion?'

'It was impossible to do the one without the other,' returned Enfield. 'And, by the way, what an ass you must have thought me, not to know that this was a back way to Dr Jekyll's! It was partly your own fault that I found it out even when I did.'

'So you found it out, did you?' said Utterson. 'But if that be so, we may step into the court and take a look at the windows. To tell you the truth, I am uneasy about poor Jekyll; and even outside, I feel as if the presence of a friend might do him good.'

The court was very cool and a little damp, and full of premature twilight, although the sky, high up overhead, was still bright with sunset. The middle one of the three windows was half-way open; and sitting close beside it, taking the air with an infinite sadness of mien, like some disconsolate prisoner, Utterson saw Dr Jekyll.

'What! Jekyll!' he cried. 'I trust you are better.'

'I am very low, Utterson,' replied the doctor drearily; 'very low. It will not last long, thank God.'

'You stay too much indoors,' said the lawyer. 'You should be out, whipping up the circulation, like Mr Enfield and me. (This is my cousin – Mr Enfield – Dr Jekyll.) Come, now; get your hat, and take a quick turn with us.'

'You are very good,' sighed the other. 'I should like to very much; but no, no, no; it is quite impossible; I dare not. But indeed, Utterson, I am very glad to see you; this is really a great pleasure. I would ask you and Mr Enfield up, but the place is really not fit.'

'Why then,' said the lawyer, good-naturedly, 'the best thing we can do is to stay down here, and speak with you from where we are?'

'That is just what I was about to venture to propose,' returned the doctor, with a smile. But the words were hardly uttered, before the smile was struck out of his face and succeeded by an expression of such abject terror and despair, as froze the very blood of the two gentlemen below. They saw it but for a glimpse, for the window was instantly thrust down; but that glimpse had been sufficient, and they turned and left the court without a word. In silence, too, they traversed the by-street; and it was not until they had come into a neighbouring thoroughfare, where even upon a Sunday there were still some stirrings of life, that Mr Utterson at last turned and looked at his companion. They were both pale; and there was an answering horror in their eyes.

'God forgive us! God forgive us!' said Mr Utterson.

But Mr Enfield only nodded his head very seriously, and walked on once more in silence.

EIGHT

❦ The Last Night ❦

MR UTTERSON WAS SITTING by his fireside one evening after dinner, when he was surprised to receive a visit from Poole.

'Bless me, Poole, what brings you here?' he cried; and then, taking a second look at him, 'What ails you?' he added; 'is the doctor ill?'

'Mr Utterson,' said the man, 'there is something wrong.'

'Take a seat, and here is a glass of wine for you,' said the lawyer. 'Now, take your time, and tell me plainly what you want.'

'You know the doctor's ways, sir,' replied Poole, 'and how he shuts himself up. Well, he's shut up again in the cabinet; and I don't like it, sir – I wish I may die if I like it. Mr Utterson, sir, I'm afraid.'

'Now, my good man,' said the lawyer, 'be explicit. What are you afraid of?'

'I've been afraid for about a week,' returned Poole, doggedly disregarding the question; 'and I can bear it no more.'

The man's appearance amply bore out his words; his manner was altered for the worse; and except for the moment when he had first announced his terror, he had not once looked the lawyer in the face. Even now, he sat with the glass of wine untasted on his knee, and his eyes directed to a corner of the floor. 'I can bear it no more,' he repeated.

'Come,' said the lawyer, 'I see you have some good reason, Poole; I see there is something seriously amiss. Try to tell me what it is.'

'I think there's been foul play,' said Poole, hoarsely.

'Foul play!' cried the lawyer, a good deal frightened, and rather inclined to be irritated in consequence. 'What foul play? What does the man mean?'

'I daren't say, sir,' was the answer; 'but will you come along with me and see for yourself?'

Mr Utterson's only answer was to rise and get his hat and great-coat; but he observed with wonder the greatness of the relief that appeared upon the butler's face, and perhaps with no less, that the wine was still untasted when he set it down to follow.

It was a wild, cold, seasonable night of March, with a pale moon, lying on her back as though the wind had tilted her, and a flying wrack of the most diaphanous and lawny texture. The wind made talking difficult, and flecked the blood into the face. It seemed to have swept the street unusually bare of passengers, besides; for Mr Utterson thought he had never seen that part of London so deserted. He could have wished it otherwise; never in his life had he been conscious of so sharp a wish to see and touch his fellow-creatures; for, struggle as he might, there was borne in upon his mind a crushing anticipation of calamity. The square, when they got there, was all full of wind and dust, and the thin trees in the garden were lashing themselves along the railing. Poole, who had kept all the way a pace or two ahead, now pulled up in the middle of the pavement, and in spite of the biting weather, took off his hat and mopped his brow with a red pocket-handkerchief. But for all the hurry of his coming, these were not the dews of exertion that he wiped away, but the moisture of some strangling anguish; for his face was white, and his voice, when he spoke, harsh and broken.

'Well, sir,' he said, 'here we are, and God grant there be nothing wrong.'

'Amen, Poole,' said the lawyer.

Thereupon the servant knocked in a very guarded manner; the door was opened on the chain; and a voice asked from within, 'Is that you, Poole?'

'It's all right,' said Poole. 'Open the door.'

The hall, when they entered it, was brightly lighted up; the fire was built high; and about the hearth the whole of the servants, men and women, stood huddled together like a flock of sheep. At the sight of Mr Utterson, the housemaid broke into hysterical whimpering; and the cook, crying out, 'Bless God! it's Mr Utterson,' ran forward as if to take him in her arms.

'What, what? Are you all here?' said the lawyer, peevishly. 'Very irregular, very unseemly: your master would be far from pleased.'

'They're all afraid,' said Poole.

Blank silence followed, no one protesting; only the maid lifted up her voice, and now wept loudly.

'Hold your tongue!' Poole said to her, with a ferocity of accent that testified to his own jangled nerves; and indeed when the girl had so suddenly raised the note of her lamentation, they had all started and turned towards the inner door with faces of dreadful expectation. 'And now,' continued the butler, addressing the knife-boy, 'reach me a candle, and we'll get this through hands at once.' And then he begged Mr Utterson to follow him, and led the way to the back garden.

'Now, sir,' said he, 'you come as gently as you can. I want you to hear, and I don't want you to be heard. And see here, sir, if by any chance he was to ask you in, don't go.'

Mr Utterson's nerves, at this unlooked-for termination, gave a jerk that nearly threw him from his balance; but he re-collected his courage, and followed the butler into the laboratory building and through the surgical theatre, with its lumber of crates and bottles, to the foot of the stair. Here Poole, motioned him to stand on one side and listen; while he himself, setting down the candle and making a great and obvious call on his resolution, mounted the steps, and knocked with a somewhat uncertain hand on the red baize of the cabinet door.

'Mr Utterson, sir, asking to see you,' he called; and even as he did so, once more violently signed to the lawyer to give ear.

A voice answered from within: 'Tell him I cannot see any one,' it said, complainingly.

'Thank you, sir,' said Poole, with a note of something like triumph in his voice; and taking up his candle, he led Mr Utterson back across the yard and into the great kitchen, where the fire was out and the beetles were leaping on the floor.

'Sir,' he said, looking Mr Utterson in the eyes, 'was that my master's voice?'

'It seems much changed,' replied the lawyer, very pale, but giving look for look.

'Changed? Well, yes, I think so,' said the butler. 'Have I been twenty years in this man's house, to be deceived about his voice? No, sir; master's made away with; he was made away with eight days ago, when we heard him cry out upon the name of God; and *who's* in there instead of him, and *why* it stays there, is a thing that cries to Heaven, Mr Utterson!'

'This is a very strange tale, Poole; this is rather a wild tale, my man,' said Mr Utterson, biting his finger. 'Suppose it were as you suppose, supposing Dr Jekyll to have been – well, murdered, what could induce the murderer to stay? That won't hold water; it doesn't commend itself to reason.'

'Well, Mr Utterson, you are a hard man to satisfy, but I'll do it yet,' said Poole. 'All this last week (you must know), him, or it, or whatever it is that lives in that cabinet, has been crying night and day for some sort of medicine and cannot get it to his mind. It was sometimes his way – the master's, that is – to write his orders on a sheet of paper and throw it on the stair. We've had nothing else this week back; nothing but papers, and a closed door, and the very meals left there to be smuggled in when nobody was looking. Well, sir, every day, ay, and twice and thrice in the same day, there have been orders and complaints, and I have been sent flying to all the wholesale chemists in town. Every time I brought the stuff back, there would be another paper telling me to return it, because it was not pure and another order to a different firm. This drug is wanted bitter bad, sir, whatever for.'

'Have you any of these papers?' asked Mr Utterson.

Poole felt in his pocket and handed out a crumpled note, which the lawyer, bending nearer to the candle, carefully examined. Its contents ran thus: 'Dr Jekyll presents his compliments to Messrs Maw. He assures them that their last sample is impure and quite useless for his present purpose. In the year 18—, Dr J. purchased a somewhat large quantity from Messrs M. He now begs them to search with the most sedulous care, and should any of the same quality be left, to forward it to him at once. Expense is no consideration. The importance of this to Dr J. can hardly be exaggerated.' So far the letter had run composedly enough; but here, with a sudden splutter of the pen, the writer's emotion had broken loose. 'For God's sake,' he had added, 'find me some of the old.'

'This is a strange note,' said Mr Utterson; and then sharply, 'How do you come to have it open?'

'The man at Maw's was main angry, sir, and he threw it back to me like so much dirt,' returned Poole.

'This is unquestionably the doctor's hand, do you know?' resumed the lawyer.

'I thought it looked like it,' said the servant, rather sulkily; and then, with another voice, 'But what matters hand of write?' he said. 'I've seen him!'

'Seen him?' repeated Mr Utterson. 'Well?'

'That's it!' said Poole. 'It was this way. I came suddenly into the theatre from the garden. It seems he had slipped out to look for this drug, or whatever it is; for the cabinet door was open, and there he was at the far end of the room, digging among the crates. He looked up when I came in, gave a kind of cry, and whipped upstairs into the cabinet. It was but for one minute that I saw him, but the hair stood upon my head like quills. Sir, if that was my master, why had he a mask upon his face? If it was my master, why did he cry like a rat and run from me? I have served him long enough. And then . . .' the man paused, and passed his hand over his face.

'These are all very strange circumstances,' said Mr Utterson, 'but I think I begin to see daylight. Your master, Poole, is plainly seized with one of those maladies that both torture and deform the sufferer; hence, for aught I know, the alteration of his voice; hence the mask and his avoidance of his friends; hence his eagerness to find this drug, by means of which the poor soul retains some hope of ultimate recovery – God grant that he be not deceived! There is my explanation; it is sad enough, Poole, ay, and appalling to consider; but it is plain and natural, hangs well together, and delivers us from all exorbitant alarms.'

'Sir,' said the butler, turning to a sort of mottled pallor, 'that thing was not my master, and there's the truth. My master' – here he looked round him, and began to whisper – 'is a tall fine build of a man, and this was more of a dwarf.' Utterson attempted to protest. 'O, sir,' cried Poole, 'do you think I do not know my master after twenty years? do you think I do not know where his head comes to in the cabinet door, where I saw him every morning of my life? No, sir, that thing in the mask was never Dr Jekyll – God knows what it was, but it was never Dr Jekyll; and it is the belief of my heart that there was murder done.'

'Poole,' replied the lawyer, 'if you say that, it will become my duty to make certain. Much as I desire to spare your master's feelings, much as I am puzzled about this note, which seems to prove him to be still alive, I shall consider it my duty to break in that door.'

'Ah, Mr Utterson, that's talking!' cried the butler.

'And now comes the second question,' resumed Utterson: 'Who is going to do it?'

'Why, you and me, sir,' was the undaunted reply.

'That is very well said,' returned the lawyer; 'and whatever comes of it, I shall make it my business to see you are no loser.'

'There is an axe in the theatre,' continued Poole; 'and you might take the kitchen poker for yourself.'

The lawyer took that rude but weighty instrument into his hand, and balanced it. 'Do you know, Poole,' he said, looking up, 'that you and I are about to place ourselves in a position of some peril?'

'You may say so, sir, indeed,' returned the butler.

'It is well, then, that we should be frank,' said the other. 'We both think more than we have said; let us make a clean breast. This masked figure that you saw, did you recognize it?'

'Well, sir, it went so quick, and the creature was so doubled up, that I could hardly swear to that,' was the answer. 'But if you mean, was it Mr Hyde? – why, yes, I think it was! You see, it was much of the same bigness; and it had the same quick light way with it; and then who else could have got in by the laboratory door? You have not forgot, sir, that at the time of the murder he had still the key with him? But that's not all. I don't know, Mr Utterson, if ever you met this Mr Hyde?'

'Yes,' said the lawyer, 'I once spoke with him.'

'Then you must know, as well as the rest of us, that there was something queer about that gentleman – something that gave a man a turn – I don't know rightly how to say it, sir, beyond this: that you felt it in your marrow – kind of cold and thin.'

'I own I felt something of what you describe,' said Mr Utterson.

'Quite so, sir,' returned Poole. 'Well, when that masked thing like a monkey jumped from among the chemicals and whipped into the cabinet, it went down my spine like ice. O, I know it's not evidence, Mr Utterson; I'm book-learned enough for that; but a man has his feelings; and I give you my bible-word it was Mr Hyde!'

'Ay, ay,' said the lawyer. 'My fears incline to the same point. Evil, I fear, founded – evil was sure to come – of that connection. Ay, truly, I believe you; I believe poor Harry is killed; and I believe his murderer (for what purpose, God alone can tell) is still lurking in his victim's room. Well, let our name be vengeance. Call Bradshaw.'

The footman came at the summons, very white and nervous.

'Pull yourself together, Bradshaw,' said the lawyer. 'This suspense, I know, is telling upon all of you; but it is now our intention to make an end of it. Poole, here, and I are going to force our way into the cabinet. If all is well, my shoulders are broad enough to bear the blame. Meanwhile, lest anything should really be amiss, or any malefactor seek to escape by the back, you and the boy must go round the corner with a pair of good sticks, and take your post at the laboratory door. We give you ten minutes to get to your stations.'

As Bradshaw left, the lawyer looked at his watch. 'And now, Poole, let us get to ours,' he said; and taking the poker under his arm, he led the way into the yard. The scud had banked over the moon, and it was now quite dark. The wind, which only broke in puffs and draughts into that deep well of building, tossed the light of the candle to and fro about their steps, until they came into the shelter of the theatre, where they sat down silently to wait. London hummed solemnly all around; but nearer at hand, the stillness was only broken by the sound of a footfall moving to and fro along the cabinet floor.

'So it will walk all day, sir,' whispered Poole; 'ay, and the better part of the night. Only when a new sample comes from the chemist, there's a bit of a break! Ah, it's an ill conscience that's such an enemy to rest! Ah, sir, there's blood foully shed in every step of it! But hark again, a little closer – put your heart in your ears, Mr Utterson, and tell me, is that the doctor's foot?'

The steps fell lightly and oddly, with a certain swing, for all they went so slowly; it was different indeed from the heavy creaking tread of Henry Jekyll. Utterson sighed. 'Is there never anything else?' he asked.

Poole nodded. 'Once,' he said. 'Once I heard it weeping!'

'Weeping? how that?' said the lawyer, conscious of a sudden chill of horror.

'Weeping like a woman or a lost soul,' said the butler. 'I came away with that upon my heart, that I could have wept too.'

But now the ten minutes drew to an end. Poole disinterred the axe from under a stack of packing straw; the candle was set upon the nearest table to light them to the attack; and they drew near with bated breath to where that patient foot was still going up and down, up and down in the quiet of the night.

'Jekyll,' cried Utterson, with a loud voice, 'I demand to see you.' He paused a moment, but there came no reply. 'I give you fair warning, our suspicions are aroused, and I must and shall see you,' he resumed; 'if not by fair means, then by foul – if not of your consent, then by brute force!'

'Utterson,' said the voice, 'for God's sake, have mercy!'

'Ah, that's not Jekyll's voice – it's Hyde's!' cried Utterson. 'Down with the door, Poole!'

Poole swung the axe over his shoulder; the blow shook the building, and the red baize door leaped against the lock and hinges. A dismal screech, as of mere animal terror, rang from the cabinet. Up went the axe again, and again the panels crashed and the frame bounded; four times the blow fell; but the wood was tough and the fittings were of excellent workmanship; and it was not until the fifth that the lock suddenly burst in sunder, and the wreck of the door fell inwards on the carpet.

The besiegers, appalled by their own riot and the stillness that had succeeded, stood back a little and peered in. There lay the cabinet before their eyes in the quiet lamplight, a good fire glowing and chattering on the hearth, the kettle singing its thin strain, a drawer or two open, papers neatly set forth on the business table, and nearer the fire, the things laid out for tea; the quietest room, you would have said, and, but for the glazed presses full of chemicals, the most commonplace that night in London.

Right in the midst there lay the body of a man sorely contorted and still twitching. They drew near on tiptoe, turned it on its back, and beheld the face of Edward Hyde. He was dressed in clothes far too large for him, clothes of the doctor's bigness; the cords of his face still moved with a semblance of life, but life was quite gone; and by the crushed phial in the hand and the strong smell of kernels that hung upon the air, Utterson knew that he was looking on the body of a self-destroyer.

'We have come too late,' he said sternly, 'whether to save or punish. Hyde is gone to his account; and it only remains for us to find the body of your master.'

The far greater proportion of the building was occupied by the theatre, which filled almost the whole ground storey, and was lighted from above, and by the cabinet, which formed an upper storey at one end and looked upon the court. A corridor joined the theatre to the door on the by-street; and with this, the cabinet communicated separately by a second flight of stairs. There were besides a few dark closets and a spacious cellar. All these they now thoroughly examined. Each closet needed but a glance, for all were empty, and all, by the dust that fell from their doors, had stood long unopened. The cellar, indeed, was filled with crazy lumber, mostly dating from the times of the surgeon who was Jekyll's predecessor; but even as they opened the door, they were advertised of the uselessness of further search by the fall of a perfect mat of cobweb which had for years sealed up the entrance. Nowhere was there any trace of Henry Jekyll, dead or alive.

Poole stamped on the flags of the corridor. 'He must be buried here,' he said, hearkening to the sound.

'Or he may have fled,' said Utterson, and he turned to examine the door in the by-street. It was locked; and lying near by on the flags, they found the key, already stained with rust.

'This does not look like use,' observed the lawyer.

'Use!' echoed Poole. 'Do you not see, sir, it is broken? much as if a man had stamped on it.'

'Ah,' continued Utterson, 'and the fractures, too, are rusty.' The two men looked at each other with a scare. 'This is beyond me, Poole,' said the lawyer. 'Let us go back to the cabinet.'

They mounted the stair in silence, and still, with an occasional awe-struck glance at the dead body, proceeded more thoroughly to examine the contents of the cabinet. At one table there were traces of chemical work, various measured heaps of some white salt being laid on glass saucers, as though for an experiment in which the unhappy man had been prevented.

'That is the same drug that I was always bringing him,' said Poole; and even as he spoke, the kettle with a startling noise boiled over.

This brought them to the fireside, where the easy chair was drawn cosily up, and the tea things stood ready to the sitter's elbow, the very sugar in the cup. There were several books on a shelf; one lay beside the tea things open, and Utterson was amazed to find it a copy of a pious work for which Jekyll had several times expressed a great esteem, anno-tated, in his own hand, with startling blasphemies.

Next, in the course of the review of the chamber, the searchers came to the cheval-glass, into whose depth they looked with an involuntary horror. But it was so turned as to show them nothing but the rosy glow playing on the roof, the fire sparkling in a hundred repetitions along the glazed front of the presses, and their own pale and fearful countenances stooping to look in.

'This glass has seen some strange things, sir,' whispered Poole.

'And surely none stranger than itself,' echoed the lawyer, in the same tone. 'For what did Jekyll' – he caught himself up at the word with a start, and then conquering the weakness – 'what could Jekyll want with it?' he said.

'You may say that!' said Poole.

Next they turned to the business table. On the desk, among the neat array of papers, a large envelope was uppermost, and bore, in the doc-tor's hand, the name of Mr Utterson. The lawyer unsealed it, and several enclosures fell to the floor. The first was a will, drawn in the same eccentric terms as the one which he had returned six months before, to serve as a testament in case of death and as a deed of gift in case of disappearance; but in place of the name of Edward Hyde, the lawyer, with indescribable amazement, read the name of Gabriel John Utterson. He looked at Poole, and then back at the papers, and last of all at the dead malefactor stretched upon the carpet.

'My head goes round,' he said. 'He has been all these days in pos-session; he had no cause to like me; he must have raged to see himself displaced; and he has not destroyed this document.'

He caught the next paper; it was a brief note in the doctor's hand, and dated at the top. 'O Poole!' the lawyer cried, 'he was alive and here this day. He cannot have been disposed of in so short a space; he must be still alive, he must have fled! And then, why fled? and how? and in that case can we venture to declare this suicide? O, we must be careful. I foresee that we may yet involve your master in some dire catastrophe.'

'Why don't you read it, sir?' asked Poole.

'Because I fear,' replied the lawyer, solemnly. 'God grant I have no cause for it!' And with that he brought the paper to his eye, and read as follows:

MY DEAR UTTERSON, – When this shall fall into your hands, I shall have disappeared, under what circumstances I have not the penetration to foresee; but my instincts and all the circumstances of my nameless situation tell me that the end is sure and must be early. Go then, and first read the narrative which Lanyon warned me he was to place in your hands; and if you care to hear more, turn to the confession of

Your unworthy and unhappy friend,

HENRY JEKYLL.

'There was a third enclosure?' asked Utterson.

'Here, sir,' said Poole, and gave into his hands a considerable packet sealed in several places.

The lawyer put it in his pocket. 'I would say nothing of this paper. If your master has fled or is dead, we may at least save his credit. It is now ten; I must go home and read these documents in quiet; but I shall be back before midnight, when we shall send for the police.'

They went out, locking the door of the theatre behind them; and Utterson, once more leaving the servants gathered about the fire in the hall, trudged back to his office to read the two narratives in which this mystery was now to be explained.

NINE

❖ Dr Lanyon's Narrative ❖

ON THE NINTH OF JANUARY, now four days ago, I received by the evening delivery a registered envelope, addressed in the hand of my colleague and old school-companion, Henry Jekyll. I was a good deal surprised by this; for we were by no means in the habit of correspondence; I had seen the man, dined with him, indeed, the night before; and I could imagine nothing in our intercourse that should justify the formality of registration. The contents increased my wonder; for this is how the letter ran:

10th December 18—.

DEAR LANYON, – You are one of my oldest friends; and although we may have differed at times on scientific questions, I cannot remember, at least on my side, any break in our affection. There was never a day when, if you had said to me, 'Jekyll, my life, my honour, my reason, depend upon you,' I would not have sacrificed my fortune or my left hand to help you. Lanyon, my life, my honour, my reason, are all at your mercy; if you fail me tonight, I am lost. You might suppose, after this preface, that I am going to ask you for something dishonourable to grant. Judge for yourself.

I want you to postpone all other engagements for tonight – ay, even if you were summoned to the bedside of an emperor; to take a cab, unless your carriage should be actually at the door; and, with this letter in your hand for consultation, to drive straight to my house. Poole, my butler, has his orders; you will find him waiting your arrival with a locksmith. The door of my cabinet is then to be forced; and you are to go in alone; to open the glazed press (letter E) on the left hand, breaking the lock if it be shut; and to draw out, *with all its contents as they stand*, the fourth drawer from the top or (which is the same thing) the third from the bottom. In my extreme distress of mind, I have a morbid fear of misdirecting you; but even if I am in error you may know the right drawer by its contents: some powders, a phial, and a paper book. This drawer I beg of you to carry back with you to Cavendish Square exactly as it stands.

That is the first part of the service: now for the second. You should be back, if you set out at once on the receipt of this, long before midnight; but I will leave you that amount of margin, not only in the fear of one of those obstacles that can neither be prevented nor foreseen, but because an hour when your servants are in bed is to be preferred for what will then remain to do. At midnight, then, I have to ask you to be alone in your consulting-room, to admit with your own hand into the house a man who will present himself in my name, and to place in his hands the drawer that you will have brought with you from my cabinet. Then you will have played your part, and earned my gratitude completely. Five minutes afterwards, if you insist upon an explanation, you will have understood that these arrangements are of capital importance; and that by the neglect of one of them, fantastic as they must appear, you might have charged your conscience with my death or the shipwreck of my reason.

Confident as I am that you will not trifle with this appeal, my heart sinks and my hand trembles at the bare thought of such a possibility. Think of me at this hour, in a strange place, labouring under a blackness of distress that no fancy can exaggerate, and yet well aware that, if you will but punctually serve me, my troubles will roll away like a story that is told. Serve me, my dear Lanyon, and save

> Your friend,
> H.J.

P.S. – I had already sealed this up when a fresh terror struck upon my soul. It is possible that the post office may fail me, and this letter not come into your hands until tomorrow morning. In that case, dear Lanyon, do my errand when it shall be most convenient for you in the course of the day; and once more expect my messenger at midnight. It may then already be too late; and if that night passes without event, you will know that you have seen the last of Henry Jekyll.

Upon the reading of this letter, I made sure my colleague was insane; but till that was proved beyond the possibility of doubt, I felt bound to do as he requested. The less I understood of this farrago, the less I was in a position to judge of its importance; and an appeal so worded could not be set aside without a grave responsibility. I rose accordingly from table, got into a hansom, and drove straight to Jekyll's house. The butler was awaiting my arrival; he had received by the same post as mine a registered letter of instruction, and had sent at once for a locksmith and a carpenter. The tradesmen came while we were yet speaking; and we moved in a body to old Dr Denman's surgical theatre, from which (as you are doubtless aware) Jekyll's private cabinet is most conveniently entered. The door was very strong, the lock excellent; the carpenter avowed he would have great trouble, and have to do much damage, if force were to be used; and the locksmith was near despair. But this last was a handy fellow, and after two hours' work, the door stood open. The press marked E was unlocked; and I took out the drawer, had it filled up with straw and tied in a sheet and returned with it to Cavendish Square.

Here I proceeded to examine its contents. The powders were neatly enough made up, but not with the nicety of the dispensing chemist; so that it was plain they were of Jekyll's private manufacture; and when I opened one of the wrappers, I found what seemed to me a simple crystalline salt of a white colour. The phial, to which I next turned my attention, might have been about half full of a blood-red liquor, which was highly pungent to the sense of smell, and seemed to me to contain phosphorus and some volatile ether. At the other ingredients I could make no guess. The book was an ordinary version book, and contained little but a series of dates. These covered a period of many years; but I observed that the entries ceased nearly a year ago, and quite abruptly. Here and there a brief remark was appended to a date, usually no more than a single word: 'double' occurring perhaps six times in a total of several hundred entries; and once very early in the list, and followed by several marks of exclamation, 'total failure!!!!' All this, though it whetted my curiosity, told me little that was definite. Here were a phial of some tincture, a paper of some salt, and the record of a series of experiments that had led (like too many of Jekyll's investigations) to no end of practical usefulness. How could the presence of these articles in my house affect either the honour, the sanity, or the life of my flighty colleague? If his messenger could go to one place, why could he not go to another? And even granting some impediment, why was this gentleman to be received by me in secret? The more I reflected, the more convinced I grew that I was dealing with a case of cerebral disease; and though I dismissed my servants to bed, I loaded an old revolver, that I might be found in some posture of self-defence.

Twelve o'clock had scarce rung out over London, ere the knocker sounded very gently on the door. I went myself at the summons, and found a small man crouching against the pillars of the portico.

'Are you come from Dr Jekyll?' I asked.

He told me 'yes' by a constrained gesture; and when I had bidden him enter, he did not obey me without a searching backward glance into the darkness of the square. There was a policeman not far off, advancing with his bull's-eye open; and at the sight, I thought my visitor started and made greater haste.

These particulars struck me, I confess, disagreeably; and as I followed him into the bright light of the consulting-room, I kept my hand ready on my weapon. Here, at last, I had my chance of clearly seeing him. I had never set eyes on him before, so much was certain. He was small, as I have said; I was struck besides with the shocking expression of his face, with his remarkable combination of great muscular activity and great apparent debility of constitution, and – last but not least – with the odd, subjective disturbance caused by his neighbourhood. This bore some resemblance to incipient rigor, and was accompanied by a marked sinking of the pulse. At the time, I set it down to some idiosyncratic, personal distaste, and merely wondered at the acuteness of the symptoms; but I have since had reason to believe the cause to lie much deeper in the nature of man, and to turn on some nobler hinge than the principle of hatred.

This person (who had thus, from the first moment of his entrance, struck in me what I can only describe as a disgustful curiosity) was dressed in a fashion that would have made an ordinary person laughable; his clothes, that is to say, although they were of rich and sober fabric, were enormously too large for him in every measurement – the trousers hanging on his legs and rolled up to keep them from the ground, the waist of the coat below his haunches, and the collar sprawling wide upon his shoulders. Strange to relate, this ludicrous accoutrement was far from moving me to laughter. Rather, as there was something abnormal and misbegotten in the very essence of the creature that now faced me – something seizing, surprising and revolting – this fresh disparity seemed but to fit in with and to reinforce it; so that to my interest in the man's nature and character there was added a curiosity as to his origin, his life, his fortune and status in the world.

These observations, though they have taken so great a space to be set down in, were yet the work of a few seconds. My visitor was indeed, on fire with sombre excitement.

'Have you got it?' he cried. 'Have you got it?' And so lively was his impatience that he even laid his hand upon my arm and sought to shake me.

I put him back, conscious at his touch of a certain icy pang along my blood. 'Come, sir,' said I. 'You forget that I have not yet the pleasure of your acquaintance. Be seated, if you please.' And I showed him an example, and sat down myself in my customary seat and with as fair an imitation of my ordinary manner to a patient as the lateness of the hour, the nature of my preoccupations, and the horror I had of my visitor would suffer me to muster.

'I beg your pardon, Dr Lanyon,' he replied, civilly enough. 'What you say is very well founded; and my impatience has shown its heels to my politeness. I come here at the instance of your colleague, Dr Henry Jekyll, on a piece of business of some moment; and I understood . . .' he paused and put his hand to his throat, and I could see, in spite of his collected manner, that he was wrestling against the approaches of hysteria – 'I understood, a drawer . . .'

But here I took pity on my visitor's suspense, and some perhaps on my own growing curiosity.

'There it is, sir,' said I, pointing to the drawer, where it lay on the floor behind a table, and still covered with the sheet.

He sprang to it, and then paused, and laid his hand upon his heart; I could hear his teeth grate with the convulsive action of his jaws; and his face was so ghastly to see that I grew alarmed both for his life and reason.

'Compose yourself,' said I.

He turned a dreadful smile to me, and, as if with the decision of despair, plucked away the sheet. At sight of the contents, he uttered one loud sob of such immense relief that I sat petrified. And the next moment, in a voice that was already fairly well under control, 'Have you a graduated glass?' he asked.

I rose from my place with something of an effort, and gave him what he asked.

He thanked me with a smiling nod, measured out a few minims of the red tincture and added one of the powders. The mixture, which was at first of a reddish hue, began, in proportion as the crystals melted, to brighten in colour, to effervesce audibly, and to throw off small fumes of vapour. Suddenly, and at the same moment, the ebullition ceased, and the compound changed to a dark purple, which faded again more slowly to a watery green. My visitor, who had watched these metamorphoses with a keen eye, smiled, set down the glass upon the table, and then turned and looked upon me with an air of scrutiny.

'And now,' said he, 'to settle what remains. Will you be wise? will you be guided? will you suffer me to take this glass in my hand, and to go forth from your house without further parley? or has the greed of curiosity too much command of you? Think before you answer, for it shall be done as you decide. As you decide, you shall be left as you were before, and neither richer nor wiser, unless the sense of service rendered to a man in mortal distress may be counted as a kind of riches of the soul. Or, if you shall so prefer to choose, a new province of knowledge and new avenues to fame and power shall be laid open to you, here, in this room, upon the instant; and your sight shall be blasted by a prodigy to stagger the unbelief of Satan.'

'Sir,' said I, affecting a coolness that I was far from truly possessing, 'you speak enigmas, and you will perhaps not wonder that I hear you with no very strong impression of belief. But I have gone too far in the way of inexplicable services to pause before I see the end.'

'It is well,' replied my visitor. 'Lanyon, you remember your vows: what follows is under the seal of our profession. And now, you who have so long been bound to the most narrow and material views, you who have denied the virtue of transcendental medicine, you who have derided your superiors – behold!'

He put the glass to his lips, and drank at one gulp. A cry followed; he reeled, staggered, clutched at the table and held on, staring with injected eyes, gasping with open mouth; and as I looked, there came, I thought, a change – he seemed to swell – his face became suddenly black, and the features seemed to melt and alter – and the next moment I had sprung to my feet and leaped back against the wall, my arm raised to shield me from that prodigy, my mind submerged in terror.

'O God!' I screamed, and 'O God!' again and again; for there before my eyes – pale and shaken, and half fainting, and groping before him with his hands, like a man restored from death – there stood Henry Jekyll!

What he told me in the next hour I cannot bring my mind to set on paper. I saw what I saw, I heard what I heard, and my soul sickened at it; and yet, now when that sight has faded from my eyes I ask myself if I believe it, and I cannot answer. My life is shaken to its roots; sleep has left me; the deadliest terror sits by me at all hours of the day and night; I feel that my days are numbered, and that I must die; and yet I shall die incredulous. As for the moral turpitude that man unveiled to me, even with tears of penitence, I cannot, even in memory, dwell on it without a start of horror. I will say but one thing, Utterson, and that (if you can bring your mind to credit it) will be more than enough. The creature who crept into my house that night was, on Jekyll's own confession, known by the name of Hyde and hunted for in every corner of the land as the murderer of Carew.

HASTIE LANYON

Henry Jekyll's Full Statement of the Case

I WAS BORN IN THE YEAR 18— to a large fortune, endowed besides with excellent parts, inclined by nature to industry, fond of the respect of the wise and good among my fellow-men, and thus, as might have been supposed, with every guarantee of an honourable and distinguished future. And indeed, the worst of my faults was a certain impatient gaiety of disposition, such as has made the happiness of many, but such as I found it hard to reconcile with my imperious desire to carry my head high, and wear a more than commonly grave countenance before the public. Hence it came about that I concealed my pleasures; and that when I reached years of reflection, and began to look round me, and take stock of my progress and position in the world, I stood already committed to a profound duplicity of life. Many a man would have even blazoned such irregularities as I was guilty of; but from the high views that I had set before me, I regarded and hid them with an almost morbid sense of shame. It was thus rather the exacting nature of my aspirations, than any particular degradation in my faults, that made me what I was, and, with even a deeper trench than in the majority of men, severed in me those provinces of good and ill which divide and compound man's dual nature. In this case, I was driven to reflect deeply and inveterately on that hard law of life which lies at the root of religion, and is one of the most plentiful springs of distress. Though so profound a double-dealer, I was in no sense a hypocrite; both sides of me were in dead earnest; I was no more myself when I laid aside restraint and plunged in shame, than when I laboured, in the eye of day, at the furtherance of knowledge or the relief of my scientific studies, which led wholly towards the mystic and the transcendental, reacted and shed a strong light on this consiousness of the perennial war among my members. With every day, and from both sides of my intelligence, the moral and the intellectual, I thus drew steadily nearer to that truth by whose partial discovery I have been doomed to such a dreadful shipwreck: that man is not truly one, but two. I say two, because the state of my own knowledge does not pass beyond that point. Others will follow, others will outstrip me on the same lines; and I hazard the guess that man will be ultimately known for a mere polity of multifarious, incongruous and independent denizens. I, for my part, from the nature of my life, advanced infallibly in one direction, and in one direction only. It was on the moral side, and in my own person, that I learned to recognize the thorough and primitive duality of man; I saw that, of the two natures that contended in the field of my consciousness, even if I could rightly be said to be either, it was only because I was radically both; and from an early date, even before the course of my scientific discoveries had begun to suggest the most naked possibility of such a miracle, I had learned to dwell with pleasure, as a beloved daydream, on the thought of the separation of these elements. If each, I told myself, could but be housed in separate identities, life would be relieved of all that was unbearable; the unjust might go his way, delivered from the aspirations and remorse of his more upright twin; and the just could walk steadfastly and securely on his upward path, doing the good things in which he found his pleasure, and no longer exposed to disgrace and penitence by the hands of this extraneous evil. It was the curse of mankind that these incongruous faggots were thus bound together – that in the agonized womb of consciousness these polar twins should be continuously struggling. How, then, were they dissociated?

I was so far in my reflections, when, as I have said, a side light began to shine upon the subject from the laboratory table. I began to perceive more deeply than it has ever yet been stated, the trembling immateriality, the mist-like transience, of this seemingly so solid body in which we walk attired. Certain agents I found to have the power to shake and to pluck back that fleshly vestment, even as a wind might toss the curtains of a pavilion. For two good reasons, I will not enter deeply into this scientific branch of my confession. First, because I have been made to learn that the doom and burthen of our life is bound for ever on man's shoulders; and when the attempt is made to cast it off, it but returns upon us with more unfamiliar and more awful pressure. Second, because, as my narrative will make, alas! too evident, my discoveries were incomplete. Enough, then, that I not only recognized my natural body for the mere aura and effulgence of certain of the powers that made up my spirit, but managed to compound a drug by which these powers should be dethroned from their supremacy, and a second form and countenance substituted, none the less natural to me because they were the expression, and bore the stamp, of lower elements in my soul.

I hesitated long before I put this theory to the test of practice. I knew well that I risked death; for any drug that so potently controlled and shook the very fortress of identity, might by the least scruple of an overdose or at the least inopportunity in the moment of exhibition, utterly blot out that immaterial tabernacle which I looked to it to change. But the temptation of a discovery so singular and profound at last overcame the suggestions of alarm. I had long since prepared my tincture; I purchased at once, from a firm of wholesale chemists, a large quantity of a particular salt, which I knew, from my experiments, to be the last ingredient required; and, late one accursed night, I compounded the elements, watched them boil and smoke together in the glass, and when the ebullition had subsided, with a strong glow of courage, drank off the potion.

The most racking pangs succeeded: a grinding in the bones, deadly nausea, and a horror of the spirit that cannot be exceeded at the hour of birth or death. Then these agonies began swiftly to subside, and I came to myself as if out of a great sickness. There was something strange in my sensations, something indescribably new, and, from its very novelty, incredibly sweet. I felt younger, lighter, happier in body; within I was conscious of a heady recklessness, a current of disordered sensual images running like a mill race in my fancy, a solution of the bonds of obligation, an unknown but not an innocent freedom of the soul. I knew myself, at the first breath of this new life, to be more wicked, tenfold more wicked, sold a slave to my original evil; and the thought, in that moment, braced and delighted me like wine. I stretched out my hands, exulting in the freshness of these sensations; and in the act, I was suddenly aware that I had lost in stature.

There was no mirror, at that date, in my room; that which stands beside me as I write was brought there later on, and for the very purpose of those transformations. The night, however, was far gone into the morning – the morning, black as it was, was nearly ripe for the conception of the day – the inmates of my house were locked in the most rigorous hours of slumber; and I determined, flushed as I was with hope and triumph, to venture in my new shape as far as to my bedroom. I crossed the yard, wherein the constellations looked down upon me, I could have thought, with wonder, the first creature of that sort that their unsleeping vigilance had yet disclosed to them; I stole through the corridors, a stranger in my own house; and coming to my room, I saw for the first time the appearance of Edward Hyde.

I must here speak by theory alone, saying not that which I know, but that which I suppose to be most probable. The evil side of my nature, to which I had now transferred the stamping efficacy, was less robust and less developed than the good which I had just deposed. Again, in the course of my life, which had been, after all, nine-tenths a life of effort, virtue and control, it had been much less exercised and much less exhausted. And hence, as I think, it came about that Edward Hyde was so much smaller, slighter, and younger than Henry Jekyll. Even as good shone upon the countenance of the one, evil was written broadly and plainly on the face of the other. Evil besides (which I must still believe to be the lethal side of man) had left on that body an imprint of deformity and decay. And yet when I looked upon that ugly idol in the glass, I was conscious of no repugnance, rather of a leap of welcome. This, too, was myself. It seemed natural and human. In my eyes it bore a livelier image of the spirit, it seemed more express and single, than the imperfect and divided countenance I had been hitherto accustomed to call mine. And in so far I was doubtless right. I have observed that when I wore the semblance of Edward Hyde, none could come near to me at first without a visible misgiving of the flesh. This, as I take it, was because all human beings, as we meet them, are commingled out of good and evil: and Edward Hyde, alone, in the ranks of mankind, was pure evil.

I lingered but a moment at the mirror: the second and conclusive experiment had yet to be attempted; it yet remained to be seen if I had lost my identity beyond redemption and must flee before daylight from a house that was no longer mine: and hurrying back to my cabinet, I once more prepared and drank the cup, once more suffered the pangs of dissolution, and came to myself once more with the character, the stature, and the face of Henry Jekyll.

That night I had come to the fatal cross-roads. Had I approached my discovery in a more noble spirit, had I risked the experiment while under the empire of generous or pious aspirations, all must have been otherwise, and from these agonies of death and birth I had come forth an angel instead of a fiend. The drug had no discriminating action; it was neither diabolical nor divine; it but shook the doors of the prison-house of my disposition; and, like the captives of Philippi, that which stood within ran forth. At that time my virtue slumbered; my evil, kept awake by ambition, was alert and swift to seize the occasion; and the thing that was projected was Edward Hyde. Hence, although I had now two characters as well as two appearances, one was wholly evil, and the other was still the old Henry Jekyll, that incongruous compound of whose reformation and improvement I had already learned to despair. The movement was thus wholly toward the worse.

Even at that time, I had not yet conquered my aversion to the dryness of a life of study. I would still be merrily disposed at times; and as my pleasures were (to say the least) undignified, and I was not only well known and highly considered, but growing towards the elderly man, this incoherency of my life was daily growing more unwelcome. It was on this side that my new power tempted me until I fell in slavery. I had but to drink the cup, to doff at once the body of the noted professor and to assume, like a thick cloak, that of Edward Hyde. I smiled at the notion; it seemed to me at the time to be humorous; and I made my preparations with the most studious care. I took and furnished that house in Soho to which Hyde was tracked by the police; and engaged as a housekeeper a creature whom I well knew to be silent and unscrupulous. On the other side, I announced to my servants that a Mr Hyde (whom I described) was to have full liberty and power about my house in the square; and, to parry mishaps, I even called and made myself a familiar object in my second character. I next drew up that will to which you so much objected; so that if anything befell me in the person of Dr Jekyll, I could enter on that of Edward Hyde without pecuniary loss. And thus fortified, as I supposed, on every side, I began to profit by the strange immunities of my position.

Men have before hired bravos to transact their crimes, while their own person and reputation sat under shelter. I was the first that ever did so for his pleasures. I was the first that could thus plod in the public eye with a load of genial respectability, and in a moment, like a schoolboy, strip off these lendings and spring headlong into the sea of liberty. But for me, in my impenetrable mantle, the safety was complete. Think of it – I did not even exist! Let me but escape into my laboratory door, give me but a second or two to mix and swallow the draught that I had always standing ready, and, whatever he had done, Edward Hyde would pass away like the stain of breath upon a mirror; and there in his stead, quietly at home, trimming midnight lamp in his study, a man who could afford to laugh at suspicion, would be Henry Jekyll.

The pleasures which I made haste to seek in my disguise were, as I have said, undignified; I would scarce use a harder term. But in the hands of Edward Hyde they soon began to turn towards the monstrous. When I would come back from these excursions, I was often plunged into a kind of wonder at my vicarious depravity. This familiar that I called out of my own soul, and sent forth alone to do his good pleasure, was a being inherently malign and villainous; his every act and thought centred on self; drinking pleasure with bestial avidity from any degree of torture to another; relentless like a man of stone. Henry Jekyll stood at times aghast before the acts of Edward Hyde; but the situation was apart from ordinary laws, and insidiously relaxed the grasp of conscience. It was Hyde, after all, and Hyde alone, that was guilty. Jekyll was no worse; he woke again to his good qualities seemingly unimpaired; he would even make haste, where it was possible to undo the evil done by Hyde. And thus his conscience slumbered.

Into the details of the infamy at which I thus connived (for even now

I can scarce grant that I committed it) I have no design of entering. I mean but to point out the warnings and the successive steps with which my chastisement approached. I met with one accident which, as it brought on no consequence, I shall no more than mention. An act of cruelty to a child aroused against me the anger of a passer-by, whom I recognized the other day in the person of your kinsman; the doctor and the child's family joined him; there were moments when I feared for my life; and at last, in order to pacify their too just resentment, Edward Hyde had to bring them to the door, and pay them in a cheque drawn in the name of Henry Jekyll. But this danger was easily eliminated from the future by opening an account at another bank in the name of Edward Hyde himself; and when, by sloping my own hand backwards, I had supplied my double with a signature, I thought I sat beyond the reach of fate.

Some two months before the murder of Sir Danvers, I had been out for one of my adventures, had returned at a late hour, and woke the next day in bed with somewhat odd sensations. It was in vain I looked about me; in vain I saw the decent furniture and tall proportions of my room in the square; in vain that I recognized the pattern of the bed curtains and the design of the mahogany frame; something still kept insisting that I was not where I was, that I had not wakened where I seemed to be, but in the little room in Soho where I was accustomed to sleep in the body of Edward Hyde. I smiled to myself, and, in my psychological way, began lazily to inquire into the elements of this illusion, occasionally, even as I did so, dropping back into a comfortable morning doze. I was still so engaged when, in one of my more wakeful moments, my eye fell upon my hand. Now, the hand of Henry Jekyll (as you have often remarked) was professional in shape and size; it was large, firm, white and comely. But the hand which I now saw, clearly enough in the yellow light of a mid-London morning, lying half shut on the bed-clothes, was lean, corded, knuckly, of a dusky pallor, and thickly shaded with a swart growth of hair. It was the hand of Edward Hyde.

I must have stared upon it for near half a minute, sunk as I was in the mere stupidity of wonder, before terror woke up in my breast as sudden and startling as the crash of cymbals; and bounding from my bed, I rushed to the mirror. At the sight that met my eyes, my blood was changed into something exquisitely thin and icy. Yes, I had gone to bed Henry Jekyll, I had awakened Edward Hyde. How was this to be explained? I asked myself; and then, with another bound of terror -- how was it to be remedied? It was well on in the morning; the servants were up; all my drugs were in the cabinet -- a long journey, down two pairs of stairs, through the back passage, across the open court and through the anatomical theatre, from where I was then standing horror-struck. It might indeed be possible to cover my face; but of what use was that, when I was unable to conceal the alteration in my stature? And then, with an overpowering sweetness of relief, it came back upon my mind that the servants were already used to the coming and going of my second self. I had soon dressed, as well as I was able in clothes of my own size; had soon passed through the house, where Bradshaw stared and drew back at seeing Mr Hyde at such an hour and in such a strange array; and ten minutes later, Dr Jekyll had returned to his own shape, and was sitting down, with a darkened brow, to make a feint of breakfasting.

Small indeed was my appetite. This inexplicable incident, this reversal of my previous experience, seemed, like the Babylonian finger on the wall, to be spelling out the letters of my judgment; and I began to reflect more seriously than ever before on the issues and possibilities of my double existence. That part of me which I had the power of projecting had lately been much exercised and nourished; it had seemed to me of late as though the body of Edward Hyde had grown in stature, as though (when I wore that form) I were conscious of a more generous tide of blood; and I began to spy a danger that, if this were much prolonged, the balance of my nature might be permanently overthrown, the power of voluntary change be forfeited, and the character of Edward Hyde become irrevocably mine. The power of the drug had not been always equally displayed. Once, very early in my career, it had totally failed me; since then I had been obliged on more than one occasion to double, and once, with infinite risk of death, to treble the amount; and these rare uncertainties had cast hitherto the sole shadow on my contentment. Now, however, and in the light of that morning's accident, I was led to remark that whereas, in the beginning, the difficulty had been to throw off the body of Jekyll, it had of late gradually but decidedly transferred itself to the other side. All things therefore seemed to point to this: that I was slowly losing hold of my original and better self, and becoming slowly incorporated with my second and worse.

Between these two I now felt I had to choose. My two natures had memory in common, but all other faculties were most unequally shared between them. Jekyll (who was composite), now with the most sensitive apprehensions, now with a greedy gusto, projected and shared in the pleasures and adventures of Hyde; but Hyde was indifferent to Jekyll, or but remembered him as the mountain bandit remembers the cavern in which he conceals himself from pursuit. Jekyll had more than a father's interest; Hyde had more than a son's indifference. To cast in my lot with Jekyll was to die to those appetites which I had long secretly indulged and had of late begun to pamper. To cast it in with Hyde was to die to a thousand interests and aspirations, and to become, at a blow and for ever, despised and friendless. The bargain might appear unequal; but there was still another consideration in the scales; for while Jekyll would suffer smartingly in the fires of abstinence, Hyde would be not even conscious of all that he had lost. Strange as my circumstances were, the terms of this debate are as old and commonplace as man; much the same inducements and alarms cast the die for any tempted and trembling sinner; and it fell out with me, as it falls with so vast a majority of my fellows, that I chose the better part, and was found wanting in the strength to keep to it.

Yes, I preferred the elderly and discontented doctor, surrounded by friends, and cherishing honest hopes; and bade a resolute farewell to the liberty, the comparative youth, the light step, leaping pulses and secret pleasures, that I had enjoyed in the disguise of Hyde. I made this choice perhaps with some unconscious reservation, for I neither gave up the house in Soho, nor destroyed the clothes of Edward Hyde, which still lay ready in my cabinet. For two months, however, I was true to my determination; for two months I led a life of such severity as I had never before attained to, and enjoyed the compensations of an approving conscience. But time began at last to obliterate the freshness of my alarm; the praises of conscience began to grow into a thing of course; I began to be tortured with throes and longings, as of Hyde struggling after freedom; and at last, in an hour of moral weakness, I once again compounded and swallowed the transforming draught.

I do not suppose that when a drunkard reasons with himself upon his vice, he is once out of five hundred times affected by the dangers he runs through his brutish physical insensibility; neither had I, long as I had considered my position, made enough allowance for the complete moral insensibility and insensate readiness to evil which were the leading characters of Edward Hyde. Yet it was by these that I was punished. My devil had been long caged, he came out roaring. I was conscious, even when I took the draught, of a more unbridled, a more furious propensity to ill. It must have been this, I suppose, that stirred in my soul that tempest of impatience with which I listened to the civilities of my unhappy victim; I declare at least before God, no man morally sane could have been guilty of that crime upon so pitiful a provocation; and that I struck in no more reasonable spirit than that in which a sick child may break a plaything. But I had voluntarily stripped myself of all those balancing instincts by which even the worst of us continues to walk with some degree of steadiness among temptations; and in my case, to be tempted, however slightly, was to fall.

Instantly the spirit of hell awoke in me and raged. With a transport of glee, I mauled the unresisting body, tasting delight from every blow; and it was not till weariness had begun to succeed that I was suddenly, in the top fit of my delirium, struck through the heart by a cold thrill of terror. A mist dispersed; I saw my life to be forfeit; and fled from the scene of these excesses, at once glorying and trembling, my lust of evil gratified and stimulated, my love of life screwed to the topmost peg. I ran to the house in Soho, and (to make assurance doubly sure) destroyed my papers; thence I set out through the lamplit streets, in the same divided ecstasy of mind, gloating on my crime, light-headedly devising others in the future, and yet still hastening and still harkening in my wake for the steps of the avenger. Hyde had a song upon his lips as he compounded the draught, and as he drank it pledged the dead man. The pangs of transformation had not done tearing him, before Henry Jekyll, with streaming tears of gratitude and remorse, had fallen upon his knees and lifted his clasped hands to God. The veil of self-indulgence was rent from head to foot, I saw my life as a whole: I followed it up from the days of childhood, when I had walked with my father's hand, and through the self-denying toils of my professional life, to arrive again and again, with the same sense of unreality, at the damned horrors of the evening. I could have screamed aloud; I sought with tears and prayers to smother down the crowd of hideous images and sounds with which my memory swarmed against me; and still, between the petitions, the ugly face of my iniquity stared into my soul. As the acuteness of this remorse began to die away, it was succeeded by a sense of joy. The problem of my conduct was solved. Hyde was thenceforth impossible; whether I would or not, I was now confined to the better part of my existence; and, oh, how I rejoiced to think it! with what willing humility I embraced anew the restrictions of natural life! with what sincere renunciation I locked the door by which I had so often gone and come, and ground the key under my heel!

The next day came the news that the murder had been overlooked, that the guilt of Hyde was patent to the world, and that the victim was a man high in public estimation. It was not only a crime, it had been a tragic folly. I think I was glad to know it; I think I was glad to have my better impulses thus buttressed and guarded by the terrors of the scaffold. Jekyll was now my city of refuge; let but Hyde peep out an instant, and the hands of all men would be raised to take and slay him.

I resolved in my future conduct to redeem the past; and I can say with honesty that my resolve was fruitful of some good. You know yourself how earnestly in the last months of last year I laboured to relieve suffering; you know that much was done for others, and that the days passed quietly, almost happily for myself. Nor can I truly say that I wearied of this beneficent and innocent life; I think instead that I daily enjoyed it more completely; but I was still cursed with my duality of purpose; and as the first edge of my penitence wore off, the lower side of me, so long indulged, so recently chained down, began to growl for licence. Not that I dreamed of resuscitating Hyde; the bare idea of that would startle me to frenzy: no, it was in my own person that I was once more tempted to trifle with my conscience; and it was as an ordinary secret sinner that I at last fell before the assaults of temptation.

There comes an end to all things; the most capacious measure is filled at last; and this brief condescension to my evil finally destroyed the balance of my soul. And yet I was not alarmed; the fall seemed natural, like a return to the old days before I had made my discovery. It was a fine, clear January day, wet under foot where the frost had melted, but cloudless overhead; and the Regent's Park was full of winter chirrupings and sweet with spring odours. I sat in the sun on a bench; the animal within me licking the chops of memory; the spiritual side a little drowsed, promising subsequent penitence, but not yet moved to begin. After all, I reflected, I was like my neighbours; and then I smiled, comparing myself with other men, comparing my active goodwill with the lazy cruelty of their neglect. And at the very moment of that vainglorious thought, a qualm came over me, a horrid nausea and the most deadly shuddering. These passed away, and left me faint; and then as in its turn the faintness subsided, I began to be aware of a change in the temper of my thoughts, a greater boldness, a contempt of danger, a solution of the bonds of obligation. I looked down; my clothes hung formlessly on my shrunken limbs; the hand that lay on my knee was corded and hairy. I was once more Edward Hyde. A moment before I had been safe of all men's respect, wealthy, beloved – the cloth laying for me in the dining-room at home; and now I was the common quarry of mankind, hunted, houseless, a known murderer, thrall to the gallows.

My reason wavered, but it did not fail me utterly. I have more than once observed that, in my second character, my faculties seemed sharpened to a point and my spirits more tensely elastic; thus it came about that, where Jekyll perhaps might have succumbed, Hyde rose to the importance of the moment. My drugs were in one of the presses of my cabinet: how was I to reach them? That was the problem that (crushing my temples in my hands) I set myself to solve. The laboratory door I had closed. If I sought to enter by the house, my own servants would consign me to the gallows. I saw I must employ another hand, and thought of Lanyon. How was he to be reached? how persuaded? Supposing that I escape capture in the streets, how was I to make my way into his presence? and how should I, an unknown and displeasing visitor, prevail on the famous physician to rifle the study of his colleague, Dr Jekyll? Then I remembered that of my original character, one part remained of me: I could write my own hand; and once I had conceived that kindling spark, the way that I must follow became lighted up from end to end.

Thereupon, I arranged my clothes as best I could, and summoning a passing hansom, drove to an hotel in Portland Street, the name of which I chanced to remember. At my appearance (which was indeed comical enough, however tragic a fate these garments covered) the driver could not conceal his mirth. I gnashed my teeth upon him with a gust of devilish fury; and the smile withered from his face – happily for him – yet more happily for myself, for in another instant I had certainly dragged him from his perch. At the inn, as I entered, I looked about me with so black a countenance as made the attendants tremble; not a look did they exchange in my presence; but obsequiously took my orders, led me to a private room, and brought me wherewithal to write. Hyde in danger of his life was a creature new to me: shaken with inordinate anger, strung to the pitch of murder, lusting to inflict pain. Yet the creature was astute; mastered his fury with a great effort of the will; composed his two important letters, one to Lanyon and one to Poole, and, that he might receive actual evidence of their being posted, sent them out with directions that they should be registered.

Thenceforward, he sat all day over the fire in the private room, gnawing his nails; there he dined, sitting alone with his fears, the waiter visibly quailing before his eye; and thence, when the night was fully come, he set forth in the corner of a closed cab, and was driven to and fro about the streets of the city. He, I say – I cannot say, I. That child of Hell had nothing human; nothing lived in him but fear and hatred. And when at last, thinking the driver had begun to grow suspicious, he discharged the cab and ventured on foot, attired in his misfitting clothes, an object marked out for observation, into the midst of the nocturnal passengers, these two base passions raged within him like a tempest. He walked fast, hunted by his fears, chattering to himself, skulking through the less frequented thoroughfares, counting the minutes that still divided him from midnight. Once a woman spoke to him, offering, I think, a box of lights. He smote her in the face, and she fled.

When I came to myself at Lanyon's, the horror of my old friend perhaps affected me somewhat: I do not know; it was at least but a drop in the sea to the abhorrence with which I looked back upon these hours. A change had come over me. It was no longer the fear of the gallows, it was the horror of being Hyde that racked me. I received Lanyon's condemnation partly in a dream; it was partly in a dream that I came home to my own house and got into bed. I slept after the prostration of the day, with a stringent and profound slumber which not even the nightmares that wrung me could avail to break. I awoke in the morning shaken, weakened, but refreshed. I still hated and feared the thought of the brute that slept within me, and I had not of course forgotten the appalling dangers of the day before; but I was once more at home, in my own house and close to my drugs; and gratitude for my escape shone so strong in my soul that it almost rivalled the brightness of hope.

I was stepping leisurely across the court after breakfast drinking the chill of the air with pleasure, when I was seized again with those indescribable sensations that heralded the change; and I had but the time to gain the shelter of my cabinet, before I was once again raging and freezing with the passions of Hyde. It took on this occasion a double dose to recall me to myself; and, alas! six hours after, as I sat looking sadly in the fire, the pangs returned, and the drug had to be re-administered. In short, from that day forth it seemed only by a great effort as of gymnastics, and only under the immediate stimulation of the drug, that I was able to wear the countenance of Jekyll. At all hours of the day and night I would be taken with the premonitory shudder; above all, if I slept, or even dozed for a moment in my chair, it was always as Hyde that I awakened. Under the strain of this continually impending doom and by the sleeplessness to which I now condemned myself, ay, even beyond what I had thought possible to man, I became, in my own person, a creature eaten up and emptied by fever, languidly weak both in body and mind, and solely occupied by one thought: the horror of my other self. But when I slept, or when the virtue of the medicine wore off, I would leap almost without transition (for the pangs of tranformation grew daily less marked) into the possession of a fancy brimming with images of terror, a soul boiling with causeless hatreds, and a body that seemed not strong enough to contain the raging energies of life. The powers of Hyde seemed to have grown with the sickliness of Jekyll. And certainly the hate that now divided them was equal on each side. With Jekyll, it was a thing of vital instinct. He had now seen the full deformity of that creature that shared with him some of the phenomena of consciousness, and was co-heir with him to death: and beyond these links of community, which in themselves made the most poignant part of his distress, he thought of Hyde, for all his energy of life, as of something not only hellish but inorganic. This was the shocking thing; that the slime of the pit seemed to utter cries and voices; that the amorphous dust gesticulated and sinned; that what was dead, and had no shape, should usurp the offices of life. And this again, that that insurgent horror was knit to him closer than a wife, closer than an eye; lay caged in his flesh, where he heard it mutter and felt it struggle to be born; and at every hour of weakness, and in the confidence of slumber, prevailed against him, and deposed him out of life. The hatred of Hyde for Jekyll was of a different order. His terror of the gallows drove him continually to commit temporary suicide, and return to his subordinate station of a part instead of a person; but he loathed the necessity, he loathed the despondency into which Jekyll was now fallen, and he resented the dislike with which he was himself regarded. Hence the apelike tricks he would play me, scrawling in my own hand blasphemies on the pages of my books, burning the letters and destroying the portrait of my father; and indeed, had it not been for his fear of death, he would long ago have ruined himself in order to involve me in the ruin. But his love of life is wonderful; I go further: I, who sicken and freeze at the mere thought of him, when I recall the abjection and passion of this attachment, and when I know how he fears my power to cut him off by suicide, I find it in my heart to pity him.

It is useless, and the time awfully fails me, to prolong this description; no one has ever suffered such torments, let that suffice; and yet even to these, habit brought – no, not alleviation – but a certain callousness of soul, a certain acquiescence of despair; and my punishment might have gone on for years, but for the last calamity which has now fallen, and which has finally severed me from my own face and nature. My provision of the salt, which had never been renewed since the date of the first experiment, began to run low. I sent out for a fresh supply, and mixed the draught; the ebullition followed, and the first change of colour, not the second; I drank it, and it was without efficiency. You will learn from Poole how I have had London ransacked; it was in vain; and I am now persuaded that my first supply was impure, and that it was that unknown impurity which lent efficacy to the draught.

About a week has passed, and I am now finishing this statement under the influence of the last of the old powders. This, then, is the last time, short of a miracle, that Henry Jekyll can think his own thoughts or see his own face (now how sadly altered!) in the glass. Nor must I delay too long to bring my writing to an end; for if my narrative has hitherto escaped destruction, it has been by a combination of great prudence and great good luck. Should the throes of change take me in the act of writing it, Hyde will tear it in pieces; but if some time shall have elapsed after I have laid it by, his wonderful selfishness and circumscription to the moment will probably save it once again from the action of his apelike spite. And indeed the doom that is closing on us both has already changed and crushed him. Half an hour from now, when I shall again and for ever reindue that hated personality, I know how I shall sit shuddering and weeping in my chair, or continue, with the most strained and fear-struck ecstasy of listening, to pace up and down this room (my last earthly refuge) and give ear to every sound of menace. Will Hyde die upon the scaffold? or will he find the courage to release himself at the last moment? God knows; I am careless; this is my true hour of death, and what is to follow concerns another than myself. Here, then, as I lay down the pen, and proceed to seal up my confession, I bring the life of that unhappy Henry Jekyll to an end.